THE MYSTERY
of the
HYPERBOREAN WISDOM

THE MYSTERY
of the
HYPERBOREAN WISDOM

or

"The Mystery of Belicena Villca"

"NOVELA MÁGICA"

or

"INITIATIC NOVEL"

IN FIVE BOOKS

by

LUIS FELIPE MOYANO CIRES
"NIMROD DE ROSARIO"

TRANSLATED INTO ENGLISH

CAINITE PUBLISHING COMPANY
2022

ISBN: 9798356935091

Note from the Translator

Contained herein is a literal translation from the author's original manuscript. No part of this translation was done in an automatic manner or put through a translating machine, but manually performed, word by word, with every intention to preserve the exactitude of the original language and the incomparable literary qualities of the author and his work, leaving no part of this translation to chance. Each word and phrase has been rigorously proofread for accuracy and grammatical and historical correctness, often adapting the names of places and personages to their English-language equivalent. No part of this work has been altered during the process, with every effort made to preserve the syntax and sentence structure of the original and the intention to allow the author's words to speak for themselves, without interpretation or editorialization. Footnotes have been added to clarify and explain either foreign, archaic, or unfamiliar terms and phrases, to increase readability.

THIRD BOOK

"In Search of Uncle Kurt"

Chapter I

he reader can give free rein to the imagination. The emotions and the state of total perturbation into which the reading of Belicena Villca's letter plunged me will never be able to be represented. It was something very strange for me; as I was reading, I experienced a plurality of moods. I thus passed from initial skepticism to surprise, from this to stupor, from there I jumped to curiosity, and successively to a thousand more sensations. Finally, a primitive and insensate enthusiasm came over me and, instead of rejecting the letter as an imposture, a logical and perfectly justified attitude, I did quite the opposite, thus sealing my fate: I decided to undertake the adventure!

I was just done with reading the letter and, almost without reflecting, I had made a decision. Why? I will try to explain it. Up until the moment of reading Belicena Villca's letter, my life was empty of ideals. I had a bright professional future and everything that I was needing for my comfort; I was lucky with women and although no one was able to win my heart, sooner or later that would occur. I was foreseeing that my life would unfold along the paths that lead to worldly success. And yet something was missing in this schema because I was not happy. I was possessing peace and material tranquility, but many times sadness was weighing me down; I was sensing that my Spirit was lacking a horizon toward which to look, an ideal, a goal perhaps, worthy of the greatest sacrifice.

That is why I was sometimes enviously contemplating Universal History, the heroic periods in which I would have liked to live: to choose this or that side, to follow this or that reformer, to commit that liberating heresy, or to ardently sink myself into that tyrannical dogma. To live, to fight, to die, to be a man! But to be a man is not only to think: it is "to feel" the Spirit. And the Spirit is "felt" when life is oriented in the search for an ideal; because ideals are not in this world, they are of another order, the same as the Spirit and related to it.

It is not easy. Being an idealist requires much valor, since reality, deceptive and cruel, holds a trap for the naïve idealist and a sepulcher for the committed idealist. I have seen how the idealistic element of my generation was systematically annihilated and its ideals qualified as "*nihilistic.*" An Argentine

Admiral who passes for a cultured person, Massera, said in a speech: *"we are combating against nihilists, against those fevered for destruction, whose objective is destruction itself, even if they disguise themselves as social redeemers."* Many of the dead and disappeared were no such thing, but idealists who believed in the infantile myth of "social revolution" as a valid means to establish a more just order in the world. Precisely for believing (being idealists), they did not see the diabolical web of interests in which they were being inserted; precisely for believing, some were indoctrinated, armed, and imbecilely launched into the adventure, by the same synarchic System that later repressed them. And I am not only thinking of those who took up arms, who were perhaps deserving to die for being stateless, but of so many others who fell without knowing the smell of gunpowder; for committing the "crime" of loving ideals that affect some interest or privilege.

That is not nihilism; unbridled repression, asphyxiating censorship, instituted mediocrity, officialized corruption, typed brainwashing, in short, implacable tyranny, obscenely cloaked in "democratic" or "liberal" language, is nihilistic.

The triumph of the System is the stability of a corrupt order of things, of a society built on usury and materialism, of a country drawn with a nib,[1] so that it is inserted into foreign geopolitics, planned in detail by the International Synarchy of the Great Imperialisms.

What does this contemporary world of dollars and steel offer us that is worth our sacrifice? Here, a decadent and cipayo culture; there, a terrorism without greatness; over there, a repressive and murderous Power; over there, a cowardly and lying Church; why go on if everything stinks?

This was my state of mind when I read Belicena Villca's letter and that is why my reaction was instantaneous: I, the insignificant Dr. Siegnagel, little more than the number on a card or ID, someone lost in the daily mediocrity of remote Salta: suddenly I am called for a risky mission, I am convoked by Fate!

My blood was boiling in my veins and something, just like a reminiscence of past battles, took hold of me. Belicena was wondering in her letter if I could be a Kshatriya:

"Well, I already was!"

---

1. The tip of a pen.

Apart from this irresponsible enthusiasm, deep down I was experiencing great stupefaction as soon as I was attempting to reason about the contents of the letter. I could not deny that a tremendous primordial force, a halo of ancient forgotten truths, was emanating from it all, as if Belicena Villca did not belong to this Epoch or, better said, as if she were independent of time.

The language was pagan and vital; "fantastic" would be the fair term, were it not that the assassination of Belicena was converting this premonitory message into something macabrely real.

Two questions were boiling in my head, jumping from one thought to the other without solution of continuity. Where was this "Sign of the Origin," of which I am bearing, clearly visible to Belicena Villca and apparently representative of a certain spiritual condition? I was perfectly remembering what Belicena had written on the Second Day: "in truth, what exists as a divine inheritance from the Gods is *a Symbol of the Origin in the Pure Blood: the Sign of the Origin, observed on the Stone of Venus, was only the reflection of the Symbol of the Origin present in the Pure Blood of the Warrior Kings, of the Sons of the Gods, of the Semi-divine Men who, with an animal body and a Material Soul, were possessing an Eternal Spirit.*" If it was true that I was possessing the Symbol of the Origin in my Pure Blood, if I was a spiritual man, then I would have the possibility of obtaining the Highest Wisdom of the White Atlanteans. Or had I misinterpreted Belicena's words? For on that Second Day she wrote: "*wisdom consists in comprehending the Serpent with the Sign of the Origin.*" According to Belicena, the Gods were affirming to man, "*you have lost the Origin and are a prisoner of the serpent: with the Sign of the Origin, comprehend the serpent and you will again be free in the Origin!*" In the light of these concepts, my reasoning was the following: *if the Sign of the Origin, "my own sign of the Origin," was found manifested and plasmated in some part of my body, in such a way that it was rapidly distinguished by Belicena Villca, that was the location that I had to discover and project into the World, onto the Serpent, as the Hyperborean Initiates once did!* And so I was feeling an interior urgency to locate that Sign and comply with the mandate of the Gods.

But I was understanding, also, that I was lacking many esoteric elements of the Hyperborean Wisdom. But, if this first question had to be left pending, the second one "that was boiling in my head," about the "familial test," I would not take long to investigate it. Belicena Villca, in effect, had assured, on the Fourth Day, that my family "was destined to produce an archetypal honey, the exquisite juice of all that is sweet." That was the first news I had on the matter and I would try, at least, to verify it with my close relatives.

Chapter II

rom the moment Mama handed me the brief-case with Belicena Villca's letter, until the moment I made the decision to comply with her posthumous request, four days had passed. Certainly, I read the letter in record time, given its length and profundity, remaining locked in my room and having, from time to time, some food brought up to me. At last, one afternoon, I quietly descended, with the mysterious briefcase in hand, and took a seat among my family, who were, as was the custom at that hour, spread out in the backyard. With my head tilted back, my gaze lost in the distance of the hills, I was in silence a long time. During that lapse no one interrupted me, accustomed for years to see me studying under the shade of the gigantic oak tree. Only the whispering of the wind among the leaves, the trill of the birds, and the scratch, scratch, of Canuto itching himself from time to time, were accompanying my meditation.

I brusquely stood up, pushing aside the concrete armchair of the garden set. Next to the lapacho trees near the house, were my parents: Mama darning[2] my nephews' socks and Papa reading a European weekly that arrived fifteen days late; while, the Angelito Vargas cassette, rewound for the umpteenth time, was enveloping us all with "Tres esquinas."

"Papa, Mama," I emphatically said, "have you had ancestors or relatives in your families who followed a trade or craft by tradition?"

"That was a very common custom in Europe," Papa thoughtfully responded, "now lamentably forgotten. In my family there were many doctors like you, Arturo, and even apothecaries like my father, but without this being a law, since we also had good farmers like me: *haw, haw, haw,*" my father was laughing, celebrating his witticism.

"On the other hand, your mother's family," he continued more calmly, "does have a tradition in the cultivation and production of sugar. You know that I met her in Egypt when my father, back in 1935, decided to open new markets in the *tannin* trade, in view of the fact that the textile industry of Europe and America was functioning subject to rigid monopolies. My

---

2. mending

father was planning to sell tannin to the flourishing Arab and Turkish textile industries, so he initiated a trip through the Middle East, the final stop of which was Egypt. I was 18 years old at that time and, contradicting the wishes of my father who was preferring to see me become an engineer, my greatest aspiration was to be a farmer. Trusting that the long trip would end up dissipating what my father was taking as a whim, he agreed to bring me with him.

"Upon arriving in Egypt, we were received by a great-uncle, Hans Siegnagel, a member of a branch of the family that lives, even today, near Cairo. The Siegnagels of Egypt live there, seemingly, since the invasion of Napoleon, together with hundreds of families of German origin, which form a strong community.

"Well, during the days that we spent in Cairo, my interest was centered on observing the great Sugar-producing Mills that stretch along the Nile and the endless expanses planted with sugar cane.

"Papa, upon seeing that my inclination for Agriculture, instead of diminishing, was becoming more intense, understood that that was my true vocation and decided to accept the kind invitation of Baron Reinhold von Sübermann, owner of a powerful sugar Refinery with his own plantations, so that I stayed at his hacienda studying the techniques of cultivation.

"I was there from '35 to '38, when the prospects of a lasting world peace were rapidly dissolving, having to give in to the insistent calls of my father to return to Argentina.

"I undertook the return voyage in June of '38, but I did not do it alone; with me was coming the daughter of Baron Von Sübermann, a beautiful Valkyrie that, by the grace of Wothan, you can presently behold here."

We all laughed, especially my mother who had rolled her eyes, while Papa was recalling his fascinating life.

"What occurred since then?" I asked, knowing that it would do my old father good to complete the story.

"The war opened painful rifts and forced definitive separations. When your grandparents (my father and the Baron) died, we never reconnected with our relatives in Egypt. Many times I have felt for your mother," his voice dropped, "who is German-Egyptian and has had to suffer a lot because of the separation.

"On the other hand," he continued, now more composed, "my patriotic sentiments are only for this country and no other place than here would I be better off. Notice that your Great-Grandfather, the first Siegnagel who came to the Americas, did so in 1860 at the request of the Government to work in the manufacturing of explosives, since he was reputed as a prestigious Chemist. In more than a century, my good Arturo, the Siegnagels have become more Argentine than maté!"

When Papa made reference to the suffering that she had experienced by staying away from her family and her native homeland, my mother approached him and began to tenderly tousle his hair while she was pouring out loving reproaches.

While the elders were cuddling each other, I was feeling my cheeks burning; I was as if spellbound, seeing my imagination already unbridled, drawing the most audacious hypotheses. The affirmation that Belicena Villca was making in her letter about the familial mission of "alchemistically working the sugar," was confirmed, in principle, by my father's account. It was an indubitable reality that the Von Sübermanns had been sugar producers since time immemorial, but how had she known it?

Poor me; I was not even dreaming that this confirmation of Belicena's correctness was only the first of many situations that, in the future, would demonstrate to me to what extent the absurd and the real were interpenetrated around her. *Ting, Ting,* the sound of the triangle, that the Indian maid was playing, calling for dinner, brought me out of such gray thoughts.

That night I was pleasantly surprised by a delicious portion of humitas; that dish constitutes, since my childhood, the most precious delicacy; so, emotionally and gastronomically gratified by my family, I soon calmed down and even managed to forget, for some moments, the obsessive matter of Belicena Villca.

Chapter III

was seriously considering Belicena's warnings, about the dangers involved in the search for her son. In light of her psychic destruction and subsequent murder, these warnings were acquiring a powerful eloquence that I was unwilling to disregard. I therefore decided to resolutely, but cautiously, act.

I had already obtained all the possible police information on the case and was harboring almost no doubts that the mysterious assassins of Belicena were the Immortals Bera and Birsha: the totality of the evidence of the crime was thus indicating it. Only beings like Them could have entered that hermetically sealed cell and ritually executed her. And the most striking of those proofs was constituting the bejeweled rope: it was evident that the "Spanish gold," of the medals, came from Tharsis, from the ancient mines of Tartessos; and that the hair "dyed with milk of lime," of the rope, was belonging to the unfortunate Tartessian Vrayas, those who were assassinated by Bera and Birsha when they saved the Wise Sword and with whose blood the Immortals had written the sentence: *"the punishment for those who offend Yah will come from the Boar."* They were undoubtedly considering a cycle closed, a millenary vengeance fulfilled, perhaps they once again believed the House of Tharsis exterminated, to have used that significant form of execution: to assassinate the last Vraya with the hair that they took from one of the first Vrayas, a macabre trophy that they were now giving back with diabolical logic. And what Mystery was being hidden in the powers of Bera and Birsha, in their incredible dominion of Time! Because from the police report it was clearly concluded that that hair *had not suffered the passing of time: the hair of the rope, in effect, was still alive, as if freshly cut from a human head, from a White-Race head, when it was braided to kill; and was in no way revealing the two thousand two hundred years gone by since then.* Where, Oh if just the thought of this question was filling me with uneasiness, where had they kept it until now without it aging? Perhaps in the same Hell where They were inhabiting, and that Belicena Villca was calling Chang Shambhala? Yes. In all probability that was the correct answer: the hair was coming from their Accursed Abodes, where Time was not passing and neither were They aging.

I had already decided to face the danger and I had to get underway as soon as possible. But I was first wanting to definitively clarify the question of the legends of the gold jewels. And no one would be of greater use to me than Professor Ramirez. I would address myself, then, to his presence.

I stopped the automobile in the parking lot of the City University and arrived at the Anthropology Department in search of Professor Ramirez. He was quite occupied, carrying out a translation, but he attended to me with courtesy.

"What brings you to see me again, Dr. Siegnagel; another Quechua delusion of your patients?" he joked.

"No, Professor, this time it's about non-American languages. I found within an old book, a paper with this drawing," I coldly lied, "and I wanted to consult you about its inscriptions." I held out the drawing that I made of the sinister golden Jewel.

His small gray eyes flashed, and for an instant it seemed that he was really going to be interested; but he immediately returned to adopt the laconic air that was characterizing him. Nothing could affect the old Scholar, admired by the Universities of half the world.

"It is the most grotesque linguistic combination I have ever seen. Is this a joke, Siegnagel?" he asked with suspicion.

"I don't know. I brought it to you just as I found it," I said without exaggerating too much.

"Well, if it is not, it seems so! Hebrew and Celtic! Come on, Arturo; either it is a joke or it is something very, very serious. For one thing, the word יהוה is the famous Tetragrammaton, God's name of four letters, of nefarious power according to the Kabbalah and that is read more or less '*YHVH*,' the '*H*' letters being those that can adopt the sound of the Greek '*ETA*,' that is to say, similar to the Castilian '*E*.' As for בינה, its translation is '*Binah*' and it means 'Intelligence'; but not just any intelligence but the 'Supreme Intelligence,' the Intelligence of God, precisely the Intelligence of *YHVH Elohim*: for the Hebrew Kabbalah, Binah is one of the ten Sephiroth or Aspects of the One God."

How familiar and meaningful those explanations of the Professor were to me then, when inevitably placing them in the context of Belicena Villca's letter and her terrible death. But the Professor was continuing:

"The phrase *'ada aes sidhe draoi mac hwch'* is undoubtedly Old Celtic or one of its multiple dialects. The Celtic language evolved, from the Indo-European tree, in two branches; one, continental, produced *Gaulish;* the other, insular, would in turn be divided into two sub-branches: 1°) *Goidelic* or *Old Irish,* mother of *Irish* and *Scottish Gaelic;* and 2°) *Brittonic,* which produced *Breton, Welsh* and *Cornish.* I would tell you that these words belong to Old Irish, just as it appears in the sagas 'The Song of Marzhin' or in the poems of the Bard Taliesin, written in the fifth century.

"It is curious, Marzhin (in Welsh 'Myrddin,' and deformed in Germanic languages, 'Merlin') was a *Druid,* just like Taliesin, and the phrase that you have brought me precisely alludes to the *Druids:* "Draoi" means *Druid* in Celtic. The complete phrase would be *"Victory to the Divine Druid, Son of the Boar,"* according to the following vocabulary:

> *ada = Victory*
> *aes sidhe = Divine*
> *Draoi = Druid*
> *mac = Son*
> *hwch = Boar*

"My dear Dr. Arturo Siegnagel," the Professor was staring at me, "what do you know about the Druids?"

The question did not take me by surprise, for I myself was thinking about it at great speed, from the very moment that the Professor completed his translation.

"I know very little," I said. "That they were forming a sort of Priestly Caste among the ancient Celts. That they were practicing magic and divination... I believe that they were reputed as Wise Men and who, in spite of their pagan origin, were possessing a not inconsiderable morality." Everything I knew about the Druids, or Golen, was from Belicena Villca's letter, and my opinion of Them, naturally, could not be worse. However, I was unaware of Professor Ramirez's opinion of them and I was not trying to embarrass myself by categorically condemning them. "I think that they disappeared with the conversion of the Celts to Christianity," I innocently concluded.

The Professor was sardonically smiling:

"Sit down, Siegnagel, let's have a chat." He got up and, after locking the office, rummaged for a few minutes in his extensive private library. He was picking out books here and there, snorting with satisfaction when he was finding one that he had resisted more than 30 seconds. At last, taking a hanging folder from a file, he settled into his armchair.

"You see, Dr.," began the Professor with a grave tone, "I will be frank: if it had been someone else who was bringing me that drawing, I would have kicked him out, without a doubt. But knowing you, who is a serious person, I will confide to you my thoughts, since something tells me that there is more behind this naïve drawing."

I smiled at the Professor's accurate intuition.

"To begin, let us remember that the best etymology seems to be *Druvid*, a word that breaks down into *Dru* = 'thing in itself' or 'such a thing' and *vid* = 'to know,' which would mean 'to know things in themselves.' The Druid would then be 'he who knows things profoundly'; but an older meaning calls them 'He who knows the truth.' You should not be surprised, Arturo, of knowing little about them, for although Druidism was an institution among the ancient Celts and many classical writers mentioned them, their origin and Doctrine remain in the darkest mystery. Some of these writers who come to my memory, are, for your example, Julius Caesar, Posidonius, Cicero, Diodorus Siculus, Strabo, Pliny, Tacitus, Lucian, Suetonius, Diogenes Laërtius, Origen, etc.

"None shed too much light on them and that, to my judgment, is for three reasons: 1º) because their teaching was oral; 2º) because their teaching was initiatic; 3º) and principally, because those most interested in hiding everything that concerns the *'Druid,'* were the Druids themselves.

"With respect to your assessment that they were constituting a kind of 'Priestly Caste,' I will tell you that they were appearing to be neither one nor the other. They were not forming a caste but an Order; and they would not be 'Priests,' since they were not publicly officiating the rituals of a Cult, as it would correspond to deserve that qualification. However, the fact that they did not officiate a Cult in public does not mean that they did not secretly possess and practice it, in the thicket of the forests, near the millenary megalithic constructions that They were adapting for such a purpose. Yes, Dr. Siegnagel. You are right on this point: the Druids were Priests, and of the worst kind that have ever been recorded in the History of Mankind.

"You also believe that they were 'wise and would have a not inconsiderable morality.' Well, of their 'Wisdom' there are few doubts, since they held all the aspects of Celtic knowledge. On the other hand, opinions are mixed, when Druid morals are referred to, a pederastic General like Julius Caesar (100–44 BC) found them agreeable and even sent the Druid Divitiacus as Ambassador to Rome. But in the moral aspect, the future consul was leaving much to be desired; instead Strabo (60 BC), famous Greek geographer, contemporary of the previous, mentions acts of tremendous cruelty *'that are opposed to our customs'* and relates how the Druids were performing auguries, 'reading' the profound pains of a victim stabbed in the back. They were also fond of human sacrifices, which they were consummating by introducing the victims into an enormous wicker mask to which they were then setting on fire.

"The Druids *'were considering it a duty to cover their altars with the blood of their prisoners and to consult the Deities in the human entrails,'* wrote Tacitus."

The Professor continued a good while, reading to me quotes from various Greek and Latin authors, some praising this or that virtue, others flatly condemning the Druidic wickedness. It was not escaping me that those who "were condemning" the Druids were also pagans, so the aberrations of the former were having to be great, capable of making an impression on men familiarized with all the barbarities of their respective Epochs. The linguistic explanation that I had gone to seek from the Professor's erudition was already satisfied. However, that man was bent on instructing me about the Druids, revealing to me how much he knew about them, and I could not be so discourteous as to refuse to listen to him. Even if his talk repeated themes already amply exposed in the letter from Belicena Villca. After all, to verify that others knew part of those truths, could only instill certainty in me, and reassure me about the mental health of the late female Initiate.

"As I already told you," continued the Professor, "no Celtic source documents exist that can be consulted, except the sagas compiled by D'Arbois de Jubainville in the nineteenth century, very rich in traditional elements of the Celts of 'Iwerzhon' or Ireland. In them we verify the great power of the Druids in favoring the successive Celtic invasions (*Fir Bolg* or Celts of Belgium; *Fir Domnann* and *Fir Gáilióin,* or Gauls, Scots, and Welsh) to Ireland, inhabited until then by the *Fomors,* giant beings and the *Tuatha Dé Danann,* Divine Hyperboreans. On more than one occasion, the Celts defeated the Fomor giants whom they exterminated and also ended up expelling the Tuatha Dé Danann in spite of the magical powers of the latter. The Druids were dominating the forces of nature, as if they had the help of Satan himself. They were producing rains, electrical storms, and fogs; they were raging the seas or calming them; they were causing beautiful women or frightful monsters "to appear" by materialization; etc.

At the time of the invasion of the Welsh, their chief, the Druid Amergin, performs the following ritual: putting his right foot on the land to conquer, he recites:[3]

God [the Druid] speaks and says:	Glosses
I am a wind of the sea,	for depth
I am a wave of the sea,	for weight
I am a sound of the sea,	for horror
I am an ox of seven fights, *or* I am a stage of seven tines,	for strength
I am a griffon on a cliff, *or* I am a hawk on a cliff,	for deftness
I am a tear of the sun,	a 'dewdrop'—for clearness
I am fair among flowers,	
I am a [ruthless] boar,	for valour
I am a salmon in a pool,	'the pools of knowledge'
I am a lake on a plain,	for extent
I am a hill of poetry,	'and knowledge'
I am a battle-waging spear,	
I am a god who forms fire for a head. *or* I am a god who forms smoke from sacred fire for a head.	[i.e. 'gives inspiration'] 'to slay therewith'

And the Druid Amergin then pronounces the following six questions:

1. Who makes clear the ruggedness of the mountains?
   or Who but myself knows the assemblies of the dolmen-house on the mountain of Slieve Mis?

2. Who but myself knows where the sun shall set?

3. Who foretells the ages of the moon?

4. Who brings the cattle from the House of Tethra and segregates them?

5. On whom do the cattle of Tethra smile?
   or For whom but me will the fish of the laughing ocean be making welcome?

6. Who shapes weapons from hill to hill?

---

3. *The White Goddess,* Robert Graves, 1961; Ch. 12, pp. 205–22. Includes all small-print text in this chapter.

Invoke, People of the Sea, invoke the poet, that he may compose a spell for you.
For I, the Druid, who set out letters in Ogham,
I, who part combatants,
I will approach the rath of the Sidhe to seek a cunning poet that together we
may concoct incantations.
I am a wind of the sea.

"Here, Arturo, is the power of the Magic Verb of these Filí Druids *(Filí = Bards):* the forces unleashed with the preceding pantheistic poem allow to win a subsequent battle against the Divine Tuatha Dé Danann, who were possessing flying chariots and death rays but were completely impotent against the black magic of the Druids."

The Professor was vividly explaining with enthusiasm, but I had been thinking about the eighth verse of Amergin where it says:

"I am a ruthless Boar." I could not help but relate it to the legend of the nefarious jewel, *"Victory to the Divine Druid Son of the Boar."* I pointed this out to the Professor.

"I was getting to that, Arturo. The principal symbols of the Druid were two: the boar and the four-leaf clover that they were wearing embroidered on their white tunic. Among the Celts, they were symbolizing, respectively, the power of the Druid and that of the warrior. Some scholars, like René Guénon, intended to equate these two symbols of power with the castes of the Brahmins and the Kshatriyas of India, that is to say, the priests and warriors, considering the profound significance that the boar and the bear have in the Indo-Aryan tradition. But this is an error, since the Druids never formed a caste (nor were there castes among the Celts) and because the meaning given to the boar (a very ancient Hyperborean symbol) by them, was tinged with a materialism that it does not even remotely possess in the Rig Veda, where it appears as the third of the ten manifestations of Vishnu in the present cycle of life or Manvantara. It is as if the Druids had 'inverted' the meaning of the symbol, giving to the boar, the expression of the *Primordial Spiritual Power* proper of the Regal Function, a representation of the *Actualized Temporal Power* that is characteristic of the Priestly Function. There is much to talk about the ancient and, until today, secret Mystery of the boar and the bear, but we would move away from our subject; let us better return to the sagas compiled by Jubainville.

"As is known, the Druids imposed on the Celts the Ogham alphabet of twenty signs, fifteen consonants and five vowels, called **Beith-Luis-Nin,** because of its **B-L-N** first three letters. Well, Dr. Siegnagel: the eminent mythologist Robert Graves sustains that the 'poem' of the Druid Amergin has been distorted in successive profane transcriptions in order to hide its esoteric meaning, but that it was originally related not only to the sacred Beith-Luis-Nin alphabet, but to the Tree Calendar that the Druids were also using. Naturally, so that the Song of Amergin 'coincides' with the sacred alphabet, it is necessary to transpose its verses in this way:

		God [the Druid] speaks and says:	*Trees of the month*	
Dec. 24–Jan. 20	B	I am a stag of seven tines, or an ox of seven fights,	Birch	Beth
Jan. 21–Feb. 17	L	I am a wide flood on a plain,	Rowan	Luis
Feb. 18–Mar. 17	N	I am a wind on the deep waters,	Ash	Nion
Mar. 18–Apr. 14	F	I am a shining tear of the sun,	Alder	Fearn
Apr. 15–May 12	S	I am a hawk on a cliff,	Willow	Saille
May 13–Jun. 9	H	I am fair among flowers,	Hawthorn	Uath
Jun. 10–Jul. 7	D	I am a god who sets the head afire with smoke,	Oak	Duir
Jul. 8–Aug. 4	T	I am a battle-waging spear,	Holly	Tinne
Aug. 5 - Sept. 1	C	I am a salmon in the pool,	Hazel	Coll
Sept. 2–Sept. 29	M	I am a hill of poetry,	Vine	Muin
Sept. 30–Oct. 27	G	I am a ruthless boar,	Ivy	Gort
Oct. 28–Nov. 24	NG	I am a threatening noise of the sea,	Reed	Ngetal
Nov. 25–Dec. 22	R	I am a wave of the sea,	Elder	Ruis
Dec. 23		Who but I knows the secrets of the unhewn dolmen?		

So the text of the first part of Amergin's song may be expanded as follows:

God speaks and says:
 I am the stag of seven tines.
 Over the flooded world
 I am borne by the wind.
 I descend in tears like dew, I lie glittering,
 I fly aloft like a griffon to my nest on the cliff,
 I bloom among the loveliest flowers,
 I am both the oak and the lightning that blasts it.
 I embolden the spearman,
 I teach the councillors their wisdom,
 I inspire the poets,
 I rove the hills like a ravening boar,
 I roar like the winter sea,
 I return again like the receding wave.
 Who but I can unfold the secrets of the unhewn dolmen?

"In his book *The White Goddess,* Robert Graves expounds a synthesis of the significance of each month of the Druid Tree Calendar. About the month of the Ivy, which corresponds to the letter (G) Gort, he says the following:

'G, the ivy month, is also the month of the boar. Set, the Egyptian Sun-god, disguised as a boar, kills Osiris of the ivy, the lover of the Goddess Isis. Apollo the Greek Sun-god, disguised as a boar, kills Adonis, or Tammuz, the Syrian, the lover of the Goddess Aphrodite. Finn Mac Cool, disguised as a boar, kills Diarmuid, the lover of the Irish Goddess Grainne (Greine). An unknown god disguised as a boar kills Ancaeus the Arcadian King, a devotee of Artemis, in his vineyard at Tegea and, according to the Nestorian *Gannat Busami* ("Garden of Delights"), Cretan Zeus was similarly killed. October was the boar-hunting season, as it was also the revelry season of the ivy-wreathed Bassarids. The boar is the beast of death and the "fall" of the year begins in the month of the boar.'

"The function of the Druid is well summarized in the poem 'Prif Gyfarch,' where Taliesin says *I am a Bard, I am a Guide, I am a Judge.'* A Bard was the Druid dedicated to art and music; A Guide was the Vates, a Druid dedicated to science; A Judge was the Druid-deacht (that is, Druid-sorcerer, magician) skilled for his power to influence the Celtic Kings and impose his law. Notice, Arturo, how strange and contradictory it sounds that the legislator of a people is not a racial member of that people and yet is 'voluntarily'(?) accepted by them. For the Druids were not Celts, despite all the attempts to falsify History that have been made in this regard. Perhaps some light can be shed on this, considering the discovery of the Frisian *'Oera Linda'* manuscript. In this document, written in runes, is recounted the ancient history of the Frisian People, which apparently is a remnant of 'Atland,' an Atlantean colony situated in Northern Europe, opposite Great Britain some 5,000 years ago. It is not the legendary Atlantis, mentioned by Plato, which would have existed 12,000 years ago; but like it, Atland also succumbed to a cataclysm."

The Professor opened the hanging folder and after leafing through hundreds of photocopies, among which I recognized "The Dead Sea Scrolls, Facsimile, published by UNESCO," he extracted a folio written in runic language, which was the copy of the *Oera Linda.* With it, was an English translation annotated by Robert Scrutton in 1977, titled *The Other Atlantis.* From this latter text he read, to my curiosity, the following:

"The implications of the *Oera Linda Book* are that some refugees from the stricken and sinking Atland reached the general area of the Low Countries and Denmark, already populated by Atland colonists since around 4000 B.C. at least.

They established themselves there and presently made contact with their other kinsfolk who, as sea-rovers and traders, had maintained communication with the Motherland, and the many Atland-colonised corners of the world.

"After a time, the Frisian descendants wrote down accounts of the Motherland, its people, its history, its religion, its law. As generation succeeded generation, some older records were lost, while others were summarised, new chapters of the history of the people added. It became thus the diary of a people renewed and updated as a sacred trust by the family which held it.

"This summarisation and addition continued through one line of the Atland descendants until the year A.D. 1256 and thus, provided the authenticity of the manuscripts be accepted, gives an unbroken testament of one people's history for just under three-thousand, five-hundred years – *a document unparalleled in human history.*

"Nothing was added after the year 1256 when Hiddo Over de Linda of Friesland recopied all the existing material on to the new cotton-based paper which the Arabs had brought to Spain and which was coming into use throughout Europe.

"This final copying was passed to the care of each further generation of the family until 1848 when an old woman, Aafjie Meylhof (*née* Over de Linden), handed it to her nephew, Cornelius Over de Linden. The latter, who became a master shipwright at the Royal Netherlands Dockyards at the Helder, finally decided to allow a copy of the document to be made by Dr. Eelco Verwijs, librarian at the Provincial Library at Leeuwarden, Friesland.

"Suddenly the record – with all its implications – entered the public domain."

The Professor continued reading Robert Scrutton's commentaries, outlining the perquisites suffered by the *Oera Linda* up to the present day. For, although almost no doubts exist about its authenticity—at least up to the year 1256—many are resistant to accept it as a historical document, since the millenary book, by shedding light on mythological episodes of History, makes bitter enemies.

I was listening, fascinated, as the Professor was implacably continuing:

"Well, let's get down to business. In one of the Frisian manuscripts, which recounts the struggle that the men of Frisia

(White) sustained with the Magyar invaders (Yellow) 2,000 years BC, is the story of Neef Teunis, a Frisian sailor who, leaving Denmark, sails to the Mediterranean with the idea of entering into the service of the Kings of Egypt:

"'In the northernmost part of the Mediterranean,' says the *Oera Linda*, 'there lies an island close to the coast. They now came and asked to buy that, on which a general council was held.*

"'The mother's advice was asked, and she wished to see them at some distance, so she saw no harm in it; but as we afterwards saw what a mistake we had made, we called the island Missellia (Marseilles). Hereafter will be seen what reason we had.*

"'The Golen, as the missionary priests of Sidon were called, had observed that the land there was thinly peopled, and was far from the mother.*

'I clarify, Arturo, that both in the *Oera Linda*, as well as in numerous traditional Nordic sagas, the term 'Mother' is utilized to call, generically, the Priestesses of the Cult of the Fire.

"'In order to make a favourable impression, they had themselves called in our language followers of the truth; but they had better have been called abstainers from the truth, or, in short, "Triuwenden," as our seafaring people afterwards called them. When they were well established, their merchants exchanged their beautiful copper weapons and all sorts of jewels for our iron weapons and hides of wild beasts, which were abundant in our southern countries; but the Golen celebrated all sorts of vile and monstrous festivals, which the inhabitants of the coast promoted with their wanton women and sweet poisonous wine. If any of our people had so conducted himself that his life was in danger, the Golen afforded him a refuge, and sent him to Phonisia, that is, Palmland [Phoenicia]. When he was settled there, they made him write to his family, friends, and connections that the country was so good and the people so happy that no one could form any idea of it. In Britain,'* Atland penal colony, 'there were plenty of men, but few women. When the Golen knew this, they carried off girls everywhere and gave them to the Britons for nothing. So all these girls served their purpose to steal children from Wr-alda in order to give them to false gods.'*

"In the *Oera Linda*, God is called Wr-alda. But this Frisian God is alternatively, in the ancient accounts, sometimes the Demiurge Jehovah Satan, sometimes the Incognizable Hyperborean God. The confusion arises, presumably, because of the fall into exotericism that the Frisians, as well as other surviving peoples of the Atlantean catastrophe, suffer with the passing of the centuries.

"On this part of the *Oera Linda,* Robert Scrutton comments:

"'*Triuwenden* [or *Druviden*] can be seen as the origin of the name, "Druids," while *"Golen"* is another form of "Galli," or the "Gauls of Phoenicia."'

"As you see, friend Arturo, this incredible document sets back, by many centuries, the news about the Druids—who would now be 'those who have no Truth'—making them come from the Middle East, which confirms the presumption that always existed about their non-Celtic origin.

"It now remains to be seen... Are you listening to me Arturo?"

Minutes before, I had been paralyzed, precisely when the Professor was reading the *Oera Linda* and pronounced the word "Golen." The bitter persecutors of the House of Tharsis, whom Belicena Villca was calling "the Golen," were definitively "Druids." That I already knew because it was implicit in the letter; but there the Professor was showing me that it was not constituting any secret, that documents and sufficient information were existing about those accursed Priests. Only my ignorance of History, and of the darkest personages of History, had caused the sensation of strangeness that I experienced when I read the letter and learned the intrigues and plans of the Golen. More than once I was on the verge, and now I was repenting of it, of doubting Belicena's sanity, of denying the fantastic reality of the Golen.

"Yes, Professor, I hear you." I responded, fearful of offending him.

"It now remains to be seen," he patiently repeated, "whether they were really Phoenicians, because, in that Epoch, Sidon was a port city, tremendously cosmopolitan."

I was understanding the question that the Professor was posing, but for the moment I was not interested in delving in that direction, in light of all the details provided by Belicena on the Hebrew origin of the Golen. On the other hand, a different question was struggling to exit my throat: I had to find out what the Professor knew about the Golen's current situation.

"Professor Ramirez, excuse me if I interrupt you, but are there Druids in this Epoch?" I vehemently asked.

The old professor resignedly sighed.

"You ask me a very concrete question and I will try to answer in an identical form; but understand that it is not easy and I will have to set it against other antecedents so that you can judge, by yourself, the validity of my answer: because although there are Celtic societies and authors dedicated to the study of Druidism, they are only historians or dilettantes and not true Filí. You will have to, then, seek the truth elsewhere.

"For several centuries, Druidism seemed eclipsed, specifically (as you said at the beginning of our chat) since the conversion of the Celtic peoples to Christianity. This conversion is very early, since Saint Patrick converts Ireland to Catholicism between the years 432 and 463. The Celtic peoples of Gaul were, in that Epoch, under the dominion of Germanic dynasties, which were embracing, in all cases, Arian Christianity, a doctrine elaborated by the Libyan bishop Arius in 318 and condemned as heretical at the Council of Nicaea of 325. Father Llorca,[4] in his monumental *Manual de Historia Eclesiástica*, says that, according to Arius:

"*There is but one God, eternal and incommunicable. The Word, Christ, is not eternal, but created from nothing* (ἐξ οὐκ ὄντων). *Therefore, a true creature, much more excellent than the others; but not consubstantial with the Father* (ποίημα τοῦ Πατρός). *Consequently, he is not God.*'

"This doctrine was making an attempt against the Catholic 'Mystery' of the Trinity, for which reason it was fiercely combated by the Roman Popes.

"Be that as it may, what is certain is that in the conversion of the Arian nobility to Catholicism, the Celtic people succumbed and had to accept the new dogma, as they had previously accepted Arianism, that is to say, by imposition.

"The Visigothic kingdom of Spain became Catholic overnight at the Third Council of Toledo in 589, with the conversion of King Reccared by Saint Leander. But the Frankish King Clovis, who converted in 496, becoming an instrument of the Church for the missionary conquest, had already taken the definitive step for the Catholicization of Celtic Gaul.

"It could be thought that the Druids—of such rude opposition to the Tuatha Dé Danann Hyperborean Gods in Ireland—would have to organize the defense against the new

---

4. Bernardino Llorca, S.J.

(lunar) faith that was displacing the ancient (solar) Celtiberian cult of the God Belenus (worshiped in Greece also as Apollo) and the Mother Goddess Belisana.

"Well, none of that happened, since the Druids advised the people of the convenience of embracing Christianity and they themselves became Christians. Druid Christians? Wise in the occult laws of material nature; possessors of a secret demonic Science; do you think that they would have converted to Christianity, subjugated by this religion?"

The Professor was intensely gazing at me.

"Just as you put it," I responded, "these conversions remind me of the *Marranos,* that is, those Jews who, forced to choose between becoming Catholics or dying, accepted the former, pretending to practice the new faith for years (or centuries if we consider that there are Marrano families who even today live a double life), but preserving the Jewish rite and customs in secret."

"Good, Dr. Siegnagel!" roared the Professor, "I was precisely referring to that; to a feigned conversion like that of the Marrano Jews. If you consider the question that I was asking you before, when reading you the text from the *Oera Linda* that situates the Druids as natives of Sidon, in Phoenicia, you will understand that there are other suspicious similitudes."

The Professor was never ceasing to astonish me with his acuteness, posing things in such a way that, like in the dialogues of the Greek Sophists, the answers were spontaneously sprouting in the interlocutor of the Philosopher.

"Yes," I affirmed, feigning surprise at the conclusions that I was guessing. "The relationship is undeniable, Professor: Jews and Druids were coming from the Middle East!"

I accompanied the comment, eloquently nodding with my head. This gesture stimulated the Professor to continue and, while in one hand he was briskly waving the book "The Mystery of the Templars," he was saying in a convincing tone:

"The great Celtist Louis Charpentier, author of this book and staunch defender of the Golen and the Templars, confirms it with substantiated research: the Druids took refuge in the Catholic Church. The opportunity is provided by Saint Benedict, a personage of great wisdom and holiness who, by founding the Benedictine Order with a rule (Ora et Labora) that exalts work and prayer, impulses the latter to the salvage of Greek and Roman Culture, threatened with death by the decadence of the Roman Empire, barbarism, and the incredible ignorance of the Popes.

"The point of contact is produced with Saint Columbanus, a File[5] from Ireland entirely dedicated to converting the Celtic peoples to the Catholic religion. Louis Charpentier cannot hide his admiration for the Druidic infiltration, when he says:

"...Saint Benedict had died in 547, seven years after the birth of Saint Columbanus. To Christendom, Saint Benedict kept a classical treasure; to the same Christendom, Saint Columbanus was going to deliver the Celtic treasure.

"Saint Columbanus was a Christian from Ireland. Ireland had come to Christianity very early, and, in all likelihood, had it not been for the more or less brutal impositions of the Roman emperors, and then of the barbarians who were Christian by name, it would have been the same in all the countries of Druidic Celticism. One can well say that the Christians of Rome and the Christians of Clovis have disgusted Gaul with Christianity.

"Ireland knew neither Rome nor the barbarians, and this explains its smooth acceptance of Christianity.

"We do not know much more about the Druids, but their ease in accepting a certain form of Christianity seems to place them, spiritually, very close to it. Nothing offended them in the new revelation, which they were waiting for with the change of era: neither the divine unity, nor the uncreated God encompassing the Universe in all its forms, nor the Divinity in three persons, nor the incarnated God, nor the divine man put onto a cross, nor the resurrection, nor the immortality of the soul which they already taught.

"Was it not Saint Benno who, in his last hour, cried out, 'I see the Trinity, and Peter and Paul, and the Druids, and the saints...'

"The Celtic whole, behind its Druids, rushed toward Christianity." [...] "Ireland, which had escaped the Roman conquest, then the barbarian conquests, remained Christian but, if one can say so, 'druidically.'"

Undoubtedly, Professor Ramirez knew how to support his arguments with the most appropriate texts, I thought with admiration.

"Around these events," the Professor was continuing, "is situated (seventh century) the 'disappearance' of the Druids in their traditional aspect, but sporadic reappearances occur throughout history, especially during the Crusades (eleventh

---

5. Singular of Fili.

to twelfth centuries), in the trials of the Templars (fourteenth century), in the Renaissance (fifteenth and sixteenth centuries), in the affirmation of the so-called currents of the Enlightenment, Freethought, Encyclopedism, and Masonry, (seventeenth and eighteenth centuries).

"As you can see, they always appear linked to the crisis or revolution, but watch out Arturo, only in relation to the Celtic Race. It seems that the presence of the Druid has a single aim: *to be the guide of the Celts,* as Taliesin was singing. Today Celtic means little, but remember that a large part of France and Italy, Portugal, Belgium, Switzerland, Ireland, Scotland, part of Spain and 50% of White America, are Celtic."

At this point in the conversation (or monologue I should say, since the Professor, with his precision, was not giving room for interruptions), I was profoundly impressed. Professor Ramirez knew much more about the subject than I had imagined at the beginning of the conversation. I decided to continue with the game and feign further astonishment. To act with conviction, I would try to bring the dialogue to a concrete level.

"I can perfectly understand the Great World Jewish Conspiracy, Professor, given that the declared objective of Rabbis or simple Hebrews, of all times, is the Domination of the World and the subjugation of Humanity to the Chosen People of Jehovah. *'Celestial Israel,'* says the Talmud, *'has as its destiny of glory to reign over the Gentile peoples.'*

"But what objective do the Druids pursue, perpetuating themselves throughout the centuries to secretly direct the Celts, by means of their accursed Science? Not an imperialistic objective, since the Celts never had an Empire, but they were establishing confederations of tribes or peoples whose decadence began with the 'Campaign of the Gauls' carried out by Julius Caesar. Nor an objective that implied some type of spiritual benefit for the Celts, for, I no longer doubt it, the Filí are impulsed by some perverse end. Why do they do it, my God, why?"

I tried to pose the question to Professor Ramirez as best I could. He remained pensive a long minute and then, with a gesture of discouragement, responded:

"I don't know, Dr. Siegnagel," he was alternately calling me Arturo or Dr. Siegnagel. "I can only conjecture something. But bear in mind this is just a conjecture! In no way would I be able to prove it. I will tell you what I think, but I would never repeat it outside of this office and this moment."

I held my breath for fear that the Professor would keep quiet.

"It is well known that the Jewish financial power began to develop at the end of the Middle Ages, when the goldsmiths in precious metals (almost always Jews), seeing themselves in the obligation to construct security chambers to keep the gold and silver of the feudal Seigniors and Nobles, begin to make loans at interest, using these foreign deposits as collateral. The first step was to issue a document, recognized by all, as a 'payment element,' true paper money that was making it possible to trade without the need to make payments in metal. Of course, this 'discovery' was rapidly adopted and utilized at will by large merchants and moneylenders, in the style of the 'Merchant of Venice' that Shakespeare so brilliantly portrayed. But the secret of their enrichment was undoubtedly in *usury,* the true origin of 'Banking.'

"In the seventeenth century there are already enough Jewish banks in the world to ensure them a good portion of power; the eighteenth century, to give an example, sees the ascension of the 'House of Rothschild,' Jewish family, owner of the Bank of the same name, of disastrous performance until the twentieth century.

"All this is well-known history, but what I mean is that obtaining control of the financial means inevitably leads to a struggle for the control of the State. And at the end of the Middle Ages, when this history begins, *the State is the Catholic Church,* which is why, between the fifteenth and twentieth centuries, the struggle for power was going to pit, on many occasions, the Catholic Church against the Great Jewish Kahal.

"These clashes, sometimes fierce, should have ended with one of the sides, had not something like an invisible hand always intervened in the course of the centuries to reconcile both opponents. Study, Arturo, History and you will clearly see what I tell you; when conflict arises on one side, whether the Church or the Catholic Monarchs or the Inquisition, etc. initiates it against the Jewish Power, or on the other side, whether the Hebrew Conspiracy launches 'the Revolution,' 'Masonry,' 'Marxism,' etc., against the Christian Power, there appears a moderating element, softening the conflict; avoiding the imminent struggle; diluting the tensions. This element, the unconscious executing arm, is the Celt, but behind the Celt is the true instigator: the Golen, the Filí, the Druid, with his incredible power!

"I know you'll think that I'm not in my right mind, Arturo; and I can't prove this fantastic conjecture that I barely dared to formulate!"

The Professor was looking at me, troubled. It was evident that he was fearing to have gone too far and that is why his eyes were trying to pierce my brain. And yet, in spite of his precautions, his hypotheses were falling short in face of the magnitude of the Golen plans indicated by Belicena Villca in her letter: it was true, just as the Professor understood it, that the Golen "were mediating" between the Church and the Synagogue; but it was no less true that They were pursuing a more ambitious objective: the Universal Synarchy and the World Government of the Chosen People. I could not help but smile upon contemplating the Scholar's worried face. That reassured him.

"Through a profound historical analysis," he continued without ceasing to observe me, "many have supposed that a secret link connects the different Vertices of Power in the World and the existence of a super-secret sect that could be Masonry, B'nai B'rith (Jewish Masonry), the Trilateral Commission, etc., or any other organization of that type, to which all men who hold Power would belong, has been affirmed. This hypothesis is too gigantic for me; instead, what I can assure, basing myself on many years of historical investigation, is that between two great Colossuses, the Catholic Church and the Synagogue, an impious occult connection exists to carry out the unconfessable aim of the World Power. And this impious connection is given through the Druids! Here is part of the truth!" the Professor almost shouted, pointing to the drawing of the jewel. "But what is this paper? Nothing, no proof, only a meaningless drawing found by a pupil, but which contains the secret of some forces that move the World."

"I think I notice, from your very significant arguments, that you have affirmatively answered my question," I said, changing the conversation and willing to reveal nothing about the crime of Belicena Villca. "Should I, then, infer that the Druids would exist today?"

"My good Dr. Siegnagel, that question is perhaps destined to be answered by yourself. I have given you enough information and it only remains to assure you that historical investigation, unless another *Oera Linda* appears or the Vatican's Private Library is opened, will yield nothing new about the Druids," he categorically affirmed.

"Why?" I asked, this time with real surprise.

"For a very simple, but inexplicable reason, **Dr. Sieg-na-gel,**" the Professor said with slowness, almost spelling my German surname. "Because between 1939 and 1945 specialist battalions of the Waffen-*SS*, the German elite corps, emptied Europe of the few documents there were on the Druids.

"Why would the *SS* want that information?" I distrustfully asked, for I was not liking the direction that the conversation was taking.

"That was never known with certainty. During those years it was believed that the documentation was taken to the most important *SS* training center, Wewelsburg Castle in Westphalia, where there was a Library specialized in Religion and Occultism of more than 50,000 volumes. But at the end of the war, part of this valuable material and the "Restricted Circle" of the *SS* (some 250 super-trained and super-secret men) evaporated as if by magic.

"You know," the Professor was saying to me with a complicit gaze, "all those stories about hidden refuges, the ODESSA group,... bah, tall tales."

"Yes," I nodded and looked at my watch. It was 20:30. I calculated that we were together five hours and felt shame for abusing the Professor's precious time in that way.

"There is no reason to be sorry, Arturo," the Professor was saying to my excuses, "it has been a pleasant conversation, in which I have recalled with you something of what, in other times, had also concerned me."

On that Summer day, only the night watchman and the cleaning staff were left in the Department. I left in the company of Professor Ramirez and accompanied him to one of the Teaching Houses that he inhabits, within the same University City. And I never saw him again... May the Incognizable guide his Spirit toward the Origin, or may Wothan lead him to Valhalla, or may Frya show him the Naked Truth of Himself, may his heart be cooled forever, may he conquer the Vril and possess the Wisdom that he sought so much during his life! And, above all: may he manage to flee from the vengeance of Bera and Birsha...

Chapter IV

I made the return to my apartment immersed in somber reflections, struggling to prevent discouragement from overcoming me. After the initial enthusiasm, the weight of the reality was heavily bearing down on my spirit and I was posing to myself an unavoidable question: how could I, relying only on my own strength, comply with Belicena Villca's request? It is true that I was feeling myself the owner of an unbreakable will, that I would not give up just like that, in my determination to reach the end, that I would put *all* my *strength*, without reserve, at the disposal of the Cause of the House of Tharsis; but it was also true, and I was humbly recognizing it, that I was not endowed with the virtues of Ulysses. No, I was definitively not the Hero Perseus who, according to Belicena, descended to Hell itself to conquest Wisdom: but not only was I not resembling those mythological Heroes, I was not even remotely approaching any of the Seigniors of Tharsis. They really knew how to resolve all kinds of situations. They had faced, for millennia, an infernal conspiracy, inconceivable to an ordinary human mind, they withstood several attempts of extermination, and they came out victorious from all the trials, they dodged all the dangers, they triumphed over all the enemies. And they succeeded because, in the words of Belicena, their hearts were harder than the Diamond Stone and they were possessing the certainty of the Eternal Spirit; and because they were experiencing an *essential hostility* toward the "Potencies of Matter," which was enabling them to exhibit an indescribable strength in the face of any enemy. They had maintained themselves "on the fringes of History," trying to preserve the inheritance of the Hyperborean Wisdom from the White Atlanteans. They were Initiates who were acting conscious of their spiritual responsibility. They were complying with the "Strategy" of their Gods and the Gods were turning to and guiding them.

I, on the other hand, was incomparably weaker. I was not so clearly distinguishing between the Soul and the Spirit as they, although the reading of the letter came to me as a revelation of the "spiritual Ego," as the undeniable intuition of the truth of the Spirit enchained in matter; but for now it was only a spiritual intuition. Neither did I receive an esoteric tradition, an inherited wisdom, and much less had I the possibility of being Initiated into the true Mystery of the Spirit: I sought, yes, the truth for many years, as I will narrate later, and I even arrived to discover for myself the reality of the Universal Synarchy, but it never occurred to me to fight against such satanic forces, *nor did I ever imagine that to do so was necessary, indispensable, inevitable, a question of Honor.* On the contrary, as the well-known tango expresses, *"I surrendered without fighting":*[6] I let sentimentalism soften my heart, I let the decadent customs of the century impregnate me, I tolerated and lived with the most abominable realities, the same ones into which Western Culture is slowly sinking, without reacting. And I never reacted because I was lacking moral reflexes, I was as if asleep, perhaps because deep down, as now, I was afraid of fighting and reacting, of confronting forces too powerful. Oh, God! They had converted me into a useful idiot, into a stupid pacifist!

But now things would change: if I had to destroy, I would destroy; if I had to kill, I would kill; I would do anything before compromising with the Enemy of the Spirit, described by Belicena Villca. I was just needing help, some type of spiritual help. In summary, I was decided on reaching the end, to wager, as I said, all my strength for the Cause of the House of Tharsis, but I was also a realist, aware of my limitations, and I knew that without help I would not be able to get anywhere. But to whom could I turn for such an assistance? That, for the moment, I could not decide, but is what I would occupy myself with thinking about over the next few hours.

I kept the car in the garage of the Tower in which I was living since a few years ago and climbed up a detestable spiral staircase of reinforced concrete to the elevator lobby. A few minutes later, I was comfortably dressed in my pajamas, ready to meditate on that which was preoccupying me.

"Three rooms is too big for a single man," my parents repeated to me ad nauseam when I acquired it, but now the Apartment was not seeming so, due to the disorderly accumulation of archaeological objects, various publications, and books. In reality, for those books I allocated a small room, which I equipped with shelves on all four walls; but soon the capacity of this library was filled to capacity and the new books were invading the other rooms like unwanted guests.

---

6. From the Argentine tango *Cafetín de Buenos Aires,* with lyrics by Enrique Santos Discépolo and music by Mariano Mores.

The only place more or less arranged with a certain order, was the spacious hall with a set of armchairs, a coffee table, and a reading lamp. Next to my favorite armchair, the window was allowing me to see the slope of a small hill, at the foot of which, imposing and majestic, stands the equestrian statue of General Martín Miguel de Güemes. There I sat down, gripped by a very special sentiment, as will be seen over the course of the story, and there I remained for several hours, until the phenomena took place.

But let us not get ahead of ourselves; it was midnight and I, picking back up the thread of previous thoughts, was obsessively asking myself: I must ask for help, but from whom?

As always occurs when man is faced with situations that overtake him and he cries out for *exterior help*, a moral problem is inevitably posed; it is the age-old confrontation between good and evil. In these cases, the fundamental principle that must prevail in the judgment on "friendship" or "enmity" of the Potencies to which we direct ourselves, is *discernment.*

When the "law" is precise, in events that must be faced juridically for example, discernment is automatic, rational we would say. In the complex legislative web, thousands of laws, qualitatively and hierarchically intertwined, regulate the conduct of man in civilized society. Juridical type "figures" exist who allow to orient the judgment and precisely determine if what a man does is good or bad: it is good if it does not juridically produce demonstrable contradictions, it is bad if it breaks the law.

This is in regard to the conduct of man collectively adjusted to the "law." In the individual sphere, the subject, generally ignorant of the great variety of laws that regulate the Law, conducts himself according to his "moral conscience." This concept alludes to that the fact of being a member of a human society, as much by the cultural transference of generations of ancestors as by education or simply the imitation of one's neighbor, capacitates man in the exercise of a kind of moral conditioned reflex that acts, in the end, as an intuition (moral conscience or "voice of conscience.") But it would not be a true intuition, but the appearance of one, and what would happen would be that a stratum of moral experiences, assimilated by the mentioned means or by any other and reduced to the unconscious level, would automatically act, guiding reason in the discernment of the established oppositions and determining the logic of judgment.

It is understood that the more "automatically" this psychological mechanism is triggered, the more the will to discern is weakened. The taste or the comfort of living in populated environments or cities, speaks about the predominance of these unconscious processes and explains the panicked fear of facing original situations or circumstances where discernment may fail. Hence the fallacy of believing that the city "habitat," the cultural environment par excellence, makes man more "equilibrated," when the truth is that the individual of rural means usually possesses a more accurate moral discernment, not rational, but emanated from the profundities of the Spirit.

The serene judgment of men whom we usually take for ignorant, could come to surprise us. Without the crust of infinite decadent customs crystallized in all the places of the mind, these simple people also experience states of transcendent consciousness, without making too much fuss and, what is good, without making "parapsychological classifications."

For the purpose of comparing both behaviors, let us suppose that they have been made (the citizen and the rural man) to choose between God and the Demon, the latter being the imitation of the former. In all probability, the rationalistic inclination of the citizen, would incapacitate him to discern between essence and Divine appearance. Perhaps neither can the simple mind of the peasant make this distinction; but, by this very simplicity or purity, he will be able to "sense" the presence of God, to have the "certainty" of distinguishing between the truth and the lie.

It may seem very unlikely that anyone be faced with such a dilemma, **but for me that was the question** when considering the necessity of receiving "exterior help." For this help would be, above all things, "spiritual help," and that aid could only come from *"beyond,"* from a World transcendent to matter and man. And here is where I had stopped perplexed in the past: *what* God rules that "other world," *which* is the true Religion of the Spirit, and *who are* its representatives on Earth? *Where is* the Door to God, to the World of God, to the Fatherland of the Spirit?

For many years I searched for the truth of these questions, but never like now was I before an extreme situation in which the necessity of *discerning* became incompatible with ordinary life. For, I was sure, I could no longer advance in my life without finding an answer; I was 36 years old, but I was seeking answers for at least 15. In that search I had transited a sinuous road that did not disdain the intellectual summits of Philosophy and Science, nor the irrational abysses of Religions and Sects.

I was remembering that at the beginning I had been proud of having a "Western" background. Prepared in an environment of crude rationalistic scientism, there were times in which I blindly came to trust that the methodologies of empirical research were the only way to obtain a certain knowledge of the Universe. But years passed, anxieties appeared that could not be reduced by any "methodology" and then I considered the possibility of exploring other routes of knowledge.

I traveled through a thousand philosophical and religious trends in that search; I read hundreds of books and practiced many rites of different Cults. But the same thing was always occurring; while the theories and dogmas, expressed in every imaginable form, were at least worthy of respect, the same could not be said of the organizations that were sustaining such ideas. Unless one was blinded by a fanatical faith, one was ending up discovering "behind" the Orders or Sects—or simply of the "Leaders"—, the subaltern[7] and unconfessable aim; the inadmissible and intolerable link.

These hidden aims, I was discovering with indignation, were obeying three operating modes of the synarchic forces: *a "military" mode, a "political" mode, and a "religious" mode,* without this classification implying any order of importance or appearance. The "Synarchic Secret Societies," I will use this generic name, could behave according to one, two, or all three of the mentioned modes, and firmly tend to the fulfillment of their secret aims. Ultimately, I began to suspect, they were all uniting in a common objective: to obtain the domination of the Planet, to favor the seizing of world Power by a hierarchical group of men. Naturally, I was unaware at the time, until reading Belicena Villca's letter, that the recipients of the universal effort of the Synarchy were the members of the Chosen People. But, here is what I was verifying: the Intelligence Services of any variety and country, the *"military" mode* of the synarchic Secret Societies, occupy themselves with infiltrating

7. secondary

all possible organizations, religious sects or Churches included, even though they do not directly control them, as, for example, it occurs with the Church of Latter-day Saints (*Mor-
mons*), which is skillfully managed by the CIA. International
Marxism, Trotskyism, Zionism, etc., the *"political" modes* of the
Secret Societies, are behind hundreds of innocent organizations that serve as a front for them. And within the *"religious"
modes* are thousands of groups or splinter groups controlled by
the Synagogue, the Protestant Churches, Islam, Buddhism,
and even the Catholic Church. And always the ultimate goal is
to form a spectrum as broad as possible to encompass all ideological variants and to capture all dissidents from the Great
International Lines. *"No one must be left outside of the Synarchy's control"* seems to be the slogan that guides them.

The discovery of this black reality, underlying false promises of elevation and spiritual progress, led me to that state of
"absence of ideal" that I defined in another part of the story.
From then on I continued living more or less normally and
even interested myself in Anthropology, but the reaction to the
deceitful past experiences induced me to systematically distrust the "good faith" of *socially organized institutions*. I came to
feel spontaneous repugnance when making contact, for the
first time, with some association, the declared aim of which—I
was immediately guessing—was veiledly betrayed in favor of
its international hidden tendencies.

I was definitely not trusting in any earthly organization as
an intermediary between a Higher Spiritual Order and the
Material World.

Considering what has been said, the *dilemma* that I was facing at that moment will be better understood: to fulfill Belicena Villca's request, I would have to confront a Secret Society of
Druids, men who were possessing terrible powers as the letter
and Professor Ramirez's statements were indicating, and I
would even run the risk of attracting the attention of the Immortals Bera and Birsha, who would liquidate me in the blink
of an eye. This was not a game! I had to, at that time, seek help
against Them; and that succor could only be spiritual, provided by beings who shared the objective of the mission, that is to
say, by supporters of the Hyperborean Wisdom. But, where
were such beings?

In truth, I was seriously believing that to undertake the mission with a possibility of success, something concrete was

needed, that it was not a question of sitting around praying or wearing oneself out in metaphysical speculations. But, I was repeating to myself, to what organizations could I turn to in seek of help? Masonry, Theosophy, Anthroposophy, Martinism, the Rosicrucians, the Gnostics, and other even more occult Secret Societies, but of the same synarchic ilk, are in essential opposition to the Hyperborean Wisdom, I was now seeing it quite clearly. And so, no matter how much I was thinking and going through the list of all the known organizations, I was always concluding that they were at least suspicious of belonging to the White Brotherhood, the occult super-organization enemy of the House of Tharsis. Oh dilemma! A Secret Society of Hyperborean Initiates was existing in Argentina, an Order of Wise Constructors, as Belicena revealed in her letter, but no one knew where they were or how to reach Them; I would try to find them, but I was fully aware that hundreds, perhaps thousands, of agents of the Synarchy would be waiting for someone to approach to mercilessly execute them. I was doubting whether I would be able to undertake this search alone and that is why I examined the possibility of turning to some "friend" organization of the Hyperborean Wisdom to request help. However, I repeat, no matter how much I was thinking, I was not coming up with the solution: *is it that the Hyperborean Wisdom was not having supporters in this World?* The answer was seeming to be "no"; at least it was not having socially organized followers; or I was unaware of the existence of any such organization.

Chapter V

y only ally,—I was thinking at the beginning of my reflection—is discernment. It will indicate to me where to go, in whom to trust. If there is some related philosophical or religious line, it will allow me to discover it; it will tell me if it is "good or bad" and how to turn to it.

But the analysis effectuated after profound meditation, was yielding a chilling conclusion: as it was eliminating possibilities, all the organizations were left on one side (enemy) and on the other, *no one.*

As much as I was attempting to Manichaeanly polarize the myriad of Religions, Sects, Associations, Secret Societies, Organizations, Groups, Orders, Leagues, Brotherhoods and Fraternities, I was unable to discern even one that displayed a ray of Uncreated Light, a glimmer of the Primordial Truth of the Spirit. However, if all that Belicena Villca was affirming about the Origin of the Uncreated Spirit was true, if the Spirit could only experience hostility toward this World, toward the Judaic Culture that today predominates in this World, the result of my reflections would not be strange. On the contrary, it would be rather logical that the White Brotherhood, being on the verge of realizing the Universal Synarchy as in the thirteenth century, that only *one* organization of Initiates in the Hyperborean Wisdom existed. Yes: in the same way that in the thirteenth century the **Circulus Domini Canis** opposed the plans of the White Brotherhood, perhaps now only existed the **Order of Wise Constructors of the Lord of Absolute Orientation.**

"Then," I was desolately saying to myself, feeling that an anguish, very similar to terror, was rising from my stomach to my throat, "then I must not wait for any concrete help to accomplish my mission. I am left to my own strength!" I was struggling to accept this.

The mission proposed by Belicena was clearly a task that was requiring the performance of a superior man, someone gifted with much more than what I was having at that moment. If I was certain of anything, however, it was that spiritual help would be indispensable to fulfill the mission. But the help, according to my recent conclusions, I should not expect from human organizations: *I could not have intermediaries be-*

tween the spiritual and Myself. It was evident, then, that spiritual help would have to be directly manifested in my interior; that God, or the "Liberating Gods," or my own Spirit, Eternal, Uncreated, Infinite, if they were responding to my request for aid, would have to do so in the depths of my psychic intimacy.

For some time I was feeling a kind of shortness of breath, a tightness in my chest to which I was not giving much importance, since I was attributing it to the torrid February. This presumption soon dissipated, because Salta's nights are usually quite cool, even in summer, and this was no exception. I immediately noticed it when I opened the window: I saw the park tenuously illuminated by the 4 o'clock twilight, while a cold breeze forced me to close the shutter. Standing by the window, strangely suffocated by an unknown anguish, I torpidly thought that in a few more minutes it would be dawn.

A sensation of *cosmic solitude* had overcome me little by little, without noticing it, and at last it managed to penetrate to the depth of my Soul. For an instant I thought that the previous analysis had solipsistically isolated me from the World; or, in other words, that the Manichean polarization to which I subjected human organizations, had unconsciously continued jumping from categories to a confrontation: Myself and the World. This could be due to my instinctive rejection of the material. But it was not so because upon thinking of my friends, my family, the beings that I admire, I immediately intuited the spiritual potency in them. And the well-known sensation of joy that the spiritual inspires in me, made my body vibrate. Yes, I was able to intuit the Spirit in some beings and therefore I was not really alone. The harrowing solitude that I was now feeling—I quickly thought—was not the product of a pathological deviation like that which the egoistic solipsists usually suffer from in their melancholies. This was a totally different sensation. Lacerating and painfully acute, it could be translated into one word: *abandonment.*

I was feeling alone and cosmically abandoned, but in that sensation of abandonment, compenetrated, there was a second sensation, more subtle but less painful: it was like a muted reproach that was vibrating in the depth of my Soul, but at an unimaginable profundity. It was the reproach of a God that was transmitting Himself through a dimensionless space and that was seeming to weep for a loss; a metaphysical amputation of His Substance that was suffered as only He is capable of suffering.

And that loss that God was reproaching, was Myself...

I who was betraying Him, who was committing a condemned and abominable heresy. I was feeling alone and cosmically abandoned, I repeat, but to such an intense degree that for an instant I thought I was dead.

It must be understood that all this very rapidly occurred, perhaps in a few minutes or seconds. And the most probable thing is that I really would have died—I realized this much later—from having let myself be totally won over by that strange animic state.

If it did not occur this way, it was because remotely, on the boundaries of the consciousness that was rapidly abandoning me, I had a certain intuition: that emotion that was killing me was external to my own being!

It was not I who was lamenting and emotively moaning with such a force that it was filling everything; that was crossing my multiple spheres of perception and diffusing itself through the surrounding reality; that was dissolving my consciousness by losing the differentiation between subject and object.

The curious thing was that when becoming conscious of this intuition, everything was all of a sudden cut off, in a silent and brilliant burst in which I believed to fleetingly distinguish a white circle that was surrounding me.

That is to say, not everything was cut off, because now the sensation had *totally* moved *outside of me,* to the concrete World.

I soon felt myself lucid and alert, while all around me, the furniture, the floor, the walls of the Apartment, everything was seeming to radiate a frightful and threatening evilness. It was something tenebrous that was being epidermically induced, *that was being perceived with the whole body, with every organ, with every atom.* The same previous state, but inverted and exacerbated: the profound *cosmic solitude* was now, pure Presence; the abandonment: a muted call, but of an irresistible violence; the reproach of God, which was seeming so Divine when springing from the depths of the Soul, had converted into a bestial roar, obscene and offensive.

It is not possible to express with words what I experienced then; I can only give a pale idea if I say that that Primordial

Force was vaguely similar to the breath of an enormous and malevolent beast.

A fetid and offensive breath that was emerging from all things, which were, in their turn, the viscera, the organs, of that bristly and dangerous Dragon. A breath that was imposing its life-filled Presence; but this Life was to the Spirit, what noise is to music: a vile imitation and miserable copy. A voluptuous breath that was inhaling and exhaling in a crude and animal cadence.

In the silence and calm of the night, this Presence was enhancing itself, vitiating the air with menace; as if, invisible and powerful, a mortal Enemy stalked me, ready to throw himself upon me; to claim my life and more than my life...

I had the impression of having fallen into a foggy precipice from which I was rescued before reaching the bottom. I was now standing on the edge of the Abyss, miraculously safe, but victim to that apprehension that only one who survives disaster experiences. That is why I remained immobile and did not flee from that atmosphere charged with an indescribable evilness, which was seeming to be aggressively directed toward me.

And that immobility, serene and reflective, was seeming to excite the dramatic tension more, elevating it to unbearable levels.

I comprehended at that moment that "what was radiating Matter," whatever you want to call this, was losing its capacity to act on me, because, in the midst of the unbearable tension, it was being perceived as an impotence to consummate the aggression. Upon arriving at this point, it was seeming that everything was going to explode, to fly in pieces through the air...

And it did.

Chapter VI

I would lie if I said that I was not expecting something paranormal.

My eyes were fixed on the objects of the room, expecting to see them jump on me at any moment.

I was waiting for it and in truth I was expecting that anything abnormal occurred, except what actually happened: everything began to move and change position; to fall and jump onto the floor.

Shelves and furniture, everything was incessantly falling and jumping, while I, absorbed, thought I was living a nightmare.

It took me a few precious seconds to realize that I was witnessing a seismic movement, and when I finally decided to make my escape, the tremor was almost over.

Chance? Synchrony? The reader may think what he wants, but he cannot help but consider the fact that the earthquake of January 21, 1980, the only building that was irreversibly damaged was the one that I was inhabiting and that had to be evacuated, as I was able to verify reading the newspapers of those days.

There were no victims, but the building was inexplicably damaged in its structure, so the municipal authorities undertook, without results, an investigation of the architectural firm that constructed it. As there was no insurance, the losses were total for the owners of the Consortium, among those was including me.

Of my belongings, I could save little because, what was strong enough to survive the earthquake, succumbed to the collapse of my ceilings. Among them my car, which, although it could be repaired from the multiple dents, would not be able to leave the garage for several days due to the entrance ramp being obstructed.

I had been ruined overnight like *Job*. But without his famous patience.

I will not deny that, at first, desperation got the better of me; anyone will find it comprehensible situating themselves in my place. After the sinister narrated experience, with the weight of a long sleepless night and the burden of the previous day when I visited Professor Ramirez, I had to be more than strong enough not to give up and go to pieces. But as a few days passed, my Spirit was recovering its usual composure, and things began to resolve themselves. I rented an Apartment in a nearby neighborhood and furnished it with the help of my sister and some friends. The things that were broken and indispensable to replace, I acquired them using my scarce savings.

I was making all these arrangements impulsed by my loved ones, who in their solidarity were concerning themselves with my abstracted and indifferent state of mind. They were thinking—unaware of the strange circumstances in which the earthquake occurred—that the disaster had plunged me into a volitive shock.

Their reasoning was not mistaken because, although I was never too attached to material goods, the loss of four years of work and sacrifices was too painful an ordeal, which on another occasion would have affected me a quite a lot. At that moment, the truth was different: my mind, from the instant that I recovered my serenity, was not ceasing to analyze the lived-through moments. Being absorbed by the memory of that infernal night, it is understood that I appeared to the sight of others as absent and dejected.

Far from being so, I was growing in my interior a voiceless rage, a blind fury that, without clouding me, was rather seeming that it was nourishing me with vital strength and valor. I would not back down! Now, more than ever!

A week after the earthquake occurred, I was prepared and ready to leave for my trip. The delay was not substantially affecting my previous plans and so, with a healthy youthful impatience, I was wanting to be off as soon as possible.

It was Monday again; I was planning to pass through Cerrillos to say goodbye to my parents and, if I was hurrying to leave, I would arrive in time to have breakfast with them.

I loaded a bag and briefcase into the battered Ford, in the end rescued from the rubble, and set off on my adventure.

Chapter VII

o say that I was not the same man seven days ago would be incorrect because, *essentially,* nothing had changed in my interior. However, I was not feeling the same and *I knew* that I would never go back to being who I was before. "Like Dante, I went down to Hell and returned," I was thinking. To live from now on with the memory of the Abyss, logically, *has to be different.*

But it was not just a sinister memory. I was seeking spiritual help and I had received it. It is true that the aid arrived at the same time as the attack from the Potencies of Matter, simultaneously with the earthquake. But that was not detracting from the fact, but was giving it a particular significance, *a meaning that for the moment I was not comprehending,* but that later, during the trip to Santa María, would absorb all my attention. What occurred, in reality? Well, I *had had a Vision: the most marvelous Vision of my existence, which was, at the same time, the sought-after help.*

I will chronologically synthesize it. Apparently, the process really began when I had that intuition of not being Me who *was suffering* and *agonizing,* who was suffering the *pain* of the extinction of life. Then, I said, *"everything moved outside."* In truth, in that instant it was clear to me that *pain* and *suffering,* the agony of life and life itself, *were alien things,* of a non-spiritual nature. That is to say, at that instant, *I had clearly distinguished between the Spirit and the Soul, between my spiritual Ego and my animal nature.* I had comprehended that the Spirit *knows neither pain nor fear, but that it is pure Joy and Valor, pure resolute Honor, pure volitive Force.* And then "to live" or "to die" meant nothing to me because I was already beyond life and death, perhaps beyond, too, good and evil. It was there when the Soul, and the God of the Soul, lost the capacity to act upon my Ego and *dissolved as an Ancient Illusion, was cut off as a Primordial Enchantment: suddenly everything animic and vital, which was likewise everything evil, moved "outside" of my Ego, to my animal body and to the World where the animal body inhabits.* For the first time *I felt Me, only Me; Me, surrounded by the Potencies of Matter; Me, besieged by the Creator God of the Universe.* And then, undoubtedly as a consequence of having sustained a battle against the Soul, and having been victorious, *the Vi-*

sion was produced and I received the sought-after help. And the telluric phenomena happened.

I will not enter into details, which would contribute little to the comprehension of my mystical experience, and would only manage to degrade it. In summary: *the vision was corresponding to a Goddess.* The Apparition came about during an infinitesimal instant, I could not say if it was inside or outside my psychic structure, but the effect was that She *raptured* my Spirit. Yes, to communicate what took place I can do nothing else but conjugate the words *rapture* and *ecstatize* as verbs and affirm that She *raptured* my Spirit, *ecstatized* my Ego and took it *out of the Soul and the World.* She *raptured* me for a second from the body, and from the Earth, and showed Herself before my spiritual Ego in all the magnificence of Her Uncreated Beauty. Because that spiritual rapture was revealing to me the one whom Belicena Villca mentioned so many times in her letter, the Virgin of Agartha, the Charismatic Advocate of the enchained Spirit. And then I comprehended, in the midst of the mystical rapture, that the Raptor[8] of the Spirit imprisoned in Matter was the *necessary* Grace, *after* the Ego of the sleeping man has fought against the Soul and has won: *only by Her intervention, by the action of Her Grace, will the sleeping man manage to maintain that Victory against the Potencies of Matter; only She will give aid to the Ego, charismatically, with the contribution of an extra volitive force that will enable It to sustain Itself independent of the Created Soul.*

It was an instant without beginning or end, because it will always be present in the intimacy of my Spirit, an absolute moment in which, without a doubt, I peeked into Eternity. She kidnapped me and held me that instant in the Uncreated Sphere of Her Own Existence, and infused me with the extra volitive force that my Spirit was needing to undertake the mission of Belicena Villca. How strong and invincible I felt then! And, above all things, I realized how free, absolutely free, the Uncreated Spirit was in its essence, *without Created limits for its Eternal Existence,* that is to say, Infinite! I felt *Me,* Uncreated, Eternal, Infinite, Free, full of Wisdom; I felt *Me,* and I noticed that outside of me had remained the psychic and the animic, the consciousness of the warm life, and the content of the warm life, the external and internal Illusion that were causing

---

8. kidnapper, taker

the spiritual stupor; I suddenly knew, I experienced its evident discovery, which was the *"Great Deception,"* of which dangerous power of enchantment Belicena Villca warned me about.

I felt *Me,* and I knew of the *non-Me-ness* of the Soul, in the rapture of spiritual inspiration that the impression of the Virgin of Agartha was causing me. The Spirit *impressioned* me, and the mark still subsists, Her Radiant Uncreated Beauty, the majesty of Her Power, Her splendid Grace. I saw in Her a Goddess, but there in the realm of rapture, I was also a God. That is why I sensed in Her a *Gottkamerad,* a Comrade, a Sister, a Companion of the Race of the Spirit; only that I had been momentarily raptured from the prison in which I was finding myself and instead She was an absolutely free Hyperborean Spirit. She was approaching me, to offer me the succor of Her Grace, motivated by Honor, which is the essence of the Uncreated Spirit. This was also evident to me, in that infinite instant, and so my own Spirit, moved by Its essential Honor, was striving to *give thanks* to the Goddess in some way, to express that Her Assistance would not be in vain, to assure that my decision would be unshakable. But I did nothing in that sense, for the Goddess marvelously smiled, making me understand that she was comprehending all my thoughts.

The Virgin of Agartha had a bunch of spikes of wheat in Her Left Hand and a grain taken from the same cereal between her index finger and thumb of the Right Hand. At the time of Smiling, She made a gesture with the latter Hand, which at first I did not interpret, and directed it toward me, toward one like the *Eye of Fire* that I was possessing in a determinate part of my Spirit: *then She opened her Divine Fingers and there dropped the magical seed.* And that act put an end to the Vision, brusquely. I felt as if a Frozen Ray, entering *through my head,* had made an impact *on my heart;* immediately the icy sensation began to spread itself through my body and a growing paralysis took hold of me. And I found myself, still standing in the room, stupidly observing how all the things were beginning to jump out of their positions and the building was threatening to collapse. The ecstasy had only lasted an infinitesimal instant, as I said, but then precious seconds passed until I understood what was occurring in the World, *coincidentally, simultaneously,* and I reacted. Then, the earthquake concluded, and I noticed that the oppressive evil that a moment before was emerging from Matter had also disappeared. On the contrary, Matter was appearing *to be subordinate to me.* There was an idea that was floating in the atmosphere, flowing equally from all things, which I perfectly grasped and that I was able to translate more or less as follows: *"Now You are a God and nothing and no one will be able to resist Your Will. What occurred here is a sign of Your terrible Power!"* This concept defines the "new sense" that, just as I mentioned at the beginning, Matter *was* now *seeming* to acquire *because of the effect* of the Vision: *there was, then, the manifest intention of causally connecting the earthquake with my recent spiritual rapture.* But I was not letting myself be deceived. I was intuiting in that idea a trap from the Potencies of Matter, a temptation, which for the moment was not clear but on which, later on, I would stop to reflect with profundity.

Essentially, then, nothing had changed in my interior, but I would never be the same again: only *the relationship of forces* that were maintaining the Spirit and the Soul were disrupted due to the effect of the extra volitive force contributed by the Virgin of Agartha. Upon regaining consciousness of the reality of the World, after seeing the Divine Image, my Ego was capable of dominating the animic nature with singular potency, in a manner never achieved before, after years of yogic practices of concentration and mental control; and I was not willing to lose such power, to have the roles reversed and the Ego be once again subjected to the *desires* of the Soul. But that would not happen, I could assure it, for it was evident that not only the Ego emerged strengthened from the spiritual rapture, but that the Soul was permanently weakened in what was constituting its very essence: the sentiments and emotions, the love of life and the things of life, *the good heart* that I had always manifested and that prevented me more than once from using violence to solve the problems that were hindering my path, all these warm passions and many more, *were* rapidly *cooling,* flickering, and extinguishing like the flame of the candle that has consumed its fuel. Certainly, if I were forced to synthesize the new state of my being, I would say that it was something very similar to a *rebirth:* yes, I am not afraid to affirm it, despite being a Psychiatric Doctor and, moreover, a man of culture. Although it is unacceptable to the official orthodoxy, I could not deny what I was certainly experiencing, and that it had already produced an appreciable transformation in my conduct: it was noticeable to almost all those who knew me, and it is why that they were supposing a post-seismic shock; that I was "suffering" a kind of psychological *regression*. Suddenly I had become "like a child": "I was laughing for any reason" and it was seeming that "nothing was mattering to me anymore," such were the reproaches of my friends and relatives, who were revealing the particular regressive change of my character. But I was also becoming cruel and merciless, I knew this myself but I was not reproaching myself, for, like never before, I was despising my life and life in general. I want to clarify that "like never before" means "like never before as an adult" since, and I professionally knew this, children, like the reborn Me, *were capable of killing without prejudice or remorse.*

Perhaps, during that spiritual rapture, in that infinite instant, I really died and was resurrected at its end, which implies a paradox because what has no end cannot end, an instant that would be eternally present in my Spirit. This being so, the infantile change of character, the strengthened volitive force, the feelings that were dying, the desires that were being extinguished, the heart that was irremediably cooling, the sensation of rebirth, the spiritual certainty of feeling saved, close to the definitive liberation from material bonds, all would be explained supposing that the true spiritual life was continuing in the ambit of the rapture, from which I never left or would leave, that is to say, in the Infinite, and that this apparent life, lived to the "end" of that which cannot end, was, in fact, a form of death, a non-existent but inevitable spiritual illusion. Perhaps, in effect, I was really dead, and because of such condition I was no longer fearing anything living, much less Death. Perhaps everything was the product of that mysterious seed that the Virgin of Agartha dropped in the Eye of Fire of the Spirit. I, still, could not know it. But what was certain, what was concrete, was that I had received the requested spiritual help, that, dead or reborn, I was feeling joyful and valorous, that I was not fearing Death nor fearing to kill, and that I was feeling that, strangely, my Ego *was participating in the actual Infinite:* yes, unmistakably, I was feeling indeterminate on the side of the Ego; all that the Universe was containing, including my own biological life, and the Universe itself, were limited and perishable: this was the finite side of my being, the Illusion; but now I knew with certainty that, in the Ego, an endless abyss was opening up: this was the Infinite side of my being, the Truth.

Perhaps resorting to a metaphor, one can partly understand what I was then experiencing.

Imagine a person accustomed to living in a beautiful solitary forest. The days smoothly go by there, without too many surprises, and, although the struggle for life imposes a permanent alertness, this same persistence makes that the attention is maintained within constant and, in the end, routine levels.

One would say that this man "masters the situation" of his daily life. Nearby, serene and gentle, the lake offers the sporadic pleasure of a refreshing and restorative bath. But the lake is not a safe place to stay for long, like the forest.

Water does not have the firmness of land and, in order to sustain oneself in it, it is necessary to have a certain control, a certain extra attention, a demand that ends up tiring the man. That is why visits to the lake are regulated by the necessity of fishing or the pleasure of bathing. One day this man, by mistake or audacity, generates a circumstance that escapes his control: the fire, which had helped him to live until then, escapes into the forest, furious and destructive. The man remains static or struggles to suffocate it or blasphemes in desperation; any attitude makes no difference; nothing can prevent the catastrophe because the fire has exceeded his control, it has overtaken him. The flames spread everywhere consuming everything and it becomes indispensable to seek salvation; but where to go? Where is safety? Suddenly, like lightning, hope appears: the lake.

An irony; the site where it would never have occurred to him to seek refuge, is now the only one that offers the possibility of surviving the brutal change of the everyday world, which dissipates, consumed by the voracious and murderous bonfire.

He runs; the desperate man runs toward the saving lake. Behind him, a fiery and relentless monster seems to closely pursue him, gnashing its teeth, roaring and spewing suffocating puffs.

But it is not possible to turn to look, he would not have another opportunity. The only thing left to gain is the lake, which never seemed to be as far away as it is now. Finally, paradisiacal vision, indescribable joy, mystical apparition, the lake emerges on the horizon.

Fantastically calm, it is, for those who flee death by millimeters, an oasis of peace. The man throws himself into the protective waters and swims many strokes, intuitively **toward the** *center.* He can only turn around, momentarily, when he is safe in the cool waters, and can thus gaze toward his, until a short time ago, also safe World.

Considering the analogies that this metaphor offers with the events that I have above narrated, you will be able to understand what my spiritual state was. Like the man in the example, upon seeing the forest burning and transforming, disappearing at times amidst the smoke, that which were constituting his World and his security, so I also saw my trusted and daily reality dissolve in a fire of unmistakable evilness.

Like the man in the metaphor who was strangely secure in the waters of the lake, fickle and unknown until yesterday, I too was now secure and firm in the, until yesterday, unfamiliar waters of the Spirit.

The man in the forest, as he was safely floating, was watching the world wasting away and was thinking, *"I have been born again."* I, too, was feeling reborn in the confines of the Soul and only by this inexpressible sentiment could it be said that I was another man, although I *essentially* remained the same.

Chapter VIII

I was heading, then, to my parents' house, imbued with that mystical optimism that only those who know themselves reborn experience. Having made the decision to leave, I was only thinking of the *phenomena* of the fateful night of January 21, trying to interpret their transcendent meaning. In a few minutes I would arrive in Cerrillos, but then, these thoughts would accompany me for many hours of the journey that I would undertake.

Thirty minutes later, I was driving the car down the two hundred meters of the driveway in the company of my faithful dog Canuto.

My parents, who were in the middle of breakfast, were happy to see me and were expressing it between greetings and laughter.

They were trying to erase, with their affection, the memory of the lived disaster. I was interiorly thankful for these compliments, for I was needing to acquire reserves of peace and tranquility, in anticipation of future misfortunes. I knew that an hour later, when leaving, my mind would be concentrated on analyzing all the details of the complicated imbroglio[9] in which I was involved.

"You have a beautiful day to travel," Papa was saying while attacking an appetizing-looking grilled sausage. "Drive carefully, son, remember that in the morning the truckers are half asleep."

"Don't worry Papa; I'll go slowly and in three hours I'll be in Tucumán," I affirmed without much conviction.

Katalina, my sister, handed me the sausage and eggs, the steaming rolls and the coffee. I was astonished to find that my mouth was watering with hunger, and it dawned on me that I had been eating poorly for several days. Feeling hungry is, if there is something to satisfy it, always a sign of good health. I thought no more and gave myself over, decidedly, to consume the breakfast.

The Finca has a large dining room with a large window oriented to the east, facing the driveway, but in the mornings we were having breakfast in the kitchen. This is located behind

---

9. A difficult or complex situation.

the dining room, occupying the southern wall that has a large fixed window of four meters long with a rustic wooden table next to it. The stove and the adjoining fireplace occupy the whole West wall of the kitchen.

Sitting in front of the window overlooking the vineyards, I was having breakfast in the company of my family and was reliving the nostalgia of many similar dawns. But a black cloud was troubling my spirit; one, like a secret voice, was warning me that perhaps this was the last breakfast eaten in that pleasant manner. And then I was struggling to chase away such gloomy forebodings, fiercely chewing the grilled sausage...

"See you soon, Arturo," my father said goodbye, "I'm going to ride through the irrigation canals."

"Ciao, Papa," I accompanied him to the back door and stood watching him as he was moving away toward the stables in search of his old horse. Minutes later I was seeing him trot away down the road that runs from east to west, parallel to the main irrigation ditch. I should have left but I was purposely delaying because I was wanting to speak to Mama alone.

She was still in the kitchen and a nod was all it took for her to solicitously come over to me. This attitude would not normally have caught her attention, but when I put a hand on her shoulder and began to speak, a gesture of surprise was painted on her face.

"Dearest Mamacita," I flatteringly said to her, "you should forgive me if what I am going to ask you causes you any pain..."

"Son, you know that what I have is yours..." she realized that I was not asking for anything material and her face was now frankly alarmed, "What can I do for you, Arturo?"

"Calm down Mama, you know I wouldn't cause you any worry if I didn't think it absolutely necessary."

"Stop beating around the bush and tell me what the hell you want," said my mother, who was beginning to lose her temper.

"In what year was I born, Mama?" I asked, cutting to the chase.

"You know it well, in '44. January 30, 1944. You are now 36."

"Well, Mama, listen attentively. We never talked about it, but I want to tell you that I remember one night, more than thirty years ago; I was three or four years old and something, a noise, I don't know what, woke me up. It was late, Katalina was sleeping in the adjacent bed, and through the window I was seeing the moon hanging in the west. I think that I heard voices because I got up without getting dressed and went down the hallway stairs, debating between the sleep that was closing my eyes and the curiosity that was opening them.

"There was Papa, you, and someone I had never seen before; a tall man with a keen eye. I still remember his penetrating gaze today and his height, taller than that of Papa, who is 1.80 meters. It was he who discovered me on the stairs and burst into that thunderous guffaw, before your anguished eyes. Anyway, what I retained in my memory is not much more. I seem to be in his arms and I believe to remember that he was giving me something shiny that completely attracted my attention. Then you put me back to bed and the following day the stranger was no longer there, nor did I ever see his gift again."

Mama had gone pale. We stopped by the garden set and I made a mute indication that we sit ourselves under the oak tree.

"As the years went by," I continued, "I used to remember that night, but without giving it much importance. Only once, I was about nine or ten years old, I dared to ask Papa and his reaction was very strange: he suffered a great obfuscation and forbade me to speak of it again, but a few minutes later he changed and tried convincing me that I was remembering a dream, a bad dream, that I had had as a child.

"So I never mentioned the matter again. Until today." Mama sighed and shook her head as if waking up from a nightmare.

"Why Arturo, why thirty-two years later, do you still remember that night?" she was asking more to herself than to me. "Why do you insist on reviving a fleeting memory that means nothing to you?"

"Mother, I repeat that I do not wish to cause you pain; hold on, I still haven't told you what I want to know," I said in a reassuring voice. "Tell me only two things: if that man was from our family and if he had to do with the war."

Here I used a firm tone that convinced Mama of the uselessness of refusing to respond.

"Look, Arturo, you are a grown man and you are not unaware of how atrocious the war was. In the years following 1945, tempers were high and many people had to live on the run. But now it is different; much time has passed... It is not in anyone's interest to dig that up...!" there was a plea in Mama's voice.

"Mama, you don't answer my questions and that's wrong. Don't you trust me?"

"......" Just a mute gaze for an answer.

"You must tell me what you know because it's very important for me, for my future, do you understand?" I firmly assured her.

It was evident that she was not understanding and I decided to be more convincing.

"I am going through a terrible spiritual crisis, Mama. Fate has put me in front of a diabolical crossroads, where an error of choice means going astray on the wrong path, full of obstacles and real dangers. Your answers would help me not to fail; believe me, Mama." I took her hands in mine in a desperate effort to instill confidence in her.

"I don't understand anything you're saying, but I sense that you're really worried, son. I'll tell you what you want to know, and God forgive me if I'm wrong in doing so," she took a deep breath and continued, "Kurt; he was the one who came that night in 1947. My brother Kurt, who was presumed dead or missing in Berlin in 1945, was in reality fulfilling a mission in Italy when the war ended. He stayed two years hidden in a Franciscan Monastery in Southern Italy, until, in 1947, he was able to come to Argentina, thanks to an assistance network for war fugitives that was functioning, supported by the government of President Perón."

"But, Mama," I interrupted, "why didn't he go back to Egypt, to the family hacienda? The Egyptian government was very protective of the Germans, especially after the founding of the State of Israel in 1948."

"It is a mystery. He never wanted to say, not even the reason for his persecution, since he was only 30 years old," Mama was naively reasoning, "and he almost always had diplomatic positions."

"But what was he during the war?" I asked, intrigued, "civilian or military?"

"Military; Officer of the *Waffen-SS*. Major or something like that. You should bear in mind that in 1938 I married your father and came to Argentina, losing contact with him for many years.

"By '32 Kurt was already a Squad Leader, that is to say, *Fähn-leinführer,* of the Hitler Youth or *Hitlerjugend,* in the German community in Egypt. Thanks to the efforts of Papa, who due to his noble title was enjoying a certain influence in Germany, in 1938 he left to study at one of the *Napola* schools, *Nationalpolitische Lehranstalt,* in Berlin. After that I only saw him on three occasions, the last one before leaving for Argentina, at Christmas 1937; then 10 years would pass until, in 1947, he appeared here. During that time I did not hear much from him, for I was receiving letters at the rate of one per year and never directly, since Kurt was writing to Egypt and from there Papa was sending them here.

"So I know almost nothing about his career; only what little that he could tell me in correspondence from his student years and less during the war, in which he was very sparing. I know that at the Napola school he excelled in his knowledge of Middle Eastern languages and this earned him to take several special courses, but I don't specifically know what they were consisting in.

"I remember that in his early years he was happy, because he had been permitted to enter a division of the Napola school called, if I am not mistaken, *Flieger-HJ,* where air training was being given; but I repeat, little is what I knew of him after his graduation in 1937. He joined some special division of the ⚡⚡, but, as far as I am aware, he never fought. His function was somewhat linked to the External Service, since he spent most of the war in Asia. And that is all. In 1945 he was officially presumed dead, as his destination, it was said, was Berlin in the month of April, when this city fell into the hands of the Russians. His cadaver was 'found' in a charred plane that couldn't take off due to receiving a Russian artillery shot.

"We were notified," Mama continued, "of his death and we mourned him a lot until 1947 when, surprisingly, he made himself present here. The rest I have already told you; he was helped by the Kameraden and with a new identity he was preparing to start 'another life' in Argentina. As he said on that occasion, it was preferable to disappear forever, since if the Allies were suspecting of his existence, they wouldn't take long to look for him. I think it's a decision we should respect, don't you agree?" She was looking at me hopeful in that my "curiosity" was satisfied. I decided to continue questioning before she reacted.

"Yes, Mama, I understand and I thank you for all you've told me, but the principal thing is missing. Where is Uncle Kurt now?" I shot it out of my mouth and it seemed that the question would provoke her fainting spell.

"Arturo, my son, you're an adult and intelligent, why do you ask what prudence advises not to know? He's well; no one has bothered him in all these years and it would be desirable that no one does so before his approaching death." Something crossed her mind and she stared at me open-mouthed. "You're not thinking of going to see him? Oh no!"

"You have to get that idea out of your head. He's lived 35 years at the same site and all know him in his new personality. It would be a stupidity to put such coverage in danger on a whim."

She had guessed my intention and responded in consequence; I realized that it would be difficult to get the address of my resurrected Uncle Kurt out of her.

"You don't understand, Mama; it's not a whim; it's important that I speak with him to obtain information that it's possible he possesses and that for me is as vital as the air that I breathe. You shouldn't worry about safety. How can a once-in-a-lifetime visit from a stranger affect him? There are a thousand justifications for welcoming a visitor who will then never come back. Because that's what I'll do, Mama, I swear it! Once I've asked him what I wish to know I'll leave and never return." I was trying to convince her with any argument and she, hesitating, was gazing toward the vineyards as if seeking my father's protection.

"Come on, Mamacita, tell me where he is. I have the right to see Uncle Kurt once in my life."

Finally she decided, although showing great contrariety, and while she was speaking, far from rejoicing at my persuasion, I was inwardly cursing the pain that I had caused her and the anguish that this confidence would undoubtedly produce in her; at least until the return from my trip.

"He is near here, in the Province of Catamarca. I have never gone to visit him, since he expressly forbade me to do so, although he gave me the address in case of an emergency."

I gave her a card and the fountain pen, making sure that my mother had memorized the data.

"In these 35 years you haven't seen him again or written to him?" I incredulously asked.

She smiled while giving me back the card and the fountain pen.

"Yes, silly. We have seen him with your father a few times, in Salta and once in Buenos Aires, for some vacations. But we never write to him. He writes to us a couple of times a year, to a PO box that your father has in Cerrillos, and he lets us know when he'll go to Salta, an occasion that we take advantage of to get together for a few hours. I have seen him less than twenty times over the years."

It was hard for me to believe that two siblings separated by only 350 kilometers could not visit each other because of events that no one remembers, occurred forty years ago, and thousands of miles away. Nevertheless, I was justifying my mother's fears and realizing the effort that she must have made to give in to my request and entrust to me her secret.

Suddenly, I remembered Papa and trembled in anticipation, calculating the wrath that would overtake him upon learning of my impertinence. Mama would not hide from him my inconsiderate claims and he would be furious. Embarrassment would cover me and I might have to promise not to go to Catamarca. I decided to avoid any discussion and immediately leave.

I kissed Mama on the forehead and headed to the car. She must not have noticed my haste because before I could start the engine she shouted at me:

"Hold on, Arturo; wait a few minutes and I'll give you something."

She entered into the house and in spite of my impatience, I had to wait for ten long minutes. At last she returned with an envelope in her hand.

"I wrote a few lines for Kurt. You're so quick to think that he knows you. He saw you for five minutes when you were a little boy. How do you think he'll remember you?"

She handed me the envelope that I gratefully received as, I was admitting, it would be of great help to identify me.

"Open your right hand and put your palm face up," Mama said between a mysterious and complicit air.

I did what she was asking me and she opened her left fist, which had been clenched the whole time. Something fell into my hand that at first I could not distinguish. It was a shiny object and I was listening in amazement while I was examining it:

"This is what Kurt gave you the night of 1947. I took it while you were sleeping out of fear that you would lose it playing and I kept it in my jewelry box. With the passing of the years it became complicated to give it to you, because you would have demanded explanations that we could not have given you. At that moment he wanted to give you a gift, but he hadn't brought anything because he didn't know he had a nephew. He was remaining single and when he saw you, he was moved and said that, not having children, it would be you, his only nephew, who should keep it."

I was astonished looking at the Iron Cross with Swastika and Oak Leaves that I was holding in my hands and I was asking myself how an Officer who never fought could obtain the highest decoration that Germany was giving to reward acts of heroism and valor.

"See you soon, Mother," I waved through the car window. "Don't worry, I'll be careful. Say hello again to Papa and Katalina. Ciao. Ciao."

I started up and a few minutes later I was on the road.

Chapter IX

I stopped at the Cerrillos Service Station to fill up with gas and took the opportunity to again look at the card with Uncle Kurt's address. It was incredible that he was so close and in good condition, a relative whom I had thought passed away 35 years ago. I read it again:

Sr. Cerino Sanguedolce
Calle Fray Mamerto Esquiú 95
Santa María - Provincia de Catamarca

"Señor?" the attendant interrupted me.

"Fill the tank with special gasoline, please; Ah! Check the oil..." I said.

My brusque departure did not allow Mama to give sufficient information about Uncle Kurt. Now the questions were beginning to arise because I did not know if he had married, if he had children and grandchildren, what he was doing for a living...

"Bah," I thought. I must concentrate on the journey and have faith. I'll know everything in a few hours.

"Thirty liters of gasoline and two of oil, Señor."

"Here, take it." I held out a bill. "Do you have a road map of Catamarca Province?"

"Yes, Señor."

He went to the booth and rapidly returned bringing a colorful fold-out map with profuse tourist information.

"There are a thousand more."

I paid him and started the engine in order to remove the car from the pump, but I parked twenty meters ahead and started to examine the map.

Going to Santa María from Salta is no problem at all but, on the contrary, it has the advantage of including one of the most beautiful tourist circuits of Northwest Argentina. It is the journey from Salta to Cafayate "the beautiful," as they popularly call this city, famous throughout the world for its exquisite wines, situated in the heart of the Calchaquí valleys.

With a recently asphalted road, Ruta Nacional 68, which facilitates the trip and makes it possible to enjoy the unique landscapes of its multicolored ridges, these two hundred kilometers can be rapidly covered. The inconveniences only appear when leaving Cafayate, upon crossing the Ravine "of the Shells"[10] and abandoning the Province of Salta. Then one penetrates into the Province of Tucumán, but only for about 40 kilometers, since there it presents a small wedge, which is embedded in the Province of Catamarca. After covering this short distance, Catamarca is accessed at a point 80 kilometers away from Santa María.

When crossing the mentioned ravine, fording it because there is no bridge, the traveler has the impression of having entered into another world.

Outside the artificial physiognomy of civilized features that the valley presents in Salta, here one is really in an autochthonous environment. The roads are dirt, neglected as one moves toward the south, and towns with adobe houses inhabited by mestizo criollos, closer to Indian than to white, abound.

Poverty makes itself evident upon entering Catamarca, a province unjustly forgotten by the rest of the country and abandoned by its own children who, year after year, undertake the inevitable exodus, who seek to overcome misery and materially progress.

The beauty of the landscape does not decrease in Catamarca, on the contrary, it becomes rugged and primitive, providing excellent visual attractions to the sinuous road, which advances bordering the Sierras de Quilmes. This name comes from the Quilmes Indians, one of the tribes of the Fierce Diaguita Race, those who at the end of the Calchaquí Wars, which lasted 35 years in the seventeenth century, were taken, in number of 300 families, to the exiled location of Buenos Aires and gave rise to the population of the same name.

Between the Quilmes and the Cajón Sierras to the west and the Calchaquí and Nevados del Aconquija Peaks to the east, the fertile Yocavil Valley opens up, longitudinally flowed through by the Santa María River, seat of the city of Santa María de la Candelaria.

I knew Santa María for having gone on a study trip to several archaeological sites in the Yocavil and Calchaquí valleys to investigate the Diaguita Culture and I was not disliking repeating the trip. Naturally, going into the region of Valleys and Ravines was making it difficult for me to cross to Tafí del Valle, in Tucumán, in the middle of the Western Forests and sepa-

---

10. *Quebrada de las Conchas* or *Shell's Ravine*

rated from Catamarca by the inhospitable Calchaquí and Nevados del Aconquija Peaks. But, fortunately, from Santa María exists a road that goes up to the north, up to Amaicha del Valle: from there one could take Route 307, which crosses the Calchaquí Peaks through the Paso del Infiernillo and directly leads to Tafí del Valle. In total, from Santa María to Tafí del Valle, one would only have to travel 80 kilometers, but that would be exhausting due to the state of the Routes and the sinuous heights at which one was reaching.

I was going at more than 100 km/h, taking advantage of the good road to Cafayate to gain time, since later the pace would be slow, at no more than 40 km/h.

I had a few hours to think and I decided to immediately take advantage of them.

The landscape, the fresh wind, the silence of the Valley, everything was contributing so that I felt lax and tranquil, predisposed to meditate. But this attitude was quite abnormal if one takes into account the amount of things that had happened to me lately. The lack of preoccupation was evidencing of a great change in my interior, which was also manifesting itself in a sensation of detachment from the things of the World. I was feeling at peace because I was not needing anything. I was materially ruined, perhaps in danger of death, and this revelation was only bringing me an insensate smile.

Yes, I had changed a lot. And all that change took place between January 7, the date on which I experienced the spiritual rapture and thought I was dying, and the earthquake that wiped out my assets synchronistically took place.

So many things had happened to me! And it was seeming that it would not end, because unusual things were still happening to me. Like the matter of Uncle Kurt.

It was undoubtedly an intuition. When I was finishing the meeting with Professor Ramirez and the sage mentioned that almost all the documents about the Druids had been looted in Europe by the ⚡⚡, I thought to myself, "Who should I ask about the Black Order and their interest in the Druids?" At that moment the memory of that night in my childhood came to my mind. No logical relationship that allows to associate both things. Nothing rational. If I had thought about it a minute I would have surely rejected this supposition as absurd. But recent events were making me distrust "reason" and lo and behold, giving in to a hunch, I asked my mother what had occurred that night 33 years earlier. And there was the key! Inexplicably, irrationally, there was a relationship; because I wanted to know about the ⚡⚡ and my Uncle, of whose existence I did not know, had been a German military man. And of the ⚡⚡!

I renounced looking for an explanation and concentrated on the night of January 21, when the narrated phenomena occurred. From then on, as I already said, I was feeling reborn, and if I was thinking about it, it was only with the purpose of analyzing the way in which two events of different order, one, my mystical experience, the other, the telluric movement, were linked. Because for me there were no doubts that a non-causal, synchronistic relationship was existing between both phenomena. That I was in a case similar to that of the assassination of Belicena, when the assassin, in an act of demented pride, leaves irrefutable evidence of a terrible Power.

On January 21, Matter, agitated toward me, synchronically explodes in an earthquake of singular violence with a mystical experience in which both events are hallucinatingly confused, giving the sensation of being causally linked. If I believed it so, I would feel tempted to think that my own psyche unleashed the "seismic phenomena" and that would be my Spirit's moral defeat.

This is precisely what Someone, the Author of the earthquake, was wanting that I believed so as to, in this way, get me lost. And this colossal trap is another demonstration of infernal pride and arrogance.

The temptation to "master phenomena" is one of the primary errors into which fall those who seek to make their way on the path of the Spirit. The only phenomena that really matter for spiritual elevation are those that personally and qualitatively occur, non-transferable and non-communicable. Concrete phenomena, of collective perception, bear the seal of the quantitative and material; it is doubtful, moreover, that they can be produced by an act of will.

About this, non-specialized people are victims of intentionally confusing information. But I, as a Psychiatrist, was familiarized with all kinds of phenomenic acts derived from psychological pathologies or hysterical crises. In Neuropsychiatric Hospitals the manifestation of phenomena of this type is common, but obviously little publicized. It can be observed, in certain cases, parapsychological phenomena occurred in relation to one or several patients. These phenomena, very attractive to the layman, do not have an adequate scientific basis and that fact is the principal reason for their concealment. They are usually of very distinct typology: elevation of an object in space without an evident force that sustains it *(levitation)*, movement of objects *(telekinesis)*, increase of the brightness of the objects in the patient's cell or change in the tone of colors *(chromatization)*, appearance of unknown objects or disappearance of others *(contribution of matter)*, etc.

Needless to say that all these phenomena are susceptible to collective verification when they present themselves, but completely irreproducible under study or laboratory conditions. This is principally because those "responsible" for such phenomena are out of their minds and are generally unconscious of the alterations that they produce.

What makes such phenomena incomprehensible are their apparent contradiction to natural laws, but it is usually accepted in academic and scientific circles that a better "comprehension of nature" (that is: a greater progress of Science) will bring, justly, the solution to these questions. It is then trusted that "Science" will give the solutions to the contradictions of "Science," a proposition that is logically inconsistent and sounds ridiculous to say the least.

The crux of the matter is in that phenomena such as the mentioned telekinesis present flaws to the law of causality. This law states that "to every effect (phenomenon) corresponds a cause that originates it." In telekinesis, for example, the object moves as if a "force of action at a distance" (of the gravitational or magnetic type) acted, without, until today, the action of any force having been proven. That is to say, it moves as if a force acted, but no force acts. It is then said that "the law of causality fails" because the effect has no cause that originates it and, consequently, the existence of the effect (phenomenon) is negated, so as to "save" the law of causality.

It would be more accurate to accept that the link (the law) that unites the cause (the patient) and the effect (the moved object) is unknown.

In Analytical Psychology, developed by C. G. Jung, a very attractive theory has been tested to overcome these difficulties and those that arise from the common case of men who, being culturally, geographically and temporally separated, without any verifiable link between them, have identical or analogous ideas. A "Principle of Synchrony" unknown to Science, due to their incorrect understanding of Time, would act here.

It is worth remembering, in this respect, what C. G. Jung says in *The Secret of the Golden Flower:*

"Some years ago, the then president of the British Anthropological Society asked me how I could explain the fact that so highly intellectual a people as the Chinese had produced no science. I replied that this must really be an 'optical illusion,' because the Chinese did have a science whose 'standard work' was the *I Ching,* but that the principle of this science, like so much else in China, was altogether different from our scientific principle.

"The science of the *I Ching* is not based on the causality principle, but on a principle (hitherto unnamed because not met with among us) which I have tentatively called the synchronistic principle. My occupation with the psychology of unconscious processes long ago necessitated my looking about for another principle of explanation, because the causality principle seemed to me inadequate to explain certain remarkable phenomena of the psychology of the unconscious. Thus I found that there are psychic parallelisms which cannot be related to each other causally, but which must be connected through another sequence of events. This connection seemed to me to be essentially provided in the fact of the relative simultaneity, therefore the expression 'synchronistic.' It seems indeed, as though time, far from being an abstraction, is a concrete continuum which contains qualities or basic conditions manifesting themselves simultaneously in various places in a way not to be explained by causal parallelisms, as, for example, in cases of the coincident appearance of identical thoughts, symbols, or psychic conditions. Another example would be the simultaneity of Chinese and European periods of style, a fact pointed out by Wilhelm."

This was the thought of the prestigious psychiatrist C. G. Jung on the theme that I was occupying myself with. With his concepts, the appearance of two identical phenomena (an idea common to two persons), separated by space, will depend on a collective Archetype (cause) and the simultaneity *(synchrony)* of the phenomenic events.

To interpret the principle of synchrony, it is necessary to keep in mind a key concept of Analytical Psychology: that of the "Collective Unconscious." This concept enables a more realistic handling of the Archetypes, which are no longer static beings like Plato's Ideas, but dynamic entities of powerful animic force, the support and sustenance of the Myths that unconsciously influence man's conduct.

The concept of Collective Unconscious has been summarized by Jung in the same work cited above:

"...just as the human body shows a common anatomy over and above all racial differences, so too, does the psyche possess a common substratum. I have called the latter the collective unconscious. As a common human heritage it transcends all differences of culture and consciousness and does not consist merely of contents capable of becoming conscious, but of latent dispositions toward identical reactions. Thus the fact of the collective unconscious is simply the psychic expression of identity of brain-structure irrespective of all racial differences. By its means can be explained the analogy, going even as far as identity between various myth-themes and symbols, and the possibility of human understanding in general."

In light of the above, an important conclusion should now be drawn: although Analytical Psychology permits interpreting synchronistic phenomena, no one has ever seriously affirmed that *it was possible to exercise any form of control over them.* This class of phenomena, very showy or attractive to the layman, correspond to the lowest on a scale of valuation of the transcendent experience. As they always present themselves in relation to highly disturbed persons, whether or not they are in the madhouse.

In general, people tend to believe that the disciplining of organic or psychic functions grants a certain type of Power over the mentioned phenomena. This belief quenches its thirst from two sources: ignorance (naïve) and disinformation (a product of the Synarchic Strategy). There is ignorance in the popular belief that the "miracles" that usually accompany the activities of Saints and Great Mystics are performed thanks to a "Power" that these would have or that would have been granted to them by a Deity. In truth the "Saints" have never said such a thing, instead stating that the miracles are "made by God" or admitting, as a maximum concession, to have been vehicles of a "Grace" or of a superior "Force" that was transcending them.

Naturally, members of the Synarchy exist, also considered "Saints," "Mystics," "Gurus," "Masters," etc., who have affirmed *the search for Power as the aim of the practice of certain disciplines, such as "transcendental meditation," "yogas," "prayers or mantrams," etc.* But it is possible to immediately suspect the true occult ends that such satanic agents pursue. On the contrary, the Hyperborean Initiates, who *are really "Saints"*—now I was able to distinguish them well, after reading the letter of Belicena Villca—have always *oriented* their disciples so that they free themselves from the bonds that their Uncreated Spirit maintains with Created Matter.

Disinformation obeys a synarchic purpose and, those who are victims of it blindly believe that "Esoteric Schools" exist where a "secret" teaching is imparted that ends up transforming the neophyte—after a few *lessons in installments*—into a Western version of Krishnamurti. But, what the disinformation presents as Esoteric Schools, are in reality "Exoteric Schools," the unconfessed aim of which is the recruitment of followers.

All these Exoteric Schools claim to possess the secret of the Great Mysteries of Antiquity that they offer to "reveal" to the unwary, if the latter conform to an *internal rule* that invariably demands, as a *first test,* "blind obedience" and "faith" in the *Unknown Masters* of the school. The teaching that they are presenting to the Guru candidate, cannot be more mysterious since its base is the plagiarism of different Ancient Traditions eclectically assembled in a supposed "Occult Doctrine" (which is only so, because of the impossibility of "uncovering" any Truth in it). The Great Mysteries of Antiquity (Persia, India, Greece, etc.) have left a sediment of Myths and Sacred Symbols—more often opposing than coinciding—which only a mediocre and ill-intentioned Soul (a Rogue, come on!) would attempt to unite into a modern syncretism.

It will be noted that, during that trip to Santa María, a sentiment of fierce cultural criticism had been installed in my heart and was threatening to break up and definitively amputate the last remnants of rationalism that I was still possessing. I was feeling empty inside, but I was ready to accept a Truth that substituted all the "useless encyclopedic information" that I had assimilated in so many years of study. What value was that pompous academic knowledge having if it was not serving me to face and solve the mysterious situations that I have narrated, situations that were metaphysically involving me? None. I was, then, ready to get rid of that burden to receive the longed-for Truth. A Truth that was consisting, and I had never before been so sure of the reality of a thing as of this statement, *in the Hyperborean Wisdom.* In effect: for me, now, *the Truth was the Hyperborean Wisdom,* the scope of which I was barely catching a glimpse of in Belicena Villca's letter.

At times a dull rage was invading me, which was at the same time a personal reproach, a kind of reclamation that my present Ego, strangely transmuted, was relentlessly making to Dr. Arturo Siegnagel of the years of search, to my past Ego, who so naively had believed that *progress* was a *logical* consequence of *education.* At one time I had accepted, almost without thinking, that a law of *evolution* was enabling the Soul to expand from certain patterns of life. I was believing that "following determinate rules of moral rectitude" and facing life with a positive outlook would inevitably result in an interior *good.* "Yes. That was the key to progress. I would live according to a 'transcendental philosophy,' I would adopt a religious 'way of life,' in the manner of the Orientals, and, in the course of my search, of the instruction, of the asceticism, *progress* would inevitably come about through *'evolution.'*" That had been my choice and now, upon realizing that all my reasoning was wrong, that I had gained nothing after so many years of discipline and useless sacrifices, I was feeling how rage was invading me and how, also, an impotent reproach was wrenching desolate moans from me.

And that all my reasoning was mistaken was clearly evident from Belicena Villca's letter. The law of evolution was existing and ruling, and facilitating, the *progress* of the created Soul, and of every created entity, according to the Plan of the Creator God. But such law had nothing to do, and no "progress" would be obtained by its intervention, with the Uncreated Spirit. I was remembering with horror the words of the Immortal Birsha: *"the Soul of the man of mud, created after the Beginning, began to evolve toward the Final Perfection."* Apparently, that evolution "was very slow" and the Traitorous Gods, to accelerate it, performed the prodigious and infernal "feat" of enchaining the Uncreated Spirit to the animal-man or "man of mud": the whole Hyperborean Race, which was Uncreated, which came from "outside the created Universe," from the same World from where the Creator came, was then bound to the *evolution* of the animal-man and to *evolution* in general, to the *progress in the immanent Time of the World.* According to the Hyperborean Wisdom, the Spirit had to liberate itself from enchainment to evolutive matter, to isolate itself from the law of evolution, and to undertake the Return to the Origin. *There was the sought-after Truth.* Certainly, my Spirit was being agitated by the effect of a certain intuition: *that Truth, capable of shining for the Spirit with an Uncreated and inextinguishable Light, would have to be conquered in a struggle of superhuman dimensions, during which it would be necessary to exhibit an unshakable determination.*

That there was an Enemy, against whom such a fight had to be waged, an Enemy that "was cutting off the path toward the Origin," that I certainly knew since the night of January 21. But the preceding reflections, and the intuition I have mentioned, was enabling me to now realize that my past errors were stemming from my *strategic weakness,* from having naively yielded to the enemy Strategy. And this Strategy, which undoubtedly affects *all* planes of human activity, and even the most unknown psychic spheres, is applied in the field of Culture by means of a Control System of colossal characteristics. According to Belicena Villca: "Culture is a strategic weapon of the Synarchy." Said Control System is in charge of fomenting confusion and deception, and was, therefore, responsible for the trap into which I had fallen. Because if I was deceived, if I participated in the enemy Strategy, it occurred because of ignorance or "strategic weakness," because I did not know the nature, and even the very existence, of the Enemy: I could never have consciously collaborated with synarchic plans, I could never have been bought by the White Brotherhood, just as the spiritual integrity of the heroic Nimrod was tempted. In synthesis, if I had yielded, in past times, to the deceptive pressure of the enemy Strategy, it was because I was then asleep, spiritually asleep. But now I had awakened, thanks to Belicena Villca's letter and the spiritual rapture of January 21, and the proof was, justly, in the unwavering determination to fight to the end, against everyone and everything, to return to the Origin and free my Eternal Spirit from its material prison. Yes, I had awakened thanks to Belicena Villca, but now I was able to formulate my own conclusions about the way of acting of the Enemy, who had the capacity of a Demiurge at its depths. The Synarchy, the expression of His Power among men, was forming a formidable array of organizations and Secret Societies impossible to completely detect; and in the midst of this offensive deployment I was finding myself, until yesterday, ignorant of those realities; an easy victim for the enemy Strategy. Because, although the totality of the Demonic Plan was escaping me, as is natural, I was quite clearly seeing the tactics applied to the field of Culture. The "modern syncretisms," that I was previously mentioning, obey that will of deception that the Synarchy demonstrates in all its Secret Societies. And the idea of *evolutive progress* of the Soul, through "Karma," the "upright life," or any similar way of atonement, is presented from the *base* of Esoteric Secret doctrines, or mere religious Syncretisms, as a truth so evident that only a fool would dare to doubt it. Outside of religion, the same idea has invaded the majority of "scientific" or "humanistic" disciplines. It is instructive, for example, to see with what ability the synarch agents have imposed geometrical concepts to induce teleological interpretations of History: with an admirable rationalistic rigor, they arbitrarily define a *geometric trajectory* for the *progress of Humanity* and then *project* this figure on History, establishing associations, analogies, and coincidences, most of the time tendentious and intentional. Progress can thus follow a *circular* ($r2 = x2 + y2$), *parabolic* ($y = x2$), *spiral* ($\rho = \alpha\theta$), *in cycles* ($y = \sin x$), *uniform* ($y = x$), *exponential* ($y = e^x$), etc., trajectory, procuring to force History so that it adjusts and corresponds to the form of such functions, "confirming," in that way, the official theory or dogma of the synarchic sect.

The utilization of Analytic Geometry in the religious interpretation of History should not be surprising: some notorious synarchs affirm that *"God geometrizes"*; others sustain *"God is the Great Architect of the Universe"*; but, in general, they all sustain that the intention of the One God is that man, and Matter, the World, Everything, *evolves*. This is one of the keys to the rationalism underlying the mentioned "Occult Doctrines." Because *to evolve* means to develop in History according to a certain *law*. *"It is the law of evolution that imprints a geometric trajectory on human progress,"* the Synarchy postulates. But, being so, what is the esoteric benefit that the Synarchy obtains by *culturally* imposing evolutionism, even esoteric, in any of its geometric variants? Very simple: if everyone believes that man evolves, that Society evolves, that the Universe evolves, that progress responds to a law, they will accept, without question, that *the future is determined by the law of evolution*. This implies that, for the sake of a *better future*, certain controls can be exerted on the present. That is to say: *"let those who know the law, control Society today, in order to have a better future tomorrow."* Vain utopia; who knows the law but the Masters of Wisdom of the White Brotherhood, besides the Elders of Zion?

Now everything becomes clear; the aim of the Synarchy is the Control of the World and, naturally, it prepares its leading cadres with a well-assembled infrastructure of indoctrination, while humanity, conveniently misinformed, awaits the "Men of Destiny" who control the levers of power and "plan" for the future. This is the reality that palpitates behind an Exoteric School and that the unwary, fanaticized and dazzled by syncretism as showy as it is hollow and rationalistic, cannot notice.

On the other hand, it should be noted that syncretisms are concretized when men have lost the capacity to perceive the Myth in all its symbolic purity. This loss is a serious injury to the capacity for metaphysical thinking and metaphysical perception, analogous, if you will, to a loss of vision or blindness. By analogy, the Dark Age or Age of Darkness is spoken of: losing vision, not seeing, is the same as "seeing" all black.

There are texts on Occult Doctrine that seem to have a sound philosophical and scientific foundation: but there are also forgeries of Leonardo Da Vinci's paintings, so perfect that they resist the examination of prestigious experts. And it is logical, in both cases, the quality of the fraud depends on the skill of the forger. In the esoteric case, disgracefully, forgers have reached a high degree of dexterity: there are those very well "prepared" for their mission, owners of a great "General Culture." Let us take, for example, "esoteric" writings of "wise" and "learned" authors such as H. P. Blavatsky, Rudolf Steiner, René Guénon, Max Heindel, etc., and let us compare the farrago of theosophism that sustains any of them with the elementary simplicity of the metaphysical symbols of the Ancient Wisdom; what emerges in this comparison? That we cannot read a symbol (see its truth) and we can read a book about the symbol, which will not reveal to us the meaning of it, but will entertain ourselves with multiple descriptions and associations, susceptible to rational interpretation, which will create for us the illusion of a comprehension and progress, such as suits the Synarchy.

"There is a sensorial and a gnoseological color blindness," once wrote the great epistemologist Luciano Allende Lezama. One

can add that "there is also a semiotic color blindness": it is that which suffer those who cannot see the truth of a symbol and that must be previously healed before the search for an "Occult Knowledge." To not be deceived. To not be used by the Synarchy.

Without a clear vision of the symbolic and an adequate moral discernment, it is impossible to access the knowledge of the Hyperborean Wisdom, which, on the other hand, is not in the Exoteric Schools. The lack of these virtues, or, the contempt for them, leads the color-blind-adept to search for "phenomena" and Power, to follow "Oriental" disciplines without comprehending them or to yield to the fascination of "scientistic research" in parapsychology (Kirlian Kamera, psycho-bioenergetics, and other lies).

The danger is that these "Occult" Schools (with Legal Status, Business Name, and telephone number) do not hesitate in promising, to people of doubtful spiritual capacity, but useful to their plans, all types of Powers and "liberating experiences." Of course: progress will come "later," after a few "Initiations," "progressing" in the "internal degrees."

"*A beggar is not helped,*" C. G. Jung says, "*by our giving him outright more or less generous alms, although he may desire it. He is much better helped if we show him the way to free himself permanently of his need by work. Unfortunately, the spiritual beggars of our time are all too inclined to accept the alms of the East in specie, that is, to appropriate unthinkingly the spiritual possessions of the East and to imitate its way blindly.*"

All these reasonings were leading me to a conclusion: In the one who seeks parapsychological phenomenic Power—*thaumaturgy*—there is always an ignorant or misinformed person. In the one who promises to grant it, there can only be a perverse will. Hence, I had decided to consider, as a "synchronistic coincidence," any possible relation between the spiritual rapture of January 21 and the simultaneous earthquake. Belicena Villca and all her ancestors of the House of Tharsis, and the Liberating Gods, and every spiritual Being who observed my conduct, could be at ease in Valhalla! For me, the end of the mystical vision was marking the end of the transcendent experience: *neither was I having a Power that operated on Matter, nor was I wishing to have one. The Powers of Matter had not succeeded in deceiving me this time and, possibly, would never be able to again.*

I was making these reflections as the kilometers were quickly passing by and Salta in its valleys and ravines were generously opening up. *"Between areas of colorful and erect peaks, the slopes follow one another with lush vegetation and are framed by rocks of rugged appearance, some famous like that of the Obispo, a truly striking mountainside for its development and variety of motifs,"* I read on the map that I had acquired in Cerrillos. I was already close to Cafayate, where I was planning to have lunch and acquire some gifts, especially the exquisite wine of the area. When making impromptu trips, like that which I was undertaking, through Provinces or regions of extreme poverty, it is always a good idea to bring edible gifts. A liter of good Torrontés[11] or some alfajores[12] can open impossible doors, control borders, and overcome all kinds of difficulties.

I entered Cafayate and after doing some shopping at a regional store, I parked in front of Plaza Libertad to have lunch at a restaurant that was promising from a chalkboard "Today's Special: Empanadas and Spicy Chicken."

---

11. Argentine wine from white grapes.

12. Argentine sandwich-like cookie with a sweet filling.

Chapter X

t 14:30 hours I was back on the road, going around Shells' Ravine and ready to embark on the second part of the trip to Santa María.

The ground was loose because it was apparently not raining for some time and the wind was sufficiently strong enough to make this journey very slow.

Two hours later I had only traveled 70 kilometers and I was about to cross through the middle of the town of Colalao del Valle, since the road was continuing along the main street. This town is located in the province of Tucumán, halfway across the geographical wedge that a bad drawing of boundaries bequeathed to the current map. It is about twenty blocks long and four or five blocks wide. While crossing it, I was observing the same syndrome that manifests itself in a thousand villages and hamlets of Northern Argentina: decadence.

Poverty is endemic in these, paradoxically, rich Provinces, forgotten by the bureaucratic centralism of the Buenos Aires Megapolis and by the idleness or impotence of local governments that usually have their hands tied by a non-existent federalism beyond their official speeches.

Poverty is a malady that hurts. But it hits harder to see decadence, that is: to contemplate that which yesterday was a splendid example, today transformed into a reprehensible vision.

While the automobile was rolling along the dirt road, I was looking at the Spanish style colonial houses, which today are shadows of what they were in the past days of splendor. Cruel caricatures of the hope and faith of their builders.

"Those who built these houses," I was compunctively[13] thinking, "believed in Argentina, they had faith in America."

The inexorable collapse of them is the conclusive answer to these delusions.

It could be seen that this town, like so many others, evolved to a height that must be situated at 50 or more years ago, and then came a period of decadence during which not a wall was raised, not even a brick was laid. Windows closed years ago,

---

13. Conscientious or sensitive to wrongdoing.

when the wooden frames rotted; walls peeling and leprous; fronts gnawed by a thousand inclemencies of time and Soul.

The decadence of an urban community, of its architecture, is a setback that unfailingly implants itself in the Soul of the inhabitants. And there they were, watching me pass by with that absent air, with that contemplative indifference so characteristic of Indigenous America.

Because decadence was starkly visible in them; in those children on foot who were spying on me from behind a corner; in those dark, slanted eyes that were candidly looking at me when offering to sell me a corn tortilla but who were becoming distrustful at the slightest question. What difference has this village, these houses, these settlers, these children, with their equivalents in other parts of America; in Bolivia, Peru, Ecuador, or Colombia? None.

In that answer was also decadence; in that, paying the high price of isolating ourselves from Latin America, one hundred years of "European Culture" have not left a trace in these Criollos, forgotten by all. We have given them nothing different from what they have received in the above-mentioned countries. They are neither more nor less civilized than them in spite of the belief to the contrary that sustains the Europeanizing Oligarchy that runs this country for a hundred years.

That is why one explanation for the general decadence that plagues the settlements of American blood, can be this: in five hundred years the European Culture did not take root in the Soul of the American because, neither those who implanted it with blood and fire, nor those who beatifically taught it, were really believing in it. Their millenary Culture, dynamized by the action of Great Myths, was replaced by the materialistic European Culture, devoid of spirituality and transcendence. And the religion of America, which was preserving the memory of the White Gods, was forbidden in favor of the *rationalist* Doctrine of Catholicism: thenceforth the natives would have to glorify the biblical history of the Chosen People, worship a crucified Hebrew-God that they had never heard of, and they would be left out of the theological discussion because their new religion was already completed, finished in its philosophical foundation. If there, in the unknown Nicaea, a Council had decided that God was threefold, what could the recently submitted pagans say here? And those who were here, did they know what the Catholic Dogma was signifying? No, they were killing and plundering *in the name* of the Catholic Dogma that no one was comprehending nor would anyone bother to explain. But the wealth would run out. The time would finally come to create new wealth, to produce cultural objects for those evangelized empires. And then, at that very moment, decadence would begin. The Church would prosper with the conquest of America, systematically destroying every vestige of the Atlantean origin of the great civilizations, every proof of the extraterrestrial nature of the Spirit of man. And the Spaniard, crazed just like the Great Mother Binah prophesied to Quiblon, would evenly spill blood and semen over the native peoples. From that Holocaust of Water would come "the Sons of Horror," the mestizo population of America, men like those whom I was now seeing when passing through their decadent settlements. Culturally indifferent men, who are determined to do nothing. If a gringo does not come with faith in something, and raise houses and villages again, they will not do it. And everything will fall, to the ground, to pieces, "puerile but effective vengeance," as their Cultures fell yesterday and as the Soul of the West will fall tomorrow if it insists on continuing divorced from the blood of America.

When passing by Fuerte Quemado, I could not help but remember that Diego de Rojas camped at that site four centuries before, when he was marching in pursuit of Lito of Tharsis. He had not been able to locate the Pukara of Tharsy, despite going deep into Tafí del Valle for months. But, would I make it? I was believing that, yes; that the indications of Belicena Villca were very precise and that I would be able to reach the Chacra; and that I would meet the Indian Segundo, the unusual descendant from the People of the Moon. And my optimism had not abandoned me upon arriving to Santa María.

When crossing the bridge over the Río Santa María, I glanced at the clock: half past seven in the evening. It had taken me five hours from Cafayate and it was already getting dark. Despite my impatience to arrive at Uncle Kurt's house as soon as possible, I had decided to wait for night in order to comply with my promises to Mama with regard to prudence and safety.

I stopped the car in front of another house of regional articles to acquire the famous products of the area: paprika, syrup, raisins, and wine. After I had paid for my purchase, I amused myself by asking the salesman about Fray Mamerto Esquiú Street. So I learned that it was going from east to west, going to its end in the Santa María River, which is one of the peripheral limits of the city and runs from north to south.

"Number 95," I was thinking, "must be near the river, perhaps on the last block."

"Are you looking for someone on Esquiú Street? I might be able to help you," the salesman surprised me with his question. Ah, small-town curiosity! But I was not impressed.

"Yes, I'm looking for a poncho saleswoman," I lied. In Salta they gave me the approximate address because they were not remembering it with exactitude.

"A poncho seller on Esquiú Street? Uhm... No, lamentably I don't know any poncho seller who lives on Esquiú Street... But, tell me, what kind of ponchos do you seek? Because I have a good assortment. And at a good price..."

A while later I was leaving with my original purchase plus a white Catamarca poncho with an Incan fringe.

I chose to dine at a second-rate restaurant that, according to the regional product salesman, was preparing the best rabbit stew in the Yocavil Valley. As soon as I sat down at a secluded table, I realized the appropriateness of my choice, for this was a place frequented by vendors and traveling salesmen in which the presence of an outsider was not surprising to anyone.

I was savoring my dessert, dulce de cayote[14] with nuts, when a boy in rags offered to polish my boots.

"There is an age," I thought with dismay, "childhood, which all animals in nature use to play and frolic, protected by their parents and other adult members of the population. Human beings, on the other hand, cannot guarantee to their children the joy of living the most beautiful age as it should be lived: enjoying fantasy."

On principle, I detest that children work for profit and my first impulse was to push that shoeshiner away; but an idea occurred to me at that instant and I extended my right foot in mute acceptance. He was a little boy of about seven years of age and of indubitable Indian ancestry. He began washing and covering my boots with shoe polish, and then, by means of

---

14. A traditional dessert of Northern Argentina, made from a gourd or pumpkin.

vigorous massages with a band of linen, trying to obtain the longed-for shine.

"What's your name?" I asked, seeking to gain his confidence.

"Antonio Huanca, Señor," he hastily responded.

"Tell me Antonio, do you live far from here?"

He raised his little disheveled head and looked at me with a questioning gesture in his eyes. At last he shrugged his shoulders and pointing to an undefined place said:

"Phew, very far away Señor, over there, on the other side of the river."

I decided that my question had been unfortunate. I should try again, but this time I would be more direct:

"Do you know Esquiú Street?"

He remained pensive a moment, but his little face immediately lit up:

"Yes, Señor; it's the one at the end of town. If you go straight down this one," he was pointing to the street of the restaurant, "you will find it when the pavement ends. Right where the pavement ends is Esquiú Street, yes Señor."

He was talking without stopping polishing and at that pace he would soon finish. I bent down a little in order to speak without raising my voice and I said to him:

"I'm going to see Cerino Sanguedolce, do you know him?"

He started laughing while he was licking his lips.

"The candy man? Who doesn't know Don Cerino, Señor?"

He stretched his little head and said to me in a tone of confidence:

"Don't tell him anything, but my little brothers and I always try to steal jars of candy from him," the boy was drooling, "there's no one in Santa María who makes them richer. Hee, hee, hee."

He was laughing like a sparrow and was, celebrating his mischief, finally a child.

Uncle Kurt is a "candy man," I marveled to myself. It occurred to me at that moment that I would be a fool for having not foreseen it, but that idea made no sense and I discarded it.

The boy had finished his work and I had sufficient information to locate Uncle Kurt. I generously paid him and he moved away to other tables to offer his services.

A wall clock, hung under a small frame with a collection of arrowheads, was reading 21:00 hours. I paid the cost of dinner and left.

The night was cool but the sky was covered with clouds and not a breath of wind was blowing. The car pulled out and I set off, following the shoeshiner's instructions.

As I was approaching Esquiú Street, the houses were spreading out and diminishing in quality, until at last I found myself in a miserable looking slum, where not only the pavement was ending but the street lights were also almost nonexistent.

I turned down Esquiú Street toward where instinct was indicating to me that the river should be, and I vainly searched for a sign, a reference point that would allow me to calculate the numbering.

Inwardly cursing the idea of visiting Uncle Kurt at night, I quickly realized that I was driving through a neighborhood made up of small properties of four or five hectares each.

In the Argentine Northwest, the properties all obey the same construction pattern: a rectangle of land properly fenced and a Sala (house of the owner or caretaker) built at a short distance from the entry gate. Variations or additions may exist, but this is the general "type," which I knew well, since our own property in Cerrillos was adapted to the same scheme. I then knew the inutility of calling from the entrance, given that the house is usually far from it and I unconsciously accepted the fact that I was going to have to enter into one of the small properties to give notice of my arrival.

The automobile was running for about five minutes along the gloomy Esquiú street that was now giving the unmistakable sensation of a steep slope. The river must be close by, but although the powerful four-quartz high beam was piercing the darkness, I could not distinguish anything beyond twenty meters. I stopped the car and set the hand brake; it would be better to conduct an exploration on foot.

I took from the glove compartment a pen-type flashlight, the meager light of which is rarely useful, and got out, taking the precaution of locking the car in case that I moved away from my spot. A moment later I was realizing the opportuneness of the decision to stop the car because, fifty meters ahead, the street was abruptly narrowing and falling into a steep ravine over the Santa María River that was running below, at a distance of one hundred or one hundred and fifty meters. Had I continued advancing with the car, I would have found it difficult to turn around and back up.

I was, at last, at the beginning of Esquiú Street, not very far from Uncle Kurt's home.

This presumption gave me new encouragement to try to orient myself; something that, I was seeing, was quite difficult.

Esquiú Street had lost its sidewalks several blocks back and, where I was now, was just an alley of coarse gravel that was extending from one wire fence to the other, the limits of unknown properties. To the east was the river, so if this was the last block, the presumed abode of Uncle Kurt, the address I sought must be on one of the two sides of the street, just a few paces from there.

I explored the north hand that was comprised of a row of three strands of wire, up to a height of one and a half meters, but lined all along its extension by ligustrum shrubs, very dense and perfectly pruned in the shape of a pillar. I traveled about one hundred and fifty meters without finding any gate or palisade, so I deduced that I was at the back of a property.

Trying to calm the displeasure that I was feeling for so unusual a situation, I crossed to the southern hand and resumed the search. This property was more restricted because I soon discovered a thick mesh of diamond-shaped wires, which was revealing the tangle of the usual ligustrum.

The night was becoming impenetrable, reducing the help of the small flashlight, and so my pace was slow and hesitant, as I was inspecting, inch by inch, that gloomy stretch of Esquiú Street. When I was losing hope of finding an entrance on that wall, a miracle took place: an enormous gate of pipe and wire mesh emerged from the darkness almost at the end of the street, about ten meters from the ravine. I oriented the flashlight beam inside but, just as I was guessing, I did not see any construction but a path, formed by two parallel tracks, which was lost in the darkness. To the left was a carefully tended plantation of vines, small and laden with clusters; to the right an infinite number of seedlings of a plentiful vegetable garden.

I checked the gate again, but did not find any bell or knocker; instead I discovered two steel rings, one on the gate and another on the concrete frame, threaded by a heavy iron padlock.

Discouraged, I leaned against the gate, trying to make a decision. The most reasonable thing would be to leave and return in the daytime, but the supposition that there were farmhands or perhaps relatives of Uncle Kurt, to whom my presence would be very strange, was holding me back. There was still the possibility of persisting in the nocturnal search, entering the property in spite of the padlock; provided that it was really my Uncle's home...

I was remaining undecided, hugging the mesh of the gate, sharpening my sight in the direction to the entrance path, when I fleetingly seemed to see the glimmer of a light. It was only a second, but sufficient to revive the hope of obtaining some result that night.

I imagined that the Sala must be quite far away, which is why no light was reaching the gate, intercepted, perhaps, by trees or other obstacles. I thought no more of it and climbed up the mesh adjacent to the gate. Except for the setback of which a portion of my "Safari" sack got caught on the barbed wires that were crowning the mesh frame, I could enter without problems. A few seconds later, I was easily moving along the interior path, following the marked vehicle tracks with my flashlight. I was walking about a hundred meters, when the trail brusquely bent to the right and went into a group of leafy trees. As soon as I took this curve, I sighted, about thirty or forty meters away, an alpine-type house, two stories high, with a half-timbered tile roof, the color of which was contrasting with the white of the walls and the black bars on the windows and balconies. Against the darkness of the night, it was ghostly resting without, seemingly, any lights on.

This vision and silence, only broken by the buzzing of the *giant cicadas,* contributed to demoralize me. I stopped an instant and contemplated the immense mass of the house, shielded by the branches of some giant willows that were swaying to the rhythm of a gentle breeze. I had an inexplicable desire to run and abandon that unreal scene, but I soon pulled myself together and advanced with great strides with the intention of knocking on the door to request the presence of Uncle Kurt or Cerino Sanguedolce.

It was then that I heard it.

I was a few meters from the house when I felt a *familiar sound* coming from behind me, to the right... It was an acute whine. A very special lament that only those who have had experience in dog breeding can immediately recognize. For this whine is the expression of the desire to attack that the dog manifests, when the master prevents him from doing so.

I was remembering that Mama had brought a small cat to the property and, in order to prevent Canuto from attacking it, she decided to make him sniff it while she was scolding him with loud voices and was forbidding him to touch it. Then Canuto was trembling, torn between the instinct to kill and the obedience that he was owing to his masters, and was letting out deceptive whines that were not expressing pain but the restrained desire to attack.

This type of whine was that which had sounded behind my back. "Dogs!" I thought in alarm, "How did I not notice the lack of dogs? God, what an imbecile! Every rural property has dogs. But... why weren't they barking? Why hadn't they barked?"

I slowly turned around. What I saw induced in me a sudden terror, paralyzing me in the spot where I was standing. Two pairs of green eyes were flashing in the shadows a few paces from me. They were animal eyes, perhaps of dogs; but I believe the panic produced in me the awareness of two things; one, the abnormal size of those beasts, and the other, also their abnormal caution. Because it was inconceivable that I had been able to transit so far through the property without the animals emitting even a bark and that instead they silently followed me, almost crawling, until situating themselves so close to me that I could touch them with the tip of my foot.

One of the beasts whined again, with the evident desire to jump on me. At the moment in which I was assailing myself with the certainty that their master must not be far away, a modulated whistle sound of doubtless human origin sounded. I did not manage to turn around this time because the beasts, upon hearing the whistle, acted as if moved by a spring and with a great leap threw themselves upon their prey.

Despite being almost paralyzed with fright, the instinct of preservation and several years of *Karate*, put me on guard. But only to find that those beasts were possessing a particular training since, instead of biting and going for the neck as combat dogs do, they were seeming to know exactly what to do: each one went for an arm and sunk its teeth into it. I felt lacerated flesh and saw that the beasts were closing their jaws with no intention of letting go. The impact of the attack made me stagger as both dogs were seeming to weigh more than my 90 kg; a second later I was falling backwards while I was feeling the bone of my left arm crunch in the mouth of the gigantic canine. I thought, as I was falling, of various tactics to get away from the dogs: I would roll over, kick their testicles, bite...

"Crack" sounded the blow to my skull and everything went dark.

FOURTH BOOK

"The History of Kurt von Sübermann"

Chapter I

hey were rushing, the turbulent waters were rushing and dragging me along without me being able to avoid it. Nearby, enveloped in a roar of noise and foam, the waterfall was absorbing torrents of water like a titanic thirsty throat. I was approaching the roaring abyss, I was seeing the edge, I was trying to uselessly swim but the water was dragging me. At the end I was falling headlong into the torrent. It was the end. I would plunge to the bottom, against sharp rocks. I had to open my eyes. I had to open my eyes...

Making a supreme effort, I opened my eyes, which were instantly hurt by a terrible glare. I was blinking trying to accustom my sight to the sun, while I was realizing that I was lying down in an unknown room. I was staring as if hypnotized at the window, adorned with white curtains, while little by little the mist in which my consciousness was enveloped was dissipating.

The first thing that I took in was the intense pain in my head, plus a kind of pressure on my scalp and forehead. I attempted to bring my hands to my head and a new pain shot through my nervous system. I could hardly move my arms, which were, both of them, bandaged up to the elbow. The left was the most affected and sensitive, for a small movement was seeming as an ordeal; the right, equally painful, was appearing to be in better condition. With the latter, I found that a bandage was covering my entire skull up to my forehead. The movement was very painful, I reflexively realized upon regaining consciousness. Despite its fleetingness, it was enough to alert the person who was seated to the right of the bed, at such an angle that it at first prevented me from perceiving his presence. It was an enormous man, with a sharp gaze and a booming voice, who was approaching toward me with a concerned and... vociferating gesture. Older than how I was remembering him from that night in my childhood, though he had not changed much: it was without a doubt Uncle Kurt!

His countenance was dejected and his voice pitiful, saying incoherencies:

"You are my only nephew and I have almost killed you. I have spilled my own blood! A curse has fallen upon me. O

God, my end is near. Why add this disgrace to my sufferings...?

"You will get well Arturo, my son," Uncle Kurt was continuing with a pained voice, "you will recover. The *Ámpej*[1] Palacios has checked you and assures that you will soon get better. How can you forgive me, child...?"

Uncle Kurt was still incessantly muttering his grievances and apologies while he was keeping that potent blue gaze fixed on me.

Enveloped in a growing drowsiness, making efforts to coordinate my ideas, I recognized, in the tense face of my interlocutor, the familiar features of my mother.

As if dazed, I was staring at him searching for something to say, when I clearly heard the canine sound of a growl. It came to my ears from outside the house and had the virtue of making the memories rush into my mind. The last thing I saw and felt when I was exploring Uncle Kurt's property came like an overwhelming avalanche.

"Wha... what were they?" I stammered, trying to contain the trembling that was shaking my whole body. A question mark was on Uncle Kurt's face.

"Sorry?" he asked puzzled.

"The... the wild beasts," I said, making an effort because I was feeling my tongue swollen and asleep.

"Ah, the mastiffs," Uncle Kurt realized. "They are dogs; dogs from Tibet. Very particular animals, authentic dogs. Perhaps the only species that deserves that name. They're extraordinary animals, capable of receiving semi-human training." Involuntarily, I opened my eyes in horror and Uncle Kurt, upon noticing it, sorrowfully apologized:

"What has occurred to you is an accident. An incomprehensible accident of which only I am to blame. The mastiffs attacked you because I ordered it. O God, I alone am responsible for the greatest crime! I have shed my own blood!..."

Uncle Kurt began to repeat the previous incoherencies while I was falling gently into unconsciousness. My eyes were closing, listening to whom I had come to visit with so much illusion, transformed into a character of a Greek tragedy, because of my imprudence and lack of foresight!

---

1. Quechua word for physician, healer, skilled in administering remedies or spells.

Suddenly, I also felt guilty; my heart squeezed; I attempted to say some apology but a saving penumbra eclipsed my consciousness, plunging me into a deep sleep.

I will try to abbreviate the details of my unfortunate intrusion into Uncle Kurt's life. It will be a concession in favor of other data that I wish to make available to the reader, for the better interpretation of this strange story. For if it occurred to anyone to think that everything that had happened to me up to that point was more than sufficient to cover a quota of mysterious events, I will tell him that he is very much mistaken. This adventure was missing important parts, I would say it was just beginning, and if remarkable "coincidences" had haunted me up to then, what would come next was not far behind. Because Uncle Kurt had a story to tell. A story so strange and unusual that, considered on its own, it was unbelievable; but which I was to take with a great deal of respect, for "that" story was part of "my" own story.

But let us not get ahead of ourselves. The day that I opened my eyes, and saw Uncle Kurt for the second time in my life, was the night following my unfortunate incursion onto the property. It was about fifteen hours that I was remaining unconscious, to the despair of Uncle Kurt, who was fearing to have given me a serious brain injury.

The blow, delivered with the butt of a *Luger* pistol, had been forceful and, according to Uncle Kurt, I should thank the abnormal hardness of my skull or a miracle for my salvation.

Why this certainty? Because he had struck with much force; in his words, enough to kill the intruder. This violence was due to the fact that Uncle Kurt was expecting an attempt, an attack at any moment.

He had reason to believe it, as will be seen, and misfortune—or another cause—wanted that I had the ill-fated idea of carrying out the suspicious nocturnal visit.

At first, after making sure that there were no other intruders, Uncle Kurt dragged me to the house and devoted himself to the task of checking my pockets in search of weapons and elements of identification. With the surprise that is to be expected, he found the Iron Cross—his decoration—Mama's letter, and the documents and ID cards that were duly proving my identity.

According to Uncle Kurt, he would have committed suicide right then and there if it were not that I was inexplicably still breathing. His first reaction was to seek help, but, aware of the irregularity of the situation, he decided to be extremely cautious in order to avoid police intervention. For this very reason, it would be inconvenient to resort to an unknown doctor who might put him in a tight spot.

I must clarify that Uncle Kurt had not married, so he was living alone in the Sala, assisted by an old and faithful Indian husband and wife, who were inhabiting a small adjacent house. Apart from those mentioned, there were never less than ten farmhands dwelling there—to tend the vines and the small factory of sweets and syrup—but these were occupying a farmhouse thirty meters away from the Sala and were not trustworthy.

Uncle Kurt called to the old majordomo, named *José Tolaba,* desperately knocking on the window of his room.

"Pepe, Pepe."[2]

"Yes, Don Cerino," answered the old man with promptness.

"Come quickly, Pepe. A misfortune has occurred," cried Kurt.

Although he only named the old man, five minutes later Pepe and his wife were appearing, because by the tone of the call, they assumed that something grave was going on. The old woman, Juana, was constantly making the sign of the cross while Uncle Kurt and Pepe were moving my inanimate body to a sofa in the **living room,** since the bedrooms were on the upper floor, by means of the staircase.

I lost a little blood from a deep gash at the level of the occiput,[3] but the most impressive thing was undoubtedly the way in which the dogs mauled my forearms. Uncle Kurt left the two elders so that they washed the wounds and took care of me and departed in search of Ámpej Palacios.

He took from the garage a brand-new **Toyota** jeep—acquired in times of "easy money"—and sped off, noticing the presence of the Ford a few meters from the gate when leaving.

The hour was untimely to seek out any doctor, but not for the Ámpej Palacios.

This personage, who is not from fiction but would deserve to be, is an Indian doctor world famous for his mastery of kinesiotherapy. Already old in these years, he still runs his

---

2. Nickname for José.

3. Back of the head or skull.

humble office without being bothered by anyone, because his prestige is as great as the fortune that he amassed thanks to the gifts that generous and wealthy patients were depositing into his hands. The Ámpej Palacios has made men and women walk who have been paralyzed for years, has made necks as stiff as an obelisk move, and has straightened so many spinal columns that have been turned away by traumatologists throughout the world, that it would be difficult to believe if there were no signature books to prove it.

These books are a second touristic source for Santa María, for there are signatures and notes from people, from all over the world, who came to Ámpej Palacios to seek hope. Rich and poor, priests and doctors, nobles and plebeians, all have signed his books to testify to the wisdom of Ámpej. There is no magic or sorcery here, but pure and simple Ancient Wisdom that dynasties of Ámpej Diaguitas have preserved and transmitted from fathers to sons. Today the children of Ámpej Palacios are Medical Doctors graduated from the University of Salta and specialized in: Traumatology! They continue the familial tradition and successfully practice a knowledge thousands of years older than the materialistic science of the West.

Accompanied by the Ámpej Palacios, Uncle Kurt returned half an hour later. This one, who is a corpulent old man with a thick white mustache and hands as big as a size-12 alpargata,[4] went to check my head and arms.

"The head is not broken," affirmed the Ámpej ten minutes later, "but we will have to wait a few hours to know if there is no injury to the brain. The left arm is broken and must be put in a cast; the right arm has a healthy bone but the flesh is badly injured."

"Look, Cerino," continued the Ámpej, "I don't think that it's serious but we have to stitch up his head and arm, and give him anti-inflammatories and antibiotics. So much for me just fixing bones; I'll send you to my youngest kid who is just visiting. He's a doctor and will better attend to him."

An hour later, Dr. Palacios was arriving grumbling, since he was due to travel to Salta at 05:00 hours and they had awakened him at 01:00.

---

4. The Argentine name for the Espadrille, footwear commonly worn by rural workers.

He fully devoted himself to his task, administering several injections, stitching up the wounds of the right arm, and casting the left.

He closed the cut in the scalp, after shaving the injured area with inert plastic hooks.

"Sure that the dogs aren't rabid?" asked the Ámpej's son with diffidence.

"I can assure you," affirmed a horrified Uncle Kurt. "They bit because I ordered it; they are very domesticated animals and they blindly obey me. They would never attack anyone on their own."

The Doctor was shaking his head while he was murmuring something about the doubts that he was harboring as to the tameness of the Tibetan mastiffs.

Three hours later Dr. Palacios was leaving and Uncle Kurt, after taking the keys that I had in the Safari sack, drove my automobile onto the property and parked it inside his garage.

The second day I attempted to get up because I came to at a moment in which no one was in the room. I felt, then, a terrible weakness and such a dizziness that I almost fell to the floor. I remained seated on the edge of the bed contemplating, not without a certain curiosity, the place in which I was finding myself.

It was a soberly furnished room, with a carved walnut bedroom set and a bed with a lace mosquito net. I deduced that it was on the second floor from the vaulted ceiling and the thick quebracho beams that were supporting it. At that moment, old Juana entered and was frightened to see me sitting down.

"Ay, Señorcito," said the old lady, "How do you do these things? You have to rest, so ordered the doctor."

She was firmly pushing me by the shoulders to force me to take the horizontal position while I was letting her do it, astonished by the attitude of the stranger.

Very soon I was lying down and again covered while the old woman was incessantly protesting:

"Señorcito, you've moved your casted arm; that's not good, he's going to be angry..."

"And... the Señor?" I timidly asked.

"Don Cerino?" He'll be here right away," responded the old woman, "as soon as I notify him that you've recovered."

She approached the door to my right—the other one was leading to a bathroom as I later learned—but before leaving she turned and said:

"Stay still Señorcito, I'll soon bring you broth and a nut horchata," she smiled. "You'll soon see how you'll recover your strength."

As the days passed, I was recovering and fifteen days later I was already going down to the dining room and taking walks in the park next to the house.

Another fifteen days later they removed my cast and, only thirty-five days after having arrived in Santa María, I was able to set off for Tafí del Valle under astonishing circumstances that I will narrate later.

At the beginning, I wrote several times to my parents, lying about a supposed archaeological investigation at the Pukara of Loma Rica to reassure them about my prolonged absence. I also spoke by telephone with Dr. Cortez in order to request an extension of fifteen days to my vacations that were expiring in those days, but he only agreed to it when I informed him that I had suffered an accident.

Things were getting difficult because I had not yet begun to find out the whereabouts of Belicena Villca's son and my vacation was already coming to an end. However, when departing from Santa María, my morale was high and I had more faith than ever. The prolonged meetings that I held with my extraordinary relative had contributed to it. But let us return to those days of convalescence, when Uncle Kurt initiated the story of his fantastic life.

Chapter II

s I am a doctor, already in the first days of convalescence, I understood that it would be long, so, having sufficient time, I was seeing no reason not to tell Uncle Kurt about my adventure. I never experienced the desire to share my affairs with anyone nor have I had confidants. But now it was different. Since the day of the earthquake, I was lamenting not knowing anyone in whom to confide; someone sufficiently "spiritual" as not to make fun of the occurred events surrounding Belicena Villca's death. But also that he had the necessary freedom to be able to accept a knowledge that was involving such grave dangers.

At one point I thought of going to Professor Ramirez, but then I was ashamed of this selfish idea that could endanger the life and mind of this exemplary man dedicated to his professorships and his family.

I was upset since then because I was feeling that I was beginning to deal with ideas that were too "big," too inhuman, that could disturb me if I was not sharing them. And lo and behold, suddenly a man *of my blood,* whom I never dreamed to meet, resurrects from the past. A *solitary* man like me; *of action.* A *bold* man of an age in which one does not fear for life, for death begins to take shape as a reality.

"Yes," I was decidedly thinking, "I would confide everything in Uncle Kurt."

At the beginning we chatted about trifles because we both were avoiding telling our secrets; I was not revealing the motive for my visit and he was keeping quiet about the brutal attack from the mastiffs and his truncheon blow. I told him about my studies and also of my parents; he explained to me the techniques to obtain a good prickly-pear *syrup.*

Thus we were gaining trust, until one day, one of the last that I stayed in bed, I told him:

"Uncle Kurt, I'd like you to hand me the briefcase that I brought with me. It was left in the car the night that I arrived."

To my surprise, Uncle Kurt opened one of the closet doors and took out from a compartment the briefcase that, apparently, had been there the whole time. I opened it and took out Belicena Villca's letter and some notes that I had taken when I dialogued with Professor Ramirez.

"I'm going to explain to you the reason for my visit," I said, trying to convey the importance that the matter was worth to me. "It's a fantastic and incredible story and I seriously think that I only dare tell it to you without reservation or fear."

Uncle Kurt arched his eyebrows, vividly interested in something that, at least to me, was seeming of extreme gravity. My words, and the tone that I used, created the appropriate mood for it.

It was three o'clock in the afternoon on an ordinary day, we both had had lunch, and the serene tranquility that was reigning in that lost country house was inviting to dialogue and confidence. We had all the time in the world at our disposal to take advantage of it as we pleased.

I began to narrate the known events and, if I was harboring any doubt about the credibility that Uncle Kurt would give to it, it was soon dispelled. Visibly upset by some passages and won over by impatience in others, he was constantly interrupting me to ask for details and, after he was getting what he was wanting, he was encouraging me to continue in an authoritative tone that was unfamiliar to him.

The case of Belicena Villca had completely captured his interest but, upon finding out about the existence of the letter, he seemed to go mad. At that moment I took it out of the briefcase and I had to make an effort to prevent him from snatching it out of my hands: it was my intention to permit that he read it, but not at that moment but later, when I had finished relating what happened. I showed him, then, and continued with the narration without perturbing myself by the anxiety of my uncle, who was finding it a great effort, evidently, to wait to read it. I explained, in general terms, the objective of that posthumous missive, without going into details about the incredible history of the House of Tharsis, mentioning only the millenary persecution that it had suffered by the Golen-Druids: I spoke of Bera and Birsha and of my conviction that They were the true assassins of Belicena Villca. At that point it was seeming that Uncle Kurt's eyes were going to pop out of their sockets; however, his lips were remaining sealed in surprise. Finally, I referred him to the translation that Professor Ramirez made of the legend *"ada aes sidhe draoi mac hwch"* and its subsequent allusions to the Golen-Druids, which in my opinion was confirming the veracity of much, if not all, of the contents of the letter.

Here the charm was cut off and Uncle Kurt, springing to his feet, shouted: "Yes, Arturo! The Druids! I was waiting for them the night that you arrived! After 35 years I perceived the unmistakable sign of their presence and I knew that at any moment I would be attacked, although I was unaware why they had waited so long, why they were now *reappearing*. And now I know: because you were coming to me, bearer of the Greatest Secret!"

It was a roar that came out of his throat when pronouncing these phrases in German, being immediately answered by two prolonged howls from the mastiffs one floor below and outside of the house. I could not but be astonished because Uncle Kurt had always spoken in Castilian, since my mastery of the German language is poor as a consequence of my parents' decision to educate me "fully Argentinean" to the point that not even among them were they using this language.

Neither was it escaping me that, no matter how loud that he had shouted, the dogs could not have heard him. How then, had they answered him?

I was now looking with "different eyes" at Uncle Kurt, whom I had hitherto regarded as a person, like so many others, tortured by the memory of the days of the war, but, otherwise, completely normal.

I was understanding, slowly, that there was something else: Uncle Kurt had a secret knowledge that was enormously weighing on his conscience, now enlivened by my story.

Uncle Kurt must have been about sixty-two years old, but he was giving the impression of appearing ten years younger. Tall to exaggeration—I was calculating him to be about 190 cm—he was burly, of athletic build, and one could see that he was keeping himself in shape. His hair, which should be black, was gray, cut very short; his light blue eyes, full eyebrows, thin-lipped mouth with a thick mustache and firm chin, were completing his description. One detail, perhaps, was the scar that was on his left cheek, enhanced by the blushing red of his cheeks, a sign of health for his age.

He was liking to dress simple but sportingly and I was always seeing him wearing thick chamois boots.

In synthesis, he was an impressive man; even more so at that moment in which he was seeming to shoot sparks out of his eyes. He spent a few minutes walking in circles all around the room, with his hands behind his back, in which he had the letter from Belicena Villca that I had just given to him.

I was keeping respectful silence although I was intrigued by this reaction. We spent several hours talking while outside it was rapidly getting dark. The room was submerged in shadows when old Juana came in and turned on the light.

"Jesus, Don Cerino, why are you in the dark? Dinner is ready. I'll bring up Señor Arturo's right away," the old lady smiled as usual before leaving.

This interruption calmed Uncle Kurt, who was still pensively circling. He stopped at the foot of my bed with his hands rested on the footboard and, in correct Castilian, he said:

"Neffe,[5] I believe that you have brought me an answer that I awaited for decades. If it is so, I can die in peace when it is all over," he mysteriously said, "but tell me, what exactly brought you to me? How did it occur to you to come to see me?"

"I was wanting to find out the motive that the ⚡⚡ had for collecting all the documentation on the Druids," I responded. "When I thought about it, the memory of that night thirty-five years ago came to my mind, when you gave me the Iron Cross. It was an intuition, because immediately, for no apparent reason, I felt sure that you would know how to respond to those questions. Then I learned through Mama that you'd been an ⚡⚡ officer... And here I am."

"Ha-ha-ha," he admiringly laughed, with that thunderous guffaw that he let out upon discovering me on the Cerrillos stairway, as a child, and that I was remembering so well.

"You've assumed right, Neffe," continued Uncle Kurt, "I can tell you some things that would be useful to you in the solution of your problems. Things regarding the *esoteric Doctrine* of the ⚡⚡ Black Order. However, by an inevitable and significant design of the Gods, it will surprise you to see to what extent the answers that you were seeking were in my hands. But before speaking of it, let's have dinner."

He departed, leaving me consumed by new questions. From his earlier exclamation another mystery was clearly emerging: how had Uncle Kurt made contact with the Druids, those who, seemingly, for years were pursuing him to the death?

---

5. Nephew in German.

Chapter III

t 21:30 hours, Uncle Kurt settled into a comfortable hammock chair next to my bed, and after remaining pensive a few minutes, he began to speak. I could tell that he had been reflecting on everything that occurred and had made a decision.

"Look, Arturo," he said with a solemn tone, trying to be convincing, "I understand that you'll be impatient to obtain the answers that have brought you here, but you must give me time to read Belicena Villca's letter. It's a lengthy manuscript and it'll take me several days to assimilate it, but it's necessary that I do so before answering your questions; in that way I'll have the background of what you know, I'll assess what you still need to know, and I'll be able to express myself with precision."

He was expecting my unconditional approval. However, I was believing that it would in no way affect him to anticipate any response from me.

"I agree, Uncle Kurt, that you should take time to read the letter. But tell me now, how is it possible that on the day of my arrival you were expecting an attack from the Druids?; I mean: how'd you know that They were coming?"

"Well, because the day before I had heard *the buzzing*, the unmistakable *buzzing of honeybees*, which reveals *the use of the Dorje on the Heart!* Yes, Neffe. From that instant an uncontrollable tachycardia, which still lasts, came over me. But once again all their tricks failed in the face of the powers with which the Gods have endowed me, and they'll find themselves forced to confront me face to face." His eyes were defiantly shining, but I was wanting to clarify things. The allusion to the buzzing and the Dorje, elements that Belicena mentioned the Twenty-fifth Day, when Bera and Birsha converted the blood of the Seigniors of Tharsis into Bitumen of Judea, *before reading her letter,* had left me frozen with astonishment.

Trembling, I asked him:

"But, then, you've heard that buzzing before?"

"Of course, Arturo. I heard it for the first time in 1938, 42 years ago."

"And where?" I inquired with growing astonishment, anticipating the surprising answer.

"In Tibet; on the border between this country and China. It was during an expedition to the Gates of Chang Shambhala."

The blood rushed to my temples, I felt confused, dizzy, and I glimpsed the possibility of losing consciousness. The room had disappeared from my sight and in my mind, together with a thousand concepts and situations that were emerging from Belicena Villca's letter, the questions were reducing to their extreme abstraction: what, how, when, where, struggling to take concrete form and strafe[6] Uncle Kurt. He, who was noticing my confusion, began to merrily laugh.

"Did you see, Neffe? I knew it! It'll be impossible for you to comprehend anything in the manner how you propose the dialogue. I'll tell you everything, fear not. But so that you can make the most of my experience, so that you can comprehend it, it's best that you know a summary of my life. I repeat: wait until I read the letter, then I'll tell you about my past and then your questions will have consistency and my answers will make sense.

"However," he continued, "as I see that your impatience isn't small, I'll give you something on which to think during these days.

"If I haven't misunderstood, you're trying to find an esoteric Order that would presumably exist in Córdoba, an Order of Wise Constructors, an Order dedicated to the study of the Hyperborean Wisdom?"

I nodded.

"Well, Neffe: I am in a condition to affirm that I very possibly have precise news about said Order. And not only about it, but also about the mysterious Initiate who has founded it."

That was the last thing I would have expected to hear and, again, my lips remained sealed while in my mind the questions were forming at great velocity.

But Uncle Kurt did not give me time to ask:

"I'll prove it to you!" he said, as he was untying a package that he had brought concealed in his jacket. Undoubtedly, Uncle Kurt had no intentions of referring to that matter, unless my impatience forced him, and that was why he hidden that package: if not necessary, he would not have shown it at that moment.

---

6. To machine-gun, or to bombard.

Upon concluding, he held between his hands a book of voluminous appearance, bound with thick covers lined with red cloth. Holding it in front of my eyes, he opened it and revealed the first page; first of all, it was announcing the title of the work and the name of the author: *"Fundamentals of the Hyperborean Wisdom"* by *"Nimrod de Rosario."* Further down, an inscription was giving indications of the book's affiliation: *"Order of Tirodal Knights of the Argentine Republic."*

When I had read those succinct sentences, Uncle Kurt turned the page and pointed out to me a "Letter to the Chosen" that was inserted as a prologue; at the end of it, three pages later, was the signature of the author, Nimrod de Rosario, and the following indication: *"Córdoba, August 1979."*

"Six months!" I exclaimed. "It was only published six months ago! How, Uncle Kurt, how the Devil did you get your hands on it?"

"Ha-ha. Not precisely by the will of the Devil but my good friend Oskar, who passed away only three months ago and took the secret to his grave." Here he became serious, upon noticing the disenchantment on my face. "I know that this part of the news will not cause you any pleasure, but it's preferable that you know the truth from the start.

"Oskar, about whom I will tell you later, was, like me, a refugee in Argentina since 1947. As with your parents and other Comrades, I used to meet with him a couple of times a year: after those secret meetings, each one was returning to their usual tasks. No letters, no telephone, nothing was to bind us if we were wishing to continue to be free. For me, it was already known that a secret organization, the orders of which were saying "execute wherever he is found" without hesitation, was pursuing me; but Oskar's case was different: they were "officially" looking for him to be tried for "war crimes," and the Soviet Union was making the claim, since Oskar Feil was from Estonia. But Oskar, who was passing for an Italian immigrant under the name of "Domingo Pietratesta," had entered into marriage in Argentina and had a beautiful family to which he had to protect above all things: in his case the possibility of getting caught by the Enemy was unthinkable. That is why we were taking extreme precautions to meet every six months. And neither could we help getting together because we were both close comrades, not only since the war, but also since many years before, since the time in which we studied together at the *NAPOLA* School.

"Ah, Oskar, Oskar," sighed Uncle Kurt. "A friend for more than a lifetime. A companion to conquer Heaven and Hell, a Comrade for Eternity."

"B-but he died?" I said stammering, to bring Uncle Kurt back to reality.

He was silent for a moment. At last he seemed to notice me, and continued his story.

"Yes, Neffe. Oskar died four months ago; of 'natural death,' according to all accounts, but it is not hidden from me that he may have been assassinated: whatever his death was, his wife would never publicly reveal the truth. The future of Oskar's three children would force her to bite her lip before speaking. So I don't know what occurred with certainty since, for obvious reasons, I won't be able to get close to his family for quite a while; a year or more.

"But let's get down to business, Arturo!" he said with energy, after deeply sighing, as if bidding farewell to his dead friend. "About eighteen months ago, more or less, we met in the Province of Jujuy, at the Provincial Hotel in Tilcara: we were both passing for tourists who were visiting the famous Pukara. There I noticed him very excited and happy: he had found, he then told me, *those who were possessing a direct contact with the Source of the Hyperborean Wisdom,* that is to say, with the same source that was nourishing the Wisdom of our Initiated Instructors of the ⚡⚡ Black Order... According to Oskar, after 35 years of 'democratic' and Judaic darkness, the Spiritual Light of the Black Sun was emerging once again: yes, after 35 years, during which the Enemy poured all kinds of calumnies upon the Wisdom of the Order, and after hundreds of impostors, often mere junior ⚡⚡ personnel who were ignorant of the Secrets of the Order, sowed confusion about the initiatory teaching that was being imparted in it. In Córdoba, Oskar explained to me, a great Initiate had appeared who was calling himself 'Nimrod de Rosario'; the 'de Rosario' was, apparently, to differentiate his nickname from the historical Nimrod, a Kassite King who lived 2,000 years BC. But this was anecdotal: the important thing was consisting in that that Initiate was mastering all the Sciences of the West, and especially the Hyperborean Wisdom, in a degree as high as Oskar had never seen outside of Germany, and since the last days of the war, 35 years ago. In truth, one would have to go back to those days and to the men who were secretly directing the Black Order, in particular Konrad Tarstein, to find an equivalent Initiate. At least that was Oskar's opinion.

"Of course, outside of the inevitable comparisons, and what they had in common, there were abysmal differences between Nimrod and our ancient instructors. Of course, there was no difference with regard to Honor or the Hyperborean Wisdom itself: in this area everything was analogous to the 𝄜... But we were no longer in the days of the Third Reich and the 𝄜, and it is logical that in organizing the adherents of the Hyperborean Wisdom, Nimrod was forced to rely on what reality, the reality of 1979, was offering him. I still remember Oskar's words referring to the spiritual incompetence of his followers: 'Believe me, Kurt, Nimrod needs a racial selection like that which was practiced in Germany, and from which we emerged. I know, I know! We are no longer in Germany, but in the mestizo Third World. I am only raising an impossible possibility, a game of imagination. It saddens me to observe how his efforts fall into a vacuum, are wasted by people who cannot detach themselves from worldly life. Nevertheless, and without even remotely bordering on the discipline of the 𝄜, he has managed to form an important support group that allows him to develop his Strategy: with persons coming out of traditional esotericism, especially many who realized that the Gnostic Church of Samael Aun Weor is just one more synarchic sect, and others coming from Argentine nationalism, that is to say, men with Nazi-fascist political training. With them he formed the Order of Tirodal Knights, in which a "Hyperborean Initiation" is granted, similar to that which we receive in the 𝄜...'

" 'But the Hyperborean Initiation, which is the First of the three that spiritual liberation and the Return to the Origin requires,' continued Oskar, 'can only be administered by one who exhibits the Second Initiation, that is to say, by a Hyperborean Pontiff. Nimrod is, therefore, a Hyperborean Pontiff. How he obtained his Second Initiation, no one knows, but you and I know very well that only the Unknown Superiors, the Lords of Venus, the Hyperborean Gods bestow it. Naturally, to comply with his mission, this Initiate has prefabricated for himself the most consistent past possible, making use of his irresistible power over the illusory structure of reality. But this does not interest us: his past, and the contradictions that can be proved in it, only interest the Enemy. For us, Dear Kurt, what is certain, what is undeniable, is that his Wisdom comes from an irreproachable Source: the Lords of Agartha.'

" 'And what is his mission?' Oskar asked himself. 'It is also an enigma: it seems to be linked to the search for certain persons whom he would have to strategically orientate in order to play a role in the coming Total War. All his efforts are put into that search, but I don't think he has been lucky because, as I was saying, his collaborators are not the most suitable for the practice of High Magic. In fact, there are very few Initiates in the Tirodal Order and none respond to the demands of the mysterious mission. This assertion is not a subjective presumption but a confidence from Nimrod himself: in effect, when I met the Pontiff for the first time, he, who demonstrated to possess the power to read the initiatic Runes, congratulated me for the degree reached in the Black Order, but evidenced a visible disenchantment. To my surprise, he immediately apologized and courteously explained that when receiving a Chosen One for the first time, he was always harboring the hope "that he was one of Those who would fulfill the Mission prepared by the Gods." This comment clarified everything for me and I understood on the spot that I, obviously, was not one of 'Those' whom Nimrod was awaiting. Nevertheless, he treated me with camaraderie and offered me to participate in the Order, performing extremely reserved functions, which would in no way endanger my position. I accepted, of course; and I took advantage of his confidence in order to inquire some more about the unfortunate search for the Chosen Ones fit to carry out the plans of the Gods, a search that would be almost impossible in the infernal context of the present Epoch.'

" 'The kind of people that you seek, Nimrod, are of superior quality to the Initiates of the ⚡⚡ Black Order?'

" 'It is not a question of quality but of strategic confusion, Señor Pietratesta. Perhaps if one managed to transplant one of those Initiates from Wewelsburg Castle to this Epoch, without him experiencing the passage of time, we would have a Comrade fit for the Mission. But now, certainly, we have no such man. Our Initiates themselves *could be fit for the mission if they completely assumed the Initiation and mastered their animic nature, if they decided to be what they are. But it is difficult, very difficult, for the spiritual men of this Epoch to have the valor necessary to stop being what they appear and definitively be what they are in truth*. Nevertheless, the Gods assure that there are men capable of such valor, that the doors of the Mystery must be kept open until they arrive or those who are, are transmuted. And this certainty is that which gives us the strength to carry on, Comrade Pietratesta.'

" 'I was in a house in the City of Córdoba,' Oskar clarified, 'belonging to the Tirodal Order. In the spacious room, furnished as an office, behind an imposing desk, was seated Nimrod attentively observing me. At last he opened a drawer and took out a red-covered book.'

" 'Señor Pietratesta,' he said with seriousness. 'No one arrives at this place if he has not been previously investigated on Earth and in Heaven. You have satisfied the requisites and that is why we offer you this opportunity: to enter the Tirodal Order and become one of its Initiates. All those who enter must perform the same acts, which are very simple: they basically consist in *comprehending and accepting* the *Fundamentals of the Hyperborean Wisdom,* which, for the benefit of the Chosen Ones, we have synthesized in this book,' he handed me the red book. 'The mechanism of admission demands that you read this book and decide if you *comprehend and accept* its contents. If the resolution is positive, you are immediately incorporated into the Order and acquire the right to access the other thirteen books, which make up the "Second Part" of the Fundamentals and contain the secret preparation for the Hyperborean Initiation. If the answer is negative, if you do not comprehend or do not accept the *Fundamentals of the Hyperborean Wisdom,* all you have to do is return the book and refrain from making copies, and you will be disassociated from the Order. I must warn you,' he said with a threatening tone, 'that failure to comply with this condition is severely punished by the Order.' "

Chapter IV

"Oskar promised to act with loyalty," Uncle Kurt said, "and he had no problem in complying. The content of the book was not unknown to us, although the novelty was the high-level philosophical language in which it was written: for a Baltic-German like Oskar, the reading of that pure Castilian was an extra test, which he nevertheless passed with youthful enthusiasm. So when finishing the reading, months later, he hastened to apply for admission to the Order of Tirodal Knights, being assigned to him a weekly day to meet in a certain hidden place with a few extremely trusted Comrades, who were studying the Second *Part* of the Fundamentals and preparing themselves for the Kairos of the Initiation. And this stage, in Oskar's own words, was constituting one of the happiest events of his life. However, if there was something that was still displeasing to Oskar, that it was my absence from the Order. As he expressed to me on that occasion, in Tilcara, he was believing that my presence and the contribution of my knowledge of the Hyperborean Wisdom were indispensable to charismatically strengthen the Order. He was also wanting that I read the book, but he was not daring to disobey the Pontiff, which is why he begged me to the point of exhaustion that I authorize him to present my name to be checked 'on Earth and in Heaven' and the book obtained through the correct way.

"I finally accepted, more to placate him than out of true interest, for, as you will understand, Neffe, I have, since 1945, the precise instructions to fulfill my own mission. *And these instructions also come from the Gods, from the same Gods of Nimrod de Rosario who, surely, are also the 'Liberating Gods' who were guiding the House of Tharsis.*

"The next time that we saw each other, the last time, was in Córdoba, in August of last year. I am not going to deny, Arturo, that I was harboring a secret desire to meet the amazing Initiate of whom Oskar spoke to me so much. And yet it was not to be, because the Pontiff was on a secret retreat writing a new book. In spite of everything, Oskar came across the significant news that there was a book for me in the Order: one of the old members gave me the copy that you now have in your hands and transmitted to me Nimrod's greeting: 'the Pontiff,' he said with respect, 'was happy to "have met me" and was assuring me a great performance in the service of the Gods of the Spirit.' Of course, that interview took place in a hotel, since no one could know the properties and meeting places of the Order before being accepted.

"Do you realize, Arturo, how close I came to entering the Order of Tirodal Knights? I was close, very close, but I did not manage to concretize the entry because the only contact that I had with the Order was Oskar and he passed away in December '79. At least that was what the telegram sent by his widow in January was announcing, to my PO Box in Salta. I do not possess more precise information, Neffe. I bought the Córdoba newspapers of those days and verified that, in effect, the burial of Domingo Pietratesta, who passed away in his bed due to a cardiac syncope, had been carried out. After such unfortunate news, unable to do anything else but await the passage of time, I have read the "Fundamentals" book many times, arriving to the conclusion that its content expresses, in the most profound and rigorous system of concepts, the ancient and simple truths of the Hyperborean Wisdom. Why Nimrod conceived such a work to regulate the access of the Chosen to his Order, I believe has to do with a super-realistic vision of the Epoch, of the present Culture, and with the *type* of Initiate that he seeks to carry out the mission proposed by the Gods. Whatever it may be, I estimate that I will not cause any harm to Nimrod's Strategy permitting that you now read it. I will only incur a Debt of Honor to the Order, which someday I will have to settle. In any case, you have already previously read a letter to which I attribute as much value to as this book, even though you have not yet allowed me to give an account of it."

Here Uncle Kurt smiled, while I was overcome with shame. Despite the momentary embarrassment, I continued laughing, as I was doing since a few minutes before. I was euphoric. My life had become entangled in a very significant way after the assassination of Belicena Villca, and it was evident that that plot *could not be casual: Someone, the Liberating Gods, not the "Guardian Angel," had arranged it as a real plot, as a script of fate, so that I would "casually" follow it and find out about these things at the right moment. In a word: I had been guided by the Gods.* And this thought, this certainty, was filling me with intimate joy.

Uncle Kurt, there were no longer any doubts, was possessing the keys that I was seeking. The fact that Oskar Feil's death
had disconnected him from the Order was not discouraging
me. With the information that I was now possessing, it was
seeming a much easier task to locate Nimrod de Rosario and
the Tirodal Order: he was the Lord of Absolute Orientation
and those were the Wise Constructors of his Order. His search
was aiming, and Uncle Kurt could not yet know it because I
had not read him the letter, to find a Noyo or a Vraya, Initiates
capable of traversing the Stones of a Valley of two Rivers and
reaching the Wise Sword, together with Noyo of Tharsis, the
son of Belicena Villca. And it was clear to me that by taking
Belicena Villca's letter to him, Nimrod would not hesitate to
put me on track to Noyo Villca, to whom he would transmit
his mother's posthumous message. Without stopping smiling
because of the joy that his revelations produced in me, my
mind was working at great velocity, while in Uncle Kurt's face
was reflecting the surprise before such an incoherent attitude.
But I was thinking, incessantly thinking, about the way to obtain the address of Oskar Feil, or Domingo Pietratesta, aware
that my uncle would never voluntarily give it to me. Finally I
found the key, simple, since it was in front of my eyes all the
time: the newspapers! That was it: I would search the newspapers of December 1979 in Córdoba and check the obituaries,
and there I would discover the address of his family!

Finally I adopted a more serious attitude and responded to
Uncle Kurt:

"Certainly, that last part of your revelation is not altogether
faustian," I said with regret. "I sincerely regret the death of
your Comrade; and I even more regret, you will understand,
that his death has disconnected you from the Tirodal Order.
Nevertheless, it is so extraordinary what you have told me of
said Order, that I could repeat your words from this afternoon:
'I believe that you have brought me something that I have
awaited a long time.' You were saying so because of the letter,
which you have not yet read, but I also believe that the information about the Order, and perhaps this book that I have not
yet read, constitute a concrete answer to the *true motive* for my
visit. Because, even though I *consciously* came to inquire about
the relationship between the ⚡ and the Druids, it is clear that
such an inquiry is inserted into the larger question of the
search for the son of Belicena Villca, *the true motive, uncon-*

scious but effective, for all my movements. And that search inevitably passes through the Order of Wise Constructors of Córdoba, of which you have referred me: do you understand why, deep down, I am happy? Because the discovery of that Order represents the most necessary thing for me, the most important thing, much more than obtaining news about the Druids.

"Yes, Uncle Kurt," I emphatically affirmed, "it is indispensable that you read that letter as soon as possible. I will not disturb you until you finish. But you have done very well in bringing forward to me that you had knowledge of the Tirodal Order: it has taken a load off me, and now I will be able to await what you have to tell me later with more peace of mind."

Chapter V

I agreed, then, to give Uncle Kurt enough time to read the letter, without imagining what he would derive from such a concession. In the first place, either because he conscientiously carried out its reading, or because, most probably, the Castilian language prevented him from more rapidly grasping the obscure concepts of Belicena Villca, or for whatever reason that it was, the truth is that he finished it in just ten days. But, secondly, the most irritating part of the case is that during that time he locked himself in his room, refusing to leave even for a minute. He delegated all the chores of the Finca to his overseer José Tolaba and ordered that food be served to him in his room by old Juana. And it was in vain that I attempted to break that determination: my notes were not answered, and I did not manage to penetrate the laconic loyalty of the old woman with my questions. In synthesis: I had to arm myself with patience and accept the strange conduct of my Uncle! And, to top my frustration, I could not advance much in the reading of the *Fundamentals of the Hyperborean Wisdom* book due to the complexity of the themes that it was dealing with: it was requiring, at least, a Philosophical Dictionary to understand, in profundity, the majority of the concepts, which were used with great precision, and I was not knowing if my Uncle was possessing any kind of copy, although it would be of no use to me if it was written in German. Naturally, I did not manage to solve the problem until Uncle Kurt reappeared, and by then the Dictionary would no longer be necessary because I would never finish reading Nimrod's book: Uncle Kurt's story, and the events that occurred afterward, inevitably prevented me from doing so.

The psychological effect that the letter produced on Uncle Kurt must have been very intense because, as an effect of the reading, he was then demonstrating a very noticeable physical change, undoubtedly a psychosomatic product of the received impression. In a few words, from the look that my Uncle was presenting, he was appearing to have retroceded several years in those ten days, he was much younger, he was showing a positive and communicative character that before I was not recognizing in him. I suspect, and I do not believe myself to be too mistaken, that the thirty-three years spent in Santa María had soured his temperament, normally jovial, and caused that unsociable and pessimistic personality that I noticed when arriving at the Finca. The personality of one who no longer too much trusts that the designs of the Gods will be fulfilled and resignedly awaits the resolution of Death. Thirty-three years is a long time to wait in Catamarca. I was understanding him better than anyone, and it was seeming logical to me that his character had eroded. And that is why I was then understanding that the change was justified, even foreseeable, since Belicena Villca's letter met his expectations, postponed for so many years. For it was clear, since he himself had confessed it, that his instructions for after the war, *"instructions from the Gods,"* obliged him to remain in that place, and that my arrival carrying the letter, and the presumed and imminent attack of the Druids, were constituting proofs that that wait was almost over.

"In truth, Neffe," was the first thing Uncle Kurt said, confirming my presumptions, "it is not the letter that has affected me to an extent that you cannot imagine, but the Mystery of Belicena Villca, that which was hidden behind her actual existence and that is now uncovered before us. Of the letter, Neffe, of its contents, it is possible to assume a merely intellectual participation; but of the Mystery that the letter and that the death of Belicena pose, of the Mystery of the House of Tharsis, it is not possible to exclude oneself without being left out of the Strategy of the Gods."

"The Mystery has arrived to us," here Uncle Kurt, decidedly, was including himself in my adventure, "and we cannot and must not try to avoid it. Now, Kairos permitting, we must make it to the end, to the Tirodal Order, to Nimrod de Rosario, to Noyo of Tharsis and the Wise Sword, to the Final Battle."

I nodded, still surprised by the firm and solidary attitude of my uncle. He continued, astounding me once again.

"Look Arturo, I have thought more these days than you can imagine, evaluating the occurred events and calculating each step that must be taken in the future. By means of that global strategic analysis, and taking into account my personal experience, which you will soon have the opportunity of knowing what it consists in, since I will narrate to you the story of my life, I have drawn some conclusions that would be good you took into consideration. Before anything else, and just as I assumed from the beginning, I have verified that you are not at all prepared to face this mission." I wanted to protest, but Uncle Kurt raised his hand in an unappealable manner and I decided to allow him to complete his exposition. "Listen well, Neffe: I didn't not say that you can't carry it out, but that you are *not yet* prepared to undertake the mission. But you very soon will be if you comprehend my arguments and follow my instructions to the letter.

"Therefore, the first thing you must understand is that a mission like this is never initiated without a prior detachment. I understand, and you don't need to explain it to me, that such non-attachment is a state of spiritual consciousness that you experienced from the moment in which you launched yourself into this adventure: right now you feel disconnected from the world, liberated from material ties. But, realistically, I must tell you, that such an attitude is completely subjective, naïve, an obstacle to achieve the spiritual objective; an attitude that does not take into consideration the enemies who will try to prevent the concretion of the mission, enemies endowed with terrible powers and who have absolute mobility; an attitude, in short, that is strategically suicidal. Because is he really 'disconnected from the world' who sets out to 'fulfill a spiritual mission' taking advantage of 'the period of his vacation'; who depends 'on money' to travel, money that is limited and that at some point may run out; who underestimates the enemy and leaves behind him, outside himself, 'weak points' that can be easily attacked and destroyed, that is to say, who travels without previously renouncing the love for the 'things of the world,' whatever these may be, family, properties, friends, the habitual context where routine life takes place, etc., all possible 'targets' of enemy blows? No, Neffe; whoever behaves in this way is pure and simple, a good man, but not a good warrior: he will never come to fulfill his mission; the Enemy will stop him, striking behind his back, threatening or destroying that which 'outside' he loves, that to which he is really connected, tied, or attached, even if he does not admit it or recognize it."

I perfectly comprehended his point of view and I immediately agreed with him: in truth, I was still remaining tied to many things and my trip could not have been more improvised. Nevertheless, little was the time that I had to decide my Fate. Rather, Fate decided for me, without giving me time to change, to awaken, to "prepare myself" as Uncle Kurt was intending. Everything had happened so fast! What was I to do now? It is what I would ask Uncle Kurt:

"What else could I do given the circumstances, considering how the events occurred?" I questioned more to myself than to Uncle Kurt, trying to justify myself. "It's true, I still have my job, but it hadn't occurred to me that I may not return. And as for money: I'm not rich and you know it; and I really don't know how I'll be able to get what I need if this adventure is prolonged too much. Affectively, on the other hand, the love for my family and friends, I suppose that I will not know to what extent I master it until put to the test: you never know with the heart, Uncle Kurt! Yes, the reproaches are fair, but you must be the one who orients me at this time, otherwise I'll have no other remedy than to continue in the same 'naïve' way as I began."

Uncle Kurt was contemplating me with pity, no doubt amazed to see the irresponsibility with which I was taking things. According to him, the Druids were fierce enemies whom one ought not fear but neither underestimate. I was not fearing and that was good; but it was seeming evident that I was underestimating the enemy, that I was not noticing that I could be destroyed at any moment, that I was throwing myself to challenge a powerful adversary "without being prepared for it." I do not know if my attitude was then reaching such a degree of foolishness, but Uncle Kurt was believing so, and that was despairing him. Thence he was ready to consider me an inexpert soldier, a soldier in training of his particular army, and instead of suggesting and discussing with me what I should do, he returned to order the measures that in his opinion I would have to take without delay.

"You will immediately send a series of telegrams canceling all your commitments. Resign from your work, your studies, clubs, libraries, or any organization to which you are connected. Say goodbye to whomever you have to, communicating to them that you are embarking on a long journey: if you discourage their expectations of seeing you or saying goodbye, they will soon forget you. If you have any property, appoint a proxy, someone whom you do not know and whom does not know you, a law firm for example, and order its liquidation. Proceed in the same way with everything that links you to your old life: cut all ties, erase all traces, remove all tracks. It is not enough that you have died to yourself; you must also die to the World!

"Money will not be a problem for now: I will provide you with enough to carry out this mission. I have spent more than thirty years amassing money and the day has arrived to use it. And it is as much yours as it is mine, Neffe (Do you know that I had you named in my will?). Of course, my money solves the problems for the time being, but it is not a definitive solution: I will try, in the future, to teach you the operational tactics so that you can always get the money or the things that you need. These are techniques, methods of self-reliance, techniques that every Hyperborean Initiate must know how to apply."

Of course, I did everything that he had ordered me. I was carrying it out while my convalescence lasted, during the days in which Uncle Kurt was narrating to me his extraordinary history. Finally, the day that we had to leave, nothing of my previous life was left intact in Salta. Everything I had done in years of effort and work, was now undone: sooner or later, Dr. Arturo Siegnagel would be only a memory; and then not even that would exist, a possibility that was exciting Uncle Kurt. I was not wanting to think about the impression that those measures would have made on Papa and Mama, on Katalina, because "my heart would slacken" and I was fearing that Uncle Kurt noticed it: in front of him, I was wanting to appear stronger than what I was, I was wanting to reassure him about my poise and courage. I was wanting to put myself at his level, at the level of his demands, because, almost without noticing it, I had begun to admire Uncle Kurt, to value his great aptitudes, to appreciate and understand him.

Chapter VI

The day after he finished reading the letter, at 21:30 hours, Uncle Kurt settled into a comfortable hammock chair, next to my bed, and after remaining pensive for a few minutes, he began to narrate to me his life.

"Just as it occurs to you now, a series of 'strange' coincidences influenced the first years of my life in a determinant manner. To appreciate this assertion with greater perspective, I must begin the story many years before my birth, at the precise moment in which my father, Baron Reinald von Sübermann, came into the world, that is to say in the year 1894, in the city of Cairo, Egypt. In the same year, in Alexandria, 130 kilometers from Cairo, was born a person who would be more important in my life than any other. I refer to Rudolf Hess, whose birth occurred on April 26, 1894.

"Despite the distances between both cities, my father and Rudolf Hess soon met, since Hess' parents sent him to study at the *Lycée Français* d'Alexandrie—the school Papa was attending—from the age of six until twelve. Childhood companions, they were united by a tender friendship that strengthened over the years.

"Upon finishing their primary studies—just as many well-to-do Germans were doing with their children—the two were placed at the *Evangelisches Pädagogium* in *Godesberg am Rhein,* a town ten kilometers from Bonn.

"When they were both sixteen years old, that is to say in 1910, they separated to pursue different careers. Papa enrolls at the *Polytechnical Institute* of Berlin for Industrial Engineering. Rudolf Hess travels to Switzerland, to the *École supérieure de commerce* in Neuchâtel, at the behest of his father, a wealthy exporter from Alexandria, who was desiring to introduce the young man to the world of commerce. Rudolf's intention was, as far as possible, to pursue a Doctorate in mathematics.

"The war of 1914 ruins all their plans. Papa is reclaimed by my family to Cairo, where he returns when the conflict breaks out and definitively remains there, since upon taking charge of the Sugar Cane Refinery he will no longer be able to finish his studies.

"Rudolf Hess, who only remained a year in Switzerland, was in Hamburg perfecting himself in Foreign Trade and did not hesitate to enlist in the 1st Bavarian Infantry Regiment. He was wounded twice, in 1916 and 1917, receiving the Iron Cross for acts of heroism. In 1918 he entered the newly formed Imperial Air Corps, being instituted as a qualified pilot, but without intervening in aerial combat, since the armistice is signed in November of 1918 and he is demobilized.

"He returns to Egypt carrying a twin sorrow: defeated Germany is torn apart by the Treaty of Versailles and his parents have died during the war. The family businesses are taken care of by his siblings, the eldest Alfred, who is an accountant, and a married sister.

"He does not wish to occupy himself with commerce and thus makes it known: he intends to return to Germany to study, no longer mathematics, but History or Philosophy.

"He dedicates the time that he spends in Egypt to seek answers to so much misfortune. Answers that only the Initiates of the great Islamic or Gnostic Sects, of which Alexandria in particular and Egypt in general is a fertile hotbed, can give.

"But I will leave for another day the account of the Esoteric Current in which Rudolf Hess was going to enter in those days of 1919, in Egypt, which would bring him alongside Adolf Hitler in 1920 and to England in 1941. I will continue with the chronological unfoldment of the principal events that interest the story and, then, we will analyze these things."

Uncle Kurt was, apparently, a precise narrator, who knew what he was wanting to say and was not straying from it. I was realizing that several days would pass until he completed his recollections, and this prospect was filling me with delight.

"In February 1919," Uncle Kurt was imperturbably continuing, "Rudolf Hess traveled to Cairo to visit Papa and another friend, Omar Nautais. They met for the first time in six years, with the consequent mutual joy and that of my mother, who also knew Rudolf from childhood.

"Papa had married in 1917 and on 11/17/1918 I was born, so on that date, February of 1919, I was three months old. Since they had not yet baptized me, Papa asked Rudolf to be my Godfather, to which Rudolf gladly agreed because he was loving my parents and wishing to give them a show of his affection.

"The ceremony was held at the Cairo Lutheran Church, on a cool February morning in 1919, the 17th to be exact.

"Here you have, Neffe, a first coincidence," Uncle Kurt was saying in a reflective tone, "for that 25-year-old war hero who was holding me in his arms, would fifteen years later be Germany's Minister of State and Chancellor Adolf Hitler's right-hand man, his *Stellvertreter*.[7]

"In Egypt, as in all foreign countries, the German community organized for the training of its children, the *Hitlerjungen*, Hitler Youth, with the veiled supervision of the military attachés to the German Embassy. Within this movement, there was a 'junior' group for children from 10 to 15 years of age called *Jungvolk*, to which I entered at the age of 10, when I was still attending primary studies at the German School in Cairo.

"I graduated in 1932 and Papa decided to send me to Germany to continue higher education. I was then 14 years old and holding the title of *Fähnleinführer* in the *Hitlerjungen*.

"The following year, in July 1933, we set off from Alexandria on a merchant ship which, with a few stops, was going directly to Venice; from there we would continue to Berlin by train.

"In those days, Rudolf Hess was a very important personage in the Third Reich and incredibly popular among the members of the German community in Egypt who were feeling gratified with the triumph of one of their own. Rudolf worked hard all those years to contribute to the Führer's victory and, except for a few trips every one or two years, he had completely abandoned his first Egyptian homeland. However, he never forgot his friends, who were not many, nor his Godson Kurt von Sübermann.

"We were invariably receiving a Christmas card every year and when in the Jungvolk we needed a drum, I remember that Papa urged me to write a letter to my prestigious Godfather, who not only kindly responded with a missive in which he was encouraging me to study and persevere within the Hitlerjungen, but took care of my childish request.

"One day we received a summons from the German Embassy to pick up a parcel, of which its dispatch note was to be signed by *Fähnleinführer* Kurt von Sübermann, that is to say by me. It was the official drum of the Hitlerjungen, painted with black and white flames, a *Rune '⚡'* (s) from the old Germanic Futhark alphabet, in the shape of a lightning bolt. The Hitlerjungen was using one Rune '⚡' but the *Schutzstaffel*[8] was authorized to use two (⚡⚡). There was also a letter from *Reichsju-*

---

7. Deputy

8. "Protective Echelon"

gendführer[9] Baldur von Schirach in which he was confirming that at the request of the Private Secretary of the *Führer,* Rudolf Hess, he was sending a drum to the distant Comrades of the Jungvolk in Egypt. It was following a long list of concepts and was ending recommending to use the **Hymn of the Hitler Youth:**

> *Vorwärts! Vorwärts! [Forward! Forward!]*
> *Schmettern die hellen Fanfaren, [Blare the bright fanfares,]*
> *Vorwärts! Vorwärts! [Forward! Forward!]*
> *Jugend kennt keine Gefahren. [Youth knows no dangers.]*

"There was Baldur von Schirach's signature and three words: **Heil und Sieg.**[10]

"That drum and that letter gave me an unwarranted fame among the German children in Cairo, while stimulating my vocation to continue in the line of the Hitlerjungen.

"In 1933 news arrived in Egypt that the Führer, on celebrating his 44th birthday, would open the *NAPOLA* schools that were dissolved by the Allies in 1920.

"They would be training schools for the future German Elite and in them the Hitler Youth cadres would be prepared. Thinking of the difficulty of getting into it as a German-Egyptian, Papa, who was possessing the bitter experience of not being considered 'true German' during his studies in Bad Godesberg, considered the possibility of turning to Rudolf Hess to facilitate my admission.

"To this end, before leaving, he sent him a letter requesting an interview and informing him of the approximate date of our arrival in Europe.

"The ports and strange cities that we were passing through were fantastic sites for a proud 15-year-old Fähnleinführer who was torn between the joy of going and the anxiety of arriving. Arriving, yes, because how marvelous was the final destination of the magical journey: Germany.

"You look at me with incredulity, Neffe," Uncle Kurt was apologizing, "and I understand you; it is difficult to understand what we young Germans, even foreigners like myself, were feeling in those days. Egypt was the beloved homeland, the land where I was born and grew up.

"But Germany was something else.

---

9. National leader of the Hitler Youth.

10. *"Hail and Victory"*

"The Land of Siegfried and the Führer; of the Rhine River and Lorelei; of the Valkyries and the Nibelungen. It was a 'Fatherland of the Spirit,' where the myth, the legend, and the tradition of our elders were being nurtured.

"An eternal and distant fatherland that would suddenly become real through that fabulous voyage. We had been educated in a mysticism, the formulation of which was: 'Blood and Soil'; we were acting accordingly.

"At the end of July, in the middle of the European summer, we arrived in Venice, the end point of our sea voyage, from where we would take a combination of trains toward Berlin. We were about to get off the ship when the Captain announced to us that we would have to stop by the offices, which the company has in the port, to pick up a message.

"We arrived there, our hearts heavy thinking of bad news from Egypt, to instead find a letter with the Third Reich's official letterhead. In it, Rudolf Hess was notifying us that he would be absent from Berlin until the second week of August but that, if we were wishing to visit him right away, we could go to Upper Bavaria. The cause of this was that the Führer had decided to rest a few days at his Chalet *'Haus Wachenfeld,'* on the *Obersalzberg,* in *Berchtesgaden,* and part of his cabinet accompanied him staying in nearby inns. Rudolf Hess and his wife Ilse would be delighted to receive us if we were deciding to go there."

"Papa could not hide his satisfaction, for this situation was very beneficial to our plans. On the one hand, we were saving ourselves from traveling hundreds of kilometers, since from Venice to Berchtesgaden there are only two hundred kilometers, while to Berlin, more than a thousand. On the other hand, we were having the possibility of meeting Rudolf, outside of any official protocol, without putting up with the interference from secretaries or assistants and having the time to converse and remember the good old days.

"The sight of legendary Venice, the passage through Austria, and the arrival to the Bavarian Alps, were the threshold of my entry into a new and marvelous world.

"From the moment in which I stepped on Bavarian soil, I noticed that the air was as if electrified, as if a hidden engine

---

11. In Reicholdsgrün, Bavaria, was the "German" house of the Hess family, constructed by Rudolf's father. However, the Stellvertreter's vacations were usually taking place in Berchtesgaden, near the Führer's residence.

sent powerful vibrations through the ether. It was something so evident in those days—or years—that anyone who was moderately predisposed, was able to perceive it.

"These vibrations, which could not be picked up by a physical organ, were carrying a message to the receiving spirit: Germany awake![12] But this two-word translation is crude; it sounds like an elementary patriotic proclamation, it does not fully transmit what that mysterious force was evoking in our Spirit. I will try to explain it. It was saying 'Germany awake!' and whoever was listening was not thinking of geographical Germany, not even of the Third Reich, but was clearly feeling himself in another world, without borders, in a Germany without Time or Space, the *only limits* of which were precisely those fixed by this same vibration.

"Germany would end only where the unifying vibration was no longer perceived, for, now everyone knew, Germany was also that immanent inaudible sound called *Volkschwingen*.[13]

"Germany awake! the transcendent message was saying and Germany, like the phoenix, was being reborn from the ashes of its last defeats; it would become the epicenter of a new *Weltanschauung*[14] in which the infamies of the world Jewish conspiracy and Marxist-Leninist subversion would have no place.

"The Brown revolution would bring about a New Order that would only admit the hierarchy of the Spirit into its ruling Elite; those who were really superior in their own right, regardless of any other condition, would be superior. This perspective was stimulating healthy competition, insufflating new hopes, and encouraging everyone to share in the adventure of the 'German awakening.' And no one was to doubt, for the New Order was guaranteed, ensured in its purity by the figure of the *Führer*.

"Yes, at last Germany had its Führer. He was the true architect of the New Order, the Chief who would lead the German people to victory.

"The year was 1933, Germany was awakening, Adolf Hitler was the Führer."

---

12. *"Deutschland erwache!"*

13. Vibration of the people.

14. Conception of the world; ideology.

Chapter VII

I was fifteen years old, my soul full of illusions and the clear perception of *volkschwingen* when, by Papa's hand, we arrived at Rudolf Hess' lodging in Berchtesgaden.

"The news had been spread that the Führer was in Haus Wachenfeld and the area was overrun with journalists and onlookers, so it was difficult for us to get settled. We finally made it to the modest 'Kinderland' inn about two kilometers from Rudolf Hess' house.

"We spent the night there and early in the morning we athletically set off on a snowy trail that was following the nearby hill in its curves. Papa, dressed in Bavarian style, was wearing the narrow cuff of his mountain pants tucked into thick wool knee-high socks. Haferlschuhe,[15] shirt, and collarless jacket were completing the outfit. I was sporting a brand-new dark gray Hitlerjungen uniform, comprised of shorts, pocketed jacket with sailor collar; belt buckle with Rune ⚡, strap crossed over the chest and a small dagger on the belt with the inscription '*Blut und Ehre*'[16] engraved on the blade; neckerchief with woggle, lace-up boots, and gray socks.

"The house where the Hess family was lodging, was an old wooden building in classic Alpine style; small but comfortable. When knocking at the door, we were attended by a sleepy officer of the ⚡⚡ who was keeping guard, sleeping in the living room, next to the burning fireplace. His name was Edwin Papp and he was ⚡⚡ *Obersturmführer*.[17]

" 'Herr Hess is still lying down,' said the ⚡⚡ officer. 'He will be glad to see you, since he has been waiting for you several days. Sit in the living room, please, while I prepare coffee.'

"Half an hour later Rudolf Hess was appearing, impeccably dressed in a gym outfit: pants, windbreaker, and blue sneakers. Tall, well-built, with a quadrate face and bushy eyebrows, his black and brilliant eyes were clearly striking and were seeming to attract attention to him.

---

15. Traditional Bavarian shoe.

16. Blood and Honor

17. Lit. ⚡⚡-*Senior storm leader.*

"Barely smiling, he paused for a moment to look at Papa and then they merged in an embrace that elicited exclamations of joy and spontaneous laughter from both of them. It was many years since I had seen him and, therefore, I was only keeping a very vague memory of him, but it surprised me to discover a timidness that I could not even imagine in the Führer's powerful deputy.

"He turned toward me and admiringly observed me.

"*'Dieser mein Patenkind?'*[18] he said as if to himself. 'How time flies! He is already a man. A new man for a new Reich.'

"'Tell me Kurt,' this time he was addressing me, 'don't you want to stay in Germany? Here you could study and serve the Fatherland.'

"'Yes, *Taufpate*[19] Rudolf,' I responded overjoyed, 'that's what I want. My greatest ambition is to enter the *NAPOLA* School.'

"'Now that's a big ambition,' Rudolf Hess said, 'we'll see what we can do.'

"At that moment Ilse Pröhl Hess entered, whom Papa did not know, but after making the introductions, she was seeming to be a lifelong friend. This was because Ilse was a simple and energetic woman, but a lady of great kindness. A former National Socialist militant, she was moving away from politics since her marriage to Hess in 1927 and was expressing, shortly after speaking with us, the desire to have children, which God was seeming to deny. Just five years later, Rudolf Hess' only son, Wolf, was born, but that is another story.

"We spent a week in Berchtesgaden during which Rudolf, Ilse, and Papa became close on several occasions, when they were not going to Haus Wachenfeld to see the Führer, who was otherwise besieged by Göring and other party members.

"On those evenings, when Papa and the Hesses were exchanging memories and anecdotes, I used to interrogate, for hours, the officer in charge of keeping guard. According to my judgment in those days, there was no goal more worthy of a young German's efforts than to arrive at belonging to the ⚡⚡ Elite Corps.

"One of the first days that we spent in Berchtesgaden, Papa and Rudolf withdrew to speak on an exterior veranda, located on a hillside and protected by a railing that was surrounding

---

18. *"This is my Godson?"*

19. Godfather in German.

the house. Normally I would have ignored them, but something in their gestures, a whispering tone in the conversation, alerted me to the possibility that they were talking about me.

"I thought they were referring to my admission to the *NAPOLA* School and a growing anxiety got the better of me. Unable to resist the temptation—an unpardonable offense, my father would say—I did something repudiable: I spied on them.

"Pretending to be standing against a window that was opened in the vicinity of Papa and Rudolf Hess, I tried to hear their conversation, which effectively unfolded around the topic of my person. But it was not about admission to the *NAPOLA* School, but about a question that filled me with astonishment.

" '...You can leave Kurt with me then,' Rudolf was saying. 'Did you speak to him about the Sign?'

" 'I didn't think it was convenient,' answered Papa. 'Besides, I wouldn't know how to explain that Mystery with the sufficient profundity. You know more about these things than I; you are the best person to speak to him.'

"Rudolf Hess was affirmatively nodding his head while he was maintaining that timid smile, so characteristic of his person, etched on his face.

" 'Let's wait a few years,' said Rudolf Hess, 'if Kurt doesn't ask first. Hasn't he ever suspected anything? Hasn't he been involved in any abnormal occurrences?'

" 'No, Rudolf, except for the *Ophite* matter, which I already told you about in my letters, nothing strange occurred to him afterward, and he even seems to have forgotten it, or at least, the memory does not affect him.'

"At this point in the conversation between Rudolf Hess and my father, what I was understanding was little, but at the mention of the *Ophites* an incredible childhood episode instantly came to my memory. When I was about ten or eleven years old, I was the victim of a kidnapping! It was not a criminal kidnapping with the aim of collecting ransom, but an abduction perpetrated by fanatics of the Ophite Order that only lasted a few hours until the Police, thanks to the data that a professional informer provided, could thwart it.

Chapter VIII

T hings happened like this: my parents had traveled to Cairo—the familial sugar Refinery is a few kilometers away from that city—in order to go shopping.

"While Mama was entertaining herself in the vast departments of the English Store, I, eager for mischief, was slyly slipping away toward the street. A moment later I was running several blocks from the Store, innocently attracted by the hustle and bustle of the 'Black Market,' a labyrinthine neighborhood of miserable street stands and a safe haven for beggars and petty criminals.

"That day the human tide was dense in the narrow streets in which the distance between two vendor stands was barely leaving a walkway for pedestrian traffic. Pottery, fruits, carpets, animals, everything imaginable was being sold there and my curious eyes were stopping before each piece of merchandise. I had no fear because I had not drifted too far and it would be easy to go back or for Mama to find me.

"Following an alley, I came to a wide cobblestone plaza, with spouting fountain, into which was leading a myriad of streets and alleys that only the irregular layout of these Cairo Neighborhoods can justify. There were hundreds of vendors, vagrants, beggars, and women with their faces covered by the *niqāb*, who were collecting water in earthenware pitchers.

"I approached the fountain trying to orient myself, without noticing a group of singing Arabs who were surrounding a snake charmer. This spectacle is very common in Egypt, so it would not have caught my attention, except for the unusual fact that upon seeing me, the Arabs were lowering the tone of their singing until completely silent. I did not notice this at first, for the charmer was continuing playing the flute while the green eyes of the cobra, hypnotized by the music, was seeming to only look at me. Suddenly, the flutist also joined the group of silent Arabs and I, realizing that something abnormal was occurring, one after the other, was taking cautious steps back.

"The spell was broken when one of them, giving a frightful shriek, shouted in Arabic, 'The Sign!' while awkwardly pointing at me. It was like a signal. All at once they were excitedly shouting and running toward me with the revealed intention of capturing me.

"There was a terrible commotion because I, being a child, was running through the crowd with greater velocity, while my pursuers were being held up by various obstacles, which they were eliminating by the expeditious system of throwing to the ground whatever crossed their paths. Fortunately, the crowd was large and many witnesses to the episode were later able to report it to the police.

"The pursuit did not last long, for the frenzied fanaticism that was animating those men was multiplying their strength, while mine was rapidly being consumed.

"Initially I took a street full of merchants, escaping in the opposite direction to the one used to reach the plaza, but after a few blocks, attempting to avoid a multitude of vendors and customers, I entered into an alley. This was not straight, but was getting narrower and narrower, until it became a path of a meter wide between the walls of two Neighborhoods that had advanced from different directions, without respecting the street.

"As I was running, the alley was seeming more clear of obstacles and, consequently, my pursuers gained ground, until a protruding stone from the uneven ground caused me to defeatedly tumble. I was immediately surrounded by the excited Arabs, who did not take an instant to wrap me in one of their cloaks and carry me imprisoned in their powerful arms. The shock was great and unpleasant and, no matter how I was shouting and crying, nothing was seeming to affect my captors, who were now running faster than before.

"A while later we arrived at our destination. Although I could not see, I was perfectly understanding Arabic and I comprehended then that the fanatics were loudly calling out for someone whom they were referring to as **Master Naassene.**

"At last they freed me from the cowl wrapping that was blinding me, depositing me on a soft silk cushion, of regular size. When I accustomed my eyes to the gloom of the place, I realized that I was in a large room, dimly illuminated by oil lamps. The floor, covered with rich carpets and cushions, had the presence of a dozen kneeling men, with their foreheads on the floor, who from time to time were looking up at me and then, folding their hands over their heads, were raising their eyes to the sky, crying out, *'Ophis! Ophis!'*

"Of course, all this frightened me, for although I had not suffered harm, the memory of my parents, and the fact that I was a prisoner, was producing great distress in me. Seated on the cushion, surrounded by so many men, it was impossible to think of escaping, and this certainty was wrenching painful sobs from me. Suddenly, a good-natured voice arose from behind me, bringing momentary hope and consolation to my sufferings. I turned around and saw an old man with a white beard, wearing a turban, coming toward me.

" 'Do not be afraid son,' the old man said in Arabic, whom they were calling Naassene. 'No one will harm you here. You are an envoy of the Serpent God, *Ophis-Lúcifer,* whom we serve. The Sign that you bear, marked for His Glory, proves it.'

"He indicated in an affectionate gesture that permitted me to be held in his arms, in order to thus 'show me the image of God.' I was really needing affectionate treatment because those fanatics were not noticing that *I was a child*. I hugged the old man and he started to walk to one end of the room— which turned out to be a cellar—where a column was rising on which pedestal was shining a small sculpture of highly polished stone. It had the shape of a cobra raised on itself with refulgent[20] eyes, perhaps due to the incrustation of more intense green stones. The image fascinated me and I would have touched it if the old man did not pull back in time.

" 'Did you like the image of God, "little envoy"?' said the Master.

" 'Yes,' I responded without knowing why.

" 'You have the right to possess the jewel of the Order,' continued the Master as he was rummaging in a small pouch of fine leather that was hanging around his neck. 'Here it is!' exclaimed Master Naassene. 'It is the consecrated image of the Serpent God. To obtain it, men pass through hard tests that sometimes take them their whole lives. You, on the other hand, need not pass any test because you are the bearer of the sign.'

"With a sharp dagger that he pulled from his belt, he cut a green cord from a bundle that was hanging on the wall and, stringing the silver replica into a loop, he placed it around my neck. Next he looked into my eyes, so intensely that I have never been able to forget it. Neither did I forget his words,

---

20. shining brightly

which he pronounced in a very loud voice, *ritually*. He had grabbed me with his left arm and was lifting me up so that I was seen by all, while with the index finger of his right hand, he was pointing to the Serpent God. He said this:

"Initiates of the Liberating Serpent! Followers of the Serpent of Uncreated Light! Worshipers of the Avenging Serpent! *Behold the Bearer of the Sign of the Origin! He who can comprehend the Serpent with His Sign; he who can obtain the Highest Wisdom that the Man of Mud is given to know!* In the interior of this Divine child, in the bosom of the eternal Spirit, is present the Mark of the Enemy of the Creator and of Creation, the Symbol of the Origin of our God and of all the imprisoned Spirits of Matter. And that Symbol of the Origin has manifested itself in the Sign that we, and no one else, have been capable of seeing: Divine child; he will be able to comprehend the Serpent *from within!* But we, thanks to him, to his liberating Sign, *have comprehended it outside,* and nothing can stop us now!"

" 'Yes, yes! Now we can depart!' the unbridled Ophite Initiates were shouting in chorus.

"The minutes passed and everything was calming down in the refuge of the Ophite Order. The Arabs were engaged in some kind of preparation, and I, enthusiastic about the serpentine gift and reassured by the good treatment from Master Naassene, was not suspicious when he brought me a glass of refreshing mint. A few minutes later I was falling into a deep stupor, probably because of a narcotic laced into the drink.

"When I awoke I was with my parents, in the British Sanatorium in Cairo, next to a doctor, in white scrubs, who was uselessly trying to convince them that I was simply sleeping.

"With the passing of the years, I was reconstructing the actions that led to my release. Apparently, the Chief of Police moved quickly, fearing that the kidnapping of a member of the wealthy and influential Von Sübermann family would lead to a purge in the Police Department, the head of which— would be the first to roll—was him. Through confidants, beggars, vagrants, or simple witnesses, they learned, without a doubt, that the perpetrators of the kidnapping were the fanatical members of the millenary 'Ophite' Gnostic Order, considered as harmless and even very wise.

"At first this puzzled the policemen, who were not managing to glimpse the motive for the kidnapping but, following some clues, they arrived at Master Naassene's house. The Arabs, in the euphoria of transporting me there, had imprudently behaved, all penetrating together amid shouts and exclamations. A beggar, an eyewitness to the strange procession, as eager to earn the reward that my family had offered, as to avoid the police batons, gave the particulars of the house where the abductors entered. This was surrounded by the authorities, but, as no one was responding to the calls, they proceeded to break in the door, finding a humble home, totally empty of people. After an exhaustive inspection, it was discovered, concealed under a carpet, the trap door that was leading, by means of a musty stone staircase, to the hidden temple of the Serpent God.

"A macabre spectacle surprised those present because, stretched out upon a silk cushion, was lying my lifeless body surrounded by cadavers with convulsed expression that, as a last gesture, were directing their rigid arms toward me.

"All the kidnappers had died by cobra venom. Master Naassene and the idol had vanished.

"The impression that the newcomers received was very bad because they thought that I was also dead, but they immediately realized their error and I was transported to the British Sanatorium together with my parents.

"I was still keeping the silver serpent hanging around my neck, it being jealously guarded by Papa, although at times, years later, he used to show it to me when we were remembering that adventure.

"At that moment, while I was listening to Papa and Rudolf Hess talking about the Ophites, all these events were crowding together in my mind.

"I had situated myself sideways against the window, so that I could only see them conversing out of the corner of my eye, but the voice was arriving clear to my ears.

"'This is the silver jewel,' Papa was saying, 'with the image of *Ophis-Lúcifer*. I kept it with the original cord; here, now you must guard it.'

"It was an extraordinary revelation—I could not help but turn a little to see better—for Papa never gave importance to the little idol and neither was I, who was not realizing its significance. It had even been erased from my mind years ago.

"And it was clear there that Papa had pretended and played down the importance of the matter, but in reality was attributing some unknown value to the silver idol! And the strangest thing was that he had brought it hidden to Germany, offering it to the custody of Rudolf Hess. This made no sense to me.

"On the other hand, they were speaking of the Sign like the Arabs. What Sign? Years after the kidnapping, I was still looking at myself in the mirror searching for the blessed Sign that had led those unfortunate ones to their deaths; and I never found anything abnormal. Neither did I suspect that Papa believed in the existence of that mark—or stigma?

"In my head a whirlwind of ideas were spinning in disorder, as I was distractedly seeing Rudolf Hess examining the silver serpent.

"Suddenly, inserting his hand through the neckline of the windbreaker, he pulled out a cord that was encircling around his neck. Hanging from it was a silver serpent, exactly like mine!

"Rudolf Hess had gathered them in his hand for my Father's contemplation and, after a few minutes, he put on his own and pocketed the other. Moments later they were both entering the warm living room without mentioning the subject of their preceding conversation.

"This reserved attitude convinced me of the inconvenience of approaching the matter in any way, since it would give away the censurable espionage committed. I did not give it much thought: I would keep quiet until I was directly spoken to, but I promised myself to do the impossible to obtain information about the mysterious Sign.

It was two in the morning and Uncle Kurt stood up with the intention of going to his room. I was not reproaching him for that attitude since he had been talking for several hours, but the story awakened inquietudes and questions in my Spirit, turning me impatient and inconsiderate.

"Uncle Kurt," I said, "I know it's late, and I also know that we can continue our chat tomorrow, but I really need that you respond to two questions before you go."

"Ha-ha-ha-ha," he laughed his terrible guffaw, "you're just like me at your age: you need to get answers in order to live. It's like a thirst. I understand you, Neffe. What do you want to know?"

"Only two things, I said. First: Is there a possibility that that Sign that the Arabs were seeing in you, is the same as that which Belicena Villca saw on me?"

"Without any doubt, Neffe," he responded. The Sign signifies many things, but it is also a *Sanguine Signum*[21] and we both have the same blood. Blood is not a determinant factor for the appearance of the Sign but it is a 'condition of quality'; if a sign appears on members of our family, *it is the same sign.*"

I had been unaware until today that there was another Von Sübermann alive with such a mark. Papa, with whom I finally spoke about it, told me that according to a familial tradition, an ancestor of ours "demonstrated" to his contemporaries by means of certain marks, "to be a chosen one of Heaven," by virtue of which King Albert II of Austria granted him the title of Baron in the fifteenth century. From that Epoch, the familial annals were recorded, everything prior to it being obscure and unknown. In the subsequent centuries, the family was always dedicated to the production of sugar, as Belicena Villca says in her letter, and remained attentive to the appearance of descendants with "special aptitudes." In fact, there were several members of the Stirp who demonstrated to possess supernatural gifts, but no one managed to solve the familial enigma. Only the last generations of the Egyptian branch were able to approach the solution of the mystery, upon discovering the existence of a mark or sign of cyclical appearance among the members of the family through the ages. But except for this news, obtained thanks to the contacts made with certain *ulamā*, wise men of Islam, little is what could be known with more precision."

To my despair Uncle Kurt was still approaching the door, with the firm intention of leaving.

"I'll ask you the second question," I said. "Have you been able to find out what the Sign is?" Uncle Kurt made a gesture of annoyance.

"Do you think that an answer that I myself searched for years can be summarized in two words? I suppose your question points to the Symbol of the Origin, which is the metaphysical cause of our sign. If it is so, I will only tell you that everything I could find out in this respect is less than what Belicena Villca exposes in her letter. I fully agree with her, and according to what was revealed to me in the ᛋᛋ Black Order, that the Symbol of the Origin is linked to the Mystery of the spiritual enchainment. The Symbol of the Origin, Neffe, *is*

---

21. Mark of blood.

analogous to a Charismatic Mark: whoever is encompassed by said mark, conscious or not, "oriented" toward it or not, remains inevitably enchained to Matter; whoever instead succeeds in embracing the mark, comprehending it or transcending it, succeeds in liberating himself from enchainment, 'is free in the Origin.' And those who procure to keep the Eternal Spirit enchained under such a mark, or Symbol of the Origin, are the Masters of the Kalachakra, the White Brotherhood of Chang Shambhala. And those who try to make the Spirit transcend the Symbol of the Origin, perhaps by comprehending the Serpent, are the Initiates of the Hyperborean Wisdom, the Liberating Gods of Agartha.

"This is, in synthesis, what I know about the Symbol of the Origin. Now, if your question refers to the Sign as a mark, I will tell you that I know even less, for the Sign, only those who already *know* it can *recognize it.*

"It is basic, Neffe, to distinguish one thing from another, one must first know it; the same principle applies to the Sign; only those who have the Truth in their interior, 'see' it, for only in this way is it possible to recognize the exterior Truth, that is why you and I cannot see the Sign even though we carry it with us, because we have yet to arrive at the Truth."

I was listening to Uncle Kurt devastated, for I had harbored the secret hope that he would know about the Sign and that perhaps he would agree to confide his secret to me, but his negative answer was simple and logical: the revelation of the Sign must be interior.

My face was reflecting discouragement and this made Uncle Kurt laugh again.

"Don't worry, Neffe, it is not so important that we see the Sign but that those who must help us recognize it. And this always occurs as your own experience proves.

"But there is something that perhaps compensates the curiosity that you feel. In the years that I spent in Asia, I obtained precise information about our Sign: its bodily location."

"Where is it?" I asked with undisguised impatience.

"In a curious place, Neffe," he answered with evident glee, "on the ears." He looked at the clock and without waiting for a response he said, "See you tomorrow, Neffe Arturo," and he went out.

At first I thought Uncle Kurt was making fun of me, but then I went to the bathroom, to the mirror, to look at my ears. There was nothing abnormal about them, small, lobeless, attached to the head, they were, mind you, the same as Uncle Kurt's.

Definitively, I was not able to "see" the famous Sign; and I went to sleep.

Chapter IX

The next morning I awoke with the present memory of the last concepts set forth by Uncle Kurt the previous night, which were slowly but effectively clarifying the Mystery in which I was finding myself immersed. For one thing, it was already certain that my uncle was sharing the same occult philosophy of Belicena Villca, the "Hyperborean Wisdom," and that the same was revealed to him during his career as an officer of the Waffen-*SS*: this was more than I could dream of when coming to Santa María!

And there was also the question of the Sign: not only was Uncle Kurt knowing the existence of the Sign, but he was confirming to me that both he and I were bearers of it! There was then no doubt that, like the Ophites, Belicena Villca had perceived it, on my ears or wherever that it was plasmated, and it had made her decide to write her incredible letter. And in the case of both the Ophites and that of Belicena Villca, death had implacably intervened, as if She were an inescapable actor in the drama of those marked by the Sign!

"Good morning, Señorcito, I come to cure your head," said old Juana, the circumstantial nurse. "I brought what you asked me for. Look, Señorcito..."

She was brandishing a shiny-edged razor, a utensil that she had requested with the intention of shaving my head, already partially depilated around the wound by Dr. Palacios.

After the treatment, which was consisting in washing the scar and dyeing it with an iodine-based tincture, old Juana devoted herself to the task of shaving my head, a concession made upon realizing the impossibility of being able to do it myself, with only one hand.

Half an hour later, sporting a perfectly shaved skull like a bonze from Indochina, I was having the hearty breakfast that the solicitous old woman served me.

"At this rate you will soon be fine, Señorcito," said the old woman, delighted by the way in which I was devouring the victuals.

"Yes, but with several extra kilos," I replied without stopping eating.

At nine o'clock, Uncle Kurt came up to my room.

"How are you, Neffe? Ready to hear another part of my story?"

"Yes, Uncle Kurt," I responded, "I'm anxious, really anxious to hear what you have to tell."

He settled into his hammock chair and began to speak.

"Well, we had left off that after catching my Father's conversation with Rudolf Hess about the Sign, I decided not to speak of it until one or the two of them took the initiative."

I nodded as Uncle Kurt was picking back up the thread of the story.

"At the end of the first week of August 1933, we left toward Berlin by train. Rudolf Hess and Ilse, on the other hand, would go to Munich by automobile and from there they would arrive in Berlin by plane, together with the Führer, Göring, and several personalities of the Third Reich, who were finishing their vacations.

"In Berlin we stayed at the Hotel *Kaiserhof,* former headquarters of the *NSDAP*[22] and awaited, as agreed in Berchtesgaden, news from Rudolf Hess. It arrived in mid-August in the form of a summons to meet Rudolf Hess at the Ministry of Education and Science. We had to be ready at 07:00 hours the following day at the hotel, since we would be picked up by an official vehicle.

"At seven o'clock, ⚡ Officer Papp, whom we knew from being Rudolf Hess' guard in Berchtesgaden, arrived in a uniformed SA car with chauffeur.

" 'Herr Hess awaits you at the Ministry of Education and Science. I left him there before I came to pick you up,' said the ⚡ man

"In a few minutes we arrived and were led by the ⚡ man to a door on which was reading, '*NAPOLA* National Directorate.' We entered.

"In a spacious, soberly furnished room, we found Rudolf Hess in SA uniform, a stern-looking man and a secretary who was typing on a typewriter. They all stopped when we arrived.

" 'Professor Joachim Haupt, I introduce to you Baron Reinald von Sübermann,' said Rudolf Hess.

" 'Baron Von Sübermann, you are before Joachim Haupt, National Director of the *NAPOLA*,' Rudolf Hess completed the introduction.

---

22. Initials of *Nationalsozialistische Deutsche Arbeiterpartei,* which means: *National Socialist German Workers' Party.*

"While they were shaking hands, Rudolf took the floor.

" 'I have been discussing Kurt's induction with Herr Professor and, despite the lack of vacancies, we arrived at an agreement. He will be incorporated into the first *NAPOLA* in *Lissa*[23] to join the "Selective Corps of Oriental Studies." '

"My Destiny was apparently resolved. Professor Haupt was carefully observing me; at last he spoke.

" 'Young Von Sübermann, it is my understanding that you are fluent in several languages. Could you tell me what they are?' he asked.

" 'Yes, Herr Professor. Apart from my native languages Arabic, English, and German, I speak French and Greek,' I timidly answered.

" 'Five languages is more than sufficient to enter *NAPOLA* in Lissa,' said Professor Haupt, 'but your mastery of Arabic interests us. Would you be willing to study other languages of the Middle East or of Asia, let us say for example, Turkish or Russian?'

" 'Yes, I would like to learn other languages and I am willing to study that which best suits to serve my country,' I responded, somewhat perplexed, for it never occurred to me that I would receive such specific training in the *NAPOLA*.

" 'Then there is no more to discuss,' said Professor Haupt. 'I will issue you an order of incorporation. Next Monday you are to present yourself in Lissa.'

"He turned to Papa.

" 'We have agreed with Herr that this would be the best career for your son. Normally at the *NAPOLA* School the official secondary school curriculum is taught with specialization in the arts, natural sciences, modern languages, etc., but by a reserved decree of the Führer, we have just created a special division for Asiatic studies. This division will be called the "Selective Corps of Oriental Studies" and there the future *Ostenführer*[24] will be trained who, later on, will serve in special missions in Asia. *Reichsführer*[25] Himmler has proposed a curriculum plan, and one of the requisites to fulfill is the mastery of Asiatic languages. We already have Professors of Tibetan and

---

23. Leszno, Poland

24. Literally, "leader of the East."

25. Lit. *Reich leader*. Highest rank of the ⚡⚡.

Mongolian dialects, and of Sanskrit. Young Kurt can be a good assistant to the Arabic Professor, which is an advantage for all.

" 'There will be three intensive years in the NAPOLA, which will then be supplemented, if our plans are realized, by a subsequent training in the ⚡⚡. This is confidential information that I disclose to you by the sole fact that Herr Hess vouches for your discretion.

" 'I understand that being in Egypt, you will not be able to duly look after your son's well-being. Have you given thought to whom you will delegate the responsibility of Guardianship?' asked Professor Haupt.

"Papa and Rudolf Hess looked at each other and the latter nodded his head in mute acceptance.

" 'I will take care of young Kurt,' said Rudolf Hess. 'Arrange the necessary papers to fulfill this formality.'

" 'Then everything is settled,' said Professor Haupt, 'Do you agree, Baron Von Sübermann?'

" 'I totally agree. I could not find another guardian better for my son, nor is there anyone in Germany in whom I trust more than Rudolf,' said Papa, who was still moved by Rudolf Hess' gesture.

"Moments later, an efficient secretary was preparing a Personal File in my name, archiving the affidavits of Rudolf Hess and of my father, and handing me a sealed envelope that I was to deliver in Lissa when presenting myself the following Monday.

" 'Heil Hitler!' said Professor Joachim Haupt and Rudolf Hess in unison, upon dismissing themselves, exchanging the old Roman salute, consisting of raising the right arm and clicking their heels together.

"On the stone stairs of the Ministry of Education and Science, another farewell took place, but this time more painful, because Papa and Rudolf Hess were deeply fond of each other. The multiple occupations of Rudolf Hess were making it very difficult for him to concretize another meeting, so they decided to say goodbye there and then.

" 'See you soon, esteemed Reinald,' said Rudolf to Papa, incapacitated by his habitual timidity to be more expressive. 'I will miss you. You're one of the few true friends that I have and it's always a great joy to be with you. Don't worry about Kurt, I'll take care of him; as his guardian, I'll be immediately notified of any news that may arise.

" 'And you, Kurt,' said Rudolf Hess addressing me, 'do not fail to let me know of any necessities or problems that you have. Take this card,' he extended to me a rectangle of cardboard with the embossed eagle of the Third Reich. 'You can call the telephone number there and request my presence or transmit your request to *ϟϟ Obersturmführer* Papp, whom you already know.'

"He descended a step, according to his custom of making distance to observe his interlocutors, and gazed at us with sad eyes, while he was barely giving a timid smile on his mouth.

" 'See you soon, Von Sübermann family, Heil Hitler!' he said and, after a hug with Papa, we departed in opposite directions.

"We spent the rest of the week acquiring clothes and various items that I would need for my internment into the *NAPOLA* in Lissa. The following Monday, after making the appropriate introduction to a secretary in a brown SA uniform, I said goodbye to my father in order to start a new life."

Chapter X

hree years I remained in *Lissa,* perfecting myself in the 'Selective Corps,' during which I only saw my family on the occasions in which I was able to travel to Egypt, that is, once a year on summer vacations. I made it a point to bother Rudolf Hess as little as possible, but the few times that I called the telephone number that he gave me, I did not manage to speak to him directly, but through the intermediary of *SS* Officer Papp.

"In any case, I was never neglected in my scarce requests, all of which the said officer kindly acceded to. But Rudolf Hess was my guardian and, therefore, the one responsible for signing report cards and other bureaucratic paperwork, as befits any parent. I never heard that this was not fulfilled, so I was supposing that Rudolf Hess would have foreseen an automatic mechanism, by which he would be informed about the development of my studies. I finally verified that this theory was correct.

"For some Christmas and special celebrations, which the Hess family was spending in privacy, I was invited to be with them, which was producing in me much joy, as they were constituting my only family in Germany.

"During those three years, apart from the normal secondary school instruction, I learned religions, languages, and customs of Asia and received intense training in expeditionary and exploration practices. Mountaineering, horsemanship, and survival techniques were separating us from the practices of conventional sports that the other student bodies of the *NAPOLA* were performing.

"It was '*vox populi*' among the students of the 'Selective Corps of Oriental Studies,' that we were being trained for future missions in Asia, but no one knew anything of the character that those would have.

"In 1936, the third year of studies in a career that was lasting four, I was selected to receive aerial instruction and transferred to the *Flieger-HJ (Flieger Hitlerjugend)* division of the Hitler Youth specialized in glider flying. However—there were twenty of us in the same conditions—we were instructed in the operation of *Messerschmitt* planes and perfected our deficient practice with offensive weapons.

"We also received at that time a course on 'The Gral and the destiny of Germany' dictated by ⚡⚡ Colonel Otto Rahn, prestigious scholar in History of the Middle Ages and author in 1931 of the book 'Crusade Against the Gral.'

"The 1937 graduation from *NAPOLA* finally arrived, and the subsequent possibility of directing a successful professional career.

"The options that were being offered to the graduates were ranging from pursuing a career in the army or the party, to the incorporation into the administration, industry, or academic life. Those who were going on to non-military careers were studying at the University and earning doctorates in Philosophy and Arts, in Law, or in Mathematics and Exact Sciences.

"A great part of the graduates were aspiring to be incorporated into the *Waffen-⚡⚡*, for which they had to undergo rigorous entrance tests. But for the Selective Corps, this entrance was automatic, since very great had been the effort that the Fatherland deposited into our training. And, besides, we were only ninety graduates, those who were aspiring to the degree of *Ostenführer* of the ⚡⚡.

"One might think that a great joy was overwhelming everyone, and that was true with respect to my eighty-nine companions. I, on the other hand, was feeling my happiness marred by a strange event that deserves to be mentioned in this account, because of the subsequent implications that it had.

"Upon completing the curriculum, the first year class of the Selective Corps—part of which I was forming—one of our Professors, Ernst Schäfer, focused himself on the task of selecting a small group for a 'special operation.' It began to circulate among us, the rumor that said operation was in reality an important mission in Asia, so a consequent state of general excitement was produced. There was no one who did not long to participate in the ultra-confidential mission that, it was being said, had been commissioned by *Reichsführer* Himmler in person.

"Professor Ernst Schäfer was dictating lectures on Eastern religions, especially Buddhism, Vedism, and Brahmanism with singular erudition, but he was not an officer of the ⚡⚡ but of the *Abwehr,* the Secret Service of Admiral Canaris. For this reason the conjectures were indicating that the mission in Asia would be an espionage operation, perhaps in India or Russia.

"Our small group of *Flieger-HJ* pilots had not been included in the selection for some reason that we were unaware of, and although the rigid internal discipline was demanding absolute obedience and subordination, I was not believing to break any regulation if I was offering myself as a volunteer. I was not knowing the destination of the mysterious mission, but the enthusiasm for being admitted was making me think that the knowledge of ten Oriental languages would be a good argument to achieve my purposes.

"In accordance with this conviction, one day I went to meet with Ernst Schäfer. He was in a classroom with a group of six comrades from the Selective Corps, giving them some type of instruction. A single glance at the blackboard, from where were hanging sheets with drawings of human bodies covered with lotus flowers, was enough for me to know that he was giving explanations on the very ancient physiological concepts of *Tantra Yoga*.

"The look of disgust that he made upon seeing me was like an omen that I was wrong about something in supposing that the Professor could include me in his plans. Notwithstanding the bad feeling that I had, I decided to play my card.

"'Heil Hitler,' I said for every greeting.

"'What do you want, Von Sübermann?' he said, ignoring the political salute.

"'Pardon me, Herr Professor. I have learned that you select personnel for an important mission in Asia and, although I do not know much about it, I wish that you consider the possibility of including me. That is to say, I voluntarily offer myself.'

"'You, Von Sübermann?' He was looking at me, narrowing his eyes, with a cynical expression. 'And why do you want to go to Asia, Von Sübermann?'

"'I believe that you have not understood me, Herr Professor. I wish to be useful to the Fatherland and this is a way to demonstrate it. Perhaps my knowledge of the customs and languages of the Middle East may serve your mission. Or my pilot's license. Or the languages of the Far East. I am willing to serve and that is why I offer myself,' I said with conviction.

"The gesture, at first sardonic, on the Professor's face, was turning aggressive and in his eyes was showing a gleam of anger. I was not entirely myself either and was already feeling the blood boiling in my veins. After all, in that year of 1937, I was 19 years old and the proud Professor, no more than 25 or

26, that is to say, ages in which it is suitable to measure words and gestures...

" 'Von Sübermann,' he said with violence, 'I must thank you for your good will, but you are the last person that I would bring to Asia, understand?'

" 'No, Herr Professor,' I contested, for I was really not understanding the reason for which Professor Schäfer was hating me to the point of not being able to conceal it.'

" 'You don't understand, Von Sübermann?' he began to uncontrollably shout. 'Well, I'll spell it out for you. You are a sinister person, bearer of an *infamous mark*. Your presence is an affront in any spiritual realm, an affront to God, who in His infinite mercy permits you to live among men. You should be marginalized, separated from us or, better, exterminated like a rat, because you, Von Sübermann, contaminate everything around you with sin, you...' Ernst Schäfer was continuing with his insults, totally out of his mind and I, who at first had been astonished upon hearing an allusion to the Sign, was rapidly reacting.

"Without thinking, I fired my right fist into the Professor's face, squarely striking him in the chin. The blow was quite strong, for it sent him staggering several meters further, onto the desks of the classroom. The six students, alerted by Schäfer's shouts, hurriedly went to his aid and, while four of them were helping him to get up, two others were holding me in order to prevent me from hitting him again.

"I was enveloped in fury, for the Professor's aggression had wounded me to the deepest depths. I was innocent; I knew nothing of Marks or Signs; I was studying with my efforts set on seeking the good of the Fatherland and that was undoubtedly a noble end.

"I was not understanding Professor Schäfer's hatred or his desire to have me 'exterminated like a rat.'

" 'No doubt he's crazy,' I was thinking as I was dragged to the door by Ernst Schäfer's chosen pupils.

" 'Take him away! Get him out of my sight!' he was shouting, completely out of his mind. 'He is a liar and a murderer! He claims not to understand but in the depth of his heart he knows everything, because he is the image of the tempting Lúcifer! His purpose is to destroy our mission with his accursed presence...!'

THE HISTORY OF KURT VON SÜBERMANN

"Minutes later, in my ears were still ringing the absurd accusations from Ernst Schäfer: Murderer, liar, infamous mark, Lúcifer... 'God, what is this?'

" 'Are you all right, Kurt?' One of the 'chosen ones' was shaking me by the shoulders, trying to make me react. I looked at him, still blinded by the fury and bewilderment that the Professor's attitude had provoked in me, and only just recognized him. It was Oskar Feil, a good comrade from *Vilnius, Lithuania*. We both struck up a friendship in the early years of *NAPOLA*, when we were the object of ridicule by our German comrades because of our 'foreign' character.

" 'Kurt, calm down,' said Oskar. 'I have to go back to the classroom, but I have to speak with you. Wait for me in the gymnasium in half an hour.'

"I watched him walk away and shook my head trying to wake myself from this nightmare. I did not know that Oskar was forming part of the group selected by Ernst Schäfer nor was I suspecting what he was wanting to talk about, but I would wait for him, since he was one of the few friends that I had in Lissa. However, that half-hour wait would be as long as a century, for my animic state was impulsing me to immediately leave from there and return to Berlin, the seat of the *Flieger-HJ*.

"After washing my face with cold water and ready to wait for Oskar, I situated myself in a secluded corner of the enormous gymnasium. I was more calm when my *kamerad* arrived.

" 'Hello, Kurt,' he said, 'I see that you're better.'

" 'Yes, Oskar. It's all over now. I'm sorry for getting out of control, but the Professor's insults left me no other alternative. What did you want to speak to me about?' I coldly asked, as I was unaware of his position on what occurred.

" 'Listen well to me, Kurt,' he said. 'You are my friend, the only one in whom I can confide. I have been chosen by Ernst Schäfer probably by mistake, for nothing binds me to him and his group. Every day that passes, the more I realize that there is something odd in all this, but I live pretending, led by the selfish desire to share the mission in Asia and obtain the professional benefit that it will bring to all its members. I would like to talk to you in full confidence so that you advise me, but you must promise me that you will not say to anyone what I tell you. Will you do it, Kurt? Can I trust you?'

" 'You know that you can, Oskar,' I said relieved, 'rest assured that no one will find out about our conversation or its contents.'

" 'I accept your word, Kurt,' he shook my hand to seal the pact. 'There are several extraordinary points in this whole affair. The first is the place of the mission: Tibet. Evidently we were wrong when we were assuming that it would be about espionage. In Tibet there is nothing to spy on; one goes there to seek something else. And that is not all. Neither is it clear the criterion put into the selection of our group, for the best have not been chosen, but those most obsequious to Professor Ernst Schäfer. What do you say to all this, Kurt?'

" 'After the incident that I have had today, I could not impartially give an opinion about Professor Schäfer, but I admit that there is something abnormal in all this,' I said, reflecting on what Oskar was confiding to me.

" 'If I was having any doubt,' he continued, 'it was dispelled a while ago, when he argued with you. He did not reject you for some professional reason, but because something in you, something spiritual, could derail the mission. And that something is for him extremely hateful. I don't like any of this madness at all. Do you think that I should resign from the group?'

" 'I no longer distinguish the good from the bad,' I said with sadness, 'but I see a good reason for you to continue in the mission to Tibet: you are the only sane person of that group and someone has to tell it like it is upon returning from the journey!'

"Oskar laughed at my answer.

" 'I think I'll take your advice,' he said, 'but it'll be you to whom I keep abreast of everything that occurs.'

"I was feeling flattered by Oskar's trust.

" 'Another thing, Kurt,' he continued. 'I know that you'll let today pass and soon forget it, for such is your generous character, but this time I will be the one to advise you: talk to your Guardian and tell him everything that occurred today! Incredible things are said about the spiritual powers of Rudolf Hess; no one better than him to analyze the unspeakable attitude of Ernst Schäfer. Promise me that you'll think about it, at least.'

" 'I'll think about it, I'll think about it,' I said, surprised by Oskar's suggestion. 'I promise you, although I'll see Taufpate in only a month's time, for graduation.'

"We said goodbye and an hour later, I was boarding the train to Berlin, immersed in somber musings.

Chapter XI

The end-of-school ceremony was being held, together with other schools, in a large festival, with multitudinous parades of the Hitler Youth, which were culminating in the Berlin Stadium. There, the top brass of the Third Reich, headed by the Führer, were establishing direct contact with the youth by means of speeches and proclamations.

"Papa had come from Egypt especially to witness the graduation, being invited by Rudolf Hess to attend a party to be held that evening at the Chancellery. It would be, in my opinion, the long-awaited opportunity to clear up many unknowns.

"At 10 on the dot at night we climbed the marble stairs of the Chancellery. Papa, elegantly dressed in a jacket, and I, in the uniform of the Hitlerjungen, were not out of place among the large gathering that was already filling the great Hall of the Eagle, forming distinct murmuring huddles of voices and laughter. We crossed the hall in the direction of the gigantic fireplace of carved marble, looking for Rudolf Hess, while over our heads a chandelier of colossal dimensions was pouring torrents of light, softly dimmed by thousands of pieces of Baccarat crystal. I had never seen so many distinguished and important people together. All the leaders of the New Germany were there, Dr. Goebbels, Marshal Göring, Reichsführer Himmler, Julius Streicher... In a secluded corner we distinguished a group formed by Rosenberg, Rudolf Hess, and Adolf Hitler. Papa, fearing to interrupt a private conversation, told me to wait a few steps away, while we were drinking a glass of champagne that solicitous waiters had handed us.

"After a moment, Rudolf Hess noticed us and, after exchanging a word with the Führer, approached smiling.

" 'How are you Reinhold, Kurt?' he said. 'Come, I will introduce you to the Führer.' "

"It was the first time that I was seeing Adolf Hitler up close, a rare honor for a foreign student, and although I was coming prepared knowing that the Führer would be at the party, it had not occurred to me that we would be introduced.

" 'Adolf: Baron Reinhold von Sübermann,' said Rudolf.

"The Führer greeted Papa by effusively shaking his hand but without uttering a word.

" '*Mein Patenkind Kurt von Sübermann,*' Rudolf continued. 'Brand-new graduate of *NAPOLA,* pilot and polyglot soldier, future *Ostenführer* of the *Waffen-ϟϟ*.'

"I could not help but blush at Taufpate Hess' laudatory introduction.

"The Führer stretched out his hand, as he was fixing an icy gaze into my eyes. I felt that an electric current was running down my spinal column, while a kind of stomachic emptiness was tickling at the level of my navel. It was a sensation of an instant, but of a terrible effect. That gaze, and the contact of the Führer's hand, had worked like an acidic agent in a bucket of milk, breaking down and dissolving my state of mind. It was an instant, I repeat, a single instant in which I felt myself explored from within.

"Once recomposed, I observed with surprise that—something unusual for him—an enigmatic smile was appearing on the Führer's face.

" 'From Egypt, eh?' said Hitler. 'I adore Egypt, a marvelous land that fascinated Napoleon and has produced an invaluable Comrade like Rudolf.' "

"Meanwhile, Rosenberg, who had already been introduced, was observing the scene with an amused expression.

" 'When seeing you, young Kurt,' Hitler continued, 'I realize that it is not a coincidence about Rudolf. Egypt really is a "Center of Spiritual Force"; the enigma of the Sphinx still holds true. You are the proof,' he took Rudolf Hess and I by one arm each, 'that a Higher Order guides the fate of Germany. Two German-Egyptians, who have breathed the Gnostic effluvia of Alexandria and Cairo, led here by Unknown Superiors, to place your great spiritual capacity at the service of the National Socialist cause.

" 'Seeing you,' continued the Führer, 'I realize how Sacred is the task that we have taken upon our shoulders, in founding the Thousand-Year Reich. Our cause is not only the best ideal for which a Germanic[26] can live and die, it is also the cause of humanity's freedom, of the struggle to save the world from the dark forces, of the final combat against the *elementarwesen...*'[27]

---

26. Here the Führer uses the word *Germanic* as a noun, atypical of its common diction in English as an adjective, in order to convey that he is not only referring to the citizens of Germany, but those descendent from the Germanic peoples.

27. Demonic elemental beings who attack the heroes in the Edda saga.

"Rosenberg and Papa were nodding their heads at each affirmation of the Führer, who was continuing to pour out mystical concepts without permitting anyone to interrupt his monologue. I distracted myself thinking about the strange power that I had experienced when greeting the Führer. A powerful Force was emanating from Hitler, I did not know whether voluntarily or spontaneously, and I was wondering to myself if he had acquired this charism by means of some secret technique, of some occult knowledge to which a privileged few can access.

" '... then tell me, young Kurt, who are ultimately the enemies of Germany? Against whom are we fighting?' Hitler was asking, addressing me.

"I reacted to the unexpected question, with the desperation of having ignored a part of the conversation. Three pairs of eyes, of Rosenberg, Hess, and Papa, were set on me, waiting for my answer. However, what I had managed to hear was sufficient for me, because the answer sprang by itself from the depths of my unconscious.

" 'The Enemy is only one,' I categorically affirmed, 'it is *YHVH-Satan.*'

"I answered intuitively and in so firm a manner that there was no room for rectifications. I looked at Papa, who instantaneously became livid, and I saw the surprise portrayed on all faces.

" 'Very good, young Kurt, very good,' Hitler was saying with an expression of intense joy. 'You have given the best answer. You could have identified as our most terrible enemies Judeo-Masonry, Judeo-Marxism, Zionism, etc., but those names only represent different Aspects of one same reality, different Faces of one same ferocious Enemy: *YHVH-Satan,* the Demiurge of this World. Only an Initiate or an enlightened one like you or Rudolf could give so precise a response. Right, Alfred?'

"Rosenberg was smiling with pleasure.

" 'I congratulate you, young Von Sübermann,' said Alfred Rosenberg, 'you are a person of clear concepts.'

"Of course, I was completely stunned by what had occurred. Suddenly, in this meeting with those notable persons, I was discovering that I was possessing an 'inner ear,' a mysterious organ that was enabling me to 'hear' concretely formulated answers. And these answers were correct! I had never experienced anything like this and could only attribute this sudden illumination to the presence of the Führer. He, with his strange magnetism, had 'awakened' my 'inner ear.'

"Adolf Hitler returned to take the floor.

" 'People who are not attuned to the *Occult Philosophy* of National Socialism, usually commit gross errors of assessment when judging many of our affirmations, believing to see in them a stupid superficiality, when generally they are synthetic ideas, *slogans,* extracted from deep systems of thought. For example, before young Kurt's affirmation that "the Enemy is Jehovah Satan," which is a synthetic idea of deep philosophical content, many ignorant minds would be tempted to suppose that such a concept stems from a crude antisemitism. They would put forward elementary arguments like these: "Jehovah is the God of Israel, a God of Race, one among hundreds of ethnic Gods; it is then exaggerated to take him for the only God or Demiurge (objection, this one is indeed antisemitic)." Or this other one: "Jehovah is the God of Israel but, because of his monotheistic character, he is the only God; then why identify him with the Demiurge? Is it because of a heretical belief of the *Gnostic* type?" (questions of those who believe that being "Christian" implies the worship of Jehovah and that his rejection signifies an "anti-Christian heresy.") Another banal argument is the following: "if we are to reject the Demiurge considering his material work as essentially "evil," why only identify him with the Jewish Jehovah, having hundreds of alternative denominations in ethnological mythology and in the religious pantheons of all the peoples of the Earth?" (questions that those usually suffer who totally ignore what Israel signifies in the History of the West and what the secret of Jewish racial dynamics is).

" 'When hearing of Jehovah Satan as "the Enemy against whom we fight," our critics would raise objections like the preceding, and, of course, the word "Satan" attached to Jehovah would surprise them, which would undoubtedly draw ironic conclusions from them.

" 'Well, such arguments rest on a common circumstance: the ignorance of those who formulate them! Of course, *we know* that the Demiurge received other names throughout History. But if we choose, among them, that of Jehovah, it is because it is the *most recent name* by which He has denominated Himself. And with said name His "Chosen People," Israel, which are nothing more than a psychic unfolding of the same "Jehovah Satan," still designate Him.

"These words of the Führer vividly surprised me by their metaphysical implications: Do the Jews not constitute a Race like the others, comprised of *individuals?* ... It was a disturbing theory that I had just heard.

"'Are you surprised, young Kurt?' asked the Führer, who no doubt immediately noticed my disturbance. But he did not give me time to respond and continued his explanation:

"'Well, you haven't heard anything yet: Israel is a "Chakra" of the Earth, that is to say, it is a *collective* psychic manifestation of the Demiurge Jehovah and that is why we affirm that the Jew *does not exist* as an individual; that he is not a man like the rest of those who make up humankind.

"'But the manifestation of Jehovah in a Chosen Race is a more or less recent event, of a few thousand years, and the *ordering of Matter* or "Creation" dates from millions of years ago. That is why, because of the "novelty" that the name "Jehovah" represents compared with other names of the Demiurge, which more ancient and culturally more important peoples were using in History, and because of the geological antiquity of the Universe, it seems *excessive* to designate a cosmic God with the name "Jehovah." But it is only an appearance. Here it is necessary to imagine a Primordial Demiurge to which we can comfortably call *The One,* just as the Stoics did. This is who orders chaos and pantheistically diffuses himself throughout the Universe (He is also the Hindu Brahma or the Arabian Allah, etc., these denominations taken in their exoteric religious sense).

"'But the Cosmic Plan, it is necessary to somehow name *the idea of the material Universe,* is based on the dream of the Demiurge, a state of quietude that nevertheless dynamizes the Cosmos, like the "Unmoved mover" of Aristotle in that Great Day of Manifestation, which is also denominated, mahamanvantara. But so that everything "functions" without requiring the intervention of The One, "who *sleeps* while everything lives in Him," it is necessary to have an "automatic correction system." This is the role fulfilled by the so-called *cosmic Hierarchies,* myriads of conscious entities *emanated* by The One to maintain the impulse given to the Universe and to carry forward its Plan. The first step of the "emanation" are the *monads,* higher Archetypes that fundament the whole cosmic structure and serve as the *matrix* of The One's plan.

" 'These *conscious entities,* Angels, Devas, solar Logos, galactic Logos, planetary Souls, etc., *are not individual beings* but form part of the same One and possess, then, the *mere appearance of existing* due to the degrees of freedom with which they are endowed during the manvantara. In order for something to individually *exist,* an entity for example, it is necessary to *suppose* (or sub-pose) the act of existing to its real being, which also supposes the *subsistence* of the entity, which prevents the communication of its substantial essence with other entities or its metaphysical participation with other beings, that is to say, it puts a formal end to the entity or grants it its natural form. The recourse to achieve said illusion of existence is the extreme mechanicity of the material reality founded on the *evolutive laws,* both referred to continuous and discrete phenomena, which maintain the progressive movement of matter and energy in the exact attainment of The One's Plan.

" 'Said evolutive laws are *preserved* by the "conscious entities," already mentioned, and *directed in the direction of the Plan.* Thus we can distinguish, for example, "solar Logos," that is to say, "conscious entities" capable of "creating" a solar system following the Plan of The One, but that in reality are *temporary unfoldments* of The One. The same can be said of the galactic Logos or "planetary Souls" and even of the simple Angels or Devas: none of them exist as such, although they "evolve" subject to universal laws. The important thing here is to comprehend that this whole grandiose spectacle that we are recreating is *pure illusion,* a metapsychic conception of colossal characteristics devised by The One for his intimate contemplation. Because the truth is that all that exists disappears in the end, when the Great Pralaya comes, the night of Brahma, in which everything is once again confused in Him, after a monstrous phagocytation.

" 'But we said that the Universe is ruled by evolutive laws. Said laws, which determine the Material Universe, according to a true "heavenly architecture," as the satanic Masons say, occasion the existence of the different planes of space or Heavens in which reality is constituted. Just as there are various "Heavens" (five? seven? nine?) there are "Kingdoms of nature" (three? five? seven?) or "planets" (five? seven? nine? twelve?) or "Root races" (three? five? seven?) etc. These deceptive aspects form part of the Plan of The One, and the Demons in charge of carrying forward said Plan form a *precise hierarchical order,* based on the famous "law of evolution" that rules the Heavens—all the *Heavens,* from the atomic, chemical, or biological to the cosmic—in which each monad "evolves" following the Archetypes of each Heaven. It is the famous "law of cause and effect" that the Synarchy teaches and that the Vedic religions of India call Karma and Dharma, but which is convenient to synthesize as the "law of evolution." This law directs the "round-trip path of the monad," which takes various bodies in the different Heavens to which it descends to "evolve"; said "path" is usually represented as the serpent that bites its own tail or "ouroboros." Of course, the famous *monadic individuation* is never reached, for that would be an authentic mutilation of the substance of The One and before such a thing happens, the whole Universe will already be phagocytized in His Holy Belly.' Here, strangely, the Führer smiled as he was looking at me intensely. I was inwardly struggling with conflicting sentiments. On the one hand, I was horrified by the theory that I was hearing, already familiar from having studied it in the *NAPOLA,* but now endowed with an impressive meaning of reality when being vehemently expounded with the Führer's irresistible eloquence. And on the other hand, I was feeling flattered by the honor of receiving from the lips of the Führer of Germany, a personal, terribly extensive, and curiously out-of-place explanation at a mundane party at the Chancellery. In any case, my exterior attitude was of respectful attention to each one of his words, for I was not wanting to distract myself again.

" 'I suppose that you already know this theosophical theory that the Synarchy teaches in its Masonic or Rosicrucian sects, and that you must *feel frightened* before a deterministic conception in which there is no *foreseen* place for *eternal* individual existence, that is to say, beyond the pralayas and manvantaras. And precisely that fright, that cry of rebellion that you *must perceive* welling up from your Pure Blood, constitutes an exception to all the rules of the deterministic mechanics of The One, because it speaks of *another reality* alien to His material Universe. How can that be if we have said that everything that exists in the Cosmos has been thought and made by Him, according to His Plan and through the intermediary of His cosmic and planetary Hierarchies? Well, young Kurt, I will

tell you briefly: because a part of Humanity, which we inte-
grate, possesses an element that *does not belong to the material
order* and that cannot be determined by the Demiurge's law of
Evolution. That element, which is called Spirit or Vril, is
present in *some men* as a *possibility of eternity.* We know of it
through the *Blood Memory,* but as long as we are not capable
of freeing ourselves from the ties that bind us to the illusory
reality of the Demiurge and retracing the Path Back to the
Origin, *we will* not really *exist* as Eternal individuals. You will
ask me how it is that in a Closed Order like that which I have
described, *spiritual elements* foreign to it can coexist, and why,
if they cannot be determined by the laws of matter and energy,
they remain subject to the Universe of The One. This is a great
Mystery. But you can consider as a hypothesis that, for *a reason
that we do not know* but that we can suppose to be *an order*
from a Being infinitely superior to the Demiurge, or an *incomprehensible negligence,* or a colossal *deception,* once a myriad of
beings belonging to a spiritual Race, that we call *Hyperborean,*
entered the material Universe. Let us suppose that such beings
had penetrated the Solar System through a "gate" opened on
another planet, for example Venus, and that here, thanks to a
ruse, a part of their Hyperborean Guides had enchained them
to the law of evolution. This enchainment, we have already
said, *cannot be real* but, nevertheless, the Traitorous Guides
manage *to confuse* the Eternal Spirits by anchoring them to
matter. Why do they do this? Another Mystery. But what is
certain, what is true, is that, from the arrival of such Guides to
the Solar System, a collective mutation will take place
throughout the Galaxy that *modifies* the Plan of The One. This
modification is built on the treason of the Guides and on the
fall of the immortal beings. In order so that you see it clear,
young Kurt, I will tell you that here, on Earth, there was a
primitive human being who "was evolving" following the laws
of the "planetary chains" and the "Kingdoms of nature."

" 'This evolution was very slow and was pursuing the final
adaptation to an absolutely animal racial archetype, endowed
with a rational mind, logically structured by cerebral functions and possessing a "Soul" made up of energy from the other, more subtle, material planes. This "man" is that whom the
Traitorous Guides found, at a still primitive stage of their development, when arriving on Earth millions of years ago.
Then, by means of an ingenious system called Chang Shamb-

hala, which you will have the opportunity of studying in our Order, they decided to mutate the human Race, enchaining the Eternal Spirits to the illusory and material human beings of the Earth. From that moment on there are three classes of men: the primitive animal-men or *Paśus*, the semi-divines or *Viryas*, to whom a Spirit was attached, and the Divine Hyperboreans or **Siddhas**, who are all those who manage **to return to the Origin** and escape from the Great Deception. A part of the Guides are also called Hyperborean Siddhas, those who **did not betray** and who, headed by Khristos Lúcifer, attempt **to save** the Viryas through the Hyperborean redemption of the Pure Blood, which consists in awakening the primordial memory of one's own lost divinity. These are the Lords of Agartha... But we deviate a little from our main theme that was about Jehovah Satan, the Enemy against whom we combat to win the right to return to the lost Origin. Then this question will become clear to you, young Kurt, for if you recall that The One was delegating to some "conscious entities" the execution of His Plan, we can now add that the Solar System has been constructed by one such "consciousness" to which we call Solar Logos, seconded by Devas of lesser hierarchy who *occupy* determinate positions in the mechanics of the system. On Earth, a "planetary entity" was infusing life into the planet and impulsing the "evolution" of the Kingdoms of nature according to the Solar Plan, inserted into the Cosmic Plan of The One. It is clear that these are hierarchically linked emanations of The One: The One ⇝ Galactic Logos ⇝ Solar Logos ⇝ Planetary Angel ⇝ Collective or group soul, etc. Who is God here? Depending on the level of consciousness and the cultural and religious norms of men, it can be any of such "conscious entities," but it is always The One. If one says that God is the Sun or conceives a "creator" God of the whole Universe, The One is being spoken of. It is the same if one believes that God is "nature" or the "Milky Way" or the Earth. The different gnoseological cosmologies that men present in their different stages of "evolution" in order to conceive the world, do not invalidate the fact that one always alludes directly or indirectly to The One when God is spoken of.

" 'But let us return to Earth. When the Traitorous Guides arrive on Earth, they establish themselves in a "center" to which they call Shambhala, or Dejung, and found what has come to be known as the Great White Brotherhood or Occult

Hierarchy of Earth. It is not a physically locatable place on the terrestrial surface, a matter about which you will have to learn more later, but is situated in a topological fold of space. But what is of interest here is to point out that the chief of the Traitorous Guides titles himself King of the World, going on to occupy the place of one of the twelve Kumaras of the Solar System. What is a Kumara? A planetary Angel, one of those "conscious entities" enchained by The One that make up the "idea of a planet." It is here where the key to the name Jehovah and his "Chosen Race" is to be found. Because the planetary Spirit was called Kumara Sanat, who after the constitution of Shambhala and the coming of the King of the World, decides to act as *regent* of The One in the execution of His Plan, now modified. For it he incarnates, in the name of The One, in a "Chosen Race" to reign over the enslaved Hyperborean Spirits. That is the Hebrew Race. That is to say that we have on the one side the Occult Hierarchy of Chang Shambhala, with its Demons: the Traitorous Guides and their chief: the King of the World, who now carry forward the "evolution" of the planet and are those who "guide" the Races by means of a sinister organization called Synarchy. And on the other we have the Hebrew Race, which is nothing but the modification of Sanat Kumara on Earth in order to occupy the highest echelon of the Synarchy, in the name of The One. The Hebrews themselves in their Kabbalah study that "Israel is one of the 10 sephiroth," the sephirah Malkuth, which is to say one of the emanations of The One. Finally, Jehovah is the kabbalistic name of The One Demiurge that Sanat Kumara represents on Earth and is, as I said at the beginning of this pleasant chat, the *most recent historical name* that we know of *Him.* That is why we, *the Ancient Hyperborean Beings* who still remain enchained in Hell, must keep in mind that "the Enemy is Jehovah Satan, the Demiurge of this World," as the young Kurt said well.'

"The Führer was enthusiastically continuing his long monologue and, although a long hour had already passed and the curious glances of many people who were wishing to be seated at the table were raining down upon us, no one in Germany would have been capable of interrupting him for so prosaic a reason as having dinner. I, for my part, was only wishing to continue listening to his incredible revelations and that is why, when he asked me if I had understood him, I did not hesitate to let him know my doubts:

" 'There is something that now worries me,' I said immediately. 'All that you have said, mein Führer, about The One Demiurge, I perfectly comprehend and accept, but I cannot help but then wonder who God is, the *true God,* or... ?'

" 'That is a question that you must not ask yourself, young Kurt,' the Führer categorically affirmed. 'Not while your mind is subject to rational logic, for then you will only arrive at irreducible paradoxes. But it is evident that doubt has already germinated in you and that you will continue meditating on it. I will then give you a provisional answer: God is *incognizable* for anyone who has not conquered the Vril. Always bear this truth in mind, young Kurt: from the miserable condition of a slave of Jehovah Satan it is not possible to know God, for He is absolutely transcendent. It is necessary to go a long way of blood purification *to know* something about God, about the "true God," as you rightly say. The majority of the great religions, when speaking of God, refer to The One Demiurge. This occurs because the Races that currently populate the world have been "worked" by the Demons of Shambhala, implanting in them synarchic ideas in the *genetic memory* of their members, in order to be able to direct them toward the great collective Archetype called *Manu.* Thus, perceiving reality behind a veil of deception, one arrives at these conceptions of a pantheistic, monistic, or trinitarian God, which are only appearances of The One, the ordering Demiurge of matter.

" 'Note what occurs with the concept of God that the different peoples of the ancient family of Indo-Germanic languages possess: almost all the names derive from the same words and it is certain that these, in the remote past, denote a God, "Creator of all that exists," that is to say, the Demiurge, The One. In Sanskrit we have the words "Dyaus Pitar," which in the Vedas are used to name the "Father which art in Heaven." Dyaus is the root that in Greek produces Zeus and Theo, with a meaning similar to Sanskrit and that becomes Jupiter, Deus Pater, or Iovis in Latin. The ancient Germanics were likewise referring to Ziu, Tyr, or Tiwaz as the "Creator" God of existence, words that also come from the Sanskrit Dyaus Pitar.

" 'Words that designate God in the Turanian and Semitic language families possess the same etymology. In this last family, of important relationship with Hebrew, we find "El" as an ancient denomination of the Demiurge in his planetary representative, "The Strong." In Babylonia, Phoenicia, and Palestine were worshiped El, Il, Enlil, names that the Arabs transformed into Ilah or Allah, etc. This etymological unity should not surprise you, young Kurt, for what is alarming is the "unity of concept" that is discovered behind the mentioned words, since in all religions and philosophies one always arrives at two or three apparently irreducible ideas of God, but that in reality refer to different aspects of the Demiurge: such is the preference for a "pantheistic and immanent God": The One; or "transcendent" but "Creator of the Earth and the Heavens": Jehovah Satan, Jupiter, Zeus, Brahma, etc.'

"The Führer was now looking at me with shining eyes and I guessed that his next words would have truly important content:

"'There was a war, young Kurt. A dreadful war, of which the Mahabharata perhaps retains a distorted memory. That war involved *various Heavens* in its theater of operations and produced as its most external expression, what has come to be called "the sinking of Atlantis." But no one knows in depth what is referred to when "Atlantis" is spoken of, since it is not only a matter of "a sunken continent." Said war has already been going on for more than a million years on this physical plane, during which several physical, continental Atlantises have sunk, and now, in our twentieth century, we can say that Atlantis is ready to "sink" again. But let us leave this Mystery for now, for you will have to return to it during your studies.

"'To conclude this conversation I will tell you one last thing, young Kurt. You should know that in that Essential War, in which one fights for the liberation of the captive Spirits, for the collective mutation of the Race, against the Synarchy and against Jehovah Satan, the Third Reich has committed all its spiritual, biological, and material potential.'

"With these terrible words, the Führer seemed to end his explanation. I looked around me and saw that Papa, Rosenberg, and Rudolf Hess were still at my side.

"An elegant waiter indicated to the Führer that when they were ready they could go into the inner courtyard for a cold supper. It was eleven at night. The Führer and Rosenberg bade us farewell and went to join Göring and Dr. Goebbels at the head of the table. Rudolf Hess invited Papa and I to join him for dinner, but I had not come out well after the conversation with the Führer and, at the risk of being offensive, I decided to speak frankly with both of them.

Chapter XII

I t's so difficult to get the two of you together,' I said. 'The last time that we were together was four years ago, when entering the *NAPOLA*. Perhaps tomorrow or the day after we leave for Egypt and I don't know when there'll be another opportunity to share a conversation. Could we not withdraw a moment?'

"Papa had started to utter a protest but Rudolf interrupted him.

" 'You are absolutely right, Kurt. Come this way,' he was pointing to a door, 'I have to talk to you too.'

"A moment later we were settled in Rudolf Hess' study, who, behind an immense ministerial desk of carved oak, was rocking in a springy chair. I hurried to initiate the conversation.

" 'First of all,' I said, 'I wish that one of you clarify for me a question on which everyone seems to be in agreement, including the Führer as I could see today, but of which I have only obscure references. I refer to a kind of spiritual quality that I would have, unknown to the majority of people, but that some persons are able to distinguish. It may be the mysterious Sign that the Arab Ophites who abducted Me as a child in Egypt were mentioning or the "great spiritual capacity" of which the Führer spoke earlier. I don't know what it is, but some seem to know it... and don't like it, like for example Professor Ernst Schäfer.' Rudolf Hess arched his eyebrows when hearing the name of the *Abwehr* man. Next I related to them the bitter experience lived days ago.

"I perceived a glint of anger in the dark eyes of my Godfather.

" 'The *Abwehr* has only produced traitors! This is something that you must bear in mind from now on, Kurt. I'll tell you a secret that only four persons in the Third Reich know, including the Führer and myself; a secret that relates to you and to what you've just told me: Professor Schäfer is not wrong to distrust you; indeed, he couldn't be sure of carrying out the *altwestenoperation* if you were included in it! But you're inevitably linked to that expedition, whether Schäfer wants it or not, and you have intuitively grasped it and approached him at a bad time. I cannot now reveal to you the reasons for such a link, but perhaps another person whom you will soon meet, one of the participants in the secret, will explain them to you. With certainty, in the future you will be a personal representative of *Reichsführer* Himmler, the fourth person in the secret, in front of Ernst Schäfer. And he can do nothing to prevent it! These were our plans but, suggestively, you have beaten us to it. Nothing that can't be repaired!

" 'You may wonder how it is that the Führer or the Reichsführer knew about you. Although you have not noticed it, all these years you have been the object of intense surveillance by me and other persons whom you do not know, for the Third Reich has prepared a path for you, appropriate to your possibilities, which will enable you to serve the Fatherland like no one else has done, while you will develop your spiritual faculties. Soon, very soon you will know everything and you will understand us!'

"I had not yet received an answer to my questions, but I was moved and excited by the promising future of successes that Rudolf Hess was announcing to me. Mind you, one thing was unconsciously intriguing me: why the curious name of Ernst Schäfer's expedition '*Altwestenoperation*,' that is to say, *Operation Old West?* The memory of this question, and its incredible answer, would take place only two years later, in the heart of Tibet.

" 'You want answers and you have every right to it,' Rudolf continued speaking, 'but it is not the appropriate time or place to discuss spiritual mysteries. In these years you will have missed my presence, but it was better for you that I did not directly intervene in your life, so that the psychological development would take place normally; we even agreed on that with your Father,' Papa nodded his head. 'Now it will be different, you will have your position and you will be close to me. But first you must know *our Philosophy*. I do not refer to the National Socialist doctrine the way it appears in the Führer's book "Mein Kampf" or Alfred Rosenberg's "The Myth of the Twentieth Century," but to an *"Occult Philosophy"* to which we, a small group, adhere, as you no doubt will too. You must understand that here we are not dealing with a sterile knowledge that can be reduced to a "code of principles" or an "operational manual" by means of which to rule our actions; on the contrary, it is about acquiring a knowledge that dynamically acts on the Spirit, internally transforming us, endowing us with a millenary Wisdom that makes us transcend the merely human plane of existence.

" 'You are especially gifted to access that semi-divine state,' Rudolf continued, responding in part to the question about the Sign, 'because you have something interior that few men possess: *"the possibility of Being."* You will soon comprehend this better, when knowing the secrets of the Order, but I can anticipate that, just as the Führer has said a moment ago, not all men are equals, not all exist, not all can "be." On the contrary, for those who have *the possibility of Being,* the struggle and effort must be put into transcending this world of illusory images and perpetuating themselves in eternity, on another plane of existence to which we can only arrive if we awaken from the demonic dream in which we are immersed. The majority of the men that you see in the world, do not really exist, or if you prefer, they live a "relative existence," illusory, which is a breath for eternity. Their consciousness is diluted by death, although many believe otherwise, and nothing survives them. Eternity, dear Kurt, is for a few, for an Aristocracy of Spirit, founded on semi-divine Heroes, on Supermen who, at the cost of fighting a hard combat with the Prince of this World, YHVH-Satan, as you have justly denominated him, transmute their lower nature and win their place in *Valhalla.*[28]

" 'All will be revealed to you, Kurt, because you are a semi-divine Hero, a Virya, the mark of Lúcifer, which concerns you so much and that only indicates the purity of your spiritual lineage, proves it.'

" 'But, Lúcifer? Is he not the Devil?' I cautiously asked.

"I should have posed this question to the Führer, but I did not have the valor for it.

" 'Lúcifer, the bearer of Uncreated Light, the Devil?' Rudolf Hess was indignant. 'That is the blasphemous calumny that Jehovah Satan has foisted upon him through his disciples, the Jews and some unenlightened Christian and Muslim imbeciles. Lúcifer is Khristos. The Khristos of Atlantis...'

"Rudolf Hess breathed deeply before continuing.

" 'Let us leave those Mysteries for now and talk about you, Kurt,' said Rudolf, changing the subject. 'You have successfully

---

28. Abode of Wothan or Odin in the Eddas. The place to which warriors killed in battle go. Celestial paradise of the heroes. For the Hyperborean Wisdom, Valhalla is a center inhabited by the Liberating Gods or, as the Führer was saying, by the "Hyperborean Siddhas."

completed a hard stage of studies and another cycle of endeavors opens for you. It is our will,' he looked at Papa who again nodded his head, 'that you enter the **Waffen-⚡⚡**, for your military and political perfectionment. But that is, let us say, an exoteric training, that is to say external, at least until you arrive at the Restricted Circle of **Wewelsburg**.²⁹ There is another parallel route that you will have to take and that also entails efforts and sacrifices. It is an occult, esoteric path, which will enable you to spiritually surpass yourself and will resolve your most secret doubts. Have you heard of the **Thulegesellschaft?**'³⁰

I thought a moment, more out of commitment than anything else, for I had the certainty that I had never heard that name mentioned before.

" 'No,' I responded.

" 'It is a secret group of Wise men,' said Rudolf Hess in a respectful tone. 'I will facilitate your entrance into the Order and they will help you to progress, but you must understand, from the beginning, the following: Hyperborean Orders like the Thulegesellschaft follow a circular layout. In worldly organizations of the Freemasonry type, or if you want to simplify: like any administrative bureaucracy, one vertically advances, step by step, from the base of a triangle to the vertex, which occupies the highest Hierarchy. In a Hyperborean Order, on the contrary, one advances by overcoming concentric circles. You, for example, when entering the Order, are a wide circle, perhaps the outer circle. I am not saying that you form part of a circle or that you occupy a place in a circle, but that "you are a circle." Like you, there are other members who are circles of greater or lesser diameter, concentrically organized around a center of Power occupied by the maximum level of Wisdom. That is why I say that one advances by "overcoming circles" and not "crossing circles" of different levels, because the Hyperborean Wisdom consists in narrowing one's own circle toward the center; in "restricting the circle" as far as our capacity permits. Do you understand, *Patenkind?*'

" 'I believe so,' I said without much conviction. 'But all this that you so kindly explain to me, brings me peace and tranquility. Rest assured that I will do everything possible not to disappoint your confidence or Papa's faith.'

---

29. It was an Ordensburg or ⚡⚡ training castle, as will be seen further ahead.

30. Thule Order. Esoteric Secret Society, the affiliation of which is dealt with in another part of the work.

" 'Well, then there is nothing more to speak of. Remember Papp, the ᛋᛋ officer whom you met in Berchtesgaden? He is now ᛋᛋ *Oberführer*.[31] You will address yourself to him when you come back from Egypt to find out the steps to follow.'

"Rudolf Hess pressed a button, obtaining the hurried arrival of a custodial officer as a response. He ordered him to arrange for champagne to be brought into the important office. He was not drinking but this was different, he said, for we were to toast to my graduation and the future of Germany. Then he engaged in a frank chat with Papa, remembering common anecdotes from their student days and Egypt.

"Thus concluded the student stage of my life, Neffe Arturo. On returning from Egypt, things took a different course, and while I was complying with the various stages of training in the Waffen-ᛋᛋ in order to arrive in 1939 at *Wewelsburg* Castle, I was also overcoming various circles of the *Thulegesellschaft*. As the events that will really surprise you, since they connect with your own experience, immediately occur, starting from 1937, I will try to summarize them in some detail. Only in 1939, upon returning from a terrible, infernal mission, which was Operation *Altwesten*, I received the instruction that in part allowed me to understand everything. The following years, especially from 1941 onwards, I spent them fulfilling missions in Asia, missions similar to that which I had carried out in Operation *Altwesten* and analogous, also, to the *esoteric mission* carried out by Rudolf Hess with his historic flight to England in 1941; missions of the same strategic characteristic as that fulfilled by Belicena Villca and her son Noyo, that is to say, missions of tactical diversion to confuse and divert the Enemy; but missions that require, for their execution, the prior Hyperborean Initiation of their agents.

"But this part of the story we will leave for later. It is 12:30 hours and good Juana must already have lunch prepared."

31. Lit. ᛋᛋ-*Senior leader.*

Chapter XIII

ffectively, an instant later, the old woman entered, bringing on a tray an appetizing native stew. Chiquizuela,[32] red chorizo, bacon, garbanzos, beans, potatoes, carrots, leek, onion, and corn, all boiled and steaming, accompanied by oil, vinegar, and mustard.

Uncle Kurt's last story filled me with expectations and curiosity. While I was spreading the corn on the cob with the yellow homemade butter, I kept thinking about the particular experiences lived by Uncle Kurt in the Third Reich and especially his predestined relationship with Rudolf Hess, Adolf Hitler's strange deputy. That period of recent history, which goes from 1933 to 1945, to me as to the majority of those who were born after the war, was escaping me in its vital dynamic. The Allies, victors in a war that is, without exaggeration, the greatest that Universal History remembers, present us a puerile image of the losing nations and of the Epoch before the war. The spokesmen of the victorious alliance, morally and intellectually unable to refute the Great Nationalist Ideologies of the pre-war period with even credible arguments, resort to the irrational system of utilizing lies, calumny, disinformation, etc. With the malicious intention of confusing and devaluing the significance of words, any South American tyrant is denominated, for example, "Fascist," closer to a Mafia **boss** than to a genial statesman like "Il Duce." Fascism, National Socialism, Japanese Traditionalism, complete Systems of Political Philosophy, appear in the pen of the Revenge Publicists, stripped of their mystical, spiritual, and intellectual content, reduced to crude totalitarian schemas, and the leaders of these movements are presented as pathological cases.

For these reasons, Uncle Kurt's story had the double virtue of enlightening me about a dark period of recent History, which he intensely lived through, and of allowing me to verify what I was suspecting ever since I began to doubt the "spiritual virtues" of some "Allied Potencies" that have plunged the world into materialism and decadence. That is: that the Great Nationalist Systems mentioned, especially National Socialism, were hiding a powerful and secret spiritual current behind the

---

32. Kneecap of cattle.

facade of their respective political organizations. In an esoteric undercurrent, jealously hidden by the ferocious victors, there was a spiritual light, an unrevealed purpose that was now coming through in Uncle Kurt's story. What did the Führer and other leaders of the Third Reich intend to do? What was Rudolf Hess trying to carry out when he flew to England in May of 1941? Many questions like these danced in my brain throughout lunch and I was shuddering with joy when considering the possibility that Uncle Kurt had the answers.

On the other hand, a modest sentiment of humility was assailing me every time that I was remembering how I had arrived there, persuaded of being embarked on a unique adventure, of being a privileged protagonist in a cosmic drama. For what had occurred to me, without underestimating the real danger that it was entailing, was child's play in light of the experience lived by my ⚡ Uncle. And upon thinking this way, I was feeling that new forces were coming to my aid to fulfill Belicena Villca's request.

Since some days ago, I was wanting to abandon my sickbed, since I was feeling quite recovered. However, something was blocking my will when I was deciding to dress myself and go down to the lower floors of the house. At first I did not know that it was what was preventing me from doing so, but later I was discovering with amazement that the idea of confronting the mastiffs that were freely roaming around the park surrounding the house was simply terrifying to me. On more than one occasion, I had observed them through the window and, despite their colossal size and fierce appearance, they were not seeming to be really aggressive. I should unreservedly accept Uncle Kurt's explanation that they attacked induced by him, but it is one thing to say it and another to face those animals after such an unpleasant previous experience.

But this time I was firmly decided to abandon the sickbed. After dressing myself, for the first time in fifteen days, in clothes that I took from my baggage, I slowly descended the beautiful onyx staircase that was leading to the spacious living room, unknown to me up to that moment. I found no one in sight and, without much desire to explore the house on my own, I seated myself on a sofa—it was the same one where I laid fainting the first night—in front of the wide windows that were overlooking the park.

I was supposing that Uncle Kurt would still be having lunch, but I soon came out of my mistake when seeing him arrive from the exterior of the house. He was at the same time surprised and glad to see me up.

"Well, well," he said, "I see that you feel good!"

"Yes, Uncle Kurt, I believe it's time to get back to a normal life," I gave a pat to the casted arm, "at least while I wait for the cast to come off."

I was smiling, with an approving expression.

"If you really feel comfortable here, we'll chat all afternoon, and then we'll have dinner in the dining room."

I nodded my head. I was happy, waiting for a new story from my Uncle and thinking that things were finally getting back on track.

Uncle Kurt sat across from me in a single armchair and chatted about a trivial topic to give time for old Juana to serve us two steaming cups of coffee.

Finally he said:

"In August of 1937, I returned from Egypt and made telephone contact in Berlin with *SS Oberführer* Papp, whom I had become, after four years of pleasant dealings, particularly fond of.

" 'Hello Edwin,' I greeted, after the operator put me through to Papp. 'Is there anything for me?'

" 'Yes, Kurt. You must come to the Chancellery to receive instructions. Where are you?'

" 'At the Central Railway Station. I can be there within thirty minutes.'

" 'Well, go to the Security Office and identify yourself to *SS Oberscharführer*[33] Krüger. He will lead you to me.'

"I deposited my baggage in a chest at the station and left to meet *SS Oberführer* Papp. I did not take lodging in a hotel, because I was wanting to make sure that I would not have to continue my journey to some military department (as effectively happened).

"*SS Oberscharführer* Krüger led me through a maze of corridors and hallways to the office from where everything concerning the Führer's security within the Chancellery was being decided.

---

33. Lit. *SS-Senior squad leader.*

"It was a small world apart that was occupying a back wing of the Chancellery Palace, passing an interior courtyard, and that was gathering under the command of *SS Oberführer* Papp, several sectors of which specific activities, so different, were converging in the common objective of Security. There they were operating a Gestapo squad, a Communications and Radio Direction Finding team, a small group of the *SS* Secret Service, a chemical laboratory, an infirmary with a doctor on permanent call 24 hours a day. All mounted, equipped, and attended to by the *SS* with personnel from the *1st SS Panzer Division Leibstandarte SS Adolf Hitler*.

" 'Hello, Kurt! I'm glad to see you, young man. Sincerely,' said *SS Oberführer* Papp. 'Sit down, please.'

"I placed myself in a chair in front of the desk occupied by Papp. The office was a recent construction of reinforced concrete so the very low ceiling was contrasting with the great height of the hallways traversed to arrive there. *SS Oberführer* Papp was observing me with visible friendliness, seated in a swivel chair. Above his head a picture was showing the Führer gazing into the distance; metal filing cabinets were flanking both sides of the desk.

" 'I, too, am glad to see you again,' I responded. 'I am tremendously happy to be in Berlin again.'

" 'Well, it won't be for long,' Papp said, smiling. 'I believe that you depart at once for the *Ordensburg Krössinsee*. I have the orders for you here. They are two envelopes...' he started to look through a file.

" 'Krössinsee is in East Prussia, is it not?' I asked.

" 'Yes, in Pomerania. Here are your orders!'

"He handed me two manila envelopes. One, larger on which was written in large letters *'Krössinsee'* was containing all the enrollment papers for the *SS Ordensburg*. On the other a handwritten inscription, in delicate Gothic characters, was ordering that the envelope was to be opened in the presence of *SS Oberführer* Papp. I proceeded to break the seal and extracted from the interior of the envelope a letter in the handwriting of Rudolf Hess. It was reading:

Berlin – August, 1937
Herr Kurt von Sübermann
Dear Patenkind,

I have arranged for you to enter the *Ordensburg of Krössinsee* and then, upon receiving the minimum instruction, be transferred to the other *Ordensburgs.* You must leave at once for Pomerania and incorporate and adapt yourself to the new life. Only when you have fulfilled this part—let at least one month pass—you will put yourself in communication with the *Thulegesellschaft.*

Your contact in Berlin is named Konrad Tarstein; you will find him at *Gregorstraße 239.* He is already informed of your entry into the Order; you only have to introduce yourself, giving your name. In principle you will join the *Thulegesellschaft* in Berlin so you will have to travel from Pomerania to Berlin on weekends, but if you should come at any other time you can go to *SS Oberführer* Papp so that he arranges the corresponding permission. Good luck, *Patenkind;* remember my advice: "advance in circles, restricting the circle."

Rudolf Hess

Note:

Memorize the name and address of your contact and handover this letter to *SS Oberführer* Papp, who has the order to destroy it. Nothing must be written that could compromise you, compromise us, or compromise the *Thulegesellschaft.*

Heil Hitler

"I read the letter twice and then handed it to *SS Oberführer* Papp who destroyed it before my eyes, setting it on fire with a lighter.

" 'Rudolf Hess is in Berlin?' I asked.

" 'No. He is in Berchtesgaden with the Führer.'

"I immediately remembered that on that very date, four years earlier, we were with Papa and Rudolf Hess in Berchtesgaden. There was, therefore, nothing more to do in Berlin and, after bidding farewell to *SS Oberführer* Papp, I departed toward the train station to start my journey to East Prussia as soon as possible.

Chapter XIV

n hour later, from the window of the northern train, I was watching the last neighborhoods of Berlin pass by. I was engrossed thinking about Rudolf Hess' letter and lamenting not having been able to meet him to transmit to him some questions that were urgently requiring an answer. Something extraordinary was happening to me for some time and, except for Rudolf Hess, I was not daring to confide it to anyone.

"Since the night of graduation, when I was introduced to the Führer, I began to experience a curious psychological phenomenon. On that occasion I responded, 'YHVH-Satan' to the Führer's questions: 'Who is the Enemy of Germany? Against whom do we combat?' and I believed to recognize that said answer had not been reasoned by me, but 'grasped' or as something 'heard' by an inner ear.

"For me it was beyond doubt that the 'Voice' I heard was alien, that is to say that it was coming from outside my consciousness. But I was also realizing the impossibility of transmitting this experience to another person without running the risk of inspiring distrust about my sanity. During the journey to Egypt, I meditated on this and arrived at the conclusion that the presence of the Führer had triggered a phenomenon of unconscious discharge, the Voice heard being simply a formal intuition. That is, I somehow 'knew' the answer and, at a time in which I was psychologically blocked by the Führer's overpowering personality, I 'guessed' it or believed I did, taking an intuition for an extrasensory perception. It was a skeptical conclusion, but I had the certainty that said phenomenon would be purely circumstantial, that it would not take place again. I was clinging to this certainty with the hidden fear that its repetition implied a loss of rational equilibrium.

"It is understandable: in a society that considers 'normal' what is common to all, that is to say, collective, and represses with alienation the one who deviates from the 'normal,' feeling different can be dangerous in many ways. Mainly because the lack of 'patterns' or 'models'—systematically eliminated or self-eliminated by fear—to compare our 'abnormality' induces us to fear a loss of reason. This fear to possess gifts or virtues that make us different from others is considered a 'saintly prudence' in a world that glorifies the mediocrity of the average man and distrusts the individual.

"So, fearful of the implications that I would have to consider that experience as a real phenomenon, I was attributing the heard Voice to a projection of the unconscious onto the conscious.

"However, the phenomenon was repeated not once but several more times, with the consequent alarm on my part, who was fearing to suffer from some kind of schizophrenia.

"But, as soon as I was discarding my doubts and serenely meditating, I could not help but recognize that this phenomenon was far from being dangerous, and I would even say that it was pleasant. The reason for such a conclusion was in the 'certainty' that I was now feeling that the Voice I heard was totally alien to my own being. Of course, one may argue that the 'certainty' that a man can have in the perception of phenomena belonging to his own sphere of consciousness is totally subjective. And it is true because, in general, 'certainty' in no way guarantees the truth of his affirmation.

"For example, when the hunter feels 'sure' of hitting his prey and misses the shot or when the student, 'sure' of having given the right answer, finds that the teacher has graded him with a zero, one can say that certainty has 'failed.' What does success then depend on if, when I am 'sure' of obtaining it, I can fail?

"To respond, one must first distinguish between 'subjective certainty' and 'objective certainty.' The former is closer to imagination and the latter to reality. Subjective certainty rests on faith; objective certainty rests on reality. He who believes to take an apple in his hand and what he really takes is an apple, undoubtedly has objective certainty. If, instead, he believes to take an apple and in reality takes something else, his certainty is subjective. There is then a gap between subjective certainty and objective certainty, which, depending on the individuals, can become a chasm.

"But it is desirable that the certainty experienced in what one does or thinks is as objective as possible. Then: what must one do to close the gap that separates subjective certainty from objective certainty? Barring the case of a natural predisposition to objective reality, the answer would be that prior 'experience' ensures greater probabilities that 'certainty,' in the concretion of an act, is objectively realized.

"If one wants to better comprehend the subject, one must also distinguish between the certainty of the dilettante and of the expert. Before the same test, both feel 'sure,' but with greater probability, only the expert arrives at success, while the dilettante fails. The 'certainty' of the expert is founded on prior experience; that of the dilettante on faith in himself; but as every expert at some initial point must have been a dilettante, it is possible that the dilettante, if he perseveres, sometimes becomes an expert.

"So certainty is all the more objective the more it is accompanied by experience. But if subjective certainty is betrayed by objective reality, if it fails, the disappointment of defeat ensues. One must conclude, then, that the capacity to overcome failures is a conditioning factor to capitalize on experience in favor of objective certainty.

"Certainty, on the other hand, is a fundamental psychological attitude to face the trials of life. He who faces the challenge of a test must count on success in advance, he must be 'sure' of winning and a failure must not discourage him from trying again. In the above cases, neither the hunter stops hunting because he misses a shot, nor the student stops studying because he fails an exam; both overcome and capitalize on the experience, increasing their objective certainty, being more 'expert.'

"Considering these concepts, my attitude toward the Voice phenomenon can now be understood: I was concluding that 'being psychically prepared for several years in a rigorous intellectual training, the certainty that I was having in the accuracy of my judgments was quite objective.' That is to say that, intellectually, when I was 'sure' of a concept, it was 'surely' correct. And with that objective certainty in judgments, I was telling myself that the Voice that I was hearing was not coming from my unconscious, was not part of my Ego, was alien to my Spirit or was, perhaps, another Spirit.

"I must emphasize that the certainty that I had of being right was accompanied by a profundity of analysis in which I was considering, among other things, the fact that the Voice was capable of emitting concepts that I was in no way familiar with. This may have a more or less psychological explanation but some concepts were very specific and yet the Voice was utilizing and structuring them with great precision. Ergo, the Voice was 'Wise' and this really has no far-fetched explanation, unless one accepts what it really is: that the Voice was belonging to a psychic entity alien to me.

"Another element of the phenomenon that I was taking into account for my analysis was the fact that I had not been spiritually 'invaded' by another entity as occurs in diabolic possession or in spiritism, but that the Voice was only arriving to my consciousness, clear and energetic, without psychosomatic consequences of any kind.

"That is to say that when the phenomenon was occurring I was not 'seeing,' or 'feeling,' or 'tasting,' or 'smelling' anything strange; I was only hearing the Voice and it was, I repeat, as if my inner ear had been 'opened.'

"The first times that I heard the Voice, I was surprised by the unexpected message that was arising in leaps, energetically and swiftly, rhythmically shot like a lightning bolt. It was not always appearing, but only when I was meditating on some question that was requiring a certain concentration. To better understand the quality of the phenomenon that was happening to me, I will give some examples. You are a psychiatrist, Neffe, and I do not want, within reason, that you doubt my sanity because what was occurring should be interpreted as an enlargement of the capacity to perceive, rather than as an 'illness.'

(I made a sign of assent and confidence to Uncle Kurt because no one as I knew how many arbitrarinesses are made about the authentic psychic virtues of man, those that develop "alone" or self-develop and exalt him without affecting his rational equilibrium at all, because they are "naturally" integrated into the personality. Psychic virtues that are spontaneously obtained, without resorting to absurd "occult methods" or "gymnastics of transcendental meditation" that end up breaking the delicate mental order and leading the disciple to madness and death.)

"I remember one day," continued Uncle Kurt, "in which I was reading the *Bhagavad Gita,* a Vedic writing belonging to the great epic of the *Mahabharata,* a mythical war that involved men, Angels, and Gods in the struggle and the memory of which the ancient Aryans of India wrote and compiled.

"The Gita is about the battle that the hero *Arjuna* must wage to regain the throne, usurped by his cousin. Arjuna is a member of the warrior caste or a *Kshatriya* and next to him is *Sri Krishna,* incarnation of the God *Vishnu.*

"In the first part called 'Arjuna's Grief,' Arjuna moves with his chariot in front of the enemy army and finds that along with his cousin, a large part of his relatives and friends have lined up:

26

Then Arjuna saw, arrayed in both the armies, fathers and grandfathers, maternal uncles and brothers, sons and grandsons, comrades and friends, fathers-in-law and teachers.

27

Casting his eyes on all these kinsmen stationed on opposing sides, Arjuna was overcome with deep pity and sorrowfully spoke.

28–30

Arjuna said: O Krishna, at the sight of these my kinsmen, assembled here eager to give battle, my limbs fail and my mouth is parched. My body is shaken and my hair stands on end. The bow Gāndiva slips from my hand and my skin is on fire. I cannot hold myself steady; my mind seems to whirl. O Keśava, I see omens of evil.

31–34

Nor do I perceive, O Krishna, any good in slaughtering my own people in battle. I desire neither victory nor empire nor even any pleasure. O Govinda, of what avail to us is empire, of what avail are enjoyments and even life itself? Our fathers and uncles, sons and grandsons, fathers-in-law and brothers-in-law, teachers and other relatives, for whose sake we desire kingdom, enjoyments, and pleasures, are arrayed here in battle, having staked their wealth and lives.

35

These, O *Madhusudana* (Krishna), I would not kill, though they should kill me, even for the sake of sovereignty over the three worlds—how much less for this earth!

36–37

O *Janārdana* (Krishna), what joy can be ours in killing these sons of *Dhritarāshtra*? Sin alone will possess us if we kill these felons. Therefore we ought not to kill our kinsmen, the sons of *Dhritarāshtra*; for, O *Mādhava* (Krishna), how can we ever be happy by killing our own people?

38–39

Though they, their understanding overcome by greed, perceive no evil in the decay of families and no sin in hostility to friends, why, O *Janārdana,* should not we, who clearly perceive the evil in the decay of families, learn to refrain from this sin?

47

Arjuna, having spoken thus on the battlefield, cast aside his bow and arrow and sank down on his chariot-seat, his mind overcome with grief.

"In the second part of the Gita, called 'The Way of Ultimate Reality,' Sri Krishna responds to the disquieting and anguished questions of Arjuna.

I

To Arjuna, who was thus overwhelmed with pity, and whose troubled eyes were filled with tears, *Madhusudana* (Krishna) spoke these words:

2

The *Lord* said: In this crisis, O Arjuna, *whence comes such lowness of spirit, unbecoming to an Āryan, dishonorable, and an obstacle to the attaining of heaven?*

3

Do not yield to unmanliness, O son of Prithā. It does not become you. *Shake off this base faint-heartedness and arise,* O scorcher of enemies!

"Sri Krishna then advises Arjuna to follow the 'Way of Action' (or Karma yoga) and comply with his Dharma, that is, with the destiny of the Kshatriya, which is to enter battle and fight for justice without worrying (a priori) about the outcome of the battle, nor about the fate of the enemy (even if they are relatives and friends).

31

Considering, also, your own dharma, you should not waver; for to a kshatriya nothing is better than a righteous war.

32

Happy indeed are the kshatriyas, O Pārtha (Arjuna), to whom comes such a war, offering itself unsought, opening the gate to heaven.

33

But if you refuse to wage this righteous war, then, renouncing your own dharma and honor, you will certainly incur sin.

"This must be so, says Sri Krishna, because reality is Maya, illusion, and the 'confrontation' is circumstantial, only perceptible to those who feel 'confronted.' On a superior, spiritual plane, oppositions are resolved, confrontations are pure illusion. *The Spirit can neither kill nor die*, that is why Sri Krishna says:

19

He who looks on the Self as the slayer, and he who looks on the Self as the slain—neither of these apprehends aright. The Self slays not nor is slain.

20

The Self is never born, nor does It ever die, nor, having once been, does It again cease to be. Unborn, eternal, permanent, and primeval, It is not slain when the body is slain.

21

He who knows the Self (Spirit) to be indestructible, eternal, unborn, and immutable—how can that man, O son of Pritha, slay or cause another to slay?

22

Even as a person casts off worn-out clothes and puts on others that are new, so the embodied Self casts off worn-out bodies and enters into others that are new.

23

Weapons cut It not; fire burns It not; water wets It not; the wind does not wither It.

24–25

This Self cannot be cut nor burnt nor wetted nor withered. Eternal, all-pervading, unchanging, immovable, the Self is the same for ever. This Self is

said to be unmanifest, incomprehensible, and un-
changeable. Therefore, knowing It to be so, you
should not grieve.

26–27

But if you think the Self repeatedly comes into being
and dies, even then, O mighty one, you should not
grieve for It. For to that which is born, death is certain, and to that which is dead, birth is certain.
Therefore you should not grieve over the unavoidable.

"It then only counts to face the conflict following the 'Way
of Action,' confronting the opposed and complying with the
Dharma. *'Fear not to kill,'* says Sri Krishna, *'they are already
killed by Me.'*

"I was meditating on the preceding paragraph of the Gita,
on the extraordinary moral implications that arise from this
very ancient Indo-Aryan text when I again 'heard' the Voice:

" 'You must not deceive yourself by the superficial meaning
of the concepts, O Kurt, man of Pure Blood. Krishna's message
is addressed to Arjuna's two natures, the animic and the spiritual. To his animic part, to his animal-man nature, Krishna
advises to continue with the dramatic argument in which he is
involved by reason of his Karma: Arjuna is human, he is incarnated and lives karmic circumstances; he must fulfill the
Dharma and resolve the conflict of the opposite Archetypes;
that way he will realize the condemnation imposed a priori by
the Lords of Karma of Chang Shambhala, the incomprehensible condemnation of the familial war that weighs on his heart.
But to his spiritual part, to his Aryan-Hyperborean nature, the
Siddha Krishna suggests transcending the opposites, not by
means of their synthesis, which could be war, but by situating
oneself in the absolute instance of the Eternal Spirit. The Spirit, "the Self," in effect, is Eternal or Uncreated, *alien* to all created opposites, which are nothing but Maya, Illusion. *For the
Spirit, there is neither Created life nor death but Illusion and,
therefore, there is neither sin nor guilt, there are no debts to pay or
Karma: if the decision proceeds from the Spirit, the action will not
produce a subsequent effect on Itself because the Illusion lacks the
capacity to act on the Reality of its Being; and this, whatever the
action performed, even killing relatives and friends.* However, the
Kshatriya must fulfill an essential condition so that his spiritual nature predominates over the animic or animal part: *he*

must harden his heart, he must *"cast out that non-Aryan weakness,"* that is to say, he must divest himself of all compassionate sentiment toward those who are but actors of a karmic storyline, pure Illusion; they do not really exist, they do not live, or as Krishna says *"they are already killed by Me."* This is the Wisdom of the Lords of Venus of Agartha: *only a true Kshatriya is one who possesses a heart as hard as Stone and cold as Ice; and only such a Kshatriya can perform any action, even killing, without Karma touching him.* That is the Power, O Kurt, man of Pure Blood, of the Hyperborean-Kshatriya-Initiate, the semi-divine man who has his Uncreated Spirit enchained to the Created Soul!'

"Those words burst like lightning into my consciousness, filling me with perplexity for several reasons. First, because I was taking hold of the certainty—as I already said—that the Voice was external to my being. Second, because of the tone of the Voice: firm and energetic, it was at the same time a trustworthy and friendly Voice. I was feeling in its presence that it was not possible for me to distrust or doubt its words because that Voice was emitted by Someone superior to myself. Someone who was 'coming' to help me and guide me. And third, because the 'content' of those words, the 'concepts' poured into my conscience, were not always clear and comprehensible.

"The latter should be understood not in the sense that they were obscure or veiled, but that said concepts were alluding to things and situations unknown or forgotten by me. I say 'forgotten' because in that sentiment of truthfulness that was inducing me to listen to the words of the Voice was coexisting as a reminiscence of a lost Knowledge, of a forgotten Truth.

"Shambhala, Agartha, Lords of Venus, briefly familiar concepts that once formed part of some vaster knowledge but that, inexplicably, I had forgotten without being able to pinpoint where or when, certainly not in this life and perhaps not in 'another life' but in a 'state of Spirit' outside of all life and manifestation.

"Of one thing I was sure: the Truth was in the past, a remote past that, nevertheless, I could almost touch with my fingertips.

Chapter XV

hen I was reacting, after receiving one of these 'messages,' my first impulse was 'to ask' something else to the Voice, to question about the 'interpretation' of the message, or about the Voice itself.

"But it was useless because the Voice was disappearing as mysteriously as it had appeared and I was only getting silence for an answer. However, when I was not thinking about it, and finding myself meditating on some question in the field of History, Philosophy, or Religion, the Fleeting Commentary was appearing, the Wise and Fulgurant Word, like a Spark of Wisdom.

"That difficulty to communicate with the Voice, far from disappointing, was stimulating my curiosity and I embarked on a brief search for information about such a strange phenomenon.

"The inner ear had been opened when I was introduced to the Führer, due to the powerful influence of his presence, and then I departed with Papa toward Egypt for a vacation, as I already said. It was during those days that I attempted to unravel the mystery of the Voice's furtive appearances. To do so, I began to read everything that was relating to cases similar to mine, finding with horror that, until a few years ago, any person who was experiencing the hearing of voices was suspected of witchcraft or demonology. The image of Joan of Arc, the 'Maid of Orléans,' burning at the stake for following the dictates of an internal Voice was not a very pleasant incentive to delve into the matter.

"But I was encouraging myself thinking that we were in another century, in an epoch open to investigation and knowledge. In spite of the fact that I was verifying at every step that in the field of psychic experience, superstition or skepticism was abounding.

"Reading the works of Allan Kardec, the founder of modern Spiritism, I verified that among the multiple forms of *Mediumship* described as 'common to many gifted people,' was an *Auditory Mediumship,* which I believed could be equated with the phenomena that I was experiencing.

"According to Allan Kardec, a *Medium* is a person who can put himself in contact with the 'World of the Spirits': 'What is a medium? It is the being, the individual who serves as a link between spirits, so that they can easily communicate with men: [...] Consequently, without a medium, there can be no tangible, mental, written, or physical communication of any kind.' And he also says: 'a Spirit is a man without a physical body.'

"Mediumship as a human faculty is presented in 'relation to the senses,' being an extension of these, such that it permits to embrace part of the 'Other World.' There is thus an Auditory Mediumship, a Writing Mediumship, etc. Without accepting the Spiritist Cosmogony that affirms, as does Gnosis, Alchemy, etc., a triple composition of man: body, Soul (or perispirit), and Spirit, one can stop to analyze the phenomena that the Spiritists mention, which are almost always real.

"That was what I uselessly did in those days in Egypt, touring various Spiritist Centers and interviewing numerous Mediums.

"The disillusionment could not be greater because, in the majority of the cases, the Medium was a person of low intellectual capacity, incapable of clearly explaining the nature of the marvels protagonized by him, or on the contrary, the Medium was a scoundrel, too clever to provide explanations and rather fond of surrounding himself with a halo of 'mystery.'

"The conclusion that I was drawing from these explorations was summarized in that, when the subject was the true protagonist of a Mediumistic phenomenon, he could not exercise any control over it, being a 'mentecatto' in the majority of the cases. The Writing Medium was not conscious of what he was writing, an abject situation that was nevertheless filling with joy the witnesses, who were affirming that it was constituting the 'proof' of the truthfulness of the marvel. The same could be said about the other kinds of Mediumship.

"The Talking Medium, totally 'possessed' by the Spirit or 'disincarnated entity'—according to the Spiritist jargon—was speaking, laughing, bellowing, or contorting himself before the contemplative ecstasy of the acolytes, as ignorant as they were insensate. And the Listening Medium, who was arousing my particular interest, was hearing, not one, but a concert of voices. And these were invading him at all times, ordering, requesting, or supplicating certain actions, many times dishonorable or rude. Something depressing that had nothing in common with my superior experience.

"Convinced that by that path I would only find sick people or fanatics, I did the most logical thing that one can do in those cases: I set out to seek a solution to my problem, using myself, my own analysis and experience.

"That way, rigorously reviewing the psychic processes that were culminating in the appearance of the Voice, I verified that the key was not in mental *questioning,* in 'asking' the Voice this or that. In my confusion, to which the contact and observation of Spiritists contributed not a little, I was believing that the Voice was responding to questions raised in my consciousness during meditation. Arbitrarily taking this belief for a truth, I was concluding that it would be possible to consciously interrogate the Voice, that is to say, that I would ask and the Voice would respond: a crass error... as you will very soon see.

"Meditation on all this allowed me to realize that 'questioning' is an intrinsically rational attitude; that is to say, that it is only possible to interrogate on the basis of that ordering that we call reason. Of all existent creatures, only man interrogates, and he does so in order to know, to obtain knowledge.

"Expression of his miserable ineptitude and of the drama of his ignorance, the questioning, from reason, from his logic, enables him to emit inferences, propositions, and to establish judgments. But the knowledge exclusively obtained from reason, through the questioning of the reality of the world, entails a violence and a concealed rebelliousness. The questioning implies the possibility of the answer and in this implication there is something haughty and arrogant. The one who interrogates proudly 'knows' that he will be satiated in his knowledge. This rebelliousness, this pride, this arrogance, in short, this violence that underlies the questioning is, of course, totally useless, since it *does not facilitate the liberation of man from his enchainment to the illusory forms of matter.*

"The moral error of questioning as a 'means to know' is evident in all its absurd contradiction when man affirms the 'right' to ask, that is to say when he establishes that obtaining knowledge by questioning is juridically and morally licit. Because if it is licit and even advisable to practice questioning, without limits or moral barriers toward the questioned thing (without taboos), we will not take long to see man fiercely standing face to face with God, interrogating Him, an absurd possibility that inevitably leads to the denial of God (atheism), to confessing the impossibility of this question (agnosticism), or to the most disturbing hypotheses that are just that, probable answers but not true answers.

"Gnosis, a philosophical current to which Belicena Villca referred quite a lot, was affirming the possibility of 'saving oneself' by means of knowledge (gnosis), but this 'knowledge' was not to be obtained in a rational manner. As Serge Hutin said: *'Gnosis,* privilege of the initiates, is opposed to the vulgar *pistis* (belief) of the simple faithful. It is thus less a "knowledge" per se than a secret and mysterious *revelation.'* '... gnosis is – once it is attained – a total, *immediate* knowledge, which the individual possesses entirely or not at all; it is "knowledge" in itself, *absolute,* which encompasses Man, the Cosmos, and Divinity. And it is only through this *knowledge* – not through faith or works – that the individual can be *saved.'*

"There is then another way to 'know' and, although an obscurantist conspiracy has erased Gnosis and its Initiatic Wisdom from Official History, it was in the 'gnostic' way that I found the solution to communicate with the Voice.

"Effectively, there is a way to obtain knowledge 'beyond' reason, without falling into the mechanics of question and answer, comparison and conclusion, analysis and synthesis, in short, dialectics. And it is extremely simple. It consists in *disposing*[34] *the Spirit to remember,* in a way analogous to the attitude assumed by the consciousness when it 'seeks' a recollection in the memory.

"In this case, it is not about adopting a contemplative posture, of a 'blank mind,' but of a dynamic action, which 'seeks' without 'asking.'

"The wisdom of comprehending this lies in accepting the fact that the consciousness is 'orientable,' 'directable' toward areas of the mind.

"When we wish *to recollect* something, reason may or may not interrogate, but the remembrance inexorably *comes.* For example, what tie did I wear at John Smith's party? And the answer automatically comes—the green tie. But let us be sincere; is the obtained a true 'answer'? Or when we wanted to know what tie we wore, we dispose the mind to 'seek' the rec-

---

34. To bring into a certain state; to incline toward.

ollection of the party at John Smith's and this recollection *appeared* in the consciousness as an image that was promptly translated by reason in the form of a proposition: the green tie.

"Because if in place of asking, we simply evoke the recollection of the worn tie, it 'will appear' without necessarily being the answer to a question or even a proposition.

"When I proved this and reliably verified that when 'remembering,' the consciousness is 'directed' toward the recollection, I analogously disposed my Spirit to 'direct' itself to the Voice.

"At first I had no success, mainly because reason was interfering with doubts and skepticism, but when I concentrated well and was able to recreate in my mind the fleeting moments in which the Voice burst in, then I began to make progress. The Voice had appeared and disappeared in an instant, with a velocity greater than the swiftest of my thoughts, to the point that, at times, I could not clearly distinguish its words.

"That is why I had to concentrate a lot, and evoke the recollection, only evoke, not interrogate, dispose the consciousness so that the recollection comes and remain in total spiritual immobility. The one who understands will comprehend that it was not a contemplative attitude but an energetic attitude (of energy), similar to that of the warrior an instant before drawing his sword, full of potential strength. In contemplation there is peace (quietude), in evocation, expectant energy.

"The successfully used procedure can be explained as follows: I was recreating in my Spirit the moment in which the Voice appeared. I was trying to make sure that this recollection was as 'exact' as possible, that is to say, that it psychologically transported me to the climax lived during the experience. Then the Voice, the recollection of the Voice, was presenting itself as quickly as 'I was remembering' that it had appeared. But then, utilizing the recently discovered 'orienting' power of the consciousness, I 'was directing' the latter 'toward' the Voice (I repeat: like one who remembers) and was thus achieving to imperceptibly 'extend' the manifestation Time of the Voice. The Voice would emerge in the recollection, and I was trying to limit the recollection around it, cutting out the incidental, concentrating only on it, trying to convert the fleetingness into permanence, without losing any of its vocal dynamics. Thus I was managing, more and more, 'to follow' the message of the Voice from its appearance to its extinction.

"The appearance (beginning) was not concerning me, but the extinction was, because I was increasingly extending the last moment of the Voice, until I came to 'hear' with total clarity the final tone, the precise limit between the Voice and the Silence. Arriving at that point, I was feeling in my consciousness—so directed toward the Voice—as if there were a *sharp conical prominence,* like a funnel seen from the side into which the liquid is poured.

"The Voice had penetrated my mind through a point—the inner ear—and toward there was pointing the vertex of the psychic cone into which my consciousness was being converted when tenaciously pursuing the instant of the final extinction of the 'message.'

"I was practicing this kind of selective evocation when, while 'examining' (one must say it somehow) the psychic cone, I suddenly saw myself precipitated into a slightly spiraled and vaporous tunnel, like a vortex of bright and milky energy that soon concluded with a perfectly defined and sharp image. *I could see it and hear it at the same time,* for from it the Voice was emanating.

"Following the Voice in its extinction, like an echo, I had arrived at its source of origin and it was dazzling and blinding. Now not only equipped with an inner ear but also with an internal vision, I was absorbedly participating in a sublime igneous image. Because that marvelous and wise Verb was not emitted by any throat, or coming from a human or even an anthropomorphic entity.

"It was simply springing forth from a tongue of fire that was rhythmically flickering, accompanying the becoming of the Verb.

"'O icy and glowing fire, God is witness that in you I have recognized the Divinity of the Hyperborean Spirit!'

"Facing that Divine Presence, made of Fire, Voice, and Wisdom, I did not commit the folly of interrogating, neither had I any surprise or desire to know or comprehend.

"A savage and primordial joy was invading me while the igneous logos was shining under my interior gaze. And that ineffable jubilation was due to a certainty: I had recovered something lost long ago, I could not say when or where. But with certainty, that was what it was all about, for the flaming Presence was not unknown to me, although in some mysterious way I had forgotten it until that moment. And the joy of the

reencounter was filling my Spirit with an indescribable pleasure.

"I do not know how long that first ecstasy lasted, but I clearly remember the knowledge that 'remained' in my consciousness as a sedimentary stratum at the end of the experience. I
say 'knowledge' because when telepathically connecting myself with the mysterious Voice, I accessed a Torrent of Wisdom—I would not know how else to call it—that upon penetrating into the Spirit, was dissolving all doubt, rendering useless any question and reuniting and synthesizing the opposites. This was happening because the Voice—authentic Logos—the substance of which was constituting the Fire and the
Verb, was transmitting His Word by the mere fact of entering
into contact with Him.

"And what was the Voice saying on that occasion? It would
be a clumsy pretension to attempt to describe in words such a
transcendent experience, but I will run this risk and briefly
and imperfectly summarize the essential parts of the message:

" 'I am a Being belonging to the Ancient Race that arrived
on Earth with Lúcifer millions of years ago. I have been called
an Angel, but that is an ambiguous denomination. I have been
one of the Great Hyperborean Guides and you have known
me as such in a remote past that, nevertheless, is always
present in the Mystery of the Pure Blood. By my Hyperborean
name you must call me: Kiev; for so shall Humanity again
"know" me at the end of the Dark Age or Kaly Yuga. You are
united to me, like innumerable other Spirits enchained by the
Symbol of the Origin, the tie that binds the Created to the Uncreated: you, and any of them, can arrive to me and to the Origin of the Race of the Spirit, solving the Mystery of the
Labyrinth, crossing the Illusion of the Created Forms, going
back along the Path of the Pure Blood, as you have now done
without realizing it. There, in the Origin, there are other Beings like Me, belonging to the Race of the Spirit, whom you
have also called Angels. But, in truth, we all come from Venus,
from the *Gate of Venus.*'

" 'You can communicate with me whenever you want now
that you know how to return to the Origin following the Path
of the Pure Blood, *but you must not do so* as long as you have
not managed to comprehend the Mystery of the Labyrinth and
are not a master of Space and Time. Otherwise my presence
will act as a drug that will numb your incipient spiritual con-

sciousness. You are a victim of the Great Deception. You believe yourself to be and you almost do not exist beyond the whim of Jehovah Satan. As long as you do not *consciously* return to the Origin, where you are now without knowing it, you must not come to me, for you could lose your way. First you must be what you already are, you must return to the Beginning from where you have never departed, recover the Paradise that you never lost. When you solve this Mystery, marching along the path of the Labyrinth and arriving at the *exit,* you will at last be able to say I Am. But fear not, you will not be abandoned, you will be charismatically guided to the end. Follow the Closed Circles of the Order of Thule but do not stop in any; always advance, until you reach the Penultimate Circle; there we will see each other again. And finally, try to wisely interpret this, my counsel and guidance: *in the planetary order, the Führer first; in the individual order, Rudolf Hess first.* Therefore, follow Rudolf Hess, be inspired by Rudolf Hess.'

"I had managed to solve the Mystery of the Voice, arriving to its hidden source, the Divine Kiev, but immediately after achieving this marvelous psychic feat, I was forbidden to reestablish contact, causing me a rare sensation of sadness. Respectfully self-prevented from contemplating the sparkling sphinx of Kiev because—I was tacitly accepting—of my imperfection, I was only wishing to overcome the obstacles that were separating me from the Penultimate Circle of the Thulegesellschaft where I would be authorized to reestablish the telepathic link with the Origin.

"I was thinking about all this while the train was quickly taking me to Pomerania, lamenting not having found Rudolf Hess in Berlin in order to confide to him what had happened and to consult him about the Divine Hyperborean Kiev."

Chapter XVI

ncle Kurt, what you have told me is marvelous! You alone, internally, that is to say, without anyone's help, reached one of the Liberating Gods!" I exclaimed, impressed by the similitude of his experience with my perception of that infinite instant, the night of the earthquake, during which I contemplated the Divine image of the Virgin of Agartha.

"And tell me, Uncle," I added, ignoring the protesting gestures of Uncle Kurt, who was intending to linearly continue with his story. "Were you able to preserve the faculty of communicating with Capitán Kiev? I mean: did you manage to listen to him later on? Do you still hear him today?"

"Yes, Neffe," he affirmed with resignation. "Although several years passed until I dared to address Him directly, His Voice guided me at all times, saving my life a short time later, in Asia, as you will see if you let me continue the story. But I anticipate an affirmative answer to your last question: I still hear Him; He still guides me. He ordered me to come to Santa María and to remain here. And even though I complied with His mandate, I did so reluctantly, and all these years, these thirty-three years, I spent in open rebellion against my Unknown Superiors. Yes, Neffe: He spoke to me many times, and still speaks to me, as He did before you arrived, when vibrated the buzzing of the bees, the sound of the Dorje of the Druids, and warned me that I would be attacked; but I have not responded to His messages. I have never done so since 1945."

"My God! Why, Uncle Kurt? How have you been able to keep silent, to remain indifferent to the Voice of the Gods?" I was not understanding his attitude and I was letting him know it, almost shouting. Pursued by the Druids, by the White Brotherhood, by a whole Hierarchy of infernal beings: how could one disregard the only possible help, the help of the Liberating Gods? Oh mein Gott, how difficult it was then for me to understand Uncle Kurt.

"I know that you cannot understand me, Arturo. But you would have to put yourself in my place, to be in my shoes in 1945, seeing Germany destroyed by the Synarchy of the Allies and verifying that the Wisest men, the Initiates of the Black Order, were disappearing without a trace in the Antarctic Oasis or through the Expanded Gates. And while They were leaving, until the Final Battle or who knows until when, I was receiving the order to stay in Hell, alone, to fulfill a mission of which I knew nothing at all and in which I was not believing. Yes, Neffe, you can call it lack of faith or whatever you want, but I was not believing that my remaining here was really important: I felt abandoned, betrayed by the Gods, left to fend for myself. What could I do in the face of the triumphant Great Conspiracy? And yet I was wrong. Now I know, and I hope it is not too late to correct my stupid position. Belicena Villca's letter has shown me an unsuspected part of History, a side that gives final meaning to my life. Because, naturally, the only thing left for me is to die with honor in order to wash away the stain of these years of ignoble quietude."

Uncle Kurt was uselessly torturing himself and, once again, I was the cause of his pain. I cursed having asked and would have wanted that the ground swallow me up right there. And there was no way of stopping his subjective self-criticism.

"I am an ⚡⚡ man, Arturo! An Initiate of the ⚡⚡ Black Order!" he said with desperation. "And I have maintained myself in a comfortable situation; hidden all these years, but safe, comfortably secure! Damn me and all the ⚡⚡ officers who have acted in the same way! We should have fought, educated young consciences, revealed the Hyperborean Wisdom! But we preferred to keep quiet, to assume a cowardly attitude that was pretending to be prudent: Imagine, Arturo: if not even the Gods were able to respond, how much less will would I have to enlighten anyone! And do you know why? Because deep down we did not believe in the new generations, or in the Triumph of the Führer, or in the Final Battle! Perhaps, and I only say 'perhaps,' we are partly excused because the hand of the Enemy, the Power of Illusion of the White Brotherhood, must have intervened in our conviction. We were incredulous and selfish, and we should not expect forgiveness from the Gods for They are not judges. In truth, we are bound by ourselves, by our honor...

"Until today, I lived adopting the role of victim, affirming with intransigence that nothing could be done against the Synarchy except to await the Final Battle, the End of the World, the Apocalypse, a Divine intervention. And this I was saying with irony, without believing that the Parousia was to occur, that I would ever live to see it. And in my disdain, and in the indifference of so many others who were perhaps acting like me, we condemned to ignorance those who shall surely participate in the Essential War, in the Final Battle of the Essential War. Oh, Gods, what fools we have been! I had not realized it until today, until you came and explained to me your predestined life, until you recounted to me your years of search and showed me the impossibility of finding the Truth somewhere: how much blind walking you could have avoided if you had known me before! Me, Oskar, or any of us who knew the Truth! Oh, Arturo, what have we done! We saved our miserable lives but at the cost of losing our honor, of abandoning the youth to their own forces, of allowing them to be corrupted and destroyed by the Enemy..."

"But Uncle Kurt," I said, trying to calm him down, "you received an order from Capitán Kiev: you were to remain hidden for strategic reasons, perhaps awaiting the letter from Belicena Villca. It may be that other ⚡⚡ men have acted selfishly, as you say, but I find your story, mine, and Belicena Villca's very significant. I see everything very synchronized, very coincidental, and it occurs to me that the Gods had calculated it beforehand. So, then, you must not embitter yourself in vain: things will make sense, your thirty-three years in Santa María will make sense, if we comply with Belicena Villca's request and find her son and the Wise Sword, if we show her letter to Nimrod de Rosario and incorporate ourselves into his Order of Wise Constructors."

"Perhaps you are right. But I have realized my error, and nothing will prevent me from paying the debt of honor that I owe to those who were coming up after me. The debt is to you, Arturo, I know it! And that is why I am ready to die if necessary; to die with honor, as an ⚡⚡ officer dies. Yes, Arturo, consider it as an oath: I will protect you from the Druids, I will put at your disposal all the faculties and powers that I developed in the Black Order, and I will die for you if necessary, so that you fulfill the mission entrusted to you by Belicena Villca!"

It was useless that I attempted to persuade Uncle Kurt that the situation was not so grave, that no one was going to die. I only managed to convince him of my naivety. Anyway, one thing was clear: incredibly, he was possessing the faculty of telepathically communicating with Capitán Kiev, one of the Lords of Venus who Belicena Villca repeatedly mentioned in her letter.

Chapter XVII

I promised myself not to interrupt Uncle Kurt anymore. His story went on like this: "According to the signed and sealed papers that the envelope delivered by *ᛋᛋ Oberführer* Papp was containing, I was already a member of the Schutzstaffeln (Protective Echelon or *ᛋᛋ*) and was to receive training at *Ordensburg Krössinsee* incorporated with the degree of *ᛋᛋ Obersturmführer*. The *ᛋᛋ* was normally entered, for a career as an officer, with the degree *ᛋᛋ Untersturmführer*,[35] but *NAPOLA* graduates, due to their previous military preparation, were incorporated with an additional degree. For this reason I was entering as *ᛋᛋ Obersturmführer* of the legendary *1st ᛋᛋ Panzer Division Leibstandarte ᛋᛋ Adolf Hitler* because the *Ostenführer* of the *NAPOLA* Selective Corps of Oriental Studies had their natural seat in the *Leibstandarte.*

"The *ᛋᛋ* officers were receiving instruction in specially prepared centers in various places in Germany for this effect. These were the *Ordensburgs,* castle-monasteries surrounded by forests and parks, self-sufficient with respect to the pedagogical purpose for which they had been arranged. Three Ordensburgs were depending on the *NSDAP* and one, *Wewelsburg* castle, was exclusively belonging to the *Waffen-ᛋᛋ*.

"*Krössinsee* in East Prussia was in charge of physical and mental training and of completing purely military instruction. *Vogelsang* in the Rhineland was imparting political and mystical teachings and, finally, *Sonthofen* in Bavaria, was in charge of the higher education of the *ᛋᛋ* officers in Politics, Diplomacy, or Military Arts. To these three burgs, *Krössinsee, Vogelsang, and Sonthofen,* one was attending in that order, being able to remain one or more years in each one of them according to the particular followed career. But to *Wewelsburg* was only entering an authentic Elite, extraordinarily selected, who were aspiring to receive the Initiation to the Most Occult Knowledge of the *ᛋᛋ* Black Order, of which Grand Master was the *Reichsführer* Heinrich Himmler.

"In my particular case, there were express orders, from Rudolf Hess, to accelerate my stay at *Krössinsee* and *Vogelsang,* so I only attended three months at the first burg and three

---

35. Lit. *ᛋᛋ-Junior storm leader.*

months at the second. I was at *Sonthofen* for six months and then I spent three months in *Bernau,* near Berlin, a secret center of the *SD* where counter-espionage techniques were taught. In total, fifteen long and hard months of study that culminated at the end of 1938 when, with the degree of *SS Hauptsturmführer,*[36] I definitively abandoned the official classrooms and libraries as a student.

"Since my arrival to Germany in 1933, six years had passed during which I received an Elite education, so specific and well conceived for what I was wanting to obtain from myself, that it is difficult to imagine how it could have been improved.

"At that date," continued Uncle Kurt, "Germany and her allies were going to enter into Total War against the Potencies of Matter, a war that was more terrible than that of the Mahabharata, and, as time ran out, I had an opportunity to act for the good of my Fatherland and Humanity. In effect, Neffe: before the conflict broke out, I received my first mission, an undertaking so strange that it would be difficult to categorize it as a military operation, especially nowadays, when 'professional' armies are well-oiled machines and soldiers simple robots. But the Waffen-*SS* was not merely a military organization but the external expression of the Black Order, an Order of Hyperborean Initiates: there were, then, alongside the classically military operations, missions of a clearly esoteric character. One of them was Operation Altwesten that Professor Schäfer had undertaken in 1937, financed and directed by the *SS*. Just as Rudolf Hess had anticipated, my Fate was tied to that expedition to Tibet and no one, not even the traitor Schäfer, would be able to prevent me from participating in it. However, in 1937 the group had already departed and only a year later I joined them in Tibet.

"The previous circumstances were no less strange, but I'll narrate them to you after we have dinner," Uncle Kurt surprisingly said. He glanced at his watch and brought his hand to his forehead with astonishment. "I am inconsiderate! For five hours I have been keeping you without contemplating that this is the first time that you left your bed in fifteen days. Are you really well? Tell me the truth, for perhaps it is better that you go to bed and I'll have your supper brought up."

---

36. Lit. *SS-Head storm leader.*

"I am very well, Uncle Kurt," I said, "and if you want to know the truth, what I now feel is hunger. So, let's have dinner!"

Uncle Kurt was joyfully laughing as we led ourselves to the dining room. An hour later we were back sitting on the armchairs after having a cold, light dinner, based on cold cuts and salads, during which we talked about diverse subjects completely unrelated to the interrupted narration.

At last, while we were drinking a cup of coffee, Uncle Kurt decided to continue the story.

"It's a beautiful summer night," he said. "Clear skies, pleasant temperatures, silence, and the fragrances of the countryside. I propose that we sit under the willows, Neffe! You'll enjoy the coolness of the evening as we advance with the story."

"Oh no," I responded. "It'd be better that we return to the living room. We'll be more comfortable there."

I was regretting spoiling Uncle Kurt's enthusiasm, but I was not wishing to confront the mastiffs. I knew that sooner or later I would have to do it, but I would procure that it was in the daytime. The mastiffs at night again? The idea was filling me with apprehension, but Uncle Kurt must not have noticed because he shrugged his shoulders and headed into the living room, followed by me.

"Three or four weeks after arriving at Krössinsee, I returned to Berlin," Uncle Kurt continued narrating, "to meet Konrad Tarstein, my contact in the Thulegesellschaft.

"Gregorstraße 239 was a very old two-story mansion that had more than two centuries of eventful existence, and its only inhabitant, Konrad Tarstein, turned out to be a typical small bourgeois Berliner, bald, of short stature, with a big belly, who was perfectly matched with the decrepitude of the place.

"It is probable that such a place and subject—I thought—had the object to mislead possible spies or to disappoint restless aspirants. I suffered the second effect when banging a moldy door knocker that was spinning within a bronze fist dubiously fixed to the rickety door.

" 'Yes?' asked a shrill voice that emerged from some undefined place.

" 'I am Kurt von Sübermann,' I said, turning to the diminutive peephole that I had at last discovered in one of the door panels, from where a pair of evasive eyes were impatiently observing me. 'Herr Rudolf Hess sends me...'

"The door opened and a chubby and small figure appeared, with his hand courteously extended in salute.

" 'I am Konrad Tarstein,' he said. 'Come in, I was expecting you.'

"The interior was not at all improving the initial impression. Furnished with manifestly bad taste, in a careless mixture of forms and styles, a few minutes in the house were enough for anyone to be discouraged that there was or could be anything important going on there. And yet I was expecting a lot from the Thulegesellschaft in which, according to Rudolf Hess, I would find the answer to all my questions.

"Seated in a ridiculous Louis XV armchair, which was seeming to have nothing to do there, in front of a Norman table and some friar chairs, I was observing with surprise that Konrad Tarstein was getting ready to fill out a form. It was the furthest thing from a spiritual activity that I was able to imagine and that is why I hesitated to give my personal data, an attitude that Tarstein erroneously interpreted as a product of fear.

" 'Fear not,' said Tarstein, 'the books of the Order would never be able to be found. I can assure you, Herr Von Sübermann, that a major leak about details of the Cult or the identity of our members has never occurred. We have suffered defections and some minor betrayals, but always at the superficial levels of the Order, and by people who were not possessing a very precise knowledge of the internal organization.'

" 'Do you receive many aspirants, Herr Tarstein?' I asked.

"Konrad Tarstein lifted his gaze from the file and observed me for a few long minutes with curiosity. Finally, as if becoming aware of an oversight or omission, he put a hand to his forehead as his face was lighting up with a smile.

" 'The paucity[37] of Rudolf Hess!' he said as if he were thinking aloud. 'His eternal and timid paucity. I should have assumed that you wouldn't be advised that this interview forms no part of any regular practice in the Thulegesellschaft. Tell me, Kurt von Sübermann, what information did you receive from Rudolf Hess to arrive here?'

"I responded to him in full about everything I knew about the Thulegesellschaft: what Rudolf Hess had said in our Chancellery chat, the night of the graduation, and the refer-

---

37. Sparingness in giving information.

ence to a 'contact' in Berlin, Konrad Tarstein, stated in his letter that arrived to my hands through *SS Oberführer* Papp.

"While he was speaking, the doubt was assailing me that an unexpected misunderstanding had arisen, due to some error committed by me in the interpretation of the instructions. But no matter how much that I was reflecting, I was not finding any reason that could have provoked Tarstein's surprise to my question about the receiving of other aspirants to the Thulegesellschaft. Or is it that, effectively, no other aspirants were ever coming to Gregorstraße 239? Konrad Tarstein, finally, confirmed this for me a few minutes later. Everything I said he approved with a nod of his bald head and, after putting away the file in a leather briefcase, he invited me to go into an interior room of the enormous mansion.

"The room where we were was connecting with the street door by means of a corridor from the small hall. To the right was a staircase of fine polished and carpeted wood, which, by a ninety degree curve, was leading to the upper floor and was continuing at the banister, which was laterally extending along a hallway, perfectly visible from below. Toward the front of the room, two doors with large carved wooden frames were opening. Taking the door on the right, we gained access, with Tarstein, to an open courtyard, surrounded by galleries with small columns under Norman arches, in each one of which doors were opening. Following the veranda on the left, we went the distance of one side of the tiled courtyard and continued through a cross door that led to another courtyard, this one enclosed with a glass window, while the veranda was extending along the length of this courtyard to end at the back wall.

"Before arriving there, we entered into the last of the countless doors that were leading to the rear verandas. The site to which we had arrived, after such a labyrinthine excursion, was in truth surprising. When closing the door that was leading to the veranda, you would say that we entered a modern apartment, more characteristic of being in a high-rise on Bernauer Straße than there, in the heart of a decadent mansion of the eighteenth century.

" 'Are you surprised, Herr Kurt?' asked Konrad Tarstein smiling. 'I had to remodel a wing of this old house in order to live in some comfort. Nothing fancy, rather simple, but comfortable for anyone who has already traveled a great part of the final road.

" '...See Kurt, this is the kitchen, modern and well installed; this is the dining and living room. This way, please. See, these are the dormitories, there are two because I usually receive a couple of old friends as guests. Come this way, Kurt; see, this is the main room, where I spend most of the day and night.'

"We were before a room of large dimensions, with the four walls covered with shelves of books. In the center, under a square, height-adjustable lamp that was hanging from the ceiling, a table covered with books, some open, others stacked, and various manuscripts, was leaving me to guess Konrad Tarstein's place of work or study.

"Somewhat overwhelmed by the particular spectacle that I was witnessing and restraining my desires of immediately going to examine the spines of the books, which were evidently very old, I curbed my anxiety and asked:

" 'Why here? Why construct a house within a house? Wasn't it more feasible to acquire another, more comfortable property in a more respectable neighborhood?'

" 'Calm down, calm down, Kurt,' said Tarstein, 'this has been done for one important reason: we cannot abandon this property that is very dear to us. Very important things for Germany and Humanity have happened on it. That is why, even though those who usually visit it are few, we maintain it intact, without changing any of its old and bewildering furnishings. Thirty years ago, in 1908, a secret group, the members of which founded, in 1912, the Germanenorden, which would later give rise to the Thulegesellschaft and the *NSDAP*, was operating here. Do you now understand why we must keep this house?'

" 'Because it all began here,' I said with admiration.

" 'Exactly, the history of the next millennium began to be written here. Here, only here, the Unknown Superiors came one day to seal the foundation of the Third Reich!! Sooner will Berlin fall from its foundations than can a pin be touched in this sacred house.'

"When Konrad Tarstein was speaking in this way, his shrill voice was acquiring prophetic tones and was becoming magnetic and attractive, at times causing one to forget the odd appearance of the one who was emitting it.

" 'Let's have a cup of tea,' Tarstein proposed, 'and I will impose on you some things that you should know about the Thulegesellschaft and the arrangement that we have made with Rudolf Hess about your admission.'

"I accompanied him, regretting to leave that fascinating library, to the brand-new kitchen. We abandoned the library through another door, adjacent to that which we had entered, and went out again on the veranda and into the courtyard. I thus understood that Konrad Tarstein's house was extended throughout that wing of the old mansion, opposite the second floor.

" 'How many rooms does the house have?' I asked while sweetening the aromatic Shanghai Tea.

" 'Counting both floors, about... thirty or thirty-two rooms,' he enigmatically responded. 'Who could know?'

"He looked at me a long moment, as if hesitating whether he should stop himself there or complete the answer. At last something in him seemed to relax, and he opted for the second alternative.

" 'Look Kurt, I don't know if you are now prepared to accept certain facts that escape the normal comprehension of the common man. Anyway, since we intend to make of you a Hyperborean Initiate, sooner or later such facts will not at all be surprising for you: it's only a matter of time before you understand them. So, I'll give you a piece of information that for any rational mind would be logically incredible, but it will not be for us because it corresponds to the most rigorous truth, perfectly verifiable by every Initiate: *in this house, today it may have 32 rooms but tomorrow, perhaps, have 35, 40, or more; or perhaps less, 20, 25, 30, who could know?'*

"Naturally, Neffe, that revelation produced in me the incomprehension that Tarstein was foreseeing. Do not forget that I was only 19 years old and that I was still shocked by my recently acquired faculty of hearing the Voice of Kiev, the Lord of Venus. However, I was not startled and took his words in stride. Konrad Tarstein continued, apparently satisfied by the null effect that his data was causing.

" 'This is not an ordinary house, Kurt. No sir, you are inside what we call a *liberated plaza,* an *oppidum,* that is to say, a space *won* from the Enemy. Although you only see walls surrounding the built-up area, they only conceal a *strategic fence* denominated *Archemon* or *vallo obsesso,* which separates and isolates the plaza from the *Valplads* or enemy territory, that is to say, from the *campus belli*. You cannot perceive the Archemon because you are not yet Initiated and your Soul blocks your spiritual vision: only your Uncreated Spirit is apt to grasp the *charismatic fence* of the Archemon. But you will see, Kurt, you will see. And then you will understand that what seems impossible is real, and that the house *is not geometrically stable* because its structure does not exclusively participate in the Created Archetypes, like every house, but that in it intervenes an uncreated element, *the Actual Infinite!'*

"After that announcement, Tarstein sighed and said:

" 'Here, Kurt, Time passes in another way, desynchronized from exterior Time, from the Time of the World. That is why, in this liberated space of the plaza, and with this time of its own, the construction *cannot be stable* and not only its sectors vary, but they do so in synchrony with the *interior Time: centuries and millennia of distance could be bridged by passing through one of these doors.* Through one of such openings of time and space, once arrived my Ancestors, the Seigniors of Tharsis of the Germanic branch, those who were belonging to a medieval Order historically known as *Einherjar:* you should know that my surname Tarstein, means *"stone of Tharsis,"* in memory of a legendary House that traces its racial origins to the White Atlanteans, the White survivors of Atlantis. I know that this will seem fantastic to you, but I descend from a Stirp that remained hidden for centuries due to the tenacious persecution, mortal persecution, to which the Potencies of Matter subjected it, that is to say, that Occult Hierarchy directed by tenebrous extraterrestrial beings based in Chang Shambhala.

" 'I will be more clear: my family, the Germanic branch of the Seigniors of Tharsis, was native to Swabia, the land where they had settled in the thirteenth century with the greatest secret, fleeing from a legendary attack of the Demons that almost exterminated our whole Stirp. There they remained for four centuries, preserving the Hyperborean Wisdom that had been entrusted to our House in ancient times. In the sixteenth century, a Hyperborean Pontiff coming from England, founded at the court of Emperor Rudolf II, in Prague, the Einherjar Order, which had as its objective to develop and apply at every moment of History an exact method to locate the advent of the Lord of Absolute Will, the Envoy of the Lord of War, that is to say, the Führer of the White Race. At that time, the Pontiff decided that the best Strategy for the sustainment and perdurability of the Order was demanding that its members always belonged to eight lineages chosen among the Pure Blood Stirps of Europe. It was the case that one of the Princes convoked by the Pontiff was belonging to my family, while another was coming from the House of Brandenburg, from a collateral lineage of the Hohenzollerns. The Order worked in secret during the following centuries, forming Hyperborean Initiates and awaiting the times of the arrival of the Great Chief of the White Race. Its most important base of action constituted the *Margraviate* of Brandenburg, which was, since the twelfth century, a hereditary principality enfeoffed to the Emperor. And justly, the presence of the Order is not alien to the subsequent rise of the House of Brandenburg over the other principalities of Europe, until obtaining the investiture of King achieved by Frederick William III in 1797. Prussia was then born, the State where the national guiding principle was honor, where the family was being organized around the authoritative and exemplary figure of the father, where order was prevailing in all social classes, nobility, bourgeoisie, and peasantry, because it was being affirmed in the strongly rooted notions of the fulfillment of duty, of saving, of the unconditional obedience of the subalterns, in the entire subordination of the functionaries, and in the most rigid military discipline.

" 'But, above all, Prussia was a military State from the beginning: two-thirds of its budget was being dedicated to the support of the powerful national army that inflicted defeats on France, Austria, Russia, etc., and imposed respect and admiration for the austere and seigniorial Prussian "way of life." And along with the art of war, philosophy, literature and music were cultivated here. But none of this revolution was occurring by chance: the Order was rehearsing, in a society of Pure Blood, the New Order that the Führer, in his next coming, would apply to all Germany and the World. That is why the Führer has never hidden his debt to Prussia and has made public his sympathy for Frederick II of Prussia and for Bismarck, the Iron Chancellor.

" 'Well, Kurt: the ancient Einherjar Order was so strong in the nineteenth century that one of its Initiates arrived to be crowned King of Prussia in 1840. I refer to Frederick William IV, courteously called "Damian of Brandenburg" for his love of Eloquence and in remembrance of the famous rhetorician of

Ephesus. It was the same King who had Marienburg rebuilt, the castle which served as residence in the Middle Ages to the Grand Masters of the Teutonic Order; this work of restoration, as you will know, is presently continued by a special division of the ⚡⚡, fulfilling direct orders from *Reichsführer* Himmler. And it was that same King who, considering that the old danger had ceded, and that the Demons would no longer be able to prevent the New Order from imposing itself on the World, authorized the creation of the surname *Tharstein* or *Tarstein,* contraction of *Tharsisstein,* accompanied by the noble title of Count and the right to exhibit the familial coat of arms in the Castle of the House. The Castle of Tarstein is very near here, Kurt, about 100 kilometers from Berlin, but I have not frequented it for many years, since I am totally devoted to work for the Thulegesellschaft and the ⚡⚡ Black Order.

"'Come, Kurt; I will show you something very secret, and related to this subject.'

"Next, he led me along the exterior corridor to a nearby room, hermetically closed with a double lock. Once inside, another rich library was revealed before my eyes: on two walls were deposited some four thousand books, many of them of evident antiquity; on another wall, a bookcase was overflowing with documents and scrolls.

"'All this material has a common characteristic,' he explained, 'it refers to the "Druids" and "Druidism." Several of these documents are very secret and have been obtained at a high price: they come from throughout Europe and correspond to all Epochs, up until today. It is, with certainty, the most complete collection that anyone has ever assembled on the Druids.'

"'But,' I exclaimed in surprise, 'were not the Druids already disappeared historical personages? You speak as if they still existed!'

"'A moment ago I mentioned to you the fact that my family, the House of Tharsis, was forced to flee seven centuries ago because of "an attack from the Demons"; well, those "Demons" were Druids, or "Golen," as my ancestors were calling them. And since then, as far as I know, their power has never diminished. On the contrary, one could affirm that today it is stronger than ever. But keep this in mind, Kurt: if the Führer's Strategy triumphs, and someday the Third Reich ends up reigning over humanity, we will have to wage one of our great esoteric battles against the Golen, who in Europe constitute the pillar of the Synarchy.'

" 'But who are they? Where are they?' I asked astonished.

" 'In the Middle Ages, their center of action was the Catholic Church,' he pensively answered, 'where, apparently, they were fiercely combated by members of my family. After the fourteenth century, more concretely after the destruction of the Knights Templar that was obeying their inspiration, they were disseminated and strengthened in various strata of European society. Nowadays, there is hardly an organization where the Golen are not infiltrated.

" 'I know that with this response I don't clarify much for you. But later on I will describe to you the complex structure of the Synarchy and then you will be able to functionally understand the role that they presently play and be able to easily identify them. If I have now shown you this library and mentioned to you the Golen, it is not to respond to the natural curiosity that it would arouse in you, but to make you a serious warning. Have you heard of *hunting by species?*'

" 'Well, I think so. Isn't it that which consists of each hunter having to bag a catch of a determinate species? Like a game, in which one hunter has to bag, for example, a hare, another a rabbit, a third a pheasant, the fourth a turkey, etc.?

" 'Exactly, Kurt,' confirmed Tarstein. 'Listen to this, then, and engrave it well into your brain: analogously to the hunt by species, *from among the hunters of the Synarchy, the Druids are in charge of bagging the catch of your species.*'

"I was staring at him without comprehending; or without wanting to comprehend. He repeated: '...*of your species, Kurt von Sübermann.*'

"I could not say what was more astonishing to me, if it was the story that Tarstein had narrated, undoubtedly true, or the knowledge that I was in front of a Count, a Nobleman of very ancient lineage: by his civic appearance, by his humble and chivalrous manner, by his outfit of dubious quality, I had hardly suspected it. I also was inheriting a noble title; however, something internal, an inexplicable intuition, was telling me that his Blood was more Pure, that his Stirp was more ancient, that his nobility was superior to mine. Of his warning, about the danger of the Druids, of course, I paid not the slightest heed.

"Before leaving he took some typed sheets of paper from the shelf of documents and handed them to me. 'They are,' he said to me, 'the transcription of the article *"Druidism"* from the Encyclopædia Britannica: read it; it will refresh your memory.' He locked the Druidic library and we returned to the kitchen.

"I was drinking another cup of tea, still confused by Tarstein's revelations, when he, who had exited a moment before, returned.

"'I went to my study to look for this manuscript,' he showed me a book, skillfully bound, and handwritten in exquisite Gothic characters. 'Its title is "Secret History of the Thulegesellschaft." I have written it using knowledge that is entirely secret and that in Germany only a few Initiates know in part. You will be able to read it later on, but you should not take it out of this house because it is the only copy that exists and the secrets contained therein could change the political organization of the Planet if they fell into the hands of the Enemy. Here it explains, for example, what the Initiates of the Einherjar Order did to determine that Adolf Hitler was the Führer of the White Race and how they guided him to Power; and the intermediate Orders that they had to found, like the Germanenorden and the Thulegesellschaft, until arriving at the Order possessing the Hyperborean Wisdom in the Highest Degree, that is, the ⚡⚡ Black Order.

"One can imagine the avidity with which I observed that manuscript, wishing to have the possibility of reading it there and then. The words were sounding mysterious in Tarstein's mouth, and this impression was being accentuated due to the unreality of the place, in where centuries were being traversed just by walking a few meters of corridor.

"'Your Taufpate Hess,' Tarstein continued, changing the subject, 'I've known him since he appeared in Munich in 1919. He was a young student of geopolitics when he joined, that year, the Thulegesellschaft. Yet we recognized in him one of the great Spirits of Germany, to whom was coming to be the Squire of King Arthur. A Parsifal whose mission this time would not be the search for the Gral but the sacrifice of sitting in the dangerous seat during the crisis of the Kingdom, that number thirteen position at the round table that only a Pure Madman can occupy, a Knight capable of performing a Madness of Love to save the Kingdom.

" 'That is why Rudolf has always been close to the Führer, awaiting his hour, as the faithful Knight.

" 'And we must all hope that his opportunity never arrives, for when Parsifal undertakes his mission it will mean that King Arthur is wounded, and that the Kingdom is **terra gasta**.'

"I nodded at Tarstein's inquisitive gaze, but this mute response did not impress him in the least.

" 'You don't completely understand what I say, do you? So it must be, for: who will be capable of comprehending the pure madman?; his mission is not earthly; the victory, if he triumphs, can only be celebrated in other Heavens. Few will be, indeed, those who applaud the anonymous hero that there is in Rudolf Hess. And, yet, the triumph of the Führer depends in great measure on him.'

"How much significance these words would have, which Tarstein was saying to me on that first visit to Gregorstraße 239, four years later, when in 1941 Rudolf was preparing to valiantly confront the **elementarwesen!** But that Saturday in 1937, the war, and all the horror that was coming, was still far away, in a future that I could not suspect.

"On the other hand, Tarstein's comments were causing me a certain pride, in my status as godson of the praised Rudolf Hess, and with a pleasant sensation I was foolishly smiling, without delving into the hidden meaning that was behind the symbolism of the Arthurian legend.

"I will not dwell on this first visit because that which we spoke about was not much else. After an hour, as I recall, I left there immersed in a sea of doubts but with the firm resolution to continue to the end.

"Rudolf Hess had interposed his influence to get me to Konrad Tarstein, whoever he was, and I was not about to let him down.

"An hour later, on the train, I was reading the Encyclopædia Britannica article: what the English were saying about the Druids was not much.

" '**Druidism** was the faith of the Celtic inhabitants of Gaul until the time of the Romanization of their country, and of the Celtic population of the British Isles either up to the time of the Romanization of Britain, or, in parts remote from Roman influence, up to the period of the introduction of Christianity. From the standpoint of the available sources the subject presents two distinct fields for inquiry, the first being pre-Roman and Roman Gaul, and the second pre-Christian and early Christian Ireland and Pictland. In the present state of knowledge it is difficult to assess the inter-relation of druidic paganism.

" 'Gaul.—The earliest mention of druids is reported by Diogenes Laertius (*Vitae,* intro., 1 and 5) and was found in a lost work by a Greek, Sotion of Alexandria, written about 200 B.C., a date when the greater part of Gaul had been Celtic for more than two centuries and the Greek colonies had been even longer established on the south coast.

" 'The Gallic druids which were subsequently described by Caesar were an ancient order of religious officials, for when Sotion wrote they already possessed a reputation as philosophers in the outside world. Caesar's account, however, is the mainspring of present information, and it is an es-pecially valuable document as Caesar's confidante and friend, the Aeduan noble Divitiacus, was himself a druid. Caesar's description of the druids (*Commentarii de bello Galli-co,* vi) emphasizes their political and judicial functions.

" 'Although they officiated at sacrifices and taught the philosophy of their religion, they were more than priests; thus at the annual assembly of the order near Chartres, it was not to worship nor to sacrifice that the people came from afar, but to present their disputes for lawful trial. Moreover, it was not only minor quarrels that the druids decided, for their functions included the investigation of the gravest criminal charges and even intertribal disputes.'

" 'Himmel!' I exclaimed, while suspending my reading a moment: Could it be that I find myself so influenced by the doctrine of the Führer, that I see Jews everywhere? Well, why deny it! Those Priest-Judges, with their white ephod, to me were appearing to be Levites of pure Hebrew Race.

" 'You are not mistaken!' affirmed the Voice of Kiev in my mind. 'The Druids are Hebrews! Someday you will know the Truth!'

"I kept reading:

" 'This, together with the fact that they acknowledged the authority of an archdruid invested with supreme power, shows that their system was conceived on a national basis and was independent of ordinary intertribal jealousy; and if to this political advantage is added their influence over ed-ucated public opinion as the chief instructors of the young, and, finally, the formidable religious sanction behind their decrees, it is evident that before the clash with Rome the druids must very largely have controlled the civil administration of Gaul.'

"This omnipotent power, both in peace and in war, this intermediation between Heaven and Earth, this capacity to 'train the people' in all their strata, this power to legislate and judge, was it not analogous to that of an Aaron, a Joshua, a Samuel, some Levites, that is, that tribe of Israel to whom Jehovah entrusted the mission to *officiate the Cult of the Law?* Unanswered questions for now; but questions that were giving rise to very suggestive intuitions. The article was thus continuing:

" 'Of druidism itself, little is said except that the druids taught the immortality of the human soul, maintaining that it passed into other bodies after death. This belief was identified by later writers, such as Diodorus Siculus, with the Pythagorean doctrine, but probably incorrectly, for there is no evidence that the druidic belief included the notion of a chain of successive lives as a means of ethical purification, or that it was governed by a doctrine of moral retribution having the liberation of the soul as the ultimate hope, and this seems to reduce the druidic creed to the level of ordinary religious speculation.'

"Very contradictory, I was thinking on the train. It is quite improbable that some barbarous peoples, as were the Celts, would submit themselves, by the millions, to the religious, moral, and judicial leadership, of Priest-Judges, withdrawn into the forests, who were only sustaining a 'mere common religious speculation.' The Druids had to exhibit something patent, something superior to a mere rational speculation, something that to the Celts was the Truth.

" 'Of the theology of druidism, Caesar tells us that the Gauls, following the druidic teaching, claimed descent from a god corresponding with Dis in the Latin pantheon, and it is possible that they regarded him as a Supreme Being; he also adds that they worshiped Mercury, Apollo, Mars, Jupiter and Minerva, and had much the same notion about these deities as the rest of the world. In short, Caesar's remarks imply that there was nothing in the druidic creed, apart from the doctrine of immortality, that made their faith extraordinary, so that it may be assumed that druidism professed all the known tenets of ancient Celtic religion and that the gods of the druids were the familiar and multifarious deities of the Celtic pantheon.'

"Here the English author of the article was overstepping the line. Nowhere, prior to this last paragraph, had he said or suggested that the Druids were anything different from the Celts, except "that they were forming an official Order of Priests." But now, clearly, he was implying that in truth he was ignorant of the beliefs of the Druids and *was supposing* that they were the same that the ancient Celts were holding. So who were the Druids, if they were not Celts? And why would the Celts have changed their Religion after the, now very probable, arrival of the Druids? Unanswered questions. Questions for Konrad Tarstein.

" 'The philosophy of druidism does not seem to have survived the test of Roman acquaintance, and was doubtless a mixture of astrology and mythical cosmogony. Cicero (*De Divin.,* i, xli, 90) says that Divitiacus boasted a knowledge of *physiologia,* but Pliny decided eventually (*Natural History,* xxx, 13) that the lore of the druids was little else than a bundle of superstitions. Of the religious rites themselves, Pliny (*N.H.,* xvi, 249) has given an impressive account of the ceremony of culling the mistletoe, and Diodorus Siculus (*Hist.,* v, 31, 2–5) describes their divinations by means of the slaughter of a human victim. Caesar having already mentioned the burning alive of men in wicker cages. It is likely that these victims were malefactors, and it is accordingly possible that such sacrifices were rather occasional national purgings than the common practice of the druids.'

"Was I wrong, or was the Encyclopædia trying, with a subjective argument, to make the murderous Druids look good? Because it is one thing to be an executioner, an unpleasant but socially necessary task, and quite another to be a sacrificing Priest of human victims: man can justify the executioners, since the executed is guilty of breaking the law; to kill the one who breaks the common law is commonly comprehensible: one simply eliminates that one who is incapable of living in a community; but the Priests kill to placate a God of whom they are his representatives, and propitiate a human sacrifice that is commonly incomprehensible; only They present it as necessary and only God can justify them. I was realizing, then, that it was a great favor that which the English were doing Him by presenting the crimes of such sinister Priests as natural acts of justice.

" 'The advent of the Romans quickly led to the downfall of the druidic order. The rebellion of Vercingetorix must have ended their intertribal organization, since some of the tribes held aloof from the conflict or took the Roman side; furthermore, at the beginning of the Christian era their cruel practices brought the druids into direct conflict with Rome, and led, finally, to their official suppression.'

"And the contradictions were continuing. A juridical people like the Romans, how were they not comprehending that the ritual murders by Druids were positive acts of justice, according to the conviction that the contributor was expressing lines before? Or perhaps the writer, a connoisseur of History, was struggling between his duty to expose the true facts *and an order from the Directors of the Encyclopædia, or from other persons of singular influence, by which he was being forced to exalt the good of Druidism, very little indeed, and to hide the bad, which was too much, or to sweeten the undeniable?* As you will see, Neffe, this was Konrad Tarstein's theory.

" 'At the end of the 1st century their status had sunk to that of mere magicians, and in the 2nd century there is no reference to them. A poem of Ausonius, however, shows that in the 4th century there were still people in Gaul who boasted of druidic descent.

" '*British Isles.*—There is one mention of druids in Great Britain as contemporaries of the Gallic clergy, and that is the reference to them by Tacitus (*Annals,* xiv, 30) from which it is learned that there were elders of that name in Anglesey in A.D. 61; but there is no mention of the druids in the whole of the history of Roman England, and it may be questioned whether there ever were any druids in the eastern provinces that had been subjected, before the Roman invasion, to German influence.

" 'On the other hand, there were certainly druids in Ireland and Scotland, and there is no reason to doubt that the order reaches back in antiquity at least to the 1st or 2nd century B.C.; the word *drai* (druid) can only be traced to the 8th century Irish glosses, but there is a strong tradition current in Irish literature that the druids and their lore (*druidecht*) were either of an aboriginal or Pictish origin. As to Wales, apart from the existence of druids in Anglesey there is little to be said except that the earliest of the bards (the Cynfeirdd) very occasionally called themselves *derwyddon.*

" 'The Irish druid was a notable person, figuring in the earliest sagas as prophet, teacher and magician; he did not possess, nevertheless, the judicial powers ascribed by Caesar to the Gallic druids, nor does he seem to have been a member of a national college with an archdruid at its head.

" 'Further, there is no mention in any of the texts of the Irish druids presiding at sacrifices, though they are said to have conducted idolatrous worship and to have celebrated funeral and baptismal rites. They are best described as seers who were, for the most part, sycophants of princes.

" '*Origin.*—Some confusion is avoided if a distinction is made between the origin of the druids and the origin of druidism. Of the officials themselves, it seems most likely that their order was purely Celtic, and that it originated in Gaul, perhaps as a result of contact with the developed society of Greece; but druidism, on the other hand, is probably in its simplest terms the pre-Celtic and aboriginal faith of Gaul and the British Isles that was adopted with little modification by the migrating Celts. It is easy to understand that this faith might acquire the special distinction of antiquity in remote districts, such as Britain, and this view would explain the belief expressed to Caesar that the *disciplina* of druidism was of insular origin.

" 'The etymology of the word druid is still doubtful, but the old orthodox view taking *dru* as a strengthening prefix and *uid* as meaning "knowing," whereby the druid was a very learned man, has been abandoned in favour of a derivation from an oak word. Pliny's derivation from Greek δρυς is, however, improbable.

" 'A great revival of interest in the druids, largely promulgated by the archaeological theories of Aubrey and Stukeley and by romanticism generally, took place in the 18th and 19th centuries. One outcome of this interest was the invention of neodruidism, an extravagant mixture of helioarkite theology and Welsh bardic lore, and another result is that more than one society has professed itself as inheriting the traditional knowledge and faith of the early druids. The United Ancient Order of Druids, however, a friendly society founded in the 18th century, makes no such claim.'

"Uncle Kurt had handed me an article from the Encyclopæ-dia Britannica, identical to that which Tarstein had made him read in Germany in 1937. Considering what I had recently learned about the Druids, since they assassinated Belicena Villca, and after reading her letter and receiving the magistral explanations of Professor Ramirez, it is natural that I shared Konrad Tarstein's opinion that that article was extremely summarized and ambiguous to justify its inclusion in so pres-tigious a work: the first edition of the Encyclopædia Britannica was dating from 1771, so it was to be expected that in 1930 they would have gathered sufficient material on the Druids to com-pose a more extensive and complete article. But it was obvious that the English were not wishing to delve into the history of some ancient and forgotten Priests, who could today kill with renewed efficacy.

"On the second visit that I made to Konrad Tarstein," re-called Uncle Kurt, "he approved my reasonings and assured me that what occurred in the article was the most common event, and that he was wishing to alert me to it; that is why he had given it to me: to put me on notice that an incredible Eu-ropean conspiracy was denying the information or distorting it, with the purpose of preventing that undesirable eyes could fall on a subject that the most powerful synarchic forces were interested in concealing. And he alerted me again to the, at the time incomprehensible, circumstance that *I was the prey that They were proposing to hunt.*

"All in all, Neffe, with respect to the information, it was easy to see that Tarstein was right and that he was not admitting a simple explanation for the Druidic concealment that was be-ing carried out in England. This will become apparent if you make a clarifying comparison. For example, read the *'Druid'* article in the Encyclopedic Dictionary of Montaner and Simón, which was published in Barcelona at the end of the nineteenth century, and you will be left with no doubt that the English publication is affected by a strange rachitism,[38] al-though in the Spanish essay one can see the same purpose of leaving the Druids in good standing."

Immediately afterwards, Uncle Kurt put in my hands Vol-ume VII of the Encyclopedic Dictionary, a 25-volume work

---

38. "Softening" (usually of the bones).

that was undoubtedly smaller in size than the Encyclopædia Britannica. I looked up the aforesaid article and read:

DRUID (from lat. *druida;* from the Cymric *druiz or deruiz,* from *dervo,* oak): m. Priest of the ancient Gauls and Britons.

– **Druid:** *Hist.* Much has been discussed about the etymology of the word *druid.* Etymologists have even turned to Hebrew dictionaries to see if they could find in them something that gave them some idea about it. The name druid is an appellative like most of the radical nouns of all languages. In the Gallic language *draoi* or *druidas* means diviner, augur, magician, and *druidheatch* divination and magic. It has also been said that this word is derived from the Greek word δρυς that means oak, because they dwelled and taught their doctrines in the groves, and because, as Pliny the Elder says, they were not making their sacrifices except at the foot of an oak tree; but this etymology, although it has in its favor the reason of antiquity, since it is from the time of Pliny, does not stop it from seeming purely capricious, for it is not very natural that the Druids were to take their name from a foreign word. Others maintain that the word *druid* is derived from the British word **dru** or **drew,** which also means oak, and that the Greek word δρυς is derived from this. Of the many Oriental etymologies that have been presented, the Sanskrit form *druwidh,* which means *poor indigent,* seems the most acceptable, because the Druids, like the priests of all nations, had to take a vow of poverty. The arguments in favor of the Oriental origin of the Druids are very worthy of being attended to, and not because it has been accepted by many writers of antiquity. Diogenes Laertius and Aristotle place the Druids and the Chaldeans side by side with the Persian Magians and the Indians, an opinion that they share with a great number of writers. The divinity of the Brahmins bears a great resemblance to Druidic divinity. The importance that the Druids were giving to oxen is another singular coincidence; the Druidic mysteries also have great analogy with the mysteries of India. In the magic rod of the Druids one sees the sacred staff of the Brahmins. Both had the same consecrated objects: they were wearing cloth tiaras, and the symbolic circle of Brahma, like the crescent moon, symbol of Shiva, were Druidic ornaments. Great were also the analogies between the idea that the Druids had of a Supreme Being and that which is found in the sacred works of India; so it does not seem very adventurous to suppose great relationships between Druids and Indian and Persian priests.

There were Druids not only in Brittany inhabited by Gallic peoples, but also in Cisalpine Gaul and in the southern valley of the Danube, also inhabited by Gallic peoples; but there were none in Germania, as those who say that the Germans are the brothers of the Gauls and denominate them with the imaginary appellation of Celts claim without any foundation; or, more clear and categorical, the priests of the Germans were not bearing the name of Druids.

According to Caesar, in his work *De Bello Gallico,* Book VI of which deals with the habits and customs of the Gauls and the Germans, the Druidic science was invented in Brittany and from there passed to Gaul. Although it is evident that Gaul was inhabited before Brittany and Ireland, it is, strictly speaking, possible that the hierarchical organization of the Druidic body and the system of its doctrine was invented in Brittany. However, it is more credible that there were several schools of Druids on the Continent and on the isles, and that one or some in Brittany enjoyed greater celebrity because of the more complete instruction that was given in it or in them. In effect, Caesar does not say that all those who were wishing to enter into the Druid class were obliged to go to study in Brittany, but that those who were wishing to receive a more complete instruction were going there. A new proof that Brittany was not the principal center of the organization of the Druids, is that they were holding their general assemblies in a consecrated forest, in the land of the Carnutes, which was considered as the center of Gaul. It has been believed that this forest was in the vicinity of Dreux, and that this city was taking its name from the Druids; but this is no more than a supposition, since the name of Dreux *(Duro-Cath or Caz)* means *a fort near a river.*

In the already cited work *De Bello Gallico,* Caesar says that all the men who were belonging to the upper classes in Gaul were either among the nobles or among the Druids. These were in charge of the religious direction of the people, as well as the principal interpreters and guardians of the laws. The Druids had the power to impose the most severe punishments on those who were refusing to submit to their decisions.

From among the penalties that they could impose, the most dreaded was that of expulsion from society. The Druids were not forming a hereditary caste, they were exempt from service in the field and from the payment of tribute, and because of these exceptions and privileges, all the young men of Gaul were aspiring to be admitted into the Order. The trials to which a novice had to be submitted were sometimes lasting twenty years. All Druidic instruction or science was orally communicated, but for certain propositions they had a written language, in which they were using Greek characters. The president of the Order, whose office was elective and for life, was exercising supreme authority over all the individuals who were forming it. The Druids were teaching that the soul was immortal. Astrology, Geography, Theology, and Physical Sciences were their favorite studies. The Gauls were not making human sacrifices except in very rare cases, and in them great criminals were being sacrificed. All that is known about the religious doctrines taught by the Druids is reduced to a few fragments that are found in various works by writers of antiquity, and particularly in Caesar, Diodorus of Sicily, Valerius Maximus, Lucan, Cicero, etc. From these fragments it results that they were believing, as has already been said, in the immortality of the soul and its existence in another world, death being no more than the point or moment of separation of two existences. It is natural that from this belief was derived that of reward and punishment in the afterlife, a belief that naturally explains the indomitable valor of the Gauls and their contempt for death. They were teaching the position and movement of the stars and the magnitude of Heaven and Earth, that is to say, they were devoting themselves to the study of Astronomy, and undoubtedly to that of Astrology. Cicero says that they were also devoting themselves to the study of the secrets of nature and Physiology. From this was born their claim of possessing the science of Divination and Magic. Their most important study was theological study, but about it no certain data are possessed, their theological system being very little known, because the Greek and Latin writers, when speaking of the name and the functions and attributes of the Druidic divinities, referred them to their own theogony; so that only conjectures can be made to which the etymological study can give some probabilities. Caesar says that their principal divinity was Mercury, who was presiding over the Arts, travels, and Commerce. Then was following, in order of importance, Apollo, Mars, Jupiter, and Minerva. Lucan and other writers place Teutates at the head of the gods, and after him Hesus, Belenus,

Taranis, and Hercules Ogmios. Caesar adds that the Druids were claiming to descend from *Dīs,* a name that he was translating as meaning Pluto, and that it was owing to this origin that they counted by nights and not by days. This opinion is evidently erroneous, and the error was born of the fact that *Dīs* or *Dia* was, among the Gauls, one of the names of the Supreme Being, whom they were also calling *Aesar* or the Eternal, and *Abaïs* or *Aiboll,* the Infinite. *Belenus* or *Beal,* was one of the names of the Sun, to which they were also calling *Atys* or *Atheithin,* the hot one, and *Grannus* or *Grian,* the luminous one. *Teutates* or *Toutatis* was the god of fire, death, and destruction.

When dealing with the religious beliefs of Gaul, it is necessary to cite the opinion of the distinguished writer Thirrey. According to him, the religious beliefs of the Gauls were related to two bodies of symbols and superstitions, to two completely different religions: one very ancient, founded on a polytheism derived from the worship of natural phenomena, and the other Druidism, recently introduced by the immigrants of the Cymric race, founded on a metaphysical and mysterious material pantheism. The main divinities of the Celtic peoples were those already mentioned and *Ogmios,* god of the science of eloquence, represented under the figure of an old man armed with mace and bow, followed by captives held by the ears with gold and amber chains that were coming out of the mouth of the god. In addition to the main divinities, the Druids had other divinities assimilated to Mars, as *Cumall, Camulus, Segomo, Belatucadros,* and *Caturix,* and to Apollo, as *Mogounus and Granus,* and also other divinities that were the deification of natural phenomena, as *Taran, Taranis,* the thunder; *Kerk Caecius,* impetuous wind of the Northeast, or the deification of mountains, forests, cities, like *Poeninus,* god of the Alps; *Vosege, Vosegus,* god of the Vosges, *Arduinna, Arduinnae,* assimilated to Diana, goddess of the forest of the Ardennes; *Nemausus, Vesontio, Luxovius, Nérios, Bornonia, Damona,* local divinities of Nîmes, Besançon, Luxeuil, Néris, Bourbon-Lancy. Epona was the protecting goddess of stable hands and horse-breakers.

The druids were highly venerated by the people; they were leading an austere life and far from the consortium with the other men; they were dressing in a singular way; they were commonly wearing a tunic that was reaching below their knee. Endowed with supreme power, they were imposing penalties, declaring war and making peace; they could depose magistrates and even the king, when their actions were contrary to the laws of the State; they had the privilege of appointing the magistrates who were annually governing the cities, and the kings were not being elected without their approval. Caesar says that only nobles could enter the Druidic order, while Porphyry maintains that it was enough to enjoy the right of citizenship. It is, however, difficult to believe that a body as powerful as the Druidic order admitted individuals into its bosom who were not belonging to a determinate caste. The Druids formed the first order of the nation; they were the judges in most public and private matters; they knew all crimes, murder, hereditary questions, questions of property, and those sentenced to this penalty were considered as infamous and impious; they were abandoned by all, even by their relatives; everyone fled from them, so as not to be seen tainted by their contact, and they lost all their civil rights and the protection of the laws and of the Tribunals. The veneration that was given to the Druids was so great, that if they presented themselves between two fighting armies, the combat immediately ceased, and the combatants submitted to their arbitration.

As was said before, according to the opinion of the writers of antiquity, the Druidic doctrine was not written, it was orally transmitted, and the novices were obliged to study for twenty years in order to possess the science. It seems, however, that this assertion is erroneous, and that the error comes from the care with which the Druids were concealing their science from the profane. With age the memory inevitably weakens, and if nothing had been written it would result, perforce, that the chiefs, that is to say, the oldest, would find themselves inferior to the youngest in the details of their doctrine. The Druids had a sacred writing which, according to tradition, was called *Ogham*. It is, then, probable that they had books written in those characters, which were perhaps, as indicated above, Greek characters, but this does not mean, as some have believed, that they wrote in Greek. Unfortunately, none of those books have come down to the present time. Those that escaped the edicts of the Roman emperors in Gaul and Britain were destroyed by the first Christian propagandists, by Saint Patrick in Ireland and Saint Columba in Scotland.

The body of the *Druids* was divided into several classes: the *Druids* proper, the *diviners,* the *Saronidae,* the *Semnothei,* the *Siloduros,* and the *Bards.* With respect to the latter, some authors are of the opinion that they should not be included among the Druids, and others affirm that the Bards were a corporation of ministers dedicated to religious worship, which preceded the order or corporation of the Druids. The *Bards,* like the *Skalds* of the Germans, were but poets attached to the chiefs, and who were commissioned to sing the great deeds of heroes, to improvise praises and eulogies, funeral orations and war songs. Did they also celebrate the mysteries of their religion as did the Skalds? This is a question to which it is not possible to answer, because among the songs of the bards that have been preserved there is none that contains anything relative to the dogmas or ceremonies of any religion. Divination was the common attribute of the Druids, they were all diviners, and there is no reason to divide them into classes, under this aspect, except for the exercise of the different functions they performed. The Semnothei, a word derived from *sainch* (ecstasy) were the ecstatics or contemplators; the *Siloduros* were the instructors or institutors, and took their name from the word *réaladh,* which means teaching, and lastly the *Saronidae* must not have formed a special class, but the chiefs must have been thus named, for the name Saronidae is derived from *sar-navidh* or *sar-nidh,* which means highly venerable; it is then to be believed that *Saronide* was a title and not a new class in the Druidic order.

There were also *Druidesses,* whether they were the women or daughters of the Druids, or simply added to the corporation, since it is not possible to admit that the Druids allowed the exercise of magic, divination, and priesthood to women who did not belong to the Druidic body and were subject to its discipline. And it is doubtless that there were, since history speaks of Gallic vestals of the Île de Sein, diviners and magicians. Those who predicted to Aurelian and Diocletian that they would be emperors, and to Severus Alexander his disastrous destiny, were Druidesses. An inscription found in Metz gives the name druidess to the priestess Arete (*Druis Antistita*).

According to the opinion of Thierry, Druidism was already in decline before the epoch of Caesar. For some time, the nobles on the one hand and the people on the other, jealous of the great power of the Druids, managed to gradually reduce their political influence.

Reynaud, one of the writers who have been best studying Druidism, maintains that the ancient Druids were the first who taught with great clarity the doctrine of the immortality of the soul, and that they had as perfect a conception of the true nature of God as the Jews themselves. If they afterwards compromised with the worship of other divinities, it was with the object of reconciling Druidism with the ideas professed by the uneducated classes more disposed to believe in demigods and divinities than to conceive of a single God. According to Reynaud himself, Druidism declined and finally disappeared, because it lacked an element of life necessary in any religion: love or charity. Christianity gave that element and Druidism disappeared; but it disappeared after having fulfilled an important mission: the preservation in a part of Europe of the idea of the unity of God. Whether this theory, supported by very incomplete data, or by reasonings more or less accurate to prove certain ideas among the Gauls about the true nature of God and his relations with man, which later degenerated into gross superstition, is or is not true, is a question that should not be discussed here.

Chapter XVIII

As you will imagine, Neffe Arturo, it is only now, upon reading Belicena Villca's letter, have I come to understand that reference made by Konrad Tarstein to which his family was constituting the 'Germanic branch' of the House of Tharsis. Evidently, he was one of the descendants of Vrunalda of Tharsis, and, according to his later confidences, which were very sparing with respect to this subject, he was also the last offspring of his House; but whether, by it, he was meaning 'the last Initiate' or was really alluding to the last member of his lineage, which he was representing, I could not say. But one thing is certain: that Capitán Kiev's prophecy, which Belicena Villca transcribes on Day 50 of her letter, had been strictly fulfilled, given that the Einherjar Order, not only administered to the Führer the Hyperborean Initiation, but that someone belonging to the 'Vrunaldine branch of the House of Tharsis,' *'What Honor theirs is!'* would be *'next to the Great White Chief when he declares Total War on the Potencies of Matter. Because the Hyperborean Wisdom of that Stirp, of that Blood of Tharsis, will cause the First Coming of the Envoy of the Lord of War!'*

"Yes, Arturo, the prophecy of Kiev was mathematically fulfilled, and there is no reason to doubt that the second prediction, which refers to the descendants of Valentina of Tharsis, has not also been fulfilled. It is worth saying that the mission of Belicena Villca and her son Noyo must succeed so that the Second Coming of the Führer propitiates: *'that Stirp of Tharsis, "what Glory theirs is!" will actively participate in the Final Battle. Because the Hyperborean Wisdom of that Stirp, of that Blood of Tharsis, will cause the Second Coming of the Envoy of the Lord of War!'*

"Belicena Villca, the last Initiate descendant of Valentina of Tharsis has been assassinated by the Druids. But her son Noyo, according to all indications, has managed to carry out his mission. If this is so, Arturo, how close we are to the Final Battle! How near is the Second Coming of the Führer! The Essential War will be waged once more upon the Earth and the Liberating Gods will return to guide the awakened men toward the Infinite Origin of their Eternal Spirit! Oh, Arturo, your presence, and the message of which you are bearing, has closed a circle of my life, opened more than forty years ago, and has restored my faith in the ideals of the Black Order! For it, I will never stop thanking you!"

"Calm down, Uncle Kurt, calm down," I supplicated. "It is not me whom you should thank but the Gods, those mysterious brothers of Race who have guided us toward the triple coincidence between Belicena Villca, you, and I. It is clear that we all participate in the same story, we play roles in the same script, we are personages in the same plot. You must finish telling me about your life in order to attempt, afterward, to plan the actual shape of our movements, to adjust ourselves to the Great Strategy of the Gods, who undoubtedly expect something from us and that is why they have brought us together, in order not to commit irreparable errors."

"You are right, Neffe. But we will continue tomorrow, for the time has passed without noticing it and it is already 2 o'clock in the morning. I will only add something about the strange reference that Tarstein made to the mystical 'madness' of Rudolf Hess. I will tell you in advance that, in effect, when my Taufpate decides to carry out his historic flight and parachute into England, his act can only be qualified as 'madness.' This from the political, and even military strategic point of view. But different will be the opinion of anyone who observes the facts with an esoteric and initiatic perspective. Because Rudolf's 'madness' is analogous to the madness of Belicena Villca when she decides to develop a distraction tactic to make the movements of her son Noyo possible: she perfectly knew that her act was extremely risky, that it would attract the persecution from the Golen and they would end up capturing and executing her: she knew it and yet she did not hesitate to act, to sacrifice her life, so that the Strategy of the Loyal Gods triumphed. In the same way, Rudolf delivers himself to the Golen Druids of the Order of the Golden Dawn, that is to say, to their representative, the Golen Duke of Hamilton, because he proposes to distract the Enemy in order to favor the movements of the Führer. What would the Führer gain after the 'madness' of Rudolf Hess? Well, *a humanly invaluable objective: after the 'capture' of Rudolf Hess, the Druids would no longer be able to 'open' a Gate to Shambhala in England, they would be left isolated from the Abodes of the Traitor Gods and the White Brotherhood, and only from Asia would they be able to reestablish that contact.*

"You will ask yourself why such an effect was produced, by virtue of what Power Rudolf achieved this miracle, and I will anticipate that it occurred *by his presence alone,* thanks to the Sign of the Origin that he, like you and I, was showing without realizing it. So it was, Neffe; and later on I will narrate to you in detail the true esoteric operation that Rudolf's journey to England signified, an event that has been stupidly interpreted after the war. But much earlier, perhaps tomorrow, will you learn the Doctrine that was sustaining the Black Order, about the Power of the Sign of the Origin."

We retired to our rooms in the greatest silence, each one of us immersed in our own thoughts. I, of course, was not coming out of my astonishment at seeing how perfectly the stories of Belicena Villca and Uncle Kurt were fitting together. And I kept wondering how that adventure would end, now that I would indubitably count on Uncle Kurt's support to seek out Belicena Villca's son.

Chapter XIX

I t was 9 in the morning and a light drizzle was falling outside.

We had both slept little and we knew it. But we were both, also, sensing that we were running out of time, that that tranquility that we were enjoying would not last long.

Uncle Kurt sipped the last of his coffee and continued with the story.

"In the Nordic *Ordensburg Krössinsee,* as I already said, I stayed for three months. After one month of being there, I visited Konrad Tarstein for the first time, and the following two months I attended Gregorstraße 239 every Saturday, thanks to the fact that *SS Oberführer* Papp had arranged a permanent commission for me in Berlin on weekends. Thus it was not difficult for me to make the trip from Prussia to Berlin, but I was fearing, in those days, I would not be able to do it with the same ease from the Ordensburg *Vogelsang* farther away, in the Western Rhine.

"In those two months, as Tarstein was instructing me in the secrets of the Thulegesellschaft, I was experiencing toward him a growing affection and admiration. Soon the poor initial impression of his fascinating personality was totally buried and I must say that I would not have hesitated in striking any insolent person who dared to express aloud anything of what I myself, the first day, had thought about Tarstein. Such is the impetuousness of youth!

"The 'arrangement' that Rudolf Hess and Konrad Tarstein had made about my person was consisting in that I was to attend Gregorstraße 239 for a certain time with the aim of being instructed in the *Hyperborean Wisdom,* which was the 'Occult Philosophy' of the *true* Thulegesellschaft. This preparation, which would capacitate me to receive the *Hyperborean Initiation,* would be given by Tarstein himself, a rare honor, as was made known to me many times, which was never granted to anyone. Tarstein was, as I was comprehending with time, one of the most important men in Germany because of his secret hierarchy in the Thulegesellschaft.

"According to Konrad Tarstein, in order to receive the Hyperborean Initiation, I had to previously purify myself. To this end, he was introducing me to the marvelous knowledge that is the Hyperborean Wisdom. But, I must clarify, this teaching does not constitute a mere knowledge, an information suspended in the memory to be utilized in rational judgments. On the contrary, Tarstein was recommending not to memorize in the least and, if possible, to forget what was discussed, since the objective of the instruction was aiming **to awaken the Blood Memory,** a phenomenon that one could only achieve if the acquired knowledge was gnostically acting on the primordial Hyperborean stock that constitutes the **Divinity of the Virya.**

"This is how I was an astonished witness, astonished in all degrees of astonishment, even fright, of accounts and explanations that were surpassing the imaginable, at least what I could imagine, in that fantastic Hyperborean Cosmogony of the Thulegesellschaft. If there were a heresiological scale to measure those ideas that were profoundly deviating from 'Western Culture' in its Judeo-Christian conception, I could affirm that many of Tarstein's expositions would occupy a prominent place in that scale of heresies. Because if a heresy is what contradicts a Dogma (that is why there are Catholic, Buddhist, Islamic heresies, etc.), what to say of a philosophy that questions the **totality** of human existence with all its Dogmas, Philosophies, Religions, and Sciences, that attempts to change the historical course, that affirms the possibility of the transmutation of the semi-divine man or Virya into an immortal Siddha, that, in short, has declared war on the material potencies of Jehovah Satan, owners of the World, of History, and of the majority of men? Let us agree that in Heresiology, such ideas would occupy a distinguished place.

"I say this because when embracing concepts that depart from or oppose 'Western Culture,' one must be aware of the degree of 'departure' or 'opposition' in which one is situated with respect to it, in order to conduct oneself prudently and avoid future evils...

"And I was aware that the things that I was hearing and the effect that they were causing in me were preannouncing irreversible changes in conduct. However, that was not worrying me because I had a goal that was eclipsing all personal precaution and was making any intention of turning back appear as pure selfishness. That goal, that objective for which I was pouring all my yearnings, was the German Fatherland: *Ein Reich, Ein Volk, Ein Führer.*[39]

"You will now comprehend, Neffe, that I was living and acting **within** a **Hyperborean Mystique** and that the **charismatic bond** with the Führer was ever increasing, to the extent that it was deepening the Mystery of the Thulegesellschaft.

"On my first visits to Gregorstraße 239 I felt so confident in Konrad Tarstein, that one evening I did not hesitate in recounting to him my strange experience with the Voice of the Hyperborean Kiev. This confidence did not seem to impress him, for he observed me a long time in silence and then said to me:

" 'Tell me Kurt, have you spoken to anyone else of that perception?'

" 'No, I responded. I was thinking of speaking to Taufpate Hess about it but I have not yet been able to see him since I returned from Egypt.'

" 'Then we will make a deal,' affirmed Tarstein, 'to no one will you reveal that you are in possession of that charism outside of *your own Circle* in the Thulegesellschaft.'

" 'I promise,' I hurriedly said, 'but who makes up my Circle?'

" 'Alas, young Kurt, you should know that a Circle in the Thulegesellschaft is not determined by the **number** of persons, as in the exoteric organizations that the Synarchy fosters, but by a **qualitative relationship** denominated **charismatic bonding**. Charismatic bonding is independent of the number and, as every closed Circle of the Thulegesellschaft exists as such thanks to the charismatic bonding, those who **experience** that relationship are members of the Circle.'

" 'But how are the members of a Circle actually recognized?' I asked a bit puzzled at such gobbledygook.

" 'The recognition is interior. **One** simply **knows** that this or that Virya belongs to his own Circle. Of course, in external Circles, constituted by **non-initiated** members, some traditional forms of Secret Societies are practiced for reunion and recognition, that is to say "the Sanctuary" and "shibboleth";[40] but this is done provisionally, attending to the urgency that certain investigations require. The true Spirit of the Thulegesellschaft is not in the external Circles, which will be promptly eliminat-

---

39. "One Reich, One Volk, One Leader."

40. A word or sign to distinguish someone belonging to a particular group.

ed after the Total War, but in the internal Circles, those that are rigorously Hyperborean. In them, I repeat, the recognition is interior, *one knows with the blood.*'

" 'So I would not be able to *recognize* the members of my Circle...'

" '... as long as you do not receive the Hyperborean Initiation,' Tarstein completed.

" '... and as I promised not to talk about *my charism*...'

" '... you will not do so,' Tarstein continued again, 'as long as you do not receive the Initiation.'"

" 'Well, I feel somewhat cheated,' I said, smiling.

" 'You mustn't take it the wrong way Kurt, but this is a matter of the *highest reserve.*'

" 'You ought to thank the confidence that you inspire in us for not arranging *your immediate separation and internment* while the instruction that we are giving you lasts. If the Enemy, that is to say, the Synarchy, simply suspected your charism, you would be executed without awaiting confirmation. And that is something that neither the Thulegesellschaft nor the ⚡⚡ can allow. What's yours is important, Kurt.'

" 'Is it so important?' I asked, impressed by the veiled threat that I was discerning behind Tarstein's kind words.

" 'Very important, Kurt. Look at it this way: you have the Sign of Lúcifer, you possess notable psychic qualities, and you are an *Ostenführer* of the ⚡⚡. Doesn't it seem too much to be by chance? Well, it's not by chance!'

"He observed me a long time as if doubting about whether he should continue. At last he said:

" 'The person that we have been waiting for twenty years to head a special mission is you. So important, Kurt, so important, that perhaps the fate of the Third Reich and, why not, that of the Aryan Race depend on it.

"I was stunned by this revelation and, in my confusion, I thought to be the victim of a joke. But no matter how closely I was scrutinizing Konrad Tarstein's impassive face, I was finding nothing that confirmed this supposition.

" 'I...' I stammered, 'I never dreamed to take part in such a mission. Besides, I don't believe I deserve it.'

" *'Take part in?'* excitedly interrupted Tarstein, 'Take part in, you say? *Ha-ha-ha,*' he frantically laughed, 'you won't *take part* Kurt, *you alone will carry out the mission.* Who else could do it?' he asked as if to himself.

" 'You'll find out everything, Kurt,' he continued, now looking at me in the eyes. 'But bear in mind that here it is not about choosing. Neither you, nor I, nor anyone, can choose because *the choice has already been made,* in another sphere of consciousness, in another World. We have nothing left to do but face our Destiny, which is also the destiny of humanity, and to be grateful for having been marked for such an august task. Our God, Khristos Lúcifer, is the Most Beautiful Lord, but he is also the Most Intrepid, the Father of Valor; we must not even dream of letting him down.'

" 'I would want nothing more than to serve the Fatherland and humanity,' I dazedly said, 'but it's just that everything you say surprises me. I don't understand how I can be so important a piece in this game and the responsibility overwhelms me. How to live knowing that obtaining something that is precious to the Third Reich and the Aryan Race is in my hands? I, like every Comrade, and more so being an ⚡⚡ Officer, am ready to die for our motto when so disposed but, from now on, I would not wish to live with the anguish of failing before the time, of not being able to comply. Do you understand, Tarstein? The time that remains until the dénouement terrifies me. If there is something so important to do, I would like to carry it out as soon as possible.'

" 'Then you must have patience!!' affirmed Tarstein, almost shouting. 'Even if there is a minute or a century left, you must not demonstrate any agitation or conduct unbecoming to a *Kshatriya.*

" 'Remember, you are a Knight, a *Monk Warrior,* you must behave accordingly. Soon you will be Initiated and then you will fulfill your Destiny.'

"I nodded, disturbed by the deserved reprimand that I received from Tarstein. But that day we spoke no more of the matter.

Chapter XX

ell, Neffe," said Uncle Kurt after lunch, with his strangely brilliant eyes, "we are approaching the most important part of my life, the moment in which I received the Initiation and was entrusted with that unusual mission, that operation that Tarstein was so highly valuing and that was still incomprehensible to me.

"At that time, with Tarstein as my instructor, I learned a lot. He was seeming to know everything and I used to feel ashamed because, after so many years at *NAPOLA*, I was only capable of attentively following him in his expositions, but I was feeling incompetent to complete anything he was saying on my own. However, Tarstein was coming to console me in his own paradoxical manner:

" 'Don't worry Kurt, it's just *confusion*, blood impurity. But you are going faster than you believe. Soon you'll know everything, *you will awaken* and, then, if you wish, you will be able to master as much Science as the greatest Sage. Of course, our Hyperborean Science is an accursed Science for this satanic world. But that should not worry you, for the Siddha is truly *one* and has no necessity for anything but Himself. For the Hyperborean Wisdom, there are three classes of men. The *Paśu*, who was conceived by the ordinating Demiurge of matter, Jehovah Satan, and who only under certain conditions can be considered "man," being more accurate to call him animal-man. There is also the *Virya*, who is basically a Paśu of *Hyperborean lineage*, that is to say, a Paśu who *has mingled his blood* with an immortal Siddha, a Mystery that you will comprehend in the course of your instruction. The Viryas are to a greater or lesser extent *astray or lost* by the confusion of Blood and only the *memory contained in the Blood* would be able to purify them. That is what the Führer's *Strategy* aims at; that and *to put an end to the Kaly Yuga* or Dark Age.

" 'Keep in mind that a Paśu can never be a semi-divine Virya, but that a Virya can *completely descend* to the level of Paśu by a definitive blood confusion. And finally are the Loyal Siddhas, those who came with Khristos Lúcifer to Earth millions of years ago and belong to a "Hyperborean" Race, another Mystery that you will comprehend with clarity later on, for the terms "Hyperborean" and "Thule" have almost nothing to do with the legends of Antiquity.

" 'Thus are Siddhas, Viryas and Paśus, in the Hyperborean meaning that I have given you and not as these terms are vulgarly understood in Tibet, the three "categories" of men with whom you will have to accustom yourself to reason out from now on. Add to this an important concept: "the Synarchy organizes and plans the world for the Paśus and lost Viryas. The Hyperborean Wisdom teaches how the Virya must purify himself in order to recover the Vril and transmute himself from a semi-divine mortal into a Divine Hyperborean Immortal.

" 'I have to tell you something, Kurt, that ought to fill you with legitimate pride. Your parapsychic analysis of "hearing the Voice of Kiev," even if you have not followed the guidelines of the Hyperborean Wisdom to conquer said charism, has led you to the correct conclusion. I refer to your affirmation that it is necessary to *dispose the Spirit to remember,"* as the best attitude, before the danger of rationalizing the psychic phenomenon by formulating an equivalent question, strictly coincides with our philosophy. It is by "disposing the Spirit to remember" that one accesses the Blood Memory. And this previous step, unavoidable to obtain the Hyperborean Initiation, you have taken it alone, a feat that should, as I already said, fill you with pride.'

"From these last words one might think that Tarstein, versed in matters of Occultism, was a dreamer and unworthy of credit in rigorous matters, as is generally the case. And nothing would be more erroneous than such an appraisal, for although I have not met anyone like him who knew about Occultism, Hermetic Philosophy, or Religions, that was only a part of his immense knowledge. In those years of the 1930s, Germany, in full industrial deployment, was a giant of Science. And Konrad Tarstein knew it all. He was a scholar of Germanic knowledge in all its nuances: he was mastering advanced mathematics at its highest level, chemistry, physics, biology, the multiple industrial technologies, etc. Not to mention the humanistic field where his dominion of ancient and modern philosophies, logic, philology, psychology, etc., was fearsome. How to define such a man? And the most difficult: how to transmit his thought without distorting it? Effectively, Neffe, I would not have been capable of explaining the Hyperborean

Wisdom to you; and if I can now speak with you about it, it is thanks to those extraordinary Initiates, Belicena Villca and Nimrod de Rosario. Remember that Oskar Feil was affirming that only the Hyperborean Wisdom of Nimrod de Rosario could compare to that of Tarstein: I am sure that Belicena Villca would have said the same. Thanks to them, Neffe, I will be able to confide to you this part of my life, which would be incomprehensible to any interlocutor who did not know the *Fundamentals of the Hyperborean Wisdom.*

"I will be brief, then, given that you perfectly understand to what I refer. Konrad Tarstein profoundly instructed me in the Hyperborean Wisdom and one day, in a subterranean room of the Castle of Wewelsburg, I received the Hyperborean Initiation. In the Hyperborean Chamber specially constructed for such ceremonies, a High Initiate of the Black Order, I suppose a Pontiff, performed the ritual in front of an audience of only eight Initiates. And there I was confronted with Death, with the Kālibur Death of Pyrena, as Belicena Villca would say. That is to say, with the Archetype of Death, the Death that kills the Warm Life; and then with the Cold Kālibur Death, the Naked Truth of Oneself that is found after the End of the Warm Life. And returning to the Warm Life, after sinking into the infinite blackness of Oneself, I found that the anguish of Death had fled from me forever. The animal fear of dying, the instinct of preservation was definitively overcome by the Wisdom of Eternal Life. A will of steel definitively took hold of my animal nature and I knew that nothing could stop me, that is to say, nothing that involved Death, the threat of Death. It was pure Resolute Will: I would advance toward wherever I was ordered and, I repeat, nothing could stop me.

"It was then when the objective of the mysterious mission for which they had prepared me for so many years was revealed to me. And once again, the one in charge of the revelation was Konrad Tarstein.

" 'It will not be difficult for you to understand in what the mission consists,' Tarstein told me, 'when I acquaint you with certain facts that are occurring. Tell me, Kurt, do you know where the forces that sustain the Synarchy, the Jewish World Conspiracy, come from? I refer to the psychic forces, naturally, since the economic or political forces are only exterior expressions of them.'

" 'Well, according to what I heard the Führer affirm, and just as you yourself have explained it to me, such forces come from an Occult Center called Chang Shambhala, where dwells a Hierarchy of Infernal Beings dedicated to impose the Plan of Jehovah Satan on Earth. In the Black Order exist proofs in this respect. For example, the participation of the Hierarchy in the foundation of Masonry, the Rosicrucian Order, the Theosophical Society, etc., is proven with documents. Without going any further, we have a copy of the letter that the High Priest of Chang Shambhala, Rigden Jyepo, sent to Lenin through Nicholas Roerich, congratulating him on the success of the Bolshevik Revolution: behind Lenin and the October conspirators, the Transhimalaya Lodge was acting, founded by the White Brotherhood. Yes, Comrade Tarstein: behind the Synarchy is Chang Shambhala, the Masters and Priests of the Occult Hierarchy or White Brotherhood of Chang Shambhala.'

" 'Correct, Kurt. And now complete the concept, please: what is Chang Shambhala? A physical place on Earth, or an extraterrestrial Construction?'

" 'As you well know, Shambhala is an extraterrestrial Construction, extended between the Earth and the Sun, over dimensions of Space that make it invisible to the ordinary man,' I responded somewhat astonished by such obvious questions. 'Its Constructors were the Traitorous Gods, the founders of the White Brotherhood, and the Initiates of the Hierarchy learn a Science called "Kalachakra" that allows them to open the Gates of Shambhala, Gates that are found everywhere.'

" 'Perfect response, Kurt! Now you will realize what your mission is: you, Kurt, *are the Key that can close those Gates.*'

"I certainly understood less then than ever before. But Tarstein was about to clarify the enigma.

" 'Strictly speaking in truth, Kurt, the Key that locks those Accursed Gates is the Sign of the Origin, the Sign that has the Power to remind the Traitorous Gods of their Primordial Treason, the Sign that can communicate to them the Symbol of the Origin and confront them with the Absolute Truth of the Spirit, the Symbol of the Origin that can dissolve the absolute Lie of Material Creation that they sustain. By that Power to reveal the Absolute Truth, those who sustain the Absolute Lie, have resolved to never confront the Sign of the Origin, that is to say, as long as the Lie of the material Universe lasts. And that is why the Sign of the Origin is the Key to the Gates of Shamb-hala, a Key that closes the Route of the Demons with its impassable seal. And you, Kurt, manifest the Sign of the Origin like no one else, even if you are not able to notice it by yourself; but that does not strategically affect your mission: *your presence alone is enough to close the Accursed Gates; the Demons are not willing to contemplate the Sign that you are capable of projecting.* Of course, they would kill you when approaching the Gate, *were it not for the fact that you are now beyond Death.* Do you understand me, Kurt? *If you situate yourself in front of a Shambhala Gate, and keep yourself out of the Demons' reach by practicing the Way of Strategic Opposition that makes you independent of Time and Space, the Gate shall be inexorably closed!'*

"Now I was understanding something: with my presence alone, I would cause the closing of one of those Gates that was leading to the Accursed City, abode of the Demons of the White Brotherhood. But I was still not comprehending the objective of the mission. To which gate was Konrad Tarstein referring? A moment later, Tarstein's explanation would fill me with astonishment.

"'And now that I spoke of your faculty, of being a Key Sign, I will go directly to the details of the mission, to what the Black Order, the Third Reich, and the Führer expect of you. Do you remember Professor Ernst Schäfer?' he asked with irony; but he gave me no time to respond. 'Yes, I don't believe that you have forgotten. Not after the incident that you protagonized last year by offering yourself as a volunteer for Operation *Altwesten* and of which I am informed in all its details. You could not know it then, but your participation in that operation is the last thing in the world that Ernst Schäfer would accept. You will verify this if you take into account the faculty that you have, to close the Gates of Shambhala, and possess the answer to this question: do you know what Operation *Altwesten* consists in?'

"'Comrade Tarstein, Ernest Schäfer already departed toward Tibet a year ago. I suppose that you'll know that a good friend of mine, Oskar Feil, who supplied me with all the information that I possess, was going on the expedition,' I said, warned on the spot that it was not a good idea for me to lie to the well-informed Tarstein. 'I'm sorry if I broke any rules, for I know that the operation is top secret, but I must not deny that my distrust toward Schäfer could not be greater: even my

Taufpate Rudolf Hess confirmed that certain suspicions were weighing on him and suggested to me that, in spite of everything, I would form part of the expedition. But lamentably that has not occurred, whether for better or for worse, I do not know, and it is now beyond repair due to the time that they've been in Asia. In any case, I would like to assume full responsibility for any fault Oskar Feil may have committed by mentioning Operation *Altwesten* to me, for only my curiosity and the doubts that I harbor about Schäfer's conduct are to blame for his confidences.'

" 'Relax, Kurt, no one is accusing you of espionage. Answer me, simply, what do you know about Operation *Altwesten?*'

" 'Well, almost nothing, Comrade Tarstein. I am only aware of the path traveled by the expedition up to now, thanks to the secret letters which Oskar has managed to send me from different parts of Asia. The last one was dispatched three months ago in Lhasa, Tibet, by a messenger who had it arrive in Germany through one of our consulates in India. In it he was informing me that they were preparing to depart toward the Northwest, guided by two mysterious "lamas of the Kurkuma Bonnet," and that they were carrying safe-conducts from the Dalai Lama. That's all I know. I did not manage to find out the final destination, since not even Oskar knows it, but it is evident that it is not an exploration toward the west, as its name indicates, but toward a site directly located in the opposite direction. It seems that Schäfer was not fully trusting him and has even isolated him from the rest of the Officers.'

" 'That is all I was wanting to hear, Kurt. I will tell you without further ado where Ernst Schäfer is headed: *toward the Shambhala Gate. He goes to request to the King of the World, in the name of the so-called "sane Forces of Germany," his intervention to put an end to the Third Reich.*'

" 'Treason!' I shouted.

" 'Ha-ha,' he nervously laughed at my exclamation. 'You would be surprised if you knew the magnitude, the multiplicity, and the scope of the betrayals that corrode the Third Reich and conspire against the leadership of the Führer. But it is natural that it occurs this way, since the confrontation that National Socialism poses to the Potencies of Matter is Total: every man is subjected to the essential tension between Spirit and Matter; and many will be those who will give in to the Illusion of Matter, facing the *Judaic form* of the Illusion of Matter, that is to say, money, peace, democracy, freedom, law, etc. Only spiritual men will be capable of overcoming this Illusion: they will overcome it with the sole force of their Gracious Will, with the act of their Honor, with the valor of their Pure Blood.

" 'That of Ernst Schäfer is one more of such betrayals. It just particularly affects us because it is an esoteric fact, of a circumstance that we can eminently understand. Yes, Kurt: that of Schäfer is an enormous treason, but it is not the greatest of the betrayals that the Führer must face. However, you are right in taking it seriously, *because it depends on you whether his disloyal Plans triumph or fail.*'

" 'How would I be able to intervene and influence Schäfer's plans, from Berlin?' I asked in a daze.

" 'For it will not be Berlin from where you will act, Kurt, but from Asia. You will immediately depart toward India! Tomorrow you will present yourself to the SD and receive orders from *ϟϟ Oberführer* Papp: he will demonstrate to you how it is possible to catch up with Schäfer's expedition before it arrives at the Kunlun Mountains! But now I will anticipate something that, I do not doubt, will deeply motivate you. Above all, I will tell you that the Black Order has, since the beginning, excellent spies in Ernst Schäfer's group: it is through their reports that we have found out about the "incident" with the professor and of your friendship with Oskar Feil. Well, it is about the latter that I was wishing to speak to you:

" 'Take it easy, Kurt, but the truth is that Oskar Feil is in mortal danger. Certainly, Schäfer has never trusted him, and if he has permitted him to join the operation it is because he plans to eliminate him in Asia: only you, if you arrive in time, will perhaps be able to save him!'

" 'But why take him to Asia? If he was distrusting Oskar, why didn't he get rid of him in Germany?' I desperately cried out.

" 'Oh, Kurt. I regret having to give you this news. Hold tight, for what you are about to hear is shocking: *your Comrade has been chosen to be sacrificed.* Yes; don't look at me like that: it is confirmed! Although it is still possible to avoid it. The fact is that, on his route to Gyaring Lake,[41] beyond the Blue River,[42] Schäfer will have to cross *the Boundary of Shambhala, the last*

---

41. Zhaling Lake

42. Yangtze River

portico before arriving at the Gate of Chang Shambhala. And said portico has been watched over for millennia by a tribe of cruel guardians, those who are led by the malevolent *Jafranpa* lamas or "lamas of the Kurkuma Bonnet," members of the White Brotherhood. In Tibet, the Dalai Lama does not exercise true religious authority, but his instructor at the highest hierarchy in the *Gelugpa* sect: a *Rinpoche,* that is to say, a *"precious"* lama. All other Lamaist groups, including the Jafranpa, are subject to the Gelugpa, or "lamas of the Yellow Bonnet": only the Bodhisattvas, the Mahatmas, the Immortals, are above them. The Gelugpa protect the lamas of the Kurkuma Bonnet and that is why Schäfer has safe-conducts from the Dalai Lama. However, such passes have relative value, for while the Dalai Lama's religious power encompasses all of Tibet, his political power is limited by Chinese borders: *and The Boundary of Shambhala is currently in Chinese territory.*

"'The lamas of the Kurkuma Bonnet are experts in the Science of the Kalachakra, or "Wheel of Time," the Wisdom that enables them to understand and master karmic connections, *rten 'brel,* and to synchronize the Wheel of Life, Bhavachakra or *srid pa'i 'khor lo,* to the rhythm of the Plans of the White Brotherhood. They are, then, fervent worshipers of the Lords of Karma and of their chief, Rigden Jyepo, the Lord of Shambhala, the King of the World, Jehovah Satan. They require every pilgrim lama who requests authorization to pass through the Boundary of Shambhala, the *Yajnavirya,* that is, a *human sacrifice.* As you will realize, Ernst Schäfer gave no reason to be exempted from such an obligation.

"'In synthesis, Kurt: *Oskar Feil was selected by Ernst Schäfer to be handed over to the Lamas of the Kurkuma Bonnet. They will offer his life to Rigden Jyepo by means of the ritual beheading, Yah-Sa.'*

"Hours after this conversation with Konrad Tarstein, while traveling to the Rhineland to collect my belongings from Wewelsburg, I looked at myself in a mirror on the train and my eyes were still bloodshot. During the meeting, when Tarstein revealed to me the death that was awaiting Oskar, I would have destroyed Ernst Schäfer with my hands, had I been able to reach him at that moment.

"Konrad Tarstein took care to warn me that the conduct that the Black Order was requesting of me was not that. On the contrary: my orders were to locate Schäfer's expedition as soon as possible and to join it without violence. For that I would go equipped with the corresponding official authorizations: a secret decree from the Führer and a pass from *Reichsführer* Himmler. In addition, two secret agents of the *SS* would accompany me. These were two *SS Hauptsturmführers* who were combining the paradoxical virtues of both possessing a doctorate in law, and having served for five years in the Gestapo, where they converted themselves into expert assassins.

"According to Tarstein, the best Strategy was demanding that I fold myself into the expedition and there *manifest* the Sign of the Origin. Such a demonstration would be sufficient to cause Operation Altwesten to fail. *And it would be achieved without performing any esoteric maneuver, without using any magical technique: the mere act of my presence would be enough for the Demons to close the Gate of Shambhala.*

Chapter XXI

berführer Papp, an old acquaintance, filled me in on the details of the mission. The departure would be in four days, since everything was ready: provisions, equipment, weapons, false documentation, etc. In truth, only then did I clearly see it, that the operation was prepared a long time ago and, apparently, was only depending on me to be put into execution. That is to say, that all those who were participating in the operation, or in its secret, the Führer included, were awaiting my Initiation, waiting for the moment in which I acquired spiritual awareness of the Key of the Sign and could explain to me the mission in Asia. I do not believe that I ever felt as much shame as I did then: I, the stupid and arrogant apprentice Initiate, had lost months, precious months, trying to rationally delve into the Hyperborean Wisdom of the Black Order; at last, realizing that I was going down a dead end, that I was prey to a trap of logic, I sought in my Spirit the ultimate Truth that reason, and rational knowledge, were denying me; ***and I thus propitiated the Initiatic Kairos,*** according to the confirmation made by the Initiates of the Black Order; then I was Initiated and Konrad Tarstein explained to me the character of the mission of the 'First Key,' such is its codified denomination, and described the faculty that I should use to 'close the Gate of Shambhala,' a gate that Ernst Schäfer was proposing to open and that perhaps was opening at that moment.

"Those thoughts, and this possibility, were greatly distressing me, and I would tell the truth if I affirmed that even those four days to depart seemed interminably long to me.

"The first stage was by plane. We would fly from Berlin to Tanzania, on the east coast of Africa, making stopovers in various African countries or colonies of German allies, such as Spain and Italy. In Tanzania, in the region of what was, until World War I, the State of Zanzibar, we would parachute onto the farm of a former German settler family who were now working for the Secret Service. Such a route had to be followed because the mission was qualified as a 'top-secret Waffen-*ᛋᛋ* operation' and because the flight was being made in a military aircraft specially adapted for the job: it was a Dornier, or *'flying pencil,'* which had its classic bomb load replaced by supplementary fuel tanks.

"In Tanzania, then, we descended without problems, alongside the load of weapons and equipment. The settlers were expecting us for some time and had acquired for us a shipment of cotton thread, in which they hastened to hide the compromising objects. A day later, and wearing an outfit of evident Levantine tailoring, very appropriate for the role of Egyptian traders that we were to play, the settlers led us to the island of Zanzibar in a barge of regular dimensions. In the port was anchored the Italian ship, Tarento, which was secretly participating in the operation and would transport us to Dacca, in the NE of India.

"In Zanzibar our identity completely changed. Both I as well as the two *ϟϟ Hauptsturmführers,* would be 'Egyptian traders' from then on. It was a risky move, since Egypt was in the hands of the English, but our passports and forged histories had few flaws and it was seeming unlikely that we aroused so much suspicion as to initiate an investigation. I myself was truly Egyptian and was speaking English as well as Arabic, a language that my comrades were also mastering, although not so the English, to which they were giving a strong German accent. However, should the need arise, it would be enough that they correctly expressed themselves in Arabic, since in Egypt no one was forced to know English.

"The Tarento crossed the Indian Ocean, with a single stopover at Ceylon, and then entered the Bay of Bengal bound for Calcutta and Dacca. She finally ascended the Dhaleswari River, which is an arm of the Brahmaputra, and anchored off its left bank, in the port of Dacca, an important city of what was once the Presidency of Bengal Proper, then the Province of Bengal, later the Islamic State of East Pakistan, and today Bangladesh. The shipment of African thread, with its precious contraband, could be unloaded without inconveniences and stored in a warehouse that we rented for that purpose.

"We weren't planning to stay too long in Dacca: just long enough to sell or trade the threads for the rich Bengali silks and muslins, stock up on supplies, and hire porters. Our next goal was the city of Punakha, the Winter capital of the Country of Bhutan. There *ϟϟ Standartenführer*[43] Karl von Grossen

---

43. Lit. *ϟϟ-Standard leader.*

and his deputy, *SS Obersturmführer* Heinz Schmidt, both from Division III of the *RSHA*,[44] called 'Foreign Information Service' or 'External SD,' were waiting for us. Von Grossen was the head of 'Operation First Key' and, although he had Schellenberg and Heydrich as immediate superiors, for this mission he was placed under the direct command of *Reichsführer* Himmler. He had already gone ahead many months ago and was keeping, in a strange way, the caravan of Ernst Schäfer under permanent observation. He had a reputation as an intelligent and tough man. He had also been a policeman, like my assistants Kloster and Hans, serving several years in the Bavarian Gestapo. Later he requested a transfer to the External SD in order to make use of his doctorate in History. He was an expert in the History and Geography of Asia, as well as a specialist in rapid deployment tactics, knowledge that explains why *Reichsführer* Himmler chose him to command Operation First Key.

"Three days later we left Dacca toward the north, taking a road that skirts the left bank of the Brahmaputra up to Bonarpara and then turns off in the direction of Rangpur, the residence of the Raja of Assam. We were in the Autumn of 1938 and the stifling climate of these boggy regions, furrowed by countless rivers and apt only for rice cultivation, was making us long for the ascent to the high, cold areas of Bhutan. The two *SS Hauptsturmführers,* Hans Lechfeld and Kloster Hagen, were marching in front, preceded by fifteen pure Aryan porters, of the Kalita Race, with all the cargo; I was at the end of the column. We were exhibiting only three Mauser rifles from the First World War, weapons in keeping with our supposed profession as traders, while we were hiding our service Luger pistols in our clothes and in our backpacks, the dreaded Schmeisser submachine guns.

"We camped a day in the Garo Hills and crossed Assam without stopping more than what was indispensable. Soon we found ourselves at an altitude of over 2,000 meters, glad to leave behind the tropical regions, infested by wild animals and by the no less savage bandits of the Aka, Mishmi, Daphla, Abor, etc., tribes. A path that was serpentining along the eastern slope of the Himalayas was slowly leading us toward Bhutan.

---

44. *Reichssicherheitshauptamt* or Reich Security Main Office.

"In the village of Daga Dzong, we were received with great jubilation, as if we were ambassadors of some Western potency, which caused us great annoyance, since we were not wishing to draw the attention of the English or any true diplomat from the nation that we were. However, the mystery was soon cleared up, upon finding that two envoys of Von Grossen were awaiting our arrival for months to guide us to Punakha: they were two Lopas, functionaries of the Deb Raja of Bhutan.

"Accompanied by the slender but vigorous Lopas, also of Aryan race, we crossed numerous small valleys, nestled between mountain ranges of enormous altitude. After each step of the Himalayan slope, we were ascending hundreds of meters, the passes, or dvara, of 4 or 5 thousand meters, not being infrequent. The Lopas spoke Khams Skad, the Tibetan language, which I, as *Ostenführer,* was perfectly understanding. In the Khams dialect they explained to us that we would not go directly to Punakha because there, next to the Deb Raja, was an English garrison: Karl von Grossen was in a nearby monastery, under the protection of the spiritual head of the Country, the Dharmaraja.

"Finally, we arrived at the Taoist monastery, constructed on a mountain covered by eternal snow and from which was starting a rough path, apt only for pedestrians, that was crossing the Himalayas and leading to Tibet. Von Grossen and his assistant came out to meet us.

" 'Heil Hitler! I was fearing that you wouldn't make it in time,' he said to us out of all greetings.

" 'Heil Hitler!' I responded, '*Hauptsturmführer Doktor* Kloster Hagen and *Hauptsturmführer Doktor* Hans Lechfeld,' I introduced my accompaniers, 'and I, *Sturmbannführer* Kurt von Sübermann. Sieg Heil, mein *Standartenführer!*'

Von Grossen attentively observed me, with scientific curiosity.

" 'So you are the mysterious Initiate on whom the Fate of the Third Reich may depend?' he asked with amazement. 'I was imagining you differently!'

" 'How?' I exclaimed, perturbed by the *Standartenführer's* indiscreet frankness.

" 'Don't take it the wrong way,' he said, smiling for the first time, 'but it's just that much has been said about you here, perhaps more so than in Germany. You know, these people have highly developed psychic faculties, and for several weeks they have perceived you as you were approaching, and I wouldn't be exaggerating in the least if I affirm to you that the whole of spiritual Tibet at this moment knows of your arrival in Bhutan! Well, Von Sübermann: you've been psychically observed and described in many diverse ways, *hence my doubts.* There are those who maintain that you're a Great Saint, and others, on the contrary, that make of you a terrible Warrior.' Again, the question mark was painted on his face. 'But *we know* you're the latter, don't we?'

"There was a hint of doubt in Von Grossen's voice that greatly annoyed me.

" 'Indeed, Kamerad Von Grossen! According to the Rule of the Black Order, *I am* a Warrior, a *Wise Warrior.* I don't know what appearance I was supposed to have, but have no doubt that *I am capable of killing in the most terrible manner. And that I will kill in this way anyone who attempts to thwart my mission.'*

" 'Bravo!' exclaimed Von Grossen with evident sincerity. 'I repeat: You must excuse my surprise but, after so many months of waiting, and hearing the most absurd stories from the lamas' mouths, I no longer knew for sure what kind of man I was expecting. I am glad that you are a complete ⚡⚡ officer, Von Sübermann!'

"Karl von Grossen and Heinz Schmidt, who said not a word, nor would he later, for he was too sparing, had caught up with us five kilometers before the monastery. At that moment we arrived and were invited into a comfortable room, where wood and guano were burning on a stone hearth; outside the temperature was ten degrees below zero.

"In reality, we were not in a simple monastery of lamas, as I had supposed, but in a small citadel surrounded by a dissuasive wall: behind the walls were three buildings of very different architecture. The most imposing was the Palace of the Dharmaraja, where the spiritual Head of Bhutan was residing in Winter. The second in importance was a very ancient Pagoda, perhaps the oldest construction of the whole. 'It is a *temple* magnificently carved from a single, colossal piece of stone,' Von Grossen explained as we walked through the outer courtyard. 'It dates from the times in which this region was dominated by the *Buddhist Priests* of Manipur: the Temple was dedicated to the Cult of Vaivasvata Manu, who rules the present manvantara or *Manuantara,* that is to say, *the cycle of existence of a Humanity of animal-men.* Subsequently, the Land was conquered by a Lopa tribe under the command of Taoist Initiates, who were profoundly iconoclastic and were hating *all* Priests, without distinction of Cult. They, naturally, closed the temple after putting its last dwellers to the sword. Had it not been so, Maitreya, the next reincarnation of Manu, who would be none other than the Messiah that the Jews await, would now be venerated here. But the Buddhist Orders of Priests have not forgotten this place and permanently lie in wait, seeking the opportunity to reconquer it.'

"The third building, in which we were, was the Monastery proper and consisting of a labyrinthine building where a large community of Tibetan monks and nuns were equally inhabiting. That composition of mixed Initiates surprised me and so I let Von Grossen know it.

" 'It is that the present occupants constitute a Secret Society that is neither Hindu, nor Buddhist, nor Taoist, but is "beyond" such religious systems: and "beyond" does not mean "above" or "over," but *outside.* That is to say, the Wisdom that they possess is *outside* of the religious systems. They do not hold, then, a mere syncretism but a true spiritual Wisdom, possibly the same that you in the Black Order, and we in the Ahnenerbe Institute, call **Hyperborean Wisdom.** In fact they totally adhere to National Socialism, although politics do not interest them so much as the philosophy of the ⚡⚡ and the terrestrial presence of the Führer, whom they call "The Lord of Will." '

"The five ⚡⚡ officers were sitting in chairs around the end of a table of notable length: a minuscule group in a place where there was room for more than fifty guests. Von Grossen was seated in the center, his back to the crackling hearth. Kalita porters were resting at a nearby dormitory. The conversation was interrupted when three monks in black yak wool tunics made their entrance. They were wearing head coverings with a hood sewn to the same tunic, which was casting a shadow over their faces, although one could detect that the three had long hair and were of Tibetan race, possibly Lopas. Two were appearing to be very young and strong, and were of different sexes: a yogi and a yogini, Initiates in Martial Arts, who were moving with feline grace. The third, an old man of indefinite age, addressed a few words to Von Grossen in Khams Skad.

"The ⚡⚡ *Standartenführer* hastened to introduce him:

" '*Kameraden:* before you is *Guru Visaraga,* head of this Monastery, together with his two principal *sadhakas.*'

"They greeted us with a nod of the head, to which we absurdly responded with the Nazi salute.

" 'Despite being the hosts,' Von Grossen clarified, 'they request permission to stay by our side. I have answered them in the affirmative, for they are people of absolute trustworthiness. Let us proceed, then, about our business.'

"The monks sat down and Von Grossen calmly continued speaking in German. And for as long as the conversation lasted, I could ascertain with displeasure that they were not taking their eyes off me, as if something in my appearance irresistibly attracted their attention and had hypnotized them.

" 'As I was saying,' explained Von Grossen, 'these monks constitute a Secret Society known as the "Kaula Circle." Their Wisdom is the Kula, the tantrism "of the Left Hand," a system of yoga that enables the transmuting and harnessing of sexual energy, but which requires the physical participation of the woman. Hence the mixed population that has surprised you, Von Sübermann. The Kaulikas are feared in Tibet, for they are considered "Black Magicians," but the way I see it, the only black thing that they have is the tunic. Jokes aside, it is evident that such a qualification comes from their bitterest enemies, the members of the White Brotherhood, a mysterious organization that is behind Buddhism and other religions, and that is very powerful in these regions: it is by opposition and contrast to the *"white"* Brotherhood that the Kaulikas are called *"blacks,"* since they are ascetics of high morals. All the men and women that you have seen here are *vamachari*[45] sadhakas.

" 'The Initiates on the Path of Kula periodically perform a Ritual denominated "the Five Defiances," in which they practice "five acts forbidden to the Masters of the Kalachakra," which explains why they are hated by the Gurus of Shambhala. Vulgarly, the secret Ritual is also known as *"Panchamakara"* or "the five Ms," because with that letter begin the five names of the "forbidden things": *madya,* wine; *mamsa,* meat; *matsya,* fish; *mudra,* parched grain; *maithuna,* sexual act. According to their Buddhist enemies, by practicing this Ritual, the Kaulikas situate themselves on the *vamamarga,* or "Path of the Left," the path of the Kshatriyas, which leads to War and not to Peace, to

---

45. Kaulika Magician or Initiate of the Left Hand.

Agartha and not to Shambhala, to the absolute unification of the Self and not to the nirvanic annihilation of the Ego identified with The One Parabrahman. What is certain is that by means of secret techniques of their sexual Tantra, the Kaulikas develop incredible power over the animal nature of the human body and, even, manage to obtain spiritual liberation.

" 'Summarizing, Von Sübermann, the Kaulikas are perfect yogis, Initiates capable of reaching, in the ecstasy of the sexual act, the Infinite and the Eternity of the Spirit, and of situating their nucleus of consciousness beyond Maya, the Illusion of the material forms.

" 'Of primitive Taoism little has remained, although formally, in order to avoid persecutions, the monks define themselves as "Taoists," a more passable religion for the Buddhist and Hindu princes of the neighboring lands. But in the shastras of Lao Tzu, which are preserved in this monastery, *the word "Tao" has been substituted by "Vrune,"* that is, by *Shakti,* the Eternal and Infinite Spirit of man. Do not forget, Von Sübermann, that here we are before a Wisdom that comes from a source other than Chang Shambhala, and that is why Shakti means "Pure Spirit," a concept similar to the "Grace" of Western theology.

" 'Vrune is an ancient Indo-Aryan word that means "Eternal, Infinite, and Uncreated Spirit": from it derive the signs that represent such meanings, that is to say, the *Runes,* revealed to the Aryans by Wothan; also the God Varuna registers the same root. However, and according to the most remote traditions of the White Race, the same "Vrune" comes in turn from the Atlantean word *Vril,* which had the same meaning. You see, Von Sübermann, that the "Vril" proposed in Germany as the spiritual ideal of the ⚡ Initiate Knight, is a state represented here by Vrune, the tantric power of situating oneself beyond Kula and Akula, and as the authentic spiritual Tao is beyond Yin and Yang. *For the spiritual man, the Vril as Vrune always takes the form of an Ancient Goddess, a Divine Shakti, who is none other than the forgotten image of the Partner from the Origin.* The Kaulikas believe that once the Vrune is attained, which is only achieved after passing through ritual death, the free Spirit finds itself facing the Truth of the Origin, is reunited with its original partner, and the Wedding of the Spirit is consummated, after which Eternity is regained. The Kaulika, living or dead, from then on experiences an icy Love that is not of this

Universe and is reintegrated into a Race of Vrunic Gods, Lords of the Vril.

" 'In synthesis, *here the Kaulikas follow the Kula Path, which begins in the woman of flesh and ends in the Original Partner, in the depths of Oneself: at the end of that dangerous path, the Kaulika, definitively confronted with the Truth, drawing back the veils of all the Mysteries, is Shiva, the Destroyer of Illusion, the Warrior par excellence. For us, Von Sübermann, Shiva is Lúcifer, is Cain, is Hermes, is Mercury, is Wothan: for us, Shiva is the prototype of the ⚡⚡ Knight.'*

" 'Guru Visaraga and his sadhakas were continuing observing me with delectation. The extraordinary report given by Karl von Grossen had just revealed to me why he had been chosen to preside over that operation: to his military skills and knowledge, the *Standartenführer* was adding a great comprehension of the customs and religious beliefs of Asia. I decided to ask him a concrete question, about the principal objective of the mission.

" 'I thank you very much for your valuable data,' I said, 'but there is something that worries me since we arrived. You then said: "I thought you wouldn't make it in time." How much time do we have, Herr Von Grossen?'

" 'Little, very little, Von Sübermann. But it'll be sufficient, if we depart as soon as possible and redouble our march, to reach Schäfer before Gyaring Lake. Are you aware that one of the members of the expedition, Officer Oskar Feil, will be handed over to a sect of murderous fanatics there?'

" 'Yes,' I responded. 'I was informed in Berlin. What intrigues me is how you have been able to know it, and what means you use to know the location of Schäfer's expedition at all times.'

" 'It is not a secret, nor is it any mysterious or supernatural procedure: it is espionage, plain and simple; the most classic case of espionage that you've studied in the Security Course. As you already know, since Operation *Altwesten* was conceived in Germany, it was infiltrated by the SD: we have two Secret Service men there who haven't aroused any suspicion in the untrusting Ernst Schäfer. However, they would not have been able to do anything if we did not count on the support of the Kaula Circle, whose tentacles extend throughout Tibet, in our favor. The faithful Kaulikas are those who transport the messages of our spies across the Himalayas and permanently provide us with the location of the expedition. I already told you, Von Sübermann, that in these lands the Kaulikas are greatly feared, and their reputation favors the collaboration of the superstitious inhabitants. A reputation that, in this sense, they are by no means undeserving of, for rather than ascetics they are warrior monks, and the traitors can be sure that sooner or later they will die at their hands. Thus, a vast network of espionage has been set up around our target.

" 'You should know, Von Sübermann, that the Dharmaraja, the spiritual Leader of the whole country of Bhutan, is a secret partisan of the Kaula Circle and that is why he has assigned the adjoining Palace as a Winter Residence. He intensely hates the English, whom he considers "representatives of the Demons," and has ordered that the greatest possible assistance be provided to us as long as we remain in his Country. The second important man is the Deb Raja, who has been in charge of the Administration and State affairs, so he must remain in Punakha and endure the English, whom he hates as much as the Dharmaraja does. In any case, we have official safe-conducts that will permit us to arrive in Tibet and even to move about in that country, presenting ourselves as functionaries and merchants in the service of the Raja.

" 'According to what was said,' continued Von Grossen, 'we have very little time. We should leave tomorrow if possible. Ernst Schäfer has left Lhasa three weeks ago, following the route to Chamdo, but his progress is slow because he does not want any misunderstanding to spoil his visit to Chang Shambhala: he knows that his movements are permanently surveilled from Kampala Tower. His caution becomes more understandable, too, if one considers that he had to stay a year in Lhasa, in the Palace of the Dalai Lama, until he received the authorization to approach Chang Shambhala: he must still cross the Boundary and persuade his Guardians that, in effect, they have the support of the Masters. It is understandable, then, that he tries to avoid errors and slowly approaches his infernal destiny.

" 'For our part, we must leave as soon as possible because Winter approaches and soon the Himalayan passes will be converted into glaciers. However, once in Tibet, we will deviate from the commercial route taken by Schäfer and go forward until we catch up with him.'

Chapter XXII

arl von Grossen had everything immediately ready to go when we arrived. However, despite our efforts, we could not initiate the march until two days later. The day following our arrival I spent, then, entertaining myself in touring the Monastery and examining the marvelous sculptural work of the Pagoda. There, a pleasant event occurred to me that, astonishingly, has affected you, Neffe Arturo, more than forty years later...

"Upon penetrating into the nave of the cyclopean carved rock, I was suddenly surrounded by a group of Kaulika monks. Up to that moment they had been chanting a mantram in front of a gigantic statue of Shiva dancing on the Yah Dragon: when noticing my presence they were gradually silencing their bījas and then, just like the Arabs who kidnapped me in Cairo, they rushed beside me as if spellbound. But then I was prepared, for I had spent too many years in the Ordensburg and in the Black Order under the instruction of Konrad Tarstein to be ignorant of what was happening to those Initiates. It was the Sign of the Origin, the Sign invisible to me that in the Kaulikas was causing the charismatic effect of spiritually elevating them toward the Origin of the Self: that is why they were wishing to situate themselves close to me, to contemplate me, to sustain the perception of the Uncreated. They were wanting nothing more than that and that is why I remained immutably in place, while those Initiates were raising themselves from the unreality of the World and accessing the Reality of the Spirit.

"We remained like that for a while, in absolute silence: a new section of statues for that icy pantheon. I was understanding their language and I had attempted to speak to them, but it was useless, for in their mystical state they were almost considering it a sacrilege to address me. After a reasonable time I began to think of a way to free myself from them, when I noticed that Guru Visaraga, unusually smiling, was approaching. All the monks moved away as he passed by and he, taking me by the left arm, led me out of such a difficult situation. Slowly he led me into the courtyard, followed at a regular distance by the amazed monks.

"In the courtyard were awaiting him the sadhakas that we saw the night before, each one holding the rein of an enormous mastiff. They were wearing a leash around their necks, without muzzles, from where the rein was attached, and yet they were not uttering even a bark: mute, silent like the monks who were surrounding me, those terrible dogs were observing me without batting an eye.

"Then Guru Visaraga spoke. And his words still resonate in my ears with strange clarity.

" 'O Jowo: For us you are a *Shivatulku,* that is to say, a manifestation of Shiva. These dogs that you see here, are a gift from our community for whoever so clearly exhibits the Sign of Bhairava: the female is called "Kula," and the male "Akula." '

"It was the last gift I would have expected to receive from the Kaulikas. I was going to protest but the Guru was not accepting a reply: I only said 'Vielen Dank!'

" 'Your colleague Von Grossen, who shared our table for several months, has confided to us that the Initiates of the ⚡⚡ are capable of stopping an enraged mastiff by means of a shout.'

"I nodded:

" 'Indeed,' I said. 'Every ⚡⚡ Initiate must demonstrate that he is capable of imposing the Lordship of the Spirit over all the animal creatures of the earth, no matter how wild they are.'

" 'Ah,' sighed the Guru. 'It is difficult for us to imagine your world, just as it is almost impossible for you to imagine ours. More than Races, a Universe of Symbols separates us, a Wall of Illusion erected by the Great Deceiver. You are often satisfied with empty words, that is to say, you are content with words that represent ideas, ideas that have little weight in reality, ideas that are as illusory as the other forms of Maya. The Sign that you bear makes you different from the rest of mortals. Yet neither you, nor your Gurus, know how to demonstrate that supremacy. Well, with this simple pair of mastiffs, O Bhattaraka, you will do what no one, unless he also bears the Sign of Shiva, is capable of doing in this World: *We will reveal to you a Kyilkhor*[46] *that will enable you to mentally command both mastiffs at the same time.'*

---

46. *Yantra* or *Mandala* (Tibetan: kyilkhor). Geometric figure for ritual or magical use. It means *"fence."* The term *"khor"* gives the idea of "enclosing" or "imprisoning." More broadly, a kyilkhor can be a wall or fortification, a meaning that also corresponds to the Sanskrit "mandala."

"Directing a dog with the mind would be effectively incredible for any rationalist mentality, but I was considering it possible and taking it with naturalness; what was incomprehensible to me was that of controlling *both mastiffs at the same time.*' Guru Visaraga, who was continuing explaining the characteristics of the sinister gift, did not take long to clear up all my doubts.

" 'Do not be deceived by their fierce appearance,' he vehemently affirmed. 'They are not common animals but a very special pair of *daiva*[47] dogs, **balanced** in our Monastery thanks to very ancient formulas that the Kaula Circle possesses: the daiva dogs are manifestations of the archetypal couple of celestial dogs; each one is the exact reflection of the other, and both perfectly emanate from the Dog of Heaven; even their etheric bodies belong to the same Group Soul. They are like *pairs of manifested opposite principles* and, normally, one would neutralize the other without remedy. During a very ancient war, perhaps prior to that which the Mahabharata narrates, the Gurus were training the daiva dogs as a weapon, so that they attacked in pairs and could not be stopped by the lower varna enemies: *only the Kshatriyas, the spiritual Heroes, those who by their Pure Blood were "beyond" the opposing principles Kula and Akula, were able to stop the daiva dogs.* It is what you, who bear the Sign of Shiva, can do today with Kula and Akula!'

" 'You see,' concluded the Guru, 'that although your power to stop an enraged mastiff by means of commanding voices may seem to you an inimitable feat, and perhaps it is in the West, you could do nothing against a pair of daiva dogs. Of course, I speak of ⚡ Initiates in general. Because you, *Sweet* Pilgrim, are different from all, you possess the ancient Tao, the active quietude of meditating Shiva: *You can dominate the daiva dogs with the mind because Your Spirit is beyond Kula and Akula!*'

"Imagine, Neffe Arturo, eight rods with a *triśūla* or trident at each end, that is to say, eight rods and sixteen tridents, arranged parallel to each other and separated by small distances. Then imagine another equal set, but with the rods ordered perpendicularly to the previous ones. Finally apply one set on top of the other to form a grid, and you will obtain the basic form of the Yantra that Guru Visaraga taught me: a

---

47. "Divine" dogs; dogs of the Gods.

quadrangular grille with eight tridents on each side and forty-nine interior squares.

"After the aforementioned explanation, the Guru, always accompanied by the pair of sadhakas and the ferocious dogs, led me to a room illuminated by hundreds of candles and of which floor was not paved in any way. From one of the multiple shelves covered with candles, he took some sacks filled with fine sand of various colors and, with singular mastery, he was pouring them on the floor until forming the described Kyilkhor.

"He asked me if I would be capable of remembering it. I nodded and then he said:

" 'Son of Shiva: do not be surprised that we know your secrets, that we know more about you than you yourself apprehend. You come from a far-off land, far more distant than the Assam Kamarupa that seems to us very remote, but you have quite a lot in common with the Kaulikas: you are of our same Race and varna, you are a Kshatriya; you fight on our same side against the same Enemy; you are Initiated in the same ancient Wisdom of Shiva, the Lord of War and Destruction of Maya, the Wisdom that is the foundation of the Kaula Tantra. And, for us, who are Initiates in the Kaula Tantra, you are a *Tulku* of Shiva, as I called you a moment ago. Do you know what a Tulku is?

" 'I believe so: I responded without much conviction, the reincarnation of a God.'

" 'No!' Guru Visaraga firmly denied, although he was compassionately smiling. 'You ought to say, in any case: one of the *simultaneous* reincarnations of a God. According to the Tantric Doctrine, when a God, in a determinate Epoch, decides to reveal himself to men, he can do it, and generally does so, in a multitude of physical manifestations: the God then possesses a plurality of bodies, he simultaneously exists as a man in different places and circumstances. These men, *like you*, express the signs of the God but sometimes ignore that they are *Tulkus*.

" 'There are, then, several Tulkus at the same time. Our Tibet was always rich in Tulkus due to the elevated spirituality of the Aryans and other Races who were also mastering the ancient Wisdom; we are perhaps the only Initiates in the World who know how to read the signs of the Tulkus. But now, at the end of the Era of Kaly, the Gods have moved to the countries of the region that you come from and to others that lie behind the dark oceans. Your homeland, Germany, where the strongest descendants of the common racial stock have gathered today, is one of the last earthly scenarios in which the Tulkus will enact the Drama of the War of the Heavens. You, you are a Tulku of Shiva! It is not by chance that you are fulfilling this mission or that we assist you: *it is the other Tulkus, who live with you in your Nation, who, with great Wisdom, have sent you to block the passage of the Asuras of Shambhala.*

" 'And because we recognize you as Tulku, we will give you the diksha in the svadi[48] Kyilkhor.'

"You can suppose, Neffe, the doubts that the beliefs of the Kaulikas were causing me. I, a Tulku? The truth was that I was feeling myself the manifestation of *a single Spirit,* but I could by no means affirm or deny that I was also its *sole manifestation.* It had never occurred to me to think of such an unsettling possibility but, in fact, at that moment I was not believing in it. Although I would not have been displeased, for example, to participate as Tulku in the essence of the Führer and thus share in his Destiny of Glory.

"The Guru offered me a cup constructed from a human skull, artistically lined on its interior with silver leaf and studded with emeralds, which was brimming with an unpleasant potion. It was containing *nang mchod,* the tantric version of *soma, amrita,* or *mead,* that is, the elixir of the Rituals of Initiation, the beverage of the Gods (Siddhas) or demigods (Viryas); nang mchod is mainly used in the Ritual of the Five Defiances, for it is made from the five 'forbidden things': five kinds of meat, including human; five fish; five grains; five wines; and five substances connected with sex, such as urine, semen, blood, feces, and marrow.

"I drank it with evident distrust and Guru Visaraga, perhaps to reassure me, expanded a little more in his explanation:

" 'There are many classes of Kyilkhor: of Death, of Liberation, of Enchantment, of Power, etc. And they all require mastery in Mantram Yoga and the perfection in the pronunciation of the magical formulas that *vivify them.* That is why there are three degrees or ways to affirm the words of power or *bījas:* the *Vachika Japa,* which consists in *shouting* the *bījas,* as *acoustic orders,* in the manner of your military "commanding voices";

---

48. Initiation in the svadi Kyilkhor, or "Kyilkhor of the dog."

this is the lowest of the japas and is that which the ᛋᛋ utilizes to subdue the mastiffs; the *Upamsu Japa,* which requires *expressing* the bījas without shouting or speaking, as astral orders; and finally, the highest of the japas is the *Manasa,* the effect of which is not causal but synchronistic, that is to say, that it makes the bījas *charismatically coincide* with the event that one wants to affect, as *uncreated orders.* As the sticks of the I-Ching *form* an uncreated meaning that reveals or uncovers the designs of the Gods, a meaning *not willed* by the Gods, a meaning that *was not* in destiny, a meaning that emerges by acausal coincidence between the Higher Unknown and the Lower Known, a meaning wrested from the Traitor Gods by the force of the Magi, in the same way the Manasa Japa acts by the sole determination of the Initiates, of those who are beyond Kula and Akula.

"'You should know, O Shivatulku, that only great Initiates are capable of acquiring mastery in the Upamsu Japa, that of the second level. They are those who possess the *tulpa* power, or *mudratulpa,* the capacity to grant reality to ordered ideas and to make them arise in the world: with the right Kyilkhor and the right Upamsu Japa, it is possible to make all kinds of material objects appear or to produce an infinity of phenomena. Right here, these daiva dogs that you see, are only *tulpas* created by us to demonstrate your Tulku power.

"'Indeed, do not be astonished; we have mentally created the mastiffs so that you put into practice the superior japa, the Manasa Japa, which is a particular virtue only of the Siddhas or viryas and that the Tulkus naturally possess. The daiva dogs of the tulpamudra are indeed real, but only you, O Shivatulku, can govern them with the japas of the svadi Kyilkhor. The Kaulikas require a dangerous diksha and only achieve to express the Upamsu Japa, but you, who are a Virya, only need that *we transmit to you the vīryayojanā Power that make it possible to "give life" to the tulpa mental projections, the angkur of the Manasa Japa.* You are not a Kaulika, but you are a Tantrika; and you already have the power of the Manasa Japa.'

"Next, *he proceeded to provide me the key to the 49 bījas that were in the corresponding sectors of the Kyilkhor.*

"The 'magical' procedure of control was the following: I was to imagine the grating of the Kyilkhor and situate in each square a bīja or *word of power;* and each bīja *was an order* that the dogs would automatically obey: one bīja was meaning 'Silence!'; another 'Advance!'; another 'Stop!'; another 'Attack!'; etc., etc., until completing forty-nine.

"Despite my initial skepticism, and to the delight of the monks, I was able to verify that the system was certainly infallible: once I had memorized the Yantra, the dogs became an extension of my own mind and the slightest insinuation from the bījas was enough for them to obey without making a sound, or better said, without barking.

"As that effect was logically surprising, I could not help but question the Guru about the way in which the mental control was being made effective.

" 'For us it is very simple,' he clarified. 'We have plasmated a Kyilkhor similar to this one in the subtle body of each dog and have established an analogical correspondence between each bīja and certain vital or motor functions of both animals. If this were done with only one animal, of any species, the Guru or the Kaulika Initiate would be able to master it without obstacles. But, as I told you before, the pair of daiva dogs is different: they participate in a single dog Archetype and both are normally equilibrated; *if the mental order is issued "below" the archetypal Plane, one neutralizes the other and it lacks effect; only he who is capable of thinking "above" the archetypal Plane, beyond the Archetype Created by the Gods of Matter, above the relative duality of the manifested and the absolute unity of the unmanifested, can make his will prevail in the action of the daiva dogs.* Never forget: neither a Master of the Hierarchy nor anyone whose thought is comprised of opposing principles, can stop the daiva dogs!'

"Kula and Akula, Neffe Arturo, were the great-great-grandparents of Yin and Yang, the mastiffs who attacked you when you so furtively entered onto the finca and I took you for an enemy. Like their ancestors, they obey the mental orders of the Yantra and *both move at the same time*, perfectly synchronized."

Chapter XXIII

hat morning Dr. Palacios removed the cast. My arm was healed but a horrible sensation of weakness was still subsisting that reminded me of the terrible efficacy of the Tibetan dogs. Uncle Kurt's last stories were clarifying everything... while plunging me into a greater Mystery. His Initiation, the mission in Tibet, the Power of the Sign of the Origin, the incredible relationship of his Instructor Konrad Tarstein with Belicena Villca, and the matter of the mastiffs. Yes, everything was clearing up, but at the same time the Mystery of my own existence was growing. At every moment new elements were being incorporated into the context of my life: unknown relatives, remote countries, unknown Doctrines, implacable enemies. But what was I? Of one thing I was now sure: I had never had the slightest chance to escape from history, I had never been free to choose my Destiny, I had never had a shred of free will. It was all illusion, all a farce. I was feeling played, like a chess piece, by inhuman beings who were evidently knowing the rules of the game and the position of the pieces: the board was the Mystery, which I was barely glimpsing, but which I could not see because I was inserted onto it.

I was comprehending that I had to get these pessimistic ideas out of my brain in order to not go mad. And paradoxically, when Uncle Kurt was not making me participate in his narration, I was entertaining myself by observing the daiva dogs, which I was no longer fearing: I was waiting, however, for Uncle Kurt to fulfill his promise to reveal to me the bījas of the Yantra. According to him, I could also control them with my mind.

Chapter XXIV

y this time," continued Uncle Kurt that afternoon, "the three days had passed and an icy dawn saw us leave the monastery en route to Tibet. The caravan was now comprised of the five ⚡⚡ officers, five of the Kalita porters from Dacca, who accepted the porterage toward Tibet, and ten Kaulika Lopas, experts in Martial Arts and Tantric Magic. The Himalayan crossing was made by a path only known to the monks, which was avoiding any population until well into the Kangri valley but that was climbing to more than 5,000 meters and passing alongside the slope of Kula Kangri, a majestic peak of 7,600 meters.

"Already on the plateau of Tibet, the land of *Pay-Yul,* we were having to march straight toward the north; Von Grossen's plan was seeming outlandish at first, although, carefully examined, it was not; and in fact it produced the expected results. It was consisting in reaching the banks of the Brahmaputra, which in the Kangri valley runs parallel to the Himalayas, from west to east, and to embark on a raft to navigate on its furious current: the indicated point to descend (if we were not sinking before) would be at 30°N and 95°E where the 'Son of Brahma' river violently twists its course to the south and heads to the Bengal valleys. With such a tactical procedure, we would recover part of the time that Ernst Schäfer's expedition was ahead of us.

"According to Von Grossen's information, Schäfer and his men traveled on the Jung-lam[49] road, which was ending its 2,000-kilometer route in China and only its mail or official Tibetan functionaries were being permitted to use it; traders, on the other hand, were utilizing the Chang-lam road. But Schäfer's operation, backed by the Dalai Lama, was almost an official mission. However, the transit along that path would not be easy because, before reaching Gyaring Lake, seat of the Boundary of Shambhala, dozens of obstacles had to be overcome; to give you an idea, Neffe Arturo, of how rugged those communication routes were, I will tell you that in only 600 kilometers of its route, from Lhasa to Chamdo, the Chang-lam

49. Two important roads lead to Lhasa, one called *Jung-lam* or "official road" (935 miles long), and other the *Chang-lam* or "northern road" (890 miles).

road was crossing more than forty mountain ranges, through passes that were rising between 3,000 and 5,500 meters; And that's not counting the innumerable torrents and rivers, often lacking bridges, that were briskly flowing through the intermediate valleys.

"At Chamdo, Schäfer's caravan would depart from the official road and take a pilgrim lama path, parallelly opened to the right bank of the Mekong River, which would take the travelers directly to Gyaring Lake. Once there, they would head toward the Monastery, or *Gompa,* of the lamas of the Kurkuma Bonnet, of the Duskha tribe, Guardians of the Boundary of Shambhala. That Monastery, known since Antiquity as 'Jafran Ashram' and that we burned down, was behind the city wall of the Duskhas, a people of Tibetan race famous for the variety of saffron, or kurkuma, that they were cultivating, from which they were extracting a narcotic drug of Ritual use and a dye with which they were staining the bonnets or tiaras of their lamas. If all was going well, that is, after they had accepted the Necessary Victim and *opened the Boundary,* the expedition would continue its journey to the vicinity of Lake Kokonor,[50] where exists one of the southern extremes of the Great Wall of China and also, *or precisely for that reason,* one of the Gates of Chang Shambhala. Our strategy, of course, was requiring that we caught up with Ernst Schäfer before his arrival at the Jafran Ashram, otherwise we would have irremediably lost Oskar Feil.

"In any case, the operation we were going to carry out had been meticulously studied by Von Grossen and Schmidt, and, although the anxiety to rescue Oskar was filling me with impatience, I had no other alternative but to trust that they were right. Thus, while Schäfer's expedition was heading toward the staggered plateaus of Eastern Tibet, crossed by dozens of mountain ranges that were extending from north to south and many other linked valleys, we were advancing at maximum velocity toward the plain of the Gangri Valley heading north, procuring to arrive as soon as possible at the Yarlung Zangbo river or Upper Brahmaputra. By that river, we would only sail four hundred kilometers but, according to Von Grossen's estimation, in four or five days we would cover a distance that, by

---

50. Qinghai Lake

land, along the Jung-lam road, was requiring a time five times longer.

"At a prearranged point on the coast, two sturdily built rafts were awaiting us, capable of transporting 10 persons and a ton of cargo each: more than enough to cover our necessities. The Kaulikas had arranged for them and the price was high, for they had to be paid for the trip to Sadiya and the cost of the tugboats that would bring them back to the Upper Brahmaputra.

"The skillful boatmen, stimulated by the promise of extra remuneration, or frightened by the dangerousness of the Kaulika monks, were deftly steering the rafts down the center of the channel, taking maximum advantage of the river's speed. And while the mighty current was rapidly bringing me closer to the objective of the mission, I was admiringly contemplating one of the most extraordinary landscapes on Earth, only comparable, to a lesser extent, to the plateau of Tiahuanaco in America. Because that 'Son of Brahma' river, which was longitudinally furrowing a cold valley situated at 4,000 meters of height, had its banks guarded by two mountain ranges as famous for the elevation of their mountains as for that of the concepts that it was owing to the most ancient religions of humanity: to the right was stretching the Himalayas, in of which system the Asiatic tradition affirms that Mount Meru, the Olympus of the Indians, is found; and to the left were rising the Kangri mountains, a range that culminates in the west with Mount Kailash, the Abode of Shiva.

"A week later we were on our way toward Yushu, in the NW, trying to accelerate the journeys through the acquisition of yaks, as there was an itinerary of passes and openings that was allowing us to advance by such animals. After traveling through an uninterrupted series of small valleys, crossing numerous mountain ranges, crossing the mighty Salween River and many other minor torrents, we arrived one day on the banks of the Mekong, about 80 kilometers from Chamdo. By this time, the Kaulikas had already found out that Schäfer's expedition was only fifteen days ahead of us: not much time for those latitudes where the duration of travel was being measured in months; a lot if it was a matter of saving Oskar Feil's life.

"Fortunately, good weather accompanied us throughout the journey and it would stay that way until the end. We passed to the right bank of the Mekong and took the Path of the Lamas, in the hope of shortening the distance that was separating us from Schäfer, marching faster than his column and only stopping to rest. Anyway, progress was slow until exasperation, for the famous 'Path' was consisting of a narrow and elevated roadway that was barely letting the yaks pass, which we often were having to unload. Somewhere on that path, at an altitude of more than 4,000 meters, we crossed the Chinese border. At last we arrived in Yushu, finding that the other group of Westerners had abandoned the city ten days before. The news, instead of cheering us for the time gained, made us despair, because that city was a point included on the Chang-lam path, through which most of Tibet's trade with China was being channeled and along which one could transit quite quickly.

"Since the previous year, July of 1937, China was suffering the invasion of the Japanese, who were already dominating Korea and Formosa since the war with Russia in 1905. In those days at the end of 1938, Japan had conquered Manchuria and the entire southern coast, threatening to extend toward the interior: Canton, Nanking, Shanghai, Peking, etc., had fallen into its power; with a formidable pincer movement they were now procuring to occupy the enormous strip between the Yangtze-kiang and Huang Ho rivers, that is to say, between the Blue and Yellow rivers. Social decomposition was reigning in the country, and, in the regions that the Japanese were not yet controlling, civil war had broken out with singular violence.

"Yushu, situated on the western border, was far from the Japanese, but not from the civil war. There was quite a lot of unrest in the city and it was by no means convenient to make ourselves too visible, so we stayed hidden in the house of a Kaulika family. They were those who provided us with information about the ten days of lead that the German expedition was ahead by.

"It would be impossible to reach them traveling by caravan as before. According to Von Grossen, only one alternative was left to us: to separate ourselves from the cargo, and to go forward on horseback; the five Germans and eight monks would carry out the advance, while two Lopas would remain to guard the five Kalitas, the daiva dogs, the yaks with their cargo, and the recently incorporated *zhos*, which are the hybrid male product of the crossbreeding of the yak with the cow. Following this variant of the plan, the Kaulikas acquired the largest specimens of small Tibetan horses that they managed to obtain, and each one took the minimum provisions for ten days, since on that traders' road, villages and resting and provisioning posts were frequently alternating. The greatest weight we were having to transport was our weapons, for which we allocated two horses.

"That same day we left from Yushu, having slept only a few hours in shifts. The next day we forded the Yangtze-kiang or Blue River and found the best road after forty days of travel, giving the horses, from then on, considerable speed.

"I suppose that to an experienced officer like Karl von Grossen, it had not escaped his attention in Yushu that we would never catch up with Schäfer before Gyaring Lake if he was ten days ahead of us. He undoubtedly procured to gratify my wish of rescuing Oskar Feil alive in the best possible way, perhaps secretly trusting in the probability that, for some imponderable reason, our pursuers would stop more than necessary at some point on their route. But no such thing occurred and they held the lead long enough to arrive at the Jafran Ashram, hand over Oskar Feil, and set off again for Lake Kokonor.

"When the Chang-lam road crosses the Huang Ho, or Yellow River, which successively forms the Gyaring and Ngoring lakes, it is only about 20 kilometers from the west bank of the former. Next to that bridge, we encountered a man who immediately got the attention of the Kaulikas monks: he was one of the spies whom the Kaula Circle had infiltrated into Schäfer's expedition and who was just escaping from a certain death at the hands of the Duskhas. From him we learned that the Germans had left the Ashram three days earlier, guided by Master Djual Khul, a hierarchical member of the White Brotherhood, who would lead them to the Shambhala Gate of Kokonor.

"According to the account of the valorous Tibetan, Ernst Schäfer sent Oskar Feil in advance, so that he explored the region of the Jafran Ashram. As soon as he left, he was captured by the Duskhas, who confined him in a temple dedicated to the Cult of Rigden Jyepo, where he would be sacrificed only four days later, when the moon made its transition to the waning quarter. Oskar was still alive! Unexpectedly, we now had precious time to study the rescue.

"Naturally, everything had been planned by Schäfer in combination with the Duskhas: in order to avoid the awkward position of openly handing Oskar over, he made him fall into an infamous trap, to such an effect that the latter was unaware that he was betrayed by his Leader. But it would not be Oskar whom Ernst Schäfer was intending to deceive, since he would die anyway, but some German officers who were evidently unaware of his plans. The scoundrel was thus ensuring a brilliant alibi, as they would report upon their return to Germany that 'Kamerad Oskar Feil had gone missing in action,' in the course of Operation *Altwesten!*

"This was what shortened the expedition's stay at the Ashram, for Schäfer was not wanting to run the risk that the deceived would by chance discover that Oskar was a prisoner of the Duskhas. Precisely, with the complicity of the Duskhas, who hypocritically lent themselves to the farce, eighteen of his Comrades searched the whole area inch by inch for two days trying to find him. Apparently, only four officers were sharing Schäfer's secret objectives.

"The efficacy of that Kaulika to spy on Schäfer was coming from the fact that he was not a mere Tibetan porter, although he acted as such by order of his Gurus, but a South African of Nepalese origin who was perfectly understanding English, German, and Dutch. His family, of the Gurkha Race, that is to say, Indo-Aryan, deserted during the Boer War and took refuge in German territories, finally fleeing to Bhutan after 1918, when Germany was stripped of its colonies. Both he, whose name was Bangi, as his brother Gangi, were entrusted as children to the care of the Kaulika monks, who initiated them in Tantra and finally stationed them in Lhasa, as secret agents at the service of the Dharmaraja of Bhutan. There they managed to be hired by Schäfer, who took them for Sherpas, without noticing the difference of Race. But they were not Sherpas but two Gurkha warriors who were professing a fundamental hatred toward the English and who were patiently awaiting a new British war in order to enlist themselves on the opposing side.

"The spies were able to hear the demands that the traitor was making to the Lamas of the Kurkuma Bonnet and heard how Master Djual Khul was intervening in his favor, agreeing to cross the Boundary of Shambhala as soon as possible. They also learned of the existence of 'an offering to Rigden Jyepo' by

Ernst Schäfer and realized that Oskar Feil had been handed over by means of a stratagem. Since their Kaulika companions were not arriving in time to prevent the sacrifice, they would try to find out where the prisoner was in order to provide him with help, something very difficult in that village inhabited by 2,000 Duskhas and 500 Lamas.

"Both brothers devoted themselves to observing the surroundings of the Monastery with the utmost care, correctly presuming that the prisoner had been locked up at a different site from which the expeditionaries were occupying. In effect, they found that one of the exterior Temples, situated on an islet of Gyaring Lake, was closed and watched over by armed guards.

"They communicated the news to the German spies in the SD, requesting their support in order to uncover the maneuver and free Oskar Feil. The response of one of them, a typical response of a Western secret agent, took the Gurkhas' breath away:

" 'We informed Germany of the plans Schäfer had for Oskar Feil months in advance, and the orders that we received were clear and conclusive, as you well know: "to await special reinforcements that will prevent Ernst Schäfer from concretizing Operation *Altwesten*. Signed: Heydrich, Himmler, Hitler." ' That is to say that nothing was indicated to us regarding Oskar Feil. We were very fond of our Comrade and felt very sorry about his fate, but in such cases the regulations of the Secret Service prevent us from acting on our own initiative, since it has been established with absolute precision that the priority of our mission is Operation *Altwesten*. The rescue of Oskar Feil conspires against the discretion that we must maintain until the end of Operation *Altwesten,* besides contradicting express orders and constituting a suicidal action, after which it is most likely that there will be three instead of one victim sacrificed by these savages. We, in synthesis, will do nothing and request that you proceed in the same manner, for there is still a long way to go and we need your help to send information through Tibet.'

"The Gurkhas assured to the satisfaction of the *SS* that they would not intervene, but upon discussing the case among themselves they concluded that the orders of the Germans were not reaching them in the same manner as the vows made to Shiva to combat treason and cowardice. What was the infraction to a cold bureaucratic rule meaning in the face of the wrath of Shiva, who was punishing the poor warriors by preventing them access to the Supreme Shakti? And had they not sworn to combat the members of the White Brotherhood to the death? Their duties as spies of the Dharmaraja, authorized by the Kaula Circle, was dispensing them from many religious obligations, but to allow that a human victim be sacrificed in holocaust to the leader of the White Brotherhood was beyond measure. No Siddha could justify that sin and they would surely be punished in the Bardo. No. If for the Germans the priority was to arrive at the Gate of Shambhala, the abode of the Demons, for them the priority was the Kula, the manifestation of the Divine Shakti. And the Kula would be lost if they were not acting as authentic Akula warriors. They would be taking a risk, then, in order to help Oskar Feil.

"On the second and last night that Schäfer's group would spend at the Jafran Ashram, the Gurkhas decided to act. Without hesitation, they slid into the icy waters of Gyaring Lake and were silently swimming around the islet to emerge at the back part of the Temple. The sentinels had noticed nothing. They quickly climbed up to a skylight in the shape of a six-pointed star that, by facing east during the day, was allowing that the sun's rays illuminated the enormous statue of Rigden Jyepo, but that, on the exact day of the summer solstice, was directing the sunlight directly at the Heart of the King of the World. Fortunately, that horrible opening, which was taken advantage of by Gangi, was allowing the passage of a man to descend by throwing a rope toward the interior; his brother would remain on guard on the exterior cornice.

"Once inside, he found that the Temple was illuminated by torches, and that, tightly bound with ropes of hemp, Oskar Feil was sleeping on the sacrificial stone. In front of him, the Chief of the Lords of Karma was anticipatingly enjoying the *yajnavirya* of his pain, as the intruder thought with a shudder, upon observing the rictus and diabolical gaze of the sinister sculpture. But he saw something else: in the interior was also a guard. It was consisting of four Duskhas, although they were at quite a distance, next to the only door of the Temple: two were sleeping on a mat, while the other two were animatedly chatting. The Gurkha began to stealthily crawl, trying to make it so that the sacrificial stone intercepted the Duskha's vision and carrying in his mouth a sharp dagger to cut the bindings.

"Momentarily hidden behind the stone altar, the Kaulika Gurkha gently sat up and watched, over Oskar's body, the behavior of the Duskhas: they were still completely distracted, now engaged in playing dice. He slid a hand over Oskar's face and tightly pressed it against his mouth, with the purpose of preventing that he spoke or emitted some unnecessary sound upon awakening. However, in spite of shaking him with singular violence, the prisoner was not coming to. He finally opened his eyes, but Gangi saw that they were white, with his pupils rolled back, and he realized with dismay that the German was suffering from the effects of a narcotic.

"Nothing could be done, except to retreat and abandon the Temple. Shiva would know how to forgive the one who had at least risked his life to rescue the victim of the Demons. But it was clear that the Gods arranged another Destiny for the Gurkha; when removing his hand from Oskar's mouth, believing him completely unconscious, the unthinkable occurred: he let out a high-pitched wail and convulsed for an instant, to immediately fall into the previous fainting spell.

"The body went inert again, but it was already too late: the sentinels were running toward the altar, hurling exclamations. The Gurkha jumped on the first one and stabbed him, but then had to surrender facing the threat of two dissuasive rifles. Another guard opened the door of the Temple and soon there was an angry crowd of Duskhas surrounding the intruder. If Gangi had had the weapons of the Kaulika warriors he would have presented a better fight, but given the role of porter that he was playing in the expedition, the most that he could carry was that knife hidden in his clothes. In that terrible moment, the only thing he wished was that his brother managed to flee.

"And his wish was fulfilled, for the other Gurkha swiftly descended from the cornice and entered into the lake, reaching the shore without being seen. Hiding behind a small wall that was following the contour of the beach, he observed how minutes later Ernst Schäfer was arriving, accompanied by two of his most faithful collaborators and six lamas of the Kurkuma Bonnet. His brother's fate was sealed.

"In case of being captured, both agreed on declaring that the raid on the Temple was solely for the purpose of robbery: 'they were supposing that in the Temple,' they would say, 'would be objects of value that could be stolen from the custody of the Duskhas in order to then trade them in China or

India, thus producing a favorable change in the lives of two poor Sherpas.' They would be executed, of course, for the sacrilege committed and, especially, because Schäfer could not leave witnesses to Oskar Feil's presence in the Temple. But the version of the robbery would dispel their suspicions and not endanger the task of the German spies.

"Now one of the Gurkhas, Bangi, was free, but there was no room to raise hopes about the fate that his brother would suffer: he would be assassinated to prevent him from talking and to thus present his cadaver to the rest of the expedition, affirming that he was killed when being caught *red-handed* committing a robbery in a temple, not that of Rigden Jyepo's, but another to which his cadaver would be transported.

"He was not mistaken, for after a while two guards came out carrying Gangi's lifeless body, followed by the Germans and the lamas: by the light of the moon, he could see his neck severed from ear to ear, and he had to grit his teeth to avoid a cry of pain. He consoled himself thinking that his brother was possessing the Kula and that he would soon dance the dance of immortality alongside Shiva.

" 'Kaly, O Kaly:' he mentally invoked, 'communicate to me thy Power of Death, turn me into *Shindje shed*,[51] the Lord of Death, into *Dorje Jikje,* the Lord of Terror, into *Shiva Bhairava;* grant me, O Parvati, the Honor of avenging the blood of my brother, thy faithful servant; help me to regain the Kshatriya dignity; transform me into *Kalybala,* the Force that destroyeth the Enemies of thy Kula Path; put into my hands a Triśūla, the Trident of Shiva, a Vajra, the Thunderbolt of Indra, and a Gandiva, the Bow of Arjuna, with Isudhi, his two quivers of arrows that never misseth the target!'

"While he was praying that way to the Black Goddess, the Gurkha was feverishly swimming to get away from the cursed Jafran Ashram, aware that he would soon be sought as his brother's accomplice and condemned to the same execution.

"Once outside the walls, he climbed a nearby mountain from where he observed the hurried departure of the expedition the following morning.

" 'The Germans,' Bangi thought, 'were now making up a retinue of Demons. Together with Schäfer, in effect, were Master

---

51. Yamantaka

Djual Khul and the *Kushok* of the Gompa, a kind of Tibetan Abbot, as well as four lamas of the Kurkuma Bonnet.'

"At that moment, he realized that he had two alternatives: either to follow the caravan at a distance, risking to die of hunger and cold in a few days; or to return to the Chang-lam road and await the announced reinforcements, then risking to lose the trail of the expedition, since the Boundary of Shambhala was signifying the entrance onto a secret path, which was perhaps crossing unknown dimensions of Space or extending into other Worlds. Nevertheless, he opted for the latter variant, only three days having passed since he was by the Huang Ho bridge.

Chapter XXV

uch was, more or less, the story that the Gurkha told us. I believe that to Von Grossen, as to his spies in the expedition, Operation *Altwesten* was more important to him than the life of Oskar Feil. According to his orders, orders that were subscribed by the highest authorities of the Third Reich, but which I was unaware, were coming from the 'éminences grises' of the regime, among them Konrad Tarstein, it was an absolute priority 'to make contact with Schäfer's expedition,' 'to get Kurt von Sübermann to incorporate himself into it.' That is to say, if it had been up to Von Grossen, we ought to have abandoned Oskar to his fate and concentrated on following in Schäfer's footsteps: that was the best strategy to fulfill the orders. But the life of Oskar Feil was mattering more to me than the blessed orders, and I would not move from there until having obtained his freedom.

"Paradoxically, the 'key' of Operation First Key was I, my *voluntary* collaboration to divert Operation *Altwesten* from its occult objectives. And my collaboration was demanding, now, the prior release of Oskar Feil. Therefore, displaying great pragmatism, Von Grossen accepted the facts without arguing and prepared to plan the rescue.

"The five Germans, the eight Lopa monks, and the Gurkha monk, camped in a narrow glen, away from the main road but situated barely five kilometers from the Jafran Ashram. There Von Grossen interrogated the Gurkha for hours about the details of the enemy plaza, finally elaborating a plan of operations in which we were all in agreement. Basically, the strategy would be the following: *the rescue would take place in the middle of a surprise attack.*

"According to local traditions, the first thing that man worshiped in that place was the islet where was later erected the Temple consecrated to Rigden Jyepo. A popular legend was assuring that in remote Epochs, Jagannath, the King of the World, the Hogmin Dorje Chang, had left Shambhala in order to travel the World under his Crane Aspect. Upon his return, he chose that half-sunken crag in Gyaring Lake to rest before embarking on the last leg of his journey to Chang Shambhala. The myth tells that on the beach, which was joined to the island by a thin stone corridor, was a Holy Lama named Dusk[52] who, taking pity on the exhausted bird, approached to feed it with the only thing that he had at hand: a sack of kurkuma flowers. Grateful, the Blessed Lord decided to reward Dusk by making him the father of a people of worshipers of the King of the World and granting them, to all the Initiates who emerged from his Stirp, the guardianship of the Boundary of Shambhala, which was precisely starting on that sacred island.

"Another version of the legend, undoubtedly more ancient, was affirming that the Divine Crane had loved the Dusk lama and was wishing to give him descendants before departing. The problem was residing in that the Crane was a male specimen, of the same sex as the lama, so there would be no possible fertilization. Then the Shambhala Crane, which in this story was fed by the blood of the lama, remembered that only intercourse with a male naga serpent is capable of achieving the miracle of procreation between members of the same sex. Still on the islet of Gyaring Lake, the Crane mentally activated his Dorje of Power, which was on the King of the World's Throne in Chang Shambhala, and transformed the lama into a male naga serpent. Then they ardently mated, leaving the Rigden Jyepo Crane pregnant by the naga serpent. After that homosexual act, before departing, the Divine Crane laid two saffron-colored eggs.

"Subsequently incubated by the Dusk lama, under the Naga Serpent Aspect, both eggs bore a pair of hybrid twins, one-third Crane, one-third man, and one-third serpent, who would be the Great Ancestors of the Duskhas.

"It should not be surprising, then, that with such a belief they claimed their kinship with the King of the World and converted themselves into his most fanatical worshipers, demanding from anyone who attempted to cross the Boundary of Shambhala the pain offering of a human victim, a welcome gift for the one who holds the titles of 'Father of Human Pain,' 'Lord of the Lords of Karma,' and 'Supreme Master of the Kalachakra.'

"Since then, the Duskhas, people descendent from the mythical Dusk, zealously looked after the region and built the Rigden Jyepo Temple on the 'White Island,' thus denominated in memory of Chang Svetadvipa, the 'White Island of the

---

52. *Dusk* means *Pain*. The Duskhas were constituting "the family of Dusk," that is, the Sons of Pain.

North,' invisible to human eyes and seat of the Gate of Shambhala, the Mansion of the Bodhisattvas. With the passing of the centuries, the people of the Duskhas grew, as well as the number of their community of lamas, seeing themselves obligated to erect the enormous Gompa Jafran Ashram, which they surrounded with beautiful Pagodas, dedicated to the cult of various Deities of the White Brotherhood. The island, with its Temple, was very close to the western shore of the lake; opposite to it, the Monastery with its ring of Pagodas was erected on the mainland; and further back, forming a wide semicircle that was covered and at the same time protecting the group of religious buildings, was the village of the Duskhas.

"The Huang Ho, or Yellow River, has always constituted in that region a triple border between the Kingdoms of Tibet, Mongolia, and China. For thousands of years the invading armies, coming from this or that Kingdom, passed by the Jafran Ashram, frequently respecting its status as a religious community but on some occasions attempting to occupy the village or subjecting it to sacking. That reality forced the Duskhas to fortify the plaza, constructing an elevated stone wall in the shape of a 'U,' which was going from shore to shore of Gyaring Lake: at the opening of the 'U,' facing the open space on the lake between the ends of the wall, was the White Island with the Temple and the prisoner that we were procuring to liberate.

"And at the base of the 'U,' which was the front of the walled city, was an enormous wooden gate, framed by two elevated towers that were serving as watchtowers, permanently occupied by armed lookouts. In the two angles of the 'U' were also towers with their respective sentinels.

"It is good to clarify that such security measures had arisen by force of circumstances, that is to say, by the necessity to protect the Temples and the Ashram from possible invaders, since the Duskhas, despite their ferocity for the Ritual Sacrifice, were absolutely lacking warrior vocation. They were, however, a people of born Priests, whose members were entering, from an early age, into the practice of the Cult and were always living ascetically, displaying an ultramontane rigorism. Not only were they not warriors, but war was causing in them an essential horror, and they were imagining it as an effect of human error, of the blindness of man, who was not seeing, as they were, the Goodness of the Creator Gods of the Universe.

"Their firearms were reduced to a scant hundred Martini-Henry rifles from the nineteenth century and six small pieces of fixed artillery, mounted on the towers of the wall: they were completely lacking handguns. On the other hand, the cutlery was abundant and varied, and they were handling it with regular dexterity.

"To these material deficiencies was being added the scarce strategic vision of those wretches, who had quartered the totality of their garrison, about one hundred troops, in two barracks situated on both sides of the main gate. Evidently, the whole weight of their defense was being based more on psychological factors than real ones, that is to say, that they were trusting in the dissuasion of their walls, and the scarce plunder that was behind them, to discourage possible attackers. The artillery pieces themselves were rather representing a dissuasive object than a real danger for the besiegers, since they would hardly function: and that is, if the ideal conditions of dry powder, ammunition, and fuse were present, and if these elements were placed in the correct way.

"In synthesis, as the region was tranquil for the moment, and they had no reason to suspect any attack, the guard was reduced to its minimum expression: one man at each tower, that is to say, six watchmen; two at the main gate and one behind each of the other four side doors, that is, six more guards; another six guards at the Temple of the White Island, two outside and four inside; and forty troops sleeping in each of the barracks, but ready to come out at the slightest alarm.

"That night, Kaly would make the Gurkha's prayers a reality. It would not be the strikes of Shiva's Trident, or the Fire of Indra's Thunderbolt, or the certainty of Arjuna's arrows, but Bangi's vengeance would be instrumented by means of other similar powers: the strikes of the bullets from our rifles, the fire of the grenades, and the certainty of the arrows of the Lopas.

For the number of troops that he was counting, the formation that Von Grossen was commanding was hardly a squadron; but, for combat morale and the awareness of its own strength, it had to be qualified as a phalanx or legion. A legion, one would say, because of its great mobility for blitzkrieg. From the outset, we would attack divided: Von Grossen would lead the bulk of the squadron, while a team led by me would operate in the Temple. In a second phase of the plan, the squadron would bifurcate into two platoons, to then all reunite, at a prefixed point, and execute the retreat.

"Only the Germans would go to the assault supplied with firearms: a Luger pistol and a Schmeisser submachine gun per head, plus two of the obsolete Mauser 1914 rifles, which would be seen what use they were going to serve. In those days, the 9mm Schmeisser were secret weapons, and only an Elite corps like ours had been permitted to carry them outside of Germany. We were counting on fifty magazines with thirty rounds each, but I would only carry two, leaving the rest for my Comrades who would sustain the bulk of the attack. Naturally, we were all carrying the ⚡ Knight's dagger, with the legend 'Blut und Ehre' carved into the blade.

"The Kaulika warriors, for their part, were using three kinds of weapons: bow and arrows, scimitar, and dagger. As I said before, those monks were experts in martial arts, and their archery skills were unrivaled in Tibet, where no one was hesitating in attributing a magical power to their arrows and it was being affirmed that they could hit the bull's eye by day as well as by night, with their eyes open or blindfolded, etc. They were all carrying fifty arrows, not one more or one less, in a quiver that they let hang against their right leg: each arrow corresponding to one of the skulls of Kaly's necklace and that is why one of the letters of the sacred Aryan alphabet was engraved on its shaft. The scimitar was a short sword, about 80 centimeters long, with a single-edged blade, curved, convexly truncated and edged, and widened at that end; the crossguard was protecting the fist with two quillons that were imitating the eagle's talon, and the hilt, made of black ivory, had an exquisitely chiseled pommel, which was representing the Face of Kaly as Mrtyu, Death. The scimitar, sheathed, was hanging from a swordbelt on the left side. And finally, in a small scabbard, fastened by the sash, was the dagger with a flamed blade and ivory hilt, similar in size to the medieval *Panzerbrecher* or its contemporary *'Misericorde.'*

"The members of the Kaula Circle were calling Shiva in their Tantra, *'Rudra',* a word that was emerging from the contraction and agglutination of *Ru* and *Duskha,* and that was meaning *'He who destroys Pain.'* Shiva was thus the Enemy of Pain, or the Enemy of Dusk; and His disciples, by extension, would be the Enemies of the Duskhas. I make this clear, Neffe, because I could not fail to consider, in the balance of one's armament, the profound hatred that the Kaulikas were experiencing for the Duskhas, as an important tactical element in their favor. The Kaulikas were regarding the Duskhas as little less than vampires who were living on human pain, and were psychologically predisposed to act with maximum rigor against 'the family of Dusk': Shiva Rudra would approve and reward the valorous demonstration of His Kshatriya Kaulikas.

"The sun went down behind the formidable Bayan-Kara mountain range and the night, impenetrable due to the scarce lunar light of the waning quarter, descended over Gyaring Lake. At zero hours, we left the well-secured horses one kilometer before the Jafran Ashram and began to advance on foot, carrying the material necessary for the attack. This had been set for one sharp, the hour at which the two groups were to be at their posts.

"The Gurkha, knowing the way toward the Temple, one of the Lopas, and I, would be in charge of rescuing Oskar, at the exact moment at which Von Grossen and the others would initiate the frontal attack. The surprise was the determinant factor of the success of our Strategy and that is why we were moving with extreme caution.

"At a quarter to one, and about three hundred meters from the watchtower, we entered into the lake. We were three Initiates and knew how to release the heat of the igneous Kundalini energy to avoid freezing, but without any doubt, in that aquatic environment of high mountains, the Kaulikas were ahead of me: the Hatha yoga practices of the ⚡⚡ were mainly focused on resisting, with the naked body, the low and dry temperatures of the Bavarian Alps. Thus, I was still shivering from the cold, when we arrived at the White Island a few minutes later, without the Duskhas hearing us.

"At the back of the Temple, the three of us invaders climbed up to the starry opening through which the unfortunate Gangi entered four days earlier. It was almost one in the morning. From then on we had to act with mathematical precision, for there was the possibility that the interior guards might try to kill Oskar upon recovering from the surprise of the attack.

"At five seconds past one, with Germanic exactitude, a powerful exterior explosion vibrated the Temple and left the guards paralyzed with terror. At that instant, while Hell was breaking loose outside, I jumped from the window, rolled across the floor in the direction of the altar, brusquely stopped, and with a single blast from the Schmeisser I got rid of the four guards. The four received bullets in the back and died without knowing what was happening, finished off against the door of the Temple toward which they were turned. The horrible idol, behind which I had taken cover in case the door was opened and other guards entered, was now receiving a fairer offering than Oskar Feil.

"The Kaulikas, who arrived seconds later at the altar, took care of cutting the ties and removing the gag that was preventing Oskar, whose the narcotic wore off, from speaking.

" 'Kurt! Kurt von Sübermann!' he shouted in a daze. 'Is it really you or am I dreaming?'

" 'It's me, it's me!' I impatiently affirmed. 'Prepare yourself, because we have to get out of here as soon as possible. I'll explain everything to you later.'

"Poor Oskar couldn't stand up.

"For seven days, they kept him tied down on the altar and only fed him enough so that he arrived alive on the day of his execution. The Lopa and I each put a shoulder under each of his arms and retreated to the back of the Temple, hoisting him up in the air. Meanwhile, the Gurkha was pressing his ear to the door and, when not noticing any danger, made sure with his dagger that the guards were good and dead.

"In truth, we could have exited through the door of the Temple, since the exterior guards ran toward the village upon hearing the explosions; but we did not know it then, and were not wanting to risk sustaining an unequal combat. What we did, instead, was climb, the four of us, through the window: first, the Lopa climbed up; then Oskar, standing on my shoulders, received help and went to the exterior cornice; and, finally, Bangi and I climbed up.

We surrounded the Temple and found that the front was unguarded. We then crossed the corridor that was joining the White Island with the beach and we hid behind the small wall to observe, fifty meters ahead, what was happening at the Monastery. In the following minutes, we would meet with our Comrades again!

Chapter XXVI

he surrounding wall had been stripped of rocks, so they had to crawl fifty meters. At five minutes to one, Von Grossen, the three ₷₷ officers, and three Lopas, were clinging to the ground twenty meters from the main gate. The remaining four monks were in charge of eliminating the lookouts, deployed in positions suitable for that purpose.

"Their action was very swift and the lookouts 'saw nothing' when the Lopas emerged from the earth with the speed of the cobra, down on one knee, and shot four arrows. Four arrows in the night, four sure targets! One would say that those sacred arrows sought the heart of the worshipers of the Lord of Shambhala.

"Von Grossen and his group then ran in the direction of the gate, joining two of the archers; the other two were marching, separately, to liquidate the sentinels of the far towers of the wall, those that were on the waters of the lake. They all pressed themselves to the wall, while Kloster and Hans were fastening, to the hinges and locks, the four demolition petards. The main entrance to the village was guarded by a heavy and enormous single-leaf gate, constructed of assembled boards and covered with iron fittings that were totally covering the cracks. It was certainly a strong barricade, which would have withstood more than one battering ram charge, but certainly ineffective in modern warfare, in the face of artillery or bombs like those that we placed. Kloster looked at the time: two minutes to one; then he ignited the two-minute delayed detonator and pressed himself against the wall, beside Von Grossen.

"Psychologically, two minutes can last an instant or an eternity, especially if there is the possibility that one dies at the end of them. The Germans, to avoid thinking about anything that was not combat, dedicated themselves to verify that the submachine guns had the safety off; in order to make sure for the umpteenth time that the magazines would easily come to hand, from the canvas cartridge compartments; and to ensure that the stick grenades would slide out of the belt and from the throat of the boots without problems. Thus, for the Germans, the two minutes were closer to the instant than to eternity. The Kaulikas, on the other hand, remained absolutely motionless, with the mind concentrated on the infinite unity of the Kula. For them, who had divested themselves of the awareness of duration, the two minutes were akin to Eternity.

"But they all equally ran when the bombs exploded. And, literally speaking, *they tired themselves out from killing.*

"The charges, distributed with singular expertise, completely blew off the main gate and destroyed it, scattering the pieces around for dozens of meters. The smoke from the entrance had not yet dissipated and already Von Grossen and Heinz were stood in front of the only two gates of the barracks.

"A great confusion was reigning inside, and only a small few managed to take up their weapon and try to get out; but such a reaction came too late to save their lives. Kloster and Heinz were running around the barracks since a minute before, throwing the grenades through the embrasures: at the fifth grenade, simultaneously, both hovels began to crumble. Desperate, those who were miraculously unharmed, were struggling to gain access to the doors and get out, only to fall over the cadavers of their predecessors, struck down by the inclement bursts of the Schmeissers. Not a single one escaped that mortal trap.

"When no more guards were appearing at the doors, Von Grossen gave an order and two Kaulikas penetrated into the ruins and dedicated themselves to finishing off the wounded and survivors with accurate stabs. The *Standartenführer* consulted his wristwatch with its luminescent hands: eight past one. In only eight minutes, and without giving them time to fire a shot, the three ⚡⚡ officers exterminated the Duskha garrison!

"From the main entrance, and up to the spacious plaza where the Monastery stood, was running a wide avenue, 300 meters long, along which Von Grossen had planned the next advance. Except for the two Lopas who were left outside, and whose mission was consisting of climbing the towers, the Kaulikas were entrusted to 'clear' the way for the Germans. With that purpose in mind, as soon as the gate blew up, three of them headed directly toward there, brandishing their scimitars and, with notably mastery, slit the throats of all the Duskhas who crossed their path. The distance had been divided up and each one was going back and forth for about a hundred meters, delivering blows left and right. The first to die were, of course, the inhabitants of the houses facing the avenue, and who committed the irreparable error of going out into the street when hearing the explosions: the elderly, men, women, children, the Kaulika scimitar was sparing no one. After ten past one, when the two Lopas, who were returning from finishing off the wounded from the garrison, were summing them up, the bodies of dozens of entire families were lying lifeless in the vicinity of their dwellings.

"But, at that point of the events, after the explosion of the bombs, the grenades, and the submachine gun fire, chaos was master of the Duskha village. In the midst of the infernal shouting, a multitude of disconcerted people were converging on that street, some in order to arrive at the walls, and others to make their way toward the Monastery. And although many were coming armed with daggers and sabers, and were offering a fleeting resistance to the Kaulika monks, the latter were inexorably cutting short their miserable lives.

"When the four ⚡⚡ officers marched off at a run toward the Monastery, the avenue had turned into a river of blood. But the road was effectively 'clear.' They fired only a few rounds when passing, over the crowd that was flowing through the side alleyways. Behind them the Kaulikas also advanced, admirably fulfilling their function of ensuring the mobility of the Germans.

"At ten past one, while the Germans were marching down the avenue, the two Lopa archers returned from the exterior and climbed up a stone stairway to the towers that were guarding the destroyed entrance gate. There they separated: one would take the corridor on the left and the other on the right, corridors that were connecting all the towers to each other and that were consisting of narrow projecting platforms, peripherally distributed on the interior side of the wall. In each tower there was a primitive stove, which was now useless to heat the definitively frozen bodies of the guards. The Kaulikas, from the first towers, were observing the conglomerate of houses that were compactly spread out in a strip of three hundred meters wide, parallel to the wall. Utilizing the different towers, it was possible to take in every detail, block, alley, house, or Temple, of the Duskha village.

"They had spent the previous day making the flaming arrows. It was not difficult: it was enough to wind a woolen thread soaked in a mixture of combustible oil and sugar on the tips of the common arrows. They had one hundred of those arrows because, according to Von Grossen, no more were required; the important thing, the *Standartenführer* explained, was not the quantity of arrows but the quality of the selected targets and the degree of accuracy of the shots. According to said tactic, the Kaulikas chose the hundred targets one by one, procuring to aim at flammable materials such as wood and cloth.

"Doors, windows, canopies, curtains, sacks of food, forage piles, and looms assembled under wide corridors, began little by little to take on different categories of combustion. In some places, the flames soon exceeded the height of the houses and sparks invaded the vicinity; the fire inexorably spread and the blaze became general.

"When the two Kaulikas reached the final towers, at twenty past one, the Duskha village had been transformed into a gigantic bonfire. The uncontrolled mobs were mostly trying to escape from the suffocating heat and get to the lake or outside the walls. The sentinels of the side gates, trapped between the flames and the crowd, cleared away and were unable to prevent the passing of hundreds of terrified villagers. At that hour, the two Kaulika monks assumed very different attitudes. The one who was in the tower on the far right lowered himself with a rope outside the wall and resolutely headed toward the place where the horses were hidden, ruthlessly cutting down, with deadly strikes of the scimitar, the disconcerted Duskhas that he was encountering in his path. The one in the tower on the left prepared the rope to descend to the exterior, but then went down the stone stairway to the interior and, converted into a whirlwind of deadly thrusts, cleared the vicinity of that place of enemies: he was awaiting the arrival of Von Grossen's squadron, which should already be there.

"Fifteen minutes past one. The large crowd of Duskhas, gathered at the entrance of the Monastery, was demanding with loud voices the presence of the lamas of the Kurkuma Bonnet. Ignoring the clamor of their brethren, the monks had barricaded themselves and were, probably, reciting prayers to Rigden Jyepo and the Gods of the White Brotherhood.

"It was improbable that there were any firearms in the interior of the Gompa, the physical headquarters of the Jafran Ashram; and it was even more improbable that any lama was willing to defend his refuge with weapons.

"The appearance of Von Grossen and the ⚡⚡ officers on the run was surprising and caused the panic of the villagers. Two grenades fell among them and completed that picture of nameless terror. The explosions, in the midst of the multitude, mutilated the nearest bodies and projected dozens of shards in all directions, metal teeth eager to bite and wound the flesh, blind and winged beasts that were killing at random. Von Grossen only had to fire twice with the submachine gun, so that the rain of bullets dispersed the maddened crowd.

"The whole group took preventive shelter under the gallery of a beautiful Tibetan-style Buddhist Pagoda, in order to prepare for the next action. Kloster and Hans, in the center of the circle of Kaulika scimitars, lowered their packs and took out the forty rifle grenades. They then took the Mauser 1914s and inserted two of them into the barrel adapter.

"The rifle grenades had a phosphorous charge, which was exploding on impact, and were constituting a highly effective tactical incendiary bomb. Fired with a rifle similar to the Mauser, it was possible to hit precise targets at 300 meters. Their targets, the windows of the Monastery, were inviting them to launch the projectiles only 25 meters ahead.

"Seated on a square base of seventy meters on each side, the Gompa was showing three rows of windows on the level above the entrance door, the main façade that we were seeing from the front. It was housing, as I said, some 500 lamas of the Kurkuma Bonnet, many of whom were peering out and haranguing the Duskhas, either supplicating, or commanding, to resist the enemy, to reorganize the defense, not to flee, etc. Perhaps the most paradoxical of such dramatic intimations was that which was assuring, in the Name of the Blessed Lord, that the intruders were not Demons but simple mortals.

"There was also a large back door, which was facing the White Island, and two small doors on either side of the building, all of which were locked from the inside. The roofs, covered with brown tiles, were inclining in a gentle hyperbolic slope, and there was a central courtyard surrounded by verandas and fine columns.

"At that moment, the lamas noticed the fire that was consuming the village and exhorted the people to combat it by using water from the ponds and interior canals, which they could flood in a matter of minutes by opening locks that were containing the pressure of the lake. One must admit that some

Duskhas kept calm in those tragic moments and ran to fulfill the orders, which the lamas were not daring to carry out by themselves; and there were others who vainly attempted to oppose the voracity of the fire. But it is one thing to stop an occasional fire, arisen by accident in this or that place, and quite another to face a hundred deliberately ignited spot fires.

"The fire became uncontrollable in certain areas and their dwellers fled in terror, some heading to the exterior, and others in the direction of the Lamasery. Without noticing the riddled cadavers that were littering the plaza, mobs coming from various directions were converging at every moment to request Divine succor from their Gods, while the lamas were ordering them to immediately fight, against the fire and against the invisible-but-lethal enemies.

"However, although the lamenting and shrieking of the desperate was deafening, over the background noise that was producing the crackling of things when burning, the sound of firearms was no longer being heard. Encouraged by such silence, the lamas were now shouting prayers and mantrams from almost all the windows.

"Sixteen past one. Von Grossen's squad suddenly emerged from the darkness of the Pagoda and marched in close two-by-two order for a few meters. An instant later, Kloster and Hans were firing the first two incendiary grenades toward two windows on the second floor: one hit the chest of the lama who was circumstantially vociferating his discourse and made him disappear under a blinding light; another cleanly penetrated through the adjoining opening and exploded in the interior of the Gompa. And through both windows, after the brightness of the explosion faded, it was seen how the flames were scorching everything.

"But the ⚡⚡ were not stopping to evaluate the effect of their attack. After the first two, they continued sending grenades against the windows at the rate of ten per side, until completing the forty. Kloster ran on the right, followed by Von Grossen and two Kaulikas, stopping at intervals to load the grenade and fire. Hans did so from the left, protected by Heinz and three Kaulikas, firing in a similar manner.

"No one had counted on the possibility that the monastery had its own guard corps, which went unnoticed by the Gurkha observer. However, it was insignificant in number, although its members were well trained in the use of the saber. There they suffered their first and only casualty, when a surprise stab wound cut short the life of a Lopa from Von Grossen's group. The guards, two or three per door, were remaining outside and tried, demonstrating a certain valor, to prevent the Monastery from being attacked. Of course, they had neither the dexterity nor the necessary knowledge to rival the Kaulikas and, when they were not eliminated by their scimitars, they fell punctured by the implacable German bullets.

"In a few seconds the Lamasery was, then, equally burned to the ground. As involuntary guests of an infernal furnace, as if the Thunderbolt of Indra had effectively fallen on the peaceful Jafran Ashram, the majority of the hypocritical Holy lamas met a horrible death in those first minutes of the attack. A death that was accompanied by a shuddering concert of howls of pain.

"After two minutes, both platoons reunited at the back door of the Monastery, that which was facing the White Island and the Temple of Rigden Jyepo. The clocks were showing eighteen past one, and down the beach a third group was approaching at a slow pace: it was the squad comprised of the Gurkha, the Lopa, Oskar Feil, and Me!

"Suddenly, the door opened and some lamas intended to exit to the exterior. They were coughing and crying from the smoke, and their simple Asiatic faces were representing the image of fright: Von Grossen mercilessly machine-gunned them and bellowed:

" 'To the other doors!'

"In effect, the remaining gates opened as well, but there were very few survivors that we had to suppress: the intense heat, and the collapse of the upper floors, wiped out most of them before they could reach the exits. Like the lookouts, like the garrison, the totality of the lamas of the Kurkuma Bonnet ended up annihilated because of our superiority in the art of war.

Chapter XXVII

wenty-one minutes past one. Karl von Grossen, Heinz, Kloster, Hans, Oskar, and I, the group of five Lopas, and the Gurkha, covered the three hundred meters that were separating us from the left tower. We had to bloodily make our way through the sparse crowd that was still chaotically running without knowing what to do, but that escape route planned by Von Grossen demonstrated to be, if not the only one possible, one of the few that were left. Another course of evasion, for example, might have considered the aquatic environment of the lake; what would not be feasible to do was to go back the way we came, that is to say, along the avenue, since it was now resembling a high-temperature tunnel due to the effect of the general fire; an effect anticipated by the farsighted Von Grossen.

"In the center of a grisly circle of cadavers, at the foot of the stairs, we found the Kaulika monk. Preceded by him, we were climbing up in a column to the tower and quickly went down the rope to the exterior of the wall.

"With no obstacles worth mentioning, we embarked on our retreat to the north. Five hundred meters ahead, we found the Kaulika monk with the horses and completed the retreat, rapidly moving away from the destroyed Duskha village. The road was ascending the slope of a hill and I could not help but turn back for a moment to contemplate for the last time the consequence of our attack. The image that I perceived, as a corollary of the operation, was Dantesque: with the tenebrous frame of the dark night, the quadrate of the interior of the wall, illuminated by the reddish glow of the fire, which was still preserving its destructive vitality, was sharply distinguishable; the fire, like a famished beast, had decided to devour everything, and was still feeding on the sinister Monastery; the building, which was the tallest in the village, freely burned and its flames were projecting a multicolor fan on the immutable mirror of Gyaring Lake; under that light, it was even possible for me to recognize the accursed Temple of Rigden Jyepo, which was constructed entirely of white stones.

"The success of the attack would have been total had it been possible to follow the course of a variant planned by Von Grossen, which was contemplating the dynamiting of that satanic Temple. But no material time was available for it; that is to say, time was used to cover the doors of the Gompa in order to prevent the lamas from escaping: to the realist Von Grossen, it seemed more practical to kill all the lamas, living enemies, than to use violence on an 'inert' symbol such as the Temple. But I was disagreeing with such a criterion, since I was considering that the Lamasery had more real weight, as an adversary, than the lamas: it was going to be much easier for the White Brotherhood to replace the lamas than to rebuild the millenary Temple! However, I would never reproach Von Grossen, since, thanks to his doubtless professionalism, Oskar Feil was now galloping at my side.

"A few potent exclamations abruptly took me away from such thoughts. It took a while to realize that they all did the same as I and turned back a second to take in the final view of the Duskha village. And now, upon descending to the other side of the hill, they were letting out uncontainable and over-joyed shouts of jubilation. Naturally, I refer to the Germans, for the Asians were remaining as indifferent as ever. Von Grossen had to allude to the authority of his military degree to prevent Baldur von Schirach's song 'Hymn to the Banner of the Hitler Youth'[53] from being sung aloud. I, too, would have liked to sing it at that moment. And, remembering my childhood in Cairo, I was mentally repeating it, as my Comrades were undoubtedly doing:

>...*Germany, you will stand shining,*
>*Even if we go down.*
>*Our banner flutters before us.*
>*Our banner represents the new era.*
>*And our banner leads us into eternity!*
>*Yes! Our banner means more than death!*[54]

---

53. Fahnenlied

54. Deutschland, du wirst leuchtend stehn,
mögen wir auch untergehn.
Unsre Fahne flattert uns voran.
Unsre Fahne ist die neue Zeit.
Und die Fahne führt uns in die Ewigkeit!
Ja! Die Fahne ist mehr als der Tod!

"Yes, our Banners were superior to Death itself; and they were unleashing Death upon the enemy, as the lamas of the Kurkuma Bonnet were just finding out. We Germans were unleashing Death because History was convoking us to do so; the Enemy of our Banners would forever regret having sunk its vile claws into the Fatherland. I then remembered 'Sturmlied' by Dietrich Eckart, that founding member of the Thulegesellschaft of whom Konrad Tarstein had tirelessly spoke to me, for he had also been one of Adolf Hitler's Initiators:

Sturm! Sturm! Sturm! Sturm! Sturm! Sturm!
Ring the bells from tower to tower!
Ring, so that sparks begin to fly.
Judas appears to win the Reich.
Ring, so that the ropes turn red with blood.
All around, burning and torturing and killing.
Keep ringing the bells, so that the earth rears up
under the thunder of redeeming revenge!
Woe to the volk who still dream today!
Germany, awake! Awake!

Sturm! Sturm! Sturm! Sturm! Sturm! Sturm!
Ring the bells from tower to tower.
Ring the men, the old men, the boys.
Ring the sleepers from their rooms.
Ring the girls down the stairs.
Ring the mothers away from the cradles.
Let it roar and ring in the air.
Rush, rush in the thunder of revenge.
Ring the dead from their graves!
Germany, awake! Awake!

Sturm! Sturm! Sturm! Sturm! Sturm! Sturm!
Ring the bells from tower to tower.
The serpent is loose, the worm of hell!
Folly and lies broke its chain,
greed for gold in the filthy bed!
The sky is on fire, red as blood.
The gables collapse with a terrible crash.
Blow after blow on the chapel!
The dragon howls as it whips it to ruins!
Ring the bells now or never!
Germany, awake! Awake!

"History was convoking the fittest to fight against Evil. And we were the fittest! At a unique moment in history we had raised the Eternal Banners, as Baldur von Schirach was calling for. And that is why the Führer was ringing the alarm bell, as Dietrich Eckart was requesting. Woe to the sleeping peoples, or those who, like the Duskhas, gave in to Evil! Woe to those who heeded not the Ringing of the Eternal Spirit! They would suffer the wrath of the Awakened Sons of Germany!

"What occurred in Tibet was constituting an example: five ⚡ officers and eight Kaulikas Initiates, lamenting a single casualty, exterminated more than a thousand fierce enemies. One for a thousand! A just proportion for the life of the fallen Initiate and that of Oskar Feil, which they were proposing to take.

"Our enemies, or better said, the Enemy of our Banners, should definitively realize that *We* were not threatening in vain!"

Chapter XXVIII

want to let the reader know that I did not have the same luck as yours, because Uncle Kurt's narration, referring to the rescue operation of his Comrade Oskar Feil, required several days. Without making mention of those interruptions, I have transcribed the main parts in correlative form so as not to cause impatience, an impatience similar to that which, as one might suppose, befell me in those days.

I will only add that, as will surely occur to the reader, that feat in which Uncle Kurt participated, immediately brought to my memory the "Feat of Nimrod," recounted by Belicena Villca. Undoubtedly, the adventure in Tibet had a stamp of *magical heroism*, a style of "intrepidness without limits," which was resembling the story of the Kassite King. Otherwise, the Enemy was the same: the Enemy of the Eternal Spirit, the Enemy of the Hyperborean Wisdom, the Enemy of "our Banners," as Uncle Kurt was calling it, that is to say, the White Brotherhood of Chang Shambhala and its earthly agents.

In the same way, I will collect, in the following chapters, Uncle Kurt's most interesting accounts without intervening. Naturally, I will use such a criterion as far as possible, that is to say, up to the Epilogue (Epilogue?), which was when Uncle Kurt's account, and every account, had to be interrupted. I, for my part, was already in good health at that point, and I was only awaiting the culmination of the story to fulfill Belicena Villca's request: every day that was passing, my determination was growing, because, at every moment, things were becoming irreversibly clearer regarding the Hyperborean Wisdom.

As I remember, Uncle Kurt continued like this one morning:

Chapter XXIX

e rode without stopping until crossing the Chang-lam road. Next to the bridge over the Yellow River, in the same place where we found him, we left the Gurkha. He would remain hidden, awaiting the rest of the expedition, that is to say, the two Kaulika monks and the five Kalita porters. We, on the other hand, would continue several kilometers to camp in the mountains to the NE.

"It was not in our best interest to be seen for the moment, since the attack on the Duskha village would cause the consequent alarm in the region and we were not knowing the reaction of the official authorities in Tibet, who perhaps suspected our intervention.

"It was beginning to dawn when we stopped, being evident that the good weather that had accompanied us until then had ended. Dense clouds were swiftly rolling in overhead and an icy breeze, which was chilling us to the bone, was unequivocally announcing the imminent storm. It was a snowstorm and the most protected place would be, paradoxically, the open country: camping against the rocks of a hill we could end up buried by an avalanche. We finally found an elevated depression, a small valley of 30 square meters surrounded by gentle slopes, and we quickly set up the high mountain tents.

"By midday, it was impossible to stay out in the open, for the breeze had turned into an outright blizzard, and we had to take refuge in the tents: only the Tibetan horses, as the sons of Zephyr that they were, were naturally resisting the inclemency of the wind. That offshoot of the NW monsoon was violently shaking the tents and whistling a high-pitched and forlorn lament, a moan that was perhaps arising from the soul of Rigden Jyepo upon mourning the fate of his worshipers.

"Within my tent, another storm was threatening to break out. But the wind was not causing this one, but Von Grossen's tempestuous attitude. For the *Standartenführer*, the operation against the Duskhas was representing a pure diversion, a waste of time. His mission, to catch up with Schäfer's expedition, had not been fulfilled; and time was uselessly passing. According to his logical assessments, we were now worse off than before: 'in the first place,' he was reasoning, 'we were not knowing the secret path that was connecting the Boundary of

Shambhala with the Gate of Shambhala, near Lake Kokonor; secondly, it was seeming evident that we could no longer follow them as before, that is to say, counting on the collaboration of the Kaulika network, since the Gurkha spies were left out of the expedition; and thirdly, it was to be expected that along that road, little or not at all frequented, there would be no villagers whom to inquire; but, fourthly, it would be very improbable that if there were, they would give us the information required, after the discovery of our affiliation against the White Brotherhood by destroying the community of lamas of the Kurkuma Bonnet.

" 'How, then, how would we catch up with them, as the orders of Division III of the *RSHA* were reading?'

"I was pretending to ignore these questions and was keeping myself content explaining to Oskar Feil the true causes of his kidnapping at the hands of the Duskhas: in truth, he had fallen into an ambush; the trap was part of a plot between Ernst Schäfer and the lamas of the Kurkuma Bonnet, whose purpose was to provide a human victim to the Cult of Rigden Jyepo; however, such a conspiracy had its roots in Germany, in the traitors who were calling themselves 'the Sane Forces of Germany,' who planned that expedition and negotiated the price of their support with the White Brotherhood. And such a price would undoubtedly be very high: just to cross the Boundary required a sacrifice, the execution of a symbol of the New Germany, the death of an ⚡⚡ man, the burnt offering of an exponent of the Blood Aristocracy of the Third Reich. Then, in Shambhala, Schäfer would know the rest of the conditions: the Occult Hierarchy would support the conspirators with their magical powers and with their, more effective, synarchic organizations, in exchange for destroying the spiritual foundations of the Third Reich. Not only would the Führer and his top brass have to die, and the National Socialist party be dissolved, but the nucleus of the tumor would have to be extirpated; that is, it was necessary to disintegrate the ⚡⚡ and demolish the ⚡⚡ Black Order, mercilessly exterminating its Initiates. Yes, the scalpel of the Brotherhood would this time be interested in the depths of the wound, scraping, if it were necessary, the bone of the German social structure: only in this way, after the major surgery, could *the Civilization of Love* be built atop the ashes of the Civilization of Nazi Hatred.

" 'But, until now, it would only be a part of the price: with the fulfillment of these guidelines, the traitors would achieve nothing more than to demonstrate their willingness to collaborate with the Plan of the White Brotherhood,' I clarified to Oskar. 'Full support would come later, if the triumphant conspirators were demonstrating to be willing to go all the way and were undertaking a profound transformation of German society that erased all traces of the Nazi Culture and the Hyperborean Wisdom: a German society that is peacefully integrated into the Universal Synarchy of the second half of the twentieth century would demand, so that it was open and reliable to the White Brotherhood, a democratic and liberal form of government, and an Official Culture in which Zionism, Judeo-Masonry and Judeo-Marxism, or the ideologies born from those synarchic trunks, would have free expression. Then yes, if the reigning traitors were carrying out these conditions of the pact, Germany would be situated on the side of God, of Good, of Love, and of Justice; and the Germans would see themselves forever separated from their malevolent ancestral Deities.

" 'That's right, Oskar,' I concluded. 'Ernst Schäfer is one more of a numerous group of traitors. His function in the conspiracy is to sign, in the name of the "Sane Forces of Germany," a synarchic Cultural Pact with the representatives of the White Brotherhood. I cannot reveal to you in what our mission consists, how we are going to frustrate their plans, but I assure you that your fate was already decided in Germany. You would never pass through the Boundary of Shambhala!'

"Oskar felt ridiculous when he learned that Ernst Schäfer had condemned him to die in Tibet from the very beginning, that perhaps only permitted him to participate in Operation *Altwesten* for that purpose, and that the espionage that he carried out for me had in turn been supervised by two professional spies from the SD, also participants in the expedition. And to top it all off, he had to learn that he had involuntarily caused Gangi's death.

" 'I've been a fool,' he embarrassedly affirmed. 'And to think that *I dared to advise you* on how you should act and suggested you to consult Rudolf Hess. They have all made fun of me!'

" 'Don't torture yourself, Oskar, at that time I was unaware of these facts. And up to the last moment I was unaware of the existence of other spies among you. Now we must only think of preventing the infamous traitor Schäfer from carrying out his infernal task. *His plans are already failing:* you are alive and that is what counts. You will come with us and will know the end of the story, you will see the failure of his vain efforts to destroy the New Order,' I assured with conviction.

" 'Very clear concepts and very admirable your faith, Von Sübermann,' intervened Von Grossen, returning to the heaviness. 'But you haven't yet told me how we're going to find Schäfer in this labyrinth of mountains, and with Winter almost upon us. How'll we find him? You believe it's possible to scour such a region at random?'

"Really, I had not even the slightest idea how to respond to these questions. Under pressure from the *Standartenführer,* I could only propose:

" 'We should inquire of the Kaulikas. Possibly they know how to locate those who move through territories that are well known to them.'

"Karl von Grossen put his head in his hands, upon realizing that his suspicions were founded: I was not possessing the solution to the problem of finding Schäfer. (Mein Gott: if they were failing in that objective, they could not even dream of returning to Germany!) That operation, Himmler and Heydrich had told him quite clearly, *could constitute a journey of no return.* Failure was not permitted. If he was failing, he had to protagonize a sort of harakiri or seppuku, the honorable ritual suicide of the Japanese Samurai.

"But Von Grossen, besides being tough, was a proverbially cold-blooded man. Despite his apprehension, he said:

" 'Good idea, Von Sübermann, we will immediately try to put it into practice.'

"Without waiting for an answer, he unhooked the tent flaps and rushed outside, vigorously leaping like a frog. Outside the snowstorm was raging. I followed him perplexed and penetrated with him into one of the neighboring tents of the Lopas. Unlike us, who were keeping ourselves warm in our sleeping bags, the five Tibetans who were ahead of us were only wearing the uniform of an English high mountain porter: green jacket, green pants, and half-boots.

"I contemplated with a blank stare as the snow on his clothes was melting and the water was dripping and running down the tarp on the floor into the waste disposal opening, while Von Grossen was interrogating the Tibetans in Khams

Skad. Naturally, inside I was invoking the Gods, reciting a prayer so that the miracle be fulfilled and that the Kaulikas knew the answers that the *Standartenführer* was obsessing over.

"Suddenly, and I can assure you that for the first time in the weeks that we were together, I saw all the Lopas smiling in unison. Yes, there was no doubt about it: they were looking at us and smiling! And after exchanging suggestive gestures of complicity among themselves, they were returning to observe us and laughing even harder. Finally they filled the tent with a chorus of uncontainable laughter.

"The stern countenance of the *ᛋᛋ* chief was showing stupefaction and mine must have shown something similar. Nevertheless, we both patiently waited for the Lopas to master the amusement that Von Grossen's question caused them, trying with hope to glimpse a positive answer in their astonished reaction.

" 'What do you think of this?' I said in German.

" 'I intuit that it's about you,' he enigmatically answered. 'I suppose they believe that you know how to follow Schäfer.'

"So it was. At the conclusion of the general hilarity, Von Grossen repeated the question: 'was there any way to find the Occidental expedition, now that they had already crossed the Boundary of Shambhala?' They again looked at each other, tempted to laugh, but at last one of the Kaulika monks took the floor:

" 'We do not mock you, although your question seems to be what you customarily call a *joke.* For it seems to us nothing but a joke to find out how one can follow something or someone in the Universe, when the one who asks it is accompanied by the master of the daiva dogs. Answer you, seriously, who could hide, and where would be such a hiding place, once the daiva dogs obey the order of the Son of Shiva and run after his steps?'

"Von Grossen didn't know how to respond and looked at me in the eyes with a hostile expression.

" 'I swear I didn't know!' I apologized, shocked at the possibility that he suspected that I was not wanting to follow Ernst Schäfer.

" 'Tell me what I must do and I will comply!' I indignantly shouted to the monks. 'Your Guru has given me no more information than an incomprehensible Yantra and only 60 days ago I had not even the remotest idea that the daiva dogs were existing. You explain to me how I should proceed to get that these beasts locate the German expedition.'

"Again the Lopas looked at each other, but their faces were now showing the usual indifference. The one who had spoken, and whom they were calling *Srivirya,* took the floor:

" 'Without a doubt you joke too, O Svami. For you must know better than anyone, you who are beyond Kula and Aku-la, how to direct the daiva dogs. And if you do not know it, or have forgotten it, it will not cost you much to learn or remember it by using the *Śrotra Karṇa,* the transcendent Ear of the Tulkus, with which you are endowed. Our Guru has revealed to you the svadi Kyilkhor, by means of which it is possible to form *any word or name of Created things;* and you know the *name* of your enemy. O Sahakaladai, Magic is Power: and words and names are the utensils of Magic. Reproduce the name toward whom you wish to direct the daiva dogs to with the magical language of the svadi Kyilkhor, and they will obey you.'

"Whether because he was really believing that it was a joke or some kind of test, or because he was not wishing to go on speaking on the subject, there was no way to obtain more information from the laconic Srivirya. His last words were:

" 'O Maheśvara, he who never argues, we fail to comprehend the reason that you have for confusing us with questions to which only you can know the answers. The Kaula Circle knows the Magic that enables the daiva dogs to exist, but no one who is not a Great Guru or a Tulku succeeds in mastering them with the mind, the only way by which they receive orders: they only listen to the Interior Voice of the Gurus and the Gods, those who are beyond Kula and Akula, those who are like Shiva; or *have his Sign, like you.* I was born in a Kaula Circle Monastery, and my father and grandfather were Kaulika Initiates; and neither I, nor my father, nor my grandfather, ever saw a Guru capable of speaking to the daiva dogs, until the Gods sent you to us. If you wish to confirm it, having known you makes us proud. But do not embarrass us further with questions that are proper to the Gods. We know of our weakness and confusion in the Hell of Maya and we do everything possible to remedy it. Believe us, O Kshatriya: some day we will emerge from the human misery into which the Spirit has sunk and be like you! We will then have the Śrotra Karṇa open, like you, and be able to know everything; and the Gods will reveal to us the secrets of Tantra; and the svadi daivas will obey us like you!

"We returned to the tent deeply impressed, although for different reasons. It was surprising Von Grossen that the fearsome Kaulikas softened in my presence and almost treated me like a God. To me, justly, that deference was causing me unconcealable displeasure, perhaps because I was not completely understanding what was occurring around me: since I was kidnapped by the Ophites, during my childhood, up to then, the phenomenon had occurred that certain particular men were perceiving in me, or because of me, a spiritual significance that was pulling them out from the material World and elevating them toward the most exalted summits of the Eternal, Infinite, and Uncreated Spirit. And that significance was coming from a Sign that was revealing itself in me, or through me, a Sign that the Ophites were calling 'of Lúcifer,' Konrad Tarstein, 'of the Origin,' and the Kaulikas 'of Shiva.' The particular men who were perceiving it, according to Tarstein, and coinciding as I now see with Belicena Villca, were sharing with me the common Origin of the Spirit and were carrying in their Pure Blood, unconsciously, the Symbol of the Origin. That is why they were perceiving the Sign of the Origin in me; in truth, they were not just now *finding out about* it, but they were then *recognizing* it, projecting it on me, and then turning it conscious, discovering the Presence of the Spirit in Themselves, revealing the Mystery of the Origin. But that significance that I was manifesting, and that those particular men were realizing, *was insignificant to me.*

"Strictly speaking, I should say *non-significant,* for the Sign was mattering very much to me in spite of not being able to comprehend it, of not being able to grasp its content with my conscious mind. And this intellectual impotence was the cause of the perturbation that was still causing me to see that certain particular men were perceiving it. I could tolerate it, as in the case of the Kaulika Pagoda, but I was always left unhappy with the experience.

"This time, to the perturbation of feeling transcended by the significance of the Sign, was added the effect of the incredible knowledge that the Kaulikas had about the Inner ear. How they learned that I was possessing that faculty, a product of the Führer's charismatic power, is something that I never found out. But the subject was fascinating to Von Grossen, his doubts dissipated after Srivirya's unusual explanation, and the matter of the Inner ear had not escaped him. As soon as we were settled in the tent, he asked at point blank:

" 'What the Devil is this Śrotra Karṇa, Von Sübermann?'

" 'I am sorry mein *Standartenführer,*' I said on the spot, and not without rudeness, 'but I cannot respond to that question. I will tell you, yes, that I will do all that I can to realize the Kaulika monks' idea. If it is true that the daiva dogs are capable of tracking Ernst Schäfer, you can be sure that we will find him. I will work from now on to find the solution of the problem, and I will use the Śrotra Karṇa if necessary. That is all I can say.'

"The eyes of Von Grossen sparked, but, as usual, he maintained his serenity and bothered me no more. Undoubtedly I could not talk to him, of the Inner ear, because Konrad Tarstein had taken my word that I would only do so with 'members of my own Circle'; and a sixth sense was loudly warning me that Von Grossen was not.

"That night, when all were asleep, I decided to 'use the Śrotra Karṇa,' that is, to communicate with the Voice of Capitán Kiev. Like the first time, as always, it did not take me long to be flooded with Wisdom. I thus realized that the bījas of the Yantra were not only allowing me to issue a set of fixed orders, as Guru Visaraga revealed to me, but that they were constituting an Alphabet of Power with which one could form 'any created thing's name': the Kaulikas, evidently, were knowing that property but were ignorant of the alphabetical key that was ordering the 49 bījas and making possible the codification of any word. However, it would not have been difficult for them to discover the Alphabet of Power by performing a cryptographic analysis of the 'command words' for the daiva dogs that were appearing in their magic formulas.

"Be that as it may, the truth is that the totality of the secret had been revealed to me. I was now knowing a symbol, similar to the plan of a labyrinth, which when applied over the Yantra was endowing the bījas with a certain order, the arrangement of which the formed words were to be adjusted to. I verified it several times with the Guru's 'command words' and, when I was sure of committing no errors, I applied myself to the task of translating the sentence *follow Ernst Schäfer*' into the language of the svadi Yantra.

Chapter XXX

y night the storm subsided and in the morning the sky was clear, without traces of it. Even the wind had completely ceased and the vāyu tattva was showing itself serene: a total silence was now reigning in the diminutive valley. The warm rays of Surya, the Sun, were just managing to melt part of the accumulated snow. But I was more radiant than the sun, for although I had not slept throughout the night, I was sure of having the solution to lead the daiva dogs in the footsteps of Ernst Schäfer, and that achievement was stimulating and overexciting me.

"Upon seeing me, Von Grossen did not need to ask anything to know that the problem was solved. He occupied himself, instead, with sending a Lopa to relieve the Gurkha and notify him of the location of our encampment; then he concentrated on studying the deficient maps of Tibet and West China. I spent the morning conversing with Oskar and the other 𝕊𝕊 officers, and at midday we had tsampa for lunch, a pot cooked by the monks, all together forming a large circle of fellow soldiers. The recent adventure had brought us closer to danger and death, and left, as a positive result, a healthy camaraderie that was reminding me of the days of the *Hitlerjugend*. Yes, I could even assure you, Neffe Arturo, that in those moments a carefree joy was overcoming us.

"It was already getting dark when arrived the Gurkha, the Lopas commanded by Von Grossen, the two Lopas that we left in Yushu, and the five Kalita porters with their yaks, the zhos, and the terrible Mastiffs. I don't believe that I ever in my life felt so content as on that occasion, upon getting back the daiva dogs. The arrival was much celebrated by the 𝕊𝕊 officers for, besides provisions, on the yaks were coming another fifty Schmeisser magazines and Luger bullets, just to replenish the ammunition expended against the Duskhas. The two Kaulika monks were bringing fresh news about the attack, picked up on the Chang-lam road.

"The whole region of Tibet was, apparently, shocked by the event. On the way, troops of a so-called 'Prince of Kokonor' had intercepted them, but after the received explanations, they permitted them to leave without problems. That incident was a consequence of the civil war: at some point in its history,

the country of Tibet was reaching as far as Lake Kokonor; subsequently, the Chinese formed the province of that name and
pushed the Tibetan border back further to the south of the
Yangtze-kiang River; and lately, after the incorporation of other small states, principalities, or Tibetan fiefdoms, they
formed the great province of Tsinghai.[55]

"At the beginning of the war between Japan and China, and
because of the absence of central power because of the occupation of the capital of the Celestial Empire, the Tibetans saw
the opportunity to regain their ancient Lordship and become
independent from China and rejoin Tibet. In that particular
case, the resurgent Prince of Kokonor was a fervent Buddhist
of the Tibetan Lubum tribe, whose members form part of the
lamaist aristocracy. His devotion and respect for the Dalai
Lama was knowing no limits, and the attack on the Duskhas
profoundly affected him: for such reason he sent several parties of armed men to search for the attackers.

" 'We are,' said the Lopas, 'servants of a rich merchant from
Bhutan, who are on our way to Sining to exchange his merchandise.'

"They were traveling with the consent of the Dharmaraja,
for whom they had to fulfill certain orders. And they showed
the Tibetan soldiers a letter from the Dharmaraja in which
was stating the list of objects to acquire.

"That was sufficient. The Lopas gave away a bottle of
Bhutanese *suja*[56] liquor and the soldiers provided an abun-
dance of information. 'You ought to be careful during the
journey because there was a gang of heavily armed bandits
who were operating in the Region. They had recently attacked
and destroyed a village of peaceful and Saintly lamas, so it was
clear that they were not Tibetans, not even religious people,
but undesirable foreigners. Unless they were members of the
clandestine Kaula sect, who were hating Buddhist or Hindu
lamas in general; but they would never have dared to go so far.
The surviving Duskhas were affirming to have been attacked
by the Asuras, but the soldiers were not so gullible and were
suspecting that the "Demons" would in reality be Western
bandits, aided by Chinese thugs. If they were right, the mis-
creants would attempt to return to China through the unde-

---

55. Also spelled *Qinghai.*

56. Fermented butter tea.

fined eastern border, which they were intending to guard from now on.'

"So they were looking for us and, as Von Grossen rightly predicted, we could not be seen for quite some time. The Kaulika monks had other news.

"Their contacts with members of the Kaula Circle enabled them to learn that a deep underground sympathy movement toward us was articulating throughout spiritual Tibet. Many were admiring that group of Initiates who were mercilessly killing the disciples of the Lord of Shambhala. It would be very difficult to return to Bhutan by the same route, but our Tibetan allies were guaranteeing us a safe escape through China to the Japanese lines. Japan was then in excellent relations with Germany, and a delegation of the ⚡⚡ Secret Service was actively operating in the German consulate in Shanghai, and if we could get there, we could embark without inconveniences. The Kaulika community in Sining would help us in that endeavor.

"But it was still premature to talk about leaving Tibet. First we had to find Schäfer and neutralize his plans.

" 'Are we ready to leave at dawn, Von Sübermann?' Von Grossen courteously asked.

" 'Jawohl, mein *Standartenführer!*' I responded with confidence.

"We left everything ready and, at dawn, we pitched our tents and set out. Von Grossen was expecting me to clearly indicate the course, but the only thing we could do would be to accompany the daiva dogs. I made him understand and situated myself in front of the column, taking the reins of the mastiffs with both hands. From the Infinity of the Spirit, beyond Kula and Akula, descended the order 'follow Ernst Schäfer' in the language of the svadi Yantra and penetrated into the Universe of Created Forms, passed through the Akasha tattva and implanted itself in the animic body of the daiva dogs. And the incredible animals, as if they were really sniffing a physical trace, stiffened and stretched their heads upward, and then departed like arrows heading north.

"We traveled several days in that way, always escorting the daiva dogs and these following the invisible tracks of the German expedition. At first Von Grossen did not make any objection, but then he began to be disquieted, to mistrust, and to openly insinuate the possibility that the dogs had gone astray.

In honor of the truth, I must say that he was not without reasons to doubt, for the erratic march of the mastiffs, which were either going toward the north, or toward the east, or returning to the south, or turning to the west, had completely disoriented him.

"His compass and maps were totally useless, he dramatically told me one day. 'We are lost in the heart of Tibet, in a place absolutely unknown to civilization! *Perhaps in a place that is not of this world!*' It was not that the rational Von Grossen had suddenly become superstitious: it was occurring that the daiva dogs actually led us along a route that was seeming not of this world. At that moment we were finding ourselves in an enormous valley, ornamented with regular vegetation and endowed with spring-like weather; everything was tranquil and perfect there: *only that that place could not exist where it was.* I observed a small bird perching in a tree, I saw a bush with yellow flowers, I took a faraway glance at a swift hare, and I understood that the circumstance had no explanation. It was only then that I became concerned and I conceded that Von Grossen's claims were right.

" 'Where the Devil are we?' I thought, while stopping the mastiffs with a mental order. Von Grossen was contemplating me with annoyance.

" 'At last you've realized the problem! For a while I have been warning you that something's wrong, but you don't listen to me. You don't listen to anyone. You only pay attention to your damn dogs. I don't deny that in all this there are supernatural events, events that perhaps I cannot or should not understand: I accept it and do not even attempt to change things. I know that the dogs will guide us along strange, illogical paths to reach those who also transit along a magical road. I know that and I do not seek to understand how they do it. But hear me well, Von Sübermann; can it not happen that, in this or in another World, the dogs become disoriented, go astray, lose track of Schäfer or follow a false trail? Can there not be, perhaps, other Magicians, our enemies, who interfere with their course?'

" 'Absolutely not!' I said to him, but now he was the one who was not listening.

" 'We've been marching for a week, supposedly toward Lake Kokonor, that is to say, toward the NE. Do you know what region we should be in?'

" 'Yes,' I reluctantly affirmed. 'In Tsinghai. This valley...'

" 'No, Von Sübermann! You know perfectly well that such a valley *doesn't exist in Tsinghai!* You're an *Ostenführer,* if I remember correctly; I read it in your file. That is to say that you know quite a bit about the geography of Asia. *We should be* in Tsinghai, and at times it was seeming that we were there, but *this is* definitely *not Tsinghai!* We don't even know if it's Tibet!'

"Karl von Grossen hysterically laughed and continued. I decided to wait for him to calm down.

" 'Look at the compass. Toward there is the east, from where we came. Remember the large lake that we saw yesterday with the binoculars, and that we agreed could be none other than Kokonor? Well, the eastern shore of this lake faces the Tsinghai valley, between the Nanshan[57] mountains to the north and the Kunlun mountain range to the south. Do you know the distance between the lake and the Kunlun mountains? If you want you can consult the map.

" 'Considering that the Kunlun range runs parallel from east to west, I believe that there are about 30 kilometers between the lake and its eastern end, the Amne Machin range,' he said from memory, 'and between the eastern edge and the western end of the Kunlun, the Altyn-Tagh range for example, there are instead about 1,000 kilometers.

" 'That's it!' he triumphantly confirmed. 'Now look to the south with the binoculars. Recognize those mountains, no more than fifteen kilometers away?'

" 'They're the Altyn-Tagh!' I exclaimed stupefied. 'The western end of the Kunlun mountain range!'

" 'And does it seem to you, Von Sübermann, that from yesterday to today we were able to cover 1,000 kilometers?'

" 'Nein!'

" 'Now you're being reasonable,' he approved. 'I'll tell you how far we walked, since I've made a precise calculation: *only twenty-five kilometers.* Understand? *We've united in only 25 kilometers two places that are normally separated by 1,000 kilometers.* What happened to the normal distance? Was it shortened? Be aware, Von Sübermann: *on the planet that we were born and we studied, Lake Kokonor is not 25 but 1,000 kilometers from the Altyn-Tagh Mountains. This place is Tibet and China at the same time!'*

---

57. Also known at the Qilian Mountains, which form the border between Kokonor (Qinghai) and Kansu (Gansu) provinces of northern China.

"Before that tangible reality, of finding ourselves facing the *Altyn-Tagh* Mountains, on the west of the Kunlun mountain range, the significance of the code name *Operationaltwesten*, which we were understanding as Operation Old West, was becoming unexpectedly clear: ingeniously, they had cut the Chinese word *Altyn* to form the German word *Alt*, old. But then, nearly at the end of the adventure, the true meaning was being realized: the ill-fated mission was actually called 'Operation *Altyn-Tagh*.' I foolishly thought of this, while Von Grossen was insisting on proposing the necessity of revising the Strategy of Operation First Key: he, who forced me a week before to use the power of the *Śrotra Karṇa* and to throw the daiva dogs on Schäfer's tracks, was now affirming the necessity of revising the Strategy itself: *Wahnsinn!*

"We began to talk apart from the rest of the caravan, but the three 🆚 officers were silently moving closer and we were now surrounded by them. Von Grossen sighed and paternally put a hand on my shoulder.

" 'Look at the Tibetans,' he indicated. 'Doesn't their expression seem unusual to you?' Indeed, here Von Grossen was not exaggerating: the attitude of the Kaulika monks was undoubtedly out of the ordinary. The natural and imperturbable tranquility had disappeared and I was noticing them nervous and alarmed. Those warriors, who did not hesitate in the face of an enemy a hundred times superior, were tirelessly looking in all directions, as if they expected that Satan himself was to rush up behind their backs! I did not notice it before because the dogs attracted all my attention, as Von Grossen reproached me.

"I inwardly cursed and just mumbled: 'It's curious...'

" 'Curious? It's incredible. You just noticed it, but they've been like this for a day. I attempted to find out what was going on but they've responded with evasions, but to you, whom they respect, they won't refuse to respond.

" 'I want to know what's going on, Von Sübermann!' he continued. 'Before continuing this insane journey I want to know what's going on: whether we are lost, or in another world, or even what's happening to the Tibetans, I want to know everything. I will not oppose resuming the march guided by the dogs, *but I believe it necessary that you reflect and be aware of what occurs in your surroundings.*'

"Evidently, my abstraction of the last few days had affected him. But Von Grossen was wrong. If he was wanting to find Ernst Schäfer, if he was intending that the daiva dogs obeyed the correct order, the worst error that he could commit, would be 'to be aware of what was occurring in the surroundings' and 'to reflect.' Precisely, the secret to control the dogs was consisting in the capacity to situate oneself *far away from all 'surroundings,'* outside of Space and Time, beyond Kula and Akula; and above all, it was required not to think, not to notice, *not 'to reflect.'*

"Without realizing it, the *Standartenführer* was wanting to force me to fall into Maya, the Illusion of the material forms that were filling our 'surroundings,' which was making up the context of the Great Deception. But he was a very cultured man, who was speaking about the Vril with fluency and demonstrating to comprehend the terms of the Spirit: Eternity, the Infinite, Absolute Freedom. How to explain to him, then, what he already knew? I opted to keep silent. I was not wanting to hurt him, for I could only attribute his forgetfulness of the basic principles of the Hyperborean Wisdom *to an intense sensation of terror.*

" 'I'll interrogate the Gurkha,' I proposed. 'It seems to me that it is he who has the greatest affinity with us.'

"Von Grossen agreed and we called him right away. As he supposed, Bangi did not refuse to respond to me.

" 'We are,' he said, 'in the "Valley of the Immortal Demons." Very close to here the Gate of Chang Shambhala is to be found. You have not developed psychic vision and that is why you do not see the Sanctuary of the Queen Mother of the West. But we approached it a day ago and we Kaulikas perceive it with greater clarity at every instant.'

"The Gurkha was pointing toward the Kunlun mountains. At times he was speaking in Khams Skad, and at times in English and German, which was demonstrating his perturbation.

" 'Yes: there is the shrine of Hsi Wang Mu, the Enemy of Kula!' he affirmed with a shudder. 'She is whom others call Dolma, Tara, Kuan Yin, and also Binah, the Mother of mortal men of mud. It is tradition that into this Valley of the Immortals only enter those whom She loves and wishes to preserve so that they worship Brahma, The Creator, and serve the King of the World, that is to say, only enter those who hate Kula, those who reject the Eternal Wedding with the Absolute Shakti, the non-men, the non-virile. Never has a Kaulika set foot on this path contrary to the *Tao, the Way, and the End at the Beginning;* never has a Kula Bridegroom trodden so wretched a path, opposed to Vrune Herself!

" 'You and the daiva dogs have led us to Hell, to protagonize, in physical body, the greatest challenge of this life. *She will try to convert us into animals, but we will fight here if necessary; for Shiva; and for you, Son of Shiva; and for your Führer, the Lord of Absolute Will. But, above all, we will fight because we know that you, who have guided us to the War against the Asuras, will not abandon us in Hell. You are a Warrior of Heaven and of Hell, a Man of Honor, and you will know how to get us out of here!'* Such conviction, it is obvious to clarify, profoundly impressed me.

" 'We're in Hell? Yes, we've come a long way,' Von Grossen commented with irony. 'It's possible then that the son of a bitch Schäfer is close by, since this is the most appropriate place for him.'

"Of course, no one imagined that Von Grossen's joke was corresponding to the strictest reality: the traitor and the German expedition were close, very close by. However, the journey was not resumed until the following morning, on my initiative. I was wanting everyone to rest and I looked for trivial excuses to justify the stop. I explained, to the no-longer-so-hurried *Standartenführer,* that I was needing to 'reflect' on what I saw and heard, and to review the orders of the daiva dogs. And I believe that for the first time on the journey, since Bhutan, everyone was internally grateful to have to miss a day at the Threshold of the Valley of the Immortal Demons.

"Camaraderie is not a quantifiable *bond,* a measurable *relationship,* a ratio between companions. It is not a mere affective nexus, like friendship, but a *spiritual coincidence, an identity of ideals that are simultaneously realized.* Camaraderie is determined by absolute instants: the time and space of the event; but it lacks an extensive temporal dimension; that is to say, camaraderie admits no category of duration, a permanent Comrade, like a friend, is inconceivable. Camaraderie produces Comrades of the act, of the coincident circumstance; it implies the encounter of two or several, in the same instant, with a common ideal that *is concretized.* Friendship, on the contrary, is temporally extensive and spatially limiting and encompassing; it consists in a thick sentimental nexus, almost measurable, which unites persons independently of the event in which they participate. Friendship is independent of any ethical norm because it springs from the heart, like every affective relationship. In camaraderie, on the contrary, Honor is always present. It is required not to question the moral conduct of a friend; it is an obligation, on the other hand, to observe the ethical attitude of a Comrade: *one could betray the Fatherland, with the help of a friend. But it is only possible to die for the Fatherland, with the help of a Comrade.*

"From the opposition between affective friendship and spiritual camaraderie, it emerges with clarity why the traitor manages to extend his treason in time, 'forever,' analogously to friendship, and why the hero must demonstrate his valor in the act of an instant, an instant that Honor, and the ethics of humility, oblige to subsequently forget: that instant of the hero, which implicitly carries all the valor in the act of its occurrence, is the absolute instance of the Comrades, the perfect coincidence of those who go to fight in favor of the same ideal. Because, and the clarification is evident, the instant of the hero is a time proper to Kshatriyas, to Warriors, that is to say, to Comrades.

"In a trench, a chief and ten soldiers are sheltered. Suddenly, a deadly grenade falls within. A soldier throws himself on it and cushions the explosion with his body: he has died but he has saved all the others; he is a *hero.* One must note, in this example, that the hero, in his absolute instance, is the *charismatic leader* of the group. Let us well observe: it is a professional army, there are hierarchies and military ranks, superiors and subordinates, chiefs and soldiers. However, this exterior organization, that superficial order, does not count in the face of the imponderable Death; the internal forces of the human order are impotent to oppose the solvent potency of Death. When the grenade falls, in the trench, only Death and the men who are going to die are real: in that instant of terror there are no superiors and subordinates, chiefs and soldiers, but men who are going to die. But someone decides to oppose Death with his body. He thinks in an instant and decides: he will stop Death, he will not let it pass beyond him. It is not a suicide: it is an act of giving one's life in favor of an ideal. 'I die so that they triumph.'

"First act: The grenade falls into the trench and the grenade is Death: in front of it, a group of men are going to die.

"Second act: A man rises from his own humanity and decides to 'die alone and save them,' 'so that they triumph.' And he who does so is neither a chief nor a soldier, for valor requires no hierarchy, but the hero. Here is the miracle: *a soldier seizes the absolute instance and stops being a soldier to become a hero. And there are no longer chiefs or soldiers, not even men who are going to die, but the hero and his Comrades.*

"His companions, chief and soldiers, are the Comrades who coincide with him in the act of Death. But, above all acts, is the objective of war, the warrior's ideal, the homeland or perhaps a national goal. The realization of the ideal necessitates, then, the event of life. Death, in that case, is the Enemy. Hence, to stop Death, to prevent it from taking the life of those who fight for the ideal, is an act of service to the ideal, outside all regulations. If it were not so, the hero's act would be a mere suicide and the survivors would save a meaningless life. But the life rescued from Death has a meaning: *the triumph of the ideal.* The hero throws himself on the grenade but clearly tells them all: *'I die so that you triumph,'* that is to say, 'I die so that we all triumph,' 'I die so that the ideal triumphs,' 'triumph!'; he does not say 'I give you my life.'

"And how does he tell them? *Charismatically.* They all hear him with the Blood; that is why they do not feel that they owe their life to the hero but that they must triumph, defeat the Enemy, *comply with his mandate.* So there is order? Yes, but not the artificial order of the military organization but the formality of the Mystique: in the instant of bravery, the hero is the *charismatic leader* of his Comrades and his last thought is an *order* that all will obey. An order given outside of the military hierarchy, unlinked from the chain of command, but endowed with greater force than any exterior disposition because it has been issued within each one, simultaneously with the explosion of Death. Under the Mystical form of the ideal, the Comrades have received, in a unique instant, the order of the charismatic leader, who is so because in that absolute instance he surpasses them all with the heroic valor of his act.

"Returning to the previous comparison, one can now better appreciate the difference between friendship and camaraderie: *friends can give us much, even all that they have; perhaps even give their life for us; but only Comrades will give us something greater than their lives, even greater than our own lives, this is, the ideal. Only a hero, or a Comrade, will believe in us as heroes or Comrades and order us to follow the ideal, will point us to the ideal, will reveal to us the ideal, will bring us closer to the ideal.*

"To be a friend is to be linked to someone else's heart. To be a Comrade is to be committed to an ideal; it means to take on, at the opportune moment, the absolute instance of the hero; if necessary, charismatically leading the Comrades, ordering the march toward the ideal, dying for the ideal. *'Germany, you will stand shining / Even if we go down / ... / Yes! Our banner means more than death!'*

"But heroes do not always have to die. A hero is also he who leads his Comrades in the absolute instant and leads them directly to victory. And they all follow him, persuaded, captivated, won over, because they charismatically know, with the Blood, that he has seen the ideal and proposes to realize it. Thus is fulfilled a universal principle of the Hyperborean Wisdom; *'one leads the Comrades and the ideal is realized.'*

"In our squad, military order was prevailing. There was a scale of command that was initiating in Von Grossen, continuing with me, proceeding with Hans and Kloster, and ending in Heinz; the Kaulika warriors also had their hierarchy, and their chiefs were receiving our directives.

"However, above the military organization, the common ideal of the Spirit, of National Socialism, of the Führer, was uniting us all. At a given instant, we were all Comrades, and then the absolute instance of the hero was able to occur. During the journey, and the attack on the Duskhas, the squadron functioned as a military corps and hierarchies and ranks were respected. However, when the sought objective became incorporeal, and Death and madness began to haunt us, and it was at last evident that neither Von Grossen nor anyone, except Me, would be able to get them out of that sinister 'Valley of the Immortal Demons,' the hierarchical order broke down and the charismatic coincidence took place: Me and the Comrades. They were all believing in me, expecting from me, trusting in me.

"The circumstance, it is clear, was requiring a hero and a leader. I was aware of it and *not willing to let the opportunity pass by.* That is why I was wanting that they rest before resuming the search for Ernst Schäfer: then there would be no more time. For, at that absolute instant, followed by my Comrades without hesitating, and in turn following the Path of Kula and Akula, we would throw ourselves into the Enemy's throat. We would die or we would triumph, but whichever the case, our death or triumph would signify for the Comrades of Germany the order of realizing the ideal, the victory of the Führer. 'We will die so that they triumph,' I was thinking, trembling with heroic resolution. The ideal? As Baldur von Schirach would say, the ideal consisted in 'our Banners.'

Chapter XXXI

From there, everything happened very rapid, and I will narrate it to you in the same way, Neffe Arturo.

"Early in the morning we were prepared to reinitiate the pursuit. The totality of the warriors readied their weapons, as if we were, at any moment, to fight a battle: the Tibetans checked their arrows and the blade of their knives, and, with one hand rested on the pommel of their scimitars, were awaiting the sound to march; the Germans provided themselves with magazines and stick grenades, and replaced the Mauser rifles with Schmeisser submachine guns. Although Konrad Tarstein's orders, identical to those that Von Grossen received from the SD, were requiring me to peacefully join Ernst Schäfer's expedition, I was doubting that it was now possible. And neither were Von Grossen and the other ⚡⚡ officers considering it possible. Not after having entered into that Valley of the Immortals, after having seen that paradisiacal region in the middle of the eternal snows, that oasis in the heights of Kunlun. Such a place could not exist without surveillance. And the guardians would not be willing to let us advance or retreat. Guardians who, we were sensing, would be terribly more dangerous than the Duskhas.

"We had barely entered on the Threshold of the Valley when we stopped and camped. If we were surveilled, the guardians of the Threshold would not take long to act; hence our preparations, the certainty that something was threatening us and we would have to confront it. We were looking for Schäfer, that was the principal objective, but then the reality was that we were in a Valley of Hell.

"'Nothing indicates to us that Schäfer has taken this course, much less that he has passed through here, but I believe that it now makes no difference whether we go forward or backward,' conceded Von Grossen. 'The truth is that this valley does not exist in our World: in any case, it makes no difference whether we go in one direction or the other!'

"The Kalita porters were refusing to continue. But neither were they knowing how to return, so it was necessary to separate again. The same two Lopas, monks of advanced age but equally dangerous, the yaks, zhos, and all the horses stayed with them. Although there was no snow anywhere, and the climate was spring-like, the peaks of the Kunlun mountains were looking too close to suppose that the horses were to be useful to us for long.

"In that way, we set out, the five Germans, the seven Lopas, and the Gurkha, Comrades of the Eternal Spirit, thirteen heroes in their absolute instance. I gave the mental order to the daiva dogs and they set off in the same direction that they were following the day before.

" 'There's no denying that you're persistent,' Von Grossen grunted upon seeing the course taken.

"But I was not having the time to attend to him or to anyone else. Kala, the Devouring Time, was now the Mrtyu Death in front of us, a definitive instant in which we would either die or triumph, with no middle ground. And in that instant of heroes, a Hero among heroes was being required, a leader who transmitted the charismatic order to fight for the ideal, 'for our Banners,' 'even if we have to die.' If the ideal was finally being realized, to die or to live was signifying an honor or a triumph, whichever was the case. None should be concerned with dying or living but with the realization of the ideal, the universal imposition of our Banners, the victory of our own Strategy. That was the charismatic order to my Comrades. To the daiva dogs I was commanding 'follow Ernst Schäfer' in the language of the svadi Yantra. And the dogs Kula and Akula were following the traitor's trail in a region that was neither on Earth nor in Heaven. And I was following the daiva dogs, beyond Kula and Akula. And my twelve Comrades were behind me, without any longer caring about anything that was surrounding them, without contemplating the possibility of dying or living, only thinking of the ideal, of the realization of the ideal, of the Final Victory of our Banners.

"Since we left the bivouac, the excitement of the mastiffs was increasing, as if their prey was getting closer and closer. They guided us with much confidence along several descending trails, until finding the bed of a torrential stream, the current of which was coming from the Kunlun mountains. For an hour, more or less, we marched parallel to its right bank, and the Kaulika monks, on several occasions, had to chop with their scimitars to clear a path through the dense thicket of thorns.

"Finally, we arrived at a magnificent 50-meter waterfall, and there we obtained the first proof that we were not going in the wrong direction. In front of us was standing the wall of a stone ravine 50 to 60 meters high, where the water of the stream was pouring down, and at the base of which were unmistakable signs of man's presence. In a small clearing there was a *mound,* one of those stone tumuli similar to the South American *apachetas,* which are formed in the 'sacred places' of Tibet by the addition that all the pilgrim lamas make of a stone painted with signs corresponding to bījas of the Kalachakra. In a niche excavated in the stone wall, was the motive for the mound: the sculpture of the Living Buddha *Maggogpa,* the Master King of Shambhala, Rigden Jyepo. They had depicted him seated in the lotus position, meditating, and in his hands, a tiny statuette of the Kakini Shakti was holding a bleeding Heart, in the center of which was the sign of the Star of David, the indicator of the Anahata chakra. The whole was corresponding to the Symbol of the Doctrine of the Heart, the Yoga of Love that all the aspirants who aspire to know the Kalachakra must practice. Its presence there was frankly threatening and intimidating: only those who were initiated adepts in the Doctrine of the Heart could continue the journey toward the Gate of Shambhala. Acceptance of such a condition was demonstrated by adding a stone with the name written in blood, to the tumulus mound.

"We only stopped for fifteen minutes in that place, as the mastiffs were spiritedly insisting on continuing the search and were requiring a superhuman effort to restrain them. During that time, my Comrades explored the site and discovered that several paths were coming and going: the daiva dogs, perhaps to shorten the way, led us through completely impassable areas. But it could be seen that that 'Gate of Shambhala' had been frequently visited, given the volume of the mounds, or at least for quite a few years.

" 'Von Grossen, Von Sübermann, look at this!' shouted Heinz Schmidt, who was entertained examining the stones of the mounds.

"He had a stone in his hand and held it out to me. I observed that it was appearing written in blood on two of its faces: one was illegible, for its signs were unknown to me, but the second inscription shook my heart: it was reading, in correct German: *Ernst Schäfer.*

"Without saying a word I passed it to Von Grossen and called to Srivirya and Bangi. 'Can you tell me what language this is?' I inquired.

"'It is *Senzar,* the sacred language of the Bodhisattvas of Chang Shambhala. The Arhat Djual Khul, who guides the Germans, must have revealed to them certain formulas of the Kalachakra to write on the stones,' explained Srivirya.

"And that was all that occurred there. Moments later the daiva dogs were climbing, two by two, the steps of a staircase carved in the stone, which was leading to the top of the ravine.

"Once the ascent was completed, one was gaining access to a wide terrace, at the edge of which was beginning the slope of a mountain belonging to the eastern end of the Altyn-Tagh system. The place was equally desolate, but with evident signs of human activity. In fact, we were all surprised by the presence of an imposing *Chorten,* a sacred Tibetan monument with a square base and a strangled body in the shape of a bell, usually topped with a truncated cone, on which top sits the image of a Deity. Placed on the upper cone of the Chorten, was standing out the horrible statue of a Goddess countlessly multiplied in herself and unfolded in hundreds of similar profiles: innumerable faces, legs, and arms, were converting her into a whirlwind of Presences, that is to say, they were undoubtedly signifying Her Omnipresence. The Goddess was expressing only one Aspect, tirelessly repeated: such an aspect, isolated, was showing her compassionately smiling at us while dancing on a bleeding Heart; she was wearing her hair loose and adorned with a Queen's crown, an eye in the middle of her forehead, and eyes in the palms of her hands and on the soles of her feet. She was delicately painted, and the predominant colors were white and blue: white body, blue garments.

"The Chorten was at least 15 meters high, and the statue of the Goddess was large enough to enable us to appreciate all its details. We Germans were observing it in silence, expressing with eloquent gestures the displeasure that it was causing us: 'Teuflisch!'

"The Tibetans were also contemplating it in silence. However, in an unusual act the Gurkha turned toward the group of ⚡️ officers:

"'The image of Kuan Yin, the Queen Mother of the West, impresses you? It equally impresses us, *but contemplating the Goddess herself* interested in the visitors of her millenary Sanctuary affects us much more. If you wish, I can translate for you in clear words what this humble Kaulika monk sees and feels when perceiving the Chorten of the Goddess of Mercy in the Valley of the Immortals.'

"We all accepted, without imagining how far the Kaulika monk's sharp vision could take us into the details of the hidden plot.

" 'Yesterday I told two of you that if you could see the subtle world you would verify that we were on our way to the Sanctuary of Hsi Wang Mu,' recalled Bangi. 'Today we have come a step closer to *Her, the Mother of the animal part of man.* But you still do not see her, *even though her presence is everywhere.* Her image impresses you? For what would become of you if you could lift the veil of Maya and contemplate Kuan Yin in all her Intelligence and Majesty, in her total *Merciful* Omnipresence? I will tell you: you would not be able to resist the Gaze of the Goddess of Animal Love, the Compassionate One of the Heart!

" 'And you would not be able to do so because hers is a gaze of many eyes, of hundreds of eyes, of millions of eyes, which observe the heart of man, or jīva, waiting for him to approach and identify himself with his atman, the Divine Archetype created by Brahma in the likeness of Himself. And for that the Kakini Shakti makes her voice heard in the anahata-shabd sound, and says *"om mani padme hum,"* "O Thou, jewel that is in the lotus," "O Mother that is in the chakra," "O Devi, that is in the Anahata chakra." And if the jīva hears this mantram, and recites it as anahata japa, he converts himself into Jīvātman; and *he also receives the kalagiya, the signal to enter Chang Shambhala and join the White Brotherhood.*

" 'At each point of actual Space there is a small archetypal globe or atom, which symbolizes with exactitude the unity of Brahma, The Creator. And in the center of each one of such atoms, there is an eye with which The One contemplates Himself from all created things. Each eye of the One Father is called *Yod,* but each pupil belongs to the Mother Kuan Yin. When the blood of man is stigmatized by the Lords of Karma, and pain penetrates the eyes of The One like a pleasant symphony, the pupils of Mother Kuan Yin soften the suffering chords with the Mercy of Her Heart. That is why She is *Avalokiteśvara,* a Bodhisattva of Compassion. Yes, Western *Kameraden:* this image that impresses you is just a dim reflection of

Kuan Yin behind the Veil of Maya. Right here, at this moment, the Goddess dances the Dance of Life and her countless eyes gaze into your Hearts seeking the warmth of Love! Kuan Yin wants to feel Your Hearts palpitating with Love for created things! She wants to feel you shudder with compassion for the pain that scourges the life of man, the pain caused by those who deviate from the harmony of the Universe, from the Law of The One! And what do the eyes of Avalokiteśvara pick up on in Your Hearts? Only Cold and Hate, instead of Warmth and Love of Life. And then the eyes of the Mother withdraw enveloped in tears, promising to help you so that you return to the animal condition, to the warm Heart of those who love the tepid Life. She is the Mother of the animal-men, of the Paśus: Her Mercy will reach you and warm your Heart with her Love, dislodging the Cold and the Hate, the hard ice! And do it she will, even if she has to spin the Kalachakra and convert you into primitive simians!

" 'But here, with you, is Ganesha, the Son of Shiva, whom you call Kurt. What has the Mother Goddess of the West seen in the Heart of the Son of Shiva? Also Cold and Hate, but forming the nest for the mask of the Cold Death, the refuge of Kaly, the Black One. Yes, in the Son of Shiva is the greater abomination, for he has harbored Death in his Heart, the Mask of Death that hides the Naked Truth of the Infinite Blackness of Himself. In the Heart of Ganesha, on the dead body of the Paśu, son of Mother Kuan Yin, Kaly the Black One dances the Dance of the Cold Death; and on the cadaver of the Paśu, which is carrion, is still living the phallus of Shiva, the diamantine lingam of Vajra: facing the symbol of absolute virility, Kaly unveils Herself and lets manifest Parvati Frya, the Truth behind the Black Death; Parvati Frya then performs the yonimudrā on the lingam of Shiva, and Bhairava resurrects in the Heart of the Son of Shiva; a Child of Vajra was abnormally born in the Heart of Ganesha! A child engendered by the Spirit of Shiva with the Truth behind the Mask of Death! A child gestated in the womb of the Infinite Blackness of Himself! A child born in the broken vulva of the dead Heart of the Paśu! A Child of Vajra, a Child of Diamond, a Child of Stone, a Child of Lightning, a Child of Cold Fire, *a Child God!* A Child who is the Uncreated Vrune and who is beyond Kula and Akula, beyond Time and Space, beyond Life and Death, beyond Good and Evil, *definitively beyond the Paśu killed by Kaly in the Heart of the Son of Shiva!*

" 'The millions of eyes of Avalokiteśvara have seen a very great evil in the Heart of the Son of Shiva. An evil for which neither Her Tears of Mercy, nor Her Compassion, nor Her Love are enough. An evil for which there is no redemption possible, neither in this nor in another life of the Sridpai Khorlo Wheel of Life.

" 'It is the evil of that one who flees the care of his Father and Mother, who disowns his Father and Mother, who discovers that he has no Father or Mother, who encounters the Naked Truth of Himself and insists on Being what He Is and not what He ought to be according to the Law. Oh what ingratitude of the one who thus cools the Heart to the Mother and harbors hatred against the Father! The Naked Truth has installed itself in the Heart of man, on a bed of ice, and he has converted himself into a Virya, into a God who competes with the One God. But She has cooled the Heart because She is the Enemy of Love and the Mother Kuan Yin cannot permit it. The Enemy of Love has caused much harm: with the Mask of Kaly, She has murdered the Paśu, Her firstborn son; and with the Power of the Naked Truth, She has procreated an abominable being who was born on the cadaver of the Paśu, a Diamond Stone Child, a child who is not and never will be human. Great is the harm caused by the Enemy, Terrible the evil that nests in the Heart of the Son of Shiva.

" 'It is the duty of the all-seeing Mother Kuan Yin, whose Mercy reaches out to all, to protect her animal-man children. Because her children, of Warm Heart and cold mind, are like sheep in the flock: they depend on the Shepherd and his staff. And because the Children of Stone, of Frozen Heart and hot mind, are like hungry wolves: they stalk the flock to kill the lambs, and only flee before the Shepherd's staff.

" 'What has the Mother Goddess of the West seen in the Heart of the Son of Shiva? A wolf, a slayer of lambs, a Child of Stone Son of Himself and Bridegroom of Naked Truth, an abominable Tāotiè Existence outside of Creation. But, above all evils, Kuan Yin has seen the one who can manifest the Naked Truth to the World, discover the Forbidden and Inebriating Beauty of the Enemy of men and propagate the evil of Wisdom like an epidemic. To the eyes of Mother Kuan Yin, the Son of Shiva is the Demon of Man's Destruction. The Naked

Truth that Ganesha can exhibit to sleeping men will cause in them a new and atrocious fall into the nothingness of the Un-created. Upon the ruins of the Humanity of Love, Ganesha transformed into Shiva, will dance the dissolution of the Cre-ated, the decomposition of Maya, the Final Death of Illusion. And in the Pralaya of Love and Mercy of Kuan Yin, upon the Death of Humanity, in the Götterdämmerung of the Brother-hood, the resurrected Heroes, the semi-divine Viryas, the God-Men, will exalt the Naked Truth of Himself, the Enemy of Love, the Spouse of the Origin. Oh, how the millions of Aval-okiteśvara's eyes weep upon realizing the evil that inhabits the Heart of the Son of Shiva!

" 'But Kuan Yin knows that the evil of Ganesha is too great to be forgiven. No; for Kurt von Sübermann there is no possi-bility of negotiation, for his Presence is humiliating to the dig-nity of the Bodhisattvas, his Presence that shamelessly exposes the Naked Truth of the Origin! No one who is on the side of The One, of Brahma, The Creator, will accept such an affront! And it will once again be the Merciful One, who speaks in the Heart of the Son of Shiva and announces to him the decision of the Gods. Thus speaks the Mother Goddess Kuan Yin into the Heart of the Son of Shiva, Kurt von Sübermann!

> As a wolf, thou wilt slay my sheep.
> As a Child of Stone, Tāotiè,
> then into wolves like thee wilt thou turn them.
> For thee there shall be no compassion!
> Serene is my loving Heart,
> dry are my many eyes!
> Monster of the Forbidden Truth
> that transmutes human Peace:
> the decision is made!
> Whither thou hast come thou shalt go!
> Out of the Path of Man thou shalt go!
> Fierce wolf, thou shalt not lie in wait for my sheep!
> Naked Truth of the Origin
> to sleeping men
> thy Sign thou shalt not reveal!
> For thou art eternal,
> though thou knowest it not, Ulfheðnar,
> thou shalt not die;
> but if thou wilt transit
> the Path of Man,

to the World of Man
thou shalt never return!
To my Sanctuary on Earth
thou shalt not enter!
I am the Mother of Mankind!
I am the attentive Shepherdess,
and I watch over my flock
with zeal without equal!
He who arriveth here seeketh Immortality!
He is the one who hath passed all trials
and is a lamb in my pen;
he is the one who hath offered a tender Heart
to Avalokiteśvara;
he is the one who loveth and suffereth,
who followeth his Dharma,
who is a perfect animal-man;
he who cometh to my Sanctuary
and goeth to worship the Father!
To him I grant Immortality!
To him I guide toward the Brotherhood!
But thou, who art a wolf in the guise of a lamb,
what dost thou come to seek?
Bearer of the Black and Cold Death,
in thine Heart of Ice,
the Hidden Enemy goeth.
The Gods cannot punish thee,
but neither do they wisheth to see thee any more.
There is no place for wolves on this property!
Through my sutratma of Mercy
the lycanthrope shall not transit!
Here I am Kuan Yin, Chenrezig,
the Goddess of the Bottom of the Sea!
I guard the Path of the Deva Yana
for the Immortals of the Brotherhood!
Thy sin of Frya Stone
hath offended mine eyes of goodness,
and I have cut thee off from the path
toward the Brotherhood.
For thine abominable evil
today I have closed
the Gate of Chang Shambhala!
I am Palden Dorje Lhamo!

"We were all left astonished and surprised by the monk's words, He was calling that 'translating his impressions of the Chorten,' when it was seeming that the Goddess Kuan Yin herself had spoken to us! Undoubtedly, Bangi was possessing a superior faculty that was enabling him to see and hear the Bodhisattvas. But I was the one most altered by that vision, for I was discovering in it aspects that were closely touching me, significances that were of interest to Operation First Key, concepts that were taking on meaning within the framework of my own Strategy. The Gurkha, in effect, had transmitted a message to me, although whether he did it consciously or unconsciously was unclear.

"In synthesis, what the Gurkha said, and that no one was able to then understand except me, was that *my presence in the Valley of the Immortals was forcing the Demons to close the Gate of Chang Shambhala,* just as Konrad Tarstein was expecting to happen. That is to say, that if Ernst Schäfer had not yet succeeded in getting through, his Operation *Altwesten* would be definitively suspended, because the Goddess Kuan Yin 'was saying in my Heart': 'the decision is made,' 'today I have closed the Gate of Chang Shambhala.'

Chapter XXXII

It was midday when we left the Chorten. The daiva dogs were demanding to climb the western slope of one of the Altyn-Taghs, but we soon discovered a concealed path that was enabling us to ascend about a thousand meters. Four tiring hours later, we arrived at the summit of the mountain, verifying that to the north, the mountain was falling thousands of meters in a vertical wall: from the base, a vast desert-like plain was extending in all directions, except to the NW, where we were sighting the blue waters of a lake of enormous surface.

" 'Teufel!' exclaimed the efficient Von Grossen. 'We have the fortune of contemplating the country from a privileged terrace of 4,000 meters. What we see, in all its expanse, is the Chinese province of Sinkiang; that plain, is none other than the Taklamakan Desert, which is connected with the Mongolian Gobi Desert at its eastern end; and the lake, with all precision, is the Lop Nor. At last a geographical area that conforms to the reality of the German maps!'

"But, if the World outside of the Valley of the Immortals was still the same, in its interior Space and Time were as distorted as before, the Traitorous Gods and the Priests of the White Brotherhood were lying in wait to block our way or attack us, and we still had to locate Ernst Schäfer. The latter occurred ahead of schedule. Effectively, while we were observing Sinkiang in awe, the Kaulika monks explored the hundred square meters of the summit and within minutes brought shocking news: at the foot of the southern slope was an encampment! We ran there and verified it with the binoculars. There was no room for doubt: it was the German encampment!

"The small ravine, which looked more like a gorge, was about 500 meters long and 50 meters wide, and in winter was fulfilling the function of transporting the snow of a gigantic glacier, like a titanic stone channel. It was oriented from east to west, and at each end, two passes were allowing entry or exit: from within, it could be observed that the western pass was flanked by the sculptures of two enormous armed bodhisattvas. For some reason, the expedition did not dare to cross that eloquently ornamented stone portal, and decided to camp at the opposite end of the ravine, next to the entrance pass. It could be seen that they were already a few days in that place, and that perhaps they were thinking to stay longer, since they had unpacked all the equipment and rationally distributed it, after a rigorous castrametation: they were even making use of two sentinels, one to the east and the other to the west of the camp.

"For the long-cherished moment of encountering Schäfer's expedition, Von Grossen had drawn up a plan of approach to which only tactical details were needing to be added according to the circumstances. Given the present case, it was only necessary to confirm the positions and functions of each one so that the squad was ready to execute the plan.

"Accordingly, we descended in silence to the entrance of the ravine, the site in which the path of the summit was leading. Already there, Von Grossen, Oskar Feil, the Gurkha, and I, with the daiva dogs, remained hidden for a few minutes, while the three ⚡⚡ officers and the eight Lopas monks, were deployed around the encampment. They were to stand guard and cover our next advance, in anticipation of a misunderstanding or something going wrong.

"Without suspecting anything, the sentinel was smoking, distracted by his own thoughts, perhaps remembering his distant Fatherland. The three Germans suddenly appeared in front of him and he believed himself to be dreaming. But it was too late to react, especially when seeing the black muzzles of the Schmeisser: the Luger, the dagger, and the MP 40 submachine gun passed into Von Grossen's hands.

" 'We are officers of the Third Reich,' Von Grossen explained, 'but we can't take chances. Heil Hitler! Now approach the encampment, very slowly, and report our arrival!'

" 'Heil Hitler!' responded the troubled sentinel.

"With exquisite delicacy, he was peeking into each of the six tents and communicating to their occupants what was occurring. Many, possibly, must have supposed that the sentinel was delirious.

"In seconds, 20 or more men were assembled, but one was not able to distinguish who was officer or non-commissioned officer because they were all dressed in civilian clothes. One of them let out an exclamation and took several steps closer:

" 'I know you! You're *Standartenführer* Karl von Grossen! What the Devil are you doing here, in the armpit of Tibet?'

" 'And I know who you are, *Standartenführer Reinhart Von Krupp*,' mischievously replied the always well-informed Von Grossen, remarking on the officer's rank and name. From his years in the Gestapo, Von Grossen was keeping the bad habit of putting a certain suggestive emphasis when naming persons, implying that he was possessing confidential or compromising information about them.

" 'We are here to...' Von Grossen was going to continue, when he was interrupted by the appearance of Ernst Schäfer.

"It is possible, and even more, very probable, that Schäfer had irreversibly lost his mind when finding himself before that unexpected spectacle. To understand this, it is necessary to imagine what it would be like for him to have arrived at the Valley of the Immortals, a step from the Sanctuary of the Queen Mother of the West and the Gate of Chang Shambhala, and to see that in place of the Arhats was appearing a group of Germans, one of them his sworn enemy. And along with this one, inexplicably, was the propitiatory victim, Oskar Feil, and the missing Gurkha.

" 'Ahahahah...!' he gave a demented shriek and cried out, 'Shoot, kill them all!'

"The ⚡⚡, officers and troops, raised their rifles but waited for their *Standartenführer* to confirm the order: Schäfer was an officer of the Abwehr and had no direct command over the Schutzstaffel. That indecision prevented an armed confrontation of unforeseeable consequences.

" 'They are Germans, ⚡⚡ men!' tried to explain Von Krupp, who was stunned by Ernst Schäfer's hallucinatory attitude.

"But the latter had already drawn his Luger and was aiming at me, with the manifest intention of eliminating me from the world of the living.

"He did not manage to shoot. In a swift movement, two of the ⚡⚡ men of his expedition rushed at him and took him hostage: one snatched his pistol and held him, while the other was holding a dagger to his throat. They were the two spies of the SD!

" 'At the first one who moves, we'll cut this man's throat!' threatened one of them. 'Come closer, mein *Standartenführer*, and disarm those four!' he added, pointing at Schäfer's henchmen.

"Von Grossen did not wait long and shouted several orders. To the general surprise, Hans and Kloster emerged from among the rocks and quickly stripped the four, who put up no resistance, of their weapons. Six figures, vested in saffron-colored tunics and with their faces and hands covered with ashes, attempted to flee in the direction of the western exit of the ravine, but they fell a few steps away riddled with arrows: they were the Kushok of the Jafran Ashram and their lamas. That was the last straw. Von Krupp bellowed an order in turn and all his men took to the ground; and it was not long before the confrontation began again.

"Von Krupp's squadron was double ours in number. However, common sense prevailed and the *Standartenführer* angrily interrogated Von Grossen:

" 'What is this, Von Grossen? You show up here, treat us as if we were enemies, and kill our Tibetan guides, who were counting on our protection. I imagine that you have a good justification for this outrage!'

" 'We have nothing against you, but against that gang of traitors,' Von Grossen vociferated. 'And if it seems to you sufficient justification, here are our orders, approved by the Führer.'

"He extended him a wax-sealed envelope that was reading: *'Operationaltwesten.'* Reinhart von Krupp tore it open and took out the letter. It was a decree of brief text. He affirmatively shook his head and commented to Schäfer:

" 'They have come from Germany to take charge of the expedition! From this moment on, *Standartenführer* Karl von Grossen is in charge of security and logistics.'

"Schäfer's face was looking whiter than the snow on the Altyn-Taghs. Von Krupp said in a tone sufficiently loud enough so that everyone heard him:

" 'It's fine by me. I accept the orders and put myself under your command. But you will have to explain to me what your accusation of treason means. And how it is that Oskar Feil happens to be with you.'

"The ⚡⚡ men eased the pressure of the knife. Von Krupp's men halted and lowered their rifles, while Heinz and the eight Kaulika monks were approaching, the latter with arrows still nocked on their bows.

" 'Treason!' cried the traitor, out of his mind. 'Treason! Damn murderers, you don't know the damage that you've caused to Germany and to Humanity! Ahahahah...! Von Sübermann, son of the Devil, I knew that you were intending to impede our mission! You've come to destroy us: we should have killed you in Germany! For your sin I will be punished: the Masters will never pardon me for your condemned presence in this Sacred Valley! When the Arhat Djual Khul left, I should have imagined that something terrible was happening! It was you!! You and your execrable Mark that offends the Holy Beings!

" 'Damned, a thousand times damned Von Sübermann, spawn of Hell, how did he find me?!' he roared, completely enraged. The two *SS* spies were holding him by the arms to prevent him from throwing himself onto me.

" 'Despicable *Herr Lehrer,* the last thing that I had wanted in my life was to see you again,' I affirmed with sincerity. 'The merit of getting this far is the exclusive work of these noble canines.'

"I then let go a little of the rein on the daiva dogs, which were still obeying the order to 'fetch Ernst Schäfer,' and the mastiffs jumped up and took two fierce bites just centimeters from his neck.

"With his eyes bulged with terror, his face distorted by anger, Schäfer was the image of madness.

" 'You see: *only an infernal being could come accompanied by the wolves of Wothan!* Do not accept that decree Von Krupp, and kill them all. There is still time to avert a terrible evil for Germany and the world. I assure you that nothing will happen to you if you listen to me. Or rather, I guarantee that you will be decorated as a hero.'

" 'You're mad, Schäfer: in Germany there is no one superior to the Führer! If I don't carry out these orders the only decoration that I'll receive will be a hemp rope with a noose,' Von Krupp excused himself.

" 'No, Comrade Von Krupp,' I clarified; 'these are not the words of a madman but those of a traitor. He does believe that there are men more powerful than the Führer: they are those who plan the demise of the Third Reich and have entrusted him with a secret mission that will help to consummate the treason. And as for you, *Herr Lehrer,* it is certain that Kula and Akula are not the wolves of Wothan, although it is true that I come from a Hell and now I am in a greater Hell; but these dogs, like Cerberus, will prevent you from reaching the worst of the Hells, the one behind that Gate at the end of the ravine, that is, your beloved Chang Shambhala, the lair of the Immortal Demons.'

" 'Blasphemy! Blasphemy! Kill them, Von Krupp! Kill them now and you'll save your Soul! Kill them before it's too late and they release Lúcifer into the World!' he was imploring, already completely losing control of his words.

"Von Grossen ordered that they lock him in a tent, under the custody of Hans and Kloster. It was already beginning to get dark and the Kaulika monks hurried to put up the tents, before the astonished gaze of Von Krupp's squadron. The latter approached us and asked without much delicacy:

" 'Can someone explain to me what is going on? I was supposed to conduct and protect a scientific expedition that was aiming to investigate the Oriental ancestors of the Aryan Race. Nothing to do with what I am hearing: "Demons," "Hells," "treason to the Third Reich." What does all this madness mean? How can one betray the Third Reich in this remote place? And the most incredible thing, where did they find Oskar Feil? How did they follow us? What is that about the wolves of Wothan?'

"For half an hour, Karl von Grossen clarified as best he could all of Von Krupp's doubts. At the end, the latter posed a question to which Von Grossen had no answer.

" 'And what will we do now?'

" 'My orders,' Von Grossen revealed, 'specify that upon making contact with the expedition I must act according to the instructions of *Sturmbannführer* Kurt von Sübermann. And since you must obey me, I will save myself the trouble of relaying such instructions to you if we are both aware of them at the same time,' he concluded with overwhelming logic. 'Well, Von Sübermann, what have you to tell us?'

" 'That we have to go back to Germany immediately!' I said without hesitation. 'Tomorrow we must embark on our return. We will put Ernst Schäfer and his four accomplices under arrest, but if they resist, we will execute them on my watch.'

"Karl von Grossen unreservedly approved of this decision, but the most relieved was Von Krupp.

" 'That's it? Back to Germany? That's the best news I've heard in over a year. I feared that you would request to continue the exploration of Tibet. I totally support that proposal! The truth is that I was already fed up with Ernst Schäfer and his mysteries.'

"Poor Von Krupp! Neither Von Grossen, nor I, then imagined that he would never return to Germany...

Chapter XXXIII

I wouldn't be able to assure you, Neffe, if the first thing that we perceived was the sound or the light, *or the unmistakable sweet and penetrating smell of sandalwood smoke,* or if we sensed both tattvas at the same time.

"Von Krupp's men were already sheltered in the tents, except for two sentinels. The Gurkha and the Lopas were finishing pitching our tents helped by Heinz. And the two *Standartenführers* and I were still talking. The sun had long since set and the dying twilight was rapidly giving way to the freezing night of the Tibetan peaks. However, in an instant, the ravine began to illuminate from the western exit, as if we witnessed the dawning of a new and dazzling Sun.

"Perplexed, stunned, hypnotized, the three of us were staring at the ball of light, which was crossing the gorge and advancing through the center of the ravine, no more than a hundred meters high. Although the halo was extending tens of meters around the glowing nucleus, it was possible to distinguish that the center was comprised of four incandescent spheres, eccentrically intersecting each other. But such an observation was only for a second, because the sound that was accompanying the resplendent apparition immediately prevented us from any other perception.

"At least for me, who spent my childhood on a farm in Cairo where honeybees were being kept, that vibration was clearly familiar: *it was the classic buzzing of a swarm in movement.* It had started as a faint buzz, just as the light was at first a soft glow, but soon became unbearable. I believe that the three of us covered our ears with our hands, to find in desperation that nothing was able to stop the sonorous penetration. With my head in my hands, and my brain drilled by the murderous wave, I fell to my knees completely dazed.

"I felt that I was going to lose consciousness and, in a supreme effort of will, I looked around me. I saw Von Grossen, still standing, convulsing and screaming, while just a few centimeters away from me was lying the inert body of Reinhart Von Krupp. I automatically put my hand on his neck, looking for a pulse, but I realized that he had ceased to exist. My mind was becoming clouded; an intense dizziness was causing me the sensation that everything was spinning around me; nausea, initiated in my stomach, shook me into a violent retching; and a growing anguish in my heart, which was already a declared tachycardia, produced in me the impression that that organ was wanting to jump out of my chest and flee. Finally, victim of a psychophysical attack, for which I was knowing no defense whatsoever, I was irremediably fainting. Laughter of the Demons, Music of the Infernos, Harmony of the Creator God of the Universe, in front of that disintegrating force of the Soul, what was left of the Hero, of the charismatic leader, of the Initiate who hours before was leading his legion ready to fight against enemies of Earth or Heaven? Very little, Neffe, very little. Barely a spark of will.

"Suddenly I was seized by a severe tremor, and it took me a while to realize that Bangi had grabbed me by the shoulders and was firmly shaking me. Through the haze, I recognized him shouting before me at the top of his voice; the eight Lopas were also there: two were dragging Oskar Feil; two others were holding Von Grossen; one was running with the daiva dogs, which were tied at one end of the encampment; and the rest were feverishly drawing circles and signs on the ground with their scimitars, while chanting mantrams and adopting warlike mudras. The ball of light was already above us and the buzzing of the bees reached its maximum intensity. Whether it was because of Bangi's shaking, or the effect of the Lopas' yantras, the truth is that I regained some lucidity; enough to understand the Gurkha's dramatic words.

" '*Shivatulku! Shivatulku!*' he was impatiently calling, still shaking me, an act that culminated in two impetuous slaps. With a nod of my head I made him understand that I was hearing him.

" 'O Pawo:[58] get us out of here! Soon or the *Vimāna* of Shambhala will destroy us!'

" 'H... how? How will I, if I cannot stand?' I despondently stammered.

" 'The daiva dogs. O Druptob![59] Order the daiva dogs to *fly* you to a destination outside of here! Do you understand me?'

"I nodded, despite not totally understanding the Gurkha's request.

---

58. Hero or "brave one."

59. Siddha or "great adept."

" 'What should I do to make the daiva dogs *fly?*' I absurdly interrogated myself, but in a voice loud enough so that Srivirya responded. The Lopa, was evidently attentive to my reactions.

" 'Name them as if they were identical to Kyung, the Garuda bird that transports the Gods; or as Lungta, the Pegasus horse that fulfills the same function! Name them, *Svadi-lung;* Kula and Akula, *Svadi-lung;* and *they will fly!'*

"Destination? What destination? My head was seeming like it was going to explode. Perhaps it was the unconscious, perhaps the Śrotra Karṇa, but the positive thing was that an Interior Voice said to me:

" 'Sining, you must go to Sining,' I thought on the Yantra, imagined it as best I could, and translated, *'To Sining, Kula and Akula Svadi-lung.'*[60]

"Some of the Lopa had put the reins of the mastiffs in my hands. They were enraged by the presence of the diabolical vimāna and were howling as if they were indeed the wolves of Wothan. When I imagined the Yantra they stiffened and threw their heads forward, prepared to depart in fulfillment of the order. And when I ordered 'To Sining, Kula and Akula svadi-lung,' the incredible wonder happened that the daiva dogs jumped into a kind of abyss that was unusually being created in front of them.

"I felt myself pulled by the reins, hoisted into the air and transported in a direction to the east, plunged into an impenetrable blackness that was now occupying the place where seconds before were the Altyn-Tagh mountains. Upon being lifted into the air, an abnormal weight in my legs put my body under tension for an instant. I turned, startled, and noticed a human chain was dangling from my extremities: the Tibetans had performed a series of *tackles* at the moment of the jump, grabbing each other and also lifting Karl von Grossen and Oskar Feil. My gaze slid downward and I stupidly contemplated the ravine illuminated by the vehicle of Shambhala and the encampment converted into a collective sepulcher: Reinhart Von Krupp, dead; the sentinels, dead; and at the entrances of the tents, were scattered the cadavers of those who managed to get out but did not get very far. The buzzing was deafening, terrifying, paralyzing; the buzzing was the call of Death!

---

60. *"Let us fly to Sining, Kula and Akula."*

Heinz, Hans, Kloster! I remembered my Comrades and I believe that I screamed with helplessness, before plunging into the blackness and losing consciousness.

THE HISTORY OF KURT VON SÜBERMANN

Chapter XXXIV

econds later I regained consciousness: no sign of the deafening sound or the diabolical gleam. The twilight was still subsisting, so I could see, without any doubt, that we were in a completely different place from the ravine where Schäfer camped. All that occurred, the attack of the deadly buzzing and the escape thanks to the daiva dogs, immediately came to my memory. By a miracle, I was still alive! But where was I? Because that was evidently not Sining, but the bank of a river, a short beach at the foot of a hill.

"I was seated on the ground, still holding in my hands the now inert reins of the daiva dogs. Centimeters from my feet, the murmuring river was intoning Nature's melody. A glow against the hillside showed me the Lopas gathering wood and stoking a makeshift campfire. Karl von Grossen and Oskar Feil had stopped and were contemplating the scene in silence, as if stunned. When the eyes of the *Standartenführer* met with mine, he reacted:

" 'Von Sübermann: Gott sei Dank! Where are we? What became of the others?'

"I sat up and responded to him with raw frankness:

" 'I don't know. I don't know what this place is. Surely we're very far from the encampment, but at least we're still alive, because if there's one thing I'm convinced of, it's that those who didn't come with us must've died in the ravine. Who could survive that attack by the Demons? Even the Kaulika monks, who are experts in such kind of Black Magic, were fearing inevitable death!

"At that moment, the three of us remembered the monks and looked for them with a glance: the eight of them were standing by the fire that they had lit under the shelter of some enormous rocks, and they were observing us in turn with tranquility. Karl and Oskar approached them. I wanted to do the same, but the reins prevented me from doing so. With horror, I discovered that one of the mastiffs had died; the other stood at its side, emitting periodic groans of pain.

"If I was owing my life in this world to anyone, other than my parents, it was to those dogs, so I was understandably moved by the loss of one of them. I let the survivor continue its woeful howls, a disconsolate requiem for the absent partner, and approached the group. Without courtesy, I addressed Srivirya:

" 'How is it that one of the daiva dogs has died? Had not Guru Visaraga assured me that both were constituting an archetypal couple, the manifested synthesis of a pair of opposite principles, the existence of which must *necessarily* be simultaneous? If that was true, shouldn't they both have died? Or, rather, why aren't they both alive?'

" 'Have patience, Son of Shiva,' the monk compassionately advised, 'and remember that these dogs are tulpas, mental creations of the Magicians of the Kaula Circle. Therefore they are not subject to natural laws but to the Will of the Gurus. I told you a few days ago that, although our Order knew the secret of the daiva dogs, they had never been projected until now because there was no Initiate like you, capable of controlling them beyond Kula and Akula. Therefore, we were lacking practical information about what would happen upon being performed by a Shivatulku. That is to say, we were not knowing how they were going to behave at this stage of the Kaly Yuga: the last time that the daiva dogs traveled the Earth was in Atlantis, thousands of years ago. Evidently, this Iron Age has somehow weakened their Power of Flight and one of them was affected by the Force of the Dorje. But if we were not knowing how long they were going to live, I can instead answer you why one of them has continued to live after the lung-svadi flight: it is due to the particular laws that rule their reproduction.

" 'You have reasoned well, but you did not contemplate the laws of reproduction. Being a perfect, archetypally balanced couple, the two dogs, indeed, should have died in unison. *But the law of reproduction established by the Gurus requires that before disintegration, the couple begets and gives birth to another pair of daiva dogs.* The process would then be the following: the death of either one of them, will mean the automatic metamorphosis of the other into an androgynous specimen; it is as if one of the archetypal principles, which was manifested outside, is incorporated within the survivor; and that which lives, will carry in its bosom the germ of a new couple of daiva dogs, which will grow, mature, and be born in the end: then, after the birth, the old specimen will fatally disintegrate. Do you now understand why one of them lives?'

"I nodded, relieved to know that in little time I would recover the couple of daiva dogs.

" 'Well then,' Srivirya added, 'do not forget that in this period, while the androgynous mastiff is in charge of gestating the new couple, you should refer to him by the name of "Vrune," since he is the unity of Kula and Akula.'

"I nodded again, given that that was undoubtedly logical. At that Von Grossen burst out.

" 'For God's sake, Von Sübermann! Always the damned dogs! You're concerned about the death of a dog? And our Comrades? You've communicated to me your suspicion that they've also died: well, you ought to be grieving for them! And you don't know where we are either. I was trying to find that out from the Tibetans when you interrupted me to talk about the blasted mastiffs.'

"I decided not to respond to Von Grossen's unjust accusations.

" 'We know nothing about the place to which the Shivatulku has brought us,' Srivirya interjected. 'It is up to him to answer, for he alone knows the order that he gave to the daiva dogs.'

"Von Grossen's expression broke down upon verifying that the subject of the mastiffs was inescapable. I did not have to reflect to raise a question that was intriguing me since I regained consciousness on that beach.

" 'To Sining! I ordered the mastiffs to go to Sining. It was the first place that occurred to me, probably because the two monks who were guiding the Kalitas affirmed that from there they would help us get to Shanghai. I can't explain why the daiva dogs didn't lead us to Sining.'

" 'Oh, how strange is the mind of the Shivatulku!' exclaimed Srivirya, who could not conceive that my actions were simply stupid, as in truth they were. 'If you were wishing to go to Shanghai, why not have the dogs lead you there directly, instead of requesting the plaza of Sining, situated 2,000 kilometers before? 'Incomprehensible are the Designs of the Gods! For now that the daivas dogs are in the process of reproduction you will no longer be able to use them for a lung-svipa flight: only the future puppies, some day, will carry you through Time and Space. Of course, now we will find out where we are. What Sining have you translated in your order?'

" 'What Sining? I don't understand what you mean,' I declared, fearing to hear what would come.

" 'Of course, Son of Shiva,' Srivirya candidly explained. 'Was the order requesting to go to Sining-fu or Sining-ho, that is, to the *City* of Sining or to the Sining *River?*'

"I let out a curse. Why had I been so imprecise when defining the imposed destination for the air travel of the daiva dogs? The answer was obvious: because the order was formulated at a critical moment, in the midst of a tremendous physical disorder that prevented me from sufficiently reasoning. In that terrible circumstance I forgot everything, I did not describe the goal with precision because I unconsciously supposed that the dogs would understand, that they would interpret my wishes exactly. And the truth was quite different: the dogs were tulpas, yidams, magical machines projected by the steel will of the Magi and that were requiring the correct control of their functions.

" 'I certainly didn't specify if it was Sining-fu or Sining-ho,' I confessed with annoyance. The Kaulika monk meditated a second and smilingly said:

" 'Then it is very likely that we are by the Sining River. Upon receiving the order, the daivas found that there were two different objectives with the same name. They chose, for reasons that would be too long to detail, the older objective that was corresponding to that name, apparently, the river. And that lack of definition would also explain the death of one of the mastiffs: the cause would be the dilemma to which the opposite principles were subjected, which worked as if a logical wedge had been attempted to split the absolute unity of the dog Archetype. I believe that the problem lies in the degrees of reality of the things in play. On the one hand, the daiva dogs were not constituting a perfect couple, they were not able to be at this stage of the Kaly Yuga, and were exhibiting a certain small degree of disequilibrium. On the other hand, the Sining River turns out to be a little more real, within the Illusion of Maya, than the city of Sining. Consequence: the daiva dogs are faced with a dilemma and are forced to choose; because of the supposed disequilibrium, one of the mastiffs *tends* toward Sining-fu and the other *tends* toward Sining-ho; as the real destiny is that which magically corresponds to the most real name, only one of the mastiffs arrives at Sining-ho, where we are, while the other dog disintegrates in order to avoid the impossible alteration of the Archetype. And since daiva dogs cannot exist except in pairs, the present androgyne will also disintegrate after the reproduction.'

" 'So the dogs have gone to the Sining River, to which the current that passes in front of us would correspond!' admitted Von Grossen, who at last was beginning to geographically get his bearings. 'Being so, Kameraden, I will present the situation to you. *Elements in favor of our Strategy:* a) three Germans and eight Tibetans, members of Operation First Key, we are still alive; b) it is possible that the city of Sining is near here and it is probable that it represents our definitive salvation, if we manage to pass the night under these conditions. *Elements against our strategy:* a) we experienced five losses, three Germans and two Tibetans, in addition to the five Kalita porters and all the equipment; b) if this site is really east of Lake Kokonor, it implies a distance of more than 1,000 kilometers away from the Valley of the Immortal Demons, which for the moment makes it impossible to return to inspect or rescue the bodies and materials. *Conclusion:* It is almost certain that the personnel in charge of Operation Altwesten have met an identical fate as the members of Operation First Key, that is to say, that they are dead or missing. This conclusion puts an end to Operation First Key, and imposes on us the delicate obligation of convincingly explaining the events at Ernst Schäfer's encampment to our superiors.'

"Von Grossen looked at me significantly, as if implying that the main person responsible for the explanations would be me. His last words were:

" 'Considering the diabolical attack that we have suffered in that Valley of Hell, in light of the orders received from Germany and the structure of Operation First Key, I have drawn certain conclusions that I will communicate to you on a strictly confidential and personal basis. I believe, Gentlemen, that our leaders in Germany had a pretty good idea of what would happen in Tibet if Kurt von Sübermann was integrated into Operation Altwesten. More clearly, I believe that they, Hitler, Himmler, Heydrich, Rudolf Hess, and God knows who else, knew that certain enemies would react with extreme violence upon discovering Von Sübermann: enemies who are perhaps extraterrestrial beings, possessors of terrible weapons, incomparable to any terrestrial arsenal. If they knew what could happen, why did they permit the enemy to lock us in a deadly trap? This is a question to which I lack an answer. I intuit that they were wishing to concretely test the efficacy of Von Sübermann in order to cause the reactions of the "Demons" of Chang Shambhala and that perhaps they underestimated the enemy: perhaps they thought that the White Brotherhood would close the damned gates of their lairs, and dismissed the possibility that the Demons were trying to kill us all. Be that as it may, I am persuaded that Von Sübermann will never reveal to us the secret that inflames the Demons. In summary, I hereby conclude Operation First Key; the corresponding General Staff in Germany will make the evaluation of its results. And, as *Standartenführer* in charge of the execution of Operation First Key, I decree that the immediate return to Germany be undertaken. Do you agree, Kameraden, with the Description of the Situation and the conclusions?'

"What else could Oskar Feil and I do but unconditionally accept Von Grossen's decisions? The Tibetan monks, for their part, were never disputing orders and, once again, were ready to support our plans.

"We would leave at dawn. Meanwhile, we formed a circle around the fire and embraced each other to transfer warmth, a posture that the mastiff Vrune also adopted. In spite of the prevailing cold at daybreak, we all managed to sleep, due to the great psychic fatigue that we accumulated during the last few days. We did not even have a blanket or cloak, just the clothes on our backs, and that is why we were pressing ourselves against each other to avoid freezing, although it was evident that it was not as cold in that site as on the peaks of the Kunlun mountains. As for our weapons, we were only keeping the daggers and the Lugers of Karl, Oskar, and I, and the two Schmeisser submachine guns that we were carrying across our backs: for this fearsome weapon, we were only having two magazines each, the same as for the Lugers. Insufficient to transit through a country in civil war, but always better than nothing.

"All the Kaulikas, on the contrary, had their daggers, scimitars, and quivers with the fifty arrows. For the rest, no food, no water, no supplies of any kind, except what we were carrying on us at the moment of fleeing from the ill-fated ravine. They were few things, very few if we had been much more lost in Tibet; they were sufficient to reach Sining-fu.

"Frozen cold, from dawn we marched parallel to the Sining-ho River. Von Grossen surprised us all when pulling out the canvas letter holder from inside his jacket and unfolding a map of the Western region of China. And from his pockets, like inexhaustible Pandora's boxes, emerged the inseparable compass,[61] a folding metric scale ruler, and a pair of compasses;[62] useless items, except for the compass and the map.

"Before departing, I made a mound of stones and buried the unfortunate daiva dog. I was not in the habit of praying, but on that occasion I concentrated for a few minutes and elevated my Ego to the sphere of the Gods, using the Śrotra Karṇa to get Them to listen to me: then I turned to Wothan, to him personally, and requested from him a glass of Mead for the feat of Heinz, Hans, and Kloster. 'Yes,' I said to the Gods, 'this time You should toast to those three warriors of Eternal Germany, receive them as Heroes in Valhalla; and, if possible, you should make room for the daiva dog, the dog of Shiva that was transporting the warriors, flying like Vāyu, the Wind!'

"Originated in the southernmost systems of Nan Shan, the Sining-ho[63] descends to the south and flows into the Tatung-ho, after passing under the bridge of the Great Wall and bathing the walls of the City of Sining: the Tatung-ho, on the other hand, continues to the SE and flows into the Huang Ho or Yellow River at the confluence of Lan-chau.[64] Around midday, we arrived at a small village, fortified and surrounded by rudimentary crops: it was Huangyuan, one of the posts on the Chang-lam road!

"In the village was a Buddhist temple, several inns for pilgrims and merchants, and a free market of respectable dimensions. The stableman was belonging to the Kaula Circle and we hurriedly made our way to his establishment. There we were reassured, while we had our first hot meal in 24 hours. According to his report, the Prince of Kokonor's men searched for us for a few days, and in the end returned to Tibet. It would be difficult for them to come back unless someone convoked them, which would not happen if we were acting with prudence and were not making ourselves seen. In any case, the power of the roused Tibetans was reaching only as far as Huangyuan, a village situated on the northern side of the

---

61. navigation instrument

62. drawing tool

63. Huangshui River

64. Lanzhou

Great Wall, in a region traditionally disputed by Mongols and Tibetans. A few kilometers ahead, after the Great Wall, was the Chinese province of Tsinghai and the City of Sining,[65] where the power of the Kaula Circle was considerable.

"Of course, if in Sining-fu we were not to fear persecution from the Tibetans, we would instead have to avoid getting involved in the continuous revolts of the bitter Chinese factions. This time, logistics and tactics were left to the Kaulikas, who knew the terrain better and were possessing a powerful support infrastructure. Their plan, otherwise, was extremely simple: we would spend the night in the stable, which was seeming like a palace after the previous night, and in the morning the Chinaman and his son would take us to Sining-ho hidden in two wagons of four oxen each.

"The Kaulika monks let us know that they planned to return to Tibet after we were out of danger on our way to Shanghai. They would not return directly to Bhutan, for they would try to find their two companions, who had been left with the Kalitas at the Threshold of the Valley of the Immortal Demons. Although they had no daiva dogs, they were knowing much about the magic of the Kyilkhor and were positively knowing that the lost Valley was in the west, in the lands of the Queen Mother Kuan Yin: either from the east, as we did, or from the west, they would find the way to enter and rescue their Comrades or, perhaps, to avenge them. Then, if they were returning, they would withdraw to the Monastery in Bhutan, or to some other belonging to the Kaula Circle, to meditate on everything that occurred on that adventure. They fought side by side with the Shivatulku, were guided to the Valley of the Immortals by the daiva dogs, and participated in their lung-svipa flight: they were certainly fortunate, the Gods had smiled upon them, and it was only remaining for them to retire to meditate and give thanks.

"Nothing could object to that admirable decision, but Karl von Grossen thought differently. He called Srivirya and Bangi aside and qualified them as 'deserters.' 'Your mission,' he told them, 'would only be concluded when *those in the know* evaluated the results of the operation.' And such persons, of course, were in Germany: it was incumbent on them, then, to accompany us to our Fatherland and give their valuable testimonies.

---

65. Xining

They would then be free to return, and he would put all the necessary means at their disposal.

"As the monks were hesitating, Von Grossen morally pressured them by assuring them that they would have to accompany us to Shanghai anyway, in order to officiate as Chinese interpreters, and, once there, 'it wouldn't cost them much' to embark for Germany, 'which was almost as far away as Bhutan.' But this was not true.

"Srivirya and the Gurkha, indeed, were speaking Chinese, but no one was knowing a word of Japanese, the language of those who were occupying half of China. By contrast, Oskar and I took Chinese and Japanese in the *NAPOLA Ostenführer* course; and the two of us were proficient in Mandarin and Japanese. But, in any case, there was always the resource of English, a discredited language in Asia but with which Von Grossen or any of us could communicate. The universal language of Asia, as the sons of Perfidious Albion had intended, would be English, but the truth was that only the colonial functionaries and the usual cipayos were speaking it; among the cultured members of the Asiatic peoples, be they Indian, Nepalese, Kashmiri, Bhutanese, Chinese, Burmese, etc., English was resisted and usually remaining unknown, if not hidden and hated.

"Although we were disapproving of Von Grossen's attitude, neither Oskar nor I denied his arguments. We were smilingly observing, instead, how the two extraordinary Initiates were little by little ceding their positions. The truth was that deep down we were all wanting that the two monks travel with us to Germany. When, the following day, we left for Sining, they were already almost convinced by the persuasive *Standartenführer.*

Chapter XXXV

hat a city, Neffe! In those days it was having no less than 130,000 inhabitants, and a perimeter of more than 20 kilometers. To its towering walls were arriving routes from all over Asia: from Mongolia, Russia, Turkestan, Dzungaria, Afghanistan, India, etc., in addition to the aforementioned Chang-lam coming from Lhasa, through which arrived the wagons that were transporting us. Our way, since the daiva dogs deposited us at the foot of the Nanshan mountain range, followed the same natural course: bordering the mountain range on one side, which was now extending into the Ma-ha-che[66] mountains, and the Sining River on the other; on its right bank was Sining-fu, at an altitude of 2,500 meters above sea level.

"The City of Sining was a gigantic market, which neither the civil war, nor the national war against Japan, had affected its feverish rhythm. The different troops that were suspiciously coexisting and that from time to time were protagonizing some incident were constituting the only alteration. Such troops were belonging to many unknown Lords or triads and were controlling, each one, a sector of the city: there were even nationalist and communist factions, in addition to the aristocratic or noble, traditionalist, religious, and mafia factions. However, Sining-fu was then a 'free plaza,' that is to say, it had not fallen under the control of the Japanese. Before an external attack, paradoxically, each troop would take care of defending his part of the wall and all differences would be forgotten in order to face the common enemy.

"The Kaulika community of Sining-fu was really significant. We verified it when entering the 'pale-faced' neighborhood, so called because of the color of the complexion of its residents, and admiring the enormous Shiva Sanctuary that they were possessing. They offered to provide us with everything necessary to initiate a new expedition to Tibet: they were especially enthusiastic about the idea of our undertaking the annihilation of other Gompas like that of the Duskhas. They were disenchanted when we explained to them that we had to return to Germany.

---

66. Minshan Mountains

" 'If our Race comes to dominate the World some day, and remains faithful to the Hyperborean Wisdom of the ⚡⚡, *there will be no place on Earth for the worshiper and servants of the Potencies of Matter:* the Eternal ⚡⚡ will destroy them without mercy and you, heroic Kaulikas, will be next to us, wearing, perhaps, the *Totenkopf* insignia,' I assured them, without suspecting that the latter would become a reality sooner than I was thinking.

"In view of our irrevocable decision, the Kaulikas agreed to support the trip to the East. Briefly, they outlined the situation to us. The two most powerful military forces in China were the 'nationalists' of Chiang Kai-shek and the communists of Mao Tse-tung. Before 1937 the two armies were fiercely fighting, but now they were facing the Nipponese enemy together. Naturally, for anyone who understands the political structure of the Synarchy, the Soviet Union was supplying Mao's communists and England and the United States, that is, Anglo-Saxon imperialism, were coming to the aid of Chiang's 'nationalists.' And fraternally united, as their foreign partners were in the Synarchy, the right and the left were allying themselves against Japanese 'fascism': *on a reduced scale, what would happen four years later in the Second World War was occurring in the Chinese war.*

"There was a sole difference, which in this case was having no importance because the awakened man is guided by facts and not by names: *it was the term 'nationalists' that the members of Chiang Kai-shek's party were adopting to define themselves.* Curiously, those 'nationalists' were not supported by us, the National Socialists, but by the extreme liberalism of the Anglo-Saxons. And it is easily explained because that is what Chiang and his partisans were: exponents of the most reactionary liberal right wing in China, that is to say, the most cipayo. In this matter of being a cipayo, a partisan of the colonialist Potencies to the detriment of his own people, one must admit that Chiang Kai-shek was almost as great as Mahatma Gandhi, that agent of the English Secret Service who handed over India to the exploitation of the *commonwealth* masters, preventing that a true nationalist revolution be concretized there, that is, National Socialist.

"That is why, to call Chiang a 'nationalist' would be a joke, a joke in bad taste, if it were not for the fact that the role that his bosses of the Synarchy made him play finally caused the fall of the millenary Chinese Culture into the miserable and narrow Marxist-Leninist Doctrine. No, Chiang was not a nationalist but simply a cipayo. And whoever doubts this should observe what he did with Formosa, the modern Taiwan, where there are no popular guilds and the ethical codes that characterize nationalism, but the rapacious action of multinational companies and World Banking, and the unlimited exploitation of the Chinese people, completely marginalized from deciding the Destiny of their 'Nation,' since it has already been determined by the Synarchy.

"If a people wishes to be imperialist, History offers them two classical models, which are not in the least understood by observers but are no less utilized throughout the ages. One is the Greco-Roman model, inherited from the very ancient concept of 'Universal Empire' of the Indo-Iranians: this model, and Rome gave us one of the last examples, only requires that the remaining peoples be militarily subdued, not culturally; thus, peoples of different idiosyncrasies could be integrated into the Roman Empire preserving their Culture, language, and customs, and, if they were valiant enough to proudly resist the *Pax Romana,* they could obtain extraordinary concessions, like the citizenship of the Gauls and Spaniards, and the control of the army, and of the whole Empire, achieved by the Germanics; it was possible because in that model of the Empire, value was paradoxically based on the actual valor of the people: the most valiant was the most valuable; this principle had an undoubtable character and no one was fearing the imperial rise of a valiant people because it was obvious that such a people were valuable for the Empire.

"That is to say, in that first model it would not be necessary to practice cultural indoctrination of the defeated, using brainwashing, morally destroying them, corrupting them, keeping them in barbarism or returning them to savagery: *that was not suiting anyone, it was against the juridical essence of the Aryan Universal Empire, that is to say, it was against Honor.* And here is the crux of the matter: the ethical support of the previous principle, and all that constitutes the Universal Empire, is the Principle of principles, the Supreme Principle that is the cornerstone of the juridical-social structure of the national State: *the Principle of Honor. The justice with which the Empire will treat a conquered or allied people, on which their existence and development will depend, will only require the guarantee of*

Honor. For example, Alexander, an imperialist with Honor, did not need to dismember Egypt, or impose the Greek language on the Egyptians, or annihilate them, or subject them to slavery, or destroy their pyramids, in order to accept them without prejudice as federates of the Macedonian Empire. And the Romans, bridging the gap, when they finally subdue the Gauls, who had bloodily resisted for centuries, proceeded in the same honorable way: and they opened the gates of the Empire to such an extent that in a short time they no longer spoke of Gauls but of Gallo-Romans.

"The other Model of Empire is the Carthaginian, *typically non-Aryan,* inherited by the Phoenicians from their Semitic ancestors of Assyria, Babylon, and Sumer. It is advisable to comprehend this concept because the English and the North Americans, peoples completely Judaized by the systematic and tireless work of the White Brotherhood, have adhered to the Carthaginian model.

"Belicena Villca already spoke of the Carthaginians in her letter: a people of merchants lacking in ethical principles; only skilled in trade and piracy, famous for the human sacrifices that they were offering to their Incandescent Iron Idol. Carthaginians, English, Yankees: like their predecessors of the Assyro-Babylonian empire, they would think that the remaining peoples of the Earth are an article of consumption for their insatiable appetites! Herein lies the principle equivalent to that of the value of peoples in the Greco-Roman model: for the Carthaginians, English, and Yankees, the subjugated peoples have no value in themselves but *to the extent in which they are useful to the Empire.* Thus, the conquered or dominated people are enslaved, humiliated, dehumanized, emptied of their own worth, *transformed into a tool, into a utensil: they are valuable as long as they are useful.* A Judaic principle of value that it is no coincidence to find at the pinnacle of Anglo-Saxon imperialism. If a 'colonial' people *serve,* then they must be exploited without limits; *if they can serve,* then they must be indoctrinated so that they provide usefulness, which represents an investment that will have to be protected and recouped with interest. If something opposes the exploitation, it must be neutralized: *if it were not done in this way, they would hypocritically justify themselves, they would not be 'helping' that people to recover their value, that is, their usefulness.* Man has a price, like commodities: *he is worth for what he does, and he can be worth more for what he is capable of doing.* The Carthaginian-Anglo-Saxon Empire will commit itself to extract the maximum utilitarian value from the peoples, granting them the possibility of being worth much by producing much. Whatever is opposed to this magnanimous concession of those who hold the Power of the World, will be destroyed: for the good of those who are subjected but can demonstrate their value; in defense of the possibility of being useful to the imperialists, a possibility to which they earnestly call 'democratic liberty.' And what is it that stands in the way of these people who are worth nothing, who value themselves by being useful to the Empire, serving, producing, allowing that the Empire take possession of their wealth, if they have it, or keeping them from spending it for their own benefit if the Empire needs it now or tomorrow?

"Is their own Culture the obstacle? For it will be reculturalized by all possible means. Is national consciousness the enemy? Well, the essence of the national Being will be attacked: it will begin by discrediting or denying its own good and will exalt the foreign good; contrarily, the foreign bad will be diminished and its own bad will be exalted to the point of exaggeration; thus confidence in the national Destiny will enter into collapse, and the people will believe, overwhelmed, that the cultural distance between their own national weakness and the strength and greatness of others is insurmountable. The second step will consist in specifically attacking the supports of the national Being: the territoriality, the patriotic symbols, the traditions, etc. They will move or threaten the borders in order to create the sensation that the Nation 'is not finished,' that it is something half-built, that it does not exist; they will slander the great men of the Fatherland, who badly or well contributed to its existence, so that the people will be ashamed of its past; instead, their imperialist contemporaries will be presented for comparison, so that the people repudiate their national heroes and admire the foreigners, and lament: 'what were we doing while they were constructing their mighty Empires?'

"Is racial unity the impediment? The people will be bastardized by favoring the immigration of inferior Races. Is it national unity? It will be disintegrated by bribing or buying leaders, pitting one against the other, and creating chaos, the evidence that 'they are a people in which their members cannot agree among themselves.'

"As you see, Neffe, the Carthaginian model demonstrates a whole *modus operandi* in the action of the imperialists. While in the Greco-Roman model 'the most valuable was the most valiant,"' and the valorous peoples could grow and develop themselves without problems, according to their own cultural patterns, in the Carthaginian-Anglo-Saxon model it is necessary to permanently apply the principle 'good as long as it serves,' which forces to subdue the defeated, or dominated, peoples by means of the most vile practices. And here we also come to the heart of the matter: the juridical support of the previous principle, and all that constitutes the Carthaginian-Anglo-Saxon Empire, is the Principle of the synarchic principles, the Supreme Principle that is the cornerstone of the juridical-social structure of the synarchic State: *the Principle of Division.*

"Division of what? Of everything, because the Principle of Division gives the Emperor or King, Carthaginian, English, or Yankee, *the right* to divide the structure of the peoples. It is necessary to immediately compare, so that the differences jump out: the Principle of Honor of the Greco-Roman imperialists was essentially *ethical* and was creating the *obligation* to procure the common good, to valorize the valor of the valorous; on the contrary, the Principle of Division of the Carthaginian-Anglo-Saxon imperialists was fundamentally juridical and amoral and was generating *the right to divide* to ensure the valor of those who serve, to protect the democratic freedom of being worth being useful, producing, serving.

"Here are the fundamental differences of the two models: the ethical versus the juridical and amoral; the moral obligation of procuring the common good, versus the amoral right to divide the common good in order to extract its utilitarian value. Greco-Roman imperialism was producing 'citizens of the Empire,' an honorable title that was in no way lessening their nationality or racial pride. Carthaginian-Anglo-Saxon imperialism models 'citizens of the World,' an ambiguous and dishonorable title that more often than not conceals unconfessable treason.

"We already know the citizens of the Empire from history. It is of interest, however, to know what the 'citizens of the World' are like, a title analogous to that of 'slave of the Synarchy'? Well, they are beings who have been shaped according to the Carthaginian-Anglo-Saxon model, that is to say, beings who have suffered all the ways of the Principle of Division. They are usually *internationalists* because their nationality has been *divided* and disintegrated: they believe that the *international* bridges the gap between peoples. They are determined *pacifists* because their psychic structure was freudianly *divided* and their warrior instinct qualified as 'primitive aggressive tendencies that originate in the cortex, the animal brain, and arise through the Unconscious': for psychoanalytic culture, the warrior instinct is a shameful, almost animal impulse, extremely dangerous 'because it can incarnate itself in the Hero Myth' and become dominant in the consciousness; those who are indoctrinated this way, identify war with savagery, and believe that peace must be achieved at any cost because in that social state it is possible to demonstrate *usefulness* by serving pacifist imperialism, World Government, Synarchy, or whatever is called the system that exploits them wants. These specimens are color blind to nationality and their warrior instinct has been blocked; therefore they lack heroism, the capacity for patriotic reaction, they are psychologically mutilated beings who believe in the union of various concepts impossible to unite under a Carthaginian-Anglo-Saxon imperialism: peace, happiness, creation, progress, liberty, civilization of love, universal fraternity, etc. Naturally, in our Epoch, they can be good communists or good liberals, indistinctly.

"But besides being *internationalists* or *pacifists*, they can be collaborators of the Carthaginian imperial system, working from within their Nations, in which they do not believe, to favor the contribution of utilitarian value that the imperialists have assigned to their people or country; or they can be international agents of imperialism and devote themselves to execute its plans. In any case, their task will consist, from within or from outside, in *dividing*, that is to say, in applying the Principle of Division wherever there exists something united that is opposed to Carthaginian-Anglo-Saxon imperialism: intrigue, corruption, Machiavellianism, bribery, insidiousness, defamation, publicity, disinformation, etc., all means and crimes will be valid to *divide* the whole and strengthen the parts that are *useful* and *serve* foreign imperialism. In the formation of lackeys of this kind, Carthaginian-Anglo-Saxon imperialism has always excelled: *the classic type is the 'cipayo.'* Naturally, I am not referring to the Indian cipayo, to the concrete man who many times with incredible courage tried to get rid of the English plunderers, but to the *type* of cipayo, to the class of man *'valuable in their service'* that the English were wanting to produce by dividing all their principles. In Carthage, there were thousands of such mercenaries of that kind. In Asia and Africa, the English would produce them by the hundreds of thousands.

"And so we come to Chiang Kai-shek, who was the classic type of cipayo in the service of the Anglo-Saxon Carthaginian colonial power, and we see that by correctly defining the terms, such a personage can have nothing of what is 'nationalist' and much of what is an imperialist agent. He, like Gandhi in India, Marcos in the Philippines, F. Duvalier in Haiti, Reza Pahlavi in Iran, Tito in Yugoslavia, Fidel Castro in Cuba, and so many countless tyrants in Asia, Africa, and Latin America, were great cipayos who systematically divided the true nationalist movements of their countries and then crushed them part by part; it is understood: nationalism is the worst enemy of Carthaginian-Anglo-Saxon imperialism.

"Now then, Neffe: I have demonstrated to you that the Supreme Principle of Carthaginian-Anglo-Saxon imperialism is the Principle of Division, and I opposed it to the Principle of Honor, which fundaments the Universal Aryan Empire. Well, it is worth adding that such a 'Principle of Division' *is essentially non-Aryan.*

"But it is not only an assumption, from the fact that the Carthaginians as well as the Phoenicians, Egyptians, Assyrians, Babylonians, etc., have profoundly employed it, because in the non-Aryan Kingdoms where priestly hypocrisy has predominated for some period, the Principle of Division has also been used, given that the Priestly castes and the Synarchy both register common interests. The proof of its non-Aryan origin is, as it could not be otherwise, in its biblical provenance. That is to say, the Principle, which gives the *Right to Divide,* although ancient and non-Aryan, finds its juridical formulation in the people who worship a God of Justice, One who lay down the Tablets of the Law; and that people are Israel, the Chosen People of Jehovah Satan.

"To present the Principle of Division, the Doctors of the Law express it by means of a metaphor in the First Book of Kings. From that figure the Principle will be extracted and legally regulated, *it will become the Divine right of Kings and Emperors;*

and, modernly, the undeclared right proper to the hierarchs of the Carthaginian-Anglo-Saxon imperialism.

"Logically, because it is a right, its sanction must be realized in the course of a trial. And a trial in which the judge is unappealable, in such a manner that the exercised right is converted into a Supreme Principle, into the First Law. A judge like this can only be 'the wisest man on Earth and in History'; and he must also be a King, because the Principle of Division will only grant the right to Sovereigns of the Carthaginian model.

"The man who was meeting these conditions was, of course, King Solomon:

" '*And Your servant is in the midst of Your people whom You have chosen, a great people who are too many to be numbered or counted. So give Your servant an understanding heart to judge Your people, to discern between good and evil. For who is capable of judging this great people of Yours?*'

" '*Now it was pleasing in the sight of Jehovah that Solomon had asked this thing. And He said to him, [...] "I have done according to your words. Behold, I have given you a wise and discerning heart, so that there has been no one like you before you, nor shall one like you arise after you"' [I Kings 3:8–12].*

"The personage is already presented: he is wise by God's disposition, his judgment is unappealable; and he is King. He must, then, exercise the *Right to Divide,* so that it becomes a Supreme Principle, a First Law. Two Jewish prostitutes who argue about the maternity of a child give him the opportunity: one of them substituted her dead son for the son of the other.

" '*Then the king said, "The one says, 'This is my son who is living, and your son is the dead one'; and the other says, 'No! For your son is the dead one, and my son is the living one.'" And the king said, "Get me a sword." So they brought a sword before the king. And the king said, "Cut the living child in two, and give half to the one and half to the other. [I Kings 3:23–25]"'*

"This is the famous 'Solomonic judgment,' which legalizes the right of the King to divide *if it is useful;* in this case the usefulness is in knowing the truth, which will value the mother with her child by re-establishing her service. It is necessary to notice that the Priestly character of the Investiture has been made quite clear: the King does not carry the Sword: he requests it; he is a Priest. Let us remember that the Bible is a Sacred Book and that in it every last iota has meaning. We daily hear evangelist preachers qualify the Bible as the 'Word of

God.' But there are those who blindly believe that it is true: they are the Kabbalist Rabbis, the same ones who, precisely, secretly manage Masonry and dozens of Secret Societies of the Synarchy, organizations in which, coincidentally, militate the 'statesmen' who direct Carthaginian-Anglo-Saxon imperialism.

"Therefore, the Principle that emerges from the biblical metaphor is something serious. What do those images mean, in rabbinical terms? That the Priest-King has the *right* to request the Sword and *to divide: and that this fact is just.* Not only just, but the source of Justice. Justice at the beginning of the trial is not manifested, it is not known who the mother is in truth: *Justice was made present a posteriori to the Priest-King exercising the right to divide.* In summary: *the Priest-King takes the Sword, 'the Power of the State,' and exercises the right to divide the body of a child, 'a small people,' and it is just, it produces Justice, the very foundation of the Priest-King;* conclusion: *the right of the King to divide his base justifies the rupture and strengthens the Throne.*

"With their customary realism, the Rabbinic Doctors have interpreted the Solomonic judgment in this way and have synthesized it in the Talmud, from where Machiavelli surely learned it: *'the King must divide in order to reign.'*

"This non-Aryan, Judaic, and amoral principle has been constituted in the guiding axiom of the Carthaginian-Anglo-Saxon imperialists. They divide everything, as I demonstrated before, and even at the moment of withdrawing, from a colony for example, they leave it divided in all possible orders, from the territorial to the political and economic, counting on, of course, their cohorts of cipayos for that task.

"Remember, Neffe, that the famous *'International Division of Labor'* is a concept of nineteenth century English liberalism. Now you can see that it is inspired by talmudic Principles: *'the King, if he is Wise, must divide his base in order to reign'; 'the King is the only whole, which none of the parts can reach'; 'the parts of the Kingdom, are of value as long as they serve.'* Naturally, this Kingdom is Malkuth, the tenth Sephiroth.

Chapter XXXVI

he communists and Kuomintang nationalists,' the Sining Kaulikas explained to us, 'while fighting united against the Japanese, were sustaining fierce confrontations among themselves in the interior regions of China. Japan was controlling the entire eastern coast, to the south of Canton, and was occupying such important cities as Shanghai, Nanking, Hankou, Peking, etc. But it has never been easy to take over China: innumerable cities were dominated by Chiang Kai-shek's troops while the Communists were notably strong in the countryside, where they were counting on the unconditional sympathy of the Chinese peasantry; this was the result of 20 years of proselytism in the countryside, contradicting the postulates of Marxism-Leninism that were affirming the revolutionary primacy of the proletariat or urban working class: that tactical political success was the work of Mao Tse-tung; and thus a small guerrilla movement, which began in the southern provinces of Kiangsi and Fukien, and spread to central Szechwan after the "Long March," was now a powerful irregular military force that had under its control three more provinces, around Yenan: Shensi, Ninghsia, and Kansu, the province of which Sining-fu was part until 1928.'

"This was meaning that the communists were reigning in the countryside and keeping watch over the roads of that region. On the other hand, Chiang Kai-shek's forces, strong in the cities, were also patrolling the roads, at times being hostile to the communists. This situation was supposing certain risks for anyone who attempted to move toward the east without being enrolled in any of the warring factions. The Shivaguru of Sining proposed to us a way of getting to Shanghai:

" 'Since you do not consider the Japanese your enemies, I am going to suggest a way to reach them without the Communists or Nationalists killing you first. A few months ago, it would have been very simple taking the roads of the Northeast and taking advantage of the navigable stretches of the Yellow River. But now a terrible misfortune has occurred, which has made that region impassable: *Tongzhi*[67] Chiang Kai-shek, may

---

67. A form of address that means "comrade," used by by both the Chinese Nationalist Party and the Chinese Communist Party.

Kuan Yin take pity on his passionate heart, has just blown up the dikes on the Huang Ho River to stop the Japanese advance, but such an action has cost a terrible sacrifice of innocent Chinese lives.'

"Indeed, Neffe: in 1938, Chiang flooded the valley of the Yellow River and condemned a whopping 880,000 persons to death by drowning. Yes, almost a million dead by a single order: *and I have not known of anyone bringing him to trial for 'crimes against humanity,' in 1945.* If it has not occurred, one must admit that he was acquitted beforehand, and that such a pardon was granted to him in recognition of his refined cipayo quality.

" 'As things stand,' continued Shivaguru, 'I advise you to travel to Lan-chau-fu, a city situated 200 kilometers to the east. From there it is possible to go to Shanghai *in different ways: they will tell you how.* I remember that in peacetime, it was possible to travel the 200 kilometers to Shanghai using the railroad. Now that cannot be done because the stretch that was taking us to Lan-chau-fu is interrupted by the blowing up of the bridge over the Yellow River; and from Lan-chau-fu, only one branch line runs that does not go beyond Chengchow, in the province of Henan. In short, you will have to ride over 200 kilometers, along a road infested with guerrillas or "nationalists" and you will, possibly, have to kill members of both sides; but do not worry, killing is a common task these days!

" 'There are eleven of you: I will reinforce you with 25 men armed with rifles, part of the troop that protects our neighborhood. Now let us talk about what you will do in Lan-chaufu. Have you heard of *the Green Gang?*'

" 'You mean the gang of bandits?' asked Von Grossen, who was evidently knowing something of the matter. The Shivaguru smiled with a compassionate gesture.

" 'Don't be hard on us. The Green Gang is a Secret Society. And Secret Societies are to China what fragrances are to flowers. The Green Gang is a Society of Initiates who share our same Tantra and agree on the same Tao: many of its members have been or are Kaulika monks. Only they, because of their particular idiosyncrasy, have chosen a path that goes much deeper into the World of sleeping men. But they, of course, could not accept or obey the laws of that world without also ending up lethargic. And they do not! They act in their own way, according to their own code of Honor, and that is why they are called "gangsters" by sleeping men. But do not underestimate them, for it requires much valor to be the Lord of Oneself in the midst of pleasures and temptations: only he who has tasted and dominated the desire of the Five Forbidden Things, has sufficient will to act in the Green Gang.

" 'That path is not for everyone, I repeat. I, for one, prefer the tranquility of our Monasteries, the serenity of the Martial Art gymnasiums, *to the permanently dangerous path of the Green Gang.* However, we all need each other if we are to march fighting toward the same goal. So the Green Gang helps the Kaula Circle with what they do best: the mastery of material values. And the Kaula Circle helps the Green Gang with what they do best: *sha.*[68] Naturally, for us, as for Krishna, the son of Indra, *to kill means nothing, if the Spirit of the killer is beyond Maya, the Illusion of Life; if when our scimitar cuts down the miserable life, the Spirit dances, alongside Shiva, the Dance of Destruction.*

" 'I know I should not explain these things to you who are enlightened by Shiva, and who have performed the marvelous feat of decimating the Duskha vampires. I asked you about the Green Gang, not to know your opinion, but to inform you that they will be the ones to lead you to Shanghai. In Lan-chau-fu we will put you in contact with the Green Gang and from then on you will be in their hands, which are absolutely trustworthy. If you wish, they can take you out of China through Hong Kong, but if you insist on dealing with the Japanese you can still go to Shanghai.'

"Before leaving, the Shivaguru of Sining gave to us a notable reflection:

" 'You, the Germans, are wrong to trust in the Japanese: they, sooner or later, will betray you! We have known them for millennia and that is why we can speak with foundation: *deep down they are miserable Buddhists, even if they boast of their Samurai tradition.* They were once valiant warriors, it is true, but only the memory of that remains; and the crippled and the elderly live on memories. *They have been worked by the Buddhist Priests of the White Brotherhood, they have been "moralized,"* that is to say, softened, weakened, tamed, pacified. Today, under apparent *austerity* palpitates the Dragon of Envy for

---

68. Killing

luxury and Western Culture; under the disguise of *humility* pants the bourgeois, desirous of all pleasures; under the mask of the *warrior* devoted to the hardships of struggle, is the pusillanimous face of the one who loves the comforts of peace; under declaimed honor hides treason. Remember my words, Shivatulku, and repeat them to your Führer if you can. *Your natural ally is not Japan but China: for here the Tao passes through!*'

"Alas, Neffe Arturo, how right that Kaulika monk was in 1938! Just as the Führer explained to me that night of the graduation, at the Chancellery, and just as it was public knowledge, he was the first who stripped the internal armor of the Synarchy and exposed its Judaic core. At the center was Zionism, esoterically sustained by the Elders of Zion of the Great Sanhedrin; in order to dominate the World, the Synarchy had two tactical wings, a right or Judeo-Liberal wing, and the other a left or Judeo-Marxist wing; the right wing was esoterically supported by Masonry and hundreds of related sects; Marxism was directly controlled by the members of the Chosen People, so its esoteric foundation would be simply rabbinic. According to the Führer, the most politically illustrious man in history, the Great Jewish Conspiracy or Universal Synarchy was organically functioning this way. But, it was one thing to affirm it and another to demonstrate it. How to get that enemy, an enemy sufficiently capable of developing a Strategy for centuries and involving peoples, countries, and nations in it, to unmask itself? How to get the Enemy to abandon all caution and expose its tenebrous alliance? How to provoke it so that it gives itself away in that manner?

"The Führer found the solution. 'If there is something that the Elders of Zion, or the Synarchy, or the White Brotherhood, or the Creator Himself, Jehovah Satan, will never permit, *it will be that communism perishes*,' was more or less the reasoning. In effect, communism, the purest political expression of the Jewish mentality, could not be lost: such a possibility, for the Synarchy, was naturally inconceivable. And from such a political point of view, 'communism,' ergo, *was the Soviet Union.* In synthesis, *a tactical strike against Soviet communism would force all the participating states of the Synarchy to rush to the aid of their ally.* To attack the Soviet Union was, thus, a strategic objective of the first order against the Universal Synarchy. The Führer was knowing this and acted consciously, foreseeing that the Total War of the Third Reich against the Synarchy would be a War of Supreme Principles: the Eternal Spirit against the Potencies of Matter. During the war he anticipated what was to come, with his usual precision: *'if we win the war, the Jewish world power will have disappeared forever; if we lose, its triumph will be short-lived, for its organization will be definitively exposed.'*

"And what did the Japanese 'Comrades' do to favor the Führer's Strategy? Let us remember. Germany invades the Soviet Union on June 22, 1941. Anyone would think that with an 'ally' like Japan occupying China since 1937, the Soviet Union would be between two fires. Well, whoever thought so would be very much mistaken, for on April 13, 1941, 'coincidentally' two months before Operation Barbarossa, Japan was signing the *'Soviet-Japanese Neutrality Pact'* which was meaning the demilitarization of Manchuria and Mongolia. It is clear, Neffe, that if Japan had really shared our *Weltanschauung* it would have simultaneously attacked the Soviet Union with the Germans: with the German armies in the West and the Japanese hordes in the East, Soviet communism would have been suffocated in a deadly National Socialist pincer.

"Logically, after 1945 I have reflected a lot on the words of the Shivaguru of Sining and it was difficult for me not to find them right, since the facts confirmed them. Of course, in the face of Japan's dishonest attitude, it would have been better for us to have the Chinese as our allies: in those years they were wanting to destroy Soviet communism almost as much as getting rid of the Japanese. Had the Führer been wrong to rely on Japan, a mistake that would have cost him the Russian Campaign and the outcome of the World War? I believe that there was no such mistake and that the Führer's Strategy was so brilliant that it was going to achieve the incredible effect of revealing the 'Jewish mentality' wherever it was, even among Germany's own 'allies.' In a war of supreme principles like that which the Führer proposed, it was of no interest to 'win' or 'lose' on Earth, on the material plane, but to impose a spiritual *Weltanschauung,* the value of which was wholly outside the material plane: if the *Weltanschauung,* the Hyperborean conception of the World, 'our Banners,' were understood by the man of Honor, the war would be won, even if a material setback were suffered; if the *Weltanschauung* were not understood, or forgotten, the war would be lost, even when the fate of arms favored us. In that war of Supreme Principles, a life without Honor would be of no interest: it would be the historic moment in which each people would demonstrate their true self and what they would wish to be. An extraordinary man, perhaps a God, one whom the Kaulikas were calling the Lord of Absolute Will, had created the circumstances that would force each people to manifest their essence, that would expose the Synarchy, that would ripen the Judaic pus and make it gush wherever its corrupting culture was incubating. Being so, was the Führer wrong or did he marvelously succeed when making Japan unmask itself before the World and History and show its hidden face, which today causes the admiration of the Synarchy?

"There are no surprises in history. Historical facts register causes that sometimes go back centuries or millennia. Japan today is a gigantic kibbutz, the 'Jewish mentality' has been imposed in all orders, in a similar way as occurs in England, and a general consensus predominates for the country to remain aligned with the Synarchy, to belong to the Trilateral Commission, the UN, NATO, etc.; everyone, there, speaks of yen, peace, consumption, tourism, brotherhood, freedom, fraternity, etc. Is this apparently 'surprising change,' given the 'warrior' vocation of the Japanese before World War II, really a change, due to the lesson of Hiroshima and Nagasaki, or the exhibition of the true nature of the Japanese, who, perhaps because of a kind of collective trauma, have for centuries wanted to be what they were not, that is, Kshatriyas, Samurai, and had ended up pretending, playing, the role of warriors? Because all historical phenomena, like this supposed 'change' of the Japanese, have ancient causes that justify it: *no one turns Jewish overnight, not even if he is circumcised; to be a good son of Israel requires many 'virtues,' like for example usury and the love of profit, which require considerable time to develop.* But in such a short time the Japanese have demonstrated to be as good Jews as the Israelites and the English. Does this not signify that in Japan the Judaic mentality was larvated and that the heat of Hiroshima and Nagasaki only produced its metamorphosis, the birth of the synarchic chrysalis that today is already one more beautiful butterfly in the kaleidoscope of the White Brotherhood?

"Dear Neffe, you are a young idealist and you know History well. Listen to this principle, ascertained by an old man who has lived too long, and that synthesizes everything that I have said to you about the attitude of the Japanese: *no people, ever, loses their Honor all at once; there is no example in History that proves the contrary. Peoples, like everything that lives, follow the laws of nature and among them, as among the inhabitants of the jungle, there are lion and sheep peoples, condor and rat peoples; and, as among animals, no lion suddenly becomes a sheep, no condor suddenly transforms into a rat: if such a 'change' were in truth possible, it would require a long, millenary evolution.* Of course, as in fables, sheep may sometimes disguise themselves as lions, rats dress up as condors. Here is what I believe: *the Führer's Strategy has marked a historic time, analogous to the agreed-upon time at masquerade balls when everyone must take off their masks, in which it has been given to us to observe the sheep and the rats, and a myriad of other vermin, under the colorful and deceptive costumes of lion, condor, and other predators.*

"I believe, Neffe, that the Japanese were already before the World War what they are today; that they did not 'change' one iota; that the Shivaguru was right in his fears, but that he was not totally understanding the Führer's Strategy; that, effectively, they betrayed us,[69] for their hearts were with the White Brotherhood, even if their lips belied the strategic acts opposed to our *Weltanschauung;* and that it was foreseeable, especially for the Chinese, who for millennia were knowing what kind of oxen that they were plowing with. But the treason did not only consist of the infamous pact, scrupulously respected, which was leaving the Soviets with their hands free to only occupy themselves with Germany. Let us also remember that on December 7, 1941, when the Germans were facing the terrible Russian Winter, trucelessly confronting the Bolsheviks, the Japanese 'Comrades' were attacking the United States at Pearl Harbor, thus giving that colossal and stupid synarchic potency the opportunity to directly intervene in the world conflict.

"According to the classical model of Judaic Justice, the 'sin' of a people toward Jehovah is redeemable through the Ritual Sacrifice of a part of their members and the submission of the rest to the Law. Although the Japanese did not directly participate in the goodness of the Judaic culture, their affection for Buddhism, and every form of religion founded on the Kalachakra of Chang Shambhala, demonstrated that their de-

---

69. This naturally arises from the previous argument. He who betrays denies his own nature. He who has never been with us betrays us only in appearance (Maya).

viation from the Law was not so great: the greatest sin was consisting, without a doubt, in their recent alliance with Nazism and fascism. But that little sin was only requiring a purgatory, of Fire, as opposed to the eternal condemnation that the Rabbis were intending to apply to German National Socialism.

"How to purge a whole people of a sin that offends the Creator? By means of lye, the Rabbis respond; washing away the sin of the whole Race by means of the human lye obtained in the One Sacrifice, and then reincorporating the whole Race from purgatory to the Paradise of the Universal Synarchy. The price to be paid would not be very expensive: 250 to 300 thousand men would be sufficient to produce enough ash. The Rabbis and the Japanese Priests of the White Brotherhood arrange the pact, and that is how on August 6, 1945 and August 9, 1945 the atomic bombs fall on Hiroshima and Nagasaki: ashes of thousands of men, salt of the Earth and Heaven, water of Heaven and Earth, human lye that washes away the sin of man against Jehovah God and against the Law of God.

Who orders the mini Holocaust of Fire of the Japanese is the Hebrew president of the United States, Harry *Solomon* Truman, whose real surname is *Shippe.* A Mason of 33rd degree, he counts on the occult advice of the Great Sanhedrin and Jews and Masons of the stature of Dean Acheson, General Marshall, Snyder, Rosenman, etc., who are unabashedly supported by the Jewish gang of Bernard Baruch, Eleanor Roosevelt, Herbert Lehman, Averell Harriman, Paul G. Hoffman, Walter Lippman, etc. Because the true synarchic work of the United States in the Second War was not developed by Truman, who only acceded to power on April 12, 1945, after the sudden death of the Jew Roosevelt: he was the authentic realizer of the Judaic plans. A descendant of Claes Martenszen van Rosenvelt, a full-blooded Hebrew who immigrated to New York in 1644, Franklin Delano Roosevelt was registering a double Jewish paternity: both his father, James Roosevelt, and his mother, Sara Delano, were belonging to the Chosen People. Also his wife, Eleanor, daughter of the Jews Elliott and Anna Hall. The Jewish mafia that unleashed the crisis of 1929 catapulted him to power: some of the collaborators of that epoch were Jews of extreme danger and nameless evil, like Bernard Baruch, Herbert Lehman, Averell Harriman, Sol Bloom, Samuel Rosenman, Henry Morgenthau, Oscar Straus, Joseph

Davies, Truman, etc., all of them of exceptional power in the White House.

"The Sacrifice fulfilled, the Japanese sin washed away with human lye at Hiroshima and Nagasaki, would come the recompense that is in sight: the reconstruction plan of the Jewish Marshall, the end of Japanese 'militarism,' the integration into the international synarchic system, the exchange of samurai for yen, the raising of their standard of living, in short, the discovery of the true face of Japan, as the Shivaguru of Sining wisely advanced.

"Of course, these charges against Japan cannot be relativized or mitigated by the certain fact that during the war many Japanese fought with unparalleled heroism, for example, the Kamikazes. We must call things by their name and recognize the exceptions to the rules: just as in loyal Germany there were countless traitors, in traitorous Japan a great many valiant loyal warriors honorably stood out.

Chapter XXXVII

f Sining-fu had astonished me by its large dimensions, what to say of Lan-chau-fu, which was four times larger? But they were two different kinds of cities: Sining-fu was representing the typical frontier city, situated on an important commercial road; its life was depending more than anything else on the traffic of goods and it was not particularly interested in production; that is why it was resembling, as I said, a huge marketplace. Lan-chau-fu, on the other hand, was constituting the classic metropolis: it was the capital of the province of Kansu and, although it was trading as much or more than Sining, it was endowed with key industries, such as textiles and iron and steel, and was stockpiling a wide variety of agricultural products. Seated on the right bank of the Yellow River, it was giving the impression of a medieval European city because of its crenellated walls and high towers, but its population density was incomparable: around 1,000,000 inhabitants. Although there were fortified suburbs of poor appearance, behind the wall was the main part of the city: some 80,000 houses of beautifully decorated wood, with all its streets paved with marble or green granite. The 'nationalists' had rushed to occupy it, billeting a regiment of 10,000 troops; the motive: to control a famous heavy cannon factory and others of gunpowder and rifles.

"Things from China. Or perhaps the rationalism of Confucius. The curious thing was that in the wall of Lan-chau-fu there was a Hei-men, or *'black gate,'* which was not receiving its name because of the color with which it was painted, but because it was belonging to the *black market.* With exemplary practical meaning, the Tsung-tu[70] negotiated with the organized crime bosses the cession of that gate. According to the arrangement, the mafiosi would be in charge of maintaining a permanent guard, coordinated with the nationalist guard at the remaining gates; they could, then, channel through the Hei-men all the contraband that they wanted, without being bothered by the police. The gain that the Tsung-tu was obtaining with this original pact was in the reassurance of his troops, whom he could occupy in the war against the Japanese or in

---

70. Governor of the Province.

fighting the communists. The criminal Secret Societies were as old as China and had always been able to live together with them: they were representing the lesser evil. But with the Communists or the Japanese it would be impossible to coexist in peace. By ceding sovereignty over the Black Gate to them, he was somehow legalizing illegal activities and gaining some supervision over the uncontrollable traffic of the Black Market. To do otherwise, and to force the Societies to operate in the underground, it would be necessary to watch over the walls 24 hours a day and have to sustain periodic armed confrontations with the contrabandists.

"The Kaulikas of Sining went directly to the Hei-men and there gave a password by word of mouth. They immediately gave way to us. But, once inside, we were not led in front of a coarse miscreant, boss of a 'guild of gangsters,' as Von Grossen's definition was leading us to presume. The boss of the Green Gang was an elderly Chinaman of exquisite manners, who by the red ruby that he was wearing on his official cap was declaring to be a Mandarin of first rate and first class: such a sign was signifying the highest hierarchy in the Chinese aristocracy; we also distinguished an image of a richly embroidered unicorn on his garb, an insignia proper to the Guan[71] military: the Guan civilians were wearing bird insignias.

"His name was Tian-ma, that is to say, Horse of Heaven, and he surprised us with his knowledge of our every step: he was knowing that we were Germans, that we were coming from Bhutan, that we explored Tibet at the same time as another German expedition coming from India, that we destroyed the Duskha village, that we mysteriously appeared in the Kancheu[72] valley and arrived in Sining, and that we were now requesting help to travel to Shanghai. He was speaking in cultured Mandarin and let a halo of intrigue form around his reports.

"We were in an enormous and luxurious house that could well pass for a palace. The servants were finishing setting the table and the Guan invited us to sit down.

" 'I will be happy to have lunch with you. I understand that you are *Doctors,* men of study, as well as warriors. So am I:

71. Or *mandarin* in imperial China, a public official and bureaucrat scholar who passed the imperial examinations administered by the Ministry of Rites.

72. Zhangye. Corresponds to Marco Polo's *Kampion.*

years ago, I attained the degree of jinshi, which is equivalent to what you call *Professor,* the most elevated title that the Ministry of Rites bestows. My specialties are Mathematics and Philosophy. I have studied Taoism in depth and profess it: ours could be considered as a Taoist Society. It is because of that affiliation that we are natural allies of the Kaula Circle of Tibet: we consider that they know the occult part of Taoism; of all the taos, the Tao; of all the ways, the Way; the strategic Path that leads the Spirit to liberate itself from its material ties. Many of the members of the Green Gang, when retiring, usually recluse themselves in the Kaulika Monasteries.'

"Von Grossen and I, upon meeting Tian-ma, agreed that a new study of Chinese Criminal Societies was being required. Evidently there was a suggestive confusion, perhaps originated in that the common source that was available to Europeans to know China were the copious reports provided by the English, which would contain malicious and false information. After all, for the English the ⚡⚡ was also a criminal Secret Society! Because the last thing that one could accuse Tian-ma of was being a typical criminal, even if the actions of his organization were at odds with the law. He, and all those of his 'Gang,' were idealists, they had a spiritual goal to achieve, and they were finding themselves in a diabolical world. In such gnostic circumstances, the solution is always the same: the spiritual end justifies any means used to forge one's way in enemy territory.

"The 25 men from Sining-fu and the six Lopas were having lunch in an adjoining house. Tian-ma was accompanied by Von Grossen, Oskar Feil, Srivirya, Bangi, and I, who were the ones who would continue on to Shanghai; the former would return to Sining that same afternoon, together with the Lopas whose destination was Tibet. The boss of the Green Gang was speaking English very well, although he was not at all proud of it and was preferring to express himself in Mandarin. It was not until very late into the meal that we learned of this, for he agreed to communicate in that language with Von Grossen. We thus spent, conversing with that elderly man, endowed with the curiosity of a child, the whole afternoon: when the philosophical and religious subject was exhausted, we naturally fell into the political question, that is to say, into reality. From there, several hours followed during which we tried to make him comprehend National Socialism and its Hyperborean essence. He had information, of course, but we gave him all the details he required.

"At last, satisfied from holding a totally infrequent conference in those regions, he assured us, he prepared to reveal to us how he was going to get us to Shanghai. But first he gave us a reflection on the situation in his homeland.

" 'Oh, Jinshi: what you tell me about your Führer, and his government supported by patriotic masses, brings to my Spirit gloomy thoughts about the future of China. The Führer has set before the Germans his heroic and glorious tradition, and they have accepted it with pride. Here, on the contrary, Mao Tse-tung indoctrinates the peasants with the theories of the Jews Marx, Engels, and Lenin, and teaches them to admire the Russians, a people who were savage when China already had a developed civilization. And on the other hand, Chiang Kai-shek has turned out to be a "soft stone,"[73] for he has converted to Christianity, disavowing our millenary traditions: perhaps if he had placed, like your Führer, the Chinese Culture in front of the Chinese, they would have supported him en masse. But instead he offers them the alluring and deceptive images of a foreign Culture. A culture that belongs to those who until only yesterday exploited us like slaves. Mao and Chiang, both Chinese disavowers, are dazzled by strange Gods, both present their foreign ideals to the people. And whom do you believe the Chinese will choose? Those who will surely oppress us again, as they already did, or those who promise to do something for the people? I do not want to respond, prematurely, to that transcendental question, but as of now I inform you that the people support Mao to a greater extent than Chiang, because Mao believes in the people and knows how to express that belief, while Chiang only believes in Jesus, in England, and in the United States.

" 'Jesus! Here is another Jew, completely alien to the History and Tradition of China. But what curse is this, that has fallen on the Middle Kingdom?[74] Was it that there was no other option for China than the Jew Jesus or the Jew Marx?' None of us answered these dramatic questions, but I promised myself to get him the English edition of Mein Kampf, the Führer's book.

---

73. Kai-shek means "hard stone." Tian-ma's affirmation made ironic sense.

74. Qin: China, The Middle Kingdom

" 'I do not wish to burden my guests with an old man's laments,' apologized Tian-ma, 'but you will realize that, despite constituting a "criminal gang," as foreigners label us, we Greens deeply love China and care about its future. We foresee that certain foreign forces, which we call Bai-long-ya,[75] will try to kill the sleeping Chinese elephant, *before it awakens.*

" 'I will tell you how you will get to Shanghai. You should know that there is a Hei-tao, or *black route,* along which contraband to the Western Sea passes in both directions. It is almost official, since all along its course there are bribed officials, and it crosses the same Japanese lines, since neither can the Nips resist earning a few extra yen. In two days' time, a train leaves here that only goes as far as Chengchow. But you will get off first, in the city of Sian,[76] province of Shensi.[77] From there you will march south, crossing the Tsing-ling[78] Mountains that separate the Yellow and Blue Rivers,[79] to the village of Han-kiang, on the right bank of the Han-kiang River. In that village, you will make contact with our men, who will embark you on a transport that usually carries contraband.

" 'You will navigate through the waters of the Han-kiang and, at the confluence with the Yangtze-kiang, take it to Shanghai. As you can see, this is a very simple plan.'

" 'Indeed, it seems so,' replied the meticulous Von Grossen. 'But permit me to pose a few questions to you.'

"He nodded with a Chinese gesture that consists of leaning his head forward.

" 'You're talking about 500 kilometers by train. Isn't it possible that someone suspects and subjects us to an interrogation? What will we do then? Because we lack official German papers and we're also in China clandestinely.'

" 'Ah, Jinshi. You must cultivate the virtue of patience!' condemned Tian-ma, with naive severity. 'I told you that the train leaves in two days: by that date, the three Germans will possess papers that affirm that they are three Englishmen accredited in China by the League of Nations, with the diplomatic mission of observing the local situation and submitting re-

---

75. The White Dragon, Jehovah.

76. Xian

77. Shen: passage, gate; Si: west; Shensi: West passage.

78. Tsing or Qin: middle; Ling: mountains; Tsing-ling: Middle Mountains.

79. The Huang Ho and Yangtze-kiang Rivers.

ports that will serve for future mediation. They will display entry stamps for Hong Kong and will be written in English and Mandarin: but fear not, no one who might question you from here to Shanghai knows enough English to notice that you are Germans! We will also give you diplomatic safe-conducts and a pass for the two Tibetans, on which it will appear that you have hired them in Sining-fu.

" 'We will also give you money, plenty of Chinese and Japanese money. All fake, the papers and the money. All of the best quality. But you will not go on alone: a Green will accompany you as far as Shanghai. He will have you enter the train through a Hei-men and will accommodate you in a car that is under our control. The only occasion on which you might be questioned would be when getting off at Sian, which is very unlikely because you will only get off if there are safety signals, or if the train is stopped on the way, something possible and quite frequent, but generally everything works itself out with a generous donation. Whether nationalists or communists, in poor China nobody resists bribery. The Bolsheviks have not been original in this either, for they integrated themselves into the old institution of bribery by a name change that left safe their dignity: they call it "contribution to the Revolution." However, if they requisition you anyway, you will assert your papers and your most valuable currency. Do you agree? If not, I will give you more details; but it is in your best interest to trust the Green Gang, who know China like no one else.'

"Von Grossen had been left dumbstruck: the logistical support with which we would count on would be analogous to that which a Secret Service provides. However, he was not intimidated and returned to the fray with another question:

" 'I suppose that the rest of the journey will be equally covered, won't it? Believe me, we trust you; my questions serve a rather... professional purpose. That's right: professional! I'm an intelligence officer and I can't avoid asking questions. In truth, in whom we completely trust is the Kaula Circle: and they've placed us in your hands. So *we must* have confidence in the Green Gang.'

" 'You are right to give us credit. We will not defraud you. And I assure you that our man will take you safe and sound to Shanghai: he knows the passage through the Tsing-ling mountains and the people of Han-kiang, as well as the Japanese border guards in Nanking. But, just in case, before leaving here I will give you a password for the contact in Han-kiang and tell you where to find him.'

"For the time being, Von Grossen was satisfied, and the five of us were ushered into a spacious guest room, attended by solicitous and discreet Chinese Dames. In the following days, there would be an opportunity for the *Standartenführer* to extract from Tian-ma all the data that was interesting him.

Chapter XXXVIII

I can say, Neffe, that the Greens placed us at the very gates of the German consulate in Shanghai without any inconvenience. The plan was realized as Tian-ma had foreseen. Six days later we were finding ourselves sailing on a stout and massive junk[80] down the boggy current of the Yangtze-kiang. We passed quietly off of Nanking and, near the city of Chin-kiang,[81] we reached the confluence of the Wusong River.[82] With great skill, the captain turned the rudder and entered into the descending current of the latter river, for 25 kilometers ahead, on its left bank, stands the populous Shanghai.

"The merchandise that that innocent junk was transporting is unimaginable. Of course, it would not be so much if one was closely inspecting it and admiring the row of cannons on the port and starboard sides, and the two heavy machine guns on the bow and stern. But precautions were not superfluous because the ship was contrabanding weapons, explosives, fine fabrics, porcelain, metals, minerals, spices, food, opium, and even deserters from both Chinese sides or common snitches, in addition to the classic cargo of Chinese prostitutes that no similar organization could do without. Along with such heterogeneous and dangerous articles, we were an insignificant nuisance. We only realized it in Han-kiang, upon boarding the junk and seeing the high volume of merchandise that the Green Gang was trafficking: like that one, our guide informed us, the Society was possessing an entire fleet on the Yangtze-kiang alone, without counting those that were floating in other Rivers and in the Sea, and that were traveling as far as Hong Kong, Canton, or Macao.

"On the Wusong river, we passed by numerous modest villages, dedicated to farming and cultivation, and the Taihu lake that it fills with its waters. After drifting 200 meters, we reached Shanghai and docked at a small private wharf, equipped with a large hut that was serving as a depot. Other

---

80. A type of Chinese vessel or river boat.

81. Zhenjiang

82. Suzhou Creek

members of the Gang, who were disciplinedly waiting, were in charge of unloading and stowage, and of taking the prostitutes and fugitives. The absence of Japanese control, which we neither saw in Nanking nor anywhere else, surprised us. 'Japanese palms already *greased*,' the guide told us in his striking *pidgin*, a slang mixture of Portuguese and English spoken in the maritime coasts of China: obviously, to call *greasing* a bribe is an irony typical of Portugal and Spain. 'Mr. Tian-ma no explain to you?' I replied yes, in the same tongue, but that the power that the Green Gang's *dough* was exerting over the *greased* persons was impressing us. He smiled and communicated to us that we would immediately go to Shanghai.

"Upon leaving the port area, taking streets that the guide was seeming to know very well, we arrived at a plaza-market of enormous dimensions, where there was a natural agglomeration of hundreds of jinrikishas, those Japanese vehicles pulled by a man, which have the shape of an individual calèche and the English were calling *rickshaw*. It seemed the height of organization and discipline to verify that six were apart waiting for us, undoubtedly notified by the Greens who had left the port earlier. I looked at Von Grossen out of the corner of my eye, but he noticed.

" 'These crooks sure know how to do things,' he grunted. 'We ought to learn from them.'

"I paid no attention to this exaggeration, as we were already going quite fast and the view of the big city was completely absorbing me: with 5,000,000 inhabitants in 1938, Shanghai for the English, Chang-haï for the French, and Xangae for the Portuguese and Spanish, it was a tremendous city for any pair of Western eyes. We were now heading for the "Model Colony," or *The Bund*, the island that the Westerners were able to raise in the middle of an unhealthy swamp, which was ceded by the Chinese in the Treaty of Nanking in 1842, signed during a gun salute by the English who in that year occupied Shanghai despite the 250 artillery batteries on the Wusong: the British hijackers disembarked the infantry, which neutralized the cannons and marched on the city, while their ships were entering through the northern Gate and the Chinese were fleeing through the southern Gate.[83]

---

83. Battle of Wusong

"On those marshy grounds, a magnificent European citadel was raised, walled, with cobblestone water channeling, and paved and illuminated streets. Gigantic buildings were constructed belonging to the three occupying powers: England, United States, and France; and soon three neighborhoods characteristic of those nationalities arose, in addition to the not-to-be-missed *Chinatown,* called Nantao by the Chinese. The three colonial potencies obtained extensive private port zones for their Foreign Trade Companies to establish trading factories. When the Germans intended to enter into this deal, the port was already completely divided up and they were forced to pay franchises to their competitors. In any case, what Germany was trading with Shanghai was not much, although it was enough to require the presence of a Consul; the Embassy was located in Nanking. Naturally, the Japanese presence in Shanghai, and their distrust toward the Carthaginian imperialist powers that had operated in the region, was opening up promising prospects for Germany to obtain a larger share of the spoils.

"The rickshaws sped past the barred fence, crossed a well-kept garden, and stopped in front of the gate of a Rhenish-style mansion. A Kriegsmarine sergeant approached us while we were getting down.

" 'Heil Hitler!' saluted Von Grossen. 'I am *⚡⚡ Standartenführer* Karl von Grossen on special assignment, Sergeant. We have to see the Consul urgently.'

" 'Yes, sir,' said the sailor. 'Do me the favor of handing me your papers and you will be attended to at once.'

" 'We have no papers, Sergeant! Here is a list with the names and military rank of these Gentlemen who accompany me and mine. We are all officers.'

"The prudent Von Grossen had drafted a note for the Consul, anticipating a possible bureaucratic blockage. It was reading as follows:

Herr Consul of the Third Reich,
Shanghai,

We present ourselves before you, and request to be repatriated immediately to Germany, *⚡⚡ Standartenführer* Karl von Grossen, *⚡⚡ Sturmbannführer* Kurt von Sübermann, *⚡⚡ Hauptsturmführer* Oskar Feil, and the men from Bhutan, the Gurkha Bangi and the Lopa Srivirya, all members of Operation First Key, *Highly Confidential*, code *AI RSHA*, authorized: Hitler, Himmler, Heydrich.

Yours faithfully,

Signed: Karl von Grossen
Commander of Operation First Key.

" 'Wait a moment, Sir,' requested the sailor, and he hurriedly went into the building. Outside was still another guard.

" 'It seems that all is well,' said the Green. 'I will leave right away, but I will still be in Shanghai for a day. You can look for me at the port if any problems arise and, in case I have departed, I will leave you the name of a contact to whom I will notify that you are under the protection of the Green Gang. Remember that we can always get you out of China.'

"Fortunately, it was not necessary to again resort to the Secret Society of the Chinese underworld. While we were waiting for the Sergeant, Von Grossen interrogated the sailor. The latter informed him that the Consulate was located at the end of the French Quarter, almost next to the Yangjingbang Creek, surrounded by the branches of the few German companies that were trading with Shanghai. He also told him that in the port were anchored two German ships, scheduled to depart three and seven days later.

"The Sergeant returned accompanied by a diplomatic Secretary.

" 'Please come in, Herren,' he ordered.

"We five entered a comfortable waiting room.

" 'Take a seat, you will be attended to shortly,' he said, and left through a panel door, not without first casting a suspicious glance at Bangi, Srivirya, and the daiva dog.

"We had to wait an hour, until the Secretary finally returned and led us to the Consul's office. He was a career diplomat from Cologne, sent to Shanghai probably to take advantage of his native knowledge of French and university English. Impeccably dressed in a black suit, he was no more than 40 years of age and was appearing to be at ease.

" 'Excuse the delay, but I had to call Nanking. You cannot imagine how the Ambassador, Baron Heinrich von Baden, has protested against what he considers an interference of the *RSHA* in the Ministry of Foreign Affairs: he accepts no excuses for not having been informed about this secret "First Key" mission.'

" 'But the operation was not to take place in China but in Tibet,' interrupted Von Grossen. 'We have arrived here on the run.'

" 'Don't worry, *Standartenführer:* Von Baden always protests,' the Consul calmed him with a smile. 'Let me finish. The military attaché was consulted, who confirmed that your names and ranks appear on the ciphered list of the *SS*. What he knew not a word about, of course, was Operation First Key. Therefore, a report request has been sent to Germany and a response is awaited. As soon as the cable arrives your situation will be resolved.

" 'And how long can that take?' I irrationally asked.

" 'How should I know? If it is true that you are who you say you are, you will understand that Berlin may respond in an hour, in a day, or not answer and *take action*. When it comes to the *RSHA,* no one can anticipate their reaction. And keep in mind that I am not making a criticism because I am also of the *SS*,' he cut himself short.

" '*Honorary SS Sturmbannführer:* I obtained that rank in 1936, thanks to the action of the present Minister of Foreign Affairs, Joachim von Ribbentrop.'

" 'Very good!' Von Grossen approved.

" 'Yes, I am of the *SS* and that is why I will advise you on what you will do from now on. If you remain here, I will be under obligation to take you into custody, which would be very unpleasant for you. Instead I will have you taken to a Hotel four hundred meters from here, where you will be comfortable until news arrives from Germany or Nanking. I will tell the Ambassador that I could not stop you and that, in any case, you are safe there. You did not have your *real* papers, but do you have other papers? Money? It occurs to me that you must be provided with them otherwise you would not have made it through China.'

" 'Indeed, *Konsul Sturmbannführer:* we have fake documentation and money at our disposal. Good money, they told us, because it is also false,' Von Grossen confirmed with sarcasm. 'We thank you for your counsel, and we will follow it to the letter for it seems very sensible. After spending months exploring Asia, we could not even endure an hour as prisoners.'

" 'I am sure that you told me that you were coming from Bhutan. By God, what a journey! And from what were you fleeing through China, may I know? From the Communists?'

"I believe, Neffe, that the five of us at that moment thought of the Valley of the Immortal Demons, of the vimāna of Shambhala, of the deadly buzzing, and we burst out laughing.

" 'Ha-ha-ha. From the Communists? *No, Herr Konsul: we were fleeing from their Chiefs,*' I responded with my eyes flooded with tears, 'Ha-ha-ha.' *But we cannot reveal to you who they are: you would not believe it!*

"Karl von Grossen laughingly nodded, a gesture that Oskar, Bangi, and Srivirya imitated. The surprised Consul opted not to ask any more questions and had the Secretary accompany us to the nearby Hotel.

"Everything was solved in the following days. Strict orders came from Germany for us to immediately embark and without discussion. Seven days later, we were leaving on a cargo ship that would make, in Macao, the first of an endless series of commercial stopovers. However, the Captain communicated to us that 'somewhere in the Indian Ocean,' the coordinates of which would be transmitted to him by radio, we would transfer to a warship. So it occurred a few miles off Sumatra: a disconcerted Admiral picked us up in his cruiser and set a direct course for Germany. The ship was heading for Argentina along with two others, executing a long-planned maneuver. Off Cape Town, he received the order to change course for the Indian Ocean to pick up five passengers. His new mission was marked as 'maximum security' and, from the moment in which the mysterious personages boarded, he was to transmit in a top-secret code and avoid all contact with other ships or ground stations. No one was to be able to locate the cruiser for, otherwise, there was the possibility of entering into operations. 'Who would attack us in peacetime?' the Admiral was mumbling. 'It must be another General Staff game, a secret test maneuver for the Kriegsmarine.'

"The Admiral was not imagining that if the synarchic forces had known the location of his ship, and the identity of its occupants, they would have sank it on the spot.

Chapter XXXIX

Twenty days after departing from Shanghai, we disembarked in Hamburg. There an external SD officer in command of a platoon was waiting for us; his orders: to drive Karl von Grossen, Oskar Feil, Srivirya, and Bangi in two cars to Berlin. I was to leave from the group and take a third car to the local airport, where a plane would also transport me to Berlin.

"We were going to separate for the first time in several months and the experience was painful. We had all lost Comrades and faced mortal dangers together; the lived adventures were bonding us. Before leaving them, Von Grossen wanted to speak to me alone.

" 'I knew it!' he said to me in a worried tone. 'Von Sübermann: You were the first key of Operation First Key! And the Thulegesellschaft will only deal with you. We, from this moment on, will be incommunicado, isolated from the rest of the ⚡ Black Order to prevent us from talking. We know a lot, Kurt, perhaps more than what the initiates of the Black Order want anyone to know! I have a feeling we may never see each other again,' he grimly concluded.

" 'You're delirious, mein *Standartenführer!*' I exclaimed in horror. 'That cannot be! We returned from fulfilling an important mission, successfully I believe, and there is no reason why, instead of receiving superior approval, anyone should be punished. You're tired, Von Grossen, I respectfully tell you! You will see how soon we will meet at a Friedrichstraße Biergarten to celebrate. It's natural that we must first report to our respective units, but after these logical formalities we'll have time to see each other again.'

"Von Grossen was shaking his head as if refusing to allow my arguments to penetrate his ears.

" 'No, no! Von Sübermann, once again you don't understand the situation. Now listen well to me because the possibility of us separating for good is real. I'm telling you this very consciously and basing it on all my previous experience in secret operations. I'm not so tired that I'm unable to foresee what may occur: *we will be eliminated.* That is, if you don't save us, Kurt. Believe me, we will live only if you assure your Chiefs that we won't speak to anyone about what we've seen. That's the guarantee that they need to let us go free: the opposite of what you assume! Ha-ha-ha: a report! You make me laugh, Von Sübermann: to whom is it of interest that I make a report on what I've seen in Tibet and what I've seen you do? You think that the Initiates of the Black Order will permit that an official report exists on the vimāna of Shambhala, or on the daiva dogs, or your Śrotra Karṇa? No, Von Sübermann: we are condemned to death because of you. And only you can save us. Contrary to what you've naively suggested: assure your Chiefs that neither Oskar Feil, nor I, will make any report, and we may thus keep our lives!'

"I reassured him the best that I could, reaffirming to him my loyalty: I would never let anything happen to them because of me! And we departed, separately, for Berlin.

"At the Berlin airport, a Chancellery Mercedes-Benz was waiting for me with a motorcycle escort. Upon seeing it, I thought that it was waiting for a Minister or a General, but my surprise was great when recognizing *ẞ Oberführer* Papp standing next to the door.

" 'Kurt von Sübermann!' he called, warmly smiling. I could not help remembering the first time that I saw him, in Rudolf Hess' cottage on the Obersalzberg in Berchtesgaden. He also remembered it, because he said, as soon as I approached:

" 'Six years, Kurt. Too long or too short? Six years and you're back from your first mission. We've feared for you, you know? It was a relief for all those who were aware of the operation to receive news of you. But from Shanghai! Ha. No one could believe it. You'll tell me how you made it across China.'

"The car crossed the Spree over the Schlossbrücke and began to circle around the *Lustgarten.* I looked at Edwin in surprise, but had no time to say anything:

" 'I thought that you'd like to go for a preliminary ride through the city, before arriving at the Chancellery; it'll revive you, after so many months in Asia!'

"Edwin Papp had correctly interpreted my sentiments. It was indescribable the happiness that I was then feeling to find myself once again in the Fatherland, from which more than once in the last few weeks I said good-bye, supposing that I would never return. The Mercedes went west and turned in front of the Brandenburg Gate, which was covered with swastika flags and garlands from the recent festivities. Now I was heading east, along the *Unter den Linden* or Linden Boulevard: I saw the Pariser Platz and the statue of Frederick the Great passing by. At the end of the avenue, we went around the Opernplatz,[84] area of the Emperor's Palace, the Royal Library,[85] the Berlin State Opera, the Catholic Church of St. Hedwig's Cathedral, the University,[86] and several military buildings. Finally, from the Lindens and the Opernplatz, the car drove into the *Friedrichstadt* neighborhood and began to ride down *Wilhelmstraße*, which is its eastern boundary. The ride was over.

" 'You can imagine who sent me to pick you up from the airport, can't you? Your Patenkind suffered a lot when we believed you lost and is enormously impatient to greet and embrace you. He didn't want anyone to divert you and that's why he sent his car to receive you and commissioned me, "under strict orders," he joked, 'to keep you safe and sound at his side.'

"Minutes later we arrived at *Wilhelmstraße* 77. At the *Reichskanzlei*,[87] indeed, the Führer's *Stellvertreter* was waiting for us.

An hour later, after bidding farewell to *Oberführer* Edwin Papp, I was leaving the Chancellery in the company of Rudolf Hess. He had been greatly moved to see me, and then I realized how much that former Comrade of Papa's was loving me. During the six years that he took care of my fate in Germany, he not only was like a father, but he professed the same affection for me. Now we were on our way to Gregorstraße 239, to visit Konrad Tarstein.

It was the first time that we would go together and, as Rudolf Hess could be easily recognized by the public and did not want to call attention to Tarstein's domicile, he had insisted that I drive the Mercedes while he was keeping himself discreetly seated in the back seat. In truth, not only with Rudolf Hess, but I was never in the mysterious mansion with anyone other than Tarstein. I even came to suspect that the Initiates of the Black Order would meet elsewhere, for there was never anyone but the two of us during the two years that I frequented the house. But this time it would be different.

---

84. Now known as *Bebelplatz*.

85. Staatsbibliothek Unter den Linden

86. Friedrich Wilhelm University, now known as the *Humboldt University of Berlin*.

87. Chancellery of the Third Reich

"As if it were the repetition of a Ritual, I struck the musty ring that was spinning inside the bronze fist and the shrill voice of Konrad Tarstein responded from some undefined place, behind the rickety door.

" 'Yes?'

" 'I am Kurt von Sübermann,' I introduced myself, speaking in the direction of the tiny peephole where the elusive little eyes of the Great Initiate were verifying my identity.

"The door opened and the squat and small figure of Konrad Tarstein appeared, his hand courteously outstretched to greet me.

" 'Kurt, Rudolf, good to see you,' he said, breaking the Ritual. 'Come in: *we were expecting you.*'

"It was January 1939. We spent the New Year on the high seas, with Von Grossen and other Comrades. I thought of them as Tarstein was guiding me toward a room into which I had never entered, situated on the upper floor. I thought of them and remembered the news that he was bringing: in my judgment, the expedition of Ernst Schäfer had failed in its purpose of sealing the pact between the 'sane forces of Germany' and the White Brotherhood of Chang Shambhala. If I was not mistaken, the Gate of Shambhala had been closed before coming to any agreement, and, consequently, the destruction of the Third Reich and the universal establishment of the Synarchy were not ensured for the Enemy.

"It was January 1939 and World War II would begin in September of that year.

"Around a strange crescent-shaped table were seated 16 initiates of the Black Order. Apart from Tarstein and Rudolf Hess, I recognized only four more as high personalities of the Third Reich: the remaining ten were until then completely unknown to me. All were in civilian clothes, but I assumed that several would be military personnel, although others must undoubtedly be citizens, especially the Asian whose presence filled me with astonishment.

"I was introduced by Tarstein, and the Initiates kindly greeted me, *but did not give their names at any time.* On the contrary, they identified themselves by pseudonyms such as *Aquilae, Leo, Serpens, Draconis, Corvus, Pavo, Cycnus,* etc. The Asian said his name was *Phoenix.*

"They invited me to sit in front of them, in an armchair located in the convex part of the crescent.

" 'So, *Lupus,* what happened to Ernst Schäfer's Operation Altwesten and the men lost in Operation First Key?' asked Tarstein, baptizing me that way.

" 'All dead or missing,' I affirmed. 'Both the members of Operation Altwesten and our own. But permit me, Gentlemen, to recount to you step by step the events that have taken place since I left Germany.'

"No one batted an eye when I brought forward the fate of the absentees. Not even during the following hours, spent in narration, in which I took great care to provide the main details and present the information as objectively as possible. Tarstein enlivened the long evening with two rounds of coffee, the last accompanied by exquisite jams. And I was hardly interrupted, except to request some concrete clarification. As I would later realize, those men were not needing to ask anything because they were all extraordinary clairvoyants; they were possessing what they were calling in the Thulegesellschaft: *Faculty of Anamnesis,* that is to say, a power proper of the Hyperborean Initiates that was enabling them *to explore the Akashic Cultural Records.*

"From there, from Gregorstraße 239, *they had seen* everything that I recounted to them of our adventures in Asia.

" 'Do not take this the wrong way, esteemed Lupus,' said Tarstein at last, 'but we are going to ask that you wait downstairs. We must hold a Council.'

"The deliberation lasted another hour, until I was once again convoked. Konrad Tarstein opened the dialogue:

" 'I congratulate you, Lupus: we have unanimously agreed that Operation First Key has been a success. In spite of the losses, which cost nothing compared to the spiritual benefit of having frustrated the plans of the Demons. The three fallen, Heinz, Hans, and Kloster, will be decorated, as well as Von Krupp and his men, since they were not participating in Schäfer's conspiracy.'

" 'Permit me to interrupt you, Kamerad Unicornis. That of decorating the dead is all very good, but what of the living? What is going to happen to Karl von Grossen, Oskar Feil, and the two Tibetans? Where are they now?'

" 'Incommunicado, of course,' Tarstein fatally confirmed. 'Look, Lupus, we would only be able to set them free, and even promote them, if you see to it that they do not speak out of place.'

" 'And how would I give such credence?'

" 'It is simple, Lupus: you would only have to form a corps directed by you. For example, Oskar Feil would from now on be your assistant; and you would be in charge of controlling his tongue. In the same way, Karl von Grossen would be dedicated to training an Elite team to support you in your future missions, and he would be in permanent contact with you. What do you think?'

" 'I am in agreement,' I affirmed relieved, 'and very pleased, because those men deserve the best treatment: they are valiant and priceless patriots. But now, Herren, after clearing up that matter that was troubling me, may I ask a few questions?'

" 'Of course,' accepted 'Unicornis' Tarstein.

" 'Well. The fact is that you seem to know what occurred in that valley of Tibet. You could then clarify some doubts for me. For example, why were we attacked and by whom? And I also have a question, perhaps not as "serious" as the previous ones, but which I am not ashamed to raise here: it is about the future of the daiva dog. I cannot deny, Herren, that it has caused me great displeasure to leave Vrune caged in Hamburg, considering that it is a unique specimen on Earth and that it is about to give birth.

" 'You are right, Lupus!' accepted Tarstein. 'Tomorrow morning we will send the best veterinary officer of the ⚡⚡, and his team of assistants, with the mission to care for and safely transport the daiva dog to Berlin. Have no doubt that we value this animal in its full measure and consider it to be a *secret weapon* of the Third Reich.

" 'And about what you first asked,' Tarstein continued, 'you were attacked by the Druids!'

" 'By the Druids?' I incredulously repeated. 'But we were in Tibet!'

" 'Yes, by the Druids. Do you remember what I warned you the first day that you came to this house: *"from among the hunters of the Synarchy, the Druids are in charge of bagging the catches of your species"* ... *of your species, Von Sübermann*. It surprises you that they have ambushed you in Tibet, but you should bear in mind that you went to meddle with "The Gate of Bera and Birsha," that is to say, the sinister opening through which the Priests of Melchizedek enter Shambhala. On that particular door, Ernst Schäfer was wishing to knock, because from there have come, for thousands of years, the Arch-Priests

and Arch-Druids of the European Orders of the White Brotherhood.'

" 'Bera and Birsha?' I asked puzzled.

" 'Indeed, Bera and Birsha,' replied the Asian, whom we
were calling 'Phoenix.'

" 'Remember, Lupus, did you not see two majestic images,
one on each side of the Gate?'

" 'I suppose that you are referring to the figures of the
winged bodhisattvas, which were carved on the walls of the
gorge, or dvara, or shen, that is to say, at the opening between
mountains at the end of the ravine. I remember them perfectly: on both walls of the exit of the gorge, and about 25 or 30
meters high, there were two bas-reliefs that were representing
Beings of Divine nature, a kind of armed "angels" or "bodhisattvas." '

"I remained in silence for a few seconds, evoking that unforgettable vision. Then I added:

" 'They had wings: the two angels were both exhibiting
spread dove wings. And they were wearing white tunics down
to their ankles: yes, it was a Druid's garb or a Levite ephod!
They were even bearing the *four-leaf clover* on their breasts;
and little stars, suns, crescent moons, on their fringes. And I
also remember their weapons: each one had his right hand
closed on a handle, from which two globes were protruding on
both sides. The scene was very suggestive and that is why I
remember it with so much clarity: I was standing at the gorge
entrance, when things had already been cleared up with Von
Krupp; then I looked toward the west, at the end of the ravine,
and I saw the vertex of the gorge, or pass, flanked by those
colossal sculptures. Both of them were pointing with the index
finger of their left hand to the exit, *as if inviting to come in, a
gesture that they were also accompanying with the expression of
their diabolical faces;* however, *their right hands were not ceasing
to point with their globes in the direction of every possible visitor,*
that is to say, toward the center of the ravine. I believe that I
was precisely looking at the gorge of the West, and at its terrible guardians, when arose from there the ball of light that the
Tibetans were calling "the Vimāna of Shambhala." '

" 'There is no doubt, then, that you have been in front of the
Gate of Bera and Birsha,' assured Phoenix. 'The mysterious
"angels" that you have described are not such, nor are they
"bodhisattvas," but Demons of the worst kind, those who are

commonly denominated "Immortals": Bera and Birsha are two Immortal Demons who for thousands of years have acted in Europe and Asia, and whose image you have had the luck, or misfortune, depending on how you look at it, of contemplating in that ravine of Tibet. Their master, Melchizedek, assigned them millennia ago to work in favor of the Universal Synarchy of the Chosen People, especially taking care of sustaining the conspiracy in the bosom of the peoples of Indo-European, Indo-Iranian, and Hindustani lineage. In the European context, They have been the Supreme Arch-Druids who were secretly directing the Druidic Order, and that is why Unicornis and other Initiates also qualify them as "Druids" or "Golen." But they are much more powerful beings than the Druids, whom they command.

"'For example, They have been distinguished by Rigden Jyepo, the King of the World, with the Power of the Dorje, the most terrible weapon in the Solar System. Dorjes: those were the weapons, similar to two globes joined by a handle, that you observed on the bas-reliefs of the Immortals! But you, Lupus, not only perceived the Dorjes carved in stone: *you experienced their deadly power in the flesh.*'

"I looked at him dumbfounded. And Phoenix further clarified what my ears were refusing to hear.

"'Concretely, Lupus: the buzzing of bees that you felt, and that caused the death of your Comrades, is nothing more than the acoustic manifestation of the Power of the Dorje, which also acts on the other four tattvas; with the Dorje it is possible to emit the *om* or the final *yod,* the monosyllable of the dissolution of Created Forms, which is identical to the bīja of the Principle of Creation. It is quite possible that it has been the Demon Bera who applied the Power of the Dorje on your heart. In synthesis, be assured that you have been in front of the Gate of Bera and Birsha, in a mountain pass of Tibet known since ancient times as *"Das Pech."* Of course, Das Pech[88] is not easy to get to, that is to say, it is not easy to reach its eastern gorge, but curiously, on many ancient maps it appears there where you found it, next to the Altyn-Tagh mountains.

"'It can't be,' I irrationally denied. 'I saw a flying vehicle, an extraterrestrial craft; I don't know what it was, but for sure the buzzing sound was emanating from it.'

---

88. *The Pitch.*

" 'So it is, valued Lupus: *the phenomenon that you saw was the Demon Bera in all his Power. It was not a flying craft, or an unknown vimāna or airplane, but an "absolute energy unit" of the Universe animated by the infernal "Intelligence" of Bera, which is the Sephirah Binah. An "absolute energy unit," "an archetypal atom," adopted by Bera to present himself and unleash the dissolving Force of the Dorje: that is what you witnessed, although you believed to see something else.'*

" 'It's not possible,' I repeated disturbed, resisting to accept that that Deadly Presence was in truth an 'Immortal' Demon, and that this Monster was finally on my tail. I was beginning to realize what Tarstein was getting at when warning me about 'the hunters of the Synarchy' who would procure to bag catches 'of my species.'

"Unperturbed, Phoenix continued explaining:

" 'The archetypal atom is the Primordial Form par excellence, the Egg of Brahma, the monad made in the image and likeness of The One: all real atoms and all atomic forms, all units, emanate from it and participate in its exemplifying existence. And do you know why Bera adopted that form to manifest himself before You and use the Power of the Dorje? *Because the only way left for a Demon like Him, traitor to the Spirit of Man, to resist the Sign of the Origin that you exhibit, is to enclose himself in the absolute unity of the Created Monad.* But you have already seen the result of that tactic, Comrade Lupus: *it has not been able to resist you, with the Sign of the Origin that you possess, and the Gates of Shambhala have been closed to our enemies.*

" 'Oh, I would not be so optimistic, Comrade Phoenix,' I suggested, at the same time that I was agitatedly shaking from old and new terrors. 'I remind you that if I preserve my life, it is not precisely due to the effect of the Sign but thanks to the intervention of those incredible warriors who are the Kaulika monks, and the invaluable collaboration of the daiva dogs that brought us out of the Altyn-Tagh ravine.'

" 'Ah, Comrade Lupus, I fear that you do not realize the situation.'

"Phoenix was giving me the same reproach as Karl von Grossen. Evidently, I was comprehending nothing, or very little, of what was going on around me. Either everyone was pretending to comprehend what was going on better than I. Or I was becoming extremely obstinate or stupid. But, whatever it was, there was something that I was comprehending, and in which I was not mistaken: the cause of all my ills, which until yesterday I was considering a marvelous privilege, was the in-apprehensible Sign of the Origin. Distinction of the Gods or Stigma? In front of me, the most important men of the Third Reich were counting on me, and on my Sign, to carry forward the Führer's plans. But, and this I was now realizing, the most terrible Forces of Hell, Forces that I had seen up close in Tibet, *were considering me a priori their mortal enemy and would deploy an unimaginable attack against me.*

"Allegorically speaking, such a situation, the only situation that I was perhaps comprehending, was that the Third Reich was preparing to march on the World, like a cyclopean phalanx, and that I would then perform the function of *banner-bearer*. Yes, I would be the *standard-bearer* of the Third Reich, and the flag that I would fly would be the Sign of the Origin, the Sign of Lúcifer, the Sign of Wothan, the Sign of Shiva, *my Sign*. And, as in every army in operations, the Enemy would try to conquer the flag, *our Banners,* procuring to strike down the banner-bearer *without prior warning,* trying to take away the Sacred Insignia of the Spirit, trying to take away his life, trying to take away his banner, trying to take away *my life,* trying to take away *my Sign*.

"I did not protest against Phoenix's commentary, and he continued:

"'Esteemed Lupus: You owe your "salvation" to no one but Yourself. Are you forgetting that if there was Operation First Key, and daiva dogs, it occurred *because there was previously an Initiate Kurt von Sübermann, who was bearing the Sign of the Origin?* The daiva dogs, and you, are the same thing, because without you there would be no daiva dogs, no Sign of the Origin, no Sign of Shiva, and no one *capable of placing his Ego beyond Kula and Akula*. The Demon Bera attacked you with the fury of a vimāna and you believe that you were saved "thanks" to the daiva dog: but know that it is your own insecurity, your lack of faith in Yourself, *your incomprehension of the situation,* the cause of which encourages such an erroneous conviction! Because if you were in reality the Initiate that you should be, *sure of Yourself in the face of Death, and beyond Death, all the way to the Origin,* you would know without hesitation that your Sign has made you invulnerable to the attack of any Created Being, even the most powerful God! If you were to find yourself alone, facing the Demons Bera and Birsha, or others like them, and They applied all the Power of the Dorje on your heart, you would easily remain out of their reach by situating yourself beyond Kula and Akula, in the Origin, *or by creating, with a tulpamudra, your own daiva dogs, or lungta "daiva horses," or any illusion of the sort!'*

"'All right! All right! I give up!' I proposed, sadly smiling; and before the claims of the Initiates of the Black Order became unanswerable. 'I will strive to understand your points of view,' I promised. 'Do you truly believe that those damned Immortals not only attacked me to death, but closed the Gate of their Lair?'

"'That's right, Lupus,' said Tarstein. 'I will tell you what has happened, according to the coincident vision of all the Initiates present here. In principle, and this will surprise you, we have reason to believe that Ernst Schäfer did not die at Das Pech. And if he had died during the attack, we are sure that the Immortals would resurrect him. What for? *So that he returns to Europe to look for your head.* Never, understand it well, Lupus, because your life is at stake, never will they permit someone like you to exist in a synarchic society. On the contrary, you being in the way, there will be no pact between the White Brotherhood and the Secret Societies of the Synarchy; and consequently, there will be no constitution of the Synarchy. Undoubtedly, Ernst Schäfer, or some other similar fool, will be delegated by the Demons to make their conditions heard in the west: *and in these new conditions will be demanded the elimination of you and all those who, like you, are bearers of the Sign of the Origin that they cannot stand.*

"'The Universal Synarchy of the End Times must see the Traitorous Gods lord over the World, as in the days of Atlantis, side by side with the Great Rabbis of the Chosen People: *but they will not be able to do so as long as there are spiritual men in the World who raise the banner of the Origin, who speak with the Runes of Wothan.* Hence we can affirm without fear of being mistaken that Operation First Key has been a success: we have brought an Initiate with the Sign of the Origin to Das Pech, in front of the Gate of Bera and Birsha of Chang Shambhala; and we have reclaimed him for the Strategy of the Third Reich. In a word, we have inflicted upon the Enemy the greatest defiance on its own ground: it is impossible for it to now want anything else but revenge. And its retaliations will no longer be of a diplomatic or political order, it will no longer bring about secret pacts that back coups d'état or palace intrigues: the Third Reich will have to prepare itself to resist a formidable military potential.

" 'And as for you, Lupus: it goes without saying what you represent for us. To count on you means to have a *strategic advantage* for the execution of the plans of the Black Order. On this basis, we should try to protect you from any danger; it would be the most logical thing to do. However, we will do the opposite: we will not neglect your safety, but neither will we prevent you from fulfilling your mission, *the mission that was entrusted to you by the Gods when they marked you with the Sign of the Origin.* You will continue, then, taking risks! We will carefully study your future operations and we will send you to close, with your Divine Sign, the Gates of Hell! Now we know that *you can* do it, will you?'

"The sixteen pairs of eyes were drilling into my brain. I looked at Rudolf Hess, almost a father to me, how could I say no to him? And to Konrad Tarstein, my Hyperborean Instructor, the Sage who revealed so many secrets to me, what would I not give to him, who was needing and asking nothing for himself? And to the remaining Initiates, the Secret Architects of the New Germany, the Chiefs of the ⚡⚡ Black Order: to deny them anything was to refuse to serve the Fatherland. At that moment, Neffe Arturo, my answer could only be one:

" 'Heil Hitler!' I shouted, and raised my right arm to unequivocally agree. My answer, Neffe, and everyone understood that, was an oath, a vow as an ⚡⚡ Knight.

"When they all withdrew, half an hour later, and only the host, Rudolf Hess, and I were left at Gregorstraße 239, we said goodbye to Tarstein and left in the Mercedes. As before, I was driving and Rudolf Hess was remaining in the back seat. I was longing to greet Ilse and ruled out that we were going to Rudolf's house, but he immediately instructed me, 'to Hotel Kaiserhof.' I looked at him in the rearview mirror, not understanding.

" 'Can't you guess who's waiting for us there?' he asked, while he was teasingly smiling. I trembled upon asking:

" 'Papa?'

" 'Yes, Kurt. Your father in person. Baron Von Sübermann has specially traveled from Egypt to see his elusive son.'

" 'Oh, what a joy; what a joy. I still can't believe it. You told him, didn't you? Tell me the truth, Taufpate?'

" 'Yes, I did. I notified him, when we heard that you were at sea, that he could come to Berlin 20 days later. And that's what he did without wasting a moment. What was the harm in that? It is good for your father to see you at least once a year. Or at the end of an operation in which you nearly lost your life. You approve of my decision, yes?'

" 'Oh, yes, Taufpate. You have given me the most beautiful gift that I could hope for.'

"That was one of the best nights of my life. With Papa, Rudolf, Ilse, and little Wolf Rüdiger, in Berlin, in January 1939, the world was seeming to be in our hands. I still remember that during dinner, Papa announced that his daughter had married a German-Argentine engineer and that they would soon depart to settle in Argentina, where the Siegnagels were the owners of a winery. And that Rudolf also announced that I would be promoted in the following days, in the hierarchy of the *ϟϟ*, with the rank of *Standartenführer*, thus skipping the intermediate rank of *Obersturmbannführer*. I would be, he said, one of the youngest *Standartenführers* or Colonels of the Waffen-*ϟϟ*.

Chapter XL

ear Neffe, thus concluded my first mission for the ⚡⚡ and the Third Reich. During it, the mysterious character of that Sign of the Origin that was causing the devotion of some and the terror of others was evidenced. By now, many of your initial doubts will have been dispelled. You will have realized, I hope, that the story of Belicena and my own history are built on the same armature, on an infrastructure called 'Hyperborean Wisdom.' And you will have realized—it is necessary that you do so!—*that both stories continue in you, that the Hyperborean Wisdom passes through you, that the Gods have marked you with the Sign of the Origin.*

"Your story and mine, Neffe Arturo, are partly parallel: to begin with, we are both members of the same family stock; we both suffered a shocking experience: I, because of the interview with the Führer, and you because of the death of Belicena Villca; and those impressions led us both to seek the truth in ourselves, in the depths of the Self: I, during the vacations in Egypt, in 1937, when the Śrotra Karṇa awakened in me, and you now, in 1980, in that infinite instant of the spiritual *rapture* by the Virgin of Agartha. Yes, Neffe: I believe that at that point we both *self-Initiated.* I know that the purpose of the Ritual of the Hyperborean Initiation is to put the chosen one in contact with the Vrunes of Navutan but, as such Signs were already in us, we were able to realize the miracle of the *self-revelation of the Naked Truth of the Self.*

"Then, the parallelism of the events lived by both of us culminates in the correlativity of our initiatic experience: we are both, from now and forever, indissolubly linked to a Spiritual, Eternal, and Infinite Source, to the Grace of the Virgin of Agartha, to the Hyperborean Wisdom of the Gods. That is why, *as I raised them at the time, you must from now on raise 'our Banners,' which are the banners of the Spirit.* You were asking yourself in your Salta apartment: to whom to turn for spiritual help? Who are the representatives of the Hyperborean Wisdom in this world? Well, now you have the clearest answer. *The Führer has given the answer: the answer is the ⚡⚡, the ⚡⚡ Black Order. Remember that the Führer will return, Neffe, even Belicena Villca was announcing it in her letter:*

" *'The Great White Chief, the Lord of Absolute Will and Valor, will come once, twice, three times, to Your World. The first time, he will break History, but he will go away, and cause the insensate laughter of the Demons* (as it seems to me Neffe, this part of the prophecy has already been fulfilled); *the second time he will raise the Final Battle, but he will go away, amidst the Roar of Terror of the Demons* (and I suppose, Arturo, that this is what will happen very soon.); *the third time he will guide the Race of the Spirit toward the Origin, but he will go away forever, leaving behind him the Holocaust of Fire in which the followers of the One God, men, Souls, and Demons will be consumed. But those who follow the Envoy of the War Lord will be Eternal!'* (And here I can only call out *'fiat, fiat,'*[89] Neffe Arturo.)

"These are Capitán Kiev's words, which will be inexorably fulfilled. You will seek the Tirodal Order and bring to their Initiates the Letter of Belicena Villca. It will be very opportune because they seek, also, the Noyo and the Wise Sword in order to initiate the Final Battle. But you will bring them something more important than the letter of Belicena Villca: the Sign of the Origin, which closes the Gates of Shambhala and opens the Gates of Agartha, through which the Führer and the Eternal One will return to unleash the Final Battle!

"That is the *true* reason for the great maneuver, Neffe! That you draw near to those who wait, at the right moment, in the Kairos of the Final Battle! That is the spiritual significance of this whole series of coincidences: *to bring the Sign of the Origin closer to the Kairos of the Final Battle!*

"*And like the House of Tharsis, and like me, Neffe, you must understand that it is all the more reason for them to attempt to get rid of you. The Druids will be after you! Perhaps Bera and Birsha in person!*

"For this reason, I want to propose that we leave as soon as possible. From my stories, although incomplete, you will already have drawn plenty of conclusions. Later on, if circumstances permit, I will give you the details of the following events up to 1947, the year in which I came to Argentina and since when I remained hidden.

"In summary, and in broad strokes, this is what happened from 1939.

---

89. Latin for *"May it happen,"* or *"Let it be done."*

"German citizenship was granted to Bangi and Srivirya and they were decorated with the Iron Cross 1st Class. They were also inducted into the Waffen-*SS* with the effective rank of *Untersturmführer*. They remained until the summer of 1939 in Berlin, where they imparted to them training in cryptography and tasks related to the Secret Service, and finally they left for Tibet, and reunited with the Lopas who left from our expedition, they diligently devoted themselves to the mission that had been entrusted to them: to prepare an Elite corps that would act as Foreign Legion within the Waffen-*SS*. From there would emerge the famous *Tibetan Legion,* which was secretly depending on the *1st SS Panzer Division Leibstandarte SS Adolf Hitler* and one of which battalions would defend, to the death, the Führer's bunker in April of 1945.

"Karl von Grossen would also return to Asia. From India and China, he would occupy himself with discreetly supplying the Tibetan Legion, the natural settlement of which would be in Assam, in the dominions of a Kaulika Prince who was a bitter enemy of the English. In that small Kingdom on the border with Bhutan, *SS* instructors especially from Germany supplemented the offensive arsenal of the Kaulika monks, comprised of arrows, daggers, and scimitars, with modern weapons of tactical purpose, such as grenades, pistols, and assault rifles. However, the maximum effectiveness of those terrible warriors, would always be accompanied by the use of their traditional weapons, for which they had no rival in Tibet. In any case, for the sake of reference, that corps never exceeded a hundred troops.

"But long before the Tibetan Legion was ready, Vrune was giving birth in Berlin to two beautiful daiva puppies, dying in labor. Another legion, this one of *SS* veterinarians, took it upon themselves under the most severe threats to make sure that the twins lived. Notwithstanding our reservations, they grew up without problems and I named them *Yum* and *Yab*. They responded well to conventional training and even better to the use of the svadi Kyilkhor, understanding and obeying my slightest wishes.

"In September, Germany invades Poland and the Second World War begins. On June 14 of the following year, 1940, the troops of the Third Reich enter Paris. Neither the Tibetan Legion nor I intervened in those actions because it was being repeated to us in the Black Order that *'the true and only front of the Third Reich was in the East.'*

"Contrary, then, to the movement of our armies, we concentrated on planning Asian operations, in everything similar to First Key, in which I obtained my baptism by fire. Finally, in August of 1940, I received the order to execute 'Operation Second Key,' which had the objective of reaching Mount Elbrus, where, according to the Indo-Aryan traditions, *the Aryans were twice-born.* But it was not about going directly to the Caucasus, but to *strategically approach with the daiva dogs to arrive at a Gate situated in other dimensions.*

"That time, I traveled from Germany with Oskar Feil, a *Hauptsturmführer* named Caesar von Lossow, and the mastiffs Yum and Yab. On the Pamir plateau, at the source of the Pyandzh River, Karl von Grossen was waiting for us with the *Gebirgsjäger* of the Tibetan Legion, about fifty men in total. From there, we initiated one of those crazy journeys that the daiva dogs would follow in order to go some place. I do not know what shortcuts they had taken, since, instead of crossing Tadzhikistan, Afghanistan, Turkmenistan, Iran, Armenia, and Georgia, and traveling 3,000 kilometers, the mastiffs found Georgia 500 kilometers away. Although it is hard to believe, 500 kilometers from the Pyandzh River we came upon Grozny, a city situated at the foot of Mount Elbrus; of course, the vicissitudes and peripeteias gone through up to then, and that I cannot narrate now, took us several months.

"Inversely to what was in Das Pech, *at Mount Elbrus there was a Path to Agartha, or to Venus, which is the same.* The mission entrusted by Tarstein, and the Initiates of the Black Order, was consisting *in locating the Caucasian Gate of Agartha and to unite such place with the locality of Rastenburg, in East Prussia.* How? With the daiva dogs; ordering the mastiffs in the Caucasus to reach Rastenburg, by means of a jump through Time and Space. In that way, according to Tarstein's assumptions, the distance between Elbrus and Rastenburg would be *eliminated* or, in other words, the Gate of Agartha 'would remain' in Rastenburg.

"What importance had Rastenburg, in order to demand such an operation? We were not knowing then, for we were only asked to execute the plan before May of 1941, but as of June 22, when the Third Reich initiates the invasion of the Soviet Union, the Führer's Headquarters would be established in Rastenburg.

"The Führer's code name was *Wolf*, and that is why his center of operations in the East, the Throne from where he would oppose the darkest Potencies of Matter with the Power of the Spirit, would be known as *Führerhauptquartier Wolfsschanze*, that is to say, the Supreme Stronghold Headquarters of the Wolf. It was in the Prussian province of Köningsberg, former plaza of the Teutonic Order, in the middle of the forests that grow on the banks of the Guber, and there Karl von Grossen, Oskar Feil, Bangi, Srivirya, and I landed one day in May of 1941: the rest of the legion was remaining camped on Mount Elbrus, 2000 kilometers away. Like their parents in Tibet, Yun and Yab had responded to the order *to fly* and bridged the established distance in an instant. Once in Rastenburg, we dedicated ourselves to marking the exact place where the daiva dogs touched down, because wherever the place was, a railroad track would be laid there to station the Führer's train car. We were under strict order not to move until being located by the troops of the ⚡⚡ that Himmler had stationed and that were constantly patrolling the region. A platoon found us and immediately a whole battalion occupied the zone in which, weeks later, the Wolfsschanze would be stationed. It is worth remembering that in the same place, on July 20, 1944, a group of traitorous Generals, the same ones who were helping Ernst Schäfer, attempted to assassinate the Führer by means of the installation of a high-powered bomb just a few meters away from him. Of course, those who do not know what the Caucasian Rastenburg Gate was, still do not understand how the Führer came away from the attack unscathed.

"When I finally returned to Berlin, in August of 1941, it was already too late to say goodbye to Rudolf Hess: on May 10, my Taufpate had flown to England to attempt to neutralize the Golen Strategy that had dominated the British High Command. His flight was concerted between members of the English Golden Dawn Secret Society and Initiates of the Thulegesellschaft, but as soon as he landed he was captured by the Druids thanks to the treason of the German Albrecht Haushofer and the British Duke of Hamilton, and confined in a military prison. For the Synarchy, peace between England and Germany and its alliance against the Soviet Union, a project that Rudolf Hess was authorized to handle, would have been a catastrophe. He was therefore incommunicado during the war years and a supposed dementia was publicized while attempting to effectively destroy his psyche with drugs similar to those that Belicena Villca mentions. Analogously, in the case of Belicena Villca, being a Great Initiate like Rudolf, the Golen did not achieve their purpose.

"Yes, Neffe, in August of 1941 the time had arrived to re-member the words that Tarstein had said to me four years ear-lier: *'we must all hope that his opportunity never arrives, for when Parsifal undertakes his mission it will mean that King Arthur is wounded... and that the Kingdom is terra gasta.'* Yes, Rudolf, the pure madman, like Parsifal, had departed for Albion, England, the White Island that was somehow representing Chang Shambhala, the Abode of the Demons: Tarstein predicted it to me because he knew that it was possible, because he was fa-miliar with an esoteric significance that was explaining the deep symbolism of the journey. That the diplomat Albrecht Haushofer was a traitor, a member of the group of the 'sane forces of Germany,' we were already knowing for years from the reports that Heydrich had written in the SD: Albrecht was the son of Professor Karl Haushofer and a Jewess by the name of Martha Mayer-Doss. And that the Golden Dawn Secret So-ciety, which at some point at the start of the century was relat-ed to the Einherjar and the Thulegesellschaft, fell into the hands of the Druids after the takeover by the priest Aleister Crowley, we were also knowing. So the result of his mission could hardly take Rudolf by surprise, but there must be a deeper and more secret reason that justified his sacrifice.

"I asked Tarstein directly, but that time he avoided direct clarification and spoke to me again in symbolic language, without a doubt so as not to affect the Myth, so that the Myth continued acting.

" 'See, Kurt,' he pointed out, 'King Arthur, the Führer, may be betrayed by Guinevere-Germany and such a dishonor can leave the Kingdom weak against the attack of the elemental beings, the *Elementarwesen* hordes coming from the east. To prevent the Kingdom from being destroyed, King Arthur needs to count on the strength of the Gral. But the Gral has not been present in the World of Sleeping Men for 700 years. What to do? As in Wolfram von Eschenbach, the Führer says:

"man mac mich dâ in strîte sehen:
der muoz mînhalp von iu geschehen."[90]

" 'And Parsifal departs for the Castle of Sigune, from where emerge the forces that animate the subhuman beings that threaten the Kingdom. And there, like Joseph of Arimathea, King Crudel captures and sentences him and his Knights to 48 years in prison. But then, in prison, Joseph of Arimathea enters into contact with the Gral and it spiritually nourishes him during the time of his confinement: and the elemental forces are, thus, to some extent restrained, because the Knight of the Gral, still locked up, possesses enough spiritual forces to transmit them to King Arthur and support him in his Regal Function. Some day the Knight Joseph of Arimathea will manage to get out from his unjust confinement and will be free with the Stone of the Gral, reading on it the Name of the Führer and restoring his sovereignty in the Kingdom. It will be at that moment that Frederick II, bearer of the Stone of Genghis Khan, will meet the Seignior of the Dog, Prester John, the Lord of Cathay or K'Taagar, that is, the Lord of Agartha. Then the elemental forces will be definitively defeated on Earth.'

"I managed to extract nothing more than symbolic affirmations of this type from Tarstein, which did not help me much to understand the hidden significance of his mission, although I was intuiting it enough. But I did not see my Taufpate again since 1940. Naturally, during the Nuremberg Trial of 1945/46, Rudolf was interrogated by the hypocritical Allied judges and, of course, he did not say a word about the Gral or King Arthur. Instead he spoke a good deal about the brainwashing and drug treatments to which the English subjected him:

• •

" '... Of course, I thought constantly how the monstrous behavior of the people around me might be explained. I eliminated the possibility that they were criminals because socially they made an extremely good impression. Also, their own past contradicted that assumption.'

....

" 'A further thought that I had was that these people had been hypnotised, although at the time I did not know that

---

90. *"It will seem that I am the one who fights, but in truth it will be you who fights me."*

there was any possibility of causing such a strong and lasting state of hypnotism. I expressed this suspicion quite frankly to Major F., who evidently regarded this a wonderful joke. He said that he and all others around me were absolutely normal, and that unfortunately I was merely the victim of auto-suggestion.'

....

" 'My headache went on constantly. I persisted in pretending that I had lost my memory. I learned from my mistakes. I assumed that I must not recognise people that I had seen more than fourteen days ago, even if it was one of the doctors who had been with me for years. From that, it can be recognised what terrible poisons they gave me, a poison for which there was no antidote [...].

....

" 'Soon I didn't make any more mistakes. I came through tests like a sudden appearance of persons whom I had known before, and I pretended not to recognise them any more, although I was in a state of hypnotic sleep. I had to be ready, day and night. Finally, I was ready to answer questions falsely even in my dreams by keeping up the pretence of loss of memory.'

....

" 'On the 19th of April, 1945, Brigadier-General Dr. Rees came to see me. He again tried to convince me that my conclusions as well as my suffering only stemmed from mental fixations. I interrupted him with the remark that there was no purpose in his speaking **because I knew what I knew.** Meanwhile, I had gained further convictions which were adequate to substantiate my suspicions. The abominable atrocities which the British perpetrated during the Boer War in concentration camps on women and children could also be ascribed **to the secret chemical.**'

" 'Brigadier-General Rees reflected with a gloomy face. Then he jumped up and hurried out with the words: "Oh well, I wish you good luck."

" 'I had been imprisoned for four years now with lunatics, and had been at the mercy of their torture without being able to inform anybody of this, without being able to convince the Swiss Envoy that this was so, not to mention my being unable to enlighten the lunatics about their condition. It was worse than being in the hands of criminals, for, with them, there is some little reasons in some obscure corner of their brain—

some feeling, and little bit of conscience in them. With my lunatics, this was one hundred percent out of the question. But
the worst were the doctors, who employed their scientific
knowledge for the most refined tortures. As a matter of fact I
was without a doctor these four years because those who so
called themselves in my entourage had the task of creating
suffering for me and if anything to make it worse. Just as I was
without medicine during all this time, because what was given
to me under this name only served the same purpose and beside that was poison. In front of my garden, lunatics walked up
and down with loaded rifles—lunatics surrounded me in the
house—when I went for a walk, lunatics walked in front and
behind me—all in the uniforms of the British Army—we met
columns of the inmates of a nearby lunatic asylum who were
led to work. My companions expressed pity for them **and did
not sense that they belonged in the same column**; that the
doctor in charge of the hospital, and who was at the same time
in charge of the lunatic asylum, should have been his own patient for a long time. They did not sense that they themselves
needed pity. I pitied them honestly—here, decent people were
made into criminals.

" 'However, what worry was this to the Jews?—they were as
little worried about that as about the British King and the
British people. **For the Jews were behind all this**—if probability alone had not argued for that then the following would
have. I was given the book of a Jew, about treatment that he
had suffered in Germany in a very significant manner—I was
given reports of the British Consulates about the treatment of
Jews in Germany according to the description by Jews. Dr. Dix
told me that my mental fixations were a consequence of bad
conscience about the treatment of Jews, for which I was responsible,—I replied that it had not been one of my duties to
decide the treatment of Jews. However, if this had been the
case, **I would have done everything to protect my people
from these criminals and I wouldn't have had a bad conscience about it.** Lt. A.-C. of the Scots Guard, who was with
me for my protection in the name of the King, told me one
day: "You are being treated like the Gestapo treats their political enemies." Dr. Dix and the nurse, Sgt. Everett, were present
and smilingly agreed. Since they had stepped out of their regular role, because it was always claimed that I was imagining

my suffering, the doctor and the officer were relieved shortly thereafter.

" 'I mentioned the expression used by A.-C. of the Scots Guard in my protest of September 5th, 1941, and added that it was typical for the Jews to claim that their enemies did what they did themselves [without the Jews giving them a motive, and to charge their enemies with the crimes that in reality they were accustomed to commit]. The Hungarian Bishop, Prohaska, had found this already after the Bolshevik domination of Hungary in 1919. He reported that during this period whole truck-loads of mutilated bodies were driven on to the bridges over the Danube in Budapest to be pushed into the river; that priests had had their caps nailed on their heads, that their fingernails had been pulled out, and that their eyes had been gouged out, and the current joke was why should they go into the other world with their eyes open. All those responsible, with Bela Kun at the head, had been Jews. The world Press had been silenced. However, when, after the collapse of the Bolshevist Government, some of the guilty were to be judged, the same world Press cried out about white terror in Hungary. It has always been like this, Prohaska concluded, whenever a people had to fight against the Jews.

" 'I could not foresee at this time that the Jews, in order to receive material for a propaganda against Germany, would go so far as **to bring the guards of the German Concentration Camps by use of the secret chemical to treat the inmates like the OGPU**[91] **did:** [every criminal act of this nature must be attributed to the use of secret drugs that the Jews employed within Germany itself]. If I asked myself what the reasons were for the crimes perpetrated on me, I suspect the following—first, the British Government had been hypnotised into endeavoring to change me into a lunatic so that I could be paraded as such if necessary, if they were to be reproached that they had not accepted my attempt at an understanding whereby England could have been spared many sacrifices. Secondly, the general inclination of Jews or of non-Jews whom they had gotten into their power to maltreat me and revenge on me the fact that National Socialist Germany had defended itself from the Jews. Thirdly, revenge on me because I had tried to end the war too early which the Jews had started with

---

91. Soviet Secret Police, whose chiefs are invariably Jews of unparalleled cruelty.

so much trouble, whereby they would have been prevented from reaching their war aims. Fourthly, it was to be prevented that I was to publish the disclosures contained in this report.' "[92]

. . . .

"The secret truth about the famous 'Holocaust of 6,000,000 Jews' may be in these declarations of Rudolf Hess. It is notable, indeed, that the members of the Chosen People were victims of a typically Jewish genocide, a mode of extermination that, just as Belicena Villca demonstrates in her Letter, is that which the Rabbis have been demanding for millennia to apply to the 'Gentiles' or 'Goyim.' But Rudolf Hess rightly exposed 'that it was typical of the Jews to claim that their enemies did what they did themselves, without the Jews giving them a motive, [and to charge their enemies with the crimes that in reality they were accustomed to commit.]' This attitude of the Jews is frequent, is confirmed by hundreds of historical proofs, and explains the incredible accusation that the ⚡⚡ would have carried out on them a mini Holocaust of Fire, projecting upon the concentration camps the image of the Final Death with which they themselves dream of destroying spiritual Humanity, that is to say, non-Jewish Humanity. In synthesis, Neffe Arturo, only a typically Jewish mentality could have conceived of such a mode of extermination, which never passed through the imagination of Heinrich Himmler or, of course, the Führer. And as for the Germans who supposedly 'confessed' to having perpetrated those crimes, besides the fact that there are many obvious explanations as to why someone would testify against himself or against his homeland, it is clear that one must seek the real cause in the secret drugs known to the Druids, whose main lair for millennia is precisely England. Rudolf Hess himself exposed it in 1945, as you have seen, when affirming that not only had the witnesses been drugged and hypnotized in order to testify against himself, but that, in the event that any crime may have truly been committed in the German KZ, it was to be attributed to the introduction of drugs before the fall of the Third Reich, with the object of disturbing the guards in order to obtain further propagandistic gains.

92. Excerpts from a statement written by Hess during his time at Maindiff Court, which was taken by him to Nuremberg and there translated.

"In the end, I never saw Rudolf Hess again after my return to Elbrus-Rastenburg, but I heard news of the accursed Ernst Schäfer: he had silently returned, just as Tarstein foresaw, and was in occupied France. Admiral Canaris' Secret Service, the Abwehr, which was outside the jurisdiction of the external SD, was protecting him. According to reports available to Walter Schellenberg, it was seeming very probable that his four henchmen also accompanied him, although one of them *would have lost his eyesight in Tibet,*' due to his eyes being exposed *'to an intense and unknown Light source.'*

"As is natural, I immediately proposed a covert operation to execute him, both him as well as his accomplices, but I was dissuaded by Tarstein, who was maintaining that the traitor was more valuable alive than dead: 'being alive, he will be able to communicate to the synarchic forces that, with the Third Reich, they have only one path: war,' Tarstein was explaining to us. The White Brotherhood will support an alliance against Germany, but only if, after its total destruction, the Universal Synarchy of the Chosen Peoples is constituted in little time. If this objective is concretized, Germany will undoubtedly be sacrificed, but that World Government will signify the end of History: Germany will be reborn once again, perhaps not as a Nation, but its Spirit, its Führer, its Wothan God, will be backed by the Gods Loyal to the Spirit of Man, *and the Final Battle will be unleashed upon the Earth.*

"Ernst Schäfer returned converted into a Master of the White Hierarchy, that is to say, spiritually dead. His initiation in Tibet earned him the recognition of numerous synarchic Secret Societies, such as the English Masonry, which granted him the 33rd degree and the position of President of the Grand Orient of the Ancient and Accepted Scottish Rite. The destruction of Operation Altwesten was attributed in the papers to common accidents in this type of exploration and Schäfer lived quietly until after the war: his relatives still reside in Argentina.

"That freedom he enjoyed under the protection of the resistance groups to the Führer, allowed him, just as we had calculated in the Black Order, to plan and launch a multitude of attacks against my person. No one knows for certain how many attacks were perpetrated against the Führer, but those that I suffered in those years were not far behind him: poisonings, bombs, snipers, ambushes, sabotage of my equipment, and permanent threats: either I was abandoning the ⚡⚡, deserting, leaving Germany for good, definitively distancing myself from the places sacred to the Priests, *or there would be no place on Earth where I could hide from the inevitable rabbinical vengeance.*

"Of course, I did not give in to threats and fulfilled my orders to the end, Neffe, even those orders that were not pleasing to me, like the last one, which obliged me to remain 35 years in Santa María de Catamarca.

Chapter XLI

I will not speak of the intermediate operations, for this will be my last reference to the intense esoteric undertakings of those years. I will only recall that in 1945 we were working in Southern Italy, in the region of Apulia, where is located the Octagonal Castle of Emperor Frederick II Hohenstaufen, who ruled from 1220 to 1250 and of whom Belicena Villca is very much concerned in her letter. Our mission had no direct relation with the war, since one could do little to revert a situation that was daily becoming more adverse. In those days, Germany was retreating on all fronts; but on all fronts, for the first time in History, the same Jewish enemy could be pointed out: Capitalists, Communists, Zionists, all the Allied Nations, regardless of their ideology, were showing the same Hebrew faces, the true profile of the Synarchy.

"And in the midst of that colossal debacle, while Germany was yielding to forces a thousand times superior, forces that were appearing united under the mask of Jehovah Satan, we no longer worked for Germany, to close the Gates of the Demons, the enemies of Germany, but *for the ⚡⚡, for the future of the ⚡⚡*. What was our mission in Southern Italy consisting in? In something unusual: we had to seek *the Stone of Genghis Khan.*

"Yes, this is not a delirium. Konrad Tarstein had specific and ancient information that was assuring that in 1221 Genghis Khan sent to Frederick II, to his court in Sicily, a Stone coming from Agartha, on which was engraved a tripartite pact to establish the Universal Empire; the three parties would be: Genghis Khan, Emperor of Asia; Frederick II, Emperor of the West; and the Loyal Gods of Agartha, for the Subterranean Forces of Earth. Before dying, in 1250, Frederick had that strange octagonal castle constructed and forever hid the Stone. Now, Konrad Tarstein was explaining to us that the Castle, in its construction, was hiding a key to locate the Stone, which would not be found very far from the plaza. Indeed, at 800 meters of distance, under a soft slope covered with grass, the daiva dogs sniffed out a stone crypt that was containing a chest of Queen Constance and the longed-for Stone of

Genghis Khan, engraved in Uighur characters and in Germanic Runes.

"It was not easy to find. We had to carry out deep excavations and trigonometric measurements with theodolites. The measurements were taken a posteriori, to try to discover the key to the construction through strategic opposition that was enabling *to protect* a valuable object, placing it *outside the walls.*

"There was no time to complete the measurements because since April 5, 1945, the Allied invasion of Italy had begun. We were retreating, then, toward the north, but at every step we were verifying the magnitude of the disaster. The war was lost for Germany and would soon be over. We decided to split up. Karl von Grossen and Oskar Feil, under protest, would remain hidden in a Franciscan monastery, the Prior of which was a sympathizer of Germany and of the Arab cause: both had to swap the black uniform for the brown *seraphic* soutane. The daiva dogs would also remain in their care.

"While our Comrades were staying at the Neapolitan Monastery, the Tibetan Legion embarked on a journey to Berlin. We were Bangi, Srivirya, fifty commandos, and myself. After multiple clashes with the communist partisans who were infesting the roads, we managed to reach Verona, from where several paths that were passing through the Alps were starting. We took the Bolzano one, which led us directly to Berchtesgaden a day later.

"On April 25, the ⚡⚡ Commandant of Berchtesgaden received a telegram from Bormann ordering him to arrest Marshal Göring. When we arrived, there was no one who could attend to or give information to us. We then headed for the Obersalzberg, but before arriving, Fate, that tragic Fate that was always pursuing me, decided to play its best role: 318 Lancaster bombers arrived first and began to unload tons of bombs on the peaceful Alpine village. Paralyzed with grief, pierced by the lacerating nostalgia, I believe that I was shouting with helplessness, I saw Rudolf Hess' house and others nearby blown into a thousand pieces. That house where 12 years ago we arrived with my father to visit the Führer's Stellvertreter and request of him help to point my career in the right direction! There Papa had entrusted him with the Ophite medal. What would have become of it? Perhaps Ilse had it, his and mine...

"How many memories! ...

"Damned English, damned Yankees, damned Russians, damned Jewish Synarchy! What need was there to destroy that Obersalzberg village? Perhaps to suppress a symbol? But it is only possible to break the form of symbols, to break their appearance, because the content is metaphysical, transcendent, and can never be broken by a Lancaster bomb.

"Finally, unable to hold back my tears, I observed the smoking ruins of the Berghof, the Führer's headquarters, empty at the time because, as the Allies were well aware, the Führer was in the bunker in Berlin, and the remains of Bormann's and Göring's houses, and of many villagers who had nothing to do with Nazism and the Third Reich. We returned to Berchtesgaden and were able to get transportation to Munich the following day. There I met General Koller who informed me of the disastrous situation in Berlin: the Russians had reached the banks of the Elbe and Eisenhower stopped the American Army near Torgau, with the confessed purpose that Berlin be razed to the ground by the Slav hordes. 'That was,' the accursed Jew justified himself, 'what had been agreed upon at Yalta.'

"Berlin was, thus, besieged by the Russians, being almost impossible to enter or exit by land. 'Then the Tibetan legion will enter into Berlin!' I affirmed with determination.

" 'It will not be necessary that you run such a risk, *Brigadeführer* Von Sübermann: orders have just arrived for you, which command that you go to Plauen. *Reichsführer* Himmler personally wishes to see you there.' General Koller, to my surprise, handed me Himmler's telegram. How did the *Reichsführer* know that we would be in Munich? There was only one answer: the SD officer in Berchestsgaden had reported our passage. I cursed to myself and questioned Koller.

" 'Is there a telephone line to the *Reichsführer?*'

" 'Only in the case of extreme urgency.'

" 'Well, this is it, mein General. This is an emergency.'

" 'Alright, *Brigadeführer*. Patch through on the radio and I'll authorize the call.'

"I sighed with relief: it was necessary to confirm my suspicions before leaving!

" 'This is *Brigadeführer* Kurt von Sübermann, mein *Reichsführer,*' I greeted, through the inaudible line.

" 'Von Sübermann! How glad I am to hear from you at this moment! I congratulate you for reaching Munich. Just in time! Well, *Brigadeführer* Von Sübermann, listen well: *things have changed here in Germany, and now I am in charge of Operation Frederick II. So, then, you must come as soon as possible and bring me the King's Relic. Come by plane.* See you soon. Put me through to General Koller so that I can give him the necessary instructions.'

" 'See you soon, mein *Reichsführer!*' I bade farewell, plunged into the blackest of apprehensions.

"I reunited with Bangi and Srivirya. As luck would have it, there were no planes available at the time. What would I do? It was evident that Himmler was planning to take possession of the Stone of Genghis Khan to utilize it for some personal end. But the Stone of Agartha was not belonging to him but to the ⚡⚡ Black Order, to the Thulegesellschaft, to Germany. To me the *Reichsführer* was worthy of the best of concepts, a Hyperborean Initiate faithful to the Führer and loyal to our Banners: if the fall of Germany had upset him, it would be understandable. But in the Black Order they would never forgive me if I was losing an object that Frederick II Hohenstaufen protected for 700 years.

" 'Comrades, I'm in trouble,' I confided in the chiefs of the Tibetan Legion. 'I will surely find myself in the necessity to disobey an order from the *Reichsführer* and I don't want you to get involved. I've thought of transferring you to the local ⚡⚡ Commandant, and continue the journey to Berlin alone. It's my duty to hand over the chest that we found in Apulia to the Initiates of the Black Order, who are also members of the Thulegesellschaft, and for that I must go to Berlin; on the contrary, the *Reichsführer* intends that I give the Relic to him alone, in the city of Plauen.'

" 'And how will you get to Berlin, Shivatulku?'

" 'Well, by land, since it's impossible to get there by air. I'll pretend to go to Plauen, but then I'll divert to the north, and somehow try to pass through the Russian fence.'

" 'Then we will follow you to Berlin. Think it through: We will be useful to you in order to carry out the feat that you plan. And besides, what do charges of disobedience matter to us, even if it means death? We have already lived too long and Death does not frighten us at all!'

"The Gurkha's words brought me back to reality. Those days were undoubtedly signaling the end of the Third Reich. And they would very likely represent our own end. Yes, it was all coming to an end, and perhaps we too would come to an end. Sooner or later, life would have to be risked against a plethora of enemies: Russians, English, Yankees, French, who, by Wothan, who would take our lives? Leaving the Tibetan Legion in Munich was only meaning prolonging their lives a day or two longer: that was the reality.

"I decided to act right away. We had to act before General Koller got the plane.

"I gathered them all in a remote courtyard and spoke to them:

" 'Tibetan Legion! In a few minutes we're going to enter into operations. Our objective is to reach Berlin, and we need to equip ourselves at once. *But we cannot officially request such equipment.* Therefore, we will seize them.

" 'First of all, we have to get hold of two artillery trucks, with spare tires and enough ammunition. Bangi and fifteen men will take care of it, trying not to cause casualties on either side, which are the same side as Germany. Capture and gag whoever you have to abduct, and keep them hidden in the trucks, as we'll release them before we leave. You have ten minutes to execute the mission and park in front of the Quartermaster depot.'

" 'Srivirya and 20 men will raid the depot, only taking what is essential for a 600-kilometer journey and 50 troops: grenades, rifles, ammunition, and minimal provisions. Immobilize everyone and, when the trucks arrive, load everything and meet us in the dormitory building, next to the mess hall. You have to be there in fifteen minutes!' I ordered.

"The fifteen Tibetans and I dedicated ourselves to gathering our equipment and clothes, and piling everything at the door of the barracks. Fifteen minutes later we were leaving the Munich quarters. The first group had taken four prisoners. The highest rank was a *Scharführer:* to him I gave the letter addressed to General Koller. In it, I was apologizing for the violation, and was informing him that '*I could not obey Reichsführer Himmler's orders because it was contradicting with a previous order that was forcing me to go to Berlin. The author of the first order was a Secret Service Chief of whom I was only authorized to mention his code name: Unicornis.'* I was requesting this message to be communicated verbatim to the *Reichsführer* and bade a kind farewell to General Koller. I was not expecting that Koller forgave me for having ridiculed his men, but I had faith that Himmler would leave everything as it was, rather than face *the hidden brains of the Third Reich*. We then released the disconcerted soldiers at the northern entrance of Munich, reiterating to them to transmit that letter to General Koller as soon as possible.

"My calculations were correct because Himmler did nothing after receiving the laconic message. We even came across ⚡⚡ troops coming from the Russian front to whom no warning had been given regarding us.

"Now then: it was April 28th and I believe that that was the last day on which there was even the slightest possibility of reaching Berlin by road. Our route was like marching along the edge of the synarchic Dragon's teeth: all were enemy vanguards along the way; first, French and Yankee vanguards that were advancing from the west, and then Russian vanguards coming from the east, which were colliding with the Yankee columns on the banks of the Elbe. Munich would fall into the hands of the Franco-Yankees on April 30, that is to say, two days after we left.

"Anyway, and sustaining periodic combat against Yankees and Russians, we reached Potsdam at nightfall. Impossible to get through the Russian lines in two German trucks and with an ⚡⚡ legion. It took another two hours to locate a suitable Russian encampment to obtain the indispensable camouflage: some 60 Russian infantrymen were sleeping in a row of tents, guarded by four sentinels. All were stabbed to death, the majority of their throats slit, as no one was wishing to spoil their disguise. However, no legionnaire wanted to take off his ⚡⚡ uniform and the Russian clothes had to be put on over it, many times helping to get it on by means of generous knife strokes.

"Thus dressed, we marched more or less openly in the direction of the Spree. Following its bank we came to the Weidendammer Bridge, which was covered by the children of Artur Axmann's Hitler Youth. It took me ten minutes to convince a 12-year-old *Obersturmführer* that we were an ⚡⚡ legion and that he should let us pass. Finally we crossed and everyone took off their Russian clothes right there, except for me who still had a ways to go.

"Because we now had decided to definitively separate. The Tibetan Legion was belonging to the Leibstandarte Adolf Hitler, the ⚡⚡ Corps that was in charge of the Führer's personal guard, and the most logical thing would be for that corps to head to the bunker to contribute to its defense. Berlin was looking catastrophic: entire blocks demolished by aerial bombardments and Russian cannon fire, the streets covered with rubble, the glow of various fires were adding to the twilight of the dawn of that fateful 29th of April 1945. We marched in silence for several blocks until reaching Friedrichstraße, or what was left of it. The idea was to follow that street up to the U-Bahn station and then descend and go underground; at Wilhelmplatz station we would go up a few meters from the Chancellery. It was not possible to carry out this simple plan because a terrible tank battle was being fought on Frederick Street. We tried, then, to race to Wilhelmstraße when Fortune, so elusive until then, came to our aid.

"Indeed, down the cross street that we took, a column of tanks began to turn toward us. In command was an ⚡⚡ *Oberführer* by the name of Otto Meyer, whom we knew because Von Grossen got him, three years earlier, to give us a lecture on armored cavalry tactics: he was a young officer of legendary valor and great professionalism for the leading of motorized troops. He had fought in France and Russia, and survived, as well as causing great losses to the enemy. When Rudolf, after my first mission, alluded to the fact that I would be one of the youngest *Oberführers* in the German Army, he was undoubtedly including Otto Meyer in his plural concept. Now they had convoked him for the Battle of Berlin, the last one, and he would surely die.

"He stopped his panzer and came out through the turret: 'Kurt von Sübermann and the Tibetan Legion! Ha-ha-ha. I never expected to find you here, *secret agent!* Where the hell do you think you're going?'

"'Otto Meyer!' I shouted with emotion. 'I didn't expect to see you again either. Oh, Otto: this is the Führer's guard. They must get to the Chancellery!'

"'But it's just a few blocks! Don't worry, they'll get there. Tell them to march protected by the panzers and I'll drop them off at the gate itself. And climb in, I want to chat with someone who hasn't gone crazy yet, like everyone else in this city.'

"Fifteen minutes later, the five panzers stopped in front of the Chancellery, which was practically no longer existing, except for the subterranean bunkers, and the Tibetan Legion assembled in the garden. The astonishment of *Brigadeführer* Mohnke, ⚡⚡ commander of the Chancellery, knew no limits, when contemplating that troop of Asiatic faces.

" 'The Tibetan Legion, special formation of the *1st ⚡⚡ Panzer Division Leibstandarte ⚡⚡ Adolf Hitler,* presents itself to take guard at the Führerbunker! Heil Hitler, mein *Brigadeführer!*' I presented and saluted in a loud voice.

"Mohnke was suspicious of that reinforcement, of which he had no news, and thought of a possible desertion from the front, but he was reassured when I proved to him that our destination was Italy, from where we logically had to withdraw, and I communicated to him that Himmler was informed of our march toward Berlin.

" 'Now, if I may, I must complete the mission that the Secret Service entrusted to me,' I requested.

" 'As far as I am concerned, you do your duty, *Brigadeführer.* There's nothing more to do here,' he affirmed in a somber tone.

"It was 10 in the morning. I heard when they were telling Otto Meyer that the Führer was resting, that he would not be able to receive him. The heroic Meyer had attempted to see Hitler before embarking on a tour from which he might never return. I signaled to him to wait for a moment and said goodbye forever to Bangi, Srivirya, and the fifty Lopa warriors of the Tibetan Legion. Why describe what that farewell was like? It suffices to add that even after 35 years, I still see them clearly in the garden of the ruined Chancellery, raising their arm to militarily salute me, and I hear the voice of the Gurkha who says 'Farewell Shivatulku! Do not suffer for us, for soon we will find ourselves in another war, fighting alongside the Gods!'

" 'Gregorstraße?' repeated Meyer, in a questioning tone. 'But that's in the Gipfelstadt: you have to go through the Brandenburg Gate and cross the Tiergarten. Look, Kurt, for a few days now the Russians are trying to occupy the Tiergarten but they have not succeeded in breaking our anti-tank artillery. Therefore, they have also mounted their own artillery. Conclusion: no one can get through because an inferno of crossfire has formed. But have no illusions: neither could you get through on foot because we have mined all the fields and roads of the Zoo.'

"I looked at him desolately and this provoked another of his usual guffaws.

" 'Calm down, Kurt, calm down, all is not lost. Even if the panzers can't get through, that doesn't mean that *nothing can* get through. Have you heard of the Kamikazes?' he asked, always joking.

" 'Yes: they're the Japanese suicide pilots.'

" 'Well, my dear Comrade! If you dare to be a *Kamikaze motorcyclist,* it's possible that we'll get you through to the Gipfelstadt!'

"I was beginning to understand.

" 'The plan is elementary; all you need is the kamikaze to carry it out,' he said smiling.

"I nodded, making clear to him that I would play the role of the suicide pilot.

" 'Well then, there's nothing more to talk about. Take a motorcycle escort, which are now completely useless, and take off down the grand avenue, cross the Brandenburg Gate, and enter into the Tiergarten; with luck, in ten minutes you'll be in Gregorstraße. Of course, you must take the Tiergarten at high speed, more than a hundred kilometers per hour, so that the Russians can not sharpen their aim. In the meantime, we'll entertain them with at-will fire. Do you agree?'

" 'I absolutely agree. The plan is truly suicidal, but the only one that gives me any chance,' I accepted.

" 'You've done well preserving that Russian getup: it's an officer's. It may be useful to you later on, since where you're going there are no Germans but Russians. And you speak the language of the subhumans, don't you?'

"I nodded. I no longer felt like talking or joking; I was only anxious to depart for the suicidal adventure. I was realizing that I had everything at stake and I was just wanting to leave.

"Otto Meyer understood this, but did not stop making jokes until the end.

" 'Goodbye Comrade,' he bade farewell smiling, 'the next time we see each other you'll take me for a ride in the sidecar. Ha-ha-ha.'

" 'And me in a panzer carousel. Ha-ha-ha.'

"At the end we both laughed, and also said goodbye forever.

Chapter XLII

I crossed the main avenue of the Tiergarten riding on a motorcycle that was going at more than one hundred kilometers per hour, dodging, with instantaneous reflexes, thousands of potholes of what was looking like a lunar landscape. The German artillery, alerted by Otto Meyer, opened fire pretending to try to hit me, which disconcerted the Russians and led them to concentrate their fire against them, allowing me to get away.

"Ten minutes later, I was entering the Gipfelstadt and driving along Gregorstraße at regular speed. I stopped in front of 239, lifted my goggles, and observed both sides of the street: not a soul. But the most curious thing was that, unlike the other blocks, which had suffered the devastating attack from the bombings, that which was containing Konrad Tarstein's house was intact, as if the war had not passed through there.

"Once again, like a Rite a thousand times repeated, I struck, the musty ring spinning in the bronze fist.

" 'Yes?' Tarstein's shrill voice was heard through some crack in the old door.

" 'I am Kurt von Sübermann; that is, Lupus, I am Lupus, Comrade Unicornis.'

"The door opened and Tarstein, at the height of serenity, repeated once again.

" 'Come in, I was waiting for you. It's 16:00 hours. You're just in time for a cup of tea, if an hour ahead of English time doesn't affect you?' he asked with irony.

" 'No, no. Tea will be fine. You don't know what I had to go through to get here: literally, I went through a pass of heavy fire. In those instants I didn't know if I was going to make it here; and I didn't know what I was going to find here either. You can imagine my surprise upon seeing that you have not departed from your usual habits.'

" 'My dear Lupus, it's not good for the health that an old man like me be changing his way of life at this point,' he explained with renewed irony. 'Come, let's go to the kitchen and drink that tea, and forget for a while what's going on outside. Leave everything on that sofa, except the saddlebag that contains the Stone of Genghis Khan. Because that's why you've come, isn't it? You've risked your life a thousand times to com-

ply with the Black Order: you are admirable, Kurt von Sübermann, a Knight worthy of the Führer, an Initiate worthy of the
Gods.'

"Like so many times before, I entered the modern kitchen
and sat myself down at a small table covered with a fine white
linen tablecloth. Tarstein prepared the infusion in a porcelain
teapot from Shanghai and filled the cups with tea from the
same place. As I was sipping it, I observed Tarstein examining
the Stone of Genghis Khan. He was seeming moved, which
was unusual for him. Finally he asked:

" 'Do you know what this is? The proof that Humanity has a
chance, the concrete testimony that the Gods of the Spirit
agreed to deal with the Great Initiates who were attempting to
make the Universal Empire a reality. If they had triumphed in
the thirteenth century, the History of Humanity would be very
different and the Enemy would not have had the chance to
constitute the Universal Synarchy in the fourteenth century:
for example, it would not have been necessary for Philip the
Fair to dissolve the Templars between 1307 and 1314 because
Frederick II would have liquidated them, in good taste, in 1227.
And do you know why this was not realized? Well, because
this Stone that you have brought was lost during seven key
years, from 1221 to 1228. In truth, it was not lost, but they mis-
placed it, due to the failure of the imperial plans. Alas, Lupus:
if this Stone had reached the hands of Emperor Frederick II in
time, perhaps my own family, the House of Tharsis, would not
have been exterminated in 1268!'

"I, naturally Neffe, was understanding very little of all this.
Only now, after reading Belicena Villca's letter, do the words of
Tarstein acquire their true and dramatic significance. At that
moment, Konrad Tarstein must have noticed the confusion on
my face because he procured to clarify with other words the
meaning of that incredible Relic.

" 'Do you remember the history of Emperor Frederick II
Hohenstaufen?' he energetically asked.

" 'Yes. That is: I remember some salient facts,' I hesitantly
responded.

" 'Well then. This fact is very salient. Do you remember
what happened with his Crusade vow?'

" 'Oh, yes!' I affirmed, pleased at not being totally ignorant.
'I believe that Frederick II was crowned at Aachen, in 1214, and
there he made the fatal vow to Innocent III to undertake a

Crusade to the Holy Land; for various reasons, he did not fulfill this promise until 1228, which cost him innumerable complications with the Popes, which resulted in excommunications and wars.'

" 'The dates are correct, Lupus. What you don't know with exactitude, because it has remained secret until now and was only in the domain of certain Secret Societies, is the *true reason* for which Frederick II was delaying his trip to Palestine. *And that reason is this: the Stone of Genghis Khan.* Frederick II was awaiting since 1221 the arrival of a Mongol Initiate who would be the bearer of a written pact between the Emperor of the East and the Emperor of the West: such Initiate never arrived in Sicily and the reason was that they assassinated him in Frankish Syria by order of the Catholic Druids. When Frederick II finally decided to travel to the Middle East, he did so with the purpose of rescuing the Stone of Genghis Khan, which was in the possession of the Lord of Beirut. But it was already too late to consummate the metaphysical pact, to submit the World Order to the Universal Empire: Genghis Khan had died in 1227 and his successors, who were not Initiates, quickly fell into the hands of the Priests of the White Brotherhood.

" 'It is worth knowing the history in all its details, because now, 700 years later, the possibility of erecting the Universal Empire has presented itself again. And like then, the true struggle takes place on the plane of the Great Initiates and the High Doctrines: the Universal Empire against the Universal Synarchy; the Hyperborean Wisdom against the Judaic Culture; the pact of the Führer with the Loyal Gods of Agartha against the pact of a handful of little men, Churchill, Roosevelt, Stalin, De Gaulle, etc., with the Traitorous Gods of Chang Shambhala. The enormous slaughtering of the fighting masses impress but they lack importance, they always lack importance, in front of the confrontation of the Initiates and the Gods. This Stone, which you have found at the Castle of Frederick II, was the pact of the Emperors with the Gods of Agartha that was going to make possible the realization of the Universal Empire in the thirteenth century. Frederick II had it hidden by Hyperborean Initiates, experts in Lithic Construction, with the order that it only be found by the future Universal Emperor. This Stone, as you will understand, belongs to the Führer.'

" 'Then I should have delivered it to him personally, when I passed by the bunker a few hours ago,' I foolishly reflected.

" 'No, Lupus! This Stone will be delivered to the Führer in the Antarctic Oasis where he is now. The Führer in the bunker, it is possible that he has died by now.'

" 'I do not understand,' I confessed, even though I knew that my words would irritate Konrad Tarstein.

" 'Then you ought to understand!' he complained with predictable annoyance. 'After all, you are a *Tulku* too! The Tulkus, my esteemed Lupus, possess several bodies. And nobody knows how many or where. As they rightly told you in Tibet, in the Third Reich there is the strange phenomenon that there are many "reincarnated Gods"; *many Tulkus,* Kurt von Sübermann. The Führer is a Tulku and there is nothing strange about him dying in Berlin and, simultaneously, living in Antarctica. To that Führer, powerful and strong as he was at the age of twenty-five or thirty, we will send the Blood Pact Stone to Agartha.'

"It got the better of me and I had to inquire:

" 'But was the Führer aware that he had this extraordinary faculty at his disposal?'

" 'Do you, "Shivatulku," know where your other, necessary, existences are occurring?'

" 'Certainly not.'

" 'Well, there is the answer that you seek. If you, so soon, are incapable of responding, how do you want me to know the process of a Tulku?

" 'However, I will give you an idea,' he conceded. 'This is how I imagine the process of the Tulkus: a special case of *metamorphosis.* Let us establish a relationship of analogy between Tulkus and lepidopterous insects, and suppose that *the whole life of a Tulku specimen, such as the Führer, you, or Rudolf Hess, is analogous to a lepidopterous butterfly.* Let us also suppose that there is a set of twin larvae that, by a particular law of the Tulkus, remain in a state of latent life while the butterfly develops its active life. And, lastly, let us suppose that the special laws of the Tulkus determine that when the butterfly dies, one of the larvae automatically resumes the process of metamorphosis and transforms into a chrysalis, generating a new active life and *a new reality.* Of course, because the larval life is latent life, and the active life, of the butterflies and Tulkus, is real life: *the reality of life corresponds then, to the Tulku-butter-*

flies; the Tulku-larvae live on a plane of existence not real, but possible: such an existence is not of the same degree as that which the Tulku-butterflies demonstrate. Only if a Tulku-butterfly dies, or if a law of the Tulkus that requires the existence of two or more Tulku-butterflies acts, will a Tulku-larva become real. But, my esteemed Lupus, who knows the laws of the Tulkus? Who knows how many Tulku-men can exist in a larval state? A common man can only make one decision to perform in a determinate time and space: if the alternatives are two, he must say without hesitation "I am going to do this" or "I am going to do that." The Tulku, on the contrary, *can opt to perform both possibilities, although for it, logically, he needs to have two simultaneous realities at his disposal.* The Tulku can, for example, say *"I am going to stay in Berlin, and I am going to die there if the Third Reich loses the war"* and also say *"I am going to retire to the Antarctic Oasis, together with the ⚡⚡ Elite, to prepare the Final Battle against the Universal Synarchy," and fulfill both statements.* For a common person it would be impossible to perform both sentences, but for a *Führertulku* it is perfectly possible.

"'Naturally, Lupus, two or three realities of the Tulku *will only coincide in the Tulku himself, in the context that confers meaning on him and that he signifies.* Outside of the Tulku, the realities of the living Tulkus may not coincide, Time may contract or expand, things may dislocate, History may contradict itself. What is in the reality of a living Tulku, that is to say, of a real, exemplary Tulku, of a Tulku-butterfly, beyond the Tulku, *may not be in the reality of another real Tulku but different from the first one; or, inversely, it may very well be in context.* I clarify this to warn you that, from now on, *the partisans of the Hyperborean Wisdom must define to which reality they refer: whether to the reality of the dead Führer in the Chancellery-bunker of Berlin or to the reality of the living Führer, always young in his Magical Refuge, where he awaits the historic times of the Final Battle.* And I anticipate that those who choose to live in the first reality will be considered traitors, no matter how much they proclaim themselves "National Socialists" or "Nazis."'

"Eyes sparkling, Konrad Tarstein paused for a second to serve himself more tea.

"'Rudolf Hess... ?'

"'Yes, Rudolf Hess is also a Tulku and that is why he is now alongside the Führer in the Secret Refuge: he is just as you know him; he has not changed at all. And because he is a Tulku, he can be with the Führer and, *moreover, be a prisoner of the English.*'

" 'But let us leave the Tulkus for the moment and return to the Stone of Genghis Khan. I was telling you before that it is worth knowing the story in detail. You have found it and you deserve more than anyone else to know that history, even if this is not the best occasion to tell it. Anyway, I will summarize it; pay attention:

" 'In Mongolia, in the Gobi Desert, there is a place that the Hyperborean Wisdom denominates *"The Tar Gate,"* which directly communicates with the Kingdom of Agartha. In the Epoch of Genghis Khan and Frederick II, the Loyal Siddhas had approved a plan of the Hyperborean Initiates, known as the *Tyr Strategy,* intended to found the Universal Empire on Earth: the Chosen One in the East for it was Prince Temüjin, who received, as a youth, the Hyperborean Initiation by some Siddhas coming from the Tar Gate. Remember that Temüjin's father, Yesügei, had died poisoned by the Tartars when the young Prince was only 9 years old and that, from then until his adulthood, he lived miserably with his mother and siblings in the deserted lands of the Upper Onon. Like all the Great Chosen Ones of History, it is during that period that the Siddhas instruct and initiate him.

" 'According to local tradition, the Great Ancestors of the Mongols were the gray Wolf and the tawny Fallow Deer, which means that their Ancestors were not human, or, in other words, that they were Gods. In the sacred cave of Erkeneqon, the Gray Wolf married the Fallow Deer, who came from the vicinity of Lake Baikal. Subsequently, the original couple moved to the sacred mountain Burkhan Khaldun, today's Khentii, the ancient abode of *Kök Kev,* God of the Infinite.

" 'If his great ancestors were Gods, his close relatives had been no less powerful: his great-grandfather was Kabul Khan, the first organizer of the Mongolic tribes and military conqueror; and his father, Yesügei, had taken the nickname of Ba'atur, that is, "the Valiant." His mother Hoelun brought him into the world in "the year of the pig" of 1167, meaning that he was 27 years older than Frederick II, born in 1194.

" 'His *Purity of Blood* was so elevated that he became worthy of *representing* the Sign of the Origin, the highest Hyperborean distinction of the thirteenth century after the Gral, which was entrusted to the Occitan Cathars. That is why when an Assembly of Mongol Chiefs and Kings gathered in 1206 in Karakorum, and elected him "Khan," Temüjin proudly exhibited the sign that his triumph over his enemies had given him and allowed him to achieve the unity of his Race: that sign, which he was displaying on his ring and banner, was none other than the *levorotatory swastika,* the same sign that seven hundred years later would be worn in the most glorious feats by another Hyperborean people, but this time of the White Race.

" 'A historic mission was entrusted to Genghis Khan and he knew how to fulfill it in all its aspects, so it is not possible to at all reproach him for the failure of the Tyr Strategy. On the contrary, this failure is due almost exclusively to the excellent counter-offensive unleashed on the West by the enemy forces, which were operating infiltrated in the Catholic Church. That historical mission was consisting in founding a Great Mongol Kingdom in the East, which completely encompassed North and Central Asia, *simultaneously* with the emergence of a Great White Kingdom in the west.

" 'When the foundation of these Kingdoms was consummated, then the moment would arrive to seal with a pact the creation of a Universal Empire in which the Mongols would be subordinated to an authentic King of the White World and where the Yellow masses would reserve themselves the right to advance toward the west and the White Elites, less numerous but more culturally qualified, would march toward the east. There, in Mongolia, the Crown of the Earth, would flourish a Hyperborean civilization not seen since the days of Atlantis. These were, in a few words, the objectives proposed by the Tyr Strategy.

" 'I will now show you, Lupus, how Genghis Khan fulfills his part in the Tyr Strategy. In 1206 he unites all the Mongol tribes and initiates the conquest of China and, in 1215, with the capture of Peking, he reaches the eastern boundary of Asia. From then on, the only thing left to do was to make contact with the "King of the West." But who is this King? How to recognize him if, toward the west, far from unity existing, a confused feudal organization can be seen? I remind you, Lupus, that according to the Hyperborean Wisdom, *the effects of the Kaly Yuga are not of the same intensity in all geographical points;* on the contrary, there is a *Route of the Kaly Yuga* that spirals around the spherical surface of the Earth and over which the Kaly Yuga is "more intense" or more present. Said zone is orientable and, in the region that we are considering, orientable "from east to west," that is to say, that the effects of the Kaly Yuga are more intense toward the west than toward the east: *going toward the east increases "spirituality" and going toward the west increases the "materialism" characteristic of the Kaly Yuga.* It is according to these principles that the Tar Gate in the Gobi Desert is also denominated the "Center of lesser intensity of the Kaly Yuga."

" 'To situate oneself in Genghis Khan's dilemma, one must consider that the "King of the West" should be "Great" by the power of the Spirit, as was Temüjin, and reflect on the difficulties *of looking* from the east of Asia toward the west of the Occident. Genghis Khan, *"to the west,"* was only *"seeing"* spiritual darkness... and Kingdoms. Many Kingdoms, but no "Great Kingdom." The Kingdom of the Persians, which would soon fall, the Kingdom of the Byzantine Greeks, which was barely resisting the Arab and Turkish siege: a very small and weak Kingdom, with Kings without Initiative who were liking to call themselves "Emperors." The Slavic Kingdoms of the Russians and Poles, they could not even dream of placing themselves at the head of the peoples of the West and, on the contrary, they would be easy prey for the Golden Horde. For the same reason, Armenia, Georgia, Bulgaria, Hungary, etc. could be ruled out.

" 'The Germanic Kingdoms of Europe were remaining, undoubtedly the strongest, but in them, according to Genghis Khan's vision, darkness was absolute. If the Great King was there, it would be necessary to distinguish him by his exterior qualities and for that he would have to count on adequate information. For this purpose he had many travelers, merchants, or the religious, brought to his presence, whom he harshly interrogated, with scarce results. But from their accounts he was able to find out that there were truly two great Christian Kingdoms, one Frankish and the other Romano-Germanic. The Frankish Kingdom was precisely that which, for a century, was waging that absurd war against the Arabs, during which they had occupied Syria and Palestine.

" 'Genghis Khan then thought that he should address the Frankish King and the German King but there was still a doubt to clear up: both Kings were calling themselves "Christians" and servants of a High Priest called "Pope." Would not this Pope be the true King of the World? To form an opinion about Christianity and the Pope he sent for Nestorian Priests from Armenia and some Greek Orthodox who were as slaves in Peking; from them he learned the story of Jesus Christ and found out that the Pope was not a warrior but a shepherd, that he was not killing but commanding to kill, and that he was not riding together with his people during wars but staying all his life in safe and distant convents. And with a grimace of disgust Genghis Khan ruled out the Pope as a worthy spiritual authority with whom he could deal.

" 'Before 1220, Genghis Khan already knew that of the two Kings, the Frankish and the German, it was suiting his plans to turn to the latter. He obtained this conviction by evaluating the religious information that one of his many esoteric confidants gave him. But it is worth making a clarification here: during the life of Genghis Khan three were the religions that surrounded him and to which he paid special attention: Nestorian Christianity, Persian Manichaeism and, fundamentally, Taoism.[93] He rejected the religion of Confucius as reactionary, and in Buddhism he immediately recognized a system based on the Kalachakra of Chang Shambhala, against which his Hyperborean instructors warned him early on.

" 'It was a Manichaean priest who informed him one Day that "beyond the Kingdom of the Franks, in fiefs of the King of Aragon, who is in turn vassal of the German King, there is a powerful Manichaean community to whom the Angels have delivered, into safekeeping, a Stone Vessel that is not of this World." This news shocked Genghis Khan, as well as the knowledge that the troops of the King of the Franks, with the blessing of the Pope, were dedicating themselves to exterminate those Manicheans of the West called "Cathars," that is to say, "pure ones." A whole "Manichaean route" was allowing that such news reached Asia: from the Languedoc to Italy, to the Cathar and Bogomil communities of Milan; from there to Bulgaria, the center of Bogomil Manichaeism; and, from the Balkans, Bogomil and Paulician missionaries were carrying the news as far as Armenia and Iran.

---

93. Manichaeism, which had managed to expand as far as China in the thirteenth century, was respected by Genghis Khan but not so by his successors who fiercely combated it until making it disappear; Taoism was later persecuted in the same way.

" 'The Cathars were sustaining that the material world had been created by Jehovah Satan with the help of a court of Demons; believing in a true God that was Incognizable from the state of spiritual impurity that incarnation was implying; likewise they were believing in Cristo Luz, whom they were calling Lucibel, and in the Paraklete or Holy Spirit, an agent absolutely transcendent to the material sphere. Consequently with these beliefs, they were rejecting the Old Testament of the Bible for considering that in it the history of the creation of the world was being narrated by Jehovah Satan, an evil Demiurge, and in which the true God was not being mentioned at all; of the New Testament, they were only accepting the Gospel of John and the Book of Revelation. About the Church of Rome, they were of the opinion that it was "the Synagogue of Satan," a refuge for the Demons and their servants in which not even a ray of spiritual light was shining

" 'Naturally, if the believers in so clear a doctrine were condemned to death by the Pope, and repressed to the point of annihilation by the troops of the Frankish King, there could be no doubt that the latter were, in turn, partisans of the Demiurge Jehovah Satan. But things were not "looking" so clear from Mongolia; indeed, it was suspicious that the Frankish King Philip Augustus did not personally participate in the Cathar massacre and, what was even more striking, that the whole of France had been put into interdict between 1200 and 1213 by Innocent III due to the cohabitation that the King was maintaining with a mistress. Which of the Kings, the German or the Frank, was, in the end, the ally that the Siddhas were mentioning?

" 'Seeing the West obscured by the darkness of the Kaly Yuga, Genghis Khan decided to send three messenger ambassadors, to Innocent III, to Philip Augustus, and to Frederick II, with the mission to initiate diplomatic relations and whom he instructed to carry out discreet prospecting intended to concretize an alliance between the East and the West. He did this to gain time, while other envoys of his were traveling to the "center of lesser intensity" to seek the longed-for answers.

" 'By 1220, Genghis Khan already knew that the deal was to be made with the German King. But such a pact, which would not be political but spiritual and that would be celebrated in several worlds at the same time, was requiring greater certainty than mere human conviction: in 1221 the Taoist sage Qiu

Chuji returned, after two years, from the expedition to the "center of lesser intensity." At the Mongol encampment, on the banks of the Onon River, the sage told of his incredible adventure to Genghis Khan: he had been authorized by the Siddhas to visit the Kingdom of Agartha; guided by some mysterious Mongol Initiates, they went hundreds of kilometers into the Gobi desert until reaching a completely desolate and barren place where it was not seeming possible that any vestige of vegetable or animal life existed; in such a place, apparently in the middle of the desert, the monks decided to camp and, although it was seeming a suicide, the Chinese sage did not dare to contradict them; they remained there several days, he lost count of the total, until one night in which he was deeply asleep, trying to recover the strength that during the day the burning sun was mercilessly taking from him, he was brusquely awakened; without coming out of his astonishment, he was invited by the monks, who were accompanying some terrible warriors, emerged from where he was not imagining, to go with them into the desert in a determinate direction; but they did not walk far, for very near to the encampment, in a place that in those days he had observed many times and in which *could be nothing but sand,* a whitish glow could be clearly distinguished rising up from the ground; it was a cloudless night, with a moon that was pouring torrents of silvery light upon the sinuous surface of the desert; however, and the sage of Shantung repeated this many times, when arriving a few steps away, *the light that was rising up from the ground was a hundred times more intense than the moon,* to the point that its blinding brightness was preventing him from distinguishing what or who was producing it; staggering, he stopped next to the light source and only a few seconds later, when his eyes had become adjusted, he could see that a perfect rectangular outline was cut out against the floor, where a heavy stone slab had been moved; the light was coming from that opening that was leading directly to a descending staircase of which steps were quickly being lost from sight into the depths of the Earth.

" 'In spite of the fantastic nature of the story, Genghis Khan accepted it without hesitation because the sage Qiu Chuji was deserving of his total confidence and, mainly, *because his mission had been successful:* he was bringing with him *a message from the Siddhas* and *an inhabitant of Agartha* was accompanying him to interpret that message to the Khan of the Mongols.

According to Qiu Chuji, after descending to incredible depths through that desert trapdoor, they arrived at a perfectly illuminated horizontal tunnel, and there they boarded "a chariot that was swiftly traveled without wheels or horses," which led them in a few minutes to the "City of Wo-Tang, the Lord of War," where "despite being underground, it is possible to see the sky and the stars." In Agartha "the Lord of War himself" received Qiu Chuji to whom, he said, "was waiting to deliver unto him *the magic formula that gives power over the peoples.*" Said formula, explained Wo-Tang, *was already known to Genghis Khan since the days of his Hyperborean Initiation.* The novelty was now consisting in that the formula "*had been endowed with a new, more intense light, so that it could be read even in the midst of the most impenetrable darkness.*"

"'In synthesis: Wo-Tang handed Qiu Chuji a green stone, similar to jade, on which were engraved two parallel columns of thirteen signs because, explained Wo-Tang, both the Uighur, spoken by Genghis Khan, and the language of the Great King of the West to whom the stone was destined, were coming from an ancient sacred language called *"H,"* that is, *Eta.* The stone, was consisting of the only *"pactio verborum,"*[94] since by the mere reading by each one of the Kings, the Mongol and that of the West, of the written formula, a metaphysical pact would be sealed that was involving not the body or material goods but the Spirit of the Peoples and that was committing the Lord of War and his army of Angels to the struggle. Such a pact was surely a thousand times more powerful and enduring than the weak and dubious alliances of men. To guard the Stone and ensure that the formula would be pronounced with the right Ritual, one of those strange inhabitants of Agartha, with Mongolian features but reddish skin, would accompany Qiu Chuji to Genghis Khan's encampment.

"'In 1221, when Genghis Khan pronounced the thirteen words in the due order and time, his part in the Tyr Strategy was definitively completed; from then on everything would depend on the White Races of the West: if they were pure enough they would not hesitate to follow a Universal Emperor from their lineage *once he had pronounced the thirteen words, which were also thirteen Runes.* Since a year before, at the time

---

94. Agreed formula; terms of agreement.

of Qiu Chuji's return from the Gobi desert, some messengers of the Khan had departed for distant Sicily to announce to the German Emperor the future arrival of an Initiate, who would carry a message "from another World." And during the following years, between 1222 and 1228, that envoy would be vainly awaited in the West, a matter that delayed the Crusade that the German Emperor was to undertake to the Holy Land on more than one occasion and that finally led to his excommunication.

" 'What had occurred to the messenger and the Stone? For four years, Frederick II fruitlessly awaited his arrival, but the "Tartar" had been swallowed up by the earth. The excellent Berber clairvoyants that the Emperor was keeping at his court in Palermo announced to him many times that the envoy of the Khan "had been arrested in the Holy Land," but Frederick II was refusing to give credence to such omens, rather attributing them to the antipathy that the Franks were arousing in the Saracens. However, he took advantage of his recent widowhood and in 1225 he married Yolande of Brienne, the daughter of John of Brienne, Frankish King of Jerusalem. Yolande was dowry for the Kingdom of Jerusalem, but Frederick II was not so much interested in that crown as in knowing where the Stone of Genghis Khan was. Through his wife he was able to find out: her uncles, John and Philip of Ibelin, encouraged by the papal legate, had seized the Messenger and his Message. But it was too late for the Tyr Strategy: Frederick II learned the truth only in 1227, the year of Genghis Khan's death, and after threatening Yolande with repudiation.

" 'Resolved to find the Stone, he set out for the Holy Land, but not before being excommunicated by Pope Gregory IX. In that same year, the unfortunate Queen Yolande died in labor, giving birth to the future King Conrad IV, father of the ill-fated Conradin. Knowing that John of Ibelin was in Cyprus, he took this island by assault with 800 Teutonic Knights and seized his sons, Balian and Baldwin of Ibelin. Arrived at the Emperor's camp to parley, Frederick II requested the return of the Stone and of the Messenger of Genghis Khan, to which John of Ibelin responded that the Mongol had died years ago and that the Stone was in his castle in Beirut, in Frankish Palestine. In view of this, Frederick placed the young Princes on the rack and threatened them with torture if the Stone was not restituted to him within a minimum period of time, to which the Lord of Beirut unconditionally acceded.

" 'Once the Stone was obtained, he was able to learn the root of the plot. It had originated in the Knights Templar: the Grand Master had assured the Pope, and many pious Frankish Knights, that Frederick II was planning an alliance with the Mongols to subjugate the World to their will; the next step would be the destruction of the Catholic Church. This information, though not totally false, was malicious and ill-intentioned, and achieved the sought-after effect of preventing that said pact be concretized. But the plot had developed six years earlier and was already beyond repair, after the death of Genghis Khan.

" 'Thus, defeated in what was constituting the spiritual objective of his life, Frederick II disembarked in the Holy Land ready to take vengeance as soon as possible. Paradoxically, that Emperor of the Christian Kings was facing a general uprising of the Frankish Lords, fomented by the Templar and Hospitaller Orders, and yet he was enjoying the high esteem of the Arabs. For years, in effect, Frederick II maintained correspondence with the Sultan of Egypt, al-Malik al-Kamil, who was considering him "the greatest Prince of Christendom" and "a Saint." On that occasion, he did not hesitate in ceding to him the three holy cities, Jerusalem, Bethlehem, and Nazareth, which were in his possession; in 1229, the Treaty of Jaffa was signed that was confirming such a cession, *provided that the Teutonic Knights were in charge of its custody.*

" 'But Frederick II was not content with humiliating the Franks in this way: he was desiring that all of Syria be passed into the possession of the Teutonic Knights and he used every resource at hand to achieve it, among them the promise made to the Sultans to share the holy places with the Muhammadans; in fact, he permitted that the mosques remain open in Jerusalem, as in the other cities that he recovered. In Jerusalem he protagonized the most irritating event when taking the King's Crown, which was over the Holy Sepulchre, and crowning Himself, placing it on his head in the presence of the Grand Master of the Teutonic Order Hermann von Salza and hundreds of German and Sicilian Knights.

" 'Not satisfied with this, he went to Saint-Jean-d'Acre, Bastion of the Templars, and occupied it with his troops. In the palace of the King, of which he took possession for being sovereign of Jerusalem, he gave a great feast to which he invited numerous chiefs of the Saracen Army, during which he exhibited dozens of Christian prostitutes rescued from brothels belonging to the Templars. This initiative exposed the hypocrisy of the Frankish Knights, who on the one hand were proclaiming chastity, and even practicing sodomy, and on the other were exposing these baptized women to all sorts of temptations and sins. Such a crude reality impressed even the not too virtuous Saracens, and the prestige of the Templars fell lower than ever.

" 'Of course, the Emperor was seeking with such denunciations that the Templars would lose their patience and offer him an excuse to battle them. And his tactic paid off because they attempted to assassinate him and he responded by attacking the House of the Temple and the "Château Pèlerin." And if they did not all end up exterminated by the wrath of Frederick II, who predictably would not take long in calling the Arabs to his aid, it was because he received the stab in the back of knowing that his father-in-law John of Brienne was invading Sicily by mandate of Pope Gregory IX and that his son Henry II, King of Germany, was betraying him by supporting the Guelphs. That bad news forced him to return to Sicily where, with far superior troops, he defeated the Pope and forced him to lift the excommunication, then marched to Germany where he deposed Henry and replaced him with the child Conrad IV.

" 'In the years following, he had the King of the World's Castle built by the Hyperborean Initiates and buried the Stone that you have now located, Lupus.

" 'But keep in mind that Frederick II was also a Tulku, something that everyone was accepting in his time, since the people never resigned themselves to his death and awaited "his return" for centuries. And where were the Ghibellines supposing that the Emperor had traveled? Well, none other than to the Kingdom of Prester John, that is, to the Kingdom of Genghis Khan, the Great Emperor of Cathay, K'Taagar or Agartha: the mythical Kingdom of Catigara, which was located "in China."

" 'In the Epoch of Frederick II, the Great Khan was also the Great "Canine," that is to say, the Lord of the Dog, the Guardian of Heaven's Stone, the King of the Universal Empire "of the East," just as I mentioned to you several years ago, on the occasion of Rudolf Hess' flight to England. When Frederick II "departed," after 1250, and especially during the Inter-regnum, hundreds of troubadours and jongleurs were singing verses in which the Emperor's journey to the Kingdom of Prester John were being narrated, and tears and laments were being shed because both Kings had not "met" after all, an event that would bring about the New Order of the Universal Empire: "nevertheless," it was being assured in the songs, "some day Frederick II, carrying his Stone of Venus, *lapis exilis,* would meet Genghis Khan in order to found the Universal Empire."

" 'In conclusion, I want to remind you that the aforemen-tioned alliance between the Romano-Germanic Empire and the Mongol Empire was an open secret in the thirteenth cen-tury, although later the synarchic obscurantism hid the truth of the facts. But it is enough to refer to the evidence to know that truth: as soon as the death of Genghis Khan and the posi-tion of his successor, Ögedei, became known in the West, nothing else was thought of than to create another alliance, this time favorable to the synarchic plans. Behind this was, of course, the White Brotherhood. In 1245, Pope Innocent IV, who had taken refuge in Lyon, the City of the Druids, fleeing from Frederick II, proclaimed a General Council with the object of excommunicating him and stripping him of his imperial in-vestiture: it was the famous Council of Lyon, a sort of "Con-gress of Basel" of the epoch, that is to say, similar to that which the Rabbis held in 1897 and that the "Protocols of the Elders of Zion" mention, in which was discussed the quickest way to put an end to the House of Swabia and implant the Universal Synarchy. Well, no one associates the fact that in that Council, exclusively convoked to deal with the topic of Frederick II, Pope Innocent IV proposed to send an embassy to the Mongol Emperor: from the Council of Lyon would emanate the direc-tives followed by the Franciscan monk John of Plano Carpini and the friars Benedict of Poland and Stephen of Bohemia, who in 1246 would arrive in Mongolia after crossing Russia. And if the synarchic counter-alliance was not then concretized it was because Ögedei had died and Güyük, his successor, was not at all convinced by the letters of the Pope, of whom his grandfather Genghis Khan warned him.

" 'Later on, the Holy See would send Friar Ascelin with the same mission of convincing the Mongols of the goodness of the Synarchy and Saint Louis himself would send Knights to

Mongolia, but only to request help against the Arabs: they were representatives of Saint Louis, among others, André de Longjumeau and the friar Guillaume de Rubrouck. They set out in 1253 and reached Karakorum by the Black Sea Route, but also failed because then was reigning Möngke Khan, whom Sartaq, great-grandson of Genghis Khan and a Nestorian Christian, had advised against the Pope of Rome.

" 'Pope Nicholas IV, pressured by the Order of Preachers, sends to Baghdad the Dominican Ricold of Monte Croce, he who establishes a fruitful deal with the Mongols and succeeds in founding a monastery in Marāgha. As a result of this embassy, the Turkish Bishop Rabban Çauma comes to Paris on behalf of the Mongol King of Persia, Arghun. The grandson of Saint Louis, Philip the Fair, a staunch Ghibelline and partisan of the Universal Empire, was then reigning in France, and that is why this time the alliance has chances of prospering. However, despite maintaining a permanent diplomatic connection with Mongolia, Philip the Fair did not manage to concretize the project due to the fall of Saint-Jean-d'Acre in 1291, at the hands of the Mamluks of Sultan Al-Ashraf, who would bring the Templars to Europe. Philip the Fair was desiring to be Universal Emperor like Frederick II of Swabia, but that would only be possible if he was first putting an end to the power of the Templars and the Popes; the terrible confrontations that he held with Boniface VIII and the very complex task of dismantling the infrastructure of the Knights Templar would keep him occupied until his death. Perhaps the historic opportunity of Frederick II was still present in the times of Philip the Fair, but the latter lacked the material time to consolidate himself in Europe and join the spiritual forces of Asia.

" 'In synthesis, Lupus, all this proves that there was a great esoteric movement between Europe and Mongolia-China long before the publicized and feuilletonesque[95] adventure of the Polo Venetian merchants in the fourteenth century: theirs was only a lucrative materialistic adventure, devoid of any transcendent content, and it is no doubt put in first place due to that. It has been tried by the usual obscurantist methods to ignore what one does not wish to accept as real, to deny or to not respond to the disquieting question of the military power of the Mongols: their tactical superiority, by invariably laying

---

95. In the style of a literary work that is serialized, similar to a soap opera.

waste to medieval formations, is undeniable but has caused a collective trauma to the Europeans. From where can come the superiority of a Strategy but from the Spirit, from a lucid Intelligence and limitless Valor? If the Mongols were the barbarians that they were made out to be, they would have never gone beyond the Urals. But of us they will also say that we were barbarians and that we were eating human flesh; or who knows what other barbarities. Do not forget that we have acted in a manner similar to the Mongols of Genghis Khan, and against the same Enemy, and displaying the same banner: even our best tactic, the *blitzkrieg,* is inspired by the swift and accurate movement of the Mongol horde.

" 'Wait a moment, Lupus, I'll go get something that I had prepared for you.'

"The master class that Tarstein had just given had made me forget the war, the imminent military defeat of the Third Reich, and even the black reality of not knowing what I was going to do from then on, whether I should go to die in the bunker, as the Tibetan Legion heroically decided, or whether I would have to flee to an uncertain fate in a World without the Third Reich, that is to say, in a synarchic World. I was not even wanting to consider this last possibility. Instead I was harboring the secret hope that the Initiates of the Black Order had decided to take me with them to the Antarctic Refuge of the Führer: did I not have sufficient merits to deserve such a distinction? Besides, Rudolf Hess, my protector, was *also* there. Would he disapprove of my presence? I was not fully comprehending the mysterious matter of the Tulkus and their faculty of possessing several bodies. I already told you, Neffe, that I was feeling that I was a unique individual, a perception that did not change until today, and back then I was not seeing what problem there could be in another Tulku joining the Tulkus who were preparing for the Final Battle.

"Before continuing with the account of what took place that day, the last day that I was there, at Gregorstraße 239, I want you to notice that the information provided by Tarstein about Frederick II makes quite clear the words of Belicena Villca written on the Nineteenth Day of her Letter: there she was saying, 'the causes (of Frederick II's hostility toward the Golen Church) were two: the positive reaction from the Inheritance of his Pure Blood *thanks to the historical proximity of the Gral, a concept that I will soon explain; and the influence of certain Hy-*

perborean Initiates that Frederick II himself made come to his Court of Palermo from distant countries of Asia and whose story I will not be able to stop to relate in this letter.'

" 'Today you have brought something very valuable to the Führer and the ⚡⚡,' Tarstein began saying upon returning, as he was holding out to me a leather case with silver fittings and a key lock, 'and I will recompense you with something incomparably lesser, but no less valuable to me. Take, Lupus, Kurt, my unpublished book "Secret History of the Thulegesellschaft": in it is narrated the history of the last 630 years of the German branch of the House of Tharsis, and contains the proof of its outstanding intervention in the foundation of the Einherjar medieval Order, which would last several centuries and would give rise in the twentieth century to the Thulegesellchaft, and then to the ⚡⚡ Black Order. I give it to you because I have consulted with the Siddhas and they have told me that you are predestined to know all the secrets of my Stirp: perhaps it will be given to you to know what even I have not achieved, that is, to follow the millenary history of the House of Tharsis and to discover the mission that your Great Ancestors entrusted to you.'

"I was noticing that for Tarstein that detachment was very significant, but I was also understanding that he was subtly sending me away, and that was what I was fearing. I was feeling for Tarstein's sensibilities but I had to clarify things. I took the book and ignored his speech.

" 'You speak as if we were never going to see each other again, but at the same time as if I were going to survive long enough to read this book,' I harshly said.

"Tarstein was undaunted and decided to respond with irony to my insolence, but with similar harshness.

" 'Very shrewd, Lupus! But we will indeed not see each other again in this life, although we will soon reunite in the Final Battle: such is the ambiguity of the Fate of the Tulkus! It was very difficult for me to communicate this to you, believe me, but I'm glad that you've cut to the chase. Now I will tell you frankly what the situation is: *You are still an ⚡⚡ officer and must carry out orders like everyone else.* And your orders are: *flee Germany immediately and hide yourself in the Argentine Republic, where your sister lives.*

" 'No!' I shouted, interrupting his directives.

" 'You can't do this to me. I've complied with everything that I've been ordered up to now, with all the loyalty and valor that I've been able, but these orders are excessive. I would rather die a thousand times than survive in a world dominated by Jews. It is not a lack of valor, it is not disloyalty, it is disgust, Comrade Tarstein, simple repugnance and horror to live in a world without Honor, where our Banners don't fly anywhere: since childhood in Egypt, when I joined the Hitler Youth, I have ceaselessly breathed the Mystique of National Socialism; no one prepared us for this! No, Comrade, we were not made to be defeated by the infernal forces and to survive under their empire. A moment ago, I was harboring the hope that I would be permitted to be evacuated to the Führer-Tulku's Refuge, as you call it; but now you leave me frozen with your orders to hide me in Argentina. I have been an ⚡⚡ officer, I have been an Initiate, I have developed amazing faculties, but now I see that I've only been an instrument of Fate, a toy of the Gods. And do you know why I feel this way? Because, in spite of all what I have been and done, the truth is that I don't comprehend anything, in the same way that I can't see the Sign that I am Myself and that you admire so much. And even less do I understand this condemnation to survive the destruction of the Third Reich. I supplicate you, Comrade Tarstein, if it's not possible that I depart with you together with the Führer, ask me to die, grant me the authorization to die with Honor, or have me killed!'

" 'You see Kurt, you are getting testy and I will have to interrupt the exposition of your orders to clarify some points. First and foremost, I already warned you that, from now on, *the partisans of the Hyperborean Wisdom will have to define to which reality they refer: whether to the reality of the dead Führer or to the reality of the living Führer.* And I anticipated that those who choose to live in the first reality would be considered traitors by the *Black Order.* You, my esteemed Kurt, by presenting to me the case of survival in a World where the Third Reich has been defeated, are participating in the first reality. Of course, I am not going to make this a syllogism and conclude that you are a traitor because I know that you are not. Only that, indeed, you "do not comprehend the situation," an accusation that, as you have said to me, other persons have already made to you. Well, I will clarify the situation in such a way that no doubts remain for you: you are not going to stay in the World that you imagine as a condemned man, *but you are going to act as a secret agent of the ⚡⚡ Black Order in an effectively Jewish World; and you are going to act as a representative of the living Führer, as his fifth column, as an Initiate infiltrated in enemy territory, nothing different from the missions that you have fulfilled up to now. Take heed, Kurt, Lupus, do not believe in the fall of the bunker and the suicide of the Führer! It is the only way in which you will be able to carry out your orders.*

" 'Secondly, and you must believe me, we would gladly take you to the Führer's Refuge but the Siddhas affirm that *you must fulfill this last mission.* As I said to you years ago, you are not only important: you are a first degree support for the Führer's Strategy. And the Strategy cannot afford to do without you in the place in which you have to be just because you suffer from nausea and Judeophobia. What we ask of you is not impossible for you and I know that you will comply: They need you here. And the Loyal Gods are the ones who decide who goes and who does not go to the Führer's Refuge: such a selection totally escapes the will of the Initiates of the Black Order.

" 'Thirdly, you have erroneously presumed that I will also depart for the Führer's Refuge, but I must repeat to you what I said at the beginning: "we will not see each other again in this life." That does not mean that I am authorized to leave from here: like you, my orders assure that I must stay in this World, in this house in East Berlin that will never be found by the Russians, not even if they search every house on the block. However, you must not come to see me, nor must you see anyone else of the Waffen-⚡⚡ except your dear Comrade Oskar Feil. About Karl von Grossen, I will tell you what the orders are. That is all, Kurt, have you understood me? If so, I will go on to give you your orders.'

" 'Suppose that years pass, and nothing occurs, and I disobey and decide to come to see you,' I interrupted.

" 'You don't understand, Kurt! *You will never find this house!* Test it when you leave, go a few blocks away in any direction, go around the block, do whatever you want and then return to Gregorstraße and try to find 239: you will find that it does not exist, you will find a different house, perhaps bombed. If you have been able to arrive here it is because I was waiting for you, but when your Presence is not necessary for the Strategy you will never coincide with me and this house: *such is the power of the absolute location that the beings consecrated to the Hyperborean Strategy possess; only the beings whose coincidence is strategically significant coincide in space and time; and that is the reality of the beings that exist; and the other created beings, although they are related to each other in space and time, they do not exist for the Spirit, they are Maya, Illusion, if they are not strategically significant.* You as an Initiate should know this; have you forgotten that this is the War between Spirit and the Potencies of Matter?'

"But I was not listening to reason. Of course I was comprehending that a Hyperborean Pontiff like Tarstein had the power to situate himself in other dimensions of the illusory reality of Maya, including the house of the Thulegesellschaft, and that I would never find him if he was not wanting that to happen. But I insisted one more time.

" 'What if I use the daiva dogs? If I track you down through the dimensions and approach you, even if it's not at Gregorstraße 239?'

"Tarstein burst into laughter.

" 'You really are stubborn, Kurt. If you use the daiva dogs you will undoubtedly find me. Likewise, if you make them *fly* to the Führer's Refuge, they will surely take you there. But I do not want to exaggerate how any of us will take such an attitude on your part. Accept it once and for all! You are a military man and will continue being so from now on, no one will discharge you from the ⚡⚡! And as a military man you must obey orders, orders that I will now transmit to you and that you will scrupulously fulfill! Orders that if you do not fulfill will be grounds for summary proceedings or a Court of Honor! If you appear by my side, or head to the Führer's Refuge, you will be liable to the penalty of summary execution, but, what is worse than death for an Initiate, *you would be expelled from the ⚡⚡ Black Order.*

" 'I know that what I tell you is tough, but you must accept it and behave like a military man, like a Wise Warrior. Earlier you were complaining that the Third Reich did not instruct you to live under the Universal Synarchy. This is true. But if we have clarified anything, it is the difference between the Heart and the egoic Mind, that is to say, between the reason of the Heart and the reason of the Ego; between the emotions or sentiments of the Heart and the pure ideas of the spiritual Ego. And in the Noological Ethics of the Hyperborean Wisdom we have demonstrated to you the spiritual superiority of the Ego over the Heart, we have taught you to dominate, with the Ego, the Heart, we have stripped it of feelings and we have forged for you a new Heart of steel.

" 'We put a Stone in your Heart, Kurt! And in exchange for the reason of the Heart, which is weak and enchanting, we made you access the Absolute Honor of the Spirit, the foundation of Camaraderie. I remind you of these noological ethical principles because, and excuse my frankness, to me your attitude is pusillanimous, the product of a miserable affective connection, of a fear of doing without the illusory relationships between Hyperborean Initiates, of a lack of faith in Yourself. The truth, the hard truth Kurt, is that *we are not friends nor will we ever be; we are, however, Comrades, partisans of the mystical ideals of the Führer's Strategy. And if we are not friends, and strategic orders demand that we never see each other again in this life, can you tell me for what spiritual motive you would want to reunite with me outside of the Kairos?*

"I was speechless. I would no longer respond to this unanswered question because I was remembering my attitude in Operation First Key, when guided by the daiva dogs I became a Charismatic Leader, a Hero, and led the Comrades into the Hell of the Valley of the Immortal Demons. How different were the morals of that time and the present. Of course, the war had not started then and the Third Reich was seeming militarily invincible. I was fully realizing that what was difficult to digest, even if one comprehended the Führer's strategic motives and shared them, was the destruction of the Third Reich and the probable constitution of the Universal Synarchy. It was not that my heart had softened, but that the war, the apparent result of the war, had confused me. And from that confusion was being formed the nihilistic attitude that I was presenting before Tarstein's orders. Then I was understanding it, Tarstein's Wisdom had made me understand. That is why his question would remain unanswered. But I would not give up my negative attitude because of that. As I told you, Neffe, the reality of 1945 was very difficult to digest, even though Tarstein advised me not to believe in it.

"Seeing that I was not replying to him, Konrad Tarstein continued without further ado with the orders.

" 'Well, Kurt: I will continue with your orders. The first thing that you will do, upon leaving from here, will be to return to

Italy, to the Monastery of our Franciscan Comrades where Von Grossen and Feil have been hidden. You three are on a secret list managed by an SS organization known by the code name of "The Spider." Such an organization has been formed to support members of the Waffen-SS who are the object of Jewish persecution after the war. Have prudence when dealing with them because they consist of an exoteric group, who know little or nothing about the Black Order, other than second-hand news. To your misfortune I will confirm that the 775 SS Initiates of the Black Order, and their Instructors, have been or will be evacuated from Western Civilization for, although not all are accepted into the Führer's Refuge, there are other appropriate Refuges to await the Final Battle: the 15,000 Pure Blood children, the product of Darré and Rosenberg's racial experiments, have been moved to those sites. You, on the contrary, are requested to remain in this World and I know of no other Initiate to whom such an order has been given, although I do not rule out that, in the future, Initiates will be sent to fulfill special missions: the Gods will know why they have determined it this way and you will have to seek them out. But in the meantime you will have to be careful, very careful, because those who remain acting on behalf of the SS will be Comrades without esoteric instruction of the Hyperborean Wisdom, many of whom have not understood and will not understand the true Strategy of the Führer. Notice that, although the Führer suggested resisting to the last drop of blood, and destroying Germany to the ground before letting it fall into enemy hands, our most valuable human capital, that is to say, the great scientists, have been made available to the Allies. The SS could have executed them all, and yet it has protected them and served them on a platter to the Allies. You may ask why? Because they have all received the Führer's order to reveal to the Enemy the secret of the most terrible weapons that the human mind can conceive, and to stimulate their construction. From the different countries where they are taken, they will foment the competition of sophisticated armaments and develop undreamed-of weapons, which will set one against the other because of the natural ignorance of the military, and will endanger the universal synarchic alliance. With the plans that are already being taken from the Third Reich, they have more than enough to initiate said tactic. Tactics that obey the strategic purpose of generating a certain state of world tension when the Universal Synarchy is declared. Then the Gods will intervene; the spiritual undercurrents of Humanity, placed in extreme tension by the permanent danger of the end of Civilization, will react to the Judaic Terror in which the Synarchy will be affirmed; and the Final Battle will ensue, during which the Führer and the Eternal ⚡ will return.

" 'You understand this simple but top-secret tactic, which constitutes an inevitable trap into which the Allies will fall, but how many others will understand it? You will see how many so-called Nazis, and even ex-members of the ⚡, will claim that our scientists are traitors. But they are incapable of comprehending the Führer's Strategy, and that is why they do not understand the actions of those who act motivated by strategic ends. *They will understand you even less, if they find out what you are, esteemed Lupus.*

" 'You must be prudent and tolerant with those Comrades *who have opted for the reality of the dead Führer.* Once they have located you, you will disconnect from them and never resume contact. It will be an elementary way to prevent unnecessary risks because, for enemies, you already have enough and terrible ones, with the White Brotherhood, the Immortals Bera and Birsha, and the Druids and Jews who will search for you to eliminate you. As I was saying, you will wait in Italy until the Argentine passports and tickets are delivered to you. The Spider will deposit a sum of money in Buenos Aires Banks that will allow each to establish yourselves without problems; you should immediately withdraw those funds in order to avoid possible traces and investigations. Regarding you, the Siddhas say that you should seek a locality consecrated to the Virgin of Agartha, not far from your family. You will be able to meet with your sister, but employing all forms of cover in the Secret Service Manual: it is for the good of both of you; think that if the Enemy discovers your sister, they may attempt to extract your whereabouts by violent means and even put pressure on you, and that if you are well covered, but give your sister away, they may take their revenge on her when faced with the impossibility of capturing you.

" 'You will adopt the same precautions in order to meet Oskar Feil, who must inhabit a place far away from your home. You are prohibited to carry out any type of commercial partnership, not even by means of third parties, and to intervene in common activities that may fortuitously relate to them. You will only meet as Comrades, to share your spiritual ideals. With respect to Von Grossen, you will have to say goodbye to him forever in Argentina. Oskar Feil will be able to maintain contact but it is convenient that he also keeps out of the way, for the old fox will not hold still and will try to wage his private war against the Synarchy. Possibly he will become an advisor in matters of Intelligence and Counter-espionage, and put himself at the service of pseudo-fascist regimes, of which abound in South America. Nothing that would be convenient for you.

" 'Lastly: keep the daiva dogs but do not use them except in case of extreme necessity. The same goes for your initiatic faculties: keep yourself alert, well trained, but do not act except in extreme cases. These are, in synthesis, your orders: *to wait*. Survive, protect yourself, and *wait!*'

" 'By all the gods!' I shouted out of my mind. 'Wait for what?'

" 'I cannot give you more information,' Tarstein impassively responded. 'Carry out your orders and you will find out!'

"He shook my hand and, as if such a greeting were not enough, he embraced me.

" 'Farewell, Kurt von Sübermann. Rest assured that your contribution has been invaluable to the cause of the ⚡⚡ Black Order. The Third Reich has decorated you with the Iron Cross, but the Order will some day award you an even more valuable distinction, which you have deservedly earned. I repeat: soon we will meet again, during the Final Battle, even if we do not meet again in this life.'

"We were at the door. I had exited and was grabbing onto the useless motorcycle, while I was hearing Konrad Tarstein say almost the same words of the Gurkha Bangi. I would have wanted to cry with helplessness in the face of that absurdity: they were all dying or leaving. Only I, a mute witness to a terrible and secret reality, had to remain in Hell. And without knowing why.

" 'Heil Hitler!' I shouted in salute, as the door of Gregorstraße 239 was closing behind me forever.

"I started up the motorcycle and, dodging the debris, turned around the block. Before completing the third block someone shot at me from a terrace. The bullet cleanly severed the fork and my front wheel suddenly crossed; I slammed on the brakes and flew several meters forward. Without stopping rolling, I hid behind the incinerated chassis of a car, pursued by a hail of bullets. 'I had forgotten that I was wearing a Russian uniform and was walking down a lonely Berlin street without any protection.' I let out several swears and ran to the corner, hugging the walls. I was back on Gregorstraße. I would be long gone by now had I not decided to take one last look at Tarstein's house. I advanced the meters that were separating me from it, looking at both corners, alternatively. It was dead of night but not silent; that 30th of April would dawn accompanied by the heaviest combat and the noise of bullets, howitzers, and bombs was deafening.

"I soon found to my dismay that Tarstein's warning was not in vain. In fact, there was *now* no 239 on Gregorstraße. But the place where I left did exist, the fresh tire tracks of the motorcycle on the sidewalk and in the street were evidencing it. But door 239, in front of those tracks, was no longer there. In its place was the closed door of a business in fairly good condition. With my hand I removed the layer of dust that was covering the plaque and read: *'Hyperboreanische Buchhandlung.*'[96] I felt footsteps that were approaching; perhaps the snipers who had shot at me minutes before. There was nothing left to do there, so I ran in the opposite direction.

"I repeat that time is of the essence, Neffe, so I will leave out the account of my adventures until arriving in Italy for another time. I will only mention that in June of 1945 I reunited with Karl von Grossen and Oskar Feil at the Franciscan Monastery in Southern Italy and that I remained there until February of 1947. On that date, our contact with The Spider introduced us to an Argentine Army officer by the name of Zapalla, who provided us passports and tickets, and, of course, new identities: I became Cerino Sanguedolce, as you know; Oskar became Domingo Pietratesta; and Karl von Grossen, Carlo de Grandi. The three of us would appear to be Italian immigrants, hence the linguistic affiliation of the names.

"Once in this country, everything happened as Tarstein had foreseen: they delivered the money to us in Buenos Aires, and each one went to live in a different Province. Von Grossen remained in Buenos Aires and, as Tarstein said, he would not take long to dedicate himself to organize a Secret Service in the company of another former Gestapo Comrade of his, *SS Standartenführer* Justin von Grosmann. Oskar Feil chose Córdoba, and it seems that the Gods had guided him because years later he found there the Order of Tirodal Knights, which oriented his last days; and I, knowing that the Siegnagels were residing in Salta, decided that 'Santa María de la Candelaria' was a good title for the Virgin of Agartha, and I acquired this finca where since then I inhabit.

"Having left the World War behind, and having to stick to 'my orders,' I resumed the traditional familial profession of candy making and remained hidden until now, meditating all these years on what had occurred in the first half of my life. My only recreations were the sporadic visits of your parents, or of Oskar, to the neutral places agreed upon in advance to hold short, very short, meetings. And the only permanent companions that I have had, faithful by the way, have been the daiva dogs: Yin and Yang are the third Argentine generation, great-grandchildren of Yun and Yab.

"And since I settled in Argentina, except for the failed attempt to make contact with Nimrod de Rosario in Córdoba by acceding to Oskar's request, no one has ever, ever convoked me to fulfill the final mission of the Hyperborean Wisdom until you appeared here with Belicena Villca's Letter. I am not ashamed to confess it: I had already lost all hope that Konrad Tarstein's announcements would be fulfilled. However, I was keeping myself on alert, as he ordered me, and as you lamentably proved. *Meine Ehre heißt Treue!*"[97]

---

97. Oath of the ⚡⚡ Black Order, also engraved on the Knight's Dagger: *My Honor is called Loyalty.*

EPILOGUE

to the fantastic book
"The Mystery of the
Hyperborean Wisdom,"
dedicated to them.

...or PROLOGUE

to the actual Mystery of the
Hyperborean Wisdom,
dedicated to us, we who feel
running through our veins

The Blood of Tharsis.

Chapter I

nd that was all Uncle Kurt managed to narrate to me about the story of his life. At that moment, he was right in feeling hurried, as events were demonstrating, but he was leaving the most interesting part untold: the details of his secret missions during the war and the mysterious mission of his godfather Rudolf Hess. Logically, he was also hoping to complete his stories on a future occasion. But it was written that such an occasion would never present itself.

However, the last night that we spoke about these topics and he recounted to me his arrival in Argentina, I managed to ask him two questions that I still clearly remember. It was already late, about eleven o'clock at night on March 21, exactly two months after the spiritual rapture of January 21, and we decided to go to sleep, after a long day of conversation. It was then when I raised a question that was causing me a lot of discomfort.

"Tell me, Uncle Kurt: if in 1945 you had received Konrad Tarstein's unpublished book 'Secret History of the Thulegesellschaft,' in which the German history of the house of Tharsis is narrated, how is it that you remained indifferent the first time that we spoke about the Letter from Belicena Villca, implying that you were unaware of its important historical contribution? I remember very well that you were only startled when hearing the name 'Tharsis,' but you expressed nothing about the German Tharsises. Nevertheless, you had to know a part of the history, perhaps as rich in nuances as that which I learned from Belicena Villca. And you were very careful not to say anything about it, even until now. Your behavior doesn't seem right to me, Uncle Kurt!" I affirmed with a tone of painful reproach.

Uncle Kurt observed me with surprise and let out one of his formidable guffaws.

"But I hadn't read it!" he apologized.

"What? After thirty-five years you hadn't read Tarstein's book?" I asked stupefied.

"I already told you, Neffe, that I was very angry about the orders that Tarstein transmitted to me! Here, in Santa María, I simply kept the book to read it on the day that Tarstein's predictions came true, that is, the day that I somehow gained access to the rest of the history of his Stirp. And that day came with your visit and the Letter from Belicena Villca. That's why I read it, in effect, during the days that I was shut away in my room, after learning the contents of the Letter: everything was coinciding, it was really the part that was missing from Belicena's story, the connection between the Vrunaldine branch of the House of Tharsis and the Thulegesellschaft! The history of the search for the Führer, initiated in the Middle Ages, and his location and Initiation in the twentieth century! But if I have said nothing to you afterward about this, it was because I was hoping to narrate to you my own life and to make you aware of the existence of that work, which I still keep. It is my wish that you read it yourself and then retain it as part of your inheritance! To whom, but to you, is it justly due? You must join it to the Letter from Belicena Villca and take it to Córdoba, so that the Tirodal Knights and, if possible, Noyo Villca, learn of it."

I was stunned by my Uncle's incredible response: thirty-five years without reading Tarstein's book! Ha! That's *what you call stubborn!*

Uncle Kurt went to his room and returned with the leather and silver hardware case that was holding the precious work. He unconditionally handed it over to me and there I fired at him the second question:

"I was left with a great curiosity to know what became of the Tibetan Legion. If you don't mind wasting a minute, synthetically tell me what happened with them."

"I'll tell you. And it's not too long to recount. The part of the Legion that was remaining at its base in Assam, on the border with Bhutan, quietly dispersed at the end of the war: some returned to the Kaulika Monasteries and others enlisted themselves as mercenaries in the subsequent wars in Asia: that of Chiang Kai-shek against Mao and those of Korea and Vietnam. Those, at the outset, survived World War II. But, surely, you ask me about the fate of Bangi, Srivirya, and the fifty legionnaires who stayed in Berlin to guard the Bunkerführer: about them I must confess to you, with pride, that they all died fighting the Russians. It's an amusing incident: according to what they informed me in those days, when I was still having to flee from Germany, on April 30 the Russians managed to take the bunker but at the terrible cost of ten to one. It is worth saying that the Tibetans wiped out an infantry battalion of more than five hundred men. And so impressive was the impact of that carnage, carried out by an Asian ᛋᛋ Legion, that Stalin himself ordered the removal and concealment of the Tibetan cadavers and negotiated with the Allies the official suppression of all news about the Tibetan Legion from the bunker. Nevertheless, many independent investigators have mentioned the existence of the Legion and its valorous determination to defend the bunker to the end. Of course, if one consults the 'official historians,' those who must live on academic or journalistic presuppositions, their version will be quite different: the Russians would have found the bunker almost unguarded; and the Tibetan Legion never existed."

Chapter II

e said goodbye until the following day, with the instruction to leave immediately for Tucumán. After all, it was almost three months since the assassination of Belicena Villca and I still had not attempted to fulfill her request. I mentally counted them: 74 days. Seventy-four days! It might be a long time; perhaps for Noyo Villca it was, and I was regretting it. But for me it would be the most fruitful seventy-four days of my life. It was causing me laughter and shame to remember who I was before January 6, in that sinister Neuropsychiatric Hospital: "Dr. Arturo Siegnagel, one of our best interns"—the nurses were introducing me. What the system had turned me into! Before January 6 I had everything, from the material point of view, but I was lacking in clear ideals: they had brainwashed me! On the contrary, now I had nothing, comparing myself with the prestigious Dr. whom I had been, *I was lacking a material future, a predictable future within the laws of the system; but I had the clear ideal of the Hyperborean Wisdom.* And with this ideal that I now had, I was not needing to possess anything else in life, least of all the determinateness of a *mediocre future!*

I got into bed, jubilantly I would say. How everything had changed for the better! How I had changed for the better! The night was starry and a little cool, perhaps heralding the beginning of autumn. At first I thought of reading Konrad Tarstein's book, but then I held myself back. I was also a bit tired and was not wanting to get completely out of control, nor was I desiring that the present joy completely dominate me: if Uncle Kurt kept himself from reading it for 35 years, why should I be impatient? Was I not capable of waiting one more day? And then, after generating such foolish thoughts, I turned off the light and went to sleep.

Oh, Gods, what a fool! That was what I had now become, apart from "enlightened by the Hyperborean Wisdom," which by the way had nothing to do with what happened. It was I, my excessive pride as a result of all what I was finding out in such a short time and that was puffing up my plumage like a peacock, the only one to blame for the Misfortune, which was lying in wait, to cast itself upon us that night. Of course; I do not rule out or underestimate the astonishing vigilance that the enemy keeps over the whole World, or "over many Worlds," according to the concepts that Capitán Kiev was using with Belicena Villca. No, I am not going to underestimate the attentive task of observation that the Demons were developing trying to locate Uncle Kurt; perhaps that watch would have borne fruit one day and they would have somehow found him. *But I was mainly responsible for what occurred that night! A hundred times, a thousand times, it would have been preferable that I read Tarstein's book, as I was "normally" desiring, instead of doing what I did!!!*

As I said, I turned off the light and went to sleep. I saw the starry sky through the glass, and closed my eyes. But, being still quite nervous, as well as tired, *I decided to lull myself to sleep by mentalizing the svadi Kyilkhor. And that would be my fatal mistake!*

Uncle Kurt revealed to me the form of the Kyilkhor and gave demonstrations on the mental mastery that it was enabling to exercise over the daiva dogs. I realized then that the "whistle" used to launch the dogs on me, when I furtively entered onto his finca, had not truly been an audible sound: it was my unconscious predisposition to grasp the symbols of the Kyilkhor, from "beyond Kula and Akula," the cause of the perception of Uncle Kurt's order. The same had happened with the whimpers of the Tibetan mastiffs who were expressing their contained desires to attack: it was all mental, extrasensory perceptions, symbols that the ignorance of my reason was translated as originated by sounds, the illusion of sounds. Of course, only I, or someone who possessed "the Sign of the Origin" as I, would have been able to hear them: any "normal" person, no matter the training that his auditory sense possessed, would have only noticed the presence of the dogs when the deadly jaws had shut on his limbs.

In short, Uncle Kurt had agreed, like so many unfinished things that remained, to permit me to use it according to his indications; but the occasion did not present itself and I did not get to carry out any kind of practice on the mastiffs. That night, fifteen or twenty minutes before 12, I entertained myself a good while, fixing the image of the Kyilkhor in my mind, and at last, without reflecting on it, I issued an order. That is to say, I composed the word of an order without imagining that it would be inexorably fulfilled. It was a simple directive, *"bark,"*

I thought, which was in no way allowing me to suppose what it would cause.

Instantly, the mastiffs emitted a wolfish, harrowing howl, and began to bark in duet, **without stopping.** The bellows that they were letting out were shuddering, and very intense, which was why I sat up in bed, frozen with fright and desperate. "They'll wake up Uncle Kurt," I stupidly thought, and I concentrated again on the Yantra, trying to form a word to stop the canine concert. I imagined that the word would be *"silence"* but how does one say *silence* in Sanskrit or Tibetan, the only languages in which one could translate the concept with the key of the svadi Kyilkhor? "Uncle Kurt had told it to me," I was assuring myself, while fruitlessly procuring to remember. And it was then that the first of the series of nefarious phenomena that would happen during that hellish night took place.

It occurred as if my consciousness had all of a sudden limitlessly expanded: I perceived **the whole room at a single glance,** but without looking, as if a will more powerful than mine compelled me to do so. Then I saw the exterior of the house, the Finca, **all at once;** and the city of Santa María, and the road to Salta, and my own Finca in Cerrillos. I saw Papa, Mama, Katalina, Enrique and Federico, my nephews, and even Canuto the dog. As if hypnotized, I was seeing everything and I could not stop seeing. Unexpectedly, from the bottom of my field of vision, right in front of me, and as if emerging from behind the Cumbres del Obispo,[1] a point began to grow at an extraordinary speed until occupying all my attention. I can never forget it! Taking the words that Princess Isa said to Nimrod, I would affirm that it was *"the most hideous and abominable monster that can be imagined in an eternity of madness,"* one *"who cannot be described by any mortal without losing his sanity."* And what saved me from that Presence of Hell? Undoubtedly the Virgin of Agartha, the Seed of Stone that She deposited on January 21 in a human and mortal heart; the Seed that, in spite of everything, had germinated and made me what I now was.

Because in the past I would have died right there, in front of the Demon who had contemplated me for an instant with a hatred that I never believed possible that anyone could experience. But now I had sufficient strength to face him and push

---

1. Bishop's Slope, a hill southwest of Salta.

him away from me. Yes, he disappeared from sight and the vision dissipated. Again I found myself in the room in Santa María, seated on the bed and listening to the mastiffs incessantly howling. I realized in an instant that my mind, when attempting to silence the daiva dogs, became "careless," offered a weak side, and was "tuned in to," captured, by a Demon of the White Brotherhood, a representative of the Potencies of Matter, maybe the Immortal Bera, maybe Rigden Jyepo, perhaps Enlil-Jehovah-Satan himself.

Evidently, I was not entirely unfocused, for I heard, or believed I heard, the voice of Uncle Kurt who was thundering the words *"niścala nirvāta svadi"* directly into the interior of my psyche, so that the dogs immediately ceased to bark. The truth was that an instant later Uncle Kurt was truly bursting into my room, shouting "Arturo! Arturo!"

"Arturo! You're all right, thank the Gods!" he exclaimed upon turning on the light and making sure that I was alive. "What have you done, Arturo? The Demon Bera has located you! For a moment I felt it like that time at Das Pech ravine, in Tibet!"

I told him about the imprudent use that I made of the Yantra.

"Oh, Arturo," he marveled, "you've been very strong in getting rid of him. But I don't believe that that's enough. I very much fear that the Druids have discovered this house. We'll have to get out of here as soon as possible."

I did not know what to say. Irrationally, I grabbed my wristwatch from the bedside table and looked at the time: "00:10 hours," I said, and turned my head toward Uncle Kurt, who was observing me with wide eyes.

I did not take long in realizing the reason for his horror: *it was the buzzing, the unmistakable buzzing of honey bees.* In truth, that euphonic sound of the Dorje was only being noticed when its complementary effects were already taking place. At first I did not notice it, but then, naturally after Uncle Kurt had perceived it, I heard it clearly, filling the environment with the sensation of the arrival of an innumerable swarm. But at that point it was impossible to react, for the pressure on my heart was not allowing distractions. I let myself fall backward, until my head hit the pillow, and I relaxed as best I could; unconsciously I covered my ears with my hands, but the deadly sound was still penetrating, each instant with more intensity;

and my heart, completely out of control, was seeming to want to burst out of my chest. And the worst was yet to come.

I was experiencing a growing paralysis in my whole body and I reasoned, already at the end of my psychic resistance, that the best mental tactic to fight against the powerful Willpower of the Demons would consist in concentrating my thought on an idea alien to the terrible reality of the Dorje. To think of something else, but of what? Oh Gods, how greedy for ideas can a fanciful imagination like mine become in such an extreme situation, when animal life is at stake! And how much more greedy it must become if, as the Hyperborean Wisdom assures us, the Created Soul is ready to betray us because its substance is part of the Creator, a participant of his Archetype in image and likeness! There I undoubtedly proved it: the Soul would always betray the Spirit, the Ego, in order to favor the Will of the Demons, who belong to the White Hierarchy in which the One-Creator unfolds and links Himself! Because at last a saving idea suddenly came to me: it was a memory of my days as a university student, when I was attending Biology classes. And I let the memory carry me away; and it seemed for a moment that I was freeing myself from the pressure of the Dorje. Yes, the Soul, owner of memory and recollections, had finally obeyed the will of the Ego and was pulling me out of that deadly reality. It was a Biology class, I was perfectly re-calling it; I was surrounded by dozens of classmates; what was the class about? Ah, yes! Physiology of insects! Now Professor Jacobo Cañás was entering the Lecture Hall and was begin-ning to teach the class. Subject: "the *common bee;* also classi-fied under the name of *Apis mellifica* by Linnaeus; *Apis domes-tica* by Réaumur; *Apis cerifera* by Scopoli; *Apis gregaria* by Ge-offroy; and many other names with which the Great Natural-ists have designated the same insect."

I was lacking the strength to get out from the memory. Someone within me, the same one who attempted to plunge me into the Abyss the night of the earthquake in Salta, had betrayed me again. Ah, if I had ascended for aid to the Virgin of Agartha, as then, if I had let myself be raptured by Her Di-vine Grace! Surely, that rapture of the Absolute Woman was what the Kaulikas were calling Kula. Kula would have trans-formed me into Akula, into a living Shiva, and the Spirit would have situated itself "beyond Kula and Akula." Surely, then, that was the true way of salvation to get out from the

Demon's siege, which I did not know how to find at first because of a manifest lack of faith in Myself, because of my distrust in the fact that my Spirit could really be loved by the Goddess of Eternal Deliverance.

Instead, I was stuck in Professor Jacobo Cañás' class: "the buzzing of *hymenoptera* is generally a combination of three distinct tones, generated in different organs. The most intense is that of the wings, although it is of the lowest frequency: for the same specimen of *Apis mellifica,* it statistically varies between a *La* of 440 cycles per second[2] and a *Mi* of the same octave of 330 cycles per second; the first tone corresponds to the bee—rested, at the moment of leaving the hive; the last, to the fatigued bee, at the end of its work day." I was precisely perceiving those tones; I was clearly hearing the sound of the flapping wings; the *hymenoptera* were flying toward me: "The second tone that comprises the characteristic buzzing, is produced by the vibration of the spiracles that lead air to the pulmonary tracheas: it is usually a *Ti* of 594 cycles per second, appreciably sharper than the tone of the wings, but less intense." I was now hearing the buzzing of a bee; the buzzing of a swarm; the buzzing was saturating my senses, paralyzing my body, invading my mind. The buzzing was taking over my heartbeat and synchronizing it with its frequency! The buzzing was killing me!

"The third tone, very weak, comes from the movement of the abdominal rings"... I would never finish remembering Professor Jacobo Cañás' class. At the paroxysm of the cardiac crisis, I suffered an unbearable sensation of heat, terrible, as if my body had been abruptly thrown into an incandescent furnace. But no; in the instant that the thermal convulsion lasted, I noticed that the Fire was not outside but inside me; that it was impregnating my whole body like an inflamed liquid that was decomposing into burning gases. And that liquid that was burning was my blood.

The heating impulse lasted an instant, which shook me to the rhythm of the bee's buzzing, but I, naturally, thought that I was dying: like a last agonizing vision, I contemplated the faces of Mama, of Katalina, of my nephews, and of many other relatives unknown until then, but whose kinship was evident. But all the faces were resembling each other, not by virtue of

---

2. Also known as hertz (Hz).

their genetic similarity, but because of the common expression that they were manifesting, probably identical to mine at that instant: *they were all agonizing faces, faces of human beings who were dying in the midst of a great pain; their expressions were reproducing the Expression of Death.* And then it was all over.

EPILOGUE

Chapter III

n other words, I mean that the phenomenon then concluded; that is, the buzzing stopped and the pressure on my heart was released. Little by little my pulse was normalizing and I was able to move at will. Still dazed, I reacted and sat up when remembering Uncle Kurt: I feared the worst.

However, he was also recovering in those moments; and I saw that he had fallen to his knees, as also occurred to him in the Tibetan Das Pech ravine, more than 40 years before. For a few minutes I was immobile, sorting out my thoughts, until I suddenly remembered the last instant of the phenomenon, when I lived through my own dying moments and those of all my relatives. *And then I realized. Then I knew that that was true, that something irreparable had happened to my family.* Panic-stricken, I interrogated Uncle Kurt with my eyes: *in the horror that I read in his eyes I knew that I was right.*

I finally managed to articulate words and cried out:

"Mama, Katalina! Oh, Uncle Kurt: something terrible has befallen the family! What has happened, Uncle Kurt, what has happened?"

"I think something horrific, Arturo. I don't want to alarm you, but it seems to me that the Demon Bera didn't actually manage to find out your whereabouts, and mine, but I fear that what he saw in your psyche was enough for him to find Beatriz's Finca in Cerrillos. If so, our family is in grave danger. We must immediately go to Salta, Arturo! Request a phone call while I prepare the *Jeep!*"

"To Salta, thirty minute delay," was the operator's laconic response. I also requested urgent communication and begged that she try it every ten minutes. She then notified me the time at which my request was being made and I could hardly believe it: it was only 00:30 hours. Everything had occurred in fifteen or twenty minutes. Could it be? Could the Demons have acted in so short a time? That doubt, inconsistent, gave me a little hope. But it was only until Uncle Kurt returned from the garage and I communicated to him my inquietude.

He shook his head in a negative and discouraging gesture, and said to me:

"I would like to confirm your hope but I cannot deceive you. We must not be optimistic in any way: the Immortals dominate Time and Space, they are Masters in the art of moving in the countless worlds of the mayic illusion. They can not find us, like they were unable to find Belicena and Noyo Villca, because Our Initiated Spirits are, in truth, isolated from Time and Space by the Runes of Wothan; or by the Vrunes of Navutan, if you prefer. They do not know our Reality, the World that the Spirit affirms from the Origin, and that confuses them, prevents them from locating us; but once *the actual reference of a determinate World is obtained, they can go and reach it at any Time and in any Space.*"

I do not know why I was asking if I knew that it was so. But I got my hopes up for a moment, trusting that my reasoning had value, vainly hoping that reason prevailed over the irrationality that was taking over my life. The ringing of the telephone bell brought me out of such bitter reflections.

"Your call to Salta," the operator said laconically. For ten long minutes I listened to the phone ringing, but no one picked up in Cerrillos. That was not normal! Even at one in the morning someone should answer in much less time: I had made similar calls a thousand times from Salta and they always answered me in three or four minutes!

"They're not picking up at your number," the operator interrupted. "Shall we repeat the call later?" I did not know what to say. I glanced sideways at Uncle Kurt and observed that he was giving me an obvious signal with his jeep keys.

"No, Señorita, cancel it now. There must not be anyone in that house," I bitterly suggested.

Chapter IV

ifteen minutes later, I was finding myself for the second time in my life riding down Esquiú Street: it was Uncle Kurt, myself, and the daiva dogs. "It's necessary to take them with us, just in case they set a trap for us," he explained to me; "but those Demons are proud and they presume that they're never going to miss a mark; it's possible that they're already in Chang Shambhala, or fulfilling another of their macabre missions." He pensively paused for a moment and then added in a somber tone:

"Heavens, Arturo: where do you suppose they'd go next, if, as we fear, they've already passed through Cerrillos?

"To Tucumán, to Tafí del Valle, to Belicena Villca's Chacra," I answered without hesitating.

That probability, and what could have happened in Cerrillos, took away our desire to talk for the rest of the ride. It was an exhausting drive, if one takes into account the night hours, the poor roads, the fact that we were going a day without sleeping, and the recent physical stress caused by the Demons' attack.

The bells of the Cerrillos church were ringing for the eight o'clock mass when we passed in front of it. And a hundred meters before reaching the gate of the Finca, we already knew that something terrible had actually happened: the rotating lights on the roof of the police cars tragically confirmed our suspicions and fears. Disregarding the policemen who were guarding the entrance, Uncle Kurt swerved the Jeep and took the path toward the house at high speed. Evidently, nothing was mattering to him now: neither his strategic cover, nor the possible persecutions if he was discovered, nor that, according to his new identity, nothing was linking him to the Siegnagel-Von Sübermanns. Poor Uncle Kurt! In thirty-five years he never dared to cross that gate to visit his only sister, and now he would have to do it for her funeral!

Because all of them had died, even my mother, that is, his sister Beatriz! And in the most horrendous manner!

Parked next to the Finca, behind the lapacho trees where I received the fateful letter from Belicena Villca from my mother's hands, were four cars: two police patrols and two ambulances. Beside a lapacho tree, my favorite one, under the shade of which I studied my university degrees and meditated on the mystery of man and on his miserable earthly life, was Canuto's lifeless body, covered by some bloody newspapers. How that place had changed in only two months! The joy and happiness of the family had turned into death and mourning! Damn Belicena Villca's letter! If only I hadn't read it! I was uselessly torturing myself. As I said in the beginning: *"there are carefully set traps in the life of certain persons: it is enough to touch a spring so that irreversible mechanisms are triggered."*

When sensing the Jeep's engine, several men came out of the house. One was the police commissioner of Cerrillos, who knew me as a child.

"Jesus! Arturo Siegnagel! Just in time!" he said without thinking, for then he regretted it, looked down, and, putting a hand on my shoulder, cautiously spoke to me, that is to say, as delicately as a policeman confronted with a mind-boggling multiple homicide can speak. Uncle Kurt remained at my side.

"Excuse me, Arturo. The truth is that *you haven't arrived in time.* I only said it thinking of the investigation, because we didn't know where to find you. I don't know how to say it, you understand that I'm a policeman, not a priest, but you should know that your whole family has been killed in a *strange way.*"

I made as if to go inside the house, seeing that they had not yet put any body in the ambulances, but the Commissioner stopped me.

"Wait a moment, Arturo, but it's my duty to question you. You knew that something had occurred here? Where are you coming from now?"

"Oh yes!" I hastily affirmed. "I knew that something was wrong because no one answered the phone at the Finca at one o'clock this morning. That's why we came out here right away."

"But from where did you make the call, where were you?" he wanted to know without excuses.

"Well, at the farm of this friend here, Señor Cerino Sanguedolce, who is a candy maker in Santa María de Catamarca and with whom I was setting up a deal to sell him our leftover must.[3] I was there for a few days."

"All right Arturo, I'll check it out," he said, while putting away the notebook on which he was writing down all the data.

---

3. Fruit juice (usually grape juice) before it has been aged into wine.

"Well, they can pass. You're a doctor and are supposed to be 'cold-blooded,' but this is different: the killer or killers are undoubtedly psychopaths, perhaps escaped from the hospital where you were working. They've committed the crimes with a savagery never seen around here. You better go in prepared."

Inside, the disorder was total, after the passing of the unknown policemen who carried out their even more unknown examinations. In the dining room, the edges of two tables had been pushed together, and on them were deposited the five cadavers. Prudent sheets were covering the exhibition of the bodies. Uncle Kurt squeezed my arm with his steely hand and uncovered the first cadaver himself.

"Beatriz!" he shouted.

"Mama, Oh Mama! What have they done to you?" I cried out in despair, when seeing that the sweet face of my mother, now contorted by a grimace of indescribable horror, was appearing with her throat slit from ear to ear."

"See?" commented the Commissioner inopportunely. "This is the most aberrant criminal act I've ever seen in my life, incomprehensible, undoubtedly the product of a sick mind."

The next bodies were those of my sister Katalina and her two sons, Enrique and Federico. These were not showing any signs of violence.

"We think they were poisoned, and we were going to take them to the local morgue to perform the autopsy when you arrived. Now that you've seen them, I'll give the order to load them into the ambulances. There'll be no need to take the others, since their death is obvious and has already been determined by the coroner: your mother's throat was slit, as you yourself have seen, and your father died of a crushed skull, probably when resisting the attack: do you have any objections to that diagnosis?"

I negatively shook my head and uncovered Papa's body: the blow *came from overhead,* delivered with a blunt object, skillfully handled, since it only penetrated two centimeters of the cranial vault, at the level of the encephalon.

Uncle Kurt was standing as if lost in thought in front of his sister's lifeless body. The ambulances had already taken Katalina and her children away, and the policemen were beginning to leave. I invited the Commissioner to a drink, and pointed out several crates of our best *Sauvignon,* indicating to him that he distribute them to his men, an act of courtesy prohibited by police regulations but that would be taken as an inhospitable gesture if it were not offered. It did not take the Commissioner long to have the crates of wine carried and join me in the kitchen. Iced *Chablis* and prosciutto were consumed in quantity, while it was loosening the policeman's tongue. Uncle Kurt joined us a while later.

"Who broke the news?" I asked.

"The staff that comes at 5 o'clock," the Commissioner responded. "It seems that a Criollo named 'Jorge Luna' was the first to arrive. He was surprised when noticing that all the lights in the house were on 'like on a party night,' as he declared; he then approached the kitchen, where your father was always having maté starting at 04:30 hours, but he saw no one. So, he began to go around the house thinking that your father would be outside. The first sign that something was wrong was when stumbling upon the body of the dog, literally split in two, near the lapacho trees. A few meters farther on, was lying the cadaver of Don Siegnagel, with his skull smashed in.

"At first glance and speculating a little," continued the Commissioner, "I'd say that at least two accomplices, maybe three, were involved. Two are essential to reconstruct the event with a certain logic, because it's evident that your father came out of the house requested by your mother, perhaps responding to a terrifying scream from her, and was surprised by the murderous blow next to the door. As soon as he looked out, he received the blow that, according to the coroner, caused his immediate death. Jorge Luna found him there and peddled with his bicycle to the police station to seek help, while warning the other workers who were arriving not to approach the Finca. We found Doña Beatriz, next to the winepress. From there she presumably called to your father, before being murdered, and we believe that she was made to leave the house under false pretenses: it was past 00:00 hours when the crime took place, an improper hour to voluntarily go outside of the house for people accustomed to getting up at 5 in the morning. Of course, this is only conjecture. Until more elements are gathered, and the results of the expert reports, we can't evaluate the facts very precisely," he said, as does every professional police officer when he does not want to involve his opinion.

I encouraged the commissioner to continue with the description of what happened, while passing around the slices of ham and glasses of Chablis.

"God forgive me; you ask and I will have to crudely answer you, Arturo. The madman, who seized your mother, dragged her to the winepress, perhaps gagged, and from there allowed her to scream in order to lure Don Siegnagel to the trap that his accomplice set for him. Once your father was dead, they both met to murder Doña Beatriz. You may wonder how can I be so sure? Because, *as the coroner deduced, it takes four hands to kill in this way; that is, two to restrain the victim and two to perform so perfect a slit from ear to ear.* Four hands would not be necessary if the victim were unconscious, but this is not the case, since no blows to the head or signs of narcotics were discovered—we have to wait for the analysis to be absolutely sure—and, more concretely, there are footprints, which reveal a desperate resistance until exhaling her last breath.

I felt that I was getting dizzy, that everything was spinning around me, that nausea was reaching my stomach, my throat... I hesitated in the chair, on the verge of vomiting.

"Drink a glass, Arturo! Come on, drink! You need it!" the Commissioner was inciting me, holding out to me the glass brimming with good white wine.

I drank it in one gulp, and I attest that I never liked one of our grape varieties so much.

"It's to be expected that you'd break down. What happened tonight in your house was too frightening and repugnant. You're sure you want to know everything now? You could rest a few hours and find out later, when you're calmer."

"No, no! Please, Commissioner!" I pleaded. "It was just a passing dizziness. Tell me everything now, the sooner the better."

Uncle Kurt supported this request with a nod.

"And here comes the worst part, Arturo: Doña Beatriz was restrained in such a way, that when slitting her throat, the murderers ensured that all her blood fell into the winepress; to the last drop!"

The Commissioner was looking at us perplexed. He was expecting to surprise us with this macabre piece of data but we were unfazed, since we were imagining the Ritual maneuvers of Bera and Birsha and we assumed that their purpose would be to take advantage of the precious Pure Blood of the Von Sübermanns in order to attempt to exterminate the entire Stirp, as they did in the thirteenth century with the House of Tharsis.

"In addition," said the Commissioner, "I'd like you to explain to us something that intrigued us all."

"Whatever you want to know, Commissioner."

"It's about the wine press; what is its capacity?"

"Well, if memory serves me, about 20,000 liters," I responded.

"And may I ask *why the Hell they filled it with Tar?*"

Chapter V

I was seated on the living room sofa, dozing. I had taken 3 mg of a tranquilizer and my nervous system was quite sedated. It was about ten at night and, in my sleep, I was hearing Uncle Kurt speaking in Arabic and German. But it wasn't a dream: at noon, Uncle Kurt requested an international call and they were just calling back. Minutes later he was coming over and harshly shaking me.

"They're all dead, Arturo! All of them! You and I are the only Von Sübermanns left alive!"

I looked at him in a haze. He continued:

"My uncles and my cousins in Egypt, even some distant cousins who were living and studying in Europe, all died this morning at 00:15 hours!"

Uncle Kurt was not raising his voice, but his gestures were revealing: he was beside himself. I tried to calm him down, to transmit to him my pharmacological calmness, but I only succeeded in getting nervous again; the fury of Uncle Kurt was contagious!

A few steps away, in the Dining Room where I saw my dead parents, were laying two caskets on pairs of trestles; wreaths, floral arrangements, candelabra with lighted candles, and crosses, were completing the ceremonial elements of the Catholic funeral. My father was known in that town since childhood and my mother since 1938, so the parade of neighbors and friends who were wishing to say their last goodbyes was incessant. Many, belonging to the humbler people, but whom we always counted on for the hard work in the fields, would stay the night.

Someone hired a few professional mourners from La Merced, famous for the sentiment and fervor that they were imposing on their laments, who were dedicating themselves at that moment to playing their role.

That terrible moment, of helplessness, of seeing the manner in which our enemies were attacking us and of not being able to respond in the same measure. Surprisingly, the tough Uncle Kurt had finally seated himself on another sofa and at times was sobbing with affliction. I was to receive the condolences of the visitors, according to the traditional custom, who, before departing, were leaving their name on a card, which was assuring them to receive later, in a period of no more than ten days, the postal thank-you. Customs, habits in practice since time immemorial, from which I could not escape without causing a great scandal.

At midnight the house was packed with people. Some neighbors kindly took charge of preparing coffee and attending to acquaintances. Various groups of friends formed huddles to comment on the horrible crimes, and the most unusual rumors were circulating from mouth to mouth in the superstitious Indian and mestizo neighborhood. Uncle Kurt and I vainly attempted that the Police turn over the bodies of Katalina and the children, fearing that in a few hours they would be decomposed as had happened to the members of the House of Tharsis. But our efforts were futile. The autopsy would not be completed until the following day. And, although the Police did not admit it, we knew the reason for that delay: the Coroners were not managing to establish the cause of death. My sister and nephews were found in their rooms, on the upper floor of the house, and presumably passed away without being aware of the gruesome murders that were taking place outside; they would have died, like the uninitiated members of the House of Tharsis, at the moment in which the power of the Dorje of Bera was transforming the blood of the winepress into Tar, that is to say, at 00:15 hours. And obviously, the Coroners did not know this.

We resigned ourselves, then, to only watch over my parents, although we commissioned the funeral services company to periodically insist on the morgue and claim the pending bodies. A car stopped and a familiar person got out, but whom I would not have imagined seeing there: Officer Maidana, the policeman who intervened in the Belicena Villca case! Upon seeing me, he hurriedly approached me and expressed his "deepest condolences," as was customary. And then he elaborated on the motives that had made him decide to attend the funeral, speaking in his particular style, simple and frank.

"Dr. Siegnagel, this case, as you can imagine, has shaken the Province: we would all like to apprehend the demented murderers of your family. But this matter is out of my jurisdiction this time: I am now Commissioner of the Investigations Department, but not the Chief of the Division. With this clarification I want to assure you that I have not come here as a policeman but as a friend. Do you understand me, Dr.?"

I nodded without understanding where he was going with this. Uncle Kurt stood next to me and looked at Commissioner Maidana with curiosity.

"Then I'll get to the point: are you in trouble? Do you need some kind of help? Whatever it is, don't hesitate to confide in me. I have friendly, valiant, and loyal people, men proven in the anti-subversive struggle, who would be willing to act, let's say outside the rules, to settle accounts with the Jews or with whoever it is that's persecuting you."

Uncle Kurt frowned and for a moment I feared that he would burst into one of his thunderous guffaws; but he was too hurt for it and instead smiled with clemency. I, for my part, was irritated and stupefied; irritated, not because of Maidana's offer, which I was appreciating because, although absurd, it was sincere, but for having to live through that whole hallucinatory situation, including the funeral; and stupefied, because I was at a loss as to how the officer had reached the conclusion that I was needing that kind of help.

"No answer?" he said in consternation. "Or is it that you don't trust me? But I know that you're being persecuted, even if you deny it. It is my profession to discover these things. I've known it since yesterday, when I received at the Department of Investigations the report on what happened in Cerrillos. Then I remembered you and the case of the patient Belicena Villca. Making a parenthesis, I'll now confess that you were right when affirming that there was an obscure point in that crime: that point was never cleared up; but it's also true that nobody was interested in clearing it up, and that the Police have more important urgencies to attend to with the taxpayers' money. I know! That doesn't matter to you: you want to see Justice triumph; Belicena Villca interests you a lot because the case touched you very closely. But we have to deal with hundreds of cases and that was just one more, one that, I repeat, no one was interested in. I'm telling you this because in a way I agree with you, Dr. Look at it this way! In truth I was wanting to bury that case because it was lacking in importance. *But now I know it isn't so!*"

"What do you mean?" I asked in spite of myself.

"Well, closing the parenthesis that I opened to apologize to you, it happens that this morning I attempted to find you at the Neuropsychiatric Hospital where *you were working* and there they informed me that you resigned two months ago, during your vacations. I then called the University and found out that you requested a leave of absence from the subjects that you were taking and that you left the medical residency. All very strange acts to come from someone as... normal?... as you. It was then, at mid-morning, that I decided to take the day off and dedicate myself to carry out a small investigation on my own. I found out that you sold your apartment in Cerro San Bernardo without telling anyone of your new address; and that your friends got word from your parents that you were 'investigating an archaeological site in Catamarca on your own'; all very vague, Dr. Siegnagel. Closed bank accounts, change of address, abandonment of work, studies, friendships: *one would say that they are the acts of someone who wants to erase his steps, of someone who is running away.* But you're not a criminal, you had no motives or enemies that forced you to flee two months ago. Or is it that the mysterious enemies then arose?"

"Yes, Dr. Siegnagel. I somewhat ceded my position and connected your strange behavior with the crime at the Neuropsychiatric Hospital. 'It could be that there was something else there, something that forced the Dr. to flee,' I said to myself, and I gave myself over to re-read the file on the murder of Belicena Villca. And what did I discover? Well, that we did not pay the slightest attention to the *Jewish* medals that the deadly rope had on its ends. I wanted to know, as soon as possible, what the inscriptions were saying and, without respecting the siesta, I went to the University and investigated in a labyrinthine section, I believe that it was called the Philology Department, until I came across an incredible personage named 'Professor Ramirez.' And what does Dr. Ramirez tell me? Well, the poor man went running when finding out that I was a policeman and when seeing the pictures of the medals. I had to convince him for hours to talk. It finally turned out that he knew you very well. That you had consulted him three months ago about the same inscriptions, but without mentioning the crime to him (you were right, because when he learned of it, his mouth automatically shut). And that there is an astounding story in which behind all this, *like I was saying Dr. Siegnagel,* are the damned Jews.

"Yes; yes. I know what you think. That I don't know how to distinguish the Druids from the Jews, nor am I capable of comprehending the universal structure of the Synarchy. You, like every German, believe that we are idiots (Druid? I think this is what Professor Ramirez was calling them). Look, it's possible that I don't know what a Druid is. But I advance to you that I've just come from being six or seven hours with Professor Ramirez in which he insisted on demonstrating to me that a Druid is the same as a Jew, if I didn't misunderstand his final synthesis. So, it amounts to the same thing, intellectual subtleties. I was right: Belicena Villca was liquidated by Jews, special Jews, but Jews nonetheless. And you were also right when telling me that the form of the assassination, the *modus operandi,* was quasi-Masonic. Yes, you were right and I didn't listen to you.

"But now I won't make the same mistake, because I've been thinking. I've reflected on what occurred three months ago, your subsequent steps, and what happened here yesterday. And do you know what conclusion I've come to?"

"I dare not imagine it," I told him with sincerity.

"Well, that the murder of your family *constitutes a Ritual crime.*"

"I cannot deny it," I agreed, for the policeman was deserving the confirmation of his conclusions.

"And of the same kind as that of Belicena Villca, perhaps committed by the same murderers?"

"I wouldn't be able to prove it, but I'm sure that the answer is yes," I conceded.

"That's better, Dr. Siegnagel! I told you I'm not here as a policeman but as a friend. I understand that for some reason you cannot denounce the truth and so I come to offer my help, mine and that of my Nationalist Comrades. I have special forces prepared to go into operation at any moment!" he said, lowering the tone of his voice to an inaudible level.

Although it seems incredible, I was still not understanding what Officer Maidana was proposing to me.

"And what is it you want to do?" I blatantly asked him.

"And you're asking me, Dr.? To help you against your enemies, who are undoubtedly our enemies, and are enemies of the country! We offer you concrete help, men, weapons, equipment! *All you have to do is give us the names of the assassins, provide us with a clue, reveal their organization.* Don't you want to avenge your family? We'll do it for you, or together with you!"

I looked at Maidana with discouragement. How could I explain to him the reality of Bera and Birsha? Undoubtedly, there was no room in the policeman's head for the possibility that there was a supernatural cause behind the murderers. He was not recognizing the real existence of magic; and in his opinion, the esoteric would only be a method of intelligence, destined to achieve "psychological action" and "cultural penetration." In summary, officer Maidana, as a good veteran of the nationalist *fragote*,[4] was only conceiving enemies of flesh and blood, solid targets, Jews, Marxists, Masons, Zionists, or whoever they might be, but enemies permeable to artillery of varied caliber and TNT.

"I appreciate your offer, Maidana. I'm deeply grateful because I know that it's honest and disinterested. But you can't help us and I can't give you any information. Believe me, it's better to leave things be. Now it's not just a mere shrink's patient: it's my family, Maidana; *my whole family.* If you were able to help me, how could I not accept? But now I'm the one who wants to leave things as they are. I know what I'm saying."

"What do you mean we can't help you?" protested Maidana. "You know what I think? That you're afraid! I don't know who committed the crimes. But it's evident that you know and don't want to share the secret. And why would you do such a thing? Well, because you suppose that the enemy is too 'powerful' for us, the clumsy South Americans. I understand; you're a German and you have a prejudice against Argentine nationalism; and perhaps you're right, because a whole fauna of imbeciles and traitors have discredited us; I can't answer for those charges. But you're wrong if you suppose that it'll always be like that! We are in another era, and there are other men: *our generation, Dr. Siegnagel, will not be stopped materially,*" he affirmed with firmness. "We are many, we have ideals, and we are fed up with corruption and materialism; the day is coming when we will inflict a great national punishment on the synarchic forces. Trust us and you won't regret it! No enemy is too strong in our Fatherland for us not to deliver an unforgettable blow. Perhaps we won't win the war, but we can partially punish them, hurt their pride, break their arrogance, prevent them from savoring the triumph of their crimes! What do you say, Dr.? Is it Mossad? The English MI5? CIA?"

---

4. military rebellion

How to respond to Commissioner Maidana?

I will only tell him this, and this only: I said, "*if the Enemy were human, I'm sure that your help would be effective.* Yes, Maidana: if the Enemy were human I assure you that I would count on your support. This should be enough for you."

"But what are you saying?" he asked with a mocking tone. "I'm surprised that you, a person whom I respect for his sincerity, demonstrate that you resort to simple escapism to evade the threat of the assassins. You're afraid and don't want to face the fact that sooner or later you'll also be attacked by the assassins! *Because otherwise, if you were in your right mind, you'd realize that the assassins are quite human.*"

"What?" I involuntarily exclaimed.

"Yes, Dr.; react," Maidana requested. "The murderers are human beings: *if they weren't, why would they use knives and bludgeons?*" he asked with irrefutable police logic.

It was a simple, absurd, and elementally simple conclusion. That is why I could not accept it, I was denying it entry into my mind; because of that, and because it was coming from Maidana, a mere policeman from Salta.

"No! No!" I stubbornly denied, "you don't understand the nature of the Enemy. You cannot help us."

I had locked myself in a lamentably infantile attitude, when Uncle Kurt's intervention surprised us both.

"You can help us!" he assured.

We stared at him dumbstruck.

"Maybe he can get us back the bodies of Katalina and the boys," he suggested.

"Ah!" sighed Maidana. "This is bureaucratic red tape. It's another type of help that I came to offer you, but don't think that I'm going to let you down if you ask me for a favor."

He looked at his watch and added:

"It's 2:15. Bad hour to make arrangements. However, I'll go to the local police station to find out what's going on with those bodies, and then I'll be back. Don't forget what I told you, Dr.! In the meantime, consider my offer."

Chapter VI

ommissioner Maidana's car climbed the slope of the exit road, and two hundred meters later entered onto the provincial route. Two fat women, who were patiently waiting, approached and embraced me, both at the same time: they were the "milk mothers" of Katalina and myself. There, it was very important to be a "milk mother," "milk child," or "milk sibling"; it was all starting when a good mother "was running out of milk" for her baby, or was not producing it in the sufficient quantity: then resorting to the help of another mother, a stronger mother, who had given birth to her child at about the same time, and her help was being required in order to breastfeed both babies. Although the milk mother was the strongest, she was often also the poorest, since she was usually a Criolla or Indian, perhaps already the mother of many children, who was willingly lending her collaboration. And, of course, she was compensated for such services. But the compensation was one thing, generally gifts for her own children, clothes and food, and the mother's love quite another: that was not able to be paid with anything and that is why bonds superior to the simple commercial transaction were being created: the "milk godmother." In fact, the milk mother was usually becoming the "co-mother" of the real mother and was enjoying a certain friendship or preference with respect to other women in the Calchaquí valley. Customs, centenary customs, that were coming from the epoch of the Spaniards, or perhaps from the Indians.

Of those two women who were embracing me, one was "my milk mother" and the other had been Katalina's. "I have nothing," said the first one, "nor do I look like Doña Beatriz, but everything of mine is yours, Arturito, all my love." I tightly clutched that Criolla who had seen me being born, and kissed her on both cheeks. "Thank you, Ñã Isabel, thank you very much," I said to her, moved, while the weeping women of La Merced were chorusing me with their painful laments.

I left the co-mothers to cross themselves by the coffins and withdrew to a secluded corner, in the company of Uncle Kurt. Since Commissioner Maidana's departure, a growing overexcitement was taking hold of me. I was having an idea, an idea arisen from the rational conclusion of the policeman, which I was eager to communicate to Uncle Kurt without delay. Naturally, if I was not wanting to accept Maidana's proposals, Uncle Kurt was not even listening to them. So, I repeated it to him:

"Uncle Kurt! Uncle Kurt!" I startled him. "Reflect on the policeman's words: they are like a syllogism. He affirmed 'the murderers are human'; why? 'Because they use knives and bludgeons, that is, material weapons,' he deduced. At that moment I flatly denied such a possibility, but now I consider Commissioner Maidana's deduction almost brilliant."

"You're crazy, Neffe, completely insane," Uncle Kurt disqualified me for my opinion. "They're Immortals! Bera and Birsha are Immortals! It means nothing that they have used a dagger: it was necessary for the Ritual of Sacrifice."

"For the sake of the Gods, Uncle Kurt, don't treat me as if I were an imbecile!" I defended myself. "I know they are Immortals: *but, as Belicena Villca said in the story of Nimrod, they are so only as long as you don't kill them, 'as long as no physical violence is exerted upon Them.' 'These Immortals, too, can die.'*"

"You're mad!" he repeated, even more closed-minded. "Did you not see the power of the Demon Bera last night? We can do nothing against them. You've done very well in discouraging the policeman!"

"Oh, *mein Gott!*" I swore. "No, Uncle Kurt! I'm not mad! It's you who are obstinate! But you are going to listen to me. And you are going to allow me to put forward my idea, *einverstanden?*"

"Ja, ja," he promised without conviction.

"Then pay attention. My concept is that there are two irreducible planes, which now, through an erroneous and subjective appraisal of reality, have been interfered with or mixed. Such planes are: *the Plane of the Reality of Spirit,* and the *Plane of Human Reality.* Between the two planes there can be no relationships or connections, but *unreasons:* every nexus or reason is illusory, not real. But there is, likewise, a law, which is *the reason of unreason,* which protects and affirms the absolute reality of the planes. And this law, which sustains the reason of unreason between such planes, is the only reference for not losing your mind and going mad. This law of sanity demands: not to transgress the planes. *Not to transfer entities proper to the plane of the Human Reality to the plane of the Reality of the Spirit;* and reciprocally: *not to project ideas proper to the plane of the Reality of the Spirit to the plane of the Human Reality.*

"In this demonic matter of Bera and Birsha, my dear Uncle Kurt, it seems to me that the planes have been confused, that we no longer know which plane is threatened by the Immortals. But I will tell you, Uncle Kurt. I will tell you so clearly that you will no longer be able to repeat that I am mad, but you will have to accept that I am too sane. That is: let us first observe the plane of the Reality of Spirit: there *the truth* is the Origin, the Symbol of the Origin; because of that truth, because of not being able to resist the weight of that truth, because of denying or not bearing the presence of that truth, the Immortals are compelled to manifest an *archetypal monadic* form, like that which you saw at Das Pech. The monad form, the unity of Light, allows them to powerfully exist *outside of the plane of Human Reality* and avoid confrontation with the reality of the Origin, with the Symbol of the Origin; and that powerful form is, with certainty, the most dangerous that one can imagine; I agree that such danger is also real.

"However, let us now go to the plane of Human Reality: there *the truth* is the Ego, that is to say, the psychic and volitive manifestation of the Spirit enchained to Matter. And the lie, the Illusion of Man, but also his animic motor, is *Pain*. The Creator God is nourished by a force called *human pain;* and man produces *pain* and *suffering* to feed the Creator of the Great Deception. The common man produces little pain because to suffer the illusion of pain, the wounded nobility of the Spirit is required. Hence, Great Men, Great incarnated Spirits, are capable of generating Great pain, Great sufferings, Great afflictions, Great anguish: *the hunger of God, of Jehovah-God, demands the contribution of pain from Great Men. And those men capable of the greatest suffering must also be capable of offering the greatest sacrifice: their pain must be sacred to God, to Jehovah-God. For this are required the representatives of Jehovah-God, the Priests of Jehovah-God, Those with the power to consecrate the Great Pain, for example, Bera and Birsha.* For it will be, always, necessary that there are, on the plane of Human Reality, Priests of God who consecrate the Great Pain of the Great Man, to the unity of God, of Jehovah-God. Only like this will it be possible *to sacrifice* the Great Man so that his consecrated Great Pain nourishes the unity of The One, of the Creator God Jehovah-God.

"In synthesis, Uncle Kurt, one thing are the Immortals confronted on the plane of the Reality of the Spirit, where they have no alternative but to monadically manifest themselves, as a unit of Light, to avoid the truth of the Origin: just as it occurred to Bera with you, he had no other alternative than *to dress himself in the Clothes of The One,* that is to say, *with his Monad of Light.* You will object to me by saying that such a manifestation also occurred on the plane of Human Reality, but I will reply that you are an atypical case, and you know it. *You are like an injured man, whose unusual wound exposes one of his most intimate bones; those who contemplate you are deeply impressioned by perceiving an intimate reality, which usually escapes all consideration: in an analogous way, those who have contemplated the Sign of the Origin that you involuntarily exhibit, have been deeply impressioned because they have sensed, in the discovery, the revelation of the other Reality, intimate and alien.* In short, Uncle Kurt, your experience has no general value, it is characteristic of someone capable of exhibiting, on the plane of the Reality of Man, signs of ideas originated in the World of the Spirit, proper to a Shivatulku, perhaps.

"But on the field of ordinary human beings, like the non-initiated members of the House of Tharsis, like Mama and Katalina and I, things occur according to the law previously mentioned: *pain must be consecrated and sacrificed to Jehovah-God; and for that you need Priests of flesh and bone.* Hence, throughout her letter, Belicena Villca always describes the Immortals as Diabolic Priests. Have you understood me, Uncle Kurt? *For the Sacrifice of Pain, one must officiate the Ritual of Death; and, to officiate the Ritual of Death, one needs sacrificial Priests!"*

"What are you getting at? Or, rather, where do you think your arguments will get me?" asked Uncle Kurt, suspecting that my intention was to make him fall into a dialectical trap.

"Very simple: *my conclusion is, and I believe to have demonstrated it, that in order to perform Ritual murders like those executed yesterday, the Immortals must present themselves in human priestly form.* In a word, it is my opinion that Commissioner Maidana is right: the murderers of my parents were human beings, Priests of Crime who must utilize a dagger and physical strength to subdue their victims."

"...Although it seems crazy, I must admit that it doesn't lack sense. Well, Neffe, let's suppose that it were so: what would we gain from it? Where would the difference in the situation be?"

"Ahhh..." I triumphantly sighed. "Your question is due to the fact that you are not even remotely considering the possibility of *attacking*, are you?"

"*Attack?* I think you've gone mad indeed," he prejudged.

"Yes! Attack, attack the Demons! What's the matter with you, little Uncle? Did the thirty-five years of forced vacations soften you?" I mocked. "You were just accepting that the Demons, when acting as Priests, transform themselves into human beings, so what prevents us from executing them, from charging, with their filthy lives, all the damage that they've caused us?"

"But how, Arturo, how would we do that. Where would we find them?" I had left Uncle Kurt virtually bewildered, not knowing what argument to make against my wild idea. "And, even supposing that we could do it, what good would it do us, how would it serve us, how would it serve the Strategy of the Siddhas? Did we not already agree that the best thing would be to follow Noyo Villca's trail, in order to fulfill Belicena Villca's request?"

"*Shhhh,*" I huffed, putting my index finger over my mouth as a sign of silence. "*Still! You will obtain all those answers yourself, when you know the plan.*"

"*What... plan?*" Uncle Kurt asked with apprehension.

"My plan! The plan that I have to attack the Demons! But for now I won't speak of it until the funeral concludes. Then I'll explain it to you and we'll discuss it."

Not at all convinced, Uncle Kurt was shaking his head with comical concern. If we were not in such tragic circumstances, I would have readily laughed at his gestures, with which he was intending to express that he was a serious person who had fallen into the hands of a madman.

EPILOGUE

1178

Chapter VII

A t 05:30 hours, two hearses arrived that were transporting Katalina and her children. The three caskets were immediately placed next to those of my parents, an event that inspired the weeping women to renew their litanies with singular pathos. Fifteen minutes later, Commissioner Maidana, the author of that incredible bureaucratic feat, was appearing

"How did you manage it, Commissioner?" I inquired.

"Well, it wasn't so difficult, considering that the forensic reports were already prepared, although they lacked a signature: no one likes to sign a report devoid of a diagnosis. Because that is what they had: *nothing.* That is, they did not know what your sister and nephews died from. My only merit was convincing the doctors, who only arrived at 5, that I had confidential information that the case would be buried by a superior order. Even so, I had to wake up a respectable Judge to obtain the verbal approval that permitted the Commissioner to deliver the bodies; however, the forensic reports being ready, there was no impediment to finalize the procedure and the Judge agreed to receive them in the morning and sign the authorization. And here are your unfortunate relatives, Dr.; and do you know with what diagnosis? *Cardiac arrest.* It's silly, since we all agree that it's a multiple homicide, but these doctors didn't manage to determine the cause of death: If I were you, I would've requested an in-depth study at the University of Salta, but since you're in such a hurry to wrap up the funeral, things will have to remain as they are."

"Indeed, Commissioner Maidana. Thus they will remain; for the good of all," I assured. "In any case, the assassins will pay for what they've done to my parents."

"I was wanting to talk to you about that, Siegnagel!" Maidana euphorically said, totally changing his attitude.

"Forgive me if I am guilty of optimism," he excused himself, "but *I love to win* arguments or bets, especially when the rival is a respectable person like you: *that fills me with pride,*" he naively confessed.

"And how did you win?" I asked perplexed.

"Perhaps to you it's not important, but before leaving I made you an offer," he recalled. "And I still keep in mind your unusual words, absurdly suggesting that *'the assassins would not be human.'* 'If they were human,' you said, 'you would accept my help.' You said it!"

"Calm down, Maidana, I'm not going to refute you! Indeed, I believed it so, although later I have modified my opinion and now I practically agree with you that the assassins would be human beings, perverse and vile human beings."

"Bravo, Dr. Siegnagel! I'm glad that you've changed your opinion; now it'll be easier for you to admit that I was right. New elements have arisen in this case, Dr.!"

"What elements?"

"Witnesses, Dr. Siegnagel. Two witnesses came forward who saw the murderers perfectly," he reported in a professional tone. "At this moment they are giving their statements and providing the description that will allow us to reconstruct the faces of the criminals: once the identikit has been drawn up, thousands of them will be distributed throughout the Province, and the rest of the country, and a tracking operation will be initiated to detect their movements."

Uncle Kurt had turned livid. I, on the contrary, was evaluating that that news was benefiting my plans.

"Who are the witnesses?" I wanted to know.

"I will tell you with total reserve, since the case is under the secrecy of the judicial summary. They were two doormen from the Tobacco Company, who were to enter at 00:00 hours, 300 meters from here, and they passed in front of the entrance gate almost at that hour. As they are neighbors, they always cover the route in company, each one with his bicycle. And like all the early mornings, that of yesterday was also seeming quiet: *until they saw the automobile upon arriving here.*

"The automobile!" we shouted as a duo, Uncle Kurt and I. "What automobile?"

"Ahaha," Maidana ironized. "Are you seeing how your assassins are very human? *So much so that they even drive around in an enormous imported car.*"

"Could you give us more details?" I frantically demanded.

"Have patience, Dr., and I'll tell you everything I know, which is not much. At approximately 11:59 or 00:00, the two men began to ride their bicycles in front of this Finca. Very soon they noticed that up ahead an enormous black car was driving slowly; it was creeping, as if it were looking for a certain house, and the cyclists did not go on ahead out of pure curiosity. So, then, they continued together until, when arriving at the gate, the automobile turned and left the road, parking at the entrance. Then they got a good look at its occupants: *they were two 'Oriental-looking' men,* impeccably dressed in black suits; one of them even got out to open the gate and was clearly observed by both of them.

"The witnesses are in custody since yesterday at noon, but they didn't inform you about the progress of the investigation. The important thing is that they ran an ethnographic program through the computer monitor, and that the doormen identified the second personage as a kind of 'Turk' or person coming from the Middle East. What did I tell you, Dr.? I was not far off the mark when I suggested that they might be members of Mossad."

No, Bera and Birsha were not members of the Israeli Mossad, but they could undoubtedly be the Chiefs of that sinister Jewish "Intelligence Service" or "Death Squadron": they were more than qualified for it. They were, indeed, natives of the Middle East, where according to Belicena Villca, they were Kings in remote times. There was no doubt, then, about the form in which the High Priests of Melchizedek had come to Cerrillos: as "human beings," wearing modern attire, and driving a luxurious automobile. Upon receiving this news, Uncle Kurt completely fell silent.

"What make was the car?" I asked.

"No make or model. Curiously, the witnesses agreed to give a detailed description of the car, but they failed to recognize the make; neither did they notice if it had a license plate. From their statements it was deduced that it was a very large car, a Cadillac or Lincoln, which, for not being a frequent type in our country, would have made identification difficult."

When Maidana finished communicating to me the police information that he obtained in so little time, he went back to his own: he was expecting that I repay him with equal loyalty and reveal to him all I knew about the murders and the mysterious assassins. Of course, I could not tell him the truth, an unbelievable truth to boot, and so I was caught in a moral bind.

At 07:05 hours, the Commissioner of Cerrillos arrived. He was coming to greet me and to comply with a request from Maidana, who had also woken him up, at 3 in the morning.

"Hello, Arturo. Good morning, Señor Sanguedolce. How are you, Maidana?" he greeted. "I didn't know that you were Arturo's friend. I've brought what you asked for, but since you're friends, remember that everything is still under wraps. The judge is trying to shed light on a matter that has become excessively strange, and only in the morning will he issue the orders that will permit us to act. Until then the contents are secret."

He handed Maidana an envelope, which he hurried to open. It was containing the identikits of the assassins and several drawings that were depicting the scenes seen by the witnesses.

The portraits were showing two faces of undoubtable Oriental appearance: round, pronounced cheekbones, sparse eyebrows, slightly slanted eyes, thick lips. They were clean-shaven and were apparently lacking hair. The latter could not be ensured with certainty *because, unusually, the criminals were wearing "bowler-type" hats, tightly pulled-down.*

"There are things that do not fit, that are not in accordance with the general patterns of Criminology," commented the Cerrillos Commissioner with vexation. "We're looking for two ferocious murderers, perpetrators of the massacre of a harmless family. Two witnesses, they see them, at the time of the crime, enter into the house. So far everything is correct, everything 'normal.' We then request that the witnesses describe the alleged criminals to us. They agree; and there ends the typological normality: the case escapes any general framework; neither the criminological casuistry, nor the antecedents, nor the accumulated experience, serve to understand the event. At first the witnesses were suspected, but then their capacity to testify was verified: they are faultless people, who never drink a drop of alcohol, given that they have to hold a surveillance post, and to top it off, they are ex-policemen, that is, retired policemen, trained to observe facts and accustomed to providing details. But their story was too unbelievable. Look at that illustration, where the passenger has gotten out to open the gate and the driver is seated behind the wheel of the big black car. What did the witnesses see? Not two 'normal' criminals, who are going to furtively murder a family, but two elegantly dressed *gentlemen*, who enter as if they were visiting the Siegnagel Finca. In fact, the Judge made psychiatrists examine them, yesterday afternoon, but the report is positive: they're in perfect mental condition. They even underwent an interrogation under hypnosis, which also yielded positive results: concretely, *they speak the truth; whatever it is that they've seen, they believe in what they say.*"

I cast a sidelong glance at Commissioner Maidana, for all of that was giving off the familiar whiff during the Belicena Villca murder. But he did not flinch; evidently he also had a rational explanation for the curious attire of the "Mossad agents."

"Look here, Señores!" the Cerrillos Commissioner was insisting. "Can there be anything more ridiculous than some assassins dressed in black three-piece suits, black shoes, black hats, (black bowler hats!), black ties, and white shirts? Yes, I know that there may be assassins like that: in Hong Kong, in Istanbul, in London, in New York, and a thousand other places in the world. *But here, in Cerrillos?* If they were another kind of people, it would even be possible to accept their presence in the area: for example, if they were executives of a transnational company who came for business, to plunder some of our raw materials. It's possible to imagine that kind of criminal without effort. However, in the case at hand, they easily escape the general pattern of farmer killers."

The Commissioner looked at his watch and said goodbye: "I must go now. See you later, Arturo; very sorry about all this. I'll see you this afternoon at the cemetery. Excuse the chitchat but it was Maidana who came to stir up the hornet's nest; I wouldn't have bothered you *until after the funeral.* Naturally, the Judge also wants to speak with you and will soon summon you; when this tragic moment passes, *naturally.*"

The last words of the Commissioner of Cerrillos caused me deep concern. What would the police want? They were murdering my family and I would be the one interrogated?

"Calm down, Dr., it's nothing," Maidana assured. "It's just routine. The police are clueless and will want to know your opinion. The same thing with the Judge; that's why he was reluctant to hand over the bodies. I could give you many hypotheses about what the Commissioner didn't say and what has probably happened: for example, it's almost certain that they've radioed the description of the black car and failed to locate its whereabouts; nor will they know if it even left the Province. That puzzles them; it's a rare car and they assume that someone should have seen it. *But they don't move forward because they investigate professionally. You and I know that, con-*

trary to what the Commissioner and the Judge affirm, this is indeed a classic case: a classic case within International Intelligence and Counterintelligence."

Maidana was convinced of his theory and I would have to give him an answer without delay.

Chapter VIII

ight thirty in the morning. I was in the kitchen of the Cerrillos Finca, having breakfast with Uncle Kurt and Commissioner Maidana. I was remembering with sadness that in that room I had seen my parents together for the last time: the last image of a reality that would no longer be repeated; as a product of the journey that I embarked on that morning, my parents were now lying in the next room, each in a casket. The memory was paining me, but according to Uncle Kurt, that was *weakness:* the Hyperborean Initiates, the ⚡ Knights, he told me in Santa María, *could not have a family;* and much less love it: that would be to make it a target for the Enemy, to expose it to certain destruction, and, what was worse, it would be our *weak point.* At that time I underestimated his warnings, but I was now fatally realizing how much truth was in his words; that was why he insisted so much: he who knew that the Enemy knew, as I now knew it, that no advice was sufficient in order to be prepared against them. He had assiduously deprived himself from seeing his sister for 35 years to protect her, and it would be I, the son, who would imprudently send her to the executioner. *It was maddening. But I could not go mad. For the death of my family, I was bearing some responsibility for the committed negligence. But I should not forget that the Enemy had executed the objective murders. We were, then, in a war: and in the Strategy of that War, I had a mission to fulfill!*

After breakfast, Maidana would stop for a moment at the Police Headquarters in Salta and then go to rest. He had promised to return at 18:00 hours for the burial. Nevertheless, he was rushing to immediately make good on his offer to help. For him, there was no time to waste, for every minute that was passing was an advantage that the assassins were taking in their tactic of escape. "Now," he suggested, "if I was not wanting to catch the material killers but was wanting to strike at the instigators, then we could talk on another, less dramatic occasion," for he was guaranteeing that his nationalist group would also support me.

It would not be necessary to wait; I had already made a decision:

"Commissioner Maidana, would you be so kind as to wait just half an hour more, and not take amiss that I converse alone with Señor Sanguedolce?" I asked him.

"I have no objections," he said with confidence. Then, while Uncle Kurt was heading toward the stairs, he came close to my ear and added, "Deliberate calmly, but don't think that I'm stupid. I have attentively observed him and would swear that he's not Italian. Maybe he's German or from some Nordic country. And maybe he's a relative of yours or one of those Nazi heroes that the Jews are seeking to liquidate. Maybe he's the hidden target of the Oriental assassins: a 'contract' of Mossad. Why not, right? ..."

I walked away without listening further. It was very difficult to deal with Maidana: he was intelligent, educated, he had intuition, but he was persisting in the erroneous attitude of covering all the facts with a superficial political concept. I should no longer think about him, but about the speech I would make to Uncle Kurt.

We met in my room, a place saturated with painful memories. Uncle Kurt laid down on the bed, and I took a chair. Before I managed to utter the first word, he made his opposition known to me. But I was prepared for his reaction, for days ago I had realized why Tarstein was calling him *stubborn.*

"I imagine what you're going to tell me, Neffe. Ever since the policeman Maidana showed up, and you gave credence to the incredible idea about the 'humanity' of Bera and Birsha, I'm dreading to hear 'your plan.' And do you know why? Because I can imagine it. But don't worry; I'll listen to your plan and consider it with my best good will. I just want to lay something out beforehand, a principle from which I will not budge no matter what: *the Immortals cannot die.*"

It is obvious, Immortals cannot die, and Uncle Kurt stubbornly standing on that principle would never go along with my plan. Nor with his best "good will." But, as I anticipated, I was prepared for his reaction and had already found a way in which the future would not be up to his "good will": I was admiring Uncle Kurt, but I was believing him quite capable of waiting another 35 years before taking action. I let out my speech:

"My dear Uncle Kurt: we find ourselves facing two points of view; and in order to be able to move, one of them must prevail over the other. However, neither of us will compromise on our position; *and it is not convenient that we do so.* You because, even though you are excessively stubborn, you possess powers that no one else has and an Initiatic knowledge that one must respect. I because, oh tautology, I may be right or I may be wrong; no one knows, not even you. There is a reason why I was now convoked by the Gods, a reason why I received the Letter from Belicena Villca, a reason why I am a Von Süber-mann, a reason why I suffer this pain, the attack of the Demons against my family; all these things must be for a reason, but they are not enough by themselves to decide whether I am right or wrong. You tend to believe that everything that happens to me is because of you, but I have a different idea of myself and I think that I also exist; and that if I exist it is for a reason: we do not know what that reason is, but perhaps it is being right in my plan, which would mean that I will also be right in fulfilling Belicena Villca's request, that I will find her son, the Noyo of the Wise Sword.

"How to know what the truth is? How to know if, after what has happened to my family and after proving that Bera and Birsha have been reincarnated to attack, I will never accept that the future steps be decided by your 'good will,' or if I will never decide for myself either? I will explain to you *how we will know.* And forgive me if I have to be hard on you, Uncle Kurt. You have laid out your principle from which you will not depart, but I will lay out mine, from which likewise I will not move: *I will only accept, and I will solely accept, the Will of the Gods!* Let them decide!

"Logically, I do not propose a 'Test from God,' an Ordeal, to find out the Will of the Gods. For there is something in which I am willing to trust; and that is in your Honor, in the Honor of your Eternal Spirit. *And you can speak with the Gods by means of the Śrotra Karṇa faculty,* although I am sure that because of stubbornness you have never used it since the Third Reich fell. Well then, speak with the Gods, with Capitán Kiev, and consult about our future, concretely ask what the steps are that we must take! Whatever answer they offer you, I will accept it. And I will accept it from you: *I will believe in what you tell me.*"

In reality, what I was trusting in was that Uncle Kurt's Honor would prevent him from deceiving me. And if, in spite of everything, he was deceiving me, that was his problem: the Führer, who was the one who communicated the Śrotra Karṇa to him, would deal with him. Rather than persuading him through eloquence, with my speech I was hoping to draw Uncle Kurt into a dialectical trap that would force him to choose between carrying out the attack on the Demons or betraying the Führer's Strategy. That is if my plan was correct. But if it was not, and if Uncle Kurt was affirming that for Capitán Kiev it was not, *I would never know.* Logically, I was as sure that my plan was good as he was sure that the conversation with Commissioner Maidana had upset my reason.

For the moment, Uncle Kurt was silent. I brought him out of his reverie because I was needing to count on his approval before explaining the plan to him. In order not to fail, I resorted to a dramatic effect.

"What do you say, Uncle Kurt? Will you speak with Capitán Kiev and receive his message? Do you wish that I beg you? I'm not ashamed to beg you: do it for me. Remember that when I came to Santa María, and you nearly made the daiva dogs kill me, you assured me that if I had died you would have committed suicide: what can be worse than that, or than what happened to us afterward, when the Demons exterminated our Stirp? Yes, Uncle Kurt, I beg you: *for once in your life, loosen your stubbornness a little!*"

"Wait a moment," he interrupted me, "it's not that big a deal. You mustn't exaggerate. Your proposition seems fair to me and I accept it with good grace. I will again avail myself of the Śrotra Karṇa, which I certainly have never used since the Second War, and will procure to inquire into the Will of the Gods. It's just that I find it hard to even conceive of the usefulness of your plan: *the Immortals cannot die.* But perhaps you're right, above all else, and it is, in truth, necessary to carry out your *demented* idea. Now, would you be able to confirm in detail what my intuition has already made me see, so that doubts about what I have to consult do not arise?"

I had convinced him! The bird was in the bag! The goat had fallen into the trap! I shuddered with joy, but I did not make a gesture that gave away my state of mind, which was comparable to that of Cicero when he convinced the Senate that Rome should wage war with Carthage: if he was picking up on my thoughts it was something that I could not avoid, but I would not try to do anything that might offend him. Although he would not miss the opportunity to point out to me that my plan could only come from a madman.

"Strategically," I explained, "my plan is based on the principle of the two Realities that I mentioned earlier to you. More clearly, I affirm that the Demons, in order to attack us, have had *to descend* to the plane of Human Reality and that has rendered them vulnerable *on said plane*. It is not much, but what more can we ask for? The Hyperborean Wisdom teaches that the nature of fear is essentially animal, that is to say, animic, human, proper to the Immortal Soul; on the contrary, the Eternal Spirit is pure valor, *it knows no fear, which is essentially alien to it*. Now then: Bera and Birsha are two highly evolved Immortal Souls, *but the nature of fear is not alien to them;* on the contrary, they must be capable of feeling fear, and very much so; when?; when they are overcome by *force*. This is because, like all animic essences, they only understand one language: *that of force*. Of course, They are conscious of their own strength, and that is why they do not fear an enemy who they know is inferior *in strength,* as are the Spirits enchained to Matter, as are spiritual men. That is why they are right in not fearing men *if They themselves are supermen;* and it is true that it represents a folly to attempt to attack Bera and Birsha *outside of the plane of Human Reality*. But now the case is different because They have situated Themselves on the plane of Human Reality by momentarily becoming human beings, offering a weak point in their Strategy: *we can now attack Them in their human weakness like They attacked us.*

"What would we gain if, as you say, in the end, *'the Immortals cannot die'*? The question seen in this way, as you solve it, that is, *from the principles,* in the case of taking away their human life, we would only achieve disincarnating their Immortal Souls. That is: we would achieve nothing. But I believe that this is not how the question should be responded to, because by clinging to a single principle other principles are being left aside, as important as that of the Immortality of the Soul, which if considered, *can give us a relative strategic advantage.* Concretely, I am referring to the *principle of fear,* already set forth, and *to the 'avalanche effect' that takes place in the terrifying phenomenon, that is, to panic:* as a professional of psychic phenomena, I know very well that the sensation of fear grows following an exponential curve, which is inverse to the volitive curve; at a determinate point, both curves cross and then fear dominates the will, or what is the same, the will weakens in the face of the instinctive force, and panic ensues, during which the animic is out of control, it becomes irrational.

"My theory is the following: normally, we would not have enough strength to attack the Immortal Souls Bera and Birsha and cause them the fear that puts them on the run. Abnormally, They have situated themselves on the plane of Human Reality, they have incarnated in human beings, they have turned themselves into Priests: diabolical Priests but human beings in the end, with their vision limited by reason and *by the instinct of fear.* Against human beings, no matter how diabolical they are, we have weapons with which to fight, *and enough strength to cause them great fear; such a fear that transforms into terror; such a terror that breaks their satanic pride, their magical certainty that they cannot be defeated by human beings, and infuses them with panic; such a panic that leaves the Immortal Souls Bera and Birsha instantly out of control: as in an avalanche, a small initial force will be amplified into a great final force; as in a cosmic panic, a small initial human fear will be amplified into a great final terror, at the level of the Immortal Souls.*

"You know what Time is, Uncle Kurt: pure illusion. The only reality of Time, on the plane of the Creator of Time, is the Beginning and the End of Time, which are identical. And you know what certainty is for the Magician: the source of his power; the Magician cannot doubt even once because his magical power is cut off; *the magician must always believe that he is powerful, more powerful at every instant: that is the 'satanic pride';* a single instant of doubt and such belief will be broken, 'broken satanic pride,' the achieved evolution lost because of the consequent metaphysical fall. And according to my theory, if we succeed in instilling that instant of panic in Bera and Birsha, *it will be equivalent to their own magical destruction and their automatic returning to the Beginning of Time because of the loss of instantaneous evolution.* I do not know if two evolved Immortal Souls like Bera and Birsha will be able to return from that situation of total involution. But, if we are to accept the Hyperborean Wisdom, one must remember that it teaches that at the Beginning of Time, as well as at the End, there is the Mahapralaya, the Non-Manifestation or the Final Death of everything animic. At the Beginning of Time, Bera and Birsha would thus have two paths: one, *not to enter Time and sink themselves into the Mahapralaya;* and two, *to enter Time, forced to recover their lost evolution 'in' Time,* that is, *monadically mani-*

festing in the elemental Worlds and then evolving toward the archetypal Final Perfection during eons, successively reaching the Mineral, Animal, and Human Kingdoms, in planetary rounds and chains, in manvantaras and kalpas.

"Conclusion of my theory: *they will never be able to attack us again.*

"Putting this theory into practice is possible by means of my plan, which I will explain to you next. It is very simple, and I will begin by defining its objective: *to kill the 'Oriental assassins,' that is to say, the Priests Bera and Birsha, in the course of a commando operation.* To achieve this objective, it is necessary to fulfill four conditions; I will name them and then tell how they can be achieved: first, to have short-range powerful weapons; second, to locate the assassins; third, to get close enough to them to ensure the shots; and fourth, to count on the factor of surprise.

"I believe I can fulfill the first condition with the help of Commissioner Maidana, whom from now on I consider, and even if you disagree with my criterion, as *an envoy of the Gods;* of course, an envoy unaware of his mission.

"The second does not require any investigation because we are both sure that they left from here in the direction of Belicena Villca's Chacra: it will be there that we will catch them; and where we must go anyway. I only ask you *to confirm* our presumption in your consultation with Capitán Kiev.

"The third depends on you, on your ability to control and direct the daiva dogs. I count on them, on the *svadi-lung* jump that allows us to approach at the right distance so as not to miss the shots on the assassins.

"The fourth, naturally, depends on the third and also on you, on how you construct the mental orders with the svadi Kyilkhor that the daiva dogs will obey. It is logical that if in said orders you mention, only mention, Bera and Birsha, they will detect you like me and will be alerted. The factor of surprise requires, then, not referring the mastiffs to Bera and Birsha. How do we approach, then? It is necessary to discard the possibility of directing the daiva dogs directly to Belicena Villca's Chacra, because we run the risk of not coinciding at the right moment, that is to say, *when both are inside the house.* We must not forget that such a moment *already passed,* that the assassins *have already been at the Chacra,* and that the dogs will have to jump not only in Space but in Time, going back to the right period in Time. How will we, then, approach by surprise? By referring the daiva dogs to *the assassins' automobile,* to the *empty* black car *situated at the Chacra.* This can be achieved in several steps, the first of which consists in making the daiva dogs identify *right here, in Cerrillos,* the trail of the black car. In this way they will possess, *in abstracto,* the 'idea' or 'name' of the black car a priori of the final order. And the final order will be a precise mathematical construction that implants the idea, or coded name, of the black car in the context of the Chacra. We have to think about solving the problem, Uncle Kurt! But I'm sure that there will be no insurmountable difficulties because the Yantra is extremely versatile to construct all types of orders, even the most complex."

Chapter IX

ncle Kurt demanded to be left alone in my room. He would consult Capitán Kiev at once with his Śrotra Karṇa about the advisability of carrying out my *demented* plan or not. I was convinced that if my theory was correct, my plan would be approved by the Gods, even if it weighed on Uncle Kurt. On the other hand, the same Uncle Kurt was seeming to have somewhat dropped his negative attitude: when I concluded the speech, he only smiled, for the first time in two days, and said:

"I was wrong, Neffe. You don't just look like me, as I estimated in Santa María. You also resemble Konrad Tarstein. And you have reminded me of him now, by providing me, as you have done, with one of his *demented* missions. Then, when listening to him, like to you today, the conviction was assailing me that I had fallen into the hands of a madman. But then all was going according to plan and I had to surrender to the one who had a 'better strategic vision than I.' Really, because you deserve it, I would wish that today the same thing occurred and that you are right. *For me, I will always perceive that these plans lack something, that they are incomplete, that they cannot bring good results.* And if they lead to a happy conclusion, *the impression will always assail me that the success was not depending on the plan, on its greater or lesser perfection, as much as on the Divine intervention, on the miracle that will save us at the last moment.*"

In the end, that was my Uncle Kurt, and no one could change him anymore. I retired to the next room, that of the late Katalina, while he was communicating with the Gods Loyal to the Spirit of Man.

No more than seven or eight minutes had passed, but I was fast asleep when Uncle Kurt came in. Perhaps because I was accumulating much tiredness, perhaps so as not to think about Katalina, who hours before was occupying that room with her children until she felt that her blood was being transformed into fire, the truth was that as soon as I rested my head on the pillow I began to dream. It was a symbolic dream, strange, but very suggestive: I was finding myself, without knowing how, in a building with many floors, connected by innumerable stairs; I was looking for something and I was going up and down the stairs without coming upon its where-abouts; suddenly, when ascending some steps of green stone, I gained access to a square platform without an exit; I was about to return when I noticed a subtle movement in one of the walls that was surrounding the platform; I turned around and, upon carefully observing, I realized that that wall was really a mirror; at first the mirror reflected me, my outward appear-ance, and that is why what happened next took me completely unawares: paralyzed with terror, I discovered that an enor-mous and frightful black spider was observing me with the same carefulness; I immediately guessed that *that spider was Myself, or something of Myself that was being reflected outside;* overcoming the apprehension that was seizing me, I timidly stretched out a hand toward the mirror, at the same time that the spider was moving forward its left front leg toward that direction; on the mirrored surface, we brushed against each other; then the spider bristled, as if it decided to bite, and in the midst of my horror, it leaped forward, jumped out of the mirror and fell upon me, inside of me, sinking into the Depth of Myself; the terrible experience forced me to close my eyes, but then I opened them again, still paralyzed, and I saw the mirror again: but it was no longer reflecting the spider but a marvelous and beautiful Sword; I recognized it at once, it was the Wise Sword of the House of Tharsis, unmistakable with its two quillons on the crossguard, its Stone of Venus, its spiraled ivory hilt of unicorn Barbel horn, and the legend "Honor et Mortis"; it was as if animated, as if provided with a life that was furtively beginning to show itself behind the symbolic form; once again I brought my hand toward the mirror, notic-ing with astonishment that I could now pass through the sur-face; I then reached for the Sword with the intention of taking it, but when touching it, it surprisingly transformed itself and also jumped toward me, entered into me, moved to the depths of Myself; but this time it was not a spider but a Dame, the most beautiful that I have ever conceived, only comparable to the Uncreated Beauty of the Virgin of Agartha, *who reentered Myself,* and whom I only furtively saw, just as She was permit-ting Her Eternal Life to be perceived under the symbolic Vrunic Vesture of the Wise Sword; at that nuptial instant, upon seeing her for the first and last time in my life, I cried out without knowing why: "I have found you again!"; and She *kissed me in passing,* losing Herself in the Infinite Blackness of

Myself, and leaving me submerged in an indescribable ecstasy, more frozen than ever, harder than ever, more complete than ever: *Stone of Ice, Man of Stone, Kālibur Woman, Wise Sword, Kāli; O Kāli!* "O Kāli!" I was murmuring, when Uncle Kurt entered and transported me to the bitter reality of the Cerrillos funeral. It was hard to regain my lucidity after so vivid a dream, and as if in between dreams I heard Uncle Kurt review Capitán Kiev's message. Of course, he did not do so without making his personal protest heard.

"I spoke with Capitán Kiev, Neffe! As I was doing 35 or 40 years ago! And you were right: *it is advisable to execute your plan, strategically advisable!* Which doesn't necessarily mean that the plan is good. So, don't rejoice too much, because the Lord of Venus gave me a warning, *ambiguous, like all warnings from the Gods.* But before I refer to it, I will tell you that *nothing has changed* after so many years, that *for me everything remains the same, that is to say, in the most opaque nebula;* and that I am fed up with this life in which I have the power but, by not comprehending my power, by not embracing the Symbol of the Origin that I Am, I fail to rationally insert myself in the Strategy, in the Grand Strategy of the Loyal Siddhas and of the Führer. History has repeated itself again; when commenting to Capitán Kiev that I had no faith in the effectiveness of that plan, and even less so after the warning that he had transmitted to me, *he said to me verbatim, 'that I was not comprehending the situation.'* Do you realize that, Neffe?" he asked with an affliction that was comical to me. "*The Gods confirm the diagnosis of Tarstein, Von Grossen, the Kaulikas, and so many others!* I don't comprehend the situation, *any situation,* it seems! That I know and it fills me with sorrow, but they don't seem to give a damn about my sorrow: it is more than enough for them that I give them my power in order to realize their *demented* plans, even if I don't comprehend them. And Capitán Kiev shares this attitude: *my function is not to comprehend but to act, to carry out orders to the letter.* To comprehend the Strategy, there are men like Tarstein and you, the emulators of Nimrod, the Kassite King, the madmen who plan and manage to continue the war in Heaven, and take Heaven by storm. Of course, with the indispensable collaboration of us, the powerful ones who ignore how to apply the power, we who do not 'comprehend the situation,' but must use all our power to save the skin of the Wise Ones."

And so he continued protesting a while, as I was patiently paying attention to him. Finally, he referred to what was urgently interesting us.

"In summary, Neffe, for lack of greater comprehension, I will stick to the principle that for me is clearer: *the Immortals cannot die.* And here goes Capitán Kiev's warning. In general, he approved what you propose to do, but he told me these enigmatic words: *'upon completing the operation, you will only see what you did not contemplate at the beginning, but if you had seen it at the beginning, it would prevent you from completing the operation.'* You, in whom the gods trust, tell me what he meant by so ambiguous a warning."

"Dear Uncle Kurt, I have to be as honest as you: I don't know for sure, but I presume that he is warning us about *a flaw* in the plan; about something, an important detail, *which I have overlooked and that, if I were to consider it, would perhaps make me desist from going forward.* But even so, he advises us to act, and that we will do. But I will not stop thinking it over; I will meditate a thousand times on the plan to try to discover what is hidden from my strategic vision: I would not like to receive a surprise at the end; and I would not risk it for anything in the world if I was not convinced that we are going to win. The assassins must receive the surprise, Uncle Kurt! We have to master all the variables of the attack in order to avoid being surprised at the same time! And I swear that I will not leave an element unconsidered until I have acquired maximum certainty in the operation!"

Forty-five minutes after going upstairs, we returned to Commissioner Maidana: he was peacefully asleep on the sofa where we left him seated. Uncle Kurt asked me, when coming down the stairs, about the tactic that I would adopt in order to obtain the particular help that we were needing from him.

"Have you thought about what you'll say to him? You're not going to give him the details of the operation, are you?" He saturated me with his doubts. "Look, Neffe: I don't trust him, or any person like him. They suffer from great ideological confusion and cannot be true Comrades: today they are with you and tomorrow you don't know whom they will answer to."

"Slow down, Uncle Kurt, slow down!" I tried calming him. "Don't despise like that the one who represents our only support. Here, in Argentina, he is the best that there is: we are no longer in the Third Reich! That's over! The Führer *is no longer in sight to awaken the limitless loyalty you feel.* Only we, the Initiates, see the Führer! And we cannot demand of them that they behave like ⚡⚡ Knights if they are forced to live in the world of the Universal pre-Synarchy: remember that you yourself were preferring to die than to survive in this world! So, then, be a little tolerant; and don't worry, *I will only tell him what he wants to hear.* You understand, Uncle Kurt, that I must not lie; but neither can I tell him *the whole truth.* I will reveal to him, then, *part of the truth, that part that he is longing to know and that does not affect us that he knows."*

I awoke Maidana, with a cup of coffee in my hand. He apologized for his "lack of control" and instantly pulled himself together. He was drinking the coffee like water and in a matter of minutes consumed three cups, while listening to my proposal.

"I will speak to you as a Nationalist Comrade, Commissioner Maidana," I clarified. "We have agreed, with my friend, that you can indeed provide us with the kind of help that we need. Logically, in order to reach an agreement, I will have to lay some cards on the table, so I will start with the assassination of Belicena Villca. First of all, I will point out the motive for the crime: *her son Noyo Villca.* The assassins were procuring to establish Noyo Villca's whereabouts. Why? Because the young man was an intelligence agent infiltrated in subversive organizations.

"I knew that there was something concrete in all this!" Maidana triumphantly exclaimed. "After so much madness, and profusion of false leads, you had to have a specific motive that you were seeking to hide."

"Indeed," I confirmed. "And do you know who Noyo Villca was working for? Well, no less than for the Argentine Army. Even more: he was an Army officer, a G2 captain."

"Mother of God!" he invoked. "And why weren't those pieces of information appearing in Belicena Villca's police dossier?"

"Because a powerful synarchic organization, which functions at all levels of the Army, took care of hiding the information. Don't forget that it was the Army that locked her up in the asylum. To said organization, made up *not only of Jews,* belong the assassins of Belicena Villca and my family. What you should know, since it will allow you to discover the nexus between both crimes, is that Noyo Villca is a fugitive due to the fact that the Synarchy attempts to suppress him in order to prevent him from **putting his ultra-confidential knowledge into practice**. And that his mother, before dying, provided me with the clues to find him."

"Now everything is clear!" Maidana believed. "I congratulate you, Dr. Siegnagel! You are a real man: you put yourself on the line for the national cause and the international assassins made you pay dearly for it! You have done well to trust me. From this moment on we can work together against that organization and help Noyo Villca as well."

"Don't get ahead of yourself, Maidana, that's not how I see things," I stopped him. "The favor that we are going to ask of you does not consist in you and your group's support, but in something else. In that sense, and **for the time being**, you will be left out of our action: that will be the basis of the deal; no discussion: **take it or leave it**. My proposal is the following: Noyo Villca was belonging to a top-secret nationalist group in the Army: I know his contact and I am willing to reveal him to you, so that your group and theirs will be able to arrange to work together. In that way you will not be left out of the case: but yes, and for the time being, I repeat, you will have to let us operate against the assassins."

"What do you mean by *'for the time being'*?" Maidana, who was not born yesterday, wanted to know.

"I mean that the restriction that I'm imposing on you is provisional, motivated by the presumption that we will have a better chance of success if we operate alone. But the contact that I am going to give you demonstrates that we trust you. And furthermore, I will give you **my word of Honor that if our action fails, and another opportunity remains, we will turn to you without hesitation**."

"In principle I accept," Maidana acceded. "Who is the contact?"

"First, you must assure me that you will comply with the favor that we will ask of you," I warned.

"Fine, then, tell me once and for all what it is all about!" he irritatedly demanded.

"Weapons, Commissioner Maidana. We need at least two weapons as soon as possible."

"What kind of weapons?" he asked hesitantly, and added, "I don't know why you don't leave this in the hands of professionals, Dr. You're acting outside your specialty; it's as if I now dedicated myself to perform psychiatric cures."

"I already told you what the terms of the deal were, Maidana: *take it or leave it.*"

"I have no choice, Siegnagel! Of course I can lend you weapons. We have all kinds of weapons! Just tell me what the hell kind of weapons you want."

"We need a type of weapon that's very effective up close, which destroys the body. Two repeating shotguns would be ideal," I suggested.

"I can deliver two Itakas[5] to you this very afternoon. What else?"

"Well... ammunition for the shotguns and... is it possible to get handguns as well?" I was realizing that I was lacking the military training to request things with clarity. Uncle Kurt, who was a specialist in the subject, was keeping quiet so as not to attract attention to his knowledge.

"Handguns? There are hundreds of handguns at your disposal; but, if you'll allow me to intervene with my experience in this matter, it seems to me that it'll be best to explain to me what you intend to do and let me take care of the equipment."

I could not, of course, explain to him the plan. But I could show him some general details.

"It's a commando operation against the assassins."

"What kind of operation?"

"An ambush," I defined.

"Well, then you don't need just any handgun, but machine pistols. And you must also carry fragmentation grenades. Look, Siegnagel: I'll prepare two SWAT outfits for you, suitable for an operation of that type. Where are you going to operate? Can you wear a combat jacket?"

"Yes... I think so," I responded. I glanced at Uncle Kurt out of the corner of my eye and saw that he was nodding. "What importance does it have?"

"It's just that the jackets that I'm going to lend you have all the necessary pockets, loops, and hooks," he explained. They carry the machine pistols, which are very small despite firing a thousand bullets per minute, in a shoulder holster, and you'll resort to them only in case of necessity, since you'll carry the Itakas in your hands. The Itakas can be used with a shoulder strap or with a leg holster, but in this case I suggest the strap. They have a capacity of 8 cartridges, which gives them a hell-

---

5. Most likely a Bataan Model 71, an unlicensed clone of the Ithaca Model 37 shotgun manufactured in Argentina.

ish firepower; a single load should be enough for an ambush, but, if you have to sustain a shootout, you'll find more cartridges in the jacket. Likewise, in other pockets will be the spare magazines for the machine pistols and the ten fragmentation grenades in the belt. Just in case you're forced to demolish something, I'll also provide you with two bricks of TNT with an electronic detonator for each of you, which will also be secured in your jacket. The equipment will be completed with two hunting knives, the sheath of which is sewn to the inside of the jacket. Agreed, Dr. Siegnagel?"

"When can you deliver such equipment to me?" I admiringly asked. "This very afternoon. Now give me the name of your contact."

"Captain Diego Fernández. In 1978, he was stationed in Tucumán. He doesn't know me and surely doesn't know what happened to Belicena Villca three months ago. He won't refuse to talk to you when he learns that we're trying to protect his Comrade."

Chapter X

t 18 hours the grueling burial was carried out. The Siegnagels were possessing a spacious mausoleum in the local cemetery and there the five coffins would be deposited: cremation would not be well seen by the priests of the town. First, the funeral procession passed by the church, as was the custom, and there a mass was officiated for "the eternal rest of their souls," a Golen formula, still de rigueur. The old priest, a friend of my parents, attempted to console me for the immense loss I suffered and veiledly insinuated that my estrangement from the Church might be connected with the present misfortune. I promised to return to Sunday masses, like when I was a child, and to confess and take communion, until the good man was satisfied.

A large crowd, both curious and sad, gathered at the necropolis to bid farewell to the mortal remains. There they were, punctually, Maidana and the Commissioner of Cerrillos. The latter handed me the predictable summons.

"I regret disturbing you at this time, Arturo, but you'll understand that we have a duty to fulfill. Tomorrow you can come give your statement at the police station. It's at 11 hours: the judge will be waiting for you, who also wishes to question you."

I promised to attend with exactitude and the Commissioner withdrew satisfied. After the prayer for the dead, the priest also went away, and after him the people dispersed, but not before repeating their condolences. When I locked up the mausoleum, only Uncle Kurt, Maidana, and I were left.

We met again at the Finca. With extreme caution, Maidana lowered four aircraft-fabric bags that were containing the SWAT equipment. He made a thousand recommendations about the prudence with which we had to handle that material, and some practical clarifications. There was everything he promised, and even more: he added the boots, pants, shirts, and berets, in short, the whole of the commando's attire, dirtied with shades suitable for bush camouflage.

"I've kept my end of the bargain," he said. "And I wish you luck in the operation. By dedicating myself to achieve this in such a short time, I haven't been able to rest, so I'm leaving now because I can't stand up. Ah, I investigated about officer

Diego Fernández! He is on active duty. He is now a G2 Major, and is stationed at the 702nd Intelligence Battalion, in Buenos Aires. Tomorrow or the day after I will personally go to speak with him.

"Well, adiós, Camaradas," he solemnly bade farewell. "Ah, another thing, which I was already forgetting! When you return, Dr. Siegnagel, will you clarify for me those two obscure points in the Belicena Villca case, those irrational events that hindered the entire investigation? I'm referring to that account of the murder within the hermetically sealed cell, and the bejeweled rope used in the strangulation. I know that Ritual crimes exist, and that those who practice them are precisely members of synarchic organizations. But why was it important to give Ritual form to the death of a poor alienated woman, or to the multiple murder of your family? That's what I don't quite understand."

I looked at him discouraged. How to explain to him that the Rituals would be effective if those who were performing them were Magi of Bera's and Birsha's quality? He must have read the disappointment in my countenance because he raised his arms in a *stop* expression and smilingly walked back to his car.

"Not now, not now, Dr. You're as tired as I am and it's not a good idea to continue with the hypotheses but rather to go to sleep as soon as possible.

"When I return," I told him.

"You'll see that then you'll find a way to explain it to me!"

He immediately left, and I never saw him again.

That night, a sepulchral silence descended on the Finca. Uncle Kurt spent an hour examining the weapons, while I was using that time to bury Canuto. My faithful dog had received a kind of lightning bolt in the middle of his body, perhaps a strike from the Dorje, and was torn to shreds: he would never again wait for me at the gate to offer me his affection, during those two hundred meters to the house that were belonging only to him. And I would never ever see my parents again, and my sister with her children, at the end of the driveway. Damned Demons Bera and Birsha! Damned Priests of The One Jehovah Satan! Damned Sacred Sacrificers! Soon, very soon we would meet again and they would be executed. Not "Bera and Birsha" for, as Uncle Kurt was repeating, "Immortals cannot die," but the "Oriental assassins" of my family, the human manifestation of Bera and Birsha. They would know my fury, that of Uncle Kurt, and that of all the members of the House of Tharsis whom they murdered, tormented, and persecuted, and who were now seeming to come to my aid and encourage me. Because if I had had the willpower to impose myself on Uncle Kurt and force him to accept my plan, it was certainly because of that: because I was certain that eliminating the Oriental assassins was a matter of Honor, above all things; and I was patently feeling that in that yearning the House of Tharsis was spiritually accompanying me. I was clearly seeing Belicena Villca; and I was hearing that she was speaking to me, referring to the last words of her letter and telling me: "Yes, Dr. Siegnagel; it is a matter of Honor to do away with Bera and Birsha! They have committed an error and you must take advantage of it; the House of Tharsis accompanies you in your decision! Now you will demonstrate that you are a Kshatriya! And then, very soon, we will meet again during the Final Battle, or in Valhalla!"

The Spirit of Belicena Villca was guiding me; I was sure of it; perhaps it was She who so opportunely brought Commissioner Maidana to Cerrillos. I finished burying Canuto at the foot of my favorite lapacho tree, and went back to the house.

Uncle Kurt had retired to the upper room, taking with him the totality of the equipment. I drank the umpteenth coffee of the day and was turning off the lights until reaching my room, that is, the room that belonged to Katalina, and quickly submerged in the restful indifference of sleep.

Chapter XI

O n January 6, 1980, Belicena Villca was assassinated.

On January 21, 1980, I experienced the spiritual rapture of the Virgin of Agartha.

On January 28, 1980, I learned that I had an Uncle Kurt von Sübermann and I departed for Santa María.

On March 21, 1980, Uncle Kurt concluded the account of his life and, that night, I was detected by the Demon Bera.

On March 22, 1980, at 00:15 hours, the demons attempt to exterminate the Stirp of the Von Sübermanns. As a result, all members of the family die, except for Uncle Kurt and myself.

On March 22, at 08:00 hours, we arrive in Cerrillos and verify a quintuple murder, according to the police version.

On March 23, at 00:30 hours, Commissioner Maidana arrives to bring me his condolences, and to bring armed protection.

On March 23, at 05:45 hours, Commissioner Maidana informed us about the existence of the "Oriental assassins" and their strange vehicle.

On March 23, at 07:05 hours, the Commissioner of Cerrillos showed us the identikits of the Oriental assassins. At that time I had already conceived my plan down to the last detail.

On March 23, at 08:45 hours, I convince Uncle Kurt to consult Capitán Kiev about my plan.

On March 23, at 10:30 hours, we close a deal with Commissioner Maidana: he will lend us material help in exchange for staying on the case.

On March 23, at 20:00 hours, Commissioner Maidana leaves Cerrillos, after delivering the commando equipment to us; I would not see him again.

On March 23, at 23:00 hours, I laid down to sleep for the first time since the ill-fated night of the 21st.

On March 24, at 11 hours, I presented myself at the Cerrillos Police Station and made my statement. What I knew about the murders was not much, and of this they were not doubting, since they had verified my alibi: for it they sent two policemen who made the inverse route to Santa María, they gathered testimonies about our trip from 00:30 to 08:00 hours, they questioned the telephone operator, who knew my voice for calling frequently to Cerrillos, and they interrogated José Tolaba and his wife, the majordomos of Uncle Kurt. No, they were not doubting about my absence at the crime scene, nor were they suspecting Uncle Kurt; *what they were presuming, both the police and the judge, was that I was knowing the motive for the crime, which they had dismissed as an ordinary offense.* Could it be an error? Was there an unknown political purpose? What was I up to? What were my ideas and activities? Why had I distanced myself from the Church? Had my parents received threats before? Was there extortion?

So, grilling me with such questions, they held me until 5 in the afternoon and promised to summon me again.

On March 24, at 10:00 hours, while I was preparing myself to go to the police station, Uncle Kurt began to work with Yin and Yang. Upon returning, in the afternoon, the daiva dogs had already succeeded in isolating the trail of the black car: Uncle Kurt designated it with a code word and, mentally affirming it, effectively demonstrated to me how the daiva dogs were heading directly for the place where it was parked.

Uncle Kurt devoted the whole of March 25 to constructing the order with the svadi Kyilkhor: the whole operation was depending on the precision of that order and his meticulousness was understandable. He only spent a few hours to coordinate with me the movements we would make in front of our enemies. For example, we agreed that he would shoot first, and always to the left, while I should cover the right.

I devoted the whole of March 25 to getting the operations of the Finca sorted out.

Some neighbors, through a share in the crop yield, willingly agreed to take care of the vineyards and the future grape harvest; it would not be a difficult task since Papa had the productive mechanisms properly oiled and all the work would be reduced to administering the field and supervising the workers. We signed an improvised contract, in which I included a clause completely out of the ordinary: they were committing themselves to clean the winepress *and to inject the 20,000 liters of Tar into one of the water wells of the Finca, of which water table dried up years ago and of which mouth was still open with a cistern.* I did this because I could not run the risk that the Pitch be sold or energetically exploited: *I was not even for an instant forgetting that that lake of asphalt was constituting an organic*

synthesis of our blood, which was representing the blood of the
Von Sübermann Stirp.

On March 25, at 18:00 hours, at last, I acquired the only element that Uncle Kurt requested to complete the tactical equipment: a Teflon carboy, with hermetic cap, filled with five liters of sulfuric acid.

On March 26, 1980, we were prepared to initiate the operation.

Chapter XII

e could have acted that very morning, but Uncle Kurt preferred to wait until nightfall and spend the day going over every last detail of "Operation Boomerang." We had christened it this way, a little tongue in cheek and a little in seriousness, considering that, analogously to those Australian weapons, Bera's and Birsha's blows would come back against those who launched them.

At 19:00 hours we were already loading the equipment and getting ready to leave. At 19:30 hours we went out of the house, since the dying twilight would prevent anyone from being surprised to see us dressed in military attire. Lying down next to the lapacho trees, the mastiffs were the image of canine tranquility. We too were keeping calm. And we were no longer thinking about anything. We knew all the details of what we had to do and our only concern was to act as soon as possible.

Uncle Kurt took the reins of the daiva dogs and put them on alert. They both brusquely stopped and, moving with prodigious synchronicity, tensed their muscles and moved their heads upward, as if sniffing an inconceivable scent in the air. I was staying behind Uncle Kurt; I was carrying on my back, fastened with ropes, the carboy of acid, and hanging from my shoulder, ready to shoot, the relentless Itaka. In the end, we had decided to wear the commando uniform, for being invaluably more practical for action, although it would later represent a problem if we were seen by other persons. But what was that risk mattering in the face of the possibility of bringing down the Oriental assassins? If the luck of arms was adverse to us, there would be no return; and if we were triumphing, we would already find a way to obtain other clothes. Or were the assassins also not disguised, without giving a damn about what the witnesses thought?

I had, then, both hands free, with the purpose of carrying out Uncle Kurt's instructions: *"you must take hold of my waist as soon as I begin to elevate myself." "And when we are in space, remember that you must concentrate your attention on me the whole time: not even for a second can you be distracted because you would run the risk of separating yourself from me and getting lost in any of the innumerable Worlds of Illusion that we will pass through." "Once out of the usual context of our life, the only way for both of us to continue together, coinciding in Time and Space, is to maintain a volitive nexus between us: and that is what you will do by keeping me under visual and tactile contact."*

It seemed that we were already departing, and I was ready to hold him by the waist as soon as he got a move on, but he again turned to me to make recommendations. "Got the shotgun handy? As soon as you set foot on the Chacra, you must let go and take the gun!"

"Yes, Uncle, yes."

"Neffe, Arturo?" he called to me in a different, strangely affectionate tone.

"Yes, Uncle Kurt."

"This may be the last time that we see each other. I don't want to be pessimistic, but just in case, let's say goodbye here."

"Nooo, no," I exclaimed in horror, trying to shoo away the ominous thoughts. After what happened to my family, I could not think without shuddering at the possibility of losing Uncle Kurt as well. "Nothing bad will happen to us, dear Uncle Kurt: triumph is certain! We will be like the boomerang that returns to the hands of the one who threw it, strikes back, and stops!"

But my arguments were of no avail. Uncle Kurt had already turned around and was effusively embracing me.

"Goodbye, Neffe," he said with nostalgia. "Life didn't give us the opportunity to get to know each other better. Nevertheless, it was very good to have you in Santa María those months. You restored my faith in the Hyperborean Wisdom by bringing me the answers that I awaited for 35 years. Now I will risk my last strength in the most demented of all the missions that they have ever entrusted me with. And this is also necessary for the Führer's Strategy; as always, I do not understand why, but I know that it is so. Goodbye, Neffe Arturo: we will see each other at the end; *at the end of Operation Boomerang or when the Final Battle is fought."*

It put a lump in my throat; I had not the courage to say goodbye to him. I just tightly embraced him.

However, Uncle Kurt was still being as stubborn as ever.

"Let's be off then," he proposed. "Just remember that, whatever happens, I will not depart from the only principle that I comprehend."

"Yes, I know, Uncle Kurt; for Wothan's sake, don't say *'the Immortals cannot die'* again!"

It was 19:45 on March 26, 1980, and it had already darkened quite a bit in Cerrillos. Uncle Kurt gave the first order to Yin and Yang and the phenomenon instantaneously began to be produced: the daiva dogs and Uncle Kurt, who were seeming to have an effective point of support under their feet, were slowly levitated upwards. Such a point of support was not enough for me, and so I hastened to grab his waist, literally hanging in space, without any base, and finding that Uncle Kurt was hunching over, bearing my dead weight.

The ascent lasted a few seconds, until I lost track of the altitude. In the meantime, I managed to make out with the corner of my eye the tops of the lapacho trees, the roofs of the Finca, and, in a snapshot, the town of Cerrillos, artificially illuminated by street lamps. We were not moving uniformly, but the ascent was accelerating as we were gaining altitude. At a given moment, Uncle Kurt, beyond Kula and Akula, plasmated the complex mental orders and the daiva dogs, without stopping their movement, performed the svadi-Lung flight. The order coming from the Eternal Spirit had the effect of a whip crack and, not only the daiva dogs: I also felt it; and I verified *the power,* the terrible power that a Hyperborean Initiate, a God Man, is capable of demonstrating.

If I had to refer to time, I would say that the flight through Time and Space lasted no more than a second. However, that sinking into the most impenetrable blackness did not transmit a sensation of temporality but of eternity, of being outside of life and death, and of everything passing by.

After that instant without time, in which without any doubt I experienced the impression of a jump, a decelerated descent began, during which I again distinguished the usual objects, skies, mountains, houses, trees, lights. The trip was comprised, then, of three phases: one, of accelerated ascent, with permanent perception of the sky and the stars; the second, of the svadi-Lung jump itself, in which I lacked any contextual vision, except for Uncle Kurt; and the third, of decelerated descent, in which I reassuringly reencountered the cosmic womb of the starry sky above me.

It was around 22 or 23 hours on March 22, 1980, when my feet touched the ground of Belicena Villca's Chacra, in Tafí del Valle. I stepped on solid ground and, nevertheless, my knees loosened a little, until Uncle Kurt landed, whose feet were at all times a meter higher than mine: I repeat that I traveled "hanging" from his waist.

But as soon as I regained my stability, I let go of Uncle Kurt and grabbed the Itaka. I was still getting my bearings and I obeyed his gesture that was indicating me to get down. Rapidly, everything was making sense to me: we were finding ourselves hidden behind an enormous black automobile, the automobile of the Oriental assassins!

Uncle Kurt communicated to me with a finger over his mouth to be silent, and then pointed in the direction of the front, beyond the car. I peered over the hood, and spotted a house no more than thirty paces away, shedding profuse light into the exterior blackness through a row of three side windows. Apparently, the car was parked parallel to the vertex of the corner of the house, allowing us to make out, in addition to the windows on one side, the front door situated on the other. The door, closed, was framed on a forty-five degree plane to the left; and there we would have to go.

Undoubtedly, we were counting on the factor of surprise. The dogs had pressed themselves against the ground like serpents, mentally commanded by Uncle Kurt, and there they would stay. We were going to advance toward the door, to begin the attack, when a human scream, a shrill shriek of pain, pinned us to the spot: they were tormenting someone inside! So we ran to the door as quietly as possible.

And as we were approaching, a penetrating and sweet smell was the first thing that caught our attention. It was an aromatic substance like sandalwood or incense, and it was so out of place there that we looked at each other perplexed. We both immediately recognized that perfume for having perceived it before, in different and dramatic circumstances: Uncle Kurt, in the Tibetan valley of Das Pech; and I in the cell of Belicena Villca, the night of her death. But this only lasted an instant, for what came next concentrated all our attention.

EPILOGUE

Chapter XIII

ut it was clear that those would not be ordinary human beings. Midway, when we had not yet separated from the viewpoint of the door and were not completely visible from it, the door burst open to make way for two men of enormous physical build. One jumped out and the other remained on the threshold: contrasted by the interior light, we had in front of us the two Oriental Gentlemen, impeccably dressed in their finely tailored English suits.

The first who came out was Bera, wielding a handle with two globes, the fatal Dorje. He instantaneously raised the weapon toward Uncle Kurt, at the same time that his face was breaking down in terror. I realized that the human Demon was not seeing Uncle Kurt but the Sign of the Origin, the Absolute Truth of the Spirit that was dissolving the Essential Lie of his own illusory existence.

Despite it all, he was going to fire the death ray, but Uncle Kurt was quicker. On the run, almost without aiming, he pulled the trigger once; and that was enough. The gunshot caught Bera in the middle of the chest, lifted him a meter high, and hurled him several meters away. Simultaneously, I, who was not exactly a professional commando, stopped, took aim, and fired twice, hitting the stomach and chest of the Demon Birsha. The eighteen rounds of ammunition, wisely dispersed by that magnificent weapon, flattened Birsha against the door frame without giving him time to do anything.

"Quick!" shouted Uncle Kurt, when seeing that I had remained motionless, refusing to believe that it was all over. "Quick, prepare the acid, Arturo! *Hurry, before Avalokiteśvara manifests herself!*"

"*Avalokiteś...?*" I asked surprised. Gods! Avalokiteśvara, the Compassionate One! *That was the flaw in my plan, about which Capitán Kiev veiledly warned us! I had forgotten Avalokiteśvara, I was now seeing it clear, and that forgetfulness could derail my plan, even cost us our lives! The Great Mother would never permit that two of her best sons be destroyed, not if She could prevent it; that was precisely one of her cosmic functions: to protect her animal-man sons, to calm the fear of their Souls! And if She was succeeding in taking away Bera and Birsha's fear, even attenuate it, my whole plan would collapse like a house of cards! We could even suffer a counterattack from the Demons, already recovered, who would then know in which World to find us!*

Evaluating these possibilities was paralyzing me. I painstakingly untied the ropes and lowered the carboy of acid from my back. Uncle Kurt, displaying extraordinary skill, had already extracted Bera's heart, leaving in its place a horrible hole through which was flowing abundant blood, which was forming a pool around his cadaver. He put the smoking heart inside the bowler hat, which was floating on the blood like a grotesque replica of Charon's boat, and swiftly knelt over Birsha's lifeless body. With accurate slashes of the hunting knife, sharp as a razor, he was cutting the vest of fine English cashmere and the no less valuable Chinese silk shirt; when reaching the flesh, he made a deep central incision, which he would later enlarge until exposing the end of the ribs and the thoracic cavity: from there he would section the arteries of the heart, which in those demons was located on the right side of the body.

"Uncle Kurt knew!" I discovered to my dismay. And to think that I dared to put his Honor to the test; he not only knew that we might fail, he also knew why we might fail. And despite having known, he kept silent in order to comply with the orders of the Lord of Venus. I remembered Capitán Kiev's warning: *"upon completing the operation, you will only see what you did not contemplate at the beginning, but if you had seen it at the beginning, it would prevent you from completing the operation."* Avalokiteśvara, She was what I had not contemplated at the beginning, for if I had supposed that Her Mercy would help the Demons to overcome the panic, I would not have undertaken Operation Boomerang! And Uncle Kurt had realized it then, he who was complaining of not comprehending anything, but had kept silent because he knew how much I was wanting to attack the Demons. That is why he made me buy the sulfuric acid without giving me further explanations: he also had a theory; he knew an alchemical way to neutralize the protection of the Great Mother Binah, or he knew how to maintain the panic of the Demons. I would soon know what the answer was.

About the sulfuric acid, he had only told me that it *"fixes organic matter in Saturn"*: "by introducing the heart, seat of the Soul, into the sulfuric acid, we are constellating the Soul in Saturn, situating it at the beginning of the Universe and contributing to its involutive regression." According to the plan, it was up to me to introduce the hearts into the carboy of acid. But I was now presuming that that recommendation was aiming at another objective, in addition to that declared by Uncle Kurt.

I sat the carboy on the threshold of the door and uncapped it; I took the bowler hat, which was just receiving the second heart, and placed it beside it; and, not without a certain repugnance, I prepared to pick up the diabolical organs. It was then when I stopped in fascination, and then I was paralyzed with fright.

It is written, *"the hearts belong to Avalokiteśvara."* The heart of the animal-man, of the Man of Mud, receives the protection of the Great Mother Binah by means of the *Intellegentia* of *YHVH;* and his crepuscular *consciousness* receives more light by means of the *Sapientia* of the Great Father Chokmah.

Chapter XIV

s I said, I was going to pick up the human hearts of Bera and Birsha, when I stopped in fascination: the cause was the *scintilla luminis,* or sparks of light, which began to burst from them. Thousands of sparks that were leaping in all directions, either spinning in a circle, or in a spiral, or tracing brilliant curves of whimsical form, preventing me from distinguishing the bottom of the hat, and even the hat itself. Fascinated by the spectacle, enchanted, perhaps bewitched, I unwittingly recalled the definition of the Alchemist Khunrath; they are, he said, *"Scintillae Animae Mundi igneae, Luminis nimirum Naturae,"* that is, *"fiery sparks of the world soul, i.e. of the light of nature."* Such *scintillae* always accompany the phases of Alchemy; and at that moment all the elements of the opus were present: in the Laboratory of Nature, there was the *prima materia* of the hearts; the *aqua permanens of the Sulphur Philosophorum;* and was present Mercury, the great transmuting *Artifex,* that is, *Shivatulku* Uncle Kurt, representative of Wothan, who is Hermes, and who is Mercury.

Whirling in a hypnotic whirlwind, the *scintillae luminis* were covering my field of vision. Golden sparks were now sprouting from everywhere and flying through space until extinguishing, a space strangely devoid of wind and sound, as if the whole of Nature was entertained in manifesting its *lumen naturae.* I took my eyes off the bowler hat and the carboy of acid, invisible under the luminous spring, and, semi-anesthetized, I looked around: *scintillae* were seeming to emerge from the entire world. From the house, from the ground, from the trees that I did not see before, but that were standing ten paces away, from all things was emerging a golden and flickering aura, comprised of myriads of *scintillae luminis.* Or was that vision signifying the sudden activity of a new sense, which was making it possible to perceive the Anima Mundi, a *luminositas sensus naturae?*

But a greater luminositas attracted my attention. Over the cadavers of the Oriental assassins, in effect, two clouds of ectoplasmic vapor were beginning to rise, also twinkling due to the emission and absorption of thousands of *scintillae;* at a meter of height, those clouds were maintaining themselves whirling in a spiral, and constantly nourishing themselves with the milky vapor that was emanating from the pools of blood. As in a painting of the impressionist school, like in a work of Henri Matisse, I was seeing Reality decomposed into millions of colored points, sparks of light that were whirling in the form of the *elementum primordiale* and of the *massa confusa,* of the *chaos naturae.* With my vision saturated by the swarming of *scintillae,* I felt that interiorly, and irrationally, a voice was speaking to me; it was saying, *"Yod, Yod, each scintilla is yod, an eye of Avalokiteśvara"; "and among all the scintillae there are two that are The One, they are the scintillae pair, the Monads of Bera and Birsha that cannot die."*

Already wary by what happened in Santa María, it was just to listen to these voices coming from the Soul, from my own Soul emotionally influenced by the Great Mother, to refer me to the Virgin of Agartha. Yes: I closed my ears as best I could, since I could not ignore the great *luminosity,* and I surrendered myself to the rapture of the Virgin of the Child of Stone, whose spiritual aid allowed me to sustain myself in that terrible moment. According to what occurred next, I would have undoubtedly lost my mind if She was not supporting my Spirit from the Origin. Because at that moment, when the quantity and multiplicity of the *scintillae* had reached their maximum exaltation, *they all opened in unison and showed an inexpressive eye, an eye that was the same eye dementedly repeated in all points of space.* All of Nature, all differentiated things, all that I could see and perceive was now boiling with inexpressive eyes, with ichthyic eyes that were undoubtedly looking at us: *and those millions of fish eyes, of oculi piscium, were the Eyes of the Compassionate One that were opening to contemplate the Souls of her Beloved Sons, the Souls of Bera and Birsha that were disembodied in the midst of a great terror.*

Think of the scene: in the general form of the entities, nothing has changed, all are distinguishable and recognizable, all are nameable as ever; the tree, the floor, the house, the Heavens, the cloud, the bodies, all the objects are still the same; *but now, they also brim with a life ebullient with Divine eyes, with eyes that look with natural Love.* Think of the tree, all comprised of eyes, and of the house, or of the Heavens, also comprised of eyes, and think that *the thousands of gazes from the tree to the house and from the house to the tree, and from both to the Heavens, are the ties that bind and rebind those entities and constitute the superstructure of reality:* a structure of objects bound together by the Will of the Creator and the natural Love of the Great Mother.

If one has imagined it, one must now think that I was finding myself in that scene, frightened by the omnipresent eyes of Avalokiteśvara, "the all-seeing one," and shaken to the root of my sentiments, agitated in my emotional nature by the intense Love of the Great Mother, by her unlimited Mercy. Thus, then, first was the fascination for the *scintillae* and then the fright from the *panoptic* ebullition; and the greatest fright was to see that my own body was constituted by millions of compassionate eyes. And this phenomenon, terrible, demented, explains why my hand stopped before picking up the hearts from the interior of the bowler hat.

"Neffe! Arturo!" the voice of Uncle Kurt was heard from several meters away. "I knew that this would occur and I know what you're seeing. Fear not, it's all an illusion: we can still fulfill our objective. Can you hear me?"

"Yes, Uncle Kurt," I dazedly responded. "I hear you as if your voice came from a great distance, and I find myself very much under the suggestion of this profusion of eyes that nature manifests, of this monster into which the world has been converted."

"Listen well, Arturo: you will do exactly what I request of you and you will respond to my questions. *You will communicate to me what you see, for here there are no eyes but those of your own: all the eyes of Avalokiteśvara are illusory, they are projections of your own emotional weakness.*"

I made an effort and turned myself toward the direction in which his voice was coming from. I saw millions of shining eyes, I saw that all Reality was continuing made up of fish eyes, but where Uncle Kurt was, where his eyes should be, I only saw two empty sockets, two craters of impenetrable blackness, two open windows to Another World: I let out a cry of horror and returned my gaze forward.

"Are you with me, Arturo?" asked Uncle Kurt unusually.

"Yes, Uncle Kurt," I once more responded.

"You will perform the Work: I will only place, at the Beginning, the Sign of the Origin on the Stone of Fire!"

I remembered the words of Birsha in the Letter from Belicena Villca: "the mortal men, Men of Mud, who were evolving from mud, from the Stone of Fire of the Beginning that was reflecting a monad similar to The One, would come to be in the End individuals identical to the Stone of Fire, like Metatron, the Heavenly Man, the realized Archetype, the Son of Binah Lamb; thus they would be when the Temple was ready, and each one occupied his place in the construction, according to the symbol of the Messiah; thus they would be in the days in which the Kingdom of *YHVH* would be concretized on Earth; and the King Messiah reigned; *and the Shekhinah manifested Herself"*... So many eyes! Yes: that manifestation of Avalokiteśvara, of the Great Mother Binah, was also the Shekhinah, as Zechariah qualified it: *"these optical roots of the Tree of YHVH represent Israel Shekhinah"*! At the Beginning of Time, the created man was like a mud structure; at the End, he would be like a Stone of Fire. Such stones, the Sign of the Origin *irreversibly plasmated* them, transforming them into Cold Stone, into Uncreated Stone, as the Demons were being scandalized, marking them with the Abominable Sign: "They, *engraved the Abominable Sign* on the Stone of Fire upon which each Men of Mud's Soul was being seated. And the Abominable Sign *cooled* the Stone of Fire, *Eben Esh,* and removed it from the End. So, Cohens, *the Stone that must be washed with lye at the End, is the Cold Stone that should not be where it is, because it was not placed at the Beginning by the One Creator."* "Accursed Stone, Stone of Scandal, Seed of Stone: They planted it in the Soul of the man of mud after the Beginning, and now is found at the Beginning."

"Transmutemini de lapidibus mortuis in vivos lapides philosophicos!"[6] I heard Uncle Kurt repeat the words of Magister Dorn.[7] "Look into the *matrix!*"[8]

"I see a golden water, aqua aurea, agitated by countless sparks of light: it is the anima panoptes!"

"Put the hearts in the *matrix!*"

Without reflecting, I felt around for the hat, extracted the viscous organs, and introduced them through the mouth of the carboy. As soon as they sank into the sulfuric acid, an emanation of toxic vapor forced me to pull my head back: through the opening of the *uterus philosophorum* the *ruby* vapor rose for a moment, giving the impression that the liquid

---

6. *Let us transmute ourselves from dead stones into living Philosopher's Stones.*

7. Gerhard Dorn

8. Referring to the carboy of acid, which is like unto a matrix or womb.

had entered into combustion; however, it soon subsided, and a new glow began to shine from the interior of the carboy, this time black. At that moment I could barely notice it because Uncle Kurt was wanting me to keep my eyes off the acid and its macabre contents, but it was evident that it substantially diminished the general *morpho-optic* manifestation.

"Now what do you see?" he asked from his post.

"The starry firmament!"

In effect, the acid had turned color and now the carboy was containing a black liquid, *nigredo,* which was presenting a shiny surface and illuminated by an infinitude of fixed *scintillae,* sparks of light that were the stars of a particular microcosm.

"Now what do you see?" he repeated.

"The Zodiac!" Hundreds, thousands of constellations, all the Archetypes of the Universe were in that Heaven!

"Now what do you see?" he insisted.

"Two stars that stand out! Two stars, brighter than all the others, move forward and situate themselves in a central place, under the foot of the Virgin of the Spica, near Corvus!"

"Now what do you see?" he asked.

"The constellations seem more alive than ever, the Archetypes vibrate in the Heavens, animals of all kinds *prepare themselves to descend!* I see them and I hear their sounds!"

In truth, the sound of the celestial animals had become so real, that it was only when taking my eyes off the matrix for an instant that I realized that certainly, some of them were present around me: with a jolt I distinguished three bellows, and so I directed that fleeting glance toward the surroundings; *they were the oink of the pig, the bark of the dog, and the roar of the bear.* With growing fright, I then verified that the ectoplasmic clouds that were floating over the corpses of Bera and Birsha had acquired the unmistakable form of the *boar:* over the cadavers of the Oriental assassins were materializing two enormous white boars, that were threateningly growling and showing in their bodies the thousand eyes of Avalokiteśvara, the thousand eyes of the Anima Mundi, the thousand eyes of The One, the thousand eyes of Purusha. The daiva dogs had approached, no doubt called by Uncle Kurt, and they were seeming to see them without problems because they were barking at them with uncontainable impetus.

But the greatest impression I got when observing Uncle Kurt, how to explain what I saw? Perhaps only by saying that *his form was changing;* that at times he was Uncle Kurt *and at times an enormous wrathful bear, an ursus terrificus.* But such an explanation would not be entirely correct because, certainly, Uncle Kurt had been converted into a *bear-Man:* it was the *fury* of Uncle Kurt, *the Fury of the Bear Warrior,* the *berserkr-gangr,* the force that was transforming him. I looked for Uncle Kurt with my gaze and discovered a *Berserkr,* a Warrior of the Einherjar Order of Wothan, a Hyperborean Initiate in the Vrunes of Navutan. And the frightened look returned to his eyes, accompanied by a most violent roar and the rhythmic movement, almost Ritual, of his powerful paws. But when he spoke; it was once again Uncle Kurt.

"Now what do you see?" he demanded.

"The two brightest stars have transformed into twin Boars!"

"Now what do you see?"

"The Boars flee in terror and seek the protection of their Mother, the Dragon of the Universe!"

"Now what do you see?"

"I see the Boars taking refuge in the lap of the Dragon! And I see the Dragon: she has a thousand heads and a thousand eyes, and on each head a Star of David, and on each head appears the Face of Binah, and her thousand mouths sing the Song of the Lamb. The Dragon cradles the Lamb in her arms, and the Boars, right and left, growl without ceasing. And in chorus to the Dragon, and to the Boars, three-fourths of the stars of Heaven thus sing:

'Avalokiteśvara. Great Mother Binah!
It is coming, it is coming,
the Final Holocaust!' "

"Now what do you see?"

"The Binah Dragon holds the Lamb with her right hand, while with her left she takes a cup brimming with human lye. Now she pours the contents of the cup upon the Earth!"

"Now what do you see?"

"The very stars, they sing.

'Avalokiteśvara, Great Mother Binah!
Thy Mercy, Thy Mercy!
Wash the Earth with the lye of Jehovah!' "

"Now what do you see?"

"The lye falls to Earth. Two White Boars fly through Heavens from east to west announcing aloud: *'The Plague, the Plague!'* All that the lye touches perishes: *the Earth becomes a Stone Desert!* Only 144,000 who belong to the House of Israel survive: but they flee from the Desert and take refuge in a valley, which will then be flooded by the lye. And the Dragon, and the Boars, are furious *because the Desert Stones still remain*, because the lye has not calcined and dissolved them like the rest of the living beings!"

"Now what do you see?"

"The Dragon then sends the Lamb guarded by his brothers, the twin Boars, to graze on the Earth! But the Earth is barren and the Lamb faints among the Stones, unable to feed!"

"Now what do you see?"

"The Dragon, master of terrible wrath, curses the Stones and the Stone Desert! And she cries out that she will seek the Lamb before the Desert causes its death!"

"Now what do you see?"

"The filthy lye fallen from Heaven, and the muck that it managed to pull up from the Earth, drained into a valley, to the east of the Stone Desert, and formed a great sea! Eden and Paradise, are the names of that sea; and Tartarus and Tharsis, are the names of the Stone Desert!"

"Now what do you see?"

"The Desert has pushed the Lamb toward its shore, which is also the shore of the sea of lye! The Dragon, in Heaven, again cries out that she will help her son, who is between Eden and Tartarus!"

"Now what do you see?"

"The thousand eyes of the Dragon, shining like Suns, concentrate on the Stone Desert and the Stones suffer mortal suffocation. The majority of the Stones soften and melt, and the Desert becomes a huge lake of boiling lava: only the hardest Stones remain in their place, tenaciously maintaining their separate form!"

"Now what do you see?"

"A terrible clamor rises from the Desert and goes up beyond the Dragon: the Stones demand help from the Incognizable against the Lamb, and against the Mother of the Lamb, the Binah Dragon, who has dumped lye from Jehovah on them and has taken the Earth from them, and intends to calcine them in the Desert *for not serving as food for the Lamb!*"

"Now what do you see?"

"A Sign appeared in Heaven: *a Virgin, Blacker than Night,* and the moon under her feet, and on her head a Crown of Thirteen Uncreated Stars!

"She is the Virgin of Agartha who came to help the Stones, in the Name of the Incognizable!"

"Now what do you see?

"The descent of the Virgin produces a mantle of refreshing blackness over the Desert, which had been transformed into a lake of burning lava, and brings immediate relief to the Stones. The Presence of the Virgin refreshes and hardens the Stones again, because she interposes herself with her darkness before the thousand burning eyes of the Dragon! And the Virgin bears a spica in her hand; and she drops the grains upon the Stone Desert; and the Stones that receive the grain become immune to the Fire of Heaven, they can no longer be softened, and they are branded with a Mark, a unique Sign that signifies the black, the hard, and the cold. And the Mark of the Virgin is called the 'Sign of the Vril.'"

"Now what do you see?"

"Now the Lamb is lost among the Darkness and the Hardness, and the Coldness of the Stones. And he calls with desperation to his Mother, the Binah Dragon, because the Stones threaten to strangle his throat *or submerge him* in the sea of lye."

"Now what do you see?"

"The Virgin is with child, and cries out being in labor and in pain to give birth. And another Sign appeared in Heaven: the Dragon of a fiery red, which has a thousand heads and a thousand eyes, and a thousand stars of David on his heads. His tail sweeps away three-fourths of the stars of Heaven and hurls them to the Earth; and they descend upon the sea of lye commanded by the star Thuban. And the Dragon also descends to look after the Lamb and attack the Virgin."

"Now what do you see?"

"The Dragon stood before the Virgin who was about to give birth, so that when she gave birth he might devour her Child. *And She gave birth to a Child of Stone, who is going to rule all the Nations with a Trident of Vajra: Führer is the name of the Child of Stone.* But her son was protected from the Dragon by being mistaken among the Desert Stones. And the Virgin took refuge in the Desert, where she has a place prepared by the

Incognizable to reside for two thousand one hundred and eighty-eight days."

"Now what do you see?"

"There is a war in Heaven. Khristos-Lúcifer, and Capitán Kiev, and the Loyal Siddhas, waged war with the Dragon. The Dragon and his Immortal Angels, his Boars and stars, did not prevail and there was no longer a place found for them in Heaven. And the Great Dragon was *cast down,* he who is called Jehovah and Satan, who organizes the whole Universe; he was *cast down* to the Earth, and his Angels were *cast down* with him."

"Now what do you see?"

"I hear a loud Voice in Heaven saying:

> 'Now the Liberation, and the Power, and the King-
> dom of the Incognizable, and the Empire of His
> Khristos have come, for the enchainer of our Com-
> rades has been *cast down,* the one who marks them
> before the Incognizable day and night. But the Loyal
> Siddhas overcame him because of the Pure Blood
> and because of the Valor of their testimony, and they
> did not love the Warm Life even when faced with
> death. For this reason, fear, you Heavens and you
> who dwell in them. Woe to the Earth and the Sea,
> because the devil has come down to you with great
> wrath, knowing that he has only a short time.'"

"Now what do you see?"

"And when the Dragon saw that he was *cast down* to the Earth, he persecuted the Virgin who gave birth to the Child of Stone. But the two wings of the Great Condor were given to the Virgin, so that she could fly into the Desert to her place, where she would resist *for a cycle, and cycles, and half a cycle,* away from the presence of the Dragon. And the Dragon hurled lye like a River out of his mouth after the woman, so that he might cause her to be swept away. But the Desert helped the Virgin. And the Desert opened its mouth and drank up the new River of lye which the Dragon had hurled out of his mouth; and it drained it into the sea of lye, where the Lamb and the 144,000 were. And the Dragon was enraged with the Virgin, *and went off to make war with the rest of Her children, who exhibit Her Mark and bear the Testimony of Khristos Lúcifer.* And the dragon stood on the sand of the shore of lye."

"Now what do you see?"

"I see a man coming up out of the Desert with the Power of a Beast! He is a being half-man and half-bear, or half-man and half-wolf; at times he is like a bear and at times he is like a wolf; when he must face the Bees of Israel he is like a bear and when he has to fight against the Lamb he is similar to the wolf! He is the Son of the Virgin of Agartha who has grown as a Stone in the Desert; he is the Führer who has returned to wage war against the Lamb and the 144,000! His roar deafens the Earth, and in his wake rise the Desert Stones, those that bear the Sign of the Vril! And the Stones frozen by the Virgin of Agartha are also wolf-men that howl with uncontainable fury!"

I do not exaggerate at all if I assure that the roar that arose at that moment from the place where Uncle Kurt was, monotonously asking "now what do you see?" *made the earth tremble.* I was describing what I was seeing on the surface of the *aqua vitae* in the carboy, but my words had acquired a prophetic formality that was directly taking shape in my unconscious. For a long time I was no longer reasoning what I was saying: I was simply expressing what was filling my mind, which at that point I could not explain whether I was really seeing it or imagining it. What, of course, was not a product of my imagination, was the transmutation of Uncle Kurt and his bestial roars and howls; or the two ectoplasmic Boars that, ever more clear and evident, were materializing over the cadavers of the two Oriental assassins.

To the roars of the bear-man, the Boars were responding with the accursed bee humming that I now also knew; but when the wolf-man was howling, the Boars were trembling with panic, their hair standing on end in terror and growling with desperation. And I, upon perceiving what was going on around me, was trying to keep my eyes hypnotically fixed on the *matrix* with the acid and the hearts, contemplating visions that, as fantastic as they might be, were less terrible than the Reality of Belicena Villca's Chacra.

"Now what do you see?" Uncle Kurt's voice clearly asked.

"I see an enormous army advancing, formed by those who bear the Mark of the Virgin and are like unto the Beast, the Enemies of the Lamb. And I see that they are led by the Führer, who is like unto a furious wolf, and accompanied by the Virgin, who flies over them bearing the banner of the Sign of the Vril and of the Spica. And the Army of wolves approaches the sea of lye! And the Lamb, and the 144,000 members of the Chosen People, settle on a White Island situated toward the center of the sea of lye, which had been formed with the summit of Mount Zion! Heavenly Jerusalem and Chang Shambhala are the names of that island."

"Now what do you see?"

"The Lamb, standing on Mount Zion, and with him 144,000 who have his name and the name of His Father written on their foreheads. And I hear voices from Heaven, which sound with the harmony of manifold Nature. And they sing a *new* song before the Throne of Jehovah, before the ten Sephiroth, before the Elders of Israel, and before the Shekhinah; and no one is able learn the Song of Creation except the 144,000 who had been purchased from the Earth. These are the ones who do not know the love of the woman because they are sodomite Priests. These are the ones who follow the Lamb wherever He goes. These constitute the Hierarchy of Souls, that range from man, to Jehovah and the Lamb. They do not know the Truth of Creation. They are perfect animal-men."

"Now what do you see?"

"I now observe a Time before the fall of the Dragon: one sees upon the Earth *the men who already had the Sign of the Vril* and some Angels of the Dragon who threaten them from Heaven. One of them, the one who flies highest in Heaven, carries the Gospel of the Lamb and announces the Holocaust of Fire to those who live on the Earth, and to every Nation, Tribe, language, and People, and says with a loud voice:

> 'Fear Jehovah and give Him glory, because the hour of His judgment has come; worship Him *who made Heaven and Earth, and Sea* and springs of waters.'

"Another Angel, a second, followed, saying:
> *'Fallen, fallen is Babylon the great, she who made all nations drink of the wine of the Universal Empire.'*

"Then another angel, a third one, followed him, saying with a loud voice:

> 'If anyone worships the Beast and its image and receives its Mark on his forehead or on his hand, *he also will drink of the wine of the wrath of Jehovah, pure wine, concentrated, human lye, poured into the cup of His anger;* and he will be tormented *with Fire and*

Brimstone in the presence of the Holy Angels and in the presence of the Lamb. *And the smoke of their torment ascends forever and ever;* they have no rest *day and night,* those who worship the Beast and his image, and whoever receives the mark of his name.'

"Here is the perseverance of the Chosen People who keep the commandments of Jehovah and their faith in the Messiah!'"

"Now what do you see?"

"Another Immortal Angel: He points to the city that is on Mount Zion, in the midst of the sea of lye, and says:

'Behold the bride, the wife of the Lamb!'

"This Angel speaks for those who worship the Lamb, and promises them salvation from the wolf-men hiding themselves in the City of Jehovah. Thus he speaks to them:

'There shall come down a city from Heaven, upon Mount Zion, from Jehovah. Its brilliance was like a very valuable stone, like a stone of crystal-clear jasper. It had a great and high wall, with twelve gates, and at the gates twelve angels; and names were written on the gates, which are *the names of the twelve tribes of the sons of Israel. There were three gates on the east, three gates on the north, three gates on the south, and three gates on the west.* And the wall of the city had twelve foundation stones, and on them were the twelve names of the twelve Apostles of the Lamb.'

"The one who spoke has a gold measuring rod to measure the city, its gates, and its wall.

'The city is laid out as a square, and its length is as great as the width.'

"And he measured the city with the rod, twelve thousand stadia; its length, width, and height are equal. And he measured its wall, 144 cubits, by human measurements, which are also angelic measurements. And the Angel says:

'The material of the wall will be jasper; and the city will be pure gold, like clear glass. The foundation stones of the city wall will be decorated with every kind of precious stone. The first foundation stone will be jasper; the second, sapphire; the third, chalcedony; the fourth, emerald; the fifth, sardonyx; the sixth, sardius; the seventh, chrysolite; the eighth, beryl; the ninth, topaz; the tenth, chrysoprase; the eleventh, jacinth; the twelfth, amethyst. And the twelve gates will be twelve pearls; each one of the gates will be a single pearl, like shining crystal. There will be no temple in it, for Elohim, Jehovah Sabaoth, and the Lamb will be its temple. And the city *will not need the Sun or the Moon to shine on it*, for *the Glory Sephirah of Jehovah will illuminate it*, and its lamp will be the Lamb. *The nations will walk by its light, and the kings of the earth will bring their glory into it. In the daytime* (for there will be no night there) *its gates will never be closed*; and they will bring the glory and the honor of the nations into it; *and nothing unclean, not consecrated by the Priests of Israel,* shall ever come into it, nor those who bear the Abominable Sign, *but only those whose names are written* in the Lamb's *book of life.'* "

"Now what do you see?"

"A River of living water, out of which all created things flow, coming from the *Kether* Trunk of Jehovah and of the Lamb. The Angel pronounces the last words:

'In the middle of its street, on either side of the River, there will be a Tree of Life, bearing twelve kinds of fruit, yielding its fruit every month; and the leaves of the Pomegranate Tree will serve to heal the Nations from the River of the Living Water. And the leaves of the Pomegranate Tree will serve to cure the Nations from the sin against Jehovah. There will no longer be any curse; and the throne of Jehovah and of the Lamb will be in it, and His bond-servants will serve Him; they will see His face, and His name will be on their foreheads. And there will no longer be any night, or infinite blackness, and they will not have need of the light of a lamp nor the light of the sun, because Jehovah Elohim will illuminate them; and they will reign forever and ever.'* "

"Now what do you see?"

"I see the Final Battle. I see the Führer and his army of wolf-men storm the Island of Zion, and surprise the Heavenly

Jerusalem, which is Chang Shambhala, and cause great slaughter among its dwellers. Not even Thuban and the three-fourths of Heaven, garrisoned, succeed in stopping the furious herd! The Lamb and the 144,000 Priests are cornered in the Accursed City, *constructed with the body of the Dragon!* And they die by the thousands: they prefer to die rather than see the Sign of the Vril of the wolf-men! And the Dragon-City palpitates and writhes, unable to shake off the wolf-men. And the immortal eyes of the Dragon shed countless tears; tears that roll toward the fourfold Wailing Wall, tears of Pity for the Children of Israel. But the wolf-men do not relent and sink their fangs into the Children of Israel, into the Lamb, and into the Dragon. And the Virgin of Agartha nails her banner into the Wailing Wall, which is like unto the Heart of Binah, the mistress of all hearts: yea, in the Heart of Avalokiteśvara has been planted the Sign of the Vril, the Mark that causes the Black, the Hard, and the Cold of the Stones, and down the Wailing Wall flow Her tears as if brought forth from a miraculous waterfall. And a hard and icy darkness falls upon Zion: it is the Cold Death of the Virgin; the Death that snatches the warmth from the hearts of the Lamb and the 144,000 Saints of Israel; the Death that those who see in the darkness unleash, the wolf-men of Stone who form the Army of the Führer."

"Now what do you see?"

"The Final Battle continues on Earth, but I can no longer see what occurs there, *for I see that the White Boars flee in panic to hide themselves in Heaven: they are pursued by the Wolf-man-Pack-Army-of-Stone! But only a fourth of the stars are left in Heaven!*"

"*The moment has arrived! The End is equal to the Beginning!*" Uncle Kurt exclaimed in surprise.

Chapter XV

I was startled by Uncle Kurt's unexpected words. However, he then asked:

"Now what do you see?"

"The twin Boars have gone up to the starry Heavens seeking the Dragon. But the Dragon is not in Heaven but in the Final Battle. And the Boars have become stars again, and have situated themselves under the feet of the Virgin, near the Raven. And in the sky many constellations are missing, like a picture book from which many pages have been torn out."

"Now what do you see?"

"The stars of Heaven, *all those that were left,* abandon their posts and revolve around the two Boar-stars. It is the *chaos primordiale,* the massa confusa!"

"I will project the Sign of the Origin on the massa confusa!" shouted Uncle Kurt. It seemed that he was now very close to me, behind my back. I was imagining his empty black sockets, deep and infinite, peering into the alchemist's vessel, of which shining surface would irremediably house *what he was: the Sign of the Origin, the Sign of the Vril, the Mark of the Virgin, the Sign of Lúcifer, the Sign of Shiva.* I imagined it, for I was not wishing to look at it and see, as before, Frya Death, the Bear-Man, and the Wolf-man.

In the *matrix,* the surface of the *Sulphur Philosophorum* was showing the image of a whirlpool of *lumen naturae* that were revolving around the twin stars, the *monads of Bera and Birsha.* When the first Rune reflected on them, they lost a great part of their brightness and began to solidify. And so they continued, darkening and *solidifying,* as the following Runes were succeeding each other. And when, at last, the thirteen Runes had been plasmated, the two stars underwent a metamorphosis and were transformed into *flowers of Stone.* Then, as if Uncle Kurt had asked me the question, I described aloud what I was seeing:

"The stars are now two flowers of stone; they are two *padmas* or lotuses: Esther is the name of those Stones. And the thirteen Runes move and associate with each other in an incomprehensible way. And the thirteen Runes form a Sign that disintegrates the whirlpool, the *chaos confusum,* and replaces it with the most impenetrable darkness; only the flowers of stone have remained in the *Sulphur Philosophorum:* and now they *fall* to the bottom of the *matrix. Opus consumatum est!*"[9]

"You now possess two *lapides philosophorum!*" said Uncle Kurt. "You have completed the Work, through the Virgin, *because you have seen the Work!* And you have received the *descensus spiritus sancti creatoris!* You are just like Me, and I am just like you! *Naturalissimum et perfectissimum opus est generare tale quale ipsum est!*"[10] Suddenly, I came to realize that the roaring, growling, and barking had been silenced. I brusquely turned around and looked for Uncle Kurt with my eyes: I did not see him anywhere. Instead, I observed two white spots that were moving away toward the sky. I sharpened my eyes and thought to distinguish two wild boars that were fleeing in panic, their fur bristling and grunting in terror. Nature had calmed down and the ectoplasmic clouds were no longer over the cadavers of the Oriental assassins. The Boars were the Souls of Bera and Birsha who were fleeing toward the Beginning of Time! Had the plan succeeded, after all, despite the intervention of Avalokiteśvara? How had Uncle Kurt managed it? How did he manage that the Pity of the *Dea Mater* did not calm the panic of the Immortals Bera and Birsha? Yes, now I was remembering: *with their hearts in the Sulphur Philosophorum, with their Souls in the vessel of alchemical projections, he had taken Bera and Birsha toward the future, toward the Final Battle, when the Dragon would lose its Power; and there they had suffered more terror than that of the death of their physical bodies by our gunshots.*

Of all possible Futures, it is feasible to hope for one that corresponds to the World *"that Wothan affirms from the Origin,"* the World that constitutes *"the Reality of the Blood of Tharsis."* To that Future, in which Spirit will triumph over the Potencies of Matter, the Souls of Bera and Birsha had been alchemistically carried: to the Battle of Chang Shambhala, to the Final Battle; to the Defeat of Chang Shambhala, to the Defeat of Zion; and the Terror of the End of Chang Shambhala, of the End of Zion, caused the return of Bera and Birsha to the Beginning of Time, to the point where all possible Futures are settled and where Chang Shambhala or Zion has not determined its End before the End of Time. Because that which I

9. *"The Work is realized."*

10. *"The most natural and perfect work is to generate its like."*

saw in the *matrix* is an Uncreated Future, not foreseen by the Creator, only possible in the World of the Blood of Tharsis, in the World of the Reality of the Führer: *and Uncle Kurt had demonstrated to have blind faith in that Uncreated Future, in which the spiritual men would rise like Wild Beasts against the Lamb and the "144,000" Priests of Israel.* I believe that the success of the alchemical transmutation, and the terror infused into the Immortals Bera and Birsha, were fundamentally owed to that unshakable faith that Uncle Kurt was professing for the Führer and his Future.

Although, he was strangely affirming that the Work was mine. But I was harboring the certainty that it was he who marked the Hot Stones, the Souls of Bera and Birsha, monads above the Primordial Chaos, with the Sign of the Origin, with the "Abominable Sign" that the Demons were fearing. And their Souls had hastened the Stone of the Beginning, the *Lapis Ignis,* and now *they were to be at the Beginning. In a panic, at the Beginning:* the goal of the plan. I forgot the Pity of Avalokiteśvara, but *thanks* to Uncle Kurt the objective had been achieved.

By the way, where was Uncle Kurt? I was beginning to worry, when I heard his voice: it was coming from above, and was sounding ironic and tranquil.

"I was right, Neffe: *Immortals cannot die.* And you were right: *their fear would make them flee toward the Beginning.* It is a tie, don't you think? I must now go after them, Bear against Bees, Wolf against Pigs, I have to pursue them to the Beginning: *only then will the End be equal to the Beginning, Potentiality will become Actuality, the Possible will become Real, the Work will be Present between the End and the Beginning; and you will be able to fulfill your mission.*"

I knew what was occurring: Uncle Kurt had elevated himself with the daiva dogs until putting himself out of my reach. His decision was, then, irrevocable. I felt myself dying from sadness and desolation. My legs went slack. I got a lump in my throat. Nevertheless, I cried out with helplessness:

"Uncle Kurt, don't go! Don't leave me here *alone!*"

Then I heard the thunderous guffaw that my uncle was emitting with inevitable spontaneity: it was not a mockery, but the expression of his mood.

"And you are the one who was questioning my *stubbornness,* when I was resisting to stay *alone* in this Hell, after the Second

War?" he asked laughing. "Well, remember that I endured 35 years: you will have to endure much less. Come on, be valiant, Neffe Arturo! Or will I have to ask you, like Belicena Villca, if you are capable of being a Kshatriya? But I know that you comprehend why I do it: *it is part of the Führer's Strategy. The hunt that I now initiate will soon be imitated by thousands of Wolf-men-of-Stone. I will have the Honor of determining the End of the Age of the Boar and the Bee, just as the Spica of the Virgin will destroy the Age of the Dove.* You are like Me and I am like you. And if I am, you are: *that was the great Strategy of the Von Sübermann Stirp,* which we could not know until now; *the secret of the Tulkus.* Today, the Sign of the Origin is on you, *on your earlobes; and those who have the Pure Blood will see it.* That is why the *lapis philosophorum* adopted the form of *flowers of stone:* because *such lotuses are the adornment of the earrings of Avalokiteśvara, the earrings that the Compassionate One places on the ears of those marked with the Sign of the Origin, in order to cover the Sign of the Origin.* You have obtained them in the *matrix* of projections because your own Sign of the Origin *has been uncovered: its covers have fallen! And that is the Great Work! You are now the Sign of the Origin, and you are in the Origin of the Eternal and Uncreated Spirit, the same as I!* I could never see the Sign of the Origin, remember?; but *we both saw it today: you in me, and I in you, in the projection on the Hot Stone.* Separated, we would never have seen it. That is why it was good to be with you, Neffe; because together we will fulfill the mission of our Stirp: *we will do it for Honor, since we saw the Origin, and we have the Origin, and we can return to the Origin when we want to.* You no longer need me; nor do you need anything or anyone. Farewell Neffe; we will meet again during the Final Battle. Heil Hitler!"

"Heil Hitler!" I mechanically responded, while the roar of an indescribable Wild Beast was thundering through space and an unearthly gust of wind, icy, was hitting me like a lash and shaking the trees and kicking up clouds of dust.

I directed my sight in the direction that the Boars had fled, that is, to the south, and I swear that I observed Uncle Kurt for the last time. Or at least I received that impression. Because I saw, or believed to see, contrasted by the starry firmament, a Beast that was running after two bright stars that were running away in dread: now it was looking like a Bear, now a Wolf; and its roars and howls were becoming less loud until they were completely extinguished. *I felt sane: it was The Plague that was moving away.*

In thought, still looking toward the Southern Cross, I recalled Belicena Villca's Letter, the part where Rabbi Benjamin was referring to Bera the Mystery of the weakness of the Chosen People: Jehovah warned the People of Israel about four kinds of evils, before which they would be **weak:** "And I will appoint over them four kinds of doom," declares Jehovah: "the sword to kill, the dogs to drag away, and the birds of the sky and the animals of the earth to devour and destroy" *[Jeremiah 15:3].* There, on the floor of the Chacra, were lying the lifeless human bodies of Bera and Birsha: they had been **weak,** strategically **weak.** And in their case, the symbols warned by Jehovah had intervened, all four, at the same time:

Sword: the Wise Sword of the House of Tharsis.

Dogs: the daiva dogs.

Birds: the Virgin of Agartha, and every Kālibur Dame, whose Infinite Blackness *devours* the light of the Souls.

Wild Beasts: the *Berserkr* and the *Ulfheðnar,* that is to say, the Bear-men and the Wolf-men, of Frya Stone.

And the "remedies" proposed by Bera were of no use to them this time: the Peace of Gold, the Illusion of Rage, the Illusion of Earth, and the Illusion of Heaven.

We had won the match against the Demons, but I never ever, to this day, saw Uncle Kurt again.

Chapter XVI

ext, a phenomenon occurred that I have decided to expose separately, due to the fact that I have not yet found a convincing explanation for it. As I said, I was still looking at the Sky, toward the Southern Cross and thinking about the things that he mentioned, trying to master the nostalgia for the departure of Uncle Kurt, attempting to overcome the nervous depression.

The blow was violent, forceful, in the center of the skull, a few centimeters above the place where Uncle Kurt applied to me his accurate hit. I fell struck to the ground, seeing stars that were not exactly the product of an alchemical process, *but aware that something had fallen from the Sky on my head, something of small size and considerable weight.* I sat up, still dazed, and began to look around with the help of the pen flashlight. It did not take long to find the projectile, the cause of the bump, the painful effects of which lasted several days and of which scar I keep: as it is easy to imagine, it was a stone.

But that was an artistically carved stone, and it was evident that it was belonging to a larger whole, from which it was fractured. *It was the hand of a child of Stone, amputated at the wrist, expressing the Bala[11] Mudra,[12] the Internal Salutation of the House of Tharsis: the index finger and thumb were stretched out forming a right angle; and the middle, ring, and little fingers were bent over the palm of the hand.*

When finding the stone hand, I instantaneously remembered the Thirty-third Day of Belicena Villca's Letter, and then I checked it by re-reading that paragraph again and again: on that day Belicena was narrating the extermination of her Stirp carried out by Bera and Birsha, by transmuting the non-initiated members of the House of Tharsis, like those of my family, into *bitumen of Judea.* It was then that the Noyo, Noso of Tharsis, arrived at the church of the Virgin of the Grotto, in Turdes, to rescue the image from the generalized plundering of Lugo de Braga. And it was upon fulfilling this task when he verified that the hand that was expressing the Bala Vrune had been amputated from the Child of Stone. *But such disappearance*

---

11. Strength

12. Gesture

happened in the thirteenth century, seven hundred years ago: it was at least seeming adventurous, if not absurd, to relate this fact with that one. And yet, against all logical arguments, to me the accident was seeming suggestive. And I have not changed my mind: I mounted the little hand on a silver *bail*,[13] added a chain to it, and hung it around my neck. How it fell on my head, or from where, I do not know; whether it is the same hand from the thirteenth century, I do not know either; and what it means that it fell against my head at that moment, is something that belongs to the field of the most obscure enigmas. But the piece pleases me and I will carry it with me until the End.

---

13. The part of a necklace that connects the pendant to the chain.

Chapter XVII

hat remains for me to add to this Epilogue, or Prologue is very little.

After the shock that Uncle Kurt's departure undoubtedly produced in me, evidenced in the abnormal serenity with which I began to reflect on the symbols of the Sword, Dogs, Birds, and Wild Beasts, and getting over the painful effect of the blow to the head, I began to become aware of the reality and my nervous system entered into a violent crisis. Inside I was feeling that I was falling apart, and I tried to keep myself armed outside, shouting a thousand insults and swears against all our enemies, and from which in the end our Comrades and allies were not excluded: Belicena Villca, her son Noyo, Capitán Kiev, the Loyal Siddhas, the Führer, and even the Incognizable, were encompassed by my irreproducible profanities. I will not justify myself, for known events explain this irrational reaction. How was my will not going to be broken, if in the span of four days my family was atrociously murdered, my entire family, close and distant relatives, and the only survivor outside of me, Uncle Kurt, had just left never to return?

I became crazy. I was hurling insults and impotently kicking the cadavers of the Oriental assassins. With irrational aggressiveness, I was about to empty the clip of the useless machine gun into those diabolical bodies, when some moans coming from the interior providentially brought me back to reality. I was not alone! I suddenly remembered that during the attack we had heard screams of pain.

With my face still distorted by fury, some demented glint in my eyes, and pistol in hand, I decidedly entered into the house, causing the consequent alarm of the person who was tied up on the dining room table. It was Segundo, the Indian descendant of the People of the Moon, whom Belicena Villca was mentioning in her Letter, and whom I had seen a couple of times as a visitor at the Salta Neuropsychiatric Hospital.

He was looking terrible, because Bera and Birsha had torn out the nails of his fingers and toes; however, he ought to be grateful to the Gods, and to Operation Boomerang, because the Demons lacked the time to cut off his tongue and ears, and empty his eyes, and finally skin him or slit his throat. When I untied him and asked if there was a first-aid kit, the Indian regained his speech.

"And the two men?" he cautiously asked.

"They were not men," I gruffly responded, "but the Demons Bera and Birsha. They're both dead, out there: we killed them with the shots that you heard. And now my uncle is pursuing them to the Bottom of the Central Abyss of the Universe, to an infernal place from which they may never return."

Now I realize that such an answer was improper and absurd to offer to an unknown Indian who would possibly not have the slightest idea what I was talking about. But I was suffering from the effects of shock and crisis and was not stopping to think about what I was saying. On the contrary, I was constantly cursing myself for all my errors: for being the cause that the Demons discovered the World and the address where my family was living; because in the plan of attack I forgot to consider the compassionate action of Avalokiteśvara; and for not heeding the bad feeling that Uncle Kurt's farewell in Cerrillos produced in me, before levitating with the daiva dogs: *Uncle Kurt knew what was going to happen, that we were going to be tested by the Maternal Passion of Avalokiteśvara, who would mercifully defend the Immortals, and that in all probability he should set out in pursuit of the Demons, to keep their fear awake; and that is why he wanted to say goodbye before going into operations!* And I was the imbecile who went through with the plan to the end, regardless of anything, underestimating Uncle Kurt's capacity! Now I was alone, more alone than Uncle Kurt was in his exile, even though he affirmed the contrary to console me and give me courage!

Such were the thoughts that were occupying my mind when I responded to the Indian in the above-mentioned manner. Fortunately, I was not entirely alone; the Indian repeated, with even greater caution:

"Beraj and Birchaj?"

It is possible that only at that moment did it dawn on me that the Indian was real.

"Beraj... ?" I repeated, trying to remember where I had heard that pronunciation before. Then I remembered Belicena Villca's Letter and the history of the People of the Moon. "You know them too, of course! Those sons of bitches exterminated your family, just like the House of Tharsis and my own Stirp!" I exclaimed with exaggerated euphoria.

"And how do you know that?" asked the Indian at the height of astonishment. "You're not from the Army?"

"Ha-ha-ha," I heartily laughed, upon discovering the impression that the commando uniform was giving. "No, man, no. I don't belong to the Armed Forces. The one who was a member of the Army was Noyo Villca, as you well know. Do you not remember me? I am Arturo Siegnagel, the psychiatrist who was treating Belicena Villca in Salta. She recounted everything to me in an extensive letter: for example, I know that you descend from the People of the Moon, who were inhabiting Koaty Island on Lake Titicaca, and that your remote ancestors were residing in Scandinavia, in the country of King Kollman, of the lineage of Skiold."

"Ah, the Doctor. Yes, I remember. I was aware that Doña Belicena was writing a letter with data about the Casa of Tharsis, but I was not knowing who its addressee would be."

"And you say," he added, "that these torturers are the same Beraj and Birchaj who guided, more than six hundred years ago, the malones[14] of the Diaguita-Hebrew Indians, under the command of Chieftain Cari, in the invasion of Island of the Sun?"

"They were," I corrected him. "Indeed, they were the same, although perhaps they used other bodies; that I don't know with exactitude. But what's certain is that three months ago they assassinated Belicena Villca in the Hospital, and only four days ago they did away with my whole family; because of these damned Demons, we only have three survivors left from three spiritual Stirps: Noyo Villca, from the House of Tharsis; Segundo, from the House of Skiold; and Arturo Siegnagel, from the Von Sübermann House. Belicena Villca requests of me in her Letter to seek out Noyo Villca in Córdoba, and assures me that you will help me. She also recommends me to be very careful with Bera and Birsha, who were powerful Demons, but you can see, in spite of the blows that they gave us, and thanks to the help of the Gods, we were able to finish them off for the time being. There will be other Demons that will no doubt pursue us, and a thousand unknown dangers, but it is improbable that Bera and Birsha will return to the World of the Blood of Tharsis; *however, they will continue existing in the other Worlds of Illusion; and woe to those spiritual men*

---

14. A rapid and surprise attack by a large party of mounted warriors against an enemy group.

who do not soon find the World of the House of Tharsis! What do you think, Segundo? Will you help me?"

"Of course I will! Know, Dr. Siegnagel, that She was a Queen for those of my Race: her wishes are orders for me. She asked me not to go to the Salta Hospital anymore because she was under surveillance and was suspecting that they were going to kill her: and I carried out her orders to the letter; I did not go to Salta anymore and I did not respond to the correspondence from the Hospital, the Judge, the Police, etc. *And no one came here because this house is very hard to find.* Your powers must be very great to have arrived this way, by surprise, and to be able *to kill* the Demons. You have saved my life, and surely you have spared me a previous terrible suffering! But I don't know up until what point to thank you, since, as you will realize, I am already fed up with living."

I was perfectly understanding him, since I too was fed up with living; and if I was going on, like that Germanic Indian, it would exclusively be for Honor, because it was an Honor to stay to fulfill the mission that the Gods, who were directing the Essential War, had assigned to one, and because after the Final Battle, once the accounts with the Potencies of Matter had been settled, we would definitively return to the Origin of the Uncreated Spirit. I saw Segundo's face distorted from pain and I ran to an adjoining storehouse to get the first-aid kit that was in the glove compartment of a pick-up truck. With patience, I disinfected the twenty fingers and toes and was bandaging them one by one. I was carrying the sedative tablets with me, and I made him swallow two: four milligrams that would make him sleep until noon.

Before concluding the cure, he was already nodding off, so I took him to his room, making him step with his heels, and left him lying on his humble carob-wood bed.

I warmed up coffee, and drank it more calmly, seated in a chair in the kitchen. The encounter with Segundo had calmed me down quite a bit and I was now meditating on the next steps to take. On the table I deposited the carboy of acid, transmuted as a very black liquid but with a light density. To recover the roses of stone, the Avalokiteśvara earrings, I would pour that unusable substance into the sink, and neutralize the residual acidity with a powerful concentrated detergent that I discovered in a cupboard. A minute later, the Esther earrings were in my pocket, already empty of weapons. Certainly, we exaggerated the artillery, and were now resting on the table, the Itaka, fifty cartridges, the machine pistol with its uncomfortable underarm holster, its magazines, the ten fragmentation grenades, the TNT bombs, and the hunting knife. Nonchalantly and discreetly, I made sure of Segundo's deep sleep, and decided to take care of eliminating the remains of the Oriental assassins. Equipped with a powerful 12-Volt flashlight, I explored the surroundings of the Chacra.

I then verified that, in effect, the construction of the house was following the layout of the ancient Pukara of Tharsy, and that the perimetric fortress was reduced to a low wall, of no more than one meter, to disguise its function of fortifying a liberated plaza. In its interior was still existing the very ancient cromlech, the stones of which were forming an enormous circle, in the area of which the plan of the Chacra was easily able to fit. But the fate of the Menhir of Tharsy, the one planted by the White Atlanteans to establish the Blood Pact with the Stirp of Tharsis and to determine its familial mission, was intriguing to me. Taking the diameters of the Cromlech, I looked for the center at its intersection, and I verified with intrigue that that central place was inside the Chacra. Finally, there were no doubts that the central site was inside a huge hermetically sealed shed. I cut the chains and padlocks with a suitable bolt cutter, and opened the doors of the shed: incredibly, after centuries and millennia, the Menhir of Tharsy was still in its place of origin. It was of green stone and was showing at its base the millenary apacheta of Vultan: *purihuaca voltan guanancha unanchan huañuy.* Over the apacheta was, for four hundred and forty three years, the Wise Sword of the House of Tharsis, guarded, as in Huelva, by tireless Noyo and Vraya descendants of Lito of Tharsis. In the face of that attitude of respect and trust in the Loyal Gods, assumed over millennia of patient guarding, what were my current anxieties, my selfish anguishes, meaning? The imposing Menhir, and its rustic stone altar, had the virtue of making me ashamed of myself, of my human weaknesses, and of strengthening my will to continue until the End.

With all the vain and cruel efforts made in the past by the Demons Bera and Birsha, the hatred that that Chacra would arouse in them, at which the members of the House of Tharsis lived outside of their reach, preserving the Stone of Venus of the Wise Sword, comes as no surprise. But they arrived late, they always arrived late to America: they failed to exterminate the Skiold lineage with the Diaguita-Hebrews, or with the Spaniards of Diego de Almagro, Diego de Rojas, and so many others; neither did the murder of Belicena Villca do them any good because she wisely misled them; nor did the extermination of the Von Sübermanns allow them to finish off Uncle Kurt. America had turned out to be fatal for them! They did not know where Noyo Villca with the Wise Sword was and wanted to take revenge on the Indian Segundo, to sacrifice him by means of horrible torture before departing from the unpredictable World of the House of Tharsis. And they had been attacked and killed when they were least expecting it. Like a boomerang, their own blows came back against them; *like in a Jiu-Jitsu strike,* their enemies took advantage of their own moves and turned their forces against them.

There were all kinds of tools in the storehouse that was storing the pick-up truck. I went there, took a wide shovel, and began to look for a suitable place to dig the graves. Fifty meters from the house was growing a dense reed bed of tacuaras[15] that seemed to me would be the ideal spot: it would be difficult to penetrate the layer of roots, but after a few days no one would discover the slightest trace of the removal. I returned to the house twice and loaded the accursed cadavers into a wheelbarrow to make transport easier; on the last trip I also carried a machete to clear the path. I looked at the clock in the house and saw that it was reading 03:00 hours on the 23rd of April. Mine, on the other hand, was showing 01:30 hours on the 26th of April. Logically, I synchronized my watch with the local dial.

So, then, at 06:00 hours, three hours later, I finished the macabre task of burying the mangled cadavers of the Oriental assassins. It was already dawning and I was feeling exhausted, psychically and physically drained. And there were still several things to do, unavoidable matters that were not admitting delay. One of them was to carry out the destruction of the assassins' black car, in order to avoid police tracking: but, for that, I was needing to count on Segundo's help.

I drank a new cup of coffee and then dedicated myself to pouring buckets of soapy water on the patio, to eliminate the traces of blood, a precaution that, more than to avoid police

---

15. Type of bamboo.

investigations, was aiming to frustrate the still more terrible action of the Tucumán flies. At daylight, I discovered next to a tree, fifteen paces away from the door of the house, the jacket and all of Uncle Kurt's weapons: evidently, he had abandoned them before departing, when he silently called the daiva dogs. At that moment, I thought that my will would break again. But I overcame and joined those objects with the rest of my equipment.

I could no longer continue dressed as a commando, especially if I had to go outside the Chacra, so I devoted myself to perform a prolix inspection of the interior of the house. I ruled out the Indian's clothes, because of his size, appreciably smaller than mine, and I trusted that Noyo Villca had a larger build and that his clothes were preserved. At last I came upon his room, after passing by that of the deceased Belicena, and found, in fact, a stocked closet: I discovered a pair of jeans, more or less my size, and a similar shirt. I decided to keep Maidana's boots, and I made two large packages with the weapons and combat clothes: I only left the four TNT bombs unwrapped.

In a shoebox, of the vilest cardboard, I deposited the nefarious Dorje, the Scepter of Power that Rigden Jyepo delivered to the Demons Bera and Birsha, together with the stone padmas, the Esther earrings of Avalokiteśvara.

And then, when I had concluded those minor jobs, I headed toward the black car to calm the understandable curiosity that it aroused in me from the moment I learned of its existence.

Seen from a distance, there was no doubt that it was a classic North American limousine. However, upon inspecting it up close, confusion was arising from not being able to establish either the make or model, like the Salta police officers were saying; because it had a mark, and well-visible: *"Aviant."* But who knew that make? To what country was it belonging? Immediately, the suspicion assailed me that the automobile was not from this World, that it was coming from a Reality parallel to that of ours, where "Gentlemen" like Bera and Birsha moved around in *"Aviant"* cars. Was it really an automobile anyway? Yes, it was. An authentic and excellent luxury car, apparently just out of the factory. I popped the hood and observed a powerful eight-cylinder *"V"* engine. The keys were in; I started it up and it ran without problems. And it was useless to check its interior because the Demons were not carrying anything with them, no papers, no baggage: nothing at all, which was indicating that the possibility of being stopped or questioned on the roads was not entering into their plans; *or that they were not in any way driving on the roads and routes of human civilization.*

At 08:30 hours, I leaned back in an armchair in the dining room and slept undisturbed until 13:30 hours. I prepared more coffee, toasted bread, and woke up Segundo for the late breakfast. He was astonished upon finding out that I worked all night and that no traces of the assassins' death were remaining. While he was drinking coffee, I checked his wounds; his feet were especially interesting me: they were very swollen:

"Do you think you'll be able to drive the pick-up?" I asked.

"I'll do whatever is necessary," he valiantly said. "No matter the pain."

"It'll be nightfall," I explained. "You'll have to drive about fifteen or twenty kilometers to get rid of the assassins' car. But first I'll bring you some medicine and painkillers: just tell me where the nearest pharmacy is."

It was in Tafí del Valle, five kilometers away. At 15 hours, after roasting a chicken and eating it together, I went to the pharmacy in the pick-up and bought the anti-tetanus vaccine, syringes, anti-inflammatories, and painkillers.

At 19:00 hours we left the Chacra. Segundo would go ahead, in the pick-up, and I would follow him in the *Aviant*. We would take secondary roads, normally untransited, because the success of the maneuver would depend on no one seeing the black automobile, no one who could report it to the police; and least of all the police, who would already have its description.

But everything went well. Segundo, with his bandaged fingers and toes, and barefoot, since he could not wear alpargatas, was deftly driving the truck in the direction of the Sierra del Aconquija. We crossed the Tafí del Valle River, the Blanco River, and entered onto an almost impassable road that was going up to the summit of Cerro Ovejería. I had to perform feats with the enormous limousine in order to round the sharp curves of the cornice road. Finally, a few kilometers before the summit, we came upon the ideal place: the edge of an abyss a thousand meters deep or more. There I parked the black car, while Segundo was driving the pick-up several meters backward: the path was so narrow that we would have to backtrack hundreds of meters until finding a widening that allowed us to turn around.

Segundo's backing up was necessary to prevent a possible collapse of the road, which would leave the pick-up isolated and unable to get down the Cerro. Because I was planning to blow up the *Aviant* and that was very likely to occur, as it actually occurred.

I poured the contents of a ten-liter can of gasoline inside the car; I programmed the electronic detonators with a time of five minutes; and I placed a bomb on the engine block, another on the interior of the cabin, another in the trunk, and another underneath the chassis. Then I closed the hood, the doors, and the trunk, and ran toward the pick-up, which was waiting for me a hundred meters farther back.

The explosion of the four kilograms of TNT was impressive in those mountains, generating prolonged echoes. The automobile would never be found, for only remnants of it remained scattered over hundreds of meters of inaccessible precipice. When the explosion ceased, we approached a little closer, and made sure that this would happen, for the road disappeared where the car was parked, and the avalanche of stones had dragged the larger debris to the bottom of the gorge, burying it forever.

I remained ten days at Belicena Villca's Chacra, during which I conversed much with Segundo and we agreed on the future steps.

I referred him to the last parts of Belicena Villca's Letter and explained to him that I had certain indications about the possible residence of Noyo Villca: it was all consisting in locating the mysterious Order of Tirodal Knights and their Pontiff, Nimrod de Rosario. Since a chapter had closed in my life and there would be no turning back, I could only continue the adventure and initiate the search for the Order in the Province of Córdoba. Segundo manifested his decision to accompany me on that mission. Besides also being a Hyperborean Initiate, a disciple of Belicena Villca, and possessing a logical spiritual interest in the matter, the Indian, who was fifty years of age, had known Noyo Villca since childhood and would do whatever possible to see him again or lend him his help.

We thus designed a simple plan destined to solve the last problems that were remaining before finally moving ourselves to Córdoba. In the Chacra there was a fortune in Inga gold, to which Belicena Villca alluded in her Letter. Segundo showed me the secret hiding place, near the Menhir, where they were keeping 250 kg of gold in ingots: originally, the Indian explained to me, the gold was constituting the tableware of the Quilla Princess, because the Ingas were not giving monetary value to said metal; already in Tucumán, and to avoid possible surprises, the descendants of Lito of Tharsis melted all the utensils in the seventeenth century and hid the ingots where they still were. The family never had need for that reserve, but we could take whatever we wanted, because such was Belicena Villca's will.

However, to my understanding that wealth was belonging to Noyo of Tharsis and it was not advisable to touch it for the moment. With what Uncle Kurt left me, we had more than enough to start. It was essential, then, to ensure the care of the Chacra, even if we were absent for a long time. Segundo occupied himself with it, bringing from Tafí del Valle a large family that at other times had already cohabited the place: they would live in the service house and would watch over the place.

Once this was arranged, we left on the 4th of May for Santa María, in Segundo's pick-up. I was never intending to return to Salta, but I had to unfailingly cancel Uncle Kurt's businesses. Apart from that, at my Uncle's Finca the two dearest things left in my life were waiting for me: Belicena Villca's manuscript, reproduced in this book, and Konrad Tarstein's manuscript, from his unpublished book "Secret History of the Thulegesellschaft," which I hope to publish in the future.

The Santa María Finca was impossible to sell because Uncle Kurt was not dead, but "missing," and his will in my favor was of no value in this case. But I could lease it and that was what I did, entering into a contract with the Tolabas, who for so many years accompanied my Uncle Kurt: they would take care of the small candy factory and store my Uncle Kurt's belongings. They would only pay a moderate annual rent. Of course, in the future, if I needed to reduce that property to cash, I would appeal to the well-known expedient of falsifying the death certificate of "Cerino Sanguedolce" and put his will into effect. But the future is still in the hands of the Gods.

What I could sell, was the Cerrillos Finca, which I was not wanting to hold on to for a minute longer. So I wrote to my lawyers in Salta so that they could immediately put it up for sale and liquidate it as soon as possible. Six months later, in Córdoba, I signed the final documents of the transaction and received a considerable amount of money. And the last day that I was in Santa María, I sent the two packages by parcel to Maidana, communicating to him in a brief note that the commando operation was a success and that it would be useless for anyone to further seek out the "Oriental assassins"; and that, not recovered from the pain because of the death of my family, I was embarking on a trip to rest and would reunite with him when I got back. A "white lie," of course, but what else could I tell Maidana? Perhaps in the future; perhaps in the future if the Gods so decide.

EPILOGUE

Chapter XVIII

A nd here we are in Córdoba, trying to find the blessed Order.

Today is May 30, 1981. It has been more than a year since I bought the apartment downtown, where I live with Segundo. I have just finished this book, in Chapter XVII of the Epilogue, or Prologue, and many will wonder how and why I wrote it. The answer is simple: this book is the product of a reflection, of a written recapitulation of my extraordinary experience with the Hyperborean Wisdom. I had to do it when all attempts at locating the Order of Tirodal Knights failed. Months ago, in the face of the null results of the search, I asked Myself if I might be the cause of the non-coincidence with the Order, if I had failed to come to a *previous* conclusion. And I decided to set the record straight for Myself. And I said to myself, "what better way than to put them on paper?" So, I began to write down my memories starting from the assassination of Belicena Villca, which was when it all began.

And now, when finishing, I realize that my intuition was right, that *it was necessary for me to come to terms with a great part of all that I assimilated in so brief a time and that was still keeping my Spirit in shock*: it would not be possible that I was permitted to find the Order with such a mental state. But writing this book has helped me, and that is why I have decided to make it known: *...so that others, now like me, find the World of the Blood of Tharsis.*

HYPEREPILOGUE

Córdoba, June 7, 1981.
To the reader of this book,

Indeed, it was my intention to conclude *The Mystery of the Hyperborean Wisdom* on the previous page. At that time I had no more to say. But today, a week later, something has happened that has shed new light on the problem that was keeping me occupied, that is, the location of the Order of Tirodal Knights: ***I believe to have obtained, at last, a sure clue.*** And I think that it is my duty of Honor to share it with the reader, to give him the same opportunity that I now have.

But, before offering such information, I will succinctly state what has happened to me yesterday.

I was seeking an interior illumination, since the exterior search was leading me nowhere. That is why I wrote the present book; and it was when finishing it that, now much more serene, I decided to try a path that I had not yet attempted. Yesterday afternoon, without warning, I went to the house of Oskar Feil, the late friend of Uncle Kurt, and who had first found the Order of Tirodal Knights. As I supposed, his wife, a kind and pleasant woman of Italian nationality, was ignorant of everything concerning the location of the Tirodal Order. She assured me that Oskar died a natural but very happy death because of the spiritual satisfactions he received in his last years.

She was finding out about the existence of the Order, and even more about Uncle Kurt's history, and was surprised that he had not mentioned it. I explained that we did not have much time to speak with Uncle Kurt, and that he had left pending many topics to which he would never give me an answer:

"But what's happened to Kurt?" she asked. "Has he died? If so, I'll tell you everything I know, which isn't enough, and much less than what you seek. Look, I know about you: I know that you're a nephew from Salta, son of his sister and of an Argentine German. And do you know how I know that? Not from Kurt, who'd never say anything, but because of good ol' Oskar, who loved him like a brother and shared with me his whole history. That's why I'll recount what he didn't tell you: I'm Italian, that's obvious; what's not so obvious is that I was a novice of the Monastery where Von Grossen and Oskar Feil had to take refuge for two years, after 1945, with the subsequent company of your Uncle Kurt. Well, Oskar and I fell in love, and when he came to Argentina, I was quick to follow and marry him in this country, where we have been very happy: we had a couple of children who already go to University. That's why I'm surprised that he didn't mention me, since your Uncle knew me almost as well as Oskar. And what's happened to him? Tell me with trust; did he have to flee from those terrible enemies who, according to Oskar, would not stop searching for him even unto his death?"

"No, Señora," I clarified. "Fortunately, Uncle Kurt hasn't died, despite being true what you suppose: those 'terrible enemies' finally found him, and exterminated his whole family, which was also mine. That is to say, my whole family, my parents, my sister, nephews, and distant relatives, were assassinated a year ago; but the assassins failed to wipe us out and which is why Uncle Kurt departed more than a year ago, assuring that he would never return. Only I am left, with the mission of finding the Tirodal Knights."

"I'm very sorry for what happened, because I knew how much he loved his sister Beatriz! Justly, he avoided encounters with her for fear of compromising her and unintentionally causing her harm."

I bit my lips when hearing that truth: Uncle Kurt protected her for 35 years and I delivered her into the hands of her executioners in an instant. The news from Señora Feil was, on the other hand, not very encouraging with regard to the Order:

"I fear that I'll be able to do nothing for you, for what Oskar revealed to me about the Order of Tirodal Knights is very little. He certainly didn't give me any data about its members or meeting places."

I looked at her without being able to hide my disappointment. My expression was comical to her, because she smiled and encouraged me to have hope: there was a chance.

"We'll do something, Dr. Siegnagel; it's the only thing that's in my hands; and pray to your Gods it works. Oskar had a safe in his desk in which he was keeping the Order's things. Several times he recommended to me that if 'something' happened to him, and someone from the Order presented himself to claim his belongings, I should return to them the contents of that chest without discussion. But up to the present, no one, except you, has requested information about the Order, which is why

I've never opened his safe. What we'll do, then, will be to examine the contents of the box and try to find some clue."

We immediately went to the study of the late Oskar and, with growing anxiety, I waited for Señora Feil to key in the combination to the lock. At last it opened and the reserved objects were in sight. The meager esoteric inheritance of Oskar Feil was consisting of two objects: a book and a vulgar magazine.

It will be difficult for anyone to imagine my perplexity at that moment. The book was a copy of *Fundamentals of the Hyperborean Wisdom* by Nimrod de Rosario, exactly the same as that which Uncle Kurt gave me to read in Santa María, and which I now had in my possession. And the magazine, it was an issue of *Spot*, three years old.

Señora Feil ended up sharing my concern and, not knowing in what way to satisfy me, or wishing that the interview concluded as soon as possible, handed me the two publications. She was convinced, she said, that Oskar Feil would approve of her course of action, since I was the nephew of his dearest Comrade, to whom he could refuse nothing.

It is needless to say that I reviewed the book page by page, and line by line, looking for some secret clue, some cryptographic message, some hidden indication, some key only destined to be interpreted by the Hyperborean Initiates. Very soon I had to rule out that the book offered such a possibility.

And it is needless to explain that I read and studied all the articles in the magazine, looking for a clue there about the Order of Tirodal Knights. Very soon I arrived at the same results as with the book: nothing, not even a hint. This last task unpleasant, since *Spot* is a sensationalist magazine of the lowest intellectual or moral level.

Crudely pro-government in its general political line, it lacks defined editorial discretion since its articles are written with the evident purpose of delivering a low blow or causing a scandal, effects that, naturally, please its 2,000,000 readers. The ethical limits of the development of the topics, as is to be expected, are determined only by the legal protections with which its victims manage to defend themselves if they are attacked or by the amount of the bribes paid by the "friends" of the cheap advertising. Logically, such a magazine cannot belong to just anyone: its editor-owner is the famous yellow journalist, not just for being "Oriental," Samuel Isaacson, an exponent of the most rancid Hebrew prostitution, and an avowed Zionist. Through the issue that had reached my hands, I learned of the details of eight separations of not very close couples of actors and actresses; I familiarized myself with the demands of the National Liberation Movement of Homosexuals; I read two different articles about UFOs, in which two "Professors in Parapsychology," were assuring that their crew members were going to save humanity; I acquainted myself with the details of five murders, three rapes, and one statutory rape; I gained access to the crimes of Nazism, thanks to a biography of Anne Frank and an abridged account of her apocryphal "diary"; I saw five review columns, which in fact were containing underhanded advertising, on films with leftist themes, and five other columns on ecology and pacifism; etc; etc. In truth, there was practically no matter in which the magazine did not dabble with its habitual and repugnant vulgarity.

Mein Gott! What a cesspool that publication was! Why the Devil would Oskar Feil have kept that issue? There had to be some reason. And this possibility was my only hope.

But what reason? I had already read it several times: seventy, or more, articles and columns with the marked synarchic tone. And I did not mention the incredible and varied series of advertisements about porn-shops and Afro-Brazilian sorcery; and the endless list of *Umbanda priests,* masters, gurus, magicians, chiromancers, tarotists, etc., who were offering every kind of "spiritual help," from a "solution to couple problems" or "impotence," to complex psychological "unblocking." Of course, I did not pay the same attention to these ads as I did to the journalistic articles: there were so many, hundreds of them!

And there was the solution to the enigma! So visible that it was seeming a joke: a practical joke from Nimrod de Rosario!

Suddenly, where I would have least expected it, on a sheet covered with posters offering the "services" of various esoteric schools and masters, on a sheet that I had looked over many times without seeing anything, the phrase "Hyperborean Wisdom" was highlighted. When I thoroughly inspected the ad, with surprise I read the following:

DON'T DESTROY A PART
IF YOU CAN DESTROY IT ALL!!!

In effect:

If your hatred toward the World is so intense that you have seriously thought about committing suicide or becoming a multiple murderer; or if you plan to destroy cultural or natural assets, or join nihilist groups that practice terrorism of any kind...

Don't do it!!

...because you would waste your effort, you would waste gunpowder on chimangos!

It is very possible that you are spiritually prepared to know the Hyperborean Wisdom. This millenary Science will reveal to you who your true Enemy is and will show you the way to work positively to achieve **the TOTAL destruction of the created Universe.** The realization of such a magnificent objective will signify the absolute and definitive liberation of your Spirit away from the malignant material Universe that You hate. Reflect and turn to us! Even if you have suffered some kind of brainwashing that has momentarily weakened your aggressiveness: we will help you to recover your hatred!

Keep in mind that **there is not much time left, that the day of the Final Battle is near: then everything will be destroyed and not mere parts.** And in that moment, we hope to have you destroying it alongside us and dancing like Shiva on the ruins of the Cosmos reduced to Chaos.

Take the finger off the trigger!

Put away the dagger!

Don't drink strychnine or give it to your relatives and friends!

Don't drop the match on the gasoline!

Don't throw your Molotov cocktail!

Stop the timer on your excellent home-made "pipe" bomb!

Just contact C.C.C. 479, Córdoba. If your spirituality is true, and your repulsion toward the present Culture, toward the present World, or toward the present Universe, is authentic, you will have the opportunity to join an Order of Wise Warriors, and become a Wise Warrior yourself, and participate in the greatest man-made effort of all Time to totally destroy the Work of the Creator God of the Material Universe.

You are not alone!!
Others share your same
aspiration and know how to do it!

C.C.C. 479, Córdoba.

Was it a joke or not? The answer can only be affirmative, and more so if one takes into account the kind of magazine in which it was published. However, nothing of what the ad was affirming or proposing was strange to the Hyperborean Wisdom: anyone who has read this book will agree with me. What was making that text absurd and unbelievable was its reading outside the context of the Hyperborean Wisdom; or in the context of synarchic journalism of the characteristic of *Spot* or other similar rags. But it was not escaping me that such an effect would be deliberately sought by the Tirodal Knights. To what end? I did not know, and I was not venturing to imagine it: perhaps the ad was a password; perhaps, in fact, it was intended for spiritual persons endowed with a high degree of intuition.

Whatever the truth was, the fact was that I had no other choice but to write to the mysterious PO Box. I have already done so, before writing this Hyperepilogue. And now I will wait for the response, which will undoubtedly clarify everything. But, as I said at the beginning, I have not wanted to end this book without giving the readers the same possibility that I possess. It is a way, also, to compensate them for the fatiguing task of assimilating the elements of the Hyperborean Wisdom here exposed; so that, whoever wants, and dares, can prolong that knowledge in Reality, which, however, is as illusory as the fiction of this book.

Summarizing, my intuition tells me that the box belongs to the Order of Tirodal Knights or communicates with them. Each one will be able to verify it by himself, in the same way that I will do. And with this discovery, which constitutes the last and only clue that I have gotten about the Order of the Tirodal Knights, I hereby conclude *The Mystery of the Hyperborean Wisdom* and I bid farewell to all readers with the hope that they will have the *courage* to write and the *spirituality* necessary to merit the Order's response.

Dr. Arturo Siegnagel

Post Scriptum
Córdoba, September 4, 1987.

Table of Contents

THIRD BOOK

"In Search of Uncle Kurt"

FOURTH BOOK

"The History of Kurt von Sübermann"

EPILOGUE

HYPEREPILOGUE

Made in the USA
Las Vegas, NV
09 September 2024